PRIME SUSPECTS

A MYSTERY GUILD LOST CLASSICS OMNIBUS

PRIME SUSPECTS:

Prime Suspect

Prime Suspect 2: A Face in the Crowd

Prime Suspect 3: Silent Victims

BY

LYNDA LA PLANTE

Mystery Guild
Garden City, New York

PRIME SUSPECT

LYNDA LA PLANTE

For Jackie,
A Guiding Light

MY THANKS TO

Elaine Causon, my researcher and assistant who deserves so much credit for *Prime Suspect*. To Jenny (Mealy Mouth) Sheridan who paid for the lunch at which *Prime Suspect* was conceived. My thanks to Sally Head, Don Leaver, Ken Morgan, Roy Stonehouse, Sheelagh Killeen, and to all the cast of *Prime Suspect,* and my admiration and sincere thanks to its director, Chris Menaul.

PREFACE

When I was commissioned to write *Prime Suspect* for Granada Television, I had no notion that it would change my life. I had been very successful writing a series called *Widows*, but it had not resulted in offers of work that I felt excited about. The plot of *Widows* pivoted on four men attempting a dangerous armed robbery, and all died when the explosives held in their truck exploded. They left four widows, who discovered the detailed plans and decided they would audaciously attempt to pull the robbery.

My meeting at Granada was to see if I had any other project they could consider. Due to offers coming in that were all similar to *Widows*, I decided that the best way to approach the possible commission was to find out exactly what the network was looking for, rather than pitch one or another of my ideas. I was told they were actually looking for a female-led police drama, but they did not want her to be in uniform.

"Ah, I have been researching exactly that, and have some great material in a treatment," I LIED! But when I was asked what the title of this proposed new show was, out came, and with no forethought, the title *Prime Suspect*.

I knew this was a great opportunity, and with nothing actually written, I had to launch into research to prepare a treatment for a possible series. I was fortunate enough to meet Detective Chief Inspector Jackie Malton. She was attached to the Metropolitan Scotland Yard murder squad, and had risen through the ranks from uniform to become one of only three high-ranking female officers. By the time I had completed a story line and treatment, we had become friends. The friendship continued as I gained a commission to write the series *Prime Suspect*.

Via Jackie, and her eagerness for me to "get it right," I went to my first autopsy. I spent time in incident rooms, pathology labs, and forensic departments. She was a never-ending source of encouragement and in many ways

Jane Tennison was created via Jackie's constant desire that for once a woman was portrayed within the police force in a realistic way. She would read every scene, make corrections and suggestions with anecdotes appertaining to her own career. She was a complex woman and had been subjected to discrimination throughout her career. As I rewrote and polished up the scripts she became quite emotional because I had acted like a sponge listening and inserting sections that she didn't recall telling me about.

The moment *Prime Suspect* aired on British television it created incredible critical acclaim. I had to fight for a number of scenes to be retained. Producers were concerned that I had written an unsympathetic woman, but I refused to change, explaining over and over that this was a character based on reality. When she examined a victim she didn't, as they wanted, show emotion but retained a professional distance. To make her ambitious was yet again not wholly acceptable, but I persisted, and again I was helped by being able to introduce Jackie Malton.

Helen Mirren was unafraid of the role and added a strong quality to the character. She was the right age, she was still a very attractive woman and yet her believability never faltered. I would never have considered another actress could take on the same role. Over the years there have been so many scripts and attempts to make a U.S. version of the show. There was a constant difficulty in finding an actress on a par with Helen, and although the scripts were well written, something didn't work as the writers moved away from the original concept. That is until Maria Bello took on the role. The series is written by Alexandra Cunningham and she has brilliantly captured the world of a New York precinct. She has cleverly snatched from the original opening series the most salient points and updated them, bringing in the discrimination that still exists and how even today a woman detective has to prove herself beyond and above her male counterparts; respect does not come easily.

The books cover *Prime Suspect 1, 2, 3* . . . and they mean as much to me as the television show. Sadly with all good things, sometimes the powers that be have their own agendas and only these three books represent my voice. I only ever wrote three episodes, and three books. The learning curve from being a writer for hire, which I was on *Prime Suspect,* became the next major change in my career. I formed a production company, so that enabled me to produce my own work, cast, edit, and choose the directors. That said, although I have produced and written numerous series, I don't think there will ever be one as close to me as *Prime Suspect.*

Sincerely,

Lynda La Plante

1

Mrs. Corrina Salbanna was woken from a deep sleep by the sound of the front door banging in the wind. She squinted at her bedside clock; it was almost two. Swearing in her native Spanish, she threw off the bedclothes and stuffed her plump feet into her slippers.

She shuffled up the steps into the hall and towards the still-open front door, wrapping her dressing-gown around her against the chill. The naked light bulb gave the seedy hallway a yellowish hue that did nothing to enhance the peeling wallpaper and brown, flaking paint. Pursing her lips, Mrs. Salbanna slammed the door hard. There was no reason why anyone else in the house should be allowed to sleep if she couldn't.

As she turned again towards her warm bed, she noticed a light beneath Della Mornay's door on the first-floor landing. She put two and two together; it must be that little tart who had left the door open. Della owed three months' rent, and had been warned about bringing men back to her room. Now was the time to catch her red-handed. Moving as fast as she could, Mrs. Salbanna returned to the basement and collected the master keys, then panted back up to the first floor.

"Della, I know you're in there, open the door!"

She waited, with her ear pressed to the door. Hearing nothing, she rattled the door handle. "Della?"

There was no response. Her face set, Mrs. Salbanna inserted the key, unlocked the door and pushed it open.

The large room was as seedy as the rest of the rundown Victorian house, which had been divided into efficiency apartments long before Mrs. Salbanna and her husband had taken it over in the sixties, and many of the rooms still had the feel of the hippie years. Only the posters in this room had changed; Jimi Hendrix had given way to more modern rock and movie heroes. The first thing Mrs. Salbanna saw was a large photograph of Madonna, lips pouting, which dominated the squalid, clothes-strewn room from above the head of the old-fashioned double bed. A red shawl had been draped over the bedside lamp; in its glow Mrs. Salbanna could see that the pillows and red satin eiderdown had been dragged to the far side of the bed, revealing the stained ticking of the mattress.

There was no sign of Della. Shivering, Mrs. Salbanna looked about her with distaste. She wouldn't put it past the little bitch to be hiding; she'd been devious enough about not paying her rent. She sniffed: stale body odor and cheap perfume. The smell was stronger when she peered into the mahogany wardrobe, but it contained only dresses and shoes.

The wardrobe door, off its hinges, was propped against the wall. Its full-length, fly-blown mirror was cracked and missing a corner, but reflected enough to show Mrs. Salbanna a leg, protruding from beneath the bedclothes on the floor. She spun round.

"You little bitch! I knew you were in here!"

For all her weight, the landlady moved swiftly across the room and crouched down to grip Della's exposed ankle. With her other hand she threw the bedclothes aside. Her mouth opened to scream, but no sound came; she lost her balance and fell, landing on her backside. In a panic she crawled to the door, dragging herself up by the open drawer of a tallboy. Bottles and pots of make-up crashed to the floor as her scream finally surfaced. Mrs. Salbanna screamed and screamed . . .

By the time Detective Chief Inspector John Shefford arrived the house in Milner Road, Gray's Inn, had been cordoned off. He was the last on the scene; two patrol cars were parked outside the house and uniformed officers were fending off the sightseers. An ambulance stood close by, its doors open, its crew sitting inside, drinking tea. The mortuary van was just drawing up and had to swerve out of the way as Shefford's car screeched to a halt just where its driver had intended to park. Shefford's door crashed open as he yanked on the handbrake. He was on the move, delving into his pocket for his ID as he stepped over the cordon. A young PC, recognizing him, ushered him up the steps to the house.

Even at two-thirty on a wintry Sunday morning, word had got round that a murder had been committed. There were lights in many windows; people in dressing-gowns huddled on their front steps. A couple of kids had appeared and were vying with each other to see how close they could get to the police cordon without breaking through it. Five Rastafarians with a ghetto-blaster were laughing together on a nearby wall, calling out remarks and jokes, as if it was a street party.

Shefford, a bear of a man at six foot two, dwarfed those around him.

He had been notorious on the rugby field in the late seventies, when he played for England. With his curly hair standing on end, his crumpled shirt and tie hanging loose he didn't look or feel in a fit state to start an investigation. He had been hauled out of the celebration bash at the end of a long and tedious murder case, and he was knackered. Now he was about to lead the investigation of another murder, but this one was different.

Many of the officers in the dark, crowded hallway he had worked with before. He scanned the faces as his eyes grew accustomed to the darkness. He never forgot a face, and he greeted each man he knew by name.

At the foot of the stairs he hesitated a moment, straightening his tie. It wasn't like him to shrink from an unpleasant duty, but he had to force himself to mount each step. He was sweating. Above the confusion of voices a high-pitched wailing could be heard. It seemed to be coming from the direction of the basement.

Hearing Shefford's voice, Detective Sergeant Bill Otley stopped pacing the landing and leaned over the banister. He gestured for his guv'nor to join him in the darkness at the far end of the landing. He kept his voice low and his eye on the men coming and going from the victim's room.

"It's Della Mornay, guv. I got the tip-off from Al Franks."

He could smell the booze on Shefford's breath. Unwrapping a peppermint, he handed it over. The boss wasn't drunk; he probably had been, but he was straightening out fast. Then Otley shook out a pair of white overalls for each of them. While they struggled to put them on, their dark recess was lit at intervals by the powerful flash of a camera from the efficiency.

As Shefford dragged on a cigarette he became aware of a familiar low, gruff voice that had been droning on all the time he had been in the house. He moved towards the door and listened.

". . . She's lying next to the double bed, on the side nearest the window and away from the door. She's half-hidden beneath a red silk eiderdown. The window is open, a chest of drawers in front of it. We have a sheet, a blanket, a copy of the *Sunday Times* dated December 1990 . . . Looks like it's been used to wrap something in. She's lying face down, hands tied behind her back. Wearing some kind of skinny-rib top, mini-skirt, no stockings. The right shoe is on the foot, the left one lying nearby . . ."

"She been raped?" Shefford asked Otley as he fastened his overall.

"I dunno, but it's a mess in there."

Mrs. Salbanna's hysterical screaming and sobbing was getting on Shefford's nerves. He leaned over the banister and had a clear view of DC Dave Jones on the basement stairs trying to calm the landlady. An ambulance attendant tried to help move her, but she turned on him with such a torrent of mingled Spanish and English with violent gestures that he retreated, fearing for his safety.

The pathologist was ready to talk, so Shefford and Otley were given the nod to enter the room. Shefford took a last pull at his cigarette, inhaled deeply and pinched it out, putting the stub in his pocket. Then he eased past the mess of broken bottles of make-up and perfume, careful where he put his size eleven feet, to stand a little distance from the bed. All he could see of Della was her left foot.

The brightly lit room was full of white-overalled men, all going about their business quickly and quietly. Flashlights still popped, but already items were being bagged and tagged for removal. The bulky figure of Felix Norman, the pathologist, crouched over the corpse, carefully slipping plastic bags over Della's hands. He was a rotund man, oddly pear-shaped with most of his weight in his backside, topped off with a shock of thick, gray hair and an unruly gray beard. Rumor had it that his half-moon spectacles had been held together by the same piece of sticking plaster since 1983, when a corpse he was dissecting suddenly reared up and thumped him. But it was just a rumor, started by Norman himself. It was his voice Shefford had heard muttering into a tape recorder.

He looked up and gave Shefford a small wave, but continued dictating. "Obvious head injuries . . . possible penetrating wounds, through her clothes, her neck, upper shoulders . . . Lot of blood-staining, blood covering the left side of her head and face. Room's damned cold, about five degrees . . ." Norman broke into a coughing fit, but he didn't bother turning the tape off. He bent over the lower end of the corpse, but Shefford could not see what he was doing. Then he glanced at his watch and continued, "Say two to three degrees when she was found, the lights and everybody tramping around must have warmed the place." He winked at Shefford, still talking. "Window half-open, curtains part-drawn, no source of heat . . . Door to landing giving a strong draft, front door had been left open . . ." He felt the corpse's arms and legs, examined the scalp, then began checking for a weapon or anything lodged in the clothing that might fall when the body was removed, without pausing for breath. "Complete absence of rigor, no hypostasis visible . . ." Again he bent over the body, then sat back, waving a thermometer. He squinted at it. "Deep rectal temperature . . . Can't bloody read it for the life of me . . . Ah, time is two-thirty-eight a.m., thirty-five point eight degrees, so assuming she started at thirty-seven that puts it back to . . ."

Shefford shifted his weight from foot to foot and swallowed hard. As Norman gently rolled the body over he could see the blood matted in the blond hair, and he had to turn away. It wasn't the sight of the blood, he had seen enough of that in his time, but how small she seemed, small and broken.

Two white-clad men moved in to examine the carpet where the dead girl had been lying. Norman had another coughing fit and Shefford took the opportunity to ask how long she had been dead.

"Well, my old son, she would have cooled off pretty quickly in here, with that window open an' no heating on . . . Any time between midnight, maybe a little later, and . . . at a rough guess, twelve-thirty."

"Was she raped, Felix?" Shefford asked, although he knew Norman wouldn't answer.

Norman just gave Shefford a foul look; he no longer bothered answering questions that presumed he was telepathic or had X-ray vision. He looked around the room and called to an assistant, "Right, body-bag!"

Two men lifted the body into the black plastic bag. Shefford winced and averted his head, shocked at the disfiguration of her face. He had seen only her profile, which was hardly recognizable as human; her nose and cheek were a mass of clotted blood and the eye was completely gone.

"Not a pretty sight," said Norman, without emotion.

Shefford nodded, but his voice was muffled as he replied, "She was, though—pretty. Her name's Della Mornay. Booked her myself when I was on Vice."

Norman sniffed. "Yeah, well, let's get her out of here an' down to the mortuary. Quicker I get at her, faster you'll get results."

Even though he had asked once, Shefford could not stop himself repeating the question, "Was she raped?"

Norman pulled a face. "Fuck off, I'll tell you everything you wanna know after the post-mortem." He stared around the efficiency while the bag was closed and the body lifted onto a stretcher. "They'll need a bloody pantechnicon to take this lot down to Forensic. You had breakfast? You'd better grab some before you schlepp over to me. Gimme a couple of hours."

With a wave, Shefford shouldered his way to the landing. He paused and turned his back to the uniformed PC as he swiftly transferred a small object into Otley's hand. No one had seen him slip it from under the mattress. Otley quickly pocketed the little book.

It was not yet dawn, but the street was just as lively when Shefford left the house. The spectators watched avidly as the stretcher was carried to the waiting mortuary van and the police brought bag after bag of evidence from the house. Mrs. Salbanna and Shefford himself had both identified the corpse.

The Scenes of Crime officers, or SOCOs, had started fingerprinting every possible surface, covering most of the room in a film of gray, shining dust. They were none too happy; many of the best spots had been carefully wiped.

・ ・ ・

After snatching a quick breakfast in the canteen and detailing Otley to make sure the Incident Room was being organized, Shefford was at the mortuary by nine o'clock. DI Frank Burkin and DC Dave Jones joined him there to discuss the day's itinerary. They sat in the anteroom of the main laboratory, all but Jones blatantly disregarding the large NO SMOKING notices.

While they waited, John Shefford used the payphone to call his home. It was his son's birthday the next day and Otley, the boy's godfather, wanted to know what to buy him. His wife, however, had more on her mind.

"Have you booked the clown for Tommy's party, John?" Sheila asked. "I gave you the number last week, remember?"

Shefford was about to confess that he had forgotten all about it when he was saved by the bell; Felix Norman's assistant came to fetch him.

"I've got to go, love, they're ready for me. See you later!"

Gowned up, masked and wearing the regulation wellington boots, Shefford joined Norman.

Two bare, pale feet protruded from the end of the green sheet, a label bearing Della Mornay's name and a number tied to one ankle. Norman started talking before Shefford had even reached the trolley.

"Death, old mate, was around twelve-fifteen—it's a classic, her watch got broken and stopped. The gold winder, by the way, is missing, so they'll have to comb the carpet. The watch face is intact, but the rope that was used to tie her wrists must have twisted the winding pin off the watch. Now, you asked if she was raped; could be. Recent deposits of semen in the vagina and rectum, and in the mouth, extensive bruising to the genital area. I sent the swabs over to Willy at the lab . . ." he checked his watch, "five hours ago. Might get a blood type this afternoon. OK, the wounds . . ."

Norman threw the green sheet over the head to expose the torso, and pointed to the puncture marks. The body had been cleaned, and they showed up clearly.

"Upper right shoulder, right breast, lung punctured here, and here. Another laceration to the throat, sixth deep wound just above the navel. The wounds are neat, made with a small, rounded object, the point narrow, flat and sharp, like a sharpened screwdriver, perhaps. Not all the same depth—one three inches, one six inches, the one in the right breast is even deeper."

Shefford examined the wounds and listened intently, nodding his head. Felix Norman was one of the best in his field, and Shefford had learned from experience to let him have his say before asking any questions.

Norman continued, "OK, she also has a deep puncture to her left eye, probably what finished her off. A real mess, wanna see?"

"No, just carry on," replied Shefford with distaste, running his hands through his hair.

Norman referred to his notes. "Oh, yeah, this is interesting. Look at her hands. They seem to have been scrubbed, with a wire brush, by the look of them. But there's a nasty little nick here, and there's a smell of chlorine, some kind of household bleach. No doubt I'll find out the exact brand when I've been given the time a man of my calibre likes to have in order to do his job thoroughly! Anyway, it looks as if the scrubbing job on her hands has eliminated any possibility of blood or tissue fragments under the nails. She probably didn't put up much of a struggle, but then, her hands were tied . . ."

Shefford avoided looking at the naked torso as much as possible. "Anything else?"

Norman sniffed. "Yeah, something strange . . ." Laying his clipboard aside, he picked up one of the corpse's arms. "See, same on both sides? Deep welts and bruising to the upper arms. At this stage I can't say what caused it, but she might have been strung up. I'll have to do some more tests, but it looks like she was put in some kind of clamp. Interesting, huh?"

Shefford nodded. Somewhere at the back of his mind a bell rang, but he couldn't capture the memory . . . Norman covered the body again and continued, peering over his glasses. "Right-handed killer, height difficult to estimate at this stage, especially if she was strung up, but four of the wounds entered the body on an upward slant and two are straight, so I reckon he's around five-ten. But don't quote me until I've . . ."

Shefford pulled a face. Norman, for all his bravado, went strictly by the rules and hated being pressed for results before he was one hundred per cent sure.

"Thanks mate. Get back to me as soon as you've got anything. When the report's ready, Bill can collect it personally. And, Felix—I really appreciate it!"

Norman snorted. He had worked fast, but then he and John Shefford were old friends. He watched as Shefford removed his surgical mask and began to untie his gown.

"You got anything, John?"

Shefford shook his head. "Looks like one of her johns was into bondage and things got out of hand. See you . . ."

At the station, Della Mornay's effects were being sorted and examined. Her handbag had been found, but it contained no keys. They were able to dismiss robbery as a motive as her purse, containing fifteen pounds, was in the bag and a jewel box on her dressing table, containing a few silver chains and a gold bangle or two, was undisturbed.

In King's Cross, Della Mornay's territory, fifteen of Shefford's men were interviewing every known prostitute and call girl. They were getting little assistance, but the feedback was that Della had not been seen for weeks. There was a suggestion that she might have gone to Leeds to visit a friend dying of AIDS, but no name was mentioned.

The painstaking task of checking every forensic sample, the tapes of fibers, the fingerprints, was barely begun, and had brought no results so far. The entire area was combed for a murder weapon without success. In that neighborhood no one ever volunteered information, especially to the police.

Shefford and Otley met up again at Milner Road and spent an hour or so interviewing and looking over the efficiency again, but they discovered nothing new. Mrs. Salbanna, recovered from her shock, was already asking when she could let the room.

Shefford was hungry and very tired. He had a few pints and a pork pie in the local, then kipped down in his office while Otley went home to his flat to fetch his guv'nor a clean shirt. Shefford often stayed over at his place and left a few items of clothing there for emergencies.

Although he could have done with putting his head down for a few hours himself, Otley sprayed the shirt with starch and ironed it, paying special attention to the collar. Pleased with his handiwork, he slipped it onto a hanger and sat down for a cup of tea. He had a system for avoiding washing up; he simply used the same cup, plate and cutlery all the time. He ate all his main meals in the station canteen, and had even given up his morning cornflakes because they were a bugger to get off the bowl if you left them overnight.

The silver-framed photographs of his wife, his beloved Ellen, needed a good polish, but he'd have to leave them until his next weekend off. They were the only personal items in the flat that he bothered with. Ellen had been the love of his life, his only love, since he was a teenager. Her death seven years ago, from cancer of the stomach, had left him bereft, and he mourned her now as deeply as the moment she had died. He had watched helplessly as she disintegrated before his eyes. She had become so weak, so skeletal, that he had prayed, anguished and alone, for her to die.

It has been obvious to everyone at work that Skipper Bill Otley had personal problems, but he confided in no one. His solitary drinking and his angry bitterness had caused many arguments, and his boys, as he called them, had at last left him to himself. In the end, John Shefford had taken him aside and demanded to know what was going on, earning his abusive response, "Mind yer own fuckin' business, my personal life's me own affair."

Shefford had snapped back angrily that when it affected his work it became the boss's business, and Otley would be out on his ear if he didn't come clean about what was tormenting him. He pushed Otley to the point where he finally cracked.

Once he understood, Shefford had been like a rock. He was at the hospital, waiting outside the ward, when Ellen died. He had organized the funeral, done everything he possibly could to help. He was always there, always available, like the sweet, beloved friend Otley had buried. When Shefford's son was born he asked Otley to be godfather; the bereaved man became part of the family, his presence demanded for lunch on Sundays, for outings and parties. He and Ellen had longed for children, in vain; now his off-duty time was filled with little Tom's laughter and nonsense. So Otley wouldn't just iron his guv'nor's shirt; he would wash it, and his socks for good measure. John Shefford meant more to him than he could ever put into words; he loved the man, admired him, and backed him to the hilt, convinced that he would make Commander one of these days. No one would be more proud of him then than Bill Otley.

With the clean shirt over his arm, Otley whistled on his way back to the station.

At eleven, Detective Chief Inspector Jane Tennison parked her Ford Fiesta and entered Southampton Row police station. It was a crisp, frosty day, and she was wrapped up well against the cold.

She was officially off-duty, but had come in to prepare some final papers for a session in court the next day.

None of the blood samples taken from the efficiency had yielded a clue to the identity of Della Mornay's killer. Hers was a very common group and the only one found at the scene. But the DNA tests on the semen taken from her body were a different matter.

The new computerized DNA system was still at the experimental stage, but already the results of thousands of tests taken in the past two years had been entered on it. As a matter of routine, Willy Chang's forensic team ran the result from Della Mornay against the existing records and were astonished to find a match; a visual check on the negatives, using a light-box, confirmed it. The man Della Mornay had had sex with shortly before her murder had been convicted of attempted rape and aggravated robbery in 1988.

Willy Chang was jubilant; here was the lever they needed to press the government into releasing funds for a national DNA profiling system. He picked up the phone.

The message caught Shefford on Lambeth Bridge, on his way home for lunch and only a stone's throw from the Home Office labs. He hung up the handset, turned the car around immediately and punched Otley's arm.

"You're not gonna believe this, we got a friggin' suspect! He's got a rare blood group and it's on the ruddy computer!"

For the past three months DCI Tennison had been working on a tedious fraud case involving a tobacconist who was being sued for non-payment of VAT. The man's ferret of an accountant had more tricks up his sleeve than a conjuror, and a long series of medical certificates exempting him from court appearances. But tomorrow, at last, Judge George Philpott would complete his summing-up. Known as the legal equivalent of Cary Grant for his good looks and slow delivery, Philpott had already taken two days; Tennison hoped he would finish quickly for once so she would have time to check her desk before the end of the day.

Not that there would be anything of interest; in all her time on the special Area Major Incident Team, known as AMIT, there had been little but desk work. She had often wondered why she had bothered switching from the Flying Squad, where at least she had been busy. The set-up of five DCIs and their teams had appealed to her, and she had believed she would be able to use her skills to the full.

Sitting at her desk, Tennison heard a screech of brakes from the car park. She glanced out of the window in time to see Shefford racing into the building.

"What's DCI Shefford doing in today, Maureen?" she asked her assistant, WPC Havers. "He's supposed to be on leave."

"I think he's heading the investigation."

"What investigation?"

"Prostitute found dead in her room in Milner Road."

"They got a suspect?" Tennison snapped.

"Not yet, but they're getting all the Vice files on the victim's pals."

Tennison bristled. "How did Shefford get it? I was here until after ten last night!"

Maureen shrugged. "I dunno, guv, I think it was a middle-of-the-night job. Probably hauled him out of the afters session in the pub."

"But he's only just finished with that shooting in Kilburn—and there were the Iranian diplomats before that."

Tennison clenched her fists and stormed out. Maureen winced at the banging of the door.

DCI Tennison paced up and down the corridor, trying to talk herself down. Eighteen months she'd been waiting for a decent case, dealing with more paperwork than in her entire time at the rape center in Reading, and now the boss had gone out of his way to give DCI Shefford the case that should have been hers. She'd known when she applied for the transfer that she would be in for a tough time; had she stayed where she was she'd have been promoted to a desk job by now.

But five years with the Flying Squad had toughened her up. She went back to her room and put a call through to the Chief's office, determined to have it out with him, but he was in a meeting. She tried to work on her statements for the court hearing but her frustration wouldn't let her concentrate.

At midday Tennison was again disturbed by the racing of engines from the car park. Shefford was off again, and in a hell of a hurry. She gave up trying to work and packed her things; it was nearly lunchtime anyway.

Tennison missed the "heat" as Shefford gathered his team together, his booming voice hurling insults as he fired orders at them. He was moving fast on the unbelievable stroke of luck that had given him his suspect on a plate.

George Arthur Marlow had been sentenced to three years for attempted rape and assault, but had served only eighteen months. He had still been protesting his innocence when he was led away from the dock.

The case had been a long-drawn-out affair as Marlow insisted he was innocent. At first he had denied even knowing the victim, referred to only as "Miss X," but when faced with the evidence he told the police that he and "Miss X" had been drinking together in a wine bar. He stated that she had blatantly encouraged his advances, but when it came to the crunch she refused him.

Marlow's blood tests at the time had shown him to have an exceptionally rare blood group; he belonged to a small percentage of AB secreters, of whom there is only one in 2,500 head of population. He had been one of the first to be entered on the new computer, and when a lab assistant ran his details through the system she hit the jackpot.

The warrant was ready. Shefford high on adrenaline, called his men together. Already he had dribbled coffee down his clean shirt, and he followed it now with cigarette ash. Otley brushed him down as he bellowed, "DCI Donald Paxman holds the record in the Met, lads, for bringing in a suspect and charging him within twenty-four hours. Gimme me raincoat . . . cigarettes, who's got me cigarettes?"

He shrugged into his coat with the effortless ability of the permanently crumpled man, lighting a cigarette at the same time and switching it from hand to hand as his big fists thrust down the sleeves. "We smash that record, lads, and it's drinks all round, so let's go! Go, go!"

Jane Tennison let herself into her small service flat which she had shared for the last three months with her boyfriend, Peter Rawlins. Six feet tall, broad-chested, his sandy hair invariably flecked with paint, he was the first man she had lived with on a permanent basis.

Peter came out of the kitchen when he heard her key in the door and beamed at her. "OK, we've got Chicken Kiev with brown rice, how does that suit?"

"Suits me fine!"

She dumped her briefcase on the hall table and he gave her a hug, then held her at arm's length and looked into her face. "Bad day?"

She nodded and walked into the bedroom, tossing her coat on the bed. He lolled in the doorway. "Want to talk about it?"

"When I've had a shower."

They had spent a lot of time talking since they had met; Peter had been in the throes of divorce and Jane had provided a sympathetic ear. Marianne had left him for another man; it had hit him hard because it was not just any other man, but Peter's best friend and partner in his building firm, And she had taken with her the little son he adored, Joey.

Jane and Peter's relationship had begun casually enough; they had been teamed together in the squash club tournament and had since met on several occasions for the odd drink or cup of coffee after a game. Eventually he had asked her to see a film with him, and on that first real date she had listened to the details of his divorce. It was only after several films that he had even made an attempt to kiss her.

Jane had helped Peter to move into a temporary flat while his house was sold, and gradually their relationship had become closer. When he started looking for a permanent place to live she suggested he move in with her for a while. It wasn't very romantic, but as the weeks passed she found herself growing more and more fond of him. He was easygoing, caring and thoughtful. When he told her he loved her and suggested they look for a bigger place together, she agreed. It was a pleasant surprise to her how much she wanted to be with him.

When she had showered, Jane sat at the table in her dressing gown and Peter presented his Chicken Kiev with a flourish. She was so grateful and happy that she had someone to share her life with that she forgot her problems for a moment.

As he opened a bottle of wine she cocked her head to one side and smiled. "You know, I'm getting so used to you, I don't know what I'd do if you weren't around. I guess what I'm trying to say in my roundabout way is—"

"Cheers!" he said, lifting his glass.

"Yeah, to you, to me, to us . . ."

Marlow seemed dazed by the arrival of the police. He stood in the narrow hallway of his flat, holding a cup of coffee, apparently unable to comprehend what they wanted.

"George Arthur Marlow, I am arresting you on suspicion of murder . . ." Otley had to repeat the caution, then remove the cup from Marlow's hand himself to put the handcuffs on him.

Moyra Henson, Marlow's girlfriend, appeared from the kitchen, followed by the smell of roasting lamb.

"What the hell's going on here? Oi, where are you taking him? He hasn't had his dinner . . ."

Ignoring her, they led Marlow out to the car as quickly as possible. In his bewilderment, he almost cracked his head on the roof of the patrol car as he was helped inside.

The uniformed officers went in to search the flat, while a WPC took Moyra into the kitchen and told her that Marlow had been arrested on suspicion of the murder of a prostitute. Moyra's eyes widened and she shook her head, disbelieving.

"There's been a terrible mistake, you can't do this to him, it's a mistake . . ." She broke away from the WPC and ran to the front door. She shrieked like a banshee when she realized the police were taking out clear plastic bags of clothing at a rate of knots. Marlow's shoes, jackets, shirts, all listed and tagged, were shown to Moyra while she protested shrilly. But she didn't attempt to stop the officers, and they remained for hours, searching and removing items. When they had finished, Moyra was taken to the police station for questioning.

She was no longer irate, but coldly angry. She hated the pigs, hated them. They had already put George inside for a crime she knew he hadn't committed, and now she was sure they were about to frame him for murder. All the whodunnits she watched on video and the moral standpoints of *Dallas* and *EastEnders* had taught her her rights, and not to trust the bastards.

Jane lay curled in Peter's arms, telling him about Shefford and his attitude to her; not quite openly antagonistic but near enough. It was pretty much the same with all the men, but Shefford was so macho that he took pleasure in sending her up, albeit behind her back.

It was still a new thing for her to have someone to listen to her problems. She had been in such a foul mood when she had arrived home, making love to him had taken all the tension away. It was good to have Peter, to feel loved and wanted. She told him how the Chief had given her the usual speech about waiting, but she had to make a decision soon. The longer she waited and accepted the cases no one else wanted, the more she knew she would be put upon. If Kernan didn't give her a break she would quit. The men gave her no respect . . .

Peter laughed. "They don't know you, do they?"

She grinned. "No, I suppose they don't. I'll get a break one day, and by Christ they'll know what's hit them then."

He bit her ear. "Get them to play a game of squash with you, they'll soon take notice of that determined little face. First time I played against you I thought: Holy shit, this one's a maniac."

She laughed her wonderful, deep, throaty laugh. When they made love it no longer mattered that her bosses had overlooked her; only Peter was important. She had said it to him that afternoon, and told him she loved him.

He cuddled her close. "I'm glad we've got each other, because things are not going too well for me. We may have to stave off looking for a bigger place, the company's in bad shape and I'm having to spend capital until I get back on my feet."

She murmured that it didn't matter, the place was big enough. She asked him then how it had felt, knowing his wife was having an affair with his best friend, a subject she had always steered clear of.

He sighed, stared up at the ceiling. "Like my balls had been cut off. I couldn't believe it at first, it must have been going on for years behind my back. Then I felt like a bloody fool, you know, that I hadn't clocked it faster. He was always round the house, but we were partners and I just accepted that he was there to see me. And he was screwing my wife in my own bed!" He punched his palm, hard; it made a satisfying smack. He sighed again. "I wanted to beat him up, have it out that way, but there was no point. I just walked away from it all. She's got half the money from the house and I bought him out of the company, that's one of the reasons why cash is so tight at the moment. I should have just told him to fuck off, but I'm not like that and there's Joey to consider. I reckoned that if I got nasty about the divorce she'd try to stop me seeing Joey. I love that kid, couldn't bear not to see him."

Jane stroked his cheek gently. "Any time you want him to stay he's welcome, you know that, don't you?"

He hugged her. "Yeah, I do, and I appreciate it. You're the best thing that's happened to me in years. I know things'll work out for you, just be patient."

She smiled, without mentioning that it was exactly what her Chief's attitude had been. But she had no intention of being patient. Peter didn't really understand how important her work was to her, but he was to find out sooner than either of them anticipated.

George Marlow was quiet and co-operative. His fingerprints were taken and he was led to the cells. He stammered a little when he asked to phone his lawyer, seeming shaken, and gave the number. Although on the point of tears, he went out of his way to be helpful, but he still kept asking why he had been arrested.

Shefford had been on the go all day. Now he was preparing himself to question Marlow. His face was flushed and he was chain-smoking, cracking jokes; it was obvious that the adrenaline was still flowing.

The men on the team were clapping him on the back, calling him a lucky bastard, what a break! Several were laying bets on the outcome.

DI Burkin suddenly remembered something. "Hey, it's his kid's birthday tomorrow! While we've all got our hands in our pockets, we gonna chip in an' buy him something? You know Otley, he's so tightfisted the kid won't even get an ice-cream cornet from him. What d'you say, fifty pence each?" In great humor, they all coughed up.

Before he went down to the interview room, Shefford called his home to tell Sheila, his wife, that he would be late and she shouldn't wait up. He was too keyed up to pay much attention to what she was saying.

"You didn't answer me this morning, John. Have you booked the clown for Tom's party?"

"Yeah, yeah, I'll get it sorted . . ." He handed the phone to Bill Otley and whispered, "Talk to the missus, mate, you're his bloody godfather, after all. I haven't got time . . ."

He lit another cigarette and turned to the files as Otley took the phone and promised faithfully that he would dress up as a clown himself if they couldn't get Biffo for the birthday party.

The lads had been wrong about their skipper; Otley had spent more time and money in Hamley's toy shop that weekend than they could credit. The train sets had cost an arm and a leg, but he was prepared to dip into his savings. He and Ellen had spent hours planning what they would spend it on when he retired; now his godson would be the one to benefit. It was making the decision that took the time, as well as wandering around enjoying himself in the store.

Otley replaced the receiver and turned to Shefford. "OK, guv? Need anything else? Marlow's brief's on his way, be about an hour. Arnold Upcher, represented him on his last caper. Tough bastard, but he's fair. Doesn't scream a lot like some of the buggers."

Shefford winked. "I want a crack at 'im before Upcher gets here. Nice one for us, eh? What a stroke of fuckin' luck! See if we can't sew up Paxman's record. Get a bottle of fizz over to Forensic lot, tell 'em I love 'em, and tell Willy to stand by for all the gear from Marlow's place. And, yeah, I'm ready, let's go for the bastard."

George Marlow was sitting in the cell with his hands in his lap, head bowed. He was wearing a blue striped shirt with the white collar open at the neck; his tie had been taken away from him. His gray flannels were neatly pressed and his jacket hung over the back of his chair.

With his Mediterranean looks it was obvious that he would have to shave twice a day, but as yet his chin was clean. He raised his head when a uniformed officer opened the door and asked him politely to accompany him to the interview room.

DCI Shefford had given instructions that Upcher was to be stalled if he arrived early. He wanted a chance to question Marlow without his lawyer present. He drew himself up to his full height, threw his massive shoulders back and strode down the corridor to Room 4C. He noticed the way Marlow actually jumped with shock when he kicked the door open.

With a gesture to Marlow to remain seated, he swung a hard wooden chair around with one hand, placing it exactly opposite the suspect, and sat down.

"George? I am Detective Chief Inspector John Shefford. This is Detective Sergeant Bill Otley, and that's DC Jones over by the door. Before we get involved with your lawyer—I mean, we might not even need him—I just want to ask you a few questions, OK?"

He drew the ashtray towards him, scraping it along the formica of the table until it squealed, then lit a cigarette. "You smoke, George?"

"No, sir."

"Good . . . Right then, George, can you tell us where you were on the night of the thirteenth of January? Take your time."

Marlow kept his head down. "January the thirteenth? Saturday? Well, that's easy. I was at home with my wife. We don't usually go out, we get a video and a takeaway . . . Yeah, I was with my wife."

"Your wife? You mean Moyra Henson, the girl you're living with? She said she's not your wife, she's your girlfriend. Which is it, George? Come on, son, don't mess us about."

"Well, she's my common-law wife, we're not actually married."

Shefford's tongue felt and tasted like an old carpet. He searched his pockets and found a wrinkled piece of Wrigley's chewing gum at the bottom. It must have been there for some time as it had lost its outer wrapper, and the silver paper was covered with fluff and ash from using the pocket as an ashtray. He picked the foil off, examined the gray gum, then popped it in his mouth and chewed furiously. Marlow watched his every move, as if transfixed.

Shefford folded the wrapper into a narrow strip, ran his fingernail down it, then tossed it aside and lit a cigarette. "What were you doing, say around ten o'clock?" he asked casually.

"I'd be at home . . . Oh, hang on, earlier . . . I know what I did earlier."

Shefford inhaled the last of his cigarette and let the smoke drift from his nostrils. "Well, want to tell me?"

With a rueful smile, Marlow shrugged his shoulders slightly. "I picked up a girl. She was on the game."

"You knew the girl, did you?"

Marlow shook his head and glanced at Otley, who was sitting a few feet away taking notes. "I'd never met her before, but I saw her outside the tube station, Ladbroke Grove. She was, you know, bending down, peering into cars as they went past . . . Ladbroke Grove tube station. I pulled up and asked her how much."

"But you didn't know her?"

"No, I'd never met her before. I asked her first how much, and she said it depends. You know they like to hustle as much as they can out of you . . ."

"Oh, yeah? But you been done before, George. You don't like hassles. Della Mornay pisses you off, right? Right?

Marlow frowned, then looked at Shefford. "Della Mornay . . . ?"

Otley checked his watch and wondered how it was all going down in the interview room. It was past seven and Shefford had been at it since four-thirty, now with Arnold Upcher sitting in on the session. Otley strolled down to the basement corridor and peered through the glass panel; he could just see Marlow, sitting with his head in his hands.

"Has he confessed yet? Only it's drinking time!"

The PC on guard raised his eyebrows. "Been a lot of shouting goin' on in there, and at the last count Shefford had consumed five beakers of coffee."

"Ah, well, he would—this is pub hours, son!"

Otley turned away and went to the pub to join the others from Shefford's team. He ordered a round and sat down with his pint, telling them there was no news as yet.

"But he had his head in his hands, looked like the guv'nor's cracked him. Gonna break that bloody record . . ."

They set about betting on how long it would take Shefford to get a confession from Marlow and whether or not he would break Paxman's record. They might not have been so confident if they had been privy to the statement that was being taken from Marlow right then.

2

Shefford was using the regulation tape recorder. Marlow craned his head forward and directed his speech at the built-in microphone.

"I dropped her off at the tube station, and paid her."

"OK, so then what did you do?"

"I went to Kilburn to get a video, and I was home by . . . about ten-thirty."

Marlow rubbed his chin. He needed a shave now, the stubble made him look darker, swarthier.

"Like I said, Inspector, I remember, when I looked back, she was peering into another car, a red . . . maybe a Scirocco, I dunno, but she was looking for the next customer. I just got the video and went home, got there at ten-thirtyish. I can't remember the exact time, you'll have to ask Moyra, she'll remember."

"And you maintain that you did not know this girl you picked up? You had never met her or seen her before?"

"No, sir. Like I said, she just came over to my car."

Shefford opened a file and held out a photograph of Della Mornay, taken from Vice records. "Is this the girl you picked up?"

Marlow leaned forward, without actually touching the photo, then sat back in his chair. "I'd never met her before, I didn't know her."

He looked to his brief, then back to Shefford. "I picked her up at about seven-thirty. It was dark, I don't remember her all that well . . ."

"You had sex with her, George! You tellin' me you didn't see her face? Come on, George . . ."

Marlow shifted his weight in his chair. "It was in the back of the car!"

"Let's go again, George, an' I want all the details."

• • •

Peter was stuffing his work clothes into the overflowing laundry basket when Jane woke up. He rammed the lid on the basket. "We need a washing machine, you know."

She yawned. "Yeah, but the kitchen's too small. Besides, the launderette does it for me, they'll even do the ironing if you want, but it's fifty pence per article. I'll get Mrs. Fry to take a load down in the morning." She yawned again. "What's the time?"

"It's nearly six. I've got some bad news." He sat down beside her. "Well, not bad news for me, but for you, maybe! It must be telepathy . . . You know, after you said Joey could stay, Marianne called. She's bringing him over to stay the night. I didn't even have to ask, she suggested it."

"That's OK! What time's he coming?"

Peter shrugged. "Oh, about seven-thirty. Look, you don't have to do anything."

Jane freaked. "Is she bringing him? I mean, will she come in?"

He shrugged again. "Look, I can take him for a hamburger, he'll be no problem."

"Bollocks! Go down to the corner Indian, they're still open, and get some fish fingers. Kids like fish fingers, and baked beans, and Mars bars . . . No, tell you what, Smarties. I'll make up the spare bed while you're gone."

"It's already done, and I've put that Anglepoise lamp by the bed, he sleeps with a light on."

"OK, I'll wash my hair and get dolled up."

"You don't have to, he's only six, for Chrissake! He won't care what you look like."

"Ah, but Marianne will be looking me over, and I want to make an impression. After all, I'm the Other Woman!"

"Not quite!"

"Oh, go on, get going . . ."

Jane rolled up the newspaper he had left on the bed and whacked him on the head with it, then dashed to the bathroom. Joey would be arriving soon, and she wanted to be ready.

At Southampton Row, Moyra Henson had been interviewed over and over again. She gave Marlow a perfect alibi and wouldn't be budged; he was at home, she insisted, as he had said in his own statement. He had been at home watching television with her. Marlow had not left the flat all evening, and they had gone to bed together.

When she was finally let go, DI Burkin was ordered back to her flat to impound Marlow's car, a brown, automatic three-liter Mark III Rover. He took two officers with him and gave Moyra a lift home.

She kept up a constant stream of abuse all the way back in the patrol car, sitting between the two officers. They didn't say a word. Burkin, uncomfortable in the front seat with his long legs cramped against the glove compartment, was also silent, though Moyra's voice was beginning to grate on his nerves and he would be glad when they got shot of her.

There was no sign of the Rover; it was not in the parking bay or anywhere in the vicinity of the flats. Sullen and uncooperative, Moyra accused the police of stealing it themselves.

As she shampooed her hair under the hot water, all Jane could think of was how John Shefford had done her out of a murder case. She had to make an effort to shake herself out of it, she was becoming obsessed. Before she knew it, Peter was back from the shop.

He yelled that he'd got a few extras. He opened the bathroom door.

"I got a chocolate cake, that one you like. It needs defrosting so I've left it on the draining board, OK?"

"Yep, just give me a few minutes to get my glad-rags on and I'll set the table."

But by the time she had dressed and dried her hair, Peter had done it all. Jane shrieked that she had wanted the best china, and started collecting the plates. Peter caught hold of her.

"Hey, this is just fine! Don't put out the best stuff, he's liable to smash something."

"Do I look OK?"

He held her at arm's length. "Yeah, nice blouse, looks Victorian."

"Well, it's not, it's cheap Laura Ashley, so I bought two, but they're my best!"

She was wearing a full skirt from Next and a pair of red suede shoes she had never worn before; every time she had put them on she had felt they were a bit too flash, so they were pristine, not a scuff in sight. It tickled Peter that she was making such an effort, even down to perfume.

When the doorbell rang Jane flushed, and he grinned. "Just relax, she'll only stay a minute."

Jane hovered near the kitchen while Peter opened the door. Joey flew into his arms, yelling, "Dad! Dad!" Peter swung him up and kissed him, then put him down, but Joey hugged his dad's legs.

Jane peered at the door, expecting the ex-wife. First came a huge bag, large enough for Joey to stay two months, then a box of toys. Finally Marianne's back was visible.

She spoke to someone who was invisible to Jane. "I won't be a sec, darling!"

Peter's face was like stone. He had not even acknowledged Marianne's new husband, his old friend.

Marianne was wearing a short, frilly evening dress. Her blond, shoulder-length hair was the type that novelists describe as silky, a real shampoo advert. To Jane's surprise she seemed much younger than her thirty-eight years.

"Hi, Pete, I've brought everything he could possibly need, and a lot he might not . . ."

Peter turned to introduce Jane. "Jane, this is Marianne."

"Hi, nice to meet you, it's good of you to have Joey."

"Oh, that's OK, nice to meet you." She bent down to the little boy, who still clung to his father's legs. "And you must be Joey? You know what we've got? Fish fingers, do you like fish fingers?"

"What else have you got?"

"Chocolate cake, you want some? Yes? Come on, then, let me show you the kitchen."

She held out a hand to Joey, who shied away at first, but then he edged forward and gripped her hand tightly. "I got a new Revenge of the Joker mask!" he confided.

"Have you? Is that from Batman, then?"

Joey nodded. Anxious to get away from Marianne's critical gaze, Jane smiled and said, "Would you like a drink, Marianne?"

"No, Steve is waiting . . ."

Duty done, Jane and Joey scuttled into the kitchen, but Jane could hear every word through the thin door. She showed Joey the cake box, opened it and reached into the top cupboard for a plate.

Marianne smiled and tossed her streaked, blond hair back. She leaned confidentially towards Pete.

"Pete, I'm pregnant." She gave him a long, direct look.

Peter swallowed. "It's not . . ." He glanced nervously toward the kitchen.

"Who knows? Anyway, I really appreciate this. You know what I was like in the early stages with Joey, I'm so sick every morning, awful."

He pulled himself together. "You look OK!"

"Well, it's all show. Underneath this I'm white as a sheet and getting hideously fat." She wasn't; as far as Peter could recall she hadn't even put on much weight with Joey. Marianne went on, "She's not at all what I expected! Is it working out?"

He nodded, and glanced again towards the kitchen door. "You'd better go, I don't want him getting upset."

"Oh, he's fine, and I should say goodbye to . . . what's her name?"

"Jane." Again Peter looked towards the kitchen door. "Jane! Marianne's leaving!"

• • •

The partly defrosted cake was halfway to the plate when it slipped off the bread knife and back into the box, showering Jane in the process. Peter opened the door to see her covered in chocolate and cream, trying in vain to wipe it off with a tea towel.

"Bit of an accident! Good to meet you, Marianne, hope you have a nice dance."

"Oh, it's not a dance, just a small dinner party."

Jane covered her astonishment with a smile. If she had got herself done up in a dress as glitzy as that, it would have been for a ball at the very least.

Joey kissed his mother, apparently unperturbed at her leaving, then ran back to the kitchen to stick his fingers in the blobs of chocolate and lick them.

As the door closed behind Marianne, Jane cocked her head to one side. "So I wasn't what she expected, huh? Next time I'll borrow a WPC's hat!"

There was a crash from the kitchen as the entire chocolate cake, box and all, fell to the floor. Joey looked crestfallen, expecting to be punished, but Jane just looked at the mess on the floor and handed Joey a spoon.

"OK, let's have tea!"

It was eleven-thirty when Shefford completed his interrogation of George Marlow. He discussed the results briefly with Arnold Upcher; he was sure he had enough evidence to charge Marlow. Upcher, tired himself, pursed his lips and gave a small shrug.

"Then if you feel you have the evidence, Inspector, there is little I can do. But he's been here since early afternoon, that means you've got twenty-four hours. You will, of course, inform me if you go for extra time?"

Shefford was confident that he could charge Marlow without having to present all his evidence to a magistrate and beg for the statutory three days' delay to consolidate his case, or "three-day lay-down", as it was known. Exhausted though he was, and a little punchy, he was still going strong. His main concern was to get the statements transcribed from the tapes.

Upcher, needing time to review Marlow's situation, had said little as he took his leave of Shefford. He knew intuitively that something was wrong, but until he had time to digest the case he wouldn't even contemplate discussing it.

None of it made sense; Marlow was a handsome, attractive male, a man with a good, steady relationship at home. He was popular, he had a job that he thoroughly enjoyed and which brought him good money and his employers had even held it open for him when he was convicted of attempted rape.

Upcher had succeeded in getting the burglary charge dropped, and in Marlow's defense at the trial he had played heavily upon the confusion about which party had made the initial approach, whether both of them had been drunk—they had been seen in the same bar, and Marlow's claim that she had led him on and subsequently refused him had rung true. In Upcher's opinion the victim was a very disturbed woman whose evidence was unreliable, and he had been shattered by the verdict. Not just from a professional point of view; his relationship with Marlow was good, he actually liked the man and believed him to be innocent.

Marlow had taken it well, although Upcher was surprised that he had requested his representation for this, a much more serious charge. He had borne Upcher no grudge about losing the case, and had even admitted that, drunk or sober, he should not have forced himself on the woman, even though he had truly believed it was what she wanted. He had said, with a rueful smile, "I'll never drink more than my limit again, so I suppose some good'll come out of it. I didn't hurt her though, Arnold, she made that up, the cops got it wrong."

Was Marlow a rapist and a murderer? Upcher thought not, and could not believe he had misjudged the man to such an extent. The question occupied his thoughts all the way back to his Queen's Gate flat.

The Arnold Upchers of this world are expensive, and anyone seeing the tall, angular man in the hand-tailored suit parking his dark green Jaguar in the residents' bay could have been forgiven for mistaking him for the famous conductor who had once lived in the elegant service block a stone's throw from Hyde Park. With the remote control he locked his car and set the alarm, allowing the chill night air to clear his head. By the time he reached his door, Upcher was convinced that the police had got it wrong again. Marlow was innocent, and he would prove it.

Jane crawled to bed at midnight. She had exhausted her stock of stories before Joey finally fell asleep, from the three little pigs to a strange mixture of Batman confronting the Ninja Turtles.

Peter was sitting up waiting for her. He flipped the bedclothes back and patted the mattress. "Come in, my beauty! And tell me a story . . ."

She snuggled into bed and gave him a blow-by-blow description of the goings-on at the police station.

"They were like kids playing at cops and robbers! I don't know what they were up to, but they stopped me working. They've got a nice juicy murder that should have been my case, and you know what I've got instead? A dyspeptic accountant who's had his bloody case adjourned four times in a row! Last time I had to wait at court all morning like a prat until he sent in some fictitious doctor's note, and then I was told to go away. Next thing, the little sod'll up and leave the country—I would, in his position. He owes ten years' income tax and VAT. I've got to know the little pest so well over the past three months that I can tell you what he'll be eating for breakfast, and even when I suggested that another adjournment would be. . . . Am I boring you?"

Peter smiled. He had only been half-listening.

She closed her eyes. "I don't think I could manage another sentence, I'm so tired . . . Oh, God, am I tired!"

Peter switched the bedside light off and reached for her, wanting to draw her close, but she muttered, "I'm afraid I'm too knackered . . . anyway, haven't you had enough for one day? Book me in for tomorrow night, OK?" She was fast asleep as she finished speaking.

Peter lay awake for about ten minutes, then put the light back on to read his book. Jane started to snore and he gently eased her onto her side. She gave a little grunt and then a pathetic, "Sorry . . . I'm sorry . . ."

John Shefford was dog-tired by the time he arrived home, but his brain was ticking like a bomb. The events of the day kept repeating themselves like a newsreel in his head and he had to drink half a bottle of Scotch before he felt the dark clouds gathering to cushion him to sleep.

It seemed only a moment before the alarm woke him. His head throbbed and he took four aspirin before he could get out of bed, crunching them between his teeth and hoping that they'd reach the parts that screamed for numbness.

Sheila had his breakfast ready. As she dished it up she reminded him of his promise about the clown for Tom's party. She had wrapped the presents and heaped them on the breakfast table, where Tom had found them at the crack of dawn, and he was beside himself, in a fever of excitement. They had both been touched by the lads' whip-round for Tom, which they had presented in cash in a large Metropolitan Police envelope to be put into his Post Office savings account.

By seven, Shefford was none too happy. He tried to show enthusiasm, but he was getting ratty trying to eat his breakfast with one hand and fend off his son's new boxing gloves with the other. His nagging headache wouldn't shift, and he had another three aspirin with his coffee. Sheila was still going on about the clown, and he gave his solemn oath that not only would there be a clown but that he would perform magic acts that would silence even Tom.

The little lad had started boxing his sister, and her screams cut through Shefford's head like a knife. Sheila removed his half-eaten scrambled eggs.

"I'm not expecting you to be here, that's why the clown's important. God forbid I should ask you to do anything so normal as to be home at half past five with Tom's godfather for his party, it'd be an act of madness on my part . . ."

"Look, sweetheart, maybe I will make it, if things go well. We had a hell of a breakthrough yesterday; we've got a suspect and I think we can charge him. If we can do it this afternoon I can get home, and Bill's promised to dress up, how's that?"

Sheila screwed up her face and snorted. "Haw, haw, promises, promises! And would you take those gloves off him, and tell him they can only be worn under supervision. I never wanted him to have them in the first place . . ."

Shefford crooked his finger at Tom, who shadow-boxed up to him, ducking and diving as his father had taught him.

"OK, Tom, off with the gloves. The rule's been laid down by the boss, you only use them when I'm around, OK? So give me a quick jab-jab, and a left hook before I go."

Tom was fast and managed to clip his father on the nose. Sheila laughed, but Shefford's eyes watered and he grabbed the gloves, pulling them off as the telephone began to ring.

"Daddy, it's for you!"

Shefford listened to Felix Norman with difficulty while his daughter wound the phone cord around her neck and Tom raced up and down the hall with his rugger ball, weaving around the defense—his father—and scoring a try in the kitchen doorway.

It was Norman's habit to get to the lab at seven each morning to escape the rush hour, though rumor had it that he was more concerned about avoiding his wife, as he was invariably found there late each night.

"What in God's name's going on there?" he yelled.

Shefford glared at his son and pointed in the direction of the kitchen. This gesture was famous in the household and was always obeyed. His daughter jabbed her lethally sharp elbow in his balls as she untangled herself from the curly cord and he grimaced, giving her a good whack on the back of the head, which had no effect at all. She hurtled after her brother, whooping at the top of her voice.

"OK, sorry about that, Felix old mate, but it's Tom's birthday. No, he got the ball last year, this year it's boxing gloves . . ." He reached automatically for his cigarettes.

"Noisy little sod's a real chip off the old block . . . Well, wish him happy birthday from me. How's your suspect measure up, by the way? Is he right-handed?"

Shefford sucked on his cigarette. "Yep . . . How's this for size; he's five feet ten and a half, well-built, looks like he works out."

On the other end of the line, Felix puffed at his cigar. When the two men were together in one room they created such a dense fog that they were known as the Danger Zone. "I'd say, John boy, you're a lucky sod. By the way, I was talking to Willy last night. Did he mention to you that he reckons there's not enough blood in that room?"

"You mean she wasn't killed there?"

"It's his department, but I'd say he's probably right."

The press release that morning said little, just that a known prostitute had been murdered. Della had no family and no one volunteered any information about her movements. It was the same story all round; none of Della's friends and associates the police had contacted so far had seen her for weeks. Of ten residents of the house who had given statements, not one could say when they last saw her. Mrs. Salbanna had been staying at her daughter's to help with the children while her newest grandchild made an appearance, and had not been home much for several weeks. Anyway, Della had been avoiding her for months because of the rent she owed. It was as if she had never existed, and, sadly, no one seemed to care.

By eight-thirty Shefford was at his desk, going over the typed-up statements from the previous day. He also had the full details he'd requested on Marlow's previous conviction. As he sifted through the information an alarm bell rang in his head, the same as on the previous day. Something was trying to breakthrough . . .

Sergeant Otley brought coffee and doughnuts on a tray.

"Otters, there's something niggling me about this guy. Can you check something out for me, but tiptoe it? A girl was murdered in Oldham when I was there; get me the information on her, but keep schtum."

Otley licked sugar off his top lip and replied, "Yeah, what you think, he maybe did others?"

Shefford nodded. "Yeah. Watch out for me on this, I knew the one in Oldham too, know what I mean?"

Otley sucked jam and sugar off his fingers and carried his beaker of coffee to his own desk. He inched a drawer open and brought out Della Mornay's diary.

"What do you want done with this?" he asked.

Shefford bit into his second sugar-coated bun. "Hang on to it, old son, I'll check it out later. I'm goin' down to the cells, then upstairs, give the boss everythin' we've got. I reckon he'll give us the go-ahead to charge the bastard. If we finish it, you gotta hire a fuckin' clown's outfit!"

Laughing, Otley replaced the diary in his desk drawer. He called out as Shefford left, "Eh, Big John, there's two hundred quid riding on us from DCI Tibbs' bunch, says we can't beat Paxman's record!" Otley could hear Shefford's big, bellowing laugh all the way down the corridor.

Shefford was still laughing while he waited for the cell door to be opened. He wanted to have a look at Marlow; he always did this just before he charged a suspect. There was something in a murderer's eyes, he had never been wrong yet.

Freshly shaved and showered, the prisoner looked somehow different this morning. Shefford was slightly taken aback; there was an eagerness to Marlow, a light in his eyes when he saw who it was at the door.

"Can I go?" Marlow asked.

Without speaking, Shefford shook his head slowly.

Jane Tennison parked her car with difficulty. DCI Shefford's dented and filthy Granada was angled across his space and hers and she had a tight squeeze to get out of the driving seat. Her pleated tartan skirt brushed against the Granada and she dusted it off in disgust, hoping that this would be the last time she would have to wear her court outfit for a while, unless the nasty little accountant engineered yet another stay of execution.

In the female locker room, she hung her smart black blazer with the brass buttons in her locker, straightened her high-necked Victorian-style blouse, ran a comb through her short fair hair and slicked some gloss on her lips, all in a matter of moments. She rinsed her hands at the row of washbasins and thumped the soap dispenser, which was empty as usual. Her irritation deepened when she caught sight of Maureen Havers, wasting time tittering with someone at the open lockerroom door and fiddling with the Alice band she often wore to keep her thick red hair off her pretty face. As she talked she whisked it off, shook her hair and replaced it, still giggling, then shut the door.

Havers started to sing as she opened her locker, then stopped short.

"Mornin', guv, didn't realize you were here."

Tennison dried her hands and stepped back from the mirror. "D'you think this skirt could do with being shorter?" she asked.

Havers peered around her locker door. "Looks OK to me. That shirt suits you."

"I'm in court this morning, remember?"

"Ahhh, it's Cary Grant Philpott, is it? In that case you'd better take the skirt up about a foot, keep him awake!"

A short time later, Havers breezed into the office with the pile of photocopying Tennison had asked her to do.

"We'll have to wait, the machine's in use."

Tennison exploded. "Tell whoever's on the bloody thing to get off it, I must have the stuff before I go to court!"

Havers beamed good-naturally. She was used to Tennison's outbursts and knew better than to answer back. She had once, and regretted it; Tennison had a very sharp tongue. A perfectionist herself, Tennison expected the same diligence and professionalism from everyone else. Her pinched, angry look warned Havers that she was brewing a real explosion.

"I'll nip down and see if it's free, boss, OK?"

"Like now, Maureen, would be a good idea!"

Havers couldn't resist a little dig. "OK, boss, but DCI Shefford's team have sort of got priority. They arrested someone yesterday for the Della Mornay murder, so the Paxman record's being challenged again. DCT Shefford's lads have started the countdown."

Tennison frowned. The name of the victim, Della Mornay, rang a bell, but before she could ask any questions Havers had ducked out of the door. She chewed her lips, drummed her fingers on the desk. "Come on, why do I know that name . . . ?" She remembered, then; in the Flying Squad two years ago she had brought Della Mornay in for questioning, but for the life of her she couldn't remember what the case was. Something to do with a pimp who had beaten up one of his girls . . . Della was a tough little bitch, blond and rather pretty. She had refused to give evidence against the man. The fact that she had once interviewed the victim made Tennison all the more angry that she had not been given a chance to handle the case. Mike Kernan, the Superintendent, was going to hear about this.

Tennison closed her office door and turned just as Sergeant Otley bumped into her.

"Oh, sorry, ma'am."

"I hear you've got a suspect, that right?" She meant to sound just interested, but she could not disguise the sarcasm.

"Yep, brought him in yesterday lunchtime. Word's out that the ink won't be dry on the warrant before the boss charges him. The DNA result was bloody marvelous."

"Yeah, and such good timing! I heard there wasn't much else happening."

Otley shrugged. This was the one he didn't like, the know-all who had been prowling around for the past eighteen months. He had studiously avoided any contact with her, just in case he was roped in to work with her.

"I wouldn't say that, ma'am. The team's pretty tough, John Shefford drives us hard."

She turned, without agreeing, and he watched her push through the swing doors in her neat jacket and skirt. As the doors slammed behind her, he gave her the finger.

Kernan toyed uneasily with a felt-tipped pen as he listened to Tennison's complaint. He had never liked her, had been against her joining AMIT from the word go, but she had been more or less forced on him. She had more experience than at least one of the other DCIs, who was already on his second case. He cleared his throat and replaced the cap carefully on the pen.

"You want a transfer, is that what this is about?"

"No, I want to be given a chance. I was available for the Mornay case, but DCI Shefford was called in from leave to take it over. I want to know why I have had not so much as a sniff of anything since I've been here."

Kernan opened his desk diary and noted that he had a lunch appointment before replying, "It was my decision. Shefford knows the area and he once arrested the victim on a prostitution charge. She was also one of his informers . . ."

"I knew the victim too, sir. I've been checking my old records and I brought her in for questioning two years ago . . ."

"I'm sorry, I was unaware of that . . ."

"Are you saying I would have got the investigation if you had been aware of it, sir?"

"Look, I'll be honest. Shefford's one of my best men . . ."

"I know that, sir, but he's just finished that big case and he had been given two days' leave. It was a long and difficult case, he needed to rest. I could easily have attended the court session today and handled the investigation, but I was overlooked. All I want to know is, why, and is this going to continue?"

Kernan looked at his watch. "As you said, you had to be in court. According to the roster you were not available, but when you are you will have your chance, along with the other four officers . . ."

"DCI McLear is on a murder case right now, sir. He has nowhere near my experience, he came here six months after me. I notice his desk isn't loaded with petty fraud and tax evasion cases. I have had nothing else since I arrived."

"Look, Jane, if you want a transfer then put in for it through the right channels."

She was spitting mad, but managed to control herself. "I don't want a transfer, I want to do the work I have been trained for, and I want you to give me your word that I will not be overlooked again."

Kernan gave her the same speech he had spouted at her the last time she had complained, and she sighed. She had the distinct feeling that he couldn't wait to get her out of the office. She looked down at her shoes and seethed as he continued, "It takes time, Jane. If you are not prepared to wait, then perhaps you should consider asking to be transferred. As I have said to you before, we all appreciate your record, and your obvious abilities . . ."

"But you are not prepared to let me put them into practice, right?"

"Wrong. Just bide your time, don't rush things."

"Rush, sir? I've been here eighteen months."

"I've said all I intend saying at this point. I am sorry you feel the way you do, but until a case comes up that I feel is right for you, then . . ."

"Then I carry on as before, is that what you were going to say, Mike? Oh, come on, don't fob me off again. You gave me the same speech last time. You know I've been treated unfairly; all I'm asking for is a chance to show you, show everyone here, what I'm capable of."

"You'll get it, I give you my word." Kernan looked pointedly at his watch. "Now, I'm sorry, but I have to get on. Just be patient, I'm sorry I can't be more positive, and your turn will come."

She walked to the door, depressed that she had failed yet again to convince him.

"Thank you for your time!"

As the door closed behind Tennison, Kernan leaned back in his chair. A few more months and she would leave of her own accord. He had never liked working with women and knew that his men felt the same way. All the same, he knew she was right. She was a highly qualified officer, it was just something about her, about all the high-ranking women he had come across. Maybe it was simply the fact that she was a woman.

Tennison had missed breakfast in the rush to get Joey ready, but her anger seemed to have sharpened her appetite. She decided to have a bite to eat in the canteen.

She ate alone, eavesdropping on the rowdy conversation from the next table. DI Burkin was cracking a joke about somebody being trapped on a mountain when the "bing-bong" went. He and DI Haskons were wanted in Administration. They stood up, laughing. Young DC Dave Jones, newly transferred from Cardiff, turned from the counter with his loaded tray to see the two DIs heading towards the exit.

"You want me along?"

Burkin pointed a finger and Jones's eager face fell. "You always interrupt my jokes, Daffy. Give yourself fifteen, then get down to the Incident Room."

Tennison watched in amazement as Jones tackled the vast amount of food he had piled on his tray: sausages, eggs, chips, baked beans, a heap of toast and two puddings with custard.

"Brunch, is it?" she asked, pleasantly.

"No, ma'am, I missed my breakfast because I had to go over to the labs for the guv'nor." He stuffed a huge forkful of food into his mouth.

"You're on Shefford's team, then?"

Unable to speak, Jones nodded vigorously.

"I hear he's going to charge the suspect this morning, is that right?"

Jones wiped his mouth on a paper serviette. "Yes, ma'am, he and Sergeant Otley are with the Super now. It looks good, the Sarge said."

Tennison sipped her coffee. "Have they found the car? I hear your suspect says his car's been stolen?"

Jones had timed his eating badly; again, he could only nod. He was relieved when the "bing-bong" went; this time it was for Tennison.

She drained her coffee cup and picked up her bag of groceries. Passing Jones, she smiled. "See you."

"Yes, ma'am."

Several officers, some of them uniformed, acknowledged her as she made her way to the door. There was an air of embarrassment; no one seemed to like her, but her rank of DCI demanded respect.

Jones waited until she had left before he burped loudly, which was received with a smatter of applause, then he continued eating at a frightening rate. He didn't want to miss the big moment. The Sarge had told him it was a dead cert that they'd charge Marlow, and Paxman's record would be smashed.

It was Maureen Havers who had put out the call for Tennison, to tell her that the photocopier was now out of order, so she was still unable to do the stuff Tennison needed for court. She asked if she should take it to another station or wait until their own machine was repaired.

Tennison dropped her bag on the desk. "I don't believe this place, can't they get a bloody mechanic to fix it? What the hell's wrong with it, anyway?"

"Someone used the wrong type of paper and it's all jammed inside. We're trying to find the guilty party, ma'am, but it's really fouled up this time."

Tennison rolled up her shirt-sleeves. "Right, I'll fix it myself, at least it'll keep me occupied for a while. We'll take all the copying, and that stuff on my desk is for the shredder, let's do something useful . . ."

With their arms full of paper, they passed the open door of the Incident Room. The men were standing around in groups, with DI Burkin in the center telling another of his shaggy dog stories.

"I hear they're charging the suspect. You heard anything, Maureen?"

Havers had to jog to keep up with her. "Yes, ma'am, they'll break the record. There's a booze-up in the pub, whole station'll be there. Kitty's over a hundred and fifty quid already."

Tennison squatted to peer inside the photocopier. "Fucking thing's jammed all right, look at the mess! How do you open it up?"

Havers knelt beside her to read the instructions on the side of the machine. "It says here, lift lever A, release spring . . ."

Tennison pushed her aside. "I'll do it, get out of my light . . . Now then, pull what where?"

She yanked the lever and the machine split itself in two. "Oh, shit, now what?"

"How about waiting for the mechanic, ma'am?"

Tennison froze her with a look. "I've started, so I'll continue . . ."

For what seemed an age, the only sounds in the office were the ticking of the clock and the flick as Kernan turned the pages of Marlow's file.

"Christ, what a stroke of luck, John, bloody marvelous. What about the blood on the jacket?" He looked from Shefford to Otley, approvingly.

Shefford grimaced. He had a weird tingling in his left arm, all the way to his fingertips. He flexed his hand, rubbed the wrist.

"Willy's working his butt off. Should . . . should come through any time now . . ." The pain was shooting down his arm now, and his chest felt as if it was being crushed . . . "It was the size of a pinprick, they're waiting for it to expand at the labs, then we can check . . . Oh, Jesus . . ."

The pain was so bad it made Shefford fight for air. Kernan looked up, concerned. "Are you OK, John?"

"I dunno," Shefford gasped, "I've got . . . like a cramp in my arm . . ."

He went rigid as a new spasm of pain hit him. He snorted, and Kernan saw blood oozing from his nose. There was a terrible look of fear in his eyes.

The pain seemed to be blowing him apart, like the bomb he had felt ticking inside his head. It was blowing up, he was blowing up! Rubbing his arm frantically, he snorted again and the blood poured down his chin. Then he pitched forward, cracking his head on the edge of Kernan's desk.

The Super was already picking up the phone, shouting for a doctor, an ambulance, as Otley grabbed Shefford and tried to ease him back into his chair. But the man was so big that Otley staggered under his weight.

Shefford's body suddenly relaxed and his head lolled on Otley's shoulder. Otley cradled him in his arms, shouting hysterically for an ambulance . . . Kernan ran round the desk to help him lower Shefford to the floor. They loosened his tie, opened his shirt, and all the while Otley was saying over and over, "S'all right, John, everything's OK, just stay calm . . . Don't move, guv, it's all being taken care of, ambulance is on its way . . ."

The photocopier throbbed into life and shot out three crumpled sheets of sooty paper. Tennison gave a satisfied sigh and stood up, brushing at the black specks on her hands.

"Right, Maureen, try it with a sheet we want to shred, just in case it eats it."

It seemed that a herd of elephants suddenly charged down the corridor outside. Tennison opened the door and stepped back to avoid being trampled as the stretcher-bearers raced along. They passed too swiftly for Tennison to see who their patient was under the oxygen mask.

The corridor suddenly filled with people, propping doors open, running to follow the stretcher. Word went round like wildfire; John Shefford had collapsed.

Tennison hurried into her office to watch the ambulance in the street below, but found the window space already occupied by two WPCs. She slammed the door.

"Get away from the window, come on, move it!"

WPC Hull whipped round. "Sorry, ma'am, but it's DCI Shefford . . ."

"Well, peering out of the window isn't going to help him! Come on, move over, lemme have a squint!"

Tennison could see the ambulance with its doors open, the stretcher being loaded. She turned back to the room.

"OK, back to work. The copier's been repaired, and we may not have a lot of work to do but we might as well clear the desk. You never know, I might be needed!"

She meant it as a joke, and it was taken as one, because they didn't know then that Shefford would never regain consciousness. He was dead on arrival at hospital.

When the panic had died down, Tennison sat alone in her office and pondered . . . She was sorry Shefford was ill, of course she was, but someone had to take over the investigation. This time Kernan had to give her the job; everyone else on the rota was busy.

Deeply shocked, Otley shut himself in the gents' toilets and wept. He couldn't face anyone, and was unable to carry the news back to the men waiting in the Incident Room. He had lost the best friend he had ever had, his only real friend.

When he was able to face the men he found them sitting in stunned silence. He tried to tell them more, but all he could say was, "It's Tom's birthday today, it's his son's birthday . . . I bought him a magic set, and . . ." He wandered over to his desk. There at the side was the big package, the train set he had taken so long to choose. He stood staring down at it. The men, deeply shocked, didn't know what to say.

Otley's voice was barely audible. "We were going to set it up, surprise Tom. It's from Hamley's . . ."

DI Burkin, head and shoulders taller than his skipper, slipped an arm around him. The big officer's tears were streaming down his face, but Otley had no more tears. He clenched his fists, shrugged Burkin away.

"Right, let's nail this bastard Marlow! We do it for our guv'nor, we break the fucking record, agreed?"

It was down to Superintendent Kernan to visit Sheila Shefford. Otley had agreed to accompany him, but Kernan didn't know if it was such a good idea, the man was so distressed. In the end he decided to take DI Burkin along. No matter which way you looked at it, it was tragic.

Anticipating a harrowing time with Sheila and her family, Kernan's mood was not receptive. When Jane Tennison asked for a few minutes with him his first reaction was to refuse, but she had insisted it was important.

When he realized what she wanted he stared at her in disbelief. He was still in shock himself and he turned on her, ordering her out of his office. But she stood her ground, fists clenched.

"Look, please, I'm sorry if I appear heartless, but all I am doing is offering to finish the investigation. John was ready to charge the suspect and someone has to take over, he's not going to be well enough. We can't hold Marlow much longer, we'll have to apply for a three-day lay-down, but either way someone has to take . . ."

Kernan gripped her tightly by the elbow. "The man's not even cold! For God's sake, I can't make any decisions now. When I do, you will be the first to hear. Now *get out of my office* . . ."

"Cold?" She stared at him. "He's *dead*? But he can't be . . ."

"I didn't realize you hadn't been told. John was dead when he reached the hospital. Now will you get out?"

Appalled, she shook her head as if to clear it, drew a deep breath, then plunged on, "But you will have to make a decision, sir, and I am offering to step in right now. I can familiarize myself with the case tonight, and if charges . . ."

"I said I would consider your offer, Jane."

"No, sir, you said you couldn't make any decisions right now. I think, however, a decision has to be made, and fast. You can't back out of this one, you know I am here. I am available and I am qualified. Someone's got to prove that bloody survey's a load of bullshit. You pass me over on this one and I warn you . . ."

Kernan's face twisted with barely controlled anger. "You don't warn me, Chief Inspector, is that clear? Now you and your feminist jargon can get out of my bloody office before I physically throw you out. A friend, a close friend, and associate of mine died in this room this afternoon, and I am just on my way to tell his wife and children. Now is not the time . . ."

"When is the time, sir? Because we don't have any to spare—if Marlow's not charged very soon he will have to be released. I am deeply sorry for what happened to John, please don't insult me by thinking otherwise, but at the same time someone has to—"

"Please leave *now*. Don't tell me my job. I will not be forced into making a decision I will regret at a later date. Please leave my office."

Maureen Havers hiccuped through her tears and Tennison put an arm around her shoulders.

"Do you want to go home, Maureen love? You can if you like, there's not much to do."

Havers wiped her eyes. "I'm sorry, I'm sorry, but he was always so full of life, and only today I heard him laughing, you know that big laugh of his . . . He said . . . he said he'd beaten Paxman's record!"

Leaving it that Havers could go home if she felt like it, Tennison left for court.

Superintendent Kernan called a two o'clock meeting with Commander Geoff Trayner to discuss the situation, particularly Tennison's request to take over the Marlow case. Neither man liked the idea, even though the file on the desk proved she was fully qualified and her exboss in the Flying Squad had given her a glowing recommendation.

Tennison had been with the Flying Squad for five years, and had taken a lot of flak from the men. Unlike two of her female colleagues in a similar position she had stayed her course. Her report noted that she had been offered a position training female officers because of her previous experience working with rape victims and her instigation of many changes which had been adopted by rape centers all over the country. She had turned the offer down, not wishing to go back into uniform, and had subsequently been transferred to AMIT. She was, as they were well aware, the only female DCI attached to a murder squad; with someone of her record it would be very difficult to bring someone in from outside to take over.

Kernan drummed his fingers on the desk. "The men won't like it, you know that, but as far as I can see we don't really have a choice. There's no one free on AMIT except her. I've checked locally, and of the usuals I know Finley's in Huddersfield, Smith and Kelvin are still tied up on that shooting last week in Shepherd's Bush . . . And she's got a mouth on her, I don't want her creating a stink. She as good as threatened to resign if she was over-looked again."

"She's one of these bloody feminists, I don't want any flak from that angle. We'll give her a trial run, see what happens, but if she puts a foot out of line we'll have her transferred and get her out of our hair. Agreed?"

Kernan nodded and slapped Tennison's file closed. "I'll get her in to see you, and I'll break it to the men." He pressed a button on his intercom and requested Tennison's immediate presence.

"DCI Tennison's in court today, sir," his secretary replied.

"Hell, I'd forgotten . . . Let everyone know I want her the moment she comes in."

Jane Tennison was lucky for once. The jury was out by two-fifteen and she was away. Still upset by John Shefford's death, she drove straight to the building site where Peter was working.

Peter was in his hut, talking to one of his workmen. Jane held herself rigid and waited until the man was gone, then rushed to Peter and sobbed her heart out.

It was a while before she was calm enough to make much sense, but he eventually pieced the events of the day together. He put his arms around her; it felt so good to have him to come to that she started crying all over again.

"You know, from everything you've said, this Shefford was well-liked, it must be a shock to everyone. Perhaps you should have given it a few days."

He bent to kiss her cheek, but she turned away. "You don't understand," she snapped, "Marlow will be released tomorrow unless we charge him. If they want extra time they have to have someone to take it before the magistrate, someone who knows what's going on. If the magistrate doesn't think there's enough evidence to hold him, he'll refuse the three-day lay-down."

Peter didn't really care if they released Yogi Bear, but he made all the right noises. At last she blew her nose and stood up, hands on hips.

"If those bastards choose someone else to take over, you know what I'll do? I'll quit, I mean it! I'll throw in the towel, because if I don't get the case—I mean, with Shefford dead it leaves only four on the AMIT team, and I know the other three are working, so they'd have to bring in someone from outside. And if they do, I quit. Then I'll take them to a fucking tribunal and show them all up for the fucking chauvinist pigs they are! Bastard chauvinists, terrified of giving a woman a break because she might just prove better than any of them! I hate the fuckers . . ."

Tentatively, Peter suggested that they go home early, have a relaxing evening, but she shot back at him, "No way, because if they should call me and I'm not hanging by that phone, then the buggers have an excuse."

"Use your bleeper."

She grinned at him, and suddenly she looked like a tousle-headed tomboy, "You're not going to believe this, but I was so pissed off I left it at the station." Then she tilted her head back and roared with laughter. It was a wonderful laugh, and it made him forget the way she had snapped at him.

That was the first time he became aware of the two separate sides of Jane Tennison; the one he knew at home, the other a DCI. Today he'd caught a glimpse of the policewoman, and he didn't particularly like her.

The moment Tennison reached her office the telephone rang. She pounced on it like a hawk. She replaced the receiver a moment later and gave it a satisfied pat. She took a small mirror from her desk drawer and checked her appearance. She suddenly realized that Maureen Havers was sitting quietly in the corner.

"Wish me luck!" she said, and gave Havers a wink as she opened the door.

Havers sat at her neatly organized desk and stared at the closed door. She'd seen Tennison's satisfaction and knew something was going down. *Wish me luck?* She put two and two together and knew that Tennison was going after John Shefford's job. She was disgusted at Tennison's lack of sensitivity; she seemed almost elated.

Havers picked up the phone and dialed her girlfriend in Records. "Guess what, I think my boss is going after Shefford's job . . . Yeah, that's what I thought, real pushy bitch."

3

Otley was the last to arrive in the Incident Room. He apologized to the Super and received a sympathetic pat on the shoulder.

The room was filled with palpable depression; there was a heaviness to every man. Some of them couldn't meet Otley's eyes but stood with heads bent. Only yesterday they had been laughing and joking with their big, burly boss. Shefford had been loved by them all and they took his death hard.

Kernan cleared his throat. "OK, I've gone over all the reports on the Marlow case and it looks in good shape. I think, when I've had time to assess it all, we can go ahead and charge him. But until that decision is made, and I know time is against us, I am bringing in another DCI to take over. You all know Detective Chief Inspector Tennison . . ."

A roar of shock and protest drowned his next words, and he put up a hand for silence. "Now come on, take it easy, just hear me out. As it stands, I reckon we'll have to try for a three-day lay-down, so I want all of you to give Inspector Tennison every assistance possible. Let her familiarize herself with the case, and then we can charge Marlow . . ."

Otley stepped forward. "I'm sorry, sir, but it isn't on. Bring in someone from outside, we don't want her. We've been working as a team for five years, bring in someone we know."

Kernan's face tightened. "Right now she is all I have available, and she is taking over the case at her own request."

"She moved bloody fast, didn't she, sir?" Otley's face twisted with anger and frustration, his hands clenched at his sides.

DI Haskons raised an eyebrow at Otley to warn him to keep quiet. "I think, sir, we all feel the same way. As you said, time is against us."

"She's on the case as from now," Kernan said firmly, unwilling to show his own misgivings. "I'm afraid I can't discuss this further. She will access the charges; just give her all the help you can, and any problems report back to me. Thank you . . ." He got out fast to avoid further argument, but he heard the uproar as he closed the door, heard Otley calling Tennison a two-faced bitch, a cow who couldn't wait to step into a dead man's shoes. Kernan paused outside the room, silently agreeing with him. But the investigation was at such an advanced stage, they wouldn't be stuck with Tennison for long.

The Commander's voice was gruff as he briefly outlined the procedure for Tennison to familiarize herself with the Marlow case and to do everything necessary to ensure that he was charged. He told her abruptly to take it easy with Shefford's team, who had been working together for so long that they would not welcome an outsider. He didn't actually say, "especially a woman," but he hinted as much. "The Superintendent will give you every assistance, so don't be afraid to use him. And . . . good luck!"

"It would help if he could handle the application for the three-day lay-down," Tennison replied, and the Commander agreed.

They shook hands and Tennison said she would do everything within her power to bring the case successfully to court. It was not until she was back in her own office that she congratulated herself, grinning like the Cheshire Cat because, at last, she had done it. She, DCI Tennison, was heading a murder case.

Late that afternoon, still stunned by his guv'nor's death, Bill Otley was clearing Shefford's desk. He collected the family photographs and mementos together and packed them carefully into Shefford's tattered briefcase. Finally he picked up a photo of Tom, his little godson, and looked at it for a long moment before laying it carefully on top of the others.

He snapped the locks on the case, hardly able to believe that John wasn't going to walk in, roaring with laughter, and tell them it was all a joke. His grief consumed him, swamping him in a bitterness he directed towards DCI Tennison, as if she were in some way responsible. He had to blame someone for the hurting, for the loss. He hugged the briefcase to his chest, knowing he now had to face Sheila and the children, he couldn't put it off any longer. Maybe it would be best if he left it till the weekend, and in the meantime he'd keep John's briefcase at the flat along with his shirts and socks . . .

He was still sitting at his desk, holding the case, when DI Burkin looked in.

"She's checking over the evidence, you want to see her?"

Otley shook his head. "I don't even want to be in the same room as that slit-arsed bitch!"

Tennison was ploughing methodically through all the evidence on the Marlow case. The ashtray was piled high and a constant stream of coffee was supplied by WPC Havers. She was just bringing a fresh beaker and a file.

"Deirdre, alias Della, Mornay's Vice record, ma'am. The reason they gave for not sending it before was that King's Cross Vice Squad's computer records are not compatible with Scotland Yard's, or some such excuse."

Flicking through the file, Tennison took out a photograph of Della Mornay and laid it beside the photos of the corpse. She frowned.

"Maureen, get hold of Felix Norman for me and find out how long he'll be there. Then order me a car and tell DC Jones he's driving me. I want to see the body tonight, but I need to interview the landlady first. And ask for another set of dabs from the victim, get them compared with the ones on Della Mornay's file."

Leaving Havers scribbling furiously, she walked out.

All the items from Della Mornay's room that Forensic had finished with had been piled onto a long trestle table. It was a jumble of bags of clothes, bedding and shoes. There was also a handbag, which Tennison examined carefully. She made a note of some ticket stubs, replaced them, then pulled on a pair of rubber gloves and turned to the clothing taken from the victim's body. The bloodstains were caked hard and black. She checked sleeves, hems, seams and labels.

Engrossed in what she was doing, she hardly noticed WPC Havers enter.

"Ma'am? Ma'am, DC Jones is waiting in the car."

Tennison turned her attention to the filthy bedclothes. The smell alone was distasteful, and she wrinkled her nose.

"Dirty little tart . . . Tell Jones I'll be with him in a few minutes. And tell all of Shefford's team that I want them in the Incident Room at nine sharp tomorrow morning—all of them, Maureen, understand?"

DC Jones sat in the driving seat of the plain police car. He had left the rear door open for DCI Tennison, but she climbed in beside him.

"Right, Milner Road first. What's your first name?"

"David, ma'am."

"OK, Dave, put your foot down. I've got a hell of a schedule."

• • •

Della's room was still roped off. Tennison looked around and noted the fine dusting left by the Scenes of Crime people, then used the end of her pencil to open the one wardrobe door that still clung to its hinges. She checked the few remaining items of clothing, then sat on the edge of the bed, opened her briefcase and thumbed through a file.

DC Jones watched as she closed the case and turned to him. "Will you bring me two pairs of shoes . . ."

She spent a considerable time looking over the dressing table, checking the make-up, opening the small drawers. By the time she seemed satisfied, Jones' stomach was complaining loudly. He suggested it was time to eat. Tennison paused on her way downstairs and looked back at him.

"I'm OK, but if you can't hold out, go and get yourself something while I interview the landlady."

When Jones got back to the house he found Tennison sitting in the dirty, cluttered kitchen in the basement, listening to Mrs. Salbanna moaning.

"The rents are my living, how long will you need the room for? I could let it right now, you know!"

Tennison replied calmly, "Mrs. Salbanna, I am investigating a murder. As soon as I am satisfied that we no longer need the efficiency, I will let you know. If you wish you can put in a claim for loss of earnings, I'll have the forms sent to you. Now, will you just repeat to me exactly what happened the night you found Della Mornay? You identified her, didn't you?"

"Yes, I've told you twice, yes."

"How well did you know her?"

"How well? You're jokin'," I didn't *know* her. I let a room to her, that's all."

"How often did you see her?"

"As often as I could, to get the rent off her. God forgive me for talking ill of the dead, but that little bitch owed me months in rent. She was always late, and it gets so if you throw her out on the street you'll never get the money back, right? She kept on promising and promising . . ."

"So you saw her recently?"

"No, because she was in and out like a snake. I hadn't seen her for . . . at least a month, maybe longer."

"But you are absolutely sure that it was Della Mornay's body?"

"Who else would it be? I told you all this, I told that big bloke too."

"And that night you didn't hear anything unusual, or see anyone that didn't live here?"

"No, I didn't come home till after eight myself. Then, because I'd had such a time with my daughter—she's had a new baby, and she's already got two, so I've been looking after them . . . Well, by the time I got home I was so exhausted, I went straight to bed. Then I was woken up by the front door banging. I put notices up, but no one pays attention. It started banging, so I got up . . ."

"You didn't see anyone go out? Could someone have just left?"

"I don't know . . . See, it's got a bit of rubber tire tacked on it to try and stop the noise, so if they didn't want to be heard . . . But it was just blowing around in the wind, it was a windy night . . . I told the other man all this."

Tennison closed her notebook. "Thank you for your time, Mrs. Salbanna."

Tennison stopped off at Forensic on her way to view the body, and sat in silence while Willy Chang explained the complex details of the DNA test that had resulted in George Marlow being picked up on suspicion of murder. She looked at the slides.

"There was a big rape and murder case up in Leicester. They did a mass screening, every man in the entire village, and they got him. The semen tests took weeks to match, but in the case of such a rare blood group it's much easier to define. He's an AB secreter and belongs to group two in the PGM tests, so it narrows the field dramatically. We've been doing test runs on a new computerized cross-matching system, just using the rarer blood groups, for experimental purposes. Your man was tested in 1988, and was actually on record."

"So you got a match from the computer, out of the blue?"

"Yes. When we got the read-out it was mayhem in here, it was such a freak piece of luck."

"So the computer is infallible, is it?"

"Not exactly, it'll give you the closest match it can find. We have to confirm the results with our own visual tests on the light-box. Want to see it?"

Tennison was shown two sets of negatives that looked like supermarket bar codes, with certain lines darker than others. The black bands on each matched perfectly. She made some notes, then asked to use a telephone.

She placed a call to her old base at the rape center in Reading and requested the records of all suspected rapists charged as a result of DNA testing. She wanted to see how the judges had reacted, if they had allowed the DNA results to be the mainstay of the evidence.

Felix Norman slammed the phone down as a corpse, covered by a green sheet, was wheeled into the lab. Five students, all masked, gowned and shod in white wellington boots, trailed in after the trolley.

He gestured for them to gather round, then lifted the sheet. "Well, you're in luck, this is a nice fresh 'un. I'm gonna have to leave you for a few minutes, but you can start opening it up without me."

He picked up a clipboard and strode out to where Tennison and Jones were waiting. Greeting them with nothing approaching civility, he led them to the mortuary. At the far end of the rows of drawers he stopped and pulled on a lever, releasing the hinge, and slid out the tray with "D. Mornay" chalked on it.

Before removing the sheet from the body, Norman reeled off a list of injuries from the clipboard, including the number and depth of the stab wounds.

"I hear you had a lucky break with the forensic results. Your suspect has a very rare blood group?"

Tennison nodded, waiting for him to draw the sheet back. He did so slowly, looking at DC Jones' pale face.

The body had been cleaned, the blond hair combed back from her face. The dark bruises remained and the gashes on the head were deep and clear. Tennison frowned, leaning forward.

"Pull her out further, will you?"

Norman drew the drawer out to its fullest extent. Tennison walked around, peering at the dead girl's face, then turned to DC Jones.

"Shefford identified her, didn't he?"

"Yes, ma'am, and her landlady, Mrs. Corinna Salbanna."

Tennison made a note on her pad, walked back again, then leaned in even closer. She stared for a long time before she asked to see the wounds on the torso. Norman pointed out the incisions, then indicated the deep weals on the tops of the arms.

"These seem to indicate that she was strung up. We'll do some tests with weights . . . And here, on her wrists, you can see the marks of the ropes, tied so tightly they left imprints, the mark of her watch strap too, see . . ."

"Where's the cut? Small cut on her hand?"

"Here." He showed Tennison the corpse's right wrist. "Small, but quite deep. Would have bled a fair bit." He continued reading from his notes. "Extensive bruising all over the front of the body, plus a good deal around the genital and anal areas, but nothing on the back or buttocks."

Tennison nodded and again peered closely at the victim's face, then turned to DC Jones.

"I asked for another set of prints, will you make sure they're on the way, and the set from Della Mornay's file."

Jones shifted his weight and muttered that he'd check it out. "We already have a set, ma'am."

Tennison snapped back, "I need another set, and fast."

Norman looked at his watch. "My students are waiting, Inspector."

Tennison was frowning. She turned again to Jones. "Go and check on those prints now, Jones." Then she addressed Felix Norman. "I've got a few more questions I can ask while you work, OK?"

Norman sighed, covered the corpse and closed the drawer while Tennison added to the notes she had made during her inspection, then he led her into the dissection room.

For the next few minutes, Tennison watched as Norman, with apparent relish, helped a student remove the specimen's heart.

"That's it, ease it out . . ."

Jones returned and stood at Tennison's side. "Prints are organized, ma'am."

She ignored him and continued scribbling in her notebook. Jones watched Norman and his students as they worked on. Blood dripped into buckets set at each end of the trolley, and the stains on their gowns and rubber gloves made them appear ghoulish. On one lens of Norman's half-moon spectacles there was a clear fingerprint in blood. DC Jones' stomach turned over.

Tennison seemed intent on her notes. She did not so much as glance at Jones, who hadn't spoken for some time.

"How soon can you do the weight tests? I need to know exactly how she was strung up."

"My dear lady," Felix replied, "we'll do them as quickly as we can, and you'll be the first to hear, though I'd have thought you had enough on your suspect to bang him up for life."

He turned to the student and gave a helping hand as he opened the heart.

"Look at this, Inspector. This poor bugger's veins were so clogged up it's a wonder he lived as long as he did. Classic English breakfast causes this; bacon, fat . . . You like a cooked breakfast, Inspector?"

Tennison glanced around the room; Jones had disappeared. She smiled to herself.

The students clustered around Norman and took notes as he went on, "Liver very dodgy, see just by the size . . . I hear through the grapevine that those wankers over at the labs can't even find the winder from the victim's watch. They've got fifteen square yards of carpet, combing it inch by inch. Right, now let's have a look at his testicles . . . Hmmm, well-endowed gent."

Tennison knew she had as much as she was going to get. "Thank you for your time, Professor Norman. As soon as you can on the—"

"You'll have my report, Inspector, but you should give us the time to do our job properly. And next time, gown-up, you know the rules."

He turned to pierce her with his gimlet eye, as though she were one of his students, but she was gone.

When the Western finished at midnight, Peter switched the television off, poured a fresh cup of black coffee and carried it to the dining area. As he set it down by Jane's elbow she looked up, her eyes red-rimmed with fatigue.

"Thanks, love. I just have to wade through this mound, then I'll come to bed . . ."

"Maybe you'd be better off having a sleep now and getting up early?"

"You must be joking, I'll have to get up at five as it is, to plough through that lot on the chair."

Peter planted a kiss on the top of her head, went back to the bedroom and settled down to sleep. In the end, Jane didn't come to bed at all.

As Tennison entered the Incident Room at nine the next morning, the men fell silent. They watched her as she walked to the table and sat in the chair their guv'nor had occupied the day before. She could feel their hatred; it prickled her skin. She had not expected such open animosity and it threw her slightly.

She kept her eyes down, concentrating on her notepad, then took out her gold pen and carefully unscrewed the cap. She raised her head.

"By now you are all aware that I am taking over from DCI Shefford, and I would like to take this opportunity to say how saddened and deeply shocked I am by this tragedy. John Shefford was a well-liked and highly respected officer." She met the gaze of each man in turn as she spoke; several of them couldn't hold her eyes, one or two others, notably Otley, glared back, challenging her silently.

"I am not attempting to step into his shoes; I am the only available DCI and as such I shall appreciate all the co-operation and assistance you can give to enable me to grasp all the details of the investigation and bring it to a successful conclusion. WPC Havers will be assisting me, and she will give you details of everything I need. I will work around the clock . . . You wanted to say something, Sergeant Otley?"

Otley was standing, rigid with anger, tight-lipped. "Yes, ma'am, I know you asked for this case specifically . . ."

She lit a cigarette and gazed at him, coldly. "If you don't like it, put in for a transfer, through the usual channels. That goes for the rest of you; anyone who wishes to move can put in a formal request. Until then, I'm afraid you're stuck with me." A murmur of resentment went around the room, but she ignored it. "I'm asking for some more manpower. We've got more officers joining the team today, including Maureen Havers and four WPCs to assist with the paperwork."

She picked up some items from the desk and began pinning them on the big notice-board. There were two photographs and two sets of fingerprints, highlighted with red and green arrows. She pointed at them as she spoke.

"Now, here's the really bad news. The photo on the right is Deirdre "Della" Mornay; on the left is the murder victim. Here are the prints taken from the corpse, and these are the ones from Della Mornay's Vice file. There are nothing like the sixteen points of similarity needed for a match. The victim's clothes are all from expensive designers such as Giorgio Armani, not Della's line at all. Della's shoes are all English size five; our victim took six and a half, from Bond Street."

She looked around as they took in the implications of what she was saying. Otley was stunned; he was aware of just how well Shefford had been acquainted with Della.

Tennison went on, "We have obviously wrongly identified the victim, which makes our suspect's statement, in which he names the girl he picked up as Della Mornay, inadmissible. If we went to court with this, the case would be thrown out. Someone's been bloody careless. The officer who interrogated Marlow—"

Recovering quickly, Otley went on the attack, interrupting her. "You know it was John Shefford! Are you tryin' to destroy him before he's even buried?"

She stared him into silence. "What I want to know is how come Marlow named the victim as *Della* when the warrant gave her proper name of Deirdre? I'm told you did not state her name at the time, you just arrested him on suspicion of murder. In the tapes of his first interrogation by Shefford, Marlow insists not just once but three times that he did not know the victim, but at the end of the second interview he refers to the victim as Della Mornay. In his written statement, made that night, he again denied knowing her. In his third statement he is calling the victim by name! This would be thrown out of court, especially as Marlow's lawyer was in the room and witnessed his denials. The cock-up is therefore down to us. DCI Shefford made a gross error in wrongly identifying our victim, just as he did in giving the name to George Marlow."

Otley frowned but kept quiet as she continued, "I want new statements all around, and we'll get it right this time! So get them all in again and find out where Della Mornay is now, and get the victim's clothes and shoes checked out. Our priorities are to find the real Della Mornay and to get an ID on the body."

She paused, stubbed out her cigarette and lit another. She was wiping the floor with them, and they knew it, hated it. No one said a word as she took a sip of water, then went on.

"So we move like hell. We haven't a snowflake's chance of getting the three-day lay-down, so if we don't come up with something today, Marlow will have to be released."

She waited, hands on hips, for the howl of protest to die down. "I'm afraid it's a fact of life! OK, anyone have any queries? No? What about Marlow's car, the brown Rover? Anything on that yet? I want it found. Right, that's it for now."

The room was eerily silent as she passed them on the way out, but the moment the door closed behind her there was an explosion of catcalls and abuse.

Otley thumped the table she had recently vacated. "Fucking tart! She was after this before he was out of the bloody station! She was in with the Super almost before he was dead, the bitch! I'll give her queries, the hard-faced tart!"

"What about Marlow's car, Bill?"

Otley turned on Burkin. "You heard her, cow wants it traced, so we trace it! Christ, how much evidence does she bleeding want, for God's sake? We got him, he did it! An' she's runnin' around familiarizin' herself, the stupid cunt!"

In the corridor outside the Incident Room, Tennison leant against the wall, eyes closed, breathing deeply to calm herself. It had been a tremendous effort to keep her cool in front of the men.

Once she was in control again, she headed for the lift to the Super's office.

The men dispersed to their appointed tasks in dribs and drabs. DC Lillie said quietly to his partner, Rosper, "If the car was nicked, we ain't gonna find it. It's been stripped down by now."

Rosper's pug-nosed face broke into a grin. "Eh, you ever see that advert wiv the monkeys? Bleedin' funny . . ."

Otley and Jones were left alone in the room. "What do you think, Skipper?" Jones asked.

"That tart's gunning for John. Well, let her try it; she bad-mouths him and I'll see her knickers are screwed . . ."

The phone interrupted him. He grabbed it. "No, she's not here. Yeah? Yeah! Right, I'll send someone over. Thanks!"

He hung up and gave his first smile of the morning. "That was Forensic. The spot of blood we got off Marlow's shirt cuff, the one they've been growing, matches the victim's! We got the bastard now . . ."

"This is a right bloody mess," said Superintendent Kernan.

Tennison ran her fingers through her hair and Kernan continued, "For God's sake don't let the press get wind of it. Can you handle it? DCI Hicock, from Notting Hill, is available now."

"I can handle it," Tennison snapped. No way would she relinquish the case to Wild Bill, even if she had to hang on to it by her teeth. "I need more men, preferably from outside. If we have to let Marlow go, we'll need someone with surveillance expertise."

"I'll see what we can do. Are you going to see him now?"

"I want a little chat with Marlow, off the record . . . OK?"

"Watch yourself, Upcher's a tough bastard."

Tennison shrugged. "But I bet he's not down in the cells now, is he?"

Kernan shook his head. "Seems to me that Marlow wouldn't have hired Upcher unless he was guilty. His type cost."

"We still can't prove he was ever in the efficiency. It's strange that there's nothing, not a single shred of evidence . . ."

"Forensic's still working on it?"

"Yes," she said, standing up. "They are, at their own pace."

As soon as she left, Kernan picked up the phone. "Put me through to the Commander."

Before seeing Marlow, Tennison listened again to a short stretch of tape from his interview with Shefford. Then she was ready to face the suspect for the first time.

Marlow had been left to kick his heels in an interview room for some time, sitting in silence, watched by a uniformed PC. DI Burkin was sitting in the corridor outside, reading the paper. He was a well-built man, a prized member of the police boxing team, and his slightly battered face showed traces of his career. He rose to his feet when DCI Tennison approached.

"Sorry to keep you waiting. It's Frank, isn't it?"

Burkin nodded and jerked his thumb towards the interview room. "He's got coffee, and he doesn't smoke."

Tennison was taken aback by Marlow's handsome looks; the photographs in his file had given her completely the wrong impression. He resembled an old-time movie star, not exactly Valentino, more Robert Taylor. His blue-black hair was combed back from his face, high cheekbones accentuated his jawline. His amber eyes and long, dark lashes beneath thickly arched brows would be the envy of any woman.

He glanced at the uniformed officer for permission to stand, then rose to his feet. His clothes were well-cut, rather formal; a blue and white striped shirt with a white collar highlighted his dark good looks. His suit jacket hung neatly on the back of his chair.

"Please stay seated, Mr. Marlow. I am Detective Chief Inspector Jane Tennison, this is Detective Inspector Frank Burkin. I suppose you have been told that the DCI in charge of this investigation—"

Marlow interrupted her in a low, husky voice with a slight northern twang. "Yes, I know. I'm very sorry, he was a nice man." He glanced at Burkin, then back to Tennison, placed his hands together on the table and half-smiled; a dimple appeared in his right cheek.

Tennison returned his smile involuntarily. "You have been very co-operative, Mr. Marlow, and I'm sorry to have to question you all over again. But you must understand that in taking over the case I need to know everything . . ."

"Yes, I understand."

Tennison was furious with herself because her hand was shaking as she placed Marlow's statement and her notebook on the table. "Would you just tell me, in your own words, exactly what occurred on the night of Saturday the thirteenth of January?"

Marlow began quietly, explaining that he had drawn some money from a cash dispenser in Ladbroke Grove. He was about to return home when he saw her standing outside the tube station, obviously touting for business.

"I'm sorry to interrupt, but who was standing?"

"Della Mornay!"

"Oh, you knew her, did you?"

"No, I didn't know her name, never saw her before. He told me, said it was a tart by the name of Della . . . He told me."

"Who, exactly, told you the girl's name?"

"Inspector Shefford."

"OK, George, go on. Tell me what happened next."

"I got into my car and drove past her, slowly. She came to the window, asked me if I was looking for someone. All I said was maybe, it depended how much. She said it was twenty-five pounds for full sex. If I wanted . . ."

Looking up, Tennison caught his strange, beautiful eyes. He looked away, embarrassed.

"Go on, Mr. Marlow. Twenty-five pounds for full sex . . ."

He cleared his throat and continued, "Masturbation fifteen. I agreed to pay the twenty-five, and she directed me to some waste ground beside the . . . the Westway, I think it is. We got into the back seat. We . . ." he coughed. "We did it, then she asked me to drop her back to the Tube. Then, as she climbed over the seats into the front she caught her hand, her left hand, on my radio. It's got a sort of sharp edge, and it was only a little nick, but I wrapped my handkerchief around it . . ."

"Er, sorry, George, you just said, 'She cut her hand on my radio'?"

"Yes."

"Which hand?"

He frowned and raised his hands, looking from one to the other. "Her right hand, yeah . . . It was her right hand, because my radio's between the seats. It's got a sharp edge."

He indicated the spot on his own wrist—exactly where the small cut was on the wrist of the corpse. "You can take the radio out, it's portable. They're always being nicked out of cars, round where I live."

He paused for a second and sighed. "You found my car yet?"

Tennison shook her head. "Go on. She cut herself?"

"Yeah. I gave her my handkerchief, wrapped it round her wrist. It's got my initial on it, G . . . Then I paid her, drove her back to Ladbroke Grove station. When I dropped her off, the last I saw of her she was picking up another punter. It was a red car, I'm not sure which make, could have been a Scirocco. I didn't kill her, I swear before God that was the last I saw of her. Then I drove home, got back about half past ten, maybe nearer eleven . . ."

Tennison had been reading his statement as he talked. It was not word for word, but slightly abbreviated, as if he was getting used to repeating only the pertinent facts. "You saw a red car stop. Was it facing towards you or in the opposite direction?"

"Oh, it was coming towards me. I was going down Ladbroke Grove towards Notting Hill Gate."

"So you would have dropped her on the pavement opposite the car? Or did you swerve across the road and deposit her on the other side?"

"Oh, I crossed the road. Then when she got out I drove straight down to the Bayswater Road."

"You live on the Maida Vale/Kilburn border, wouldn't you have gone the other way? It's a quicker route, isn't it?"

"I suppose so. I never thought about it, really. I went straight along to Marble Arch, into Edgware Road and straight to Kilburn to get a video."

"Have you picked up girls in that area before?"

Marlow shook his head and looked down at his hands. "No, and I wish to God I hadn't picked this one up either, but . . ."

"But?"

He looked up, and again she was caught by the strange color of his eyes. "She was very attractive, and I thought, why not . . ."

"George, had you picked this particular girl up before?"

"No, and I must have been crazy, after what happened up north. But I paid for that. I was drunk, and I swear to you she came on to me, I swear I was innocent . . . I served eighteen months, and when they released me I swore I wouldn't mess around with other women."

"Mess around? It was a little more than that two years ago, wasn't it? You were also charged with aggravated burglary."

"Like I said, I was drunk. I just snatched her handbag . . . It was a stupid thing to do, and I lived to regret it."

"So you never knew this girl you picked up?"

There was a tap on the door and Sergeant Otley peered through the window. Irritated, Tennison went out to talk to him.

"The lab came through, that speck of blood on his jacket, it's the victim's. Thought you'd like to know. Oh, and the Super wants to see you."

"That's it? Nothing else? They can't place him in the efficiency?"

Otley shook his head. Tennison said, very softly, "Not enough . . ."

She turned and went back into the room, leaving Otley cursing to himself.

"How much more does she need, for Chrissake . . ."

Tennison spent another three-quarters of an hour with Marlow. At the end of that time she stacked her files and notebooks and thanked him for his co-operation. Seemingly intent on putting her things away, she asked, as if it was an afterthought, "You drove home, Mr. Marlow? Is that correct?"

"Yes."

"Do you have a garage? Did you put the car in a garage?"

"No, I left it outside my flat. There's a parking bay, under cover, for residents. They say they can't find it, has it been stolen, do you think? Only, I should get on to my insurance broker if it's true."

Without replying, Tennison turned to walk out. He stopped her.

"Excuse me, am I allowed to leave yet?"

"No, I'm sorry, Mr. Marlow, you are not."

Tennison was exhausted, but she hadn't finished yet by a long chalk.

Burkin had been falling asleep. He snapped to attention when Tennison knocked to be let out.

"Marlow can go back to his cell. Then I need a search warrant for his flat. We'll go together," she told him.

"Right, ma'am . . . I'll get the warrant."

"Meet me in the Incident Room ASAP." Tennison went down the corridor almost at a run.

• • •

For once the Incident Room was fairly quiet. Otley was sitting staring into space when Burkin joined him.

"She interviewed Marlow, then she went to see the Super."

Otley smirked. "An' she'll be interviewing all afternoon, I got girls comin' in from all over town. Keep her out of our hair!"

He fell silent as Tennison walked in with a big sandy-haired man and introduced him as DI Tony Muddyman, "Tony will be with us as from tomorrow. I've given him the gist of the case, but you'll have to help fill in the details."

Otley had met him before and wasn't too sure about him, but several of the others greeted him like a long-lost cousin.

"Anything on Marlow's car?" Tennison asked Otley.

"No, not yet. There's a roomful of girls waiting for you."

"What?"

"All known associates of Della Mornay. You asked for them to be reinterviewed and they're comin' in by the carload. There were seventeen at the last count . . ."

"I haven't got time to interview them! Why don't you take their statements and leave them on my desk?"

To cover his fury, Otley crossed the room to the notice-board and pinned up a large poster. It advertised a benefit night for DCI Shefford's family.

"Is this the list of girls reported missing?" Tennison had picked up a sheet of paper from his desk.

"Yeah, it's got "Missing Persons Report" on the top, hasn't it?"

"Cut it out, Sergeant."

"One in Cornwall Gardens, another in Brighton, one in Surrey looks promising . . ."

"Fine, I'll take them, shall I?"

"Why not, I've got seventeen slags to interview."

"Should have staggered them!" Tennison retorted. She beckoned Jones to her side. "Can you check if there's a handkerchief among Marlow's things? He said he bandaged the victim's hand with it, initial G on the corner."

She reached for the phone as it rang. "Tennison . . ." Peter was calling her; she gave a quick look around the room. Only Jones was close by, thumbing through the log book and shaking his head.

"OK, put him through."

She turned to face the wall while she spoke, unaware that Otley was mimicking her behind her back, to the amusement of the men.

"I'm sorry, I can't really talk now, is it important?"

Burkin was waiting for her at the door. Otley stolled over to him.

"What's goin' on, are we chargin' Marlow?"

"You're joking . . ." Over Otley's head, Burkin called, "Ma'am, we've got the search warrant!"

"What's this for?" asked Otley.

"Marlow's flat, now we're looking for a handkerchief!" replied Burkin contemptuously.

With a promise to call Peter later, Tennison put the phone down and joined Burkin. As they left, Otley was at it again.

"Yeah, a bloody handkerchief, for that snot-nosed cow! Doesn't she know we've only got ten hours before that bastard has to be released?"

As Tennison and Burkin mounted the steps towards flat 22, the curtains of number 21 twitched.

Burkin knocked on the door. They waited a considerable time before they heard a lock turn and the door was flung wide open.

Moyra Henson glared at them, then looked to Tennison, who was sizing her up fast. It was the first time she'd seen Marlow's common-law wife. She knew Moyra was thirty-eight years old, but she looked older. Her face had a coarse toughness, yet she was exceptionally well made-up. Her hair looked as if she'd just walked out of the salon, and her heavy perfume, "Giorgio," was strong enough to knock a man over at ten yards.

"Yes?" Henson snapped rudely.

"I am Detective Chief Inspector Tennison . . ."

"So what?"

Tennison was noting the good jewelery Moyra was wearing: expensive gold bangles, lots of rings . . . Her nails were long and red. She replied, "I have a warrant to search these premises. You are Miss Moyra Henson?"

"Yeah. Lemme see it. Your lot shell out these warrants like Smarties, invasion of privacy . . ."

She skimmed through the warrant. Tennison clocked her skirt, the high heels and fluffy angora sweater with the tiger motif. Miss Henson might come on as a sophisticated woman, but she was a poorer, taller version of Joan Collins, whom she obviously admired judging by the shoulder pads beneath the sweater.

"I would like to ask you a few questions while Detective Inspector Burkin takes a look around."

Moyra stepped back, looking past Tennison to the broad-shouldered Burkin. "I dunno why he doesn't move in, he spends enough time here."

Tennison was growing impatient. "Could we please come in?"

Moyra turned with a shrug and walked along the narrow hall. "I don't have much option, do I? Shut the door after you."

The flat was well decorated and exceptionally clean and tidy. The cosy sitting room contained a three-piece suite which matched the curtains and a fitted carpet.

Tennison looked around. "This is very nice!"

"What d'you expect, a dump? George works hard, he earns good money. Found his car yet, have you? It's down to you lot, you know. This estate stinks, somebody must have seen him being taken away and nicked it."

"I'm sorry, I can't give you any information on that. Really, I'm just here to have a chat with you. You see, I'm taking over the investigation. The previous Inspector died, tragically."

"Good! Less of you bastards the better. Oi, what's he up to? Hey, sonny! You can put that laundry back, that's my dirty knickers! Are you some perverted crotch sniffer?"

"How do you feel about your boyfriend picking up prostitutes?"

"Wonderful, it gives me a friggin' night off!"

"I admire you for standing by him while he was in jail."

"That bitch asked for it! She was coming on to him, and he'd had too much to drink . . ."

"Was he drunk when he came home on Saturday night?"

"No he was not!"

"And he arrived home at what time?"

"Half past ten. We watched a video, then we went to bed."

Tennison took a photograph from her briefcase and laid it on the coffee table, facing Moyra. "This is the girl he admitted to picking up, admitted having sex with in his car. Now look at her."

"What am I supposed to do, have hysterics? I feel sorry for the girl, but he only fucked her! Half the bloody government's been caught messing around at some time or other, but their wives have stuck by them. Well, I'm doing the same. Now, if you've finished wrecking my flat, why don't you get out of here?"

"I haven't finished, Moyra. Just one more question; did you know Della Mornay?"

"No, never heard of her."

"Never?"

"No."

"And George didn't know her, you're sure of that?"

Moyra folded her arms. "I have never heard of her."

Tennison put her notebook into her briefcase. "Thank you for your time, Miss Henson."

While she waited for Burkin to finish, Tennison had a good look around the flat. There were no handkerchiefs with the initial "G" on the corner, either in the bedroom drawers or the laundry basket. Enquiries at the laundry Moyra had told them she used came to nothing.

The flat was very much Moyra's and only her things were in evidence; pots of make-up, knickknacks, magazines. Just one small corner of the dressing table held a neat, old-fashioned set of bone-handled brushes with George's initials in silver. Moyra, who followed them from room to room, told them they had belonged to his father.

Tennison was struck by the neatness of Marlow's clothes in the wardrobe. They took up only a quarter of the space, the rest of which was crammed with Moyra's things. His suits were all expensive, in tweeds and grays, nothing bright, and the shirts were of good quality.

The small bookcase in the lounge contained paperbacks, mostly by Jackie Collins, Joan Collins and Barbara Taylor Bradford. It was as if Marlow didn't really live there. Tennison looked again; there were a few thrillers that were more likely to be his, such as James Elroy and Thomas Harris, plus a hardback edition of *Bonfire of the Vanities* that she guessed belonged to him.

Finding nothing of interest, Tennison and Burkin left to start checking on the missing girls. They headed for Cornwall Gardens to question a Mrs. Florence Williams.

Sergeant Otley had a feeling this was a good one, which was why he and Jones were there instead of Tennison. The report had only been in a few hours, but the description matched their victim.

The basement area of the flat in Queen's Gate, Kensington, looked as if a cat-fight had taken place in the dustbins, spewing rubbish among the broken furniture and bicycles that cluttered the approach to the door.

Otley peered through the filthy window. "Are you sure this is the right address, Daffy?"

"Yeah. Knock on the door, then."

"Christ, place looks like a dossers' pad, you seen in here?"

Jones shaded his eyes and squinted through the iron grille over the sash window. "I thought this was a high-class area," he muttered.

"It is," snapped Otley. "And shut your mouth, someone's coming."

The door was opened by a tall, exceptionally pretty girl with blond hair hanging in a silky sheet to her waist. She was wearing pink suede boots, a tiny leather miniskirt and a skimpy vest.

"Yes?"

"I am Detective Sergeant Otley, this is Detective Constable Jones. You made a missing persons report?"

"Oh, yeah, you'd better come in. It might all be a dreadful mistake, you never really know with Karen, it's just odd that Michael hasn't seen her either . . ."

Otley and Jones exchanged glances as they followed the leggy creature into the dark, shambolic hallway.

"Trudi! Miffy! There are two policemen . . ."

The blond turned to them and pointed to an open door. "If you want to go in there, I'll get them. They're in the bathroom."

The room contained a large, unmade double bed with two cats fast asleep in the middle of the grubby sheets. The furniture was a mix of good antiques and fifties junk, but the room was as much a mess as the rest of the flat. On the fireplace wall a large, moth-eaten stag's head hung at a precarious angle, with door-knockers hanging from its antlers.

"Do you want coffee or tea?" The blond hovered in the doorway.

"Cup of tea would be nice, thank you."

"Indian, China or herbal?"

"Oh, just your straight, ordinary tea, love, thanks."

Jones perched on a wicker chair until he noticed one of the legs was broken and it was propped on a stack of books. He moved a heap of clothes from a winged armchair and sat down.

Otley whispered, "What a bloody dump! Place looks as if it's not been cleaned in years.

Jones flipped open his notebook. "The girl that came in to the station is Lady Antonia Sellingham . . . So if Trudi's in the bathroom with Miffi, unless that's another cat, the blond's a titled aristo. Typical, isn't it?"

Cornwall Gardens was a total waste of time. Edie Williams, reported missing by her mother, Florence, was a thirty-five-year-old mental deficient with a passion for watching trains at Euston Station. She had returned home that morning.

Otley sipped from the cracked mug of terrible-tasting tea, prompting the three girls to remember exactly when they had last seen their flatmate, Karen. It was quite normal for her to spend several days at a time with her boyfriend, Michael Hardy, but he had been away, skiing. Antonia at last decided she had not seen Karen since Friday—no, Saturday.

"Do you have a photograph of her?"

"Oh, yes, lots. There's her modeling portfolio, would you like to see that?"

Miffy, a short, plump girl with a wonderful, chortling laugh, bounced out of the room. Lady Antonia asked if the police were worried that something had happened to Karen. Otley didn't reply but made a note of Karen's boyfriend's name and phone number. He glanced at Jones, whose eyes constantly wandered back to Antonia's legs.

The doorbell rang and Antonia strolled out, pausing to ask if anyone would care for more tea. None of them showed fear for Karen; they did not really believe that anything could have happened to her, it was just a bit odd that no one had seen her around.

Miffy returned and shrugged her shoulders. "Can't find it, but we have got some photos of when we were in St. Moritz, they'd be the most recent. I'll see if I can find them."

She went off again in search of them as the leggy Antonia returned with a large cardboard box. "It's my new pet, a chinchilla. Would you like to see it? It's just adorable . . ."

Before Jones could take up the opportunity to get closer to Antonia, Miffy came back with a large, expensive-looking album. She flipped through the pages, then stopped.

"Oh, here's a goodie, this is Karen."

Otley took the book, stared at the photograph, then silently passed it to Jones. The atmosphere in the room changed in an instant; the girls picked up on the glance between the two officers. Suddenly they were afraid.

"Is something wrong? Has something happened?"

Otley sighed and passed Jones his notebook, in which he had jotted down Michael Hardy's details. "Could DC Jones use your telephone? And I suggest you get your coats, ladies. We'll need you to accompany us to the station."

The girls left the room. Jones hovered. "Er . . . Who do I call, Skipper?"

Otley gave him an impatient stare. "You call the boyfriend, and we pick him up on our way back to the station."

"Oh, right! His number's in the book, is it?"

"In the book in your friggin' hand, you fruit!"

The house in Brighton was a late Victorian building with a fish and chip shop on the ground floor. Elaine Shawcross, daughter of the proprietors of the shop, had been missing for ten weeks. Her parents were upstairs in their flat; while Tennison went to see them, Burkin ordered fish and chips for them both.

As he carried them back to the car he was surprised to see Tennison leaving the house. She climbed into the car and slammed the door.

"I've salted and peppered them, ma'am, did you want vinegar?"

"Yeah, I'd like to smother that Otley's head in it, might make his hair grow. Either Detective Sergeant Otley needs his friggin' head seeing to, or he's deliberately sending me on a wild-goose chase. Give us me chips, then!" She crammed chips in her mouth and continued, "He's pissed off with me because he's back at the station interviewing hundreds of toms! Ha, ha, ha!"

As they drove back towards London, Tennison stared out of the window. "That snide bugger Otley did it on purpose! Sending us all the way down here, he's just stirring it at every opportunity."

Burkin did not respond, and she gave him a sidelong look. "So, Frank, what do you think of Marlow?"

"I'm sorry, ma'am?"

"I said, what do you think of the prime suspect? George Marlow?"

Burkin shrugged. He stopped the car at a red light and she could almost see the brain cells working as he chewed his lips.

"Well, spit it out! You do have some personal thought on the matter, don't you?"

"Yes, ma'am."

"So, tell me . . ."

"Well, I think he did it. There's something about him, I don't know what, maybe just intuition. But I think he's our man."

She lit a cigarette and Burkin opened his window. She felt the cold blast of wind, inhaled deeply and wound her own window down. Burkin promptly closed the one on his side.

Tennison gave him a sidelong look. "Draft too much for you, is it?"

"No, ma'am, just thought it might be too much for you!"

She stared out of the window, talking more to herself than to him.

"You know, being a woman in my position is tough going. I mean, I have intuition, but it's probably very different from yours. As a man, you feel that Marlow did it. Are you saying that your intuition tells you that Marlow is a perverted sexual maniac? Because this girl was tortured, strung up, beaten and raped . . . And you just *feel* it's George Marlow?"

"It's more than that, ma'am. I mean, he had sex with her."

"So? That doesn't make him the killer. You've got to find the gaps, the hidden areas. His common-law wife is his alibi; she stood by him before, when he was convicted of a serious sex assault. He snatched the woman's handbag, knocked her about a bit, then he freely allowed them to take samples for DNA testing to see if they could find anything else against him. They didn't, so it was his first offense. His girlfriend must have gone through hell over that. No matter how hard-faced she seems, she's still a woman! She was betrayed by him, but they both used the excuse of drink. He had been drinking, and a lot of men do things when drunk that they'd never consider doing when sober, right? But our killer is a cold-blooded, calculating man. He scrubs his victim's hands . . ."

"Well, I agree with what you're sayin', ma'am, but there is something about him . . ."

"You can't bloody charge a man because there's something about him! You can only do that with evidence, proof, and we have not got enough proof to hold George Marlow."

The radio crackled and Tennison went to answer it, saying, "Maybe this will be it, fingers crossed!"

Control patched through a call from Forensic. It was Willy Chang, though Tennison could hardly tell. His voice was breaking up over the air.

"Inspector? We've *crackle* the carpet, every inch of *crackle, crackle* . . . have nothing. There's not one shred of evidence to prove your man was ever there. We'll keep at it, but I'm not hopeful."

Tennison leaned back in her seat. "Well, that confirms it. As I was saying, we have nothing, not a hair, a fragment of material, to put Marlow in that efficiency. She was covered in blood, but we've got not so much as a pinhead on a pair of his shoes . . . How did he get her in there and walk away without so much as a single stain?"

"But there was one, ma'am, on his sleeve."

"Ah, yes, but he has a plausible explanation for that. The only thing that might possibly finger him is his car. If he killed her in his car he has to have left something . . . And by the by, Burkin, would you stop calling me 'ma'am', makes me feel like a ruddy queen. I like 'boss' or 'guv'nor,' take your pick. Kingston Hill coming up on the right . . ."

Otley led the three bewildered girls and the handsome, tanned young man to the canteen, pushing the door open to allow them to pass in front of him. Michael Hardy paused politely, and Otley waved him on, taking a good look at the boy's high-heeled cowboy boots and heavily studded biker's jacket. But it was the ponytail that got him; his eyes gleamed.

"Take the ladies to a table, sir, at the far end out of everybody's way, and I'll arrange some refreshments." He watched, shaking his head, as the four of them seated themselves, then turned to the counter.

The two canteen workers were about to haul the shutter down, but he scuttled over. "Hang about, Rose! I want four coffees for this lot, on the house. I'll get you a docket later."

The other woman walked off in a huff, not even attempting to serve him. The charming Rose muttered to herself as she turned to the steaming urn and drew four cups of pale brown liquid, banged them on the counter. Otley loaded them onto a tray. "Thanks, darlin'!"

He plonked the tray on the table, slopping the contents of the cups, and told them they would have to wait for Inspector Tennison to return. Then with a brief apology he wandered off.

He passed Maureen Havers, who had stopped to chat to DC Lillie.

"Have you heard, they're bringing in Hicock to replace her?"

Otley's ears flapped. "What was that? Hicock?"

"Yeah, I got it from the Super's secretary."

Otley nearly danced for joy. "Great! Now we need a get-together, get a report done . . ."

DI Muddyman joined them. "What am I missing?"

"Word's out that they're bringing in Hicock, Tennison's gonna get the big E . . ." Otley beamed. "We better give them a little assistance, I'll get a vote of no confidence going. That'll teach the pushy bitch."

He was almost rubbing his hands in glee as he headed out of the canteen. DC Lillie was more interested in the group of girls in the corner. He nudged Jones.

"Eh, I thought all the toms were downstairs? I wouldn't mind interviewing that lot. Who's the puff with the ponytail?"

Jones prodded Lillie in the chest. "They're the victim's flatmates, you prat!"

"What, you got an ID on her?"

"Not official, we gotta wait for the Queen Mother! Skipper's sortin' it out, sent her off to Brighton."

The men laughed amongst themselves, while Karen's four friends waited and waited for someone to tell them why they had been brought in, tell them anything at all. Officers came and went, but no one approached them. Michael was growing impatient, but he realized the long wait meant something terrible had happened. No one answered his questions, no one would tell him if Karen had been found.

"Was it Coombe Lane, ma'am?"

"Yep, should be off to the left . . . Yes, this is it. Oh, yeah, very posh."

Tennison licked her fingers, then sniffed them. They smelt of fish and chips. She took a perfume atomizer from her bag and sprayed herself quickly.

They cruised slowly along Coombe Lane and stopped at a barred gate with a sign, "The Grange." Tennison hopped out to open it. The tires crunched on the gravel drive and they both looked around, impressed.

The Tudor-style house, all beams and trailing ivy, stood well back from the road. There was a golf course behind.

"Obviously loaded, and no doubt Otley has sent us on another wild-goose chase," commented Tennison. "OK, we both go in—and straighten your tie, Burkin!"

Large stone eagles and huge urns of flowers and ivy flanked the heavy oak door. There was an old-fashioned bell-push and, next to it, a modern plastic bell.

The deep bellow of a large dog was the first response to Tennison's ring. She stepped back and waited, hearing footsteps on a stone-flagged floor. Then the door was opened wide.

"Major Howard? I am Detective Chief Inspector Tennison and this is Detective Inspector Burkin. Do you think we could ask you a few questions?"

With a slight frown he replied, "Yes, of course. Do come in."

They followed the major through the echoing hall into a vast drawing room with french windows overlooking a rolling, immaculate lawn. There were oil paintings and ornate statues in abundance, elegant sofas and chairs covered in rose silks. Even Tennison could tell that the thick, sculptured Chinese carpet was worth several years' salary. The whole place smelt of money.

A little over-awed, Tennison watched the major closely as he apologized for his shirt-sleeves and put his jacket on over his dark green cords and checked shirt. Tall and well-built, he had obviously been a very handsome man in his youth. Now, with iron-gray hair and a back straight as a die, he still exuded the sort of easy charm that comes with total confidence.

He turned to DI Burkin. "Sit down, Inspector. Now, what can I do for you? Is there something wrong?"

Tennison stepped forward. "Thank you, sir, I'll stand. I am Detective Chief Inspector Tennison. I hope we will not take up too much of your time, but we are enquiring about your daughter. She has been reported missing?"

The major looked surprised. "By whom?"

Tennison was annoyed at herself for having to check her notebook. "A young man by the name of Michael Hardy. He gave this address."

The major frowned. "Well, I hope this isn't some practical joke, that's her boyfriend. My daughter Karen doesn't actually live with us, she shares a flat with some girls in Kensington. I'd better call my wife, see if she can get to the bottom of this. Reported missing? Are you sure? I haven't heard the first thing about it. To be honest, I thought it was about Karen's car. She got a new Mini for her birthday and her parking tickets are always being sent here. We've had some fair old arguments about that. But please, I won't be a moment, excuse me."

As soon as he was out of the room, Tennison walked across to the grand piano on which stood a number of family photographs. One, in a particularly large frame, showed a girl holding the reins of a pony and smiling into camera. She would be about ten years old. The next photograph was of a family Christmas, with everyone in paper hats roaring with laughter. Tennison's heart started thumping and she moved along to the photo that had caught her eye.

The beautiful, sweet young face, the wondrous hair . . . She was the epitome of youth and health, a smiling, vibrant, free-spirited girl. Tennison turned slowly towards Burkin.

"We've found her . . ."

Mrs. Felicity Howard handed Tennison two large, professional photographs of her daughter, taken in the past year. They confirmed Tennison's suspicion. The major, knowing without being told that something was dreadfully wrong, moved to his wife's side and held her gently.

Quietly, Tennison said, "I'm sorry to have to tell you that I believe your daughter may be dead. It will be necessary for one of you to come with us to identify the body."

The major sat without speaking throughout the journey. He sat stiffly, staring straight ahead. Tennison did not attempt to make conversation; when she had radioed in to say that she was bringing Major Howard to identify the victim, she lapsed into silence.

Otley, Jones and Muddyman spent the rest of the afternoon interviewing prostitutes and call girls for the second time. They were all unhelpful, uncooperative, and one or two even had the cheek to complain about loss of earnings.

None seemed able to recall when they had last seen Della Mornay. It seemed that she was reasonably well-liked, but no one admitted to mixing with her when not on the streets.

The story was the same from the pimps and the patrons of the clubs and cafés frequented by Della Mornay. By late afternoon there was no evidence of any recent sighting of Della; it appeared that no one had seen her for weeks. At last, one very young girl volunteered the information that a friend of Della's, known only as Ginger, had contracted Aids and returned to Manchester. Perhaps Della had gone to visit her.

A few girls hinted that Della had the odd S & M client, but when asked for names their faces went blank; the reaction was the same when Otley enquired if anyone else had ever been picked up by any of Della's special clients. No one was interested.

Otley was gasping for a cup of tea, or something stronger, but the canteen was closed. He jerked a thumb at Muddyman and winked. Muddyman followed him out.

"Let's take a little break. We can use the office, she won't be back yet."

Two of the tarts he had interviewed passed him on their way out. They waved; he gave them the finger.

"You know," he said viciously, "when you start talkin' to them all it makes my skin creep. They're like an alien species, opening their legs for any bastard that'll pay up. I'd like to get a water cannon, wash the lot of them off the streets."

Muddyman shrugged. "Well, if the johns weren't there, they wouldn't be on the streets in the first place. Hose them and you've gotta hose the guys doin' the kerb-crawling after their skinny, dirty little cunts."

Otley opened the office door carefully and looked around it; it was empty. He closed the door softly behind them.

Tucked at the back of one of his desk drawers was a half-bottle of whisky. He unscrewed the cap and offered it to Muddyman.

"Fuckin' toms, I tell you, we had this Marlow done up, we'd have sent him down if it wasn't for that bitch Tennison. Now we got to crawl through the gutters, makes me puke."

"Maybe the one we found wasn't a tom?"

"Bullshit! She was in Mornay's flat, why else was she there, you tell me that? Don't give me any crap because she was wearing designer knickers, I've had girls come in dripping with mink, wearing high-class gear, but they're all the same, open the legs, drop in yer money!"

Muddyman thought it best to keep quiet as Otley was really sounding off. His face was twisted with anger and pent-up frustration.

"My wife, the most decent woman you could ever wish to meet, never done a bad thing in all her life, died of cancer, screamin' in agony. She was goodness itself, and she was a bag of bones. These slags, tartin' around, passing on filthy diseases . . . Why my wife? That's what I ask myself over and over, why does a decent woman die like that and they get away with it?"

Wisely, Muddyman decided there was no answer to that. Instead, he enquired for the third time what they were going to do about the three girls and Michael Hardy.

"What d'you think, we keep them here until ma'am comes back. I get their statements, I can't whip 'em over to the morgue, she's got a family . . . We wait, but it'll be worth it, because it's all going down on my report sheet!"

"The canteen's closed, Skipper, they're in one of the interview rooms— not the one with the tarts. They've been here for hours, an' I think Lillie's taken a fancy to the tall blond one!"

Muddyman was referring to the youngest member of the team, DC Lillie, nicknamed Flower. He took the brunt of their wisecracks when Jones wasn't around.

Otley sucked in his breath and prodded Muddyman's chest. "I'm doin' the report, an' I know how long they've been here, OK? When the canteen reopens we'll wheel 'em back up, an' you tell Lillie no chattin' up the blond Puss in Boots, savvy?"

Muddyman bristled. Sometimes Otley got right under his skin, seeming to forget who was the senior officer. But he replied, "I savvy, Sarge!"

• • •

In the mortuary, the wait for the body to be brought out seemed interminable, yet it was no more than a few minutes. The major stood in the small waiting room, tense and unspeaking.

After putting out a DO NOT DISTURB sign, Felix Norman opened the door of the waiting room and gestured to Tennison that everything was ready. He held the door open as Tennison led the major out, followed by Burkin. They formed a small group around the open drawer where Karen lay covered with a green sheet. Tennison looked at the major.

"Are you ready?"

He nodded. His hands were clenched at his sides as the sheet was drawn back.

"Major Howard, is this your daughter, Karen Julia Howard?"

He stared as if transfixed, unable to raise his eyes. He did not attempt to touch the body. Tennison waited.

After a long, terrible pause, the major wrenched his eyes from the body.

"Yes, this is my daughter," he whispered.

His work forgotten, Otley was still holding forth to Muddyman. The only way to get rid of Tennison, who he instinctively associated with the tarts, was a vote of no confidence. He had spread the word to any who would listen, and was sure the team would back him. Suddenly, he remembered that he had intended to see the Super to tell him they thought the victim had been identified.

Tennison had many questions she needed to ask the major, but before she could phrase the first one, he said bluntly, without looking at her, "How did my daughter die? I want to know the facts. I want to know how long she has been dead, and why I have not been contacted before this. I want to know when I can have my daughter's body, to give her a decent funeral . . . And I want to know who is in charge of this investigation . . ."

Tennison interrupted. "I am in charge of the investigation, sir."

He stared at her, then looked at Burkin. "I am a personal friend of Commander Trayner's, I must insist on speaking to him. I do not . . . I will not have a woman on this case, is that clear? I want to speak to the Commander . . ."

Tennison sighed. "I am in charge of this investigation, sir. If there is anything you wish to discuss with me, please feel free to do so. I assure you we will release your daughter's body as soon as it is feasible. The only problem is if you want to have her cremated . . ."

"Cremated? Good God, no, a Christian burial is what I want for my daughter . . ."

"Then the delay should be minimal, Major. I'll see to it personally," Tennison promised. "I think perhaps the questions I need to ask you can wait until you have had a chance to recover. I will arrange for a car to take you home . . ."

"I want to speak to Commander Trayner. If I didn't make myself clear in the first place, woman, then let me repeat to you, I refuse . . . I will not have . . . I will not have a female in charge of this case."

Tennison was about to reply when Burkin caught her eye. He gripped her elbow and whispered, "Leave the room, let him cry, leave him . . ."

She allowed herself to be steered from the room. She stood in the corridor, angry at first, then looked through the small glass panel in the door. She could see the major; he slammed his fist into the top of the bare table.

"I have many friends, I know many people who could take over this investigation . . ." Then he disintegrated like a helpless child, his body sagged and he held out his arms, in desperate need of comfort from anyone, a stranger, even the Detective Inspector . . .

Gently, Burkin held the heartbroken man as he sobbed his daughter's name over and over.

Tennison felt inadequate and ashamed of herself for being so eager to question the major. In his grief and rage he had turned to the young Inspector, not to her. For a long time he wept in Burkin's arms.

Listening to him, Tennison was flooded with sympathy.

Eventually the door opened and Burkin emerged.

"He's ready to go home now. I'm sorry, ma'am, if I was rude, but I could see the old boy was . . ."

"You were quite right, Frank. Don't worry about it."

He started back into the room, then paused and turned. "Oh, Sergeant Otley wants you at HQ."

"Did he just call you?"

Burkin evaded her gaze. "Came in while we were in Brighton. Karen's boyfriend and flatmates have been brought in for questioning. Sorry . . ."

"I see! In future, pass on any information immediately, no matter the circumstances. I'll go there now, you see to the major. Was there anything else?"

Burkin shook his head. She watched him closely as she said, "Otley stirring it up, is he? Next thing, he'll be going for a vote of no confidence."

His sudden flush was enough to tell her she'd hit the nail on the head.

Burkin had been greatly moved when the major, with a tremendous effort, had pulled himself together and said he was ready to go home, ready to tell his wife, and that he would be available the next morning to answer any questions. He had even asked Burkin to apologize to Inspector Tennison on his behalf for his rudeness.

As Burkin helped him out to the car the major's back was ramrod straight. He shook the younger man's hand and was gone to break the news to his wife.

4

Otley was furious to discover that Tennison had beaten him to it; her report on the identification of the murdered girl was already on Superintendent Kernan's desk. He couldn't think for the life of him how she had managed it.

It was out of order for Otley to come direct to the Chief Super but, knowing how the Sergeant felt, Kernan said nothing. He waited; Otley was still hovering.

"Something else, Bill?"

After a moment's hesitation, Otley blurted out that the men felt that Tennison wasn't sufficiently experienced. "It's out of control, guv! The big interview room's full of toms bein' questioned for the third time, and not one's seen hide nor hair of Della Mornay. The Incident Room's full of blokes sitting around waiting for her . . ."

"Is this a consensus?"

"We all feel it, guv. She's just not right, she's not handling the men at all well. She's smug, she doesn't fit in, we all feel it. We've only got a few hours left, and the way she's going we'll have to let him go!"

Kernan pursed his lips and nodded a fraction. "It's not entirely up to her, the situation's under constant review. Leave it with me, Bill, OK?"

Arnold Upcher sorted through some documents, then pushed them across the desk to Chief Superintendent Kernan.

"I thought these might interest you. They're cases from the last three years where the evidence depended solely on DNA tests. You can see for yourself, in every instance the judge threw the case out. I think my client and I have been most patient; if you have any further incriminating evi-

dence then we'll discuss it, but I am not prepared to let him stay here another night if you cannot substantiate your suspicion of murder. And that's
all you're holding him on—suspicion. It's not on; he has a solid alibi, he has
been co-operative and totally honest with you. Come on, Superintendent!
You've got the wrong man."

Convinced that the Super was going to take Tennison off the case, Otley
watched with a gleam of triumph in his eye as she entered the Incident
Room, obviously harassed and sweating, with Burkin at her heels.

"Anything on Marlow's car yet?" she demanded.

Ken Muddyman answered her from the far side of the room. "Not yet,
ma'am, but we've got you a slot on the Shaw Taylor program!"

"That's a good idea!" She heard Lillie sniggering behind her but ignored
him.

"I was joking, ma'am!"

"I'm not! Laugh away, DI Muddyman, but time's almost up and Marlow's
lawyer's with the Super now. Get on to the Press Office . . ."

Muddyman couldn't work out if she was kidding or not. Lillie interrupted them.

"Ma'am, Records sent this in, about Moyra Henson. She was picked
up for soliciting fifteen years ago. I dunno if it's of any interest, but she's
been on the dole for four years."

"You never know. Stick it on the file."

Otley chipped in, "We've got twenty-two statements from the toms,
and there's more of 'em upstairs. Nothing worthwhile yet. Plus her boyfriend and flatmates are waiting to be interviewed. What's goin' on, are we
gonna charge him?"

It was coming at her too fast; Tennison floundered for a moment.

"I'd better see the girls first. Keep the Super off my back for a while.
And I want to see everyone in here when I'm finished." She looked around
the room to see who was there. "Ken, you'd better organize a WPC for the
girls . . ."

Otley perched on the edge of his desk, watching with delight while she
tried to cope, and failed.

"There was something else . . ." Tennison continued. "Oh, the identification. Her name's Karen Julia Howard."

"We know," said Otley.

"Oh . . . yes, of course you do. Right, I'm off."

Following her, Ken Muddyman minced from the room, camping it up
and blowing Otley a kiss as he went. The hoot of laughter could be heard
all the way down the corridor.

The three girls' vagueness about Karen was infuriating; Tennison terminated the session after half an hour. By that time she knew that Karen had often spent days, even weeks, at her boyfriend's flat, but the couple had recently had a disagreement and had not seen much of each other since. When Karen had not returned for a couple of nights they presumed she had made it up with him.

On the other hand, Miffy conjectured, Michael obviously didn't make contact because he thought Karen didn't want to see him, but eventually he had called round. Discovering that no one had seen Karen, and she wasn't with her parents or any other friends, Antonia had reported her missing.

The last time the girls had seen Karen she had driven off in her white Mini to Ladbroke Grove for a modeling job. It was a knitwear advert, she had told them. She had taken her large portfolio and her Filofax. Perhaps Karen's agent would know the name of the firm.

The girls constantly looked at each other as if to confirm every detail. A couple of times they broke into tears; Tennison was patient with them but she kept pushing for the information she needed.

"Was there any mention of a new man in her life?"

They could think of no one. Miffy, her eyes red from crying, believed that Karen had loved Michael more than she pretended, but got fed up because he was a bit possessive.

"So they used to argue about it, did they?"

"Just sometimes. You know, she wanted to let her hair down a bit, but they had been going out together for years . . ."

"Did she drink a lot?"

"Oh, no! She didn't drink at all, or smoke. She was a fitness freak, always dieting, and her room at the flat was a no-smoking zone."

Tennison stubbed out her fifth cigarette of the session, not that she was counting. "What about drugs?"

They shook their heads in unison, Tennison thought a little too eagerly.

"You mean never? Not just a little grass or speed?"

Lady Antonia twisted her hands in her lap. "Karen didn't like drugs, hated any of us having stuff in the flat. She wouldn't touch anything like that."

"Not even coke? Did she use cocaine?"

"No, honestly. We've known each other for years, since school, and she got quite uptight about that sort of thing."

Tennison sighed. "OK, so what about Michael, she was a virgin as well, I suppose?"

Lady Antonia crossed her long legs and fiddled with the top of her boot. "That was her business, I have no idea what she did in private."

"Now it's my business, love. Karen was found in a prostitute's room, and I have to find out how she got there. Come on, what do you take me for? Are you trying to tell me that four girls, living in the same flat, never even mentioned sex?"

Lady Antonia pursed her lips. "I don't think you have any right to ask us that sort of question."

Tennison was getting more irritated by the second. "I have every right, as I said before. Anyway, that's it for now, but I might need to talk to you all again before you leave. This officer will show you the way back to the canteen, go and have some coffee."

Lady Antonia faced Tennison. "I am going to complain about the way we have been treated, as if we were criminals. And we don't want to go back to that awful canteen. Please would you call my father, if you need to speak to us we are perfectly willing, but we have been here for . . . we really . . . I would like to go home."

Tennison never took her eyes off the girl's face. The bravado disappeared fast, and Antonia blinked back the tears. "Please, let us go home. We've been here for hours."

Tennison pursed her lips. "Antonia, isn't it? Yes? Well, all I can do is apologize for keeping you here for so long. You are free to go at any time, but I need to question Michael Hardy. As you all came together, perhaps you'd like to leave together. I'll order you a car. Your girlfriend has been brutally murdered, we are just trying to find out how she came to be in that efficiency . . . OK? And any assistance you can give us, give me, is really appreciated. So have a cup of tea or coffee, anything, just for a while longer . . ."

She watched the round cheeks flush, and the girl blinked rapidly. Her whole face seemed to be moving, trying to say something, but unable to form the words. Then she burst out, "She was always happy . . ."

Antonia left the room, and Tennison could hear her sobbing outside in the corridor. She felt dirty, her hands were grubby, and she sniffed her armpits then made a quick exit for the locker room. Next was Karen's boyfriend, Michael Hardy, and though she was sure he was innocent he had to be checked out, eliminated completely. To do that she was going to have to be tough.

The cold water felt good as she splashed it on her face. She washed her hands, scrubbed them, then stared into the soapy water. The killer had used a wire brush on the victim's hands, scratched them raw . . .

Michael, obviously distraught, was sitting with his elbows on the table and his head in his hands. His voice was muffled.

"I can't believe she's dead, I can't believe it . . ."

"You said the reason you hadn't seen Karen was because you'd had a row, is that right?" Tennison asked him.

"I agreed not to see so much of her—" He stopped, too choked to continue.

"She was murdered, Michael, and we found her in a prostitute's efficiency apartment. Now, take a look at this photograph and tell me if you've ever seen this man, ever seen Karen with him. Come on, Michael, look at the photograph."

He raised his head and stared at the mug shot of George Marlow. "No, I've never seen him."

"OK, now what I need to know is when you last saw or spoke to Karen."

He coughed and ran his hands over his ponytail. "I, er, I phoned her, the day before I went to Switzerland. The fifth of January."

"Did you call her from there? While you were away?"

"No . . ."

"And you came back when?"

"I came home on the thirteenth, a week early. There wasn't much snow about."

Tennison sat slightly straighter in her chair. "Did you see her when you got back?"

"No. I went round to her flat yesterday. Miffy said Karen wasn't at home, they'd presumed she was with me. Then I called her parents' house. The housekeeper told me Karen hadn't been home since Christmas, so I rang round a few other friends. When I ran out of places to look for her, I went to the local police station and told them."

"When was that?"

"Er, first thing this morning. I just said no one had seen her lately."

"Ah, so we got two separate reports . . . Now, Michael, her car, the Mini. Have you any idea where it might be?"

"No . . ." He thought for a moment. "It wasn't outside the flat."

All through the interview, Tennison was aware of a lot of coming and going outside. Faces popped up in the small window, but no one knocked. One of them was the Super, but he waved at her not to bother. She found it all distracting, so it was almost a relief when Michael burst into tears and she was able to pace around the room for a few moments.

Eventually Michael blew his nose in his handkerchief. Tennison sat down again.

"So let's get back to this argument you had with Karen."

"It wasn't really an argument, it was just . . . just that she decided we were getting too involved, she wanted more time to herself. I agreed, but we didn't argue."

"But you didn't like it?"

"No, I wanted to marry her. But she was only . . . she . . ." His eyes filled up and he turned away, shrugging his shoulders helplessly as his voice cracked, "She was only twenty-two years old . . ."

"So, you agreed not to see so much of her. Did you find out if there was someone else?"

"No, she didn't have anyone else."

"How can you be so sure?"

"Because I know . . . She would have told me if there was something . . . someone else. I'm sorry . . ."

"So you don't think she had other boyfriends?"

"She had a lot of acquaintances, men friends, but most of them I knew. She didn't have anyone else, wasn't seeing anyone else."

"But you were in Switzerland, maybe she met someone else while you were away?"

He shook his head and looked at the table. Tears trickled down his face and Lillie felt even more sorry for him. The boy kept looking at Lillie as if he could stop Tennison's stream of questions.

"Did you and Karen have a good sexual relationship?"

Michael's voice was a whisper. "Yes."

"Did she like anything . . . unusual? Was she a bit kinky?"

"No."

"Do you know if she took drugs?"

"She didn't drink and she didn't take drugs."

"Do you?"

"Pardon?"

"I asked you if you take drugs, do you use hash or cocaine?"

"I have . . . but not recently."

"Did you score it?"

"How do you mean?"

"Did you buy it for yourself? Go out and score from people?"

"No . . . when I say I've used . . . I was offered some cocaine once, and grass quite a few times, but I've never bought any. Do you mean do I go out to a dealer?"

"Yes?" He shook his head.

"Michael, are you sure? We found Karen in an area where a lot of drug dealers hang out. You sure she wasn't using anything, or maybe going to get some for you?"

"No!"

"Did she pick up men?"

"No! No . . . Karen would never . . . Karen . . ."

He started to sob, hunching his shoulders, and Tennison leaned closer.

"Tell me, Michael, come on. If she was scoring for you it would make sense of where we found her, why we found her!"

Michael stood up, shaking with anger and grief, his face red with frustration. "*No*! She was a sweet, innocent girl, and you're making her out to be something dirty, something sick! You disgust me . . ."

"Sit down, Michael, *sit down*! Come on, now. You said that on the night of the thirteenth of January you . . ."

He gritted his teeth. "I was at my parents' house, I went straight from the airport. We had dinner and I stayed the night. I've told you this, I've told you this three times!"

Tennison closed her notebook. "Yes, you have, and thank you for being so co-operative. If you'd like to have a wash there's a gents' just along the corridor, and then DC Lillie will take you up to the canteen."

He was slumped in his chair, silent. He didn't look up. She walked to the door.

"You can go, Michael, and the girls are free to go with you. Thank you . . ."

Tennison leaned back and lit another cigarette as Michael followed Lillie along the corridor, standing aside to allow Superintendent Kernan to pass. The Super stopped at the door of the interview room.

"Anything?"

Tennison shook her head. "No," she replied wearily, "her car might give us a clue, if we can find it. None of them know where it is."

"Sergeant Otley reckons you've got enough to charge him."

She stood up and faced him. "Detective Sergeant Otley is wrong."

Kernan shut the door. "What do you want to do?"

She pushed her fingers through her hair. "We have to release him, we can't hold him any longer. In my opinion we don't have enough to make it stick . . . Let him go!"

At six-fifteen, Chief Superintendent Kernan left the Commander's office and spoke briefly to Tennison. He had agreed to the release of George Marlow.

Reluctantly, Tennison went to the interview room and told the men the bad news.

"We will keep at it until we have the evidence to arrest him and keep hold of him."

Otley, as tired as everyone else, shouted that it was lunacy, Marlow was guilty. Tennison didn't even attempt to argue, but when Otley stood up in front of everyone, jabbed an aggressive forefinger at her and told her that if

Marlow killed again it would be down to her, she snapped. "That's enough, Sergeant! I've taken a lot of flak from you, but I've had you right up to here! You start acting like bloody cowboys and this is what happens. This investigation has been a cock-up from the word go. If anyone should be yelling and pointing the finger, it should be me! You all fucked up, so now we take it, we eat it, and start again from scratch. I want us on that bastard night and day. We'll get him back and we'll keep him. Now, I don't know about anyone else, but I need some sleep, so let's take a break. Tomorrow we'll reassess everything we've got."

She packed her briefcase and left. Only a few murmured "goodnights" marked her departure, but she was too tired to care.

Burkin and Jones remained at their desks, but the atmosphere in the room was thick with fatigue. Everyone was knackered, but above all, they felt defeated. Marlow had beaten them.

Otley sat for a few moments, devastated. He had been so certain that they had Marlow.

When his phone rang it took him a second to recognize the sound. He answered automatically, then sat bolt upright.

"Yeah, I got that! Thanks, mate, I owe you one!"

He jumped up and ran from the building.

It was drizzling as Tennison unlocked her car. She chucked her case inside and sat for a moment, trying to raise the energy to drive home.

The rain increased to a downpour as she drove slowly out of the car park and past the main entrance to the police station. George Marlow stood there with Upcher, waiting for a taxi. A cab pulled up, and as they stepped from the doorway Marlow spotted Tennison. He ran in front of her car, then to her window. Upcher put out a hand as if to stop him, but he ignored it and tapped on the glass.

"Excuse me . . . Excuse me, miss!"

She did not want to face him, but there was no way out of it. She lowered the window.

"I'd just like to say thank you, I really appreciate it. I knew you'd help me."

She looked once again into those wide amber eyes. She said nothing, just gave him a stiff nod of her head and raised the window again. She didn't see Otley run out of the station towards her until he shouted to her. Then he saw Marlow stepping into the waiting taxi and stopped dead. He stood in the rain as the taxi did a U-turn and slowly headed back towards him. As it passed he could see Marlow's face pressed against the window, smiling.

Otley tapped on the passenger window of Tennison's car, gestured for her to open the door. He climbed in and shook his head, showering her with water, and wiped his balding head with a crumpled handkerchief.

"Is this important, Sergeant?"

"Yes, ma'am. I just got a call from DS Eastel at Sunningdale, They've found another one, about two hours ago. He's given me the tip because her hands are tied behind her back and she's been stabbed and beaten. He reckons, from our description, that it's Della Mornay."

By the time Tennison and Otley reached Sunningdale golf course it was after eight. They were directed away from the clubhouse towards a crescent of exclusive houses. There were many cars parked at one end, where a narrow private gateway led directly onto a small wooded area at the perimeter of the golf course.

A uniformed officer in a shiny black cape dripped water over their identification as he checked it, then sent them towards arc lights which had been placed around a nearby bunker on which the silhouettes of a few men could be seen. As Tennison drew nearer she could see more men sheltering beneath the trees.

Otley strode ahead, his shoulders hunched against the downpour. The ground was a shifting mud bath and Tennison gave up picking her way among the puddles. Her shoes were already sodden. As she reached the group on the bunker she found Otley already deep in conversation with his friend, DS Eastel.

Eastel shook her hand, then turned to a man taking shelter beneath the trees. "He was walking his dog. The rain must have washed some of the soil away, exposing her arm. The dog made a pretty good job of digging her up. You want to take a look?"

Tennison stared at the dog-owner, who was obviously agog at what was going on. His dog still strained on his lead, barking continuously.

Neither Eastel nor Otley assisted her up the muddy bank and she slithered the last two feet. She clutched Eastel's arm to stop herself falling.

Eastel handed her a long stick. "Take a look, see if you can make out her features, but keep off the sheeting if you can. They're almost ready to lift her."

Tennison craned forward and gently lifted the matted hair away from the girl's face. Everyone stopped what they were doing to watch as Tennison peered at the pitiful face of the victim. She crouched down, then knelt on the plastic sheeting for an even closer look. The stench of decomposed flesh made her nostrils burn, but she forced herself to study what she could see of the girl's profile, trying to match it with the photographs of Della Mornay.

Eventually she let the hair fall back into place and accepted help to rise to her feet. She slithered as she tried to climb the bank and Eastel gave her a hand.

"I can't be a hundred per cent sure, but I think you're right. It looks like Della Mornay."

The body was eased onto the plastic sheeting and lifted onto a stretcher, face downwards. The rain still pelted down as four men carried the stretcher up the bank and passed directly in front of Tennison. She stepped back to let them by, then asked them to wait a moment; she could see the rope that bound the corpse's hands. She turned to Otley.

"Is it the same rope?"

"I don't know, ma'am, but I think if she is our girl we should have her sent to our patch, get Felix Norman on it."

Tennison nodded. Despite the mud she could see marks on the victim's arms, deep weals that looked similar to those on Karen Howard.

"Yes, get Felix. I'll go back to the station and wait for him to contact me, but I want him out here tonight."

Otley nodded agreement. He watched as they carried the body away. "You should never have released Marlow. Any money on it, that bastard did this one as well."

She bristled. "I had no option but to release him. If he's guilty, I'll get him back."

"There's no *if*, you know it, we all know it. Why d'you think my guv'nor was so desperate to book him? He *knew* . . ."

"Like I said, Sergeant, when I've got the evidence we'll make an arrest, and this time we'll go by the book. This time there'll be no cock-ups!"

"Yeah, you do that, love! Go by the book, and if he kills again you can say, "I hadda stick to the rules!" That bastard is guilty, and my guv'nor knew it!"

"If he knew so much why did he foul up the way he did? Don't give me that bullshit! Right now it's the last thing I need. And you tell me, if a male officer of my rank had taken over this team, would you call him 'love'?"

"I'm sorry, ma'am, slip of the tongue. But if you blacken my guv'nor's name, you start raking up the dirt on him, then . . ."

"Then what?"

"If you were a man I'd punch that snotty look off your face, I'd do it and wouldn't give a shit about the consequences. Right now I'm off duty . . ."

Tennison wanted to shriek, but she controlled the impulse to land a punch on Otley's sharp nose. She snapped, "I don't give a damn whether you are off or on duty, Sergeant Otley. If Shefford hadn't been so damned eager to try and beat that bloody stupid Paxman's record, then maybe he wouldn't have fucked up!"

Otley looked at her with loathing. "There was never any such person as

Paxman, ma'am, it was a joke. The guv'nor just made it up to gee the lads up a bit, there was no record. If you'd known him you would have sussed that out! Just as he sussed that George Marlow was our man. He even reckoned Marlow'd done a girl up north . . ."

Tennison turned quickly to face Otley. "What did you say?"

"The boss reckoned Marlow had done a girl up north, years ago. That's why he wanted him nailed, wanted him banged up. And if he bent a few rules, so fuckin' what? Because Marlow's gonna kill again . . . and when he does, it's down to you and your fuckin' rules and your precious book."

She clenched her fists to control her fury. "You're telling me that Shefford believed Marlow had killed before? And said nothing? Is that what you're saying?"

Otley backed off, shrugged his shoulders. "I'm not saying anything. I got a lift back with Eastel, I'm on my way . . ."

Tennison followed him. "If what you say is true, why isn't it in the records? Or in Shefford's memos? Why?"

"As I said, ma'am, it was just supposition. He died before he could take it any further, he died, ma'am, remember? That's how come you're here!"

"I want your report on my desk first thing in the morning. And Otley, I've told you before, if you don't like working for me, then you can put in for a transfer."

He stared at her and she was taken aback by the loathing in his small, dark eyes. "You mean like the rest of the lads? Fine, I'll think about it. Good night."

As he stomped off, Tennison became aware that their conversation had been overheard. She gave Eastel a cursory nod of thanks, then turned back to repeat her thanks to the officers still searching the area. She was very close to the edge of the bunker; she teetered and lost her footing, landed on her backside in the mud. There were sniggers. Two uniformed men jumped to assist her and she gave a grin. It was all she could do under the circumstances.

"Ah, well, they say mud's good for the complexion!"

It was the wrong thing to say and she knew it as soon as it was out. No one laughed; they had all seen the body of the girl, stripped, tortured and covered in the filthy, slimy mud.

5

At ten o'clock Peter put a pizza in the oven as it didn't look as though Jane would be home. While he was eating it she phoned to tell him not to wait up as she had to go over to the morgue. She sounded tired and depressed.

"Things bad, are they, love?"

"Yeah, you could say that. We found another girl tonight. I'll tell you all about it in the morning."

He knew she must be exhausted, she couldn't have slept for more than about thirty-six hours, but he couldn't help feeling slightly irritated as he put the phone down. He was having a tough time at work himself; things were going from bad to worse and he needed someone to sound off at. He had tendered for a major building project that would have put him back on his feet financially; had gone in as low as possible, but had been pipped at the post.

He sat down to finish his pizza, which he'd overcooked and was hard as a rock, but he ate it anyway. Then he ploughed through his accounts, getting more depressed by the minute.

He was on the edge of bankruptcy and there seemed no way out. His share of the proceeds from the house had virtually been swallowed up by maintenance payments and business debts. He slammed the books shut and opened a bottle of Scotch.

A few minutes later the phone rang again. It was his ex-wife, asking if Peter could have their son to stay for the weekend now that he was settled. The thought cheered him up; Marianne had never been keen to allow Joey to stay overnight. His few Saturdays with the boy had left him feeling low.

"If he could maybe stay next weekend? Would that be convenient?"

"Yeah, sure! I mean, I'll have to sort it out with Jane, she's very busy at the moment, but I'm sure it'll be OK."

"How's it going with the new woman in your life, then?"

"Going fine, Marianne."

"Good. Oh . . . Nearer the time for the baby, early days yet, but later on perhaps Joey could stay longer. It'd help me out, and it's good for Joey to get to know you."

"Marianne . . ."

"Yeah?"

"Marianne . . . Look, were you trying to tell me something the other day?"

"When?"

"Come off it! When you told me you were pregnant . . ."

"Oh, that! No . . . why, what's the matter?"

"Nothing," he replied shortly, "OK, talk to you soon." He wanted her off the phone, he wanted to think . . .

"All right, then, bye!"

He put the phone down, absently. He didn't like her saying that he should get to know his own son, but it was more than that. He was trying hard to remember the date, the time he had gone to the house to pick up some of his things. Yes, it must have been about the time he had moved into Jane's . . .

Then it all came back to him; Steve not being there, Marianne a little tipsy . . . He knew it was madness, but when she wrapped herself round him the way she used to, teasing him, there had been no stopping . . . It could be. He knew her so well, that look . . . Or was she just trying to wind him up for some obscure reason? Was she jealous of Jane, angry that he was getting himself together? Could she be that small-minded? He tried to dismiss it, but the thought kept returning.

There were always so many things he should have said, things that should have been said months ago, but he never had. He never mentioned her new husband, who had once been his friend; the pain and humiliation of that betrayal were still too fresh. He found himself wishing that Jane would come home, and wondered how to tell her that his son might be coming to stay, not just for the odd weekend, but perhaps for weeks at a time.

In the Incident Room, Tennison was munching on a sandwich as her tired eyes searched the notice-board. The tickets for Shefford's benefit night was selling well. Her eyes came to rest on Karen Howard's face.

She heard a door bang and jumped, then got up to see if Otley had come back after his drink with Eastel. It might be a good time to attempt to iron out the ill feeling between them and to question him further about the other murder, the one "up north." She went through to the room Otley shared with the two DIs, but there was only the night cleaner emptying the wastepaper baskets.

The only thing on Otley's desk was a framed photograph of a rather austere-looking woman standing by a cherry tree, a white Yorkshire terrier at her feet. Tennison wondered if Otley had, as he said, put in for a transfer. She wiped the remains of her sandwich from her fingers and opened the top drawer.

There were a few photos of Shefford and his family, which made her feel guilty for snooping, but she continued. In the third drawer was a familiar file; Della Mornay's Vice record . . . She knew her copy was on her desk; the cover was almost identical, but a bit more dog-eared and perhaps a shade darker.

As she pulled it out a paper-clip caught onto the sheet beneath it. She took the whole lot out and detached the clip; underneath was a small red 1989 diary with thin cardboard covers. It had been doodled on and covered with cartoon faces, but the remarkable thing about it was the name, ornately decorated in felt-tip pen: Della. She knew there was no record of a diary having been found at Della's efficiency.

Tennison carried her finds back to her own office and flipped through the little book, slowly. It contained misspelled notes, appointments for hospital checkups, lists of cash against rent and expenditure. One entry read "New dress, new shoes, streaks." There were a number of pages missing throughout the year; they had been roughly torn out, in some cases leaving chunks of paper behind.

Was there also a diary for 1990? Tennison went back and searched Otley's desk again, but found nothing apart from a near-empty whisky bottle.

She left everything as she had found it, apart from the file and diary, collected her copy of the file from her desk and returned to the Incident Room. She laid the files side by side on the desk and began to compare them, fighting to keep her eyes focusing.

The box room felt airless. Tennison tossed and turned, got up to open the window. She had decided to sleep there so as not to wake Peter.

She lay down again, but kept seeing Della Mornay's face and hearing Otley's voice as he told her that Shefford had believed there was another murder . . . Going over and over her conversation with Sergeant Otley she dozed off at last.

At five-thirty in the morning Peter shot out of bed. He could smell burning.

He rushed into the kitchen and checked that everything was off, then followed his nose along the hallway. On the radiator near the door was Jane's raincoat; the back was singed, leaving a large dark brown stain.

He looked into the spare room. The window was wide open and Jane lay sprawled face down, arms spread wide. He felt as if he was intruding and he gently closed the door, afraid to wake her.

At six-thirty Peter brewed coffee. He was due on the building site by seven. He carried a cup into the spare room.

"Jane . . . Jane!"

"What . . . What? *What?*"

"Hey, it's OK, it's me. Brought you some coffee. There's more in the pot, but I've got to go."

"Oh, shit, what time is it?"

"Just after six-thirty."

"Oh, God, I've got to get cracking. I've got to . . . I've got . . ."

She flopped back on the pillow. "I am knackered, completely and utterly knackered . . ."

"So's your raincoat. You left it on the radiator in the hall and it's singed. I'll have to look at the heating when I get home tonight, shouldn't get that hot."

"Oh, I turned it up, my coat was sopping wet."

"Well, it's dry now . . . What time will you be home tonight?"

"Oh God, don't ask me."

"Well, I am. I've hardly seen you for three days. I was thinking you might like to have dinner somewhere."

It was the last thing she could think of. Still half-asleep, she gulped her coffee and flopped back on the bed.

"Do you think it would be OK if Joey came over, stayed the weekend? Marianne phoned last night . . ."

"Yeah, sure. You don't have to ask me, and I promise I'll try and get back by, say, eight? Is that OK?"

He leaned over and kissed her. "Tell you what, call me when you're awake, then if you know for sure you'll be free I'll book a table at Bianco's, OK?"

"Sounds good to me . . ."

Tennison was showered and dressed, her hair washed but not dried, and on her way to the station by seven-thirty. She thought her raincoat smelt a bit off, but hadn't noticed the dark stain on the back . . .

For once the Incident Room was empty, so Tennison spent some time in her own office, checking the work rota for the day. Then she skimmed through the surveillance report on Marlow. Each shift consisted of four men; two occupied an empty flat opposite Marlow's and the other two a plain car.

The team reported little movement; after work Marlow had visited a video club and then gone straight home, remaining there with Moyra for the rest of the evening. There were one or two photographs of him leaving the flat; Tennison stared at his handsome face and noted again how well dressed he was. There was still no trace of his car, the brown Rover.

It was eight-thirty; the men would start to arrive soon. She fetched herself another mug of coffee and lit her fifth cigarette of the day. At eight forty-five she gave up waiting and set off for the mortuary.

She was just getting into her car when she saw Jones arrive on his moped. She yelled across the car park, "About time, too, Jones! Come on, we're going to the mortuary!"

Mumbling about having had no breakfast, Jones climbed into her car, still wearing his crash helmet.

Felix Norman turned the sheet back carefully. "She took one hell of a beating, poor little soul. Died about six weeks ago, so we won't get any results on vaginal swabs. Lots of blood, I've sent samples over to the forensic girls. She's got similar wounds to your first victim, made by a long, thin, rounded instrument with a razor-sharp point. All the wounds are clean, and hellish deep. Could be a screwdriver, but it's longer than the weapon used on the other victim."

Tennison was wearing a mask, but the stench of the body combined with the disinfectant fumes made her sick to her stomach. "Any hope of getting anything from beneath her nails? You said she put up a struggle?"

"Well, she did that all right, but she had false nails. A couple have snapped clean off, and three are missing altogether. She had deep scratches on her hands, similar to the other one—her hands were scrubbed."

Tennison nodded. "And what about the marks on her upper arms, are they the same?"

Norman nodded but, as always until he had made out his report, he would not commit himself. "They're similar. I've not compared them as yet, so don't quote me. Maybe he strung her up to clean her, I won't know until I've made more tests. He seems to have gone to great lengths to remove any traces of himself."

He drew the sheet back from the corpse's face, revealing the side Tennison had not seen before. She had to turn away.

"Cheek smashed, jaw dislocated . . ."

"Can you give me any indication of his size? I mean, is he a big man, or . . ."

"I'd say he was medium height, five-ten, maybe a little more, but he's very strong. These lower wounds were inflicted with one direct lunge, those to the breasts and shoulders are on an upward slant, which again indicate that she was strung up . . ."

Tennison swallowed, trying to remove the taste of bile from her mouth. "Off the record, then, and I won't quote you, you think we're looking for the same man?"

Norman chortled. "Off the record, and I mean that because I've worked my butt off to give you this much, until bloody two o'clock this morning . . . Yeah, I think it might be the same man. But until I've had more time, you mustn't jump the gun. It was a different weapon, longer, but the same shape."

Tennison patted his arm, then turned to the row of seats by the doors. DC Jones was sitting there, looking very pale. As she watched, he put his head between his knees. Norman suddenly snapped his fingers and dug a hand into his back pocket.

He brought out a screwed-up bundle of notes. "Eh, Daffy, I've got to give you some money, boyo!"

Jones looked up. "Don't mind if you do," he managed to reply.

"For the benefit night, man. What was it, a pony?"

Jones looked completely blank.

"Sorry, forgot you're an ignorant Welsh git! Twenty-five quid, was it?"

Jones nodded, still confused and sick. Norman handed him the cash with a flourish.

Tennison said cheerfully, "OK, if you're feeling better, DC Jones, you can drive me back to the station!"

"Yes, ma'am. Sorry about this, but I was up half the night. The wife cooked a curry, must have turned my stomach. Sorry!"

She smiled and winked at Norman as she removed her mask. "You'll call me with anything I can quote? And . . . thanks for coming out to Sunningdale. Bye!"

Jones followed Tennison through the main doors into the station, on his way to Forensic, and noticed the stain on her raincoat. It was in a most unfortunate position, as if she'd sat in something nasty. Embarrassed, he would have let it go, but WPC Havers, coming out of the ladies', spotted it.

"Oh, boss, just a minute . . ."

"Whatever you've got, it'll have to wait."

Havers blushed. "It's your coat, you've got a terrible stain on the back!"

Tennison pulled her coat round to look. "Oh, bugger, it singed! I got soaked last night and left it on the radiator. Can you take it and sponge it down, see if you can do anything with it? It's a Jaeger, really expensive . . ."

While Havers inspected the coat, Tennison looked at Jones. "It's in a pretty unfortunate position, wouldn't you say, Jonesey? What did you think it was, menstrual cycle? Or curry tummy?"

He flushed and replied, "I didn't notice it, ma'am."

Tennison snorted. "Oh, yeah, pull the other one! Thanks, Maureen."

At nine o'clock George Marlow, looking extremely smart, left his flat and made his way to the paint factory he worked for. His shadows kept watch on both entrances to the building.

The main part of the factory with the massive vats for mixing the colors was as big as an aircraft hangar. The narrow lanes between the vats stretched from one end of the building to the other. The offices were ranged along the far side and all the windows looked out over the factory floor.

There were some outrageous stories spread among the workers about some director or other who had been caught giving his secretary a seeing-to on the desk. The embarrassed man discovered, too late, that he had neglected to draw the blinds. The entire factory had viewed the deflowering of the poor woman, Norma Millbank, who was so mortified that everyone had seen her thrashing on the desk-top that she quit her job on the spot. Since then the workers had lived in hope, but the blinds were usually kept lowered. But the offices were known from then on as the "Fish Tank."

The office George Marlow used when he was in London was at the far end. He shared it with three other salesmen, one of them a fresh-faced boy called Nicky, who had only been with the firm for sixteen months. A huge chart nearly covered one wall, and the men vied with each other to plot their progress in brilliant colors, like bolts of lightning. The bulletins were a great encouragement and stirred up the competition, not just among the four men in Marlow's office but all the salesmen. Every month there was a bonus for the highest sales, and George Marlow won it as often as not. He was known as the champion.

Marlow prided himself on being number one, and yet he was a very generous man with his contacts. He had trained and helped young Nicky Lennon, giving him introductions and special hints. Nicky was working on his accounts when the word went round that George Marlow had been picked up and charged with murder, and that he was on the factory floor right now!

They all knew that he had been in prison for rape, and that his job had been held open for him. When he had returned to work he had thrown a big champagne party, inviting all of them to ask anything they wanted, to discuss it and get it out in the open. He talked of his trial, the prison, and still he claimed he was innocent.

It had taken him a few months and some obvious ill-feeling and embarrassment before he was again the champion, accepted and fighting to regain the best-salesman sash. Never mind the bonus, it was the sash he wanted, and he won it fair and square the year he returned. He also won the respect of his colleagues, and because he was such a good worker and always ready to give assistance to the others, no one ever mentioned his spot of trouble.

Marlow was a known collector of jokes, he could outjoke the professionals and keep on going. He was the man who knew everyone by name, their wives and their sisters, their troubles. There was always a special joke, and one their mothers could be allowed to hear. The secretaries flirted with him, a few had even dated him, he was so attractive, but Moyra was a strong woman who made it known that he was her man.

The men loved Moyra, because she was as good as Marlow with the wisecracks, and they socialized quite a lot, although Marlow's frequent trips north meant that they had few close friends as a couple. There were occasional dinners and parties at the factory.

When Marlow crossed the factory floor, the cat-calls and shouts that usually filled the cavernous building were ominously missing. Secretaries appeared around the sides of the vats, then vanished. Marlow could see police everywhere he looked, talking to the paint mixers, the sales personnel, the accountants . . . He couldn't find a joke inside him even if he tried.

He kept his head down and hurried towards the Fish Tank. He was pink with embarrassment, hearing the whispers following his progress, and he was glad to make it to his office, especially when he found it empty. He peered through the blinds, wondering why they were doing this to him. Echoing footsteps hurried past his window, the distant giggles made him sweat. Was he dreaming it, or were they all watching him, whispering about him?

It was no figment of his imagination. As the morning wore on it grew worse, and no one came to his office. The worst moment was when he spotted young Nicky, who stared at him with unabashed distaste, so obvious that Marlow thought he was joking. When he approached the boy he turned his back and walked away. Not one person spoke to him or looked him in the face.

He sat in his office and typed out his own resignation, as the group's secretary insisted she was too busy. He licked the envelope and stuck the flap down, then went to see the manager. But Edward Harvey was in a meeting with all the salesmen. Marlow could see them through the window; as he walked in they fell silent. He went straight to Mr. Harvey and handed him the envelope.

"It's just a conference about the new paint for European distribution, George, not your territory, but you can stay if you want."

At least when Harvey spoke to him he looked him in the eye, even though he was lying. When Marlow walked out they started to talk again, a low hubbub at first, but it grew louder. The blinds were lifted a crack and they watched him, the champion fallen from grace. This time he had fallen too far to be picked up.

Marlow hurried among the paint vats, then turned towards the offices. He shouted, and his voice echoed around the factory floor.

"I didn't do it, you bastards!"

DC Rosper and WPC Southwood followed Marlow as he hurried from the factory. Southwood suddenly nudged her partner as she saw DI Muddyman waving to them from the main entrance.

"He's just quit his job," Muddyman said as he came close. "I was just interviewing that little cracker from their accounts department, and he handed in his notice. Instructions are to keep on him, OK?"

Rosper turned this way and that. Marlow was nowhere to be seen. "Where the hell is he?"

Southwood pointed. Way up ahead, Marlow was just crossing the main road, heading for the tube station. Rosper and Southwood took off at a run.

When Jones returned from booking Della's clothing into Forensic, Otley took him aside. "Look, my old son, she's tryin' to rake up the dirt on our old guv'nor, so stick with her. You're young an' a good-looking lad; try an' get into her good books. Anything you find out about the old slag, report back into my shell-likes." He tapped his ear, and continued, "We're lookin' for anything to needle her, know what I mean? We want her off this case . . ." He clocked Tennison heading towards them and shut up.

Tennison was talking fast. "She was naked, hands tied behind her back, dead approximately six weeks. Like Karen, she wasn't killed where she was found. You'll get all the info as soon as I do. The rope's not the same type, but the knot is! We're going to have to talk to all those toms all over again!"

The Incident Room door opened and Otley waltzed in, closely followed by the Super. All twelve people in the room turned their heads to look.

Kernan gestured to Tennison to continue, then found a chair at the back of the room.

"Right, what you got, Muddyman?" she asked.

"Marlow's made several visits to Chester Paints, the last one this morning while I was here. He's just quit his job."

"What was he doing in the first week of December? Was he in the London area?"

"Yes, it's a pretty slack period in the paint trade, he didn't go on the road again until . . ." He flicked through his notes, but Tennison was off on another track.

"So we've established that Marlow was in London for both murders. Is there anything on his car yet? No? What about his neighbors?"

"My lads have questioned most of the ones in the block. He seems to be pretty well-liked, uses the local pub regularly. Several people remembered the car, but couldn't say when they last saw it."

"You'd better turn your attention to Sunningdale. I want the biggest team you can muster, do all the houses bordering the golf course. Someone must have seen him, or at least the car. It's a collector's item, and an unusual color, so go out there and ask them."

The meeting broke up. As the room emptied, Otley said to Tennison, "Did you arrange for the release of Karen's body? The morgue said they were finished, everyone else has finished with her, Pathology and Forensic. It was all waiting on you, and her parents have asked God knows how many times . . ."

"I'm sorry, yes, I've finished with her. Will you arrange it?"

Otley pursed his lips. "Not my job, but if that's what you want . . ." Kernan came up behind Tennison. "I'll see you in your office, OK?" Tennison didn't have time to reply. Otley and Kernan walked off together and she gazed after them. She was going to look for one of those gigantic wooden spoons, and present it to Otley.

George Marlow inserted his key in the front door and pushed. The door opened about two inches and stopped dead; the chain was on.

He rang the bell and waited; nothing happened. "Moyra? Moyra! Let me in!" he called. He had to ring and shout again before the door eventually swung open.

As Marlow walked into the hall, Moyra stuck her head out of the door and looked around, saying loudly, "That old cow next door is going to do herself a mischief one of these days, glued to that bloody door all day!"

Suddenly she looked across at the block of flats opposite, stared for a moment. Then she unbuttoned her blouse, crossed the walkway and opened it wide.

In the surveillance flat DI Haskons, bored rigid, had been chatting on the radio with the two officers in the unmarked car. He sat bolt upright.

"Well, chaps, I think she's spotted us—I don't suppose anyone got a shot of her titties?"

Tennison found the Super sitting at her desk. Otley was with him. She asked Kernan about the press release.

"So we're not mentioning the weals on the arms this time either?"

"No, I kept it to a minimum." He flicked a glance at Otley. "Your decision to release Marlow could backfire . . ."

Tennison was furious, but she kept her temper. "My decision? You backed me up, have you changed your mind?"

Kernan ran his fingers through his hair and said to Otley, "You want to give us a minute?"

"No, I want him to stay . . . sir."

"OK . . . The consensus seems to be that this case is getting a little heavy for you to handle."

Tennison couldn't hold back. "Bullshit! I can—"

"Just let me finish, will you?"

"I'm sorry, sir, but I want to ask the sergeant a question." She turned to face Otley. "How well did Detective Chief Inspector Shefford know Della Mornay?"

Otley replied with a shrug, "He knew her, nobody ever denied that. She was an informer . . ."

"So you agree he knew her well?"

Otley flashed a puzzled look at Kernan and shook his head.

Tennison banged on, "Why did DCI Shefford wrongly identify the first victim?"

"Because they bloody looked alike," snapped Otley. "Her face was beaten to a pulp!"

"You knew her too, didn't you? Then why wasn't it realized until after I took over the case that the body identified as Mornay was, in fact, Karen Howard?"

"What's this got to do with anything?" Kernan demanded impatiently."

Tennison opened a drawer and slapped two files on the desk. She stood directly in front of Kernan.

"When I took over the case, I requested Della Mornay's file from Vice. I was told that the delay in sending it was due to the computer changeover, leading me to believe that DCI Shefford had not had access to the records. I was mistaken." She slapped the file. "He did have it, but it was not recorded in the case file."

"This is a bloody waste of time!" Otley protested, uneasily.

"Is it? Here's the one I received from Vice. And here's the one Shefford received. Two supposedly identical files, but in mine there was no mention of Della Mornay being used as an informer, no record of the fact that DCI Shefford was her arresting officer when he was attached to Vice."

Otley pointed to the files. "I don't know anything about that, but I do know that you've got some personal grudge against a man that was admired—"

Tennison cut him short. "Shefford was so damned eager, even desperate, to make an arrest, judging by this . . ." She stopped, realizing her voice had climbed almost to a shriek. She went on more calmly, "I still want to know, if both you and Shefford knew Della Mornay personally, how the body was wrongly identified."

Otley stared at her with loathing, tried to face her down. But she had him backed into a corner; his eyes flicked from side to side as he said, "Why don't you leave it alone! The man is dead!"

Tennison pointed to two photographs on the wall. "So are they! Karen Howard and Della Mornay! So explain this, Sergeant . . ."

Opening her desk drawer again she produced Della Mornay's diary. "It was in your desk along with the original Vice file."

Otley had no reply to make. Kernan thumped the desk. "What the hell is going on?"

"This, sir, is Della Mornay's diary, not tagged, not logged in. There are pages missing, obviously torn out." She turned to Otley and asked icily, "Do you know what happened to those pages?"

"I can explain about the diary. I gave it to John . . . er, DCI Shefford. I presumed he would have . . ." He dropped his gaze to the floor. "I found it when I was clearing out his desk. He must have removed the pages."

Through gritted teeth, Kernan whispered, "Jesus Christ!" He looked at Tennison. "You realize what this means? You are accusing a senior officer of doctoring evidence."

"Marlow made two statements. In the second one he stated that he picked up *Della* Mornay. He has to have got her name from Shefford. Yes, I know what I'm saying. If I discover any further irregularities . . ."

"Any so-called irregularities, Chief Inspector, you bring straight to me. I will decide if the matter is to be taken further."

"Until I have verification that both women were murdered by the same man, I'd like to keep the discovery of Mornay's body under wraps."

"Marlow still your main suspect?"

"Yes, sir. I want him kept under pressure, round-the-clock surveillance. I know it's expensive, but if he's killed twice . . ."

Kernan nodded, and she continued, "I'd also like to handle the press releases myself from now on, sir—reporting to you, of course."

She had won, and she knew it. She walked out and left them there, closing the door quietly behind her.

There was a moment's silence. Otley just stood there, still looking at the floor, waiting for the explosion.

"You bloody idiot! She's effing wiped the floor with the lot of you! You were lucky this time, *she* let you off the hook, not me!"

Otley dug into his pocket and brought out his wallet. "It was just the days John went to see her, nothing to do with the case."

His face set, Kernan held out his hand. Otley laid a few crumpled pieces of paper on his palm.

"He was fond of her . . ." When he looked up, Kernan was gone. He turned to face the photograph of Della on the wall. "He was very fond of her."

George Marlow was looking at the TV guide in his *Evening Standard*. He paid no attention to the large photograph of Karen Howard on the front page.

"You're home early," Moyra commented from the doorway.

"Did you get a video?" he asked.

"Yeah . . . The cops've been here again, they took the rest of your shoes. I said they'd better bring them quick or you'd be selling paint in your stocking feet."

"No I won't," he answered, "I quit today before they could sack me."

Moyra walked to the window, the tears pricking her eyes. She moved the curtain slightly to look across at the dark windows of the surveillance flat.

"Bastards! You'd think we were the spies, the way they carry on. I'm keeping the chain on the door all the time now. They've had all our keys, and I don't trust them. They could have had them copied . . ."

He looked up. He couldn't say anything to comfort her, and she was trying hard not to cry as she said, "It's getting me down, George, like we're prisoners . . ."

"I'm sorry . . ." He put his hand out for her, but she held back, folding her arms.

"Moyra, don't you turn against me. No one said a single word to me in the factory, except Edward Harvey, and even he didn't want to look me in the eye . . . I love you, Moyra, but I don't know how much more of this I can take."

"I have to take it too, George. With you not earning, what are we going to do?"

He stood there looking forlorn and his voice cracked as he said, "I won't let them beat me, I'll find another job . . ." He shook his fists in the air in frustration and yelled, "I didn't do it, I didn't do it! So help me God, I didn't do it . . ."

The telephone rang and he nearly jumped out of his skin. He stared at it as it continued to shrill.

Moyra sighed. "I'll get it. If it's another of those filthy bloody perverts . . . And those kids next door . . ."

She picked up the phone but said nothing for a second or two, then, "Oh, hallo, Doris . . . Yes, just a minute."

She turned to George. "It's your mum, it's a payphone."

He shook his head, unable to face speaking to her.

"You'll have to talk to her, come on, love."

He pulled himself up and took the receiver. Moyra was astonished that he could sound so bright.

"Hallo, Mum! I'm fine, yeah. How's your hip? It is?" He whispered to Moyra, "She's only using one stick now!"

He listened awhile, then answered, "Thanks, Mum, I wish the cops felt the same way. You know what they're like . . . I'm sorry, they're talking to everyone I know."

Moyra watched him closely until he put the phone down and stood there, dejected.

"You never even mentioned you've no job, you should have told her."

"It wasn't necessary."

"It will be when you can't pay for her 'residential home.'" Moyra couldn't keep the sarcasm out of her voice.

"I'll manage, man with my experience can always get work. Things'll be OK, I'll go and see her. Will you get me the perfume she likes?"

Moyra wanted to weep; his whole life was turned upside-down, and hers, and he was asking her to buy perfume.

"She must have a drawerful."

"I like to take her something, you know that. I'm all she's got."

"You're all I've got too, George!"

He gave her a sweet, gentle smile, showing his perfect teeth, his slanting, wonderful eyes. She loved him to bursting sometimes.

"I'll get us a cup of tea." She didn't mean to sound abrupt, it just came out that way.

When Jane arrived home that night, later than she had promised, she wanted nothing more than a hot bath and to crash out.

As she walked into the bedroom, Peter took one look at her face. "I suppose you don't want to go out to eat? Want me to get a takeaway?"

"Oh, yeah, but first I want a shower."

"I booked a court, didn't the message get to you?"

She looked at him and realized that he had been playing squash. "I'm sorry, love, I've been in and out of the station. I meant to call, but I kept getting waylaid."

"You gonna be waylaid over this dinner?"

"What? The takeaway?"

"No, I told you, I asked you for a date when I could invite Frank King and his wife, and Tom and Sheila, to dinner. I told you."

"I know, and I haven't forgotten. I've even arranged for Pam to come over tomorrow to help me sort out the menu!"

"Well, there's no need to go mad!"

"With my culinary expertise, darlin', I doubt it, but I'll have a go."

He tipped her chin up and kissed her, looking into her eyes. "It's important to me. I lost out on a contract; if I pull off this deal with Frank King we'll set up a partnership. He's got a big yard, employs fifty guys, and then Tom supplies the paint. We cut cost all round. I don't know if they want me with them, but it'd be a big plus for me, so the dinner's important."

"I know, it's no problem, but my hunger is! Lemme have a shower, you get the nosh."

The hot water felt good. Wrapped in a big toweling dressing gown, Jane switched on the television and lay on the bed to watch it. She could have gone to sleep there and then, but Peter arrived with the Chinese takeaway. She could hear him banging around in the kitchen but didn't have the energy to get up and help him.

The telephone rang and Peter appeared at the door. "If that's for you to go out, I quit! *I quit!*"

It was Jane's mother on the line to remind her of her father's birthday and to invite her to a small party. Jane covered the mouthpiece and called Peter, "Pete! Pete, it's Mum! Are you free next Monday? It's Dad's seventy-fifth and she's having a little do! Pete?"

Peter brought the tray with the cartons of food and a bottle of wine. "Sounds OK," he said.

Jane listened to her mother carrying on about her sister Pam's pregnancy and pulled a face. "Pam's got water retention!"

Already tucking in to the food, Peter gestured that it would get cold.

"Mum, I'll have to go, we're just having dinner. Yes! I'll be there, and Peter . . . OK . . . Give Pop my love!" She put the phone down, "Dear God, don't let me forget Dad's birthday card, remind me to send it off."

It was almost ten. They settled back to watch TV as they ate, but Jane had no sooner lifted the fork to her mouth than the phone rang again. She pushed the tray away.

"I'll get it."

Peter continued eating. He could hear excitement in Jane's voice, then her laughter. At least it sounded like good news. She came back into the bedroom, beaming.

"Guess what, I'm going to be on TV!"

"What? I thought *Opportunity Knocks* was defunct?"

"Ho, ho! No, I'm going on *Crime Night*, the police program, and I will be the first female murder officer they've ever had on!"

"Oh, great! Finish your dinner, the crab and noodle's good."

Jane twirled around, suddenly no longer tired. "I pulled every string I could muster. Mind you, the Chief's got to give the go-ahead, but he can't refuse. I mean, to date we've got bugger all, but I know this'll bring us something, I just know it. I'm gonna get that bastard . . .

"When is it?"

"The twenty-second, they need a while to organize the mock-up film, and I've got to put together all the evidence we can use . . . Oh, shit! It's Dad's birthday!"

"Well, maybe they can have it another day?"

"Don't be stupid, the program goes out at the same time every week . . ."

Peter threw his fork down. "I didn't mean the bloody TV program, I meant your Mum could change the party night!"

"Oh, sorry. It'll be OK, I'll just have to make a late entrance."

"I'm not that dumb. Do you want to finish your dinner or not?"

"No, I'm not hungry."

"Fine, then I'll clear away."

He snatched up the tray. As he passed her she put out a hand. "I'm sorry, I guess I'm not hungry."

"That's OK, suit yourself, you usually do!"

"What's that supposed to mean?"

"It's Saturday night, Jane. I thought that just for one night, just one, you wouldn't be on the bloody phone!"

She sighed and flopped back on the bed. She was so hyped up about the TV program that she hadn't given Peter a thought. But by the time he came back into the room she was sitting cross-legged, with that tomboyish grin he liked so much. For a moment he thought it was for him, but then she clapped her hands.

"I am going to nail him, Pete, I know it!"

"I'm going to the pub, see you later."

When Peter got home she was asleep. He stumbled around the bedroom in the dark, cursing as he stubbed his toe. Past caring if he woke her up, he threw himself into bed and thumped his pillow.

Half-asleep, she rolled towards him and muttered, "I'm sorry, Pete, but I get so tired . . ."

He looked at her shadowy face, then drew her into his arms. "You're gonna have to start making time for us, Jane, you hear me?"

"Mmmm, yeah, I know . . . and I will."

"Is that a promise?"

"Yes. I love you, Pete."

She was asleep again, her head resting on his shoulder. He eased her gently back to her side of the bed and then turned over. He was more than worried about his business, and he needed the deal with Frank King to come off. He knew he wouldn't be able to keep afloat for much longer, he'd be bankrupt.

Moyra eased the bedroom curtain aside. She could see the small red dot of a police officer's cigarette. There were two of them; bored with sitting in the car they were taking a breather, walking around the estate. She let the curtain fall back into place.

"There's two of them still prowling around outside, George!"

Marlow lay face down on the bed, his naked body draped in a sheet that just covered his buttocks. He was lean, taut, muscular.

He banged his pillow. "Just ignore them."

"It's tough, they're outside day and night, and I know there's another two in the flat opposite us. I've seen them, I know they're cops, and they've got a camera."

"You'd think they'd have better things to do with ratepayers' money."

"Yeah, but it makes my skin crawl. And her from next door is in and out, talking to everyone! I feel everybody looking at me when I go out. Bastards, this is harrassment! I'd like to get them, the bastards. Why?"

"They've got nothing better to do. It's the way they work, look at the way they treated me over that other business. They stitched me up over that! I just hope to God they find some other sucker and lay off us."

"You hope! Jesus Christ, am I going nuts?"

"Then come here . . . Take your dressing gown off and come to bed."

Moyra slipped off her Marks and Sparks satin robe. It was sexy, like the old film stars used to wear. Beneath it was a matching nightdress with thin ribbon straps.

"You look good, Moyra. That color suits you, and it looks expensive."

"Yeah, well, it was cheap, like me!"

"Don't say that! Come here . . ."

She sighed and sat on the edge of the bed. She wanted to cry, she wanted to bang on the window and scream at the pigs. "I don't feel like it, George."

"Then just lie with me, let me hold you."

He took her gently in his arms and rested his head on her breast. She stroked his hair.

"Why, George, why did you pick that bloody girl up?"

"Because . . . because she was there, Moyra, and if you think I wouldn't give anything to turn the clock back . . . I wish to God I'd never picked her up."

"But you did."

He propped himself on his elbow and traced her cheek with his fingers. "I know I did, and I know I have to make it up to you, but if I swore to you now I'd never have another woman you wouldn't believe me. I've always told you, I've never lied to you, Moyra, never! I don't cheat on you like some guys would. I don't screw your friends."

"What friends? I don't see anyone, especially not now. They can't get away from me fast enough."

"I'm sorry . . ."

"I know, love . . ."

"I love you, Moyra, and if you ever left me, and I know you have every right, but if you were to finish with me . . ."

"I'm here, aren't I? I'm not going anyplace."

She turned to him then, and he kissed her, a sweet, loving kiss. His beautiful eyes were so close that she could feel the long lashes on her cheeks. He covered her face with childish kisses, her lips, her eyes . . . She tried not to cry, but her body trembled.

"Oh, no, please don't cry, Moyra! Please don't cry!"

"I love you, George, I love you, but sometimes I just can't cope, and I don't want to lose you . . . You'll have to promise me, no more girls, please . . . please!"

He rolled onto his back and stretched his arms above his head. "OK."

"Promise me?"

He smiled and turned to her, cupping his head in his hand. "I promise, Moyra Henson! And after the trouble I'm in, do you really think I would? I'll tell you something, I don't think I could, and I'm not joking. It's made me impotent, I can't do a thing!"

She pushed his chest and giggled. "Wanna bet?"

He caught her to him then, hugging her tight, with his wonderful, gurgling laugh. "Oh, my darling, I am a lucky man!"

6

Karen Howard's coffin was completely smothered beneath wreaths of flowers, many of them from sympathetic people who had never even met her.

The funeral drew considerable media attention. Television news cameras followed the grieving parents and friends as they left the church. Tennison held back from the crowd and gestured for Jones and Otley to join her as Major Howard turned towards her.

He thanked them courteously for coming, and suggested that they might like to join the family at their home after the burial. Tennison thanked him for the invitation but declined. He seemed not to hear her, being more intent on sheltering his wife from the prying eyes of the reporters as he helped her into their car. Felicity Howard wore a wide-brimmed hat which only partially concealed a face etched with grief.

All Tennison could think of was how did a respectable girl like Karen end up in a sleazy tart's hovel. There was no hint of her being addicted to drugs, the usual reason someone like Karen did a bit of ducking and diving.

She spoke quietly to the two officers. "I'll have to make a move. You go to the graveside and then back to the station, OK?"

Jones nodded and gave her a quick grin. "Break a leg!"

She gave a short laugh and eased herself away from the mourners towards her parked car. Otley watched her departure with a smirk; a moment later he was approached by a newscaster seeking further news of the murder investigation. He replied that there was none, and that they would be informed as soon as anything developed.

The media had still not linked the Karen Howard case with the murder of Della Mornay. The report of the discovery of the body of a prostitute on Sunningdale golf course had merited only half a column in the nationals, and Tennison wanted it to stay that way. The press release had simply identified the victim and included a routine appeal for information.

The make-up department at the television center was a small room off the main studio floor. Tennison had spent a busy hour with the producer, discussing the questions she would be asked and running through the mock-up of Karen's last known movements; now that she was sitting in Carmen rollers and protective gown, with no one to talk to, she had time to worry. She began to sweat; it was six-thirty and the program would go out live at eight-fifteen. Would she make a fool of herself? Would she stutter? The more she thought about it, the more nervous she became.

The PA to the floor manager came in to go over a few last-minute notes. He reminded her that she was to pause after the third question to allow for the footage of the funeral that had taken place that afternoon. Two officers from her team were already in the telephone control room, running through the hot-line procedure before relaxing for a while in the hospitality room. As the time drew closer, Tennison found herself longing to join them. Her mouth was dry and she kept clearing her throat, but she wouldn't accept anything alcoholic. She clutched a glass of water and went over and over the questions and answers, knowing how important it was to get it right. She was very conscious of being the first female officer in her position ever to appear on the program, and she couldn't foul it up.

Jane's father was sitting right in the center of the sofa opposite the television, his hand on the remote control. Her mother was settling her grandchildren for the night, or trying to. They were dashing up and down the hall of the flat, screaming their heads off. She was getting a headache.

Jane's sister, Pam, yelled at them to be quiet and go to bed, but they paid no attention to their mother. Their father, Tony, glared at her over the evening paper and she told him to go and see to them. Peter, sitting on the arm of the sofa, gave the harassed Tony a wink and opened a bottle of wine.

"Can I give you a refill, Mr. Tennison?"

"Thanks . . . Everyone should get in here, it's going to start in a minute."

Peter poured the wine. The birthday cake and champagne were all on hold for Jane's arrival. Mrs. Tennison came rushing in with more plates of sandwiches.

"Peter, check he's got the right channel for the video, she wants us to record it."

Her husband looked daggers at her. "Just come in and sit down, she'll be on in a minute."

Peter looked at the video machine. "Are you on the right channel, Mr. Tennison?

The *Crime Night* theme started and everyone took their seats. Mr. Tennison, ignoring Peter's question, turned up the volume on the TV and sat back. "Right, no talking . . ."

All of John Shefford's team were gathered around the bar, off the main hall where the benefit dinner was to take place. The MC stood in the doorway, bellowing himself hoarse.

"Take your seats for dinner, gentlemen, please! Dinner is now being served, please take your seats for dinner . . ."

No one paid him the least attention, especially Sergeant Otley, who was leaning over the bar tugging at the sleeve of the harassed barman.

"Is the TV set up in the back? I want to see the start of the program."

Dave Jones nudged him. "Come on, let's go and eat. Someone'll have taped it."

Otley shrugged him away. "Go on in, we're on the center table. I'll be a few seconds, go on . . . Oi, Felix! you want a quick one before we go in?"

Felix Norman had appeared in the doorway, still in his overcoat. "I can't find a bloody parking space!" he yelled.

The MC had got hold of a microphone and his voice boomed, "Please take your seats, gentlemen, dinner is now being served!" He was obviously under pressure from a row of aged waitresses who were giving him foul looks. "Please go in to dinner!"

At last there was a slow surge into the main hall where the tables had been set up around a central boxing ring. Norman downed his double malt and grinned at DI Muddyman.

"How's our man? I hope he's not been in here; he can't box and drink. When I was the amateur middleweight champion of Oxford, did I tell you, I had ten bouts . . ."

Someone yelled, "How many years ago was that now, Felix?" Everyone had heard of his boxing prowess, sadly cut short by a hand injury, and no one paid any further attention in the crush as they all tried to get into the main hall at once. Superintendent Kernan was laughing at some joke, the tears rolling down his cheeks, and Otley whistled to him, pointing towards the hall.

"We're on table six, Mike, right up against the ring!"

As the men sorted themselves out and filtered into the hall, Otley scuttled round the bar and headed for the back room, where there was a small portable TV set. A little unsteadily, Otley propped himself near the door, and was squashed against the wall as the barman came through with a crate of bottles.

Tennison was on screen. Otley squinted. "That's her, she's on! What's she think she's come as, Maggie Thatcher?"

He inched further into the room to get a better view. As he had organized the benefit night he had been propping up the bar since six-thirty, and the small screen made his eyes water. He could see six of Tennison, six of the bitch! And one was bad enough.

Tennison paused on cue for the footage of Karen's funeral. She was in fact coping very well. She was now halfway through her discussion with Brian Hayes; she was clear, concise and very direct.

"We know Karen left the offices of the MacDonald Advertising Company soon after six-thirty on the evening of the thirteenth of January this year. She told the people she was working with that she was going home to her flat in Kensington. No one was seen to meet her. She turned left into Ladbroke Grove, towards the side street where she had parked her white Mini."

The picture cut to Brian. "Karen Howard never returned to her flat. Were you in Ladbroke Grove that night, Saturday the thirteenth of January, at around six-thirty? Did you see Karen?"

Again the picture cut. The screen showed WPC Barbara Morgan, dressed in the dead girl's clothes, walking away from the film company's offices.

As Jane was no longer the center of attention, her mother got up from her seat to get a glass of wine. She was told to sit down again and not interrupt the program. She gave Peter a look and pointed to the video machine, whispering, "Is it on the right channel, Peter?"

Mr. Tennison pounded on the arm of the sofa. "Be quiet!"

"Jane's not on, and I was just asking if you'd checked it's on the right channel."

"I *have*! Now be quiet!"

Mrs. Tennison sighed. The recreation of the dead girl's movements meant nothing to her; she was a stranger.

Major and Mrs. Howard were sitting in front of their television set, holding hands tightly. The major had not wanted his wife to see the program, but she had quietly insisted. They had been told so little, they knew only the bare essentials about the death of their beloved daughter.

WPC Barbara Morgan was wearing a blond, shoulder-length wig and a jacket similar to the one worn by the real Karen on the night she had been murdered. The jacket had never been traced. The WPC also wore sheer black stockings, a leather mini-skirt and identical black ballet pumps. She actually carried Karen's own portfolio containing her modeling pictures.

On screen, Barbara Morgan began acting out the last known movements of Karen Howard. Walking casually along Ladbroke Grove, she headed towards the Mini.

The major and his wife watched the last known movements of their daughter, the last hours of her life.

"She looks like her." The major's voice was very low and he gripped his wife's hand more tightly.

"No," Felicity said, "Karen was prettier."

The tears streamed down her cheeks as WPC Morgan turned a corner into a side street, stopped by a white Mini and unlocked it. After putting the portfolio in the back she sat in the driving seat and tried to start the car, but the engine would not turn over.

Brian Hayes's voice accompanied the film. "Having arrived for work at the film studio early in the morning, Karen had left her car lights on, and the battery was flat. A man working on the building site opposite was backing his truck into the street while Karen was trying to start her car. He stated that it was almost six forty-five."

On the screen, the driver hopped down from his cab and crossed the road to offer his assistance.

"Got a problem, have you, love?"

"Yes, I think the battery's flat."

"You need jump leads, love. Sorry I can't help, but hang on a mo."

He called across to his mates, asking if they had any jump leads, and was told they had not. The driver suggested that he and his pals could give the car a push, but he had to return to his truck as he was blocking a van from leaving the building site.

"Thanks for your help, but I think I'd better call the AA."

Brian Hayes's voice again took up the story. "Karen locked her car and waved to the driver as he moved off. Then she walked back to the main road."

George Marlow was standing directly in front of the television screen, his hands stuffed in his pockets, his face expressionless, as Moyra entered the room.

"Turn it off, George. What are you watching it for? Turn it off!"

She didn't wait for George, she turned it off herself. "What are you watching it for?"

With a sigh, Marlow asked, "Why do you think?"

"You tell me?"

"Because somebody out there might have the fucking evidence that'll get me off the hook, that's why. I didn't kill her, but somebody did, and they're trying to make out that it was me. I want to see if there's anything I can help them with. Now turn it back on!"

"No!"

"Jesus Christ, Moyra! You don't believe me, do you?"

"I just don't want to see her."

"It isn't her, she's dead. That's a policewoman."

"I know that," Moyra snapped. "Why don't you go out and bloody pick her up while you're at it?"

Marlow shook his head in disbelief. "Look, how many more times? If I could turn the clock back, if there was any way I could . . . But I can't. I picked that girl up and now they're saying that I killed her. I swear before God that I didn't, and maybe, just maybe, there's something in that program that'll make me remember more. Somebody killed her, Moyra, but not me!"

"I don't want to see it."

"Then leave the room."

He bent to switch the set on again but she broke down. "Why? Why did you do it, George? Why?"

"You mean why did I pick her up? Why did I fuck her?"

"Yes! Yes, tell me why!"

"Because she was there, and I was there, and she . . . She gave me the come-on, and she was . . . I don't know why! If I was to say to you that I'd never have sex with another woman, you wouldn't believe me. She was a tart. I picked her up, we did the business, I paid her. It meant nothing, it never means anything. I don't cheat on you, Moyra, and I never have."

"You don't what? You don't cheat on me? *Jesus Christ, What do you call it?*"

"*Wanking off! And no, I don't call that cheating!* It's fast, clean and finished, and I pay for it."

You can say that again . . ."

"Yeah, I'm paying for it, I'm paying, Moyra. All I want is for them to find out who did it, find him and let me off the hook."

Moyra snapped the TV set on. "You want him found, what d'you think I want?"

The telephone rang. Moyra turned and looked as if she would yank it from the wall and hurl it across the room. Marlow gripped his hands together, trying to concentrate on the television.

"Don't answer it, Moyra, just leave it."

Moyra marched to the phone. "If this is another crank bitch, then I'm ready for her. I'm bloody ready for anyone."

She snatched up the phone but said nothing, just listened. Then she sighed and held the receiver out to Marlow.

"It's your mother. George, it's Doris."

She handed the phone over, not even bothering to say hallo to Mrs. Marlow. She stood with her hands on her hips, watching the way he swallowed, closed his eyes for a moment as if trying to calm himself, make himself sound relaxed.

He said brightly, "Hallo, my old love? Mum? Eh, eh, now what's this? You crying, sweetheart?"

Moyra sighed and turned back to the TV set, arms folded, only half-listening to George's conversation.

"Yes . . . Yes, Mum, I'm watching. We've got it on. Yes, I know . . . Look, I don't want to talk about it, can I call you back? Because I want to see it! No, no . . . I was released, Mum, it was just . . . No, they don't want to see me again, no, they released me. It was a big mistake . . ."

Moyra turned the volume up and turned to George. "Jesus Christ, they got a car identical to yours! Look, look at the TV! They're giving out your number plate! George!"

Marlow dropped the phone back on the hook and stared in shock at the screen. Moyra shouted for him to get on to his lawyer, but he slumped in his chair, hands raised helplessly. "How can they do this to me? Why . . . ? Why are they doing this to me?"

"Oi, Otley, what the fuck're you doin' in here? You've missed the soup and the chicken frisky . . . mind, I don't blame you, we'll all be salmonellaed by tomorrow!"

Otley ignored the well-flushed Jones as he chuntered on. The barman had started the glass-washing machine, and the din from the main hall was drowning out the TV program.

"Come on, Burkin's on first! He's matched against the Raging Bull of Reading!"

Otley pointed drunkenly at the screen. "Look at this bull dyke, Jesus, hate her guts . . . She's comin' on like bleedin' Esther Rantzen! Look, d'you believe it? And I'm tellin' you, she's really done herself in."

Jones stared at the small screen. "Shit, it's Marlow's car, isn't it? I mean, the make?"

"Yeah, an' if that's not an infringement of personal privacy, she's given out his fuckin' registration number!"

Otley chortled, choked and drained his glass. Tennison, on screen, was discussing the Rover with Brian Hayes, then the camera zoomed in on her face for a close-up.

"Did Karen have a handbag with her on the night she died? Her portfolio was found in her car, but no bag. There was also her Filofax; it could be that she carried it in a handbag, and it has not been found. The witness who saw her stop at a cardphone and directed her to a payphone on Ladbroke Grove couldn't tell us if she had a bag or not . . ."

Otley exploded. "Oh, that's bloody marvelous! By tomorrow mornin' we'll have every soddin' lost bag in the London area . . . This bloody woman is a total fuckin' idiot . . ."

On screen, Tennison was still talking. ". . . Telecom tell us that the coinbox was out of order that night. The AA have no record of a call from Karen . . ."

The bellowing of the Master of Ceremonies cut through the singing and shouting from the main room. "Gentlemen, in the red corner we have DI Burkin, weighing in at sixteen stone fifteen pounds, let's hear it for him . . . And in the blue corner, the Raging Bull of Reading!"

Boos and cat-calls drowned Brian Hayes and Tennison. DC Jones gave up on Otley and returned to the hall to watch the fight. This was his first benefit, being the fresh man on the team, and he was having the time of his life. He seemed unaware that the orange juice was well and truly laced with vodka, but he'd know by the end of the evening. He was well on his way to getting totally plastered for the first time in his life.

Otley did not join table six until *Crime Night* was over and the fight was in the fourth round. Burkin looked very much the worse for wear, his nose streaming blood and one eye nearly closed.

During the break, Felix Norman climbed into the red corner, screaming instructions as if he was Burkin's second. "Keep your fists up! Up, man! You're flayin' around like a bloody oik! Hit him with a good body, then one, two, one, two . . ."

Felix hauled out of the ring as the bell rang for the next round. Men were bellowing from the back of the room for Felix to sit down, they could not see through his bulk.

Otley cheered loudly as he poured himself a large Scotch from one of the many bottles in front of him. Kernan was whistling and thumping on the table; Otley leaned across to him.

"'Ere, Tennison's done 'erself in tonight, guv! Wait till you see what she bloody went on about in the telly program. How she wangled that I'd like to know!"

"Yeeessssss!" Kernan was on his feet, fists in the air, as Burkin landed a good uppercut to his opponent's chin. The entire room erupted and chants of "Blood . . . blood . . . blood . . ." mingled with a pitiful request over the public address system for whoever had parked in front of the fire escape to move his car. The chanting mounted in a crescendo as Burkin staggered as if he was going to keel over, but he planted his elbow in the Raging Bull's ribs, and a small but visible head butt gave an opening for his right hand. The cheers were deafening as Burkin was proclaimed the winner.

The tiny blast of a worn-out record of *The Eye of the Tiger* started playing for the next bout as the buckets for donations to Shefford's family were being passed around. Otley sat back in his chair with a grin like the Cheshire Cat; he knew Tennison was in the shit, knew it, because he also knew that Marlow's car had not been reported stolen. To give out his registration number on live national television was going to create a nasty scene with Marlow's legal adviser. Otley's hands itched for his wooden spoon . . .

DC Jones was propped against the table, insisting on singing a solo, demanding to be let into the ring. His young face was flushed an extraordinary red, his shirt was undone . . . Otley chuckled; they'd got the poor lad well and truly pissed. He stood up to give Jones a helping hand and slithered beneath the table, where he remained for the rest of the evening.

Jane drove straight from the television studios to her parents' flat. The follow-up would not go on air for another hour and a half, and she was not required to wait for the phone-in. The two officers left in charge had her number, and she was ready to act immediately on any information that came in.

Her family had waited long enough, so the champagne was open and the candles on her father's birthday cake were lit when she rang the bell, just in time to join the chorus of *Happy Birthday*. She had forgotten to post his card, but presented it with a flourish with the two bottles of champagne she had picked up on the way from the television center.

Her father hugged her tightly, proud of her achievements, although he never said much about it. She kissed him while her mother looked on, surreptitiously removing the supermarket price labels from the champagne bottles, but not before she noticed they were bought locally. Jane couldn't even spare the time to buy her dad a present!

"Well, was I OK? What do you think, did I look OK?"

She was asking generally, but her eye caught Peter's and he gave her the thumbs-up. "Well, come on, put the video on, let me see meself!" She sat down with a glass of champagne.

Her father leaned against the back of the sofa. "What's this Brian Hayes bloke like, then? I listened to him on the radio, you know."

"Oh, he's great! Did you think I was OK, Dad?"

"Course you were, love. Do you want a sandwich?"

"No, thanks, I just want to see what I looked like. The second part'll be on soon."

Peter started the video and ice skaters zapped across the screen in fast forward. Then came a snatch of *Dallas*, then back to the skating.

"Is this the video? Peter? Is it on?"

Peter straightened and flashed a look at Jane's father. "Sorry, love, I think we recorded the wrong channel . . ."

"What! Oh, shit, no, you haven't, have you?"

The ice spectacular continued. As Peter looked on, Jane threw a beaut of a tantrum, only interrupted by the ringing of the telephone.

The second part of the program reviewed the number of calls that had been received and mentioned further evidence in the Karen Howard case.

There had actually been ten calls connected with the murder, but only one was to prove worthwhile. Once the cranks and hoaxers had been weeded out, one caller remained. Helen Masters, a social worker, had seen Karen in Ladbroke Grove on the night of the murder; she had seen a man picking her up, a man who, she was sure, knew the victim.

It was almost midnight when two officers arrived at Miss Masters' house in Clapham to take a statement. She had seen a man she was able to describe in detail, and was sure she would be able to recognize again. She described the man as five feet nine to ten, well dressed, rather handsome, with very dark hair; she described George Arthur Marlow.

Jane and Peter argued all the way home from her parents' flat. They were still rowing when they reached their door. Peter was furious at her behavior; they had all been waiting for her to cut the birthday cake, but as soon as she had arrived she had caused a terrible argument over her father not recording the program. Her tantrum, which was how he described her tirade against her father, was disgusting, especially when she knew that they had recorded it at home anyway.

Jane refused to back down, it was important to her and her father had known it.

"Do you think he did it on purpose, for God's sake?"

"That's not the point! They all knew how important it was to me, but they didn't give a fuck! The stupid old sod should have let someone else do it! He always gets it wrong!" She stormed into the bedroom.

"Of course they bloody cared!" Peter slammed the front door so hard that it sprang open again and hit him on the shoulder. "You arrive late, scream about the bloody telly, then get on the phone for the rest of the night!" He strode into the bedroom, still yelling, "I don't know why you bothered turning up, you're a selfish bloody cow! He'd been waiting to see you, he's proud as punch about you!"

"Oh, yeah? Well, I've never heard him say it. If you must know, Mother has never even approved of me being in the Force, when I was in uniform she used to make me take my bloody hat off so the neighbors would know it was me! But Pam, oh, Pam could never do anything wrong, all she's done is produce children at such a rate she looks ten years older than she should . . ."

Peter sighed and chucked his coat on the bed. Jane's followed, so hard that it flew across the room. She kicked off her shoes and sat down grumpily on the bed.

"Actually," said Peter, "it was quite funny, watching you and your dad, with Torville and whatsit whizzing round on the screen . . ."

Jane grinned like the sun coming out. "He's never got the hang of that video recorder. He taped bits of a football match over Pam's wedding film . . ." She giggled and hummed a snatch of *Here Comes the Bride*, then shrieked, "Goal!"

She threw herself back on the bed, laughing hysterically, while Peter stood shaking his head in wonder at her sudden change of mood.

"I'm going to have a drink," he said.

"Great, me too, and make it a large one!"

When Peter brought their drinks to the bedroom he found Jane glued to the TV screen as the opening theme of *Crime Night* faded into Brian Hayes's voice.

"I only want to see myself, I'm sure that make-up they put on me looked appalling."

She wound the film forward and stopped it; Peter heard her recorded voice. At the same moment the phone rang in the hall. Jane jumped to her feet and hurried to answer it. Peter sat on the bed and sipped his Scotch, watching Jane on the program sitting a little stiffly, but looking very calm and together. The screech that emanated from the hall could hardly be anything to do with that cool woman on screen . . .

She banged open the door, fist in the air. 'We've got a witness who called in after the program. She says she saw Karen Howard picked up by a man. She says the man kenw her, because she's sure he called her name . . . And, Pete, the description, she described bloody George Marlow!"

Her fist shot into the air again. "We got him! We got him, Pete!"

Pete held up her drink. "You wanted to see your performance? Well, you're missing it."

"Sod that, I'm gonna pick him up tonight."

Peter looked surprised and glanced at his watch. "Tonight? Are you going to the station?"

"You're kidding, I'm on my way right now . . ."

It was a while before she did leave; there were hurried phone calls while she was changing her clothes. She wiped the make-up off and gave Peter a perfunctory kiss, then grabbed her bag and bleeper and was gone.

Peter continued to watch her on screen, until he grew bored and switched the video off. He lay back on the bed and sighed . . . Sometimes, more times than he cared to think about, she made him feel inadequate.

But tonight he didn't just feel that way, he was also irritated by her, annoyed by her attitude, her temper, her ambition. He started counting all the emotions she aroused in him, and it was like counting sheep. There were too many, too many to remember. He fell asleep.

7

"I was outside Ladbroke Grove underground station," Helen Masters was telling DCI Tennison, "waiting to meet one of the girls from the Hammersmith halfway house, Susan Lyons. She'd absconded a few days earlier, then she called to ask me to meet her. But she was late."

Tennison nodded. Helen Masters was a terrific witness, a social worker, calm and unruffled, with, most important of all, a retentive memory.

"Were you standing on the pavement, or in the entrance? Tennison asked.

"Mostly in the ticket area, it was a pretty cold night, but I kept checking outside in case I'd missed her. That was when I saw them."

"And who did you see?"

"The man, at first. I just watched him for something to do. There's a bank across the road, a few yards down, and he was standing near the cash dispenser. He had dark hair . . . Then I saw Karen, the girl who was murdered. I'd seen her photographs in the newspapers, but it didn't register until I saw them in color, on the TV program. For a second I thought it was Susan, she's blond too. I stepped forward . . ."

"How close were you?"

"Oh, about five yards . . ." She looked around and pointed to a WPC on the other side of the room. "She was about there."

"And then what?"

"The man over the road walked to the edge of the pavement and called to Karen."

Tennison leaned forward and watched Helen closely as she asked her next question. "You heard him clearly, calling her name?"

Helen nodded. "There was quite a lot of traffic noise, but he definitely called out her name."

Tennison relaxed a little. "Can you tell me what he was wearing?"

"A brownish jacket, with a light shirt underneath."

There was a brief knock on the door and a uniformed DI entered. He gave Tennison a nod. "We're ready for you, Miss Masters," he said.

DI Sleeth led Helen Masters to the observation room next door, explaining the procedure as he did so.

"You will be able to see them, but they can't see you, it's one-way glass. Anything you want them to do, tell me and I'll give the instructions over the address system. Take your time, and don't worry. Any questions?"

She shook her head. DCI Tennison had already told her that another officer had to accompany her for the identity parade, to avoid any suggestion of bias. Helen gave Sleeth a nervous smile and sat in the chair he indicated, facing the one-way glass and the twelve men in the line-up. Sleeth gave Helen a small wink as he tested the microphone that linked them to the identification room.

The twelve men stood in a row, facing the observation window. Each man held a number in front of him; George Marlow was number ten. They were all dark haired and more or less of a size with Marlow, and two, like him, had a deep six o'clock shadow.

"Would you all please turn to your right," Sleeth said into the microphone.

Helen looked at each man in turn, frowning, then made another request. Sleeth announced it.

"When I call out your number, please take one pace forward and say the name "Karen" clearly. Number one, step forward please."

Number one turned slowly and obeyed. "Karen!"

Helen shook her head and Sleeth said, "Thank you, number one, you may step back." He consulted with Helen and continued, "Number eight, please step forward and say the name 'Karen'."

The eighth man's voice was indistinct. "Louder, please, number eight," said Sleeth.

"Karen!" shouted number eight.

In the corridor outside the observation room, Tennison and Otley waited nervously. She was pacing up and down, smoking. The door opened and DI Sleeth came out.

"She wants a closer look," he told Tennison, and led Helen to the main room. Tennison made no attempt to speak to her.

Otley tapped Tennison on the arm and gestured towards the observation room. It was against the rules, but she couldn't resist. They scurried furtively inside to watch.

Helen was moving slowly down the line of men. She paused in front of number two, but only for a second. She stopped at number ten, George Marlow.

"Come on, Helen, that's the one!" Tennison almost shouted in her excitement. Sudden panic made her check the sound system; it was set to receive only. She sighed with relief and whispered through gritted teeth, "Come on, number ten, number ten . . ."

George Marlow stepped out of the line, holding his card in front of him and staring straight ahead. Tennison's spine tingled; it was as if he knew he was looking directly into her eyes.

"Karen!" he called loudly.

Tennison dragged on her cigarette as the tension in the viewing room built up. Otley leaned forward, gritting his teeth. She was staring too long at Marlow, taking too long . . . He drummed his fingers on the table.

"Come on, sweetheart, that's him, yes . . . You've got him!"

The reception area of Southampton Row nick was a hive of activity. A woman was in tears because her Saab Turbo had been either towed away or stolen, and she swore to the desk sergeant that it had been legally parked. Two punks, wearing torn jeans and leather jackets, were being released after a night in the cells. The mother of one of the boys, a Princess Anne looka-like in a camel coat and Hermès scarf, was berating him in a voice that could have shattered glass.

"How could you be so stupid? This will ruin your chances of university! How could you do it . . . Do you know how long I've been waiting?"

Three of the men from the identity parade were leaving, pocketing their eight quid expenses, and in the midst of it all DCI Tennison was thanking Helen Masters, thanking her when she could have screamed the place down with frustration.

Arnold Upcher was guiding George Marlow through the crowd, but suddenly Marlow turned back and pushed his way past the punks towards Tennison.

"Excuse me, Inspector," he said softly, and touched her arm.

Refusing to look at him, Tennison moved quickly, through the door which led behind the reception desk, reappearing next to the desk sergeant. Marlow faced her across the broad counter.

"Inspector Tennison! You're making my life a misery! I was dragged out of bed at four o'clock this morning with no explanation. You've got people watching me night and day, tell me why? You know I'm innocent. If you've got something personal against me, tell me now, what did I ever do to you?"

Upcher, disapproving, grabbed his arm to drag him away. Tennison gave Marlow a long, hard stare, then turned her head to find two men taking great interest in the transaction.

"Inspector Tennison? *Daily Express,* can you spare us a few seconds?"

With a gesture to the desk sergeant, Tennison said, "Get them out of here!" The reporter was moved on by a uniformed officer at the same time as George Marlow, protesting, was being manhandled out of the door by Upcher.

"She's got something personal against me! I *didn't do it! I didn't do it!*"

Scenting a story, the reporter turned his attention to Marlow.

Everywhere Tennison went that day she encountered men with sore heads and matching tempers. Burkin was the worst for wear; his triumph the night before had been paid with a cut eye and lip. Tennison found the resulting lips irritating.

"Where the hell is Jones?" Tennison demanded. "I need him with me."

Otley's piggy eyes were bloodshot and seemed smaller than ever. "Dunno, ma'am." He was having difficulty looking his guv'nor in the face; he had just been telling everybody that their great witness had picked out a tax inspector who'd been hauled in off the street. They were all at it; every time she turned her back one of them would purse his lips and run his hands through his hair in imitation of Tennison on TV.

Three minutes later Jones arrived, belching from the Alka-Seltzer he'd just forced down himself. His head throbbed, his tongue felt like rubber and he looked very pale and shaky. Totally unsympathetic, Tennison told him not to bother sitting down, they were going out.

WPC Havers came rushing in. "The Super wants to see you, ma'am, right away."

"Tell him you can't find me."

"Marlow's lawyer's with him, screaming about you giving details of the car last night. Marlow's never reported it stolen."

"Shit! Well, someone had better get it sorted, and before I get back. We all know how careless filing clerks can be, don't we? The Vehicle Theft Report's probably just been misfiled, hasn't it, Burkin?"

The DI was standing in the center of the room, yawning. "We keeping you awake?" asked Tennison.

"Sorry, ma'am, got a bit of a headache."

"I just hope you won."

He started to nod but thought better of it. On top of his injuries, the bevvies he had consumed after the fight didn't help.

"It was in a good cause, ma'am. I got him in the last round—at least, I think I did. Old Felix was virtually in the ring with me, he used to box for . . ."

Otley smirked. "Made a nice little packet for the Sheffords, at twenty-five quid a ticket."

"Yes, I know. I bought four tickets myself, I'm just sorry I couldn't be there."

She jerked her head to Jones to follow her as she walked out. Otley pursed his lips; nobody had told him that split-arse had chipped in!

"It was George's decision to give notice," said Edward Harvey, George Marlow's boss at the paint factory he represented. "He was getting a lot of stick from the others. I'd never have asked him to leave, he's too good at his job, been with us ten years apart from the time he was in jail."

"He told you all about that, did he?"

"Yes, came straight out with it. I know he was found guilty, but . . ."

"But . . . ?"

"Well, he was always a bit of a lad, popular with the girls. He swears he's innocent, and I really can't see why such an attractive bloke would go and do a thing like that. He was very distressed about it."

"You're entitled to your opinion, Mr. Harvey. Now, could you show us around? If you have time."

"My pleasure."

Mr. Harvey, a cocky little man in his fifties, showed them the well-equipped production line, stopping now and then for a word with the men on the floor.

"We employ three hundred salesmen up and down the country," he told Tennison, while Jones all but disappeared head-first into one of the mixing vats. "We guarantee to match any color you want; the difficult shades are still mixed by hand."

Tennison looked around with interest. "George Marlow always worked from London?"

"He started with the firm in Manchester. We moved our headquarters down here in eighty-two, and George came with us, but he kept his old routes. Had all the contacts, you see, and of course they still had family and friends up north . . ."

"They? Did Marlow travel with someone else?"

"Moyra always went with him on his trips . . ."

"How far back do your staff records go?" asked Tennison.

"Since we moved here. We had a computer system installed, but we've got all the files . . ."

"Would they include the hotels your salesmen used, expenses and so on?"

"This company is run like clockwork," said Harvey proudly. "We like to know where our men are and what they're doing."

"We will need to examine them," Tennison said, clocking Jones' incredulous reaction. "Just Marlow's, of course."

Harvey looked puzzled, but said mildly, "Just so long as we get them back."

Tennison was starving when she arrived back at the station. She grabbed a sandwich and tried to eat it in her office, but she was interrupted by Maureen Havers, who had contacted the Rape Center about Marlow's earlier victim and managed to find out who she was.

"She wanted her identity kept secret, but it's Miss Pauline Gilling, ma'am, from Rochdale. She's been having counselling after a nervous breakdown, and the people in Rochdale say it would only aggravate the situation if we started asking questions."

Tennison spoke through a mouthful of sandwich. "I could be in line for a breakdown myself . . ." She took a sip of coffee. "Get back on to them and don't take no for an answer."

She finished the rest of her sandwich and started gathering items for the team meeting. "Oh, and Maureen, you don't know where I am if the Super asks, OK?"

They were all there. Otley was pinning black-and-white photographs of Della Mornay's and Karen Howard's bodies on the notice-board. There were also blow-ups of the marks on their arms. He turned to the waiting men.

"Right, you can see the similarities of these marks. We got a DNA match on George Marlow's sperm with the blood samples from when he went down for rape, but that's no help with Della. It also doesn't help that he admitted having sex with Karen, and gave a very plausible reason, which seems to check out, for the spot of Karen's blood on his sleeve. We're sure his car's the key; find that and I reckon we've got 'im. So keep at it."

He moved on to the photos of the bodies. "The clearest evidence linking the girls, apart from the marks on the arms, is the way their 'ands were tied. Not the rope itself, but the knots."

"Ah, *knot* the rope, eh, Sarge?" Burkin put in, still lisping.

Otley gave him the finger and replied, "Yeah, very funny . . . The knots are the same, but any boy scout could tie 'em. Now it's your turn, Inspector . . ."

Tennison entered the room, munching a packet of crisps. Burkin waited while she sat down, then picked up from Otley.

"The sack that covered Della Mornay's body was the usual type of hessian, no markings, but there were traces of sump oil on it. There was also sump oil found on Karen's skirt. It doesn't mean a lot, Karen could have got it off her own car." He nodded to Tennison. "All yours," and sat down.

She crunched the last few crisps and screwed the bag up, tossing it at the wastepaper basket and missing. As she bent to retrieve it they all saw the edge of pink lace. Otley, who never missed a trick, pursed his lips and crossed his legs like an old queen.

"Karen didn't put up much of a struggle," Tennison began, spitting a piece of crisp onto her jacket and brushing it off. "Her nails were short, clean, no skin or blood beneath them, but her hands had been scrubbed with something similar to the kind of brush used on suede shoes. Gimme Della's . . ."

Otley passed her a blow-up of Della's hands and she put it up beside the others. "I asked for this because you can see scratch marks on the backs of the hands and fingers. Now, Della did fight, and her nails, unlike Karen's, were long and false. She lost them from the thumb, index and little fingers of her right hand."

Burkin asked, "Did Marlow have any scratches on him when he was stripped?"

"No, he didn't. George Marlow is still the prime suspect, but we have no evidence to put him in that efficiency, no eye witness to link him with either Karen or Della, no mention of him in Della's diary. The list of what we don't have is endless. But if Marlow killed Della before he killed Karen, then he knew her room was empty. He might even have known that the landlady was away, probably hoped that Karen's body wouldn't be found for weeks. His mistake there was in leaving the light on. Mornay's handbag was in her room, but there were no keys."

Always ready to needle her, Otley piped up, "That reminds me, ma'am—handbags. We got a good selection an' they're still comin' in; blue ones, green ones, big 'uns an' little 'uns. What d'you want me to do with 'em?"

Tennison responded quite calmly, considering. "Get one of her flatmates in, let her go over them to save time. Right, the good news is, I'm going home. Sergeant Otley will now tell you the bad news."

As she left the room, she could hear the moan that went up in response to the bad news; all weekend leave was cancelled.

"All leave, that is, apart from 'er own. We got to check through all that gear from the bleedin' paint factory, an' there's a lot. It's a wonder they 'aven't computerized their salesmen's bowel movements . . . Get to it!"

When he went to Superintendent Kernan's office later that evening, Otley found him sitting at his desk, writing memos. Kernan pushed his work aside and poured Otley a large Scotch.

Otley sat down, took a swig and sighed. "We're gettin' nowhere, guv, we've 'ad nothing for days now," he said bitterly. "It's demoralizing, an' it's takin' good men off the streets."

"Most of them have been on the streets, and we've still got nowhere," Kernan replied. "But now she's digging up unsolved murder cases on Marlow's sales routes. He covered the Manchester area, Rochdale, Burnley, Oldham."

Otley shook his head in disgust and opened his mouth to speak, but Kernan wouldn't let him.

"And I've OKed it, so cool off, Bill. I know what you're after, but unless there's good reason for kicking her off the case, she stays put."

"It's because she's a woman, isn't it? If it'd been any of my lads that done that cock-up on telly, given out Marlow's registration number . . . You know he never reported it stolen! There's no report in the log, and I heard his brief was in here creating about it . . ."

Pissed off with Otley's attitude, Kernan cut him short. "Records had the report all the time, Bill. It was misfiled. She's off the hook, and so am I." He paused to let it sink in and wagged a warning finger. "Bill, a word of advice. Make it your business to get on with her."

Otley downed his whisky and stood up. "That an order?" he asked through clenched teeth.

Kernan didn't reply and he walked to the door, stopped with his back to the Super. "John Shefford was the best friend I ever 'ad. When my wife died, he pulled me through. I miss him."

Kernan said gently, "We all do, Bill."

Otley's back was rigid as he replied, "Good night, sir, an' thanks for the drink."

Outside the office, Otley stopped and shook out his old mackintosh, folded it neatly over his arm. *Jesus Christ, Otley, where the fuck did you get that raincoat, when you were demobbed? I'll start a whip-round, get you a decent one, fancy one of those Aussie draped jobs?* He could hear Shefford's voice as if it were yesterday and he ached with grief. He missed his friend more than he could ever put into words, especially to men like Kernan.

Maureen Havers tumbled through the double doors, carrying a vast stack of files, and gave him a glum smile.

"You seen what's coming in? We need a new trestle table for this lot . . . I thought you were on nine to three, Skipper? Haven't you got a home to go to?"

After a moment's hesitation, he offered to give her a hand, and as they walked along the corridor he said casually, "Do me a favor, would you, Maureen? If anything comes in from Oldham, let me have a shufti first, OK?"

"Sure! You got relatives up there? You know, I was almost transferred to Manchester, but I failed my driving test . . ."

They passed through the second set of swing doors and suddenly Otley felt better, because he had something to do. He was off-duty, but had nowhere to go, not now John Shefford was gone.

It was a struggle for Jane Tennison to open the front door. The files she carried were slipping out of her arms, and she dropped her briefcase to save them. When she finally made it into the hall she shut the door behind her and leaned against it, exhausted but glad to be home.

Joey's voice wailed from the spare bedroom, "Nooo-o-o-o! Daddy, don't go!"

"OK, Joe, just one more story," Peter replied patiently.

Grateful that the door was closed, Jane tip-toed past it and into her own bedroom. She was in bed before Peter had finished the last story.

"And then, what do you suppose he did then?"

Silence. Peter peered at his son in the dim light of the Anglepoise lamp; he was asleep at last. He tucked the duvet around Joey's shoulders and sat for a moment, staring at the gleam of his ash blond hair and the long blond lashes lying on his pale cheeks. He loved the boy so much, if only Marianne . . . But he mustn't think like that, the past was done, buried.

Sitting in the semi-darkness, he was unable to stop himself going over and over it in his mind; the anger and hatred, the terrible things that were said, the dragging sense of loss . . . and the last time he had seen Marianne alone. She was so flippant, sometimes he could strangle her . . . He knew he could never let it rest until she told him the truth. She was pregnant again and, from Peter's calculations, he knew that he could be the baby's father.

Jane was asleep as soon as her head touched the pillow. When Peter came to bed, needing her, needing someone, he found her flat out, snoring lightly. Suddenly angry, he threw his dressing-gown off, climbed in beside her and thumped his pillow.

She shot up, blinking in panic, then collapsed with a moan. With her eyes still closed, she mumbled, "Whassa-matter with you?"

"Every night's the same. You're exhausted, asleep before I've even cleaned my teeth . . ."

She rolled towards him and opened her eyes. "I'm sorry, Pete."

"You make me feel guilty if I so much as touch you. We haven't made love for . . . I dunno how long, I hardly see you. And when I do see you, you're always knackered. Our relationship stinks!"

Tentatively, Jane put out a hand and stroked his chest. "I love you."

"You do? But if this—" he lifted her pillow and brought out her beeper—"If this goes off, I don't exist! You're always either giving someone a bollocking on the phone or buried in files."

He switched off his bedside light, plunging them into darkness, and lay down, not touching her. Jane giggled, "You're right! I'm sorry, I will make more time for us. . . ."

He felt her moving beside him. A moment later, her nightdress flew across the room.

"There! Just to prove I'm not a frigid old bag . . ."

Peter smiled and propped himself on one elbow, reached for her.

"Daddy?" said a little voice. Framed in the light from the hall, Joey peered into the room. "Daddy . . . ?"

Pulling the duvet over her head, Jane cracked up, with laughter. "Ignore him, he'll go away . . . Go back to bed, Joey!"

Thinking it was a game, Joey snorted with laughter and jumped on the bed, trying to pull the quilt away from her.

"Don't, Joey! Go back to bed! *Joey!*"

He tried to climb into the bed, but Jane hung on. "Joey, will you pass me my nightdress?"

"Why?"

"Because I don't have any clothes on, that's why."

Peter lifted the duvet on his side. "Come on, get in . . ."

As he snuggled down, Joey demanded in his piped voice, "Tell me a story, about bums and titties!"

"Where did you learn those words?" Peter tried to sound angry, but Jane's sniggers didn't help.

"At school. My mummy goes to bed without any clothes on, sometimes, but sometimes she . . ."

He fell asleep mid-sentence. Peter lifted him into his arms. "I'll just carry him back to his own bed. Jane? Jane . . . ?"

All he could see was the top of her head, but he knew she was asleep. He sighed; the pair of them were out cold, but he was wide awake . . . Wide awake and thinking about Marianne, naked, in bed with his ex-best friend.

8

Maureen Havers was complaining bitterly to Sergeant Otley. It was the third Sunday she had worked in a row, and she didn't like it. She dumped a pile of boxes on the desk.

"These are unsolved murders from the entire Manchester area, every location visited by George Marlow since nineteen eighty-bloody-four!"

Otley was unraveling a huge computer print-out from the paint factory. Its end trailed in a heap on the floor.

"Ma'am needs her rest, Maureen! You got anythin' from Oldham?"

She pointed across the room. "It's on your desk, Skipper. Want some coffee?"

Otley grinned. "Do I! And keep it comin', it looks like we got a real workload."

The rest of the team began to appear in dribs and drabs, looking pretty unenthusiastic about being there. Then Burkin came racing in, the only one who seemed to have any life in him. Grinning, he waved a copy of the *News of the World* under Otley's nose.

"Wait till you see this! All is avenged!"

The two sisters didn't resemble each other in any way. Jane, older by three years, was a nightmare in the kitchen. She had chosen woodwork at school instead of domestic science, and actually preferred M&S ready-to-serve dinners to anything she attempted herself.

Pam, on the other hand, loved cooking. She had done a brief stint behind the counter at Boots the Chemist, then married and produced two children. Her third baby was due within the month. She was easygoing, sweet-natured and boringly happy squashed into Jane's tiny kitchen. Sunday mornings in her household were reserved for preparing the big lunch, but she had managed to send Tony and the kids off to Hampstead Heath so she could come round and help. Yet it was Jane who was brewing the coffee, Jane who set out the cups and saucers, who had brought out the well-thumbed cookery books and was frantically searching for a suitable dish for Peter's big dinner party. Everything Pam had so far suggested had been greeted by groans from Jane; she couldn't attempt a roast, she'd never get the joint ready at the same time as all the vegetables, and she'd never made proper gravy in her life.

"For Chrissakes, Pam, just something simple that looks like it's not, easy to cook but doesn't look like it, know what I mean? I've got the starters organized, just avocados with some prawns bunged in, but it's the main course I'm worried about."

"How many is it for?"

"There'll be six of us. It's got to be something simple, I haven't cooked for so long I don't think I could cope."

"Tell you an easy one—fresh pasta, a little cream and seasoning, then strips of smoked salmon. Plenty of good crusty bread, and fruit and cheese to follow. Are any of them vegetarians?"

The front door banged open and Peter appeared, with the *News of the World* open at the center pages.

"Are any of your friends vegetarian, Pete?"

Ignoring her, Peter read aloud from the paper: "'George Marlow opened his heart to our reporter. He wept, saying he was an innocent man, but the police are making his life a misery . . .'"

Jane tossed her head, thinking he was joking. "Very funny!"

He laughed. "I'm serious! They've got a terrible picture of you, like something out of a horror movie. Dragon Woman!" He dodged her as she grabbed for the paper, and continued reading in a Monty Python voice. "'This is the woman detective in charge of the murder investigation. To date, her only words have been "No comment."' Should be at home with me, mate!"

Jane's next attempt to get the paper from him succeeded, but she tore it in half in the process. "Now look what you've done!" he teased.

But she wasn't listening. Her mouth hung open as she scanned the article. She screamed, "My God, they've got pictures of my surveillance lads!"

Still laughing, Peter was reading over her shoulder. "'Marlow states that he is being hounded by a woman with an obsession—to lock him up . . .'"

"It's not bloody funny! It's buggered everything! We can't have any more line-ups, with his face plastered all over the papers. Not to mention the boys; I'm going to have to pull them off him now their cover's blown!"

She stormed out to the telephone, leaving Pam and Peter staring at each other. Pam whispered, "I think I'd better go."

George Marlow walked quickly up the steps of a large, detached house in Brighton and through the open front doors. A pair of glass swing doors admitted him to the hallway.

Following the directions of the receptionist, Marlow entered a high-ceilinged, airy room with windows overlooking the sea. Several elderly people were quietly playing draughts or chess, while one or two just sat silently in armchairs, their eyes focused on a future that no one else could see.

He knew where he would find her; alone in her wheelchair by the window, gazing out towards France. He walked silently towards her, stopped two or three feet away.

In a low voice that could not be heard by the other residents, he began to sing, "When you walk through a storm, hold your head up high . . ."

His mother turned in her chair, her face lit with joy. As her son kissed her gently on both cheeks, she picked up the refrain.

". . . And don't be afraid of the dark; at the end of the storm there's a golden sky, and the sweet, silver song of a lark . . ."

Mrs. Marlow, or Doris Kelly as she used to be known, had spent the entire morning getting ready for his visit. Her make-up was perfect, her lipstick and eye shadow perhaps a trifle overdone, but she was still a beauty, retaining a youthfulness in her face that was, sadly, not mirrored in her once-perfect body. She had grown heavy, and the scarves and beads, chosen carefully to disguise the fact, didn't help. Her tiny hands, perfectly manicured with shell-pink varnish, glittered with fake diamonds.

"Hallo, my darling!"

When he kissed the powdery cheek, he could feel the spikes of her mascaraed eyelashes. She smelt of sweet flowers. The big china-blue eyes roamed the room as if acknowledging the other residents' prying eyes.

"Take me somewhere special for lunch, George, I'm ravenous, simply ravenous. How about the Grand Hotel? Or we can have morning coffee, I'd like that. They're so kind at the Grand."

He gathered her things into a carrier bag and hung it on the back of her chair, then wheeled his mother out, pausing beside gray-haired docile old women for Doris to smile and wave gaily, and elderly gentlemen who begged her to sing their favorite songs that evening.

"Oh, we'll have to see, Mr. Donald . . . Goodbye, William, see you later, Frank . . ."

She loved the fact that even here she was a star. On Sunday evenings they hired a pianist, and she would sing. "The old fools love to be entertained, George, but the pianist has two left hands. Do you remember dear

Mr. McReady? What an ear he had, pick up any tune . . . But now, without sheet music, this young man can't play a note."

She sang snatches of songs as George tucked her blanket around her swollen legs, and called and waved until they reached the end of the driveway. Then she fell silent.

"Shall we have our usual stroll along the front, work up an appetite, Ma?"

Doris nodded, drawing her blanket closer with delicate pink-nailed fingers. George started singing again, "When you walk through a storm . . ." but Doris didn't join in.

"Come on, Ma, let's hear you!"

"No, darling, my voice isn't what it was." She put a hand to her head. "Did you bring me a scarf?"

It was high tide, and the spray was blowing onto the promenade. He parked the chair beside a bench and brought out a silk square. Folding it carefully, he handed it to her.

"Thank you, darling. I was asking Matron if we could get a better hairdresser, only I need a trim, but I don't like the young girl that comes in. Oh, she's very sweet, but she's an amateur . . ."

George watched her tie the square over her head, carefully tucking in the hair. "You have to watch these girls, they cut off far too much . . ."

George could see the reflections of her past beauty as she tilted her head coquettishly. "All ship-shape, am I, darling?"

He nodded, and gently pressed a stray curl into place. "All ship-shape. Now, how about singing me 'Once I had a secret love, that dwelt within the heart of me' . . . ?"

Sitting in her wheelchair, wrapped in her rug, she swayed to the rhythm, her hands in the air like an old trouper. Being together like this brought the memories flooding back to both of them, and they were laughing too much to finish the song.

"You always like the old ones best. Remember that Elvis medley I used to do?" She sat up straight and played an imaginary piano as she sang, "Love me tender, love me true, all my dreams fulfil; for, my darling, I love you, and I always will . . . That was your Dad's favorite. I don't know what he would think about this . . . What does that Moyra think of it all?"

George's face fell. "Now, Mum, don't start. Moyra's a good woman, and she's stood by me."

He took a newspaper from the carrier bag. It was folded so that the article about him was on the outside. Managing to grin at her, he asked, "What did you give them this photo for? I hated that school."

Mrs. Marlow pulled a handkerchief from her sleeve. "Your dad would turn in his grave . . ."

"Don't cry, Mum, don't . . . I'm innocent, Mum, I had to do something to prove it. They'll lay off me now, and I got paid a fair bit. I'll get a new job—they gave me good references. Things'll turn out, don't you worry."

He walked to the railings at the edge of the promenade and threw the paper into the sea. When he turned a moment later to face her, his hands were in his pockets.

"Which one's got a present in?" he demanded. "I want a song, though, you must promise me a song."

She made a great performance out of it, finally fooling him into giving her a clue to which pocket his gift was in. He presented the perfume with a flourish and she made him bend down for a kiss. Her warmth and her love for him shone out, despite her fears.

On the way back to the home they sang, "Why am I always the brides-maid, never the blushing bride?" vying with each other to sing the silly bits and breaking into giggles.

Moyra was doing the ironing. While George put the kettle on he was sing-ing "Why Am I Always the Bridesmaid?"

"Every time you go to see her you come back singing those stupid songs," Moyra complained.

"That was by way of a proposal," he said as he put coffee in their mugs and poured the boiling water. "I reckon it's time I made an honest woman of you."

"Not if your mother has any say in the matter; I was never good enough for you in her eyes!" Moyra retorted. "And I notice she gave the papers that photo of you in your posh school uniform . . ."

He handed her a mug of coffee. "Did I ever tell you about—"

She interrupted him. "How beautiful she looked at the school prize-giving? How all the lads said she looked like a movie star? Yes, you did!"

"But I've never told you about afterwards, after the prize-giving."

"I dunno why you go on about it, you were only at the school two min-utes."

"I walked Mum and Dad to the gates. They were all hanging out of the dormitory windows, giving her wolf-whistles. Mum was being all coy, you know, waving to the boys. She didn't want them to know we didn't have a car, that they were going to catch the bus. And then, just as we got to the gates, the wind blew her wig off. They all saw it . . ."

Moyra spluttered through her mouthful of coffee. "You're kidding me! Blew her wig off!" She laughed aloud.

Offended, he blinked. "It wasn't funny, Moyra. My dad ran down the road to get it back, and she just stood there, rooted to the spot . . ." He raised his hands to his own hair. "I didn't know her hair had fallen out. Dad helped her put the wig back on, but the parting was all crooked. Underneath all the glamour she was ugly; an ugly stranger."

"And everybody saw it? Did she ever talk about it?"

"She never even mentioned it."

"I always thought it was just old age, you know. I've never said anything to her, but it's so obvious. How long has she been bald, then?"

"I don't know. She still pretends it's her own hair, even to me, says it needs trimming and so on."

"Well what do you know! Underneath it all the Rita Hayworth of Warrington is really Yul Brynner in disguise!"

He looked at her for a moment, then laughed his lovely, warm, infectious laugh. He slipped his arms around her and kissed her on the neck.

"Did you mean it, George? About getting married?"

He lifted her in his arms and swung her around. "I love you, Moyra—what do you say, will you marry me?"

"Will I? I've had the license for two years, George, and you won't get out of it."

He smiled at her. Sometimes his resemblance to his mother took her breath away. He was so good-looking, every feature neat and clean-cut. Doris had been a real looker, and George was the most handsome man Moyra had ever known. Held tight in the circle of his arms she looked up into his dark eyes, eyes a woman would pray for, with thick dark lashes. Innocent eyes . . .

"I love you, George, I love you."

His kiss was gentle and loving. He drew her towards the bedroom.

"George! It's nearly dinnertime!"

"It can wait . . ."

DCI Tennison stared at the headline, furious. Then she ripped it down from the Incident Room door. She took a deep breath, crumpled the paper into a ball and entered the room.

The men fell silent, watching her. She held the ball of paper up so they could all see, then tossed it accurately into a waste-paper basket.

"OK, we've all read it, so the least said about it the better. But it's not just me with egg on my face."

She crossed to her desk and dumped her briefcase. "It makes our surveillance operation look like a circus."

"Any word on what their readers' survey came up with, ma'am?" asked Otley with a snide smile. "For or against female officers on murder cases?"

She gave him an old-fashioned look. "Oh, you're a biased load of chauvinists, and there's thousands more like you!"

"Don't worry, ma'am," chipped in Dave Jones, "you could always get a job in panto!"

He was holding up the photograph of her from the paper, but it had been added to in felt-tip. She started laughing and clipped him one.

Maureen Havers walked in as he raised his hands to defend himself. She tapped Tennison on the back.

"Why me? I didn't draw all over it. It was him!" Jones pointed to Burkin, who hung his head, although he couldn't really give a fuck. When she'd gone, Jones would get a right clip round the earhole.

Tennison turned to Havers, who told her she was wanted on the top floor.

"Oh well, here it comes. See you all later."

Otley claimed everybody's attention as soon as she had gone. "Right, we've all had a jolly good laugh, now get yer pin-brains on this lot. We want all these unsolved murders on the computer, so we can cross-check them for any that occurred when Marlow was in the vicinity."

As they went reluctantly to work, Maureen Havers had a word with Otley.

"You finished with the Oldham files? Only they haven't been put on the computer . . ."

"I'll sort 'em, love. Haven't had a chance to look through them yet."

Havers began to distribute more files around the Incident Room, which was greeted with moans and groans. Otley rapped his desk.

"Come on, you lot, settle down. Sooner you get this lot sorted, sooner we're in the pub. As an incentive, first round's on me!"

But a pint wouldn't compensate for the tedious slog of sifting through hundreds of unsolved murders. Otley opened the Oldham file he had already checked over; he knew there was a problem, and now he had to work out the best way to deal with it.

The bar was full of familiar faces. At one of the marble-topped tables several of the lads were discussing the unsolved murders.

"I've looked at twenty-three cases," Muddyman said, "all around Rochdale, Burnley, Southport; and I've got one possible but unlikely . . ."

Rosper cut in, "There was a woman found in a chicken run in Sheffield. Reckon she'd been there for months. The chickens were knocking out record numbers of eggs!"

"You know they've been feeding the dead ones to the live ones, that's why we've had all this salmonella scare. Got into the eggs," Lillie contributed.

"This woman was seventy-two, an old boiler!" Rosper chuckled.

They were suddenly all aware that Tennison had walked in. She looked around, located Jones and went to lean on the back of his chair.

"Next round's on me, give us your orders," she told them. "The bad news is: I'm asking for volunteers. They've withdrawn the official surveillance from Marlow, so I want four men to cover it."

Lillie stood up. "Excuse me . . ."

"Great, that leaves three . . ."

"I was just going for a slash . . ."

Rosper laughed and she nailed him. "Two! Come on, undercover's a piece of cake. Two more . . ."

She handed Rosper a twenty and sent him to the bar. "Let's get those drinks in. I'll have a large G and T."

Lillie pulled out a chair for her. "How did it go, boss?"

The others pretended not to listen. Tennison said quietly, "If I don't pull something out of the bag very soon, I'm off the case."

Her gin and tonic arrived. She thanked Rosper and he handed her back her money.

"What's this?"

Rosper shrugged. "It's OK, Skipper coughed up."

"Is this a truce? Ah well, cheers!" She raised her glass to them, but Muddyman and Rosper were looking towards Otley, who was sitting at the bar.

"Cheers, Skipper!" Muddyman called.

Otley turned and grinned, as if he had got one over on Tennison, even in the pub.

With a few drinks inside them they returned to the Incident Room to work. The stacks of paperwork did not seem to have diminished much, despite the busy atmosphere. The room was thick with tobacco smoke and littered with used plastic cups. Tennison, a cigarette dangling from her mouth, was double-checking and collating results.

At nine o'clock, Muddyman stood up and announced that he was going home. Many of the others started to make a move and Otley approached Tennison.

"We've got several cases that need looking into: one at Oldham, another at Southport, an' we're checking one in Warrington. Ma'am . . . ?"

Tennison looked up. "Sorry."

"Who do you want checking these unsolved cases?"

"Oh, anyone who's been cooped up here all day, give them a break."

"OK," Otley muttered. He made a few notes on a pad. "I'll do the Oldham . . . Muddyman, Rosper and Lillie are on Marlow, so that leaves . . . Can you take the Southport case?"

"OK, just pin it up for me."

Otley put the list up on the notice-board and picked up his coat. As he left he passed WPC Havers.

"You'll be able to retire on your overtime, gel!"

"Night, Sarge!" she replied as she passed some telephone messages to Tennison. "Why don't you take a break, boss?"

"Because I've got more to lose, Maureen." She rose and stretched, yawning, then went to examine the list on the notice-board. "I've lost track," she sighed.

Only three of the men were left working. "Go on home, you lot," she told them. "Recharge your batteries."

DC Caplan put his coat on and asked, "Anyone for a drink?"

I've had enough liquid for one day, mate," replied Jones. I'll be bumping into the mother-in-law in the night, she spends more time in the lavvy than a plumber . . ."

There was a metamorphosis taking place right in front of them, not that anyone noticed. DC Jones, of the polished shoes and old school tie, had taken to wearing striped shirts with white collars and rather flashy ties, similar to those favored by DI Burkin. He was also knocking back the pints, was even the first in the bar at opening time. It was taking time, but he was at last becoming one of the lads.

As they left, still joking, Havers asked Tennison casually, "What's with Oldham, then? He got relatives there or something?"

"What?"

"Skipper asked for anything from Oldham. I wondered what the attraction was . . . Mind if I push off?

It slowly dawned on Tennison what she was talking about. "He's doing it to me again!" She shook her head in disbelief and muttered a vague goodnight to Maureen, intent on getting to the bottom of it. Maureen saw her uncover one of the computers and start tapping the keyboard as she closed the door.

Tennison muttered to herself, "Right, Otley, let's find out just what your game is! Jeannie Sharpe . . . March nineteen eighty-four . . ." She moved the cursor down the screen, read some more, then picked up the phone to make an internal call. There was no reply; she put the receiver down and went across to the large table in the center of the room where all the files were stacked in alphabetical order. Whistling softly, she selected the Oldham file and flipped through it, then carried it back to the computer.

"Ah . . . Jeanie Sharpe, aged twenty-one, prostitute . . ." She compared the entry on the computer with the notes in the file. "Head of investigation, DCI F. G. Neal . . . Detective Inspector Morrell and . . . DI John Shefford!"

She pushed her chair back, staring at the computer screen. Why was

Otley so intent on taking the Oldham case? It had to be something to do with Shefford; it was too much of a coincidence. He had put her down for Southport with DC Jones; she snatched the list down from the notice-board. By the time she had retyped it she was seeing spots before her eyes. It was time to call it quits; but she, not Otley, was now down for Oldham.

"My car'll be here any minute! I was too tired to drive last night." Dressed and ready for work, Jane was rushing around the kitchen. Peter, still half-asleep, stumbled in.

"'Morning!"

"I got in a bit late, so I slept in the spare room. Feel this—d'you think it'll soften up by tonight?" She handed him an avocado.

"It's fine." He stood in the middle of the kitchen and stretched. The avocado slipped from his grasp and Jane caught it deftly.

"I'll be back early to get everything ready for tonight. I'm doing what Pam suggested: pasta and smoked salmon. Prawns and mayonnaise in the avocados . . . Ah!" She whipped round and jotted "Mayonnaise" on her notepad. The doorbell rang. "And cream. Give us a kiss. I'll see you about seven. If anyone calls for me, I'll be in Oldham."

She left Peter standing in the kitchen. "Oldham, right . . ." He woke up suddenly. "Oldham?" But he was talking to himself.

Tennison and Jones followed the uniformed Sergeant Tomlins through a makeshift door in a corrugated iron fence. Tomlins was still trying to make up for his error at Manchester Piccadilly station, where he had assumed Jones to be the Chief Inspector.

"In nineteen eighty-four all this part was still running," he said as he led them into the cavernous, empty warehouse. "It was shut down soon after-wards, and hasn't been occupied since. The only people that came here were the tarts with their customers, and I think some still do."

"We got the call at four in the morning, from a dosser who'd come in for the night." He pointed to an old cupboard against a wall, minus its doors. "He found her in there."

Tennison inspected the cupboard. "Actually inside?"

"Yes. The doors were still on then, but not quite closed. She was lying face down, her head that way . . . This shed was used for dipping parts; the vats used to fill the place." He spread his arms to indicate the whole area. "They all went for scrap, I suppose. They lowered the stuff on pulleys—you can still see the hooks—then raised them again to dry."

Dozens of rusty hooks still hung from the ceiling. Tennison looked around and asked, "Hands tied behind her back, right?"

"Yes. Savage beating, left half-naked. Her face was a mess. Her shift was found outside, and her coat over there."

They started to leave but Tennison turned back to stare at the spot where Jeannie Sharpe was found.

"Nasty place to end up, huh?"

"Well, these tarts bloody ask for it."

She snapped at him, "She was twenty-one years old, Sergeant!" but he was moving ahead, heaving the rubbish aside. He waited for them at the door.

"You wanted to have a word with her friends? Slags isn't the word for it . . ." He pushed the corrugated iron aside for Tennison to pass. "We clean up the streets and back they come, like rodents."

She let the door slam back in his face. "Sorry!" she said.

The flat was damp, with peeling wallpaper, but an attempt had been made to render it habitable. The furniture was cheap: a single bed, a cot, a painted wardrobe and a few armchairs, and it was fairly tidy, apart from the children's toys scattered everywhere.

Tennison was sitting in an old wing-chair beside a low table on which were two overflowing ashtrays, a teapot and a lot of biscuit crumbs. She was totally at ease, smoking and sipping a mug of tea.

Carol, a drably dressed but attractive blond woman in her early thirties, was telling her about the last time she had seen her friend Jeannie alive.

"We were all together, just coming out of the pub, our local, y'know. We'd had a few . . ."

Linda, plump and cheerful with dark hair, interrupted her. "I hadn't! I was on antibiotics, can't drink with them."

"His car was parked, er . . . You know where the pub is?" Tennison shook her head. "Well, it's right on a corner, y'know, so there's a side street . . ."

Finishing her tea, Tennison suggested they go and look.

The three women stood on the corner outside the pub. It wasn't easy to tell by looking at them which were the prostitutes and which the senior policewoman.

"See, there's the side street. He was parked just there. You could only see a bit of the car," Carol was saying.

Tennison offered her cigarettes round. "You couldn't tell me the make of it? The color?"

"It was dark, I reckon the car was dark, but it had a lot of shiny chrome at the front, y'know, an' like a bar stuck all over with badges an' stuff. He called out to Jeannie . . ."

Tennison grabbed the remark. "He called out? You mean he knew her name?"

"I don't think it was her name. It was, y'know, "How much, slag?" I said to her, hadn't she had enough for one night . . ."

Carol put in: "Ah, but she was savin' up, wanted to emigrate to Australia if she could get enough."

"So Jeannie crossed the road? Did you see her get into the car?"

Linda replied, "She went round to the passenger side."

"I looked over, y'know, to see, but he was turning like this . . ." Carol demonstrated. "I only saw the back of his head."

Tennison stepped to the kerb and peered around the corner as Linda said, "We never saw her again. She had no one to even bury 'er, but we had a whip-round."

"Fancy a drink?" asked Tennison.

They piled into the pub and found an empty booth. Carol went to the bar while the locals sized up Tennison. They were mostly laborers in overalls.

Linda had produced a photograph of herself and Jeannie. "Lovely lookin', she was. That's me—I was thinner then, and blond. Cost a fortune to keep it lookin' good, so I've gone back to the natural color. Set me back twenty-five quid for streaks! We used to get cut-price, mind, at the local salon, but they've gone all unisex, y'know. I hate having me 'air done with a man sitting next to me, don't you?"

Tennison opened her briefcase to take out her copy of the *News of the World*, but was interrupted by a man in dirty, paint-splashed overalls who strolled across from the juke box. He put a hand on Tennison's shoulder and leaned down to whisper, "I've got fifteen minutes, the van's outside . . ."

Turning slowly, she removed his hand from her shoulder. "I'm busy right now." He made no move to go, so she looked him in the eye. "Sod off!"

He looked in surprise at Linda, who mouthed "Cop!" and shot out before anyone could draw breath. Tennison carried on as though nothing had happened.

Carol returned with the drinks as Tennison placed the newspaper on the table.

"The barman says you just missed the London Express, but there's a train at four minutes past five."

"I'll be cutting it fine . . ." Tennison checked her watch and smiled. "Dinner party! Is this like him?" She pointed to the newspaper photo of Marlow and took a sip of her drink.

"He's a bit tasty, isn't he?" Carol commented, and glanced at Linda. "He was dark-haired . . ."

"You thought he had a beard, didn't you?" Linda said.

"Beard? You never mentioned that in your statement."

"She couldn't get out of the nick fast enough, they're bastards," Carol informed her. "An' I'll tell you something for nothing—they never gave a shit about Jeannie. We're rubbish, until they want a jerk-off! Four kids we got between us, and no one's interested in them. An' that inspector geezer, y'know, him . . ." She nudged Linda. "I'm not sayin' any names, but . . ."

"I will," said Linda. "It was that big bloke, John Shefford. They got rid of him faster than a fart."

Tennison asked, deadpan, "What do you mean?"

"I reckon they found out about him an' Jeannie," Carol told her confidentially. "Next thing we knew, he was on his bike, gone to London. He was as big a bastard as any of 'em—bigger. Jeannie never had a chance: her stepdad was screwin' her from the time she was seven. She was on the streets at fourteen, an' that Shefford used to tell her he'd take care of her. Well, he never found out who killed her; they never even tried."

"Poor kid, strung up like that, like a bit of meat on a hook!" Linda said. "You have to be really sick . . ."

Tennison jumped on her. "What? What did you say?"

"The dosser who found her, he told me."

"You know this man? He got a name?"

"Oh, he's dead, years back, but he told me all about it. Hanging by her arms from a hook in the ceiling."

It was getting late. Peter checked his watch anxiously and started to lay the dining table. Where the hell was she?

The front door crashed open and Jane rushed in, yelling, "Don't say a word, I've got it timed to the second. Don't panic!"

True to her word, everything was just about ready by eight o'clock, and she had put on a nice dress, though her hair was still damp. She ran quickly around the table, distributing place mats.

"Water's on, what else can I do?" Peter asked.

She stood back to look at the table. "Right, glasses for red, glasses for white, starter plates, teaspoons . . . Napkins! Shit, hang on . . ."

She shot out to the kitchen, returning to fling a packet of paper napkins at him, then disappeared again, shouting, "Bread, bread!"

The doorbell rang as she came back with the basket of rolls. She gave Peter the thumbs-up.

"All set! Let them in!"

Peter grabbed her and kissed her cheek, then they both headed for the hall.

When they had finished eating, Jane cleared the table and went to make the coffee, taking her glass of wine with her. The kitchen was a disaster area with hardly a square foot of clear work surface. She tidied up a little while she waited for the percolator.

Peter rushed in, obviously panicking. "You're taking your time! Where are the liqueur glasses?"

"We haven't got any! You'll have to use those little colored ones Mum gave me.' She drained her glass of wine. "How's it going?"

He relaxed a little. "Just getting down to business. Can you keep the women occupied? I'll take the tray."

As he hurried back to his guests, Jane yawned and pressed the plunger on the percolator. The hot coffee shot from the spout, all over her dress. "Shit!" Then she shrugged, wiped herself down as best she could, fixed a smile on her face and marched out with the coffeepot.

Frank King was obviously the dominant male, the one with the money and the big ideas. He had spread some plans on the table and was explaining them to Peter and Tom.

Frank's wife, Lisa, and Tom's wife, Sue, were sitting in the armchairs at the other end of the room, drinking apricot brandy from tacky little blue and green glasses. They were both dressed to the nines, perfectly coiffed and lip-glossed, but Lisa was the one with the really good jewelery. Jane poured them coffee.

"It's nice, isn't it? I like sweet liqueurs," Lisa was saying to Sue. "We spent three months in Spain last year; the drinks are so cheap, wine's a quarter of the price you pay here. Oh, thanks, Jane. Mind you, the price of clothes—all the decent ones are imported, that's what makes them so expensive."

Jane moved on to the men. Neither Tom nor Frank thanked her for the coffee and Peter, intent on what Frank was saying, refused it.

"Like I said, no problem. Get the bulldozers in and they're gone before anyone's woken up. Don't know why they make such a fuss about a few trees anyway. So, we clear this area completely, but leave the pool, which goes with this house here. The other we build at an angle, the two of them have to go up in less than three-quarters of an acre . . ."

"What sort of price are we looking at?" Tom wanted to know.

"The one with the pool, four ninety-five. The one without we ask three fifty. That's low for an exclusive close . . ."

Leaving them to it, Jane found a small glass that Peter had poured for her on the dresser. She carried it over to the women and sat down.

She took a sip from the glass. "Christ, it's that terrible sweet muck!" Up again, Jane fetched a wine glass and went looking for the brandy. It was on the table beside Frank's elbow, and she helped herself to a generous measure. She had been drinking since lunchtime: gins in the pub, on the train, wine throughout dinner. She was tying one on, but it didn't show, yet. She captured a bowl of peanuts and sat down again. It seemed as though Lisa hadn't stopped talking.

"She goes on and on, she wants a pony. I said to Frank, there's no point getting her one if she's going to be the same as she was over the hamster. The poor thing's still somewhere under the floorboards . . ."

Sue took advantage of the pause to speak to Jane. "Tom was telling me you have Joey at weekends."

Jane was searching for her cigarettes. She nodded and opened her mouth to speak, but Lisa got in first.

"What I wouldn't give to have mine just for weekends! Au pairs have been the bane of my life . . ."

"Oh, I've never had any troub—"

Lisa steamed on regardless. "I've had German, Spanish, French and a Swedish girl. I was going out one day, got as far as the end of the drive and realized I'd forgotten something, so I went back. She was in the Jacuzzi, stark naked! If Frank had walked in . . ."

"Probably would have jumped on her!" At last Tennison had got a word in edgeways, She grinned.

Sue nearly laughed, but remembered in time that she wanted to stay in Lisa's good books. She changed the subject.

"You're with the Metropolitan Police, Jane? Peter was telling . . ."

Lisa broke in: "Well, I'd better tell Frank to ease up on the brandy, can't have you arresting him . . ."

"That's traffic, not my department," Jane replied, knocking back her brandy.

"Oh, so what do you do? Secretary? I was Frank's before we got married."

"No, I'm not a secretary." The day was beginning to catch up on Jane, or rather the tragic little Jeannie. *There was no one to bury her, so we had a whip-round . . .*

If Lisa had heard Jane's reply she paid no attention. Her peanut-sized brain was now fixed on wallpaper, and she was holding forth about which was best, flock or fabric. In her opinion, fabric held its color better . . .

The three men were still sitting around the table, hogging the brandy bottle. As Jane helped herself to another large one, Frank pushed his glass forward without pausing for breath.

"I put my men on the main house, Pete's men on the second, and the two of them go up neck and neck. I'm looking for a quick turnover, so we do a big color brochure with artist's impressions and start selling them while we dig the foundations. Tom does the interiors, and we split the profits . . ."

Jane was unused to being ignored. She downed the brandy and poured another to carry back to her perch on the arm of the only really comfortable chair which, oddly enough, no one had sat in. She knocked over the bowl of peanuts into the chair and spent a few minutes eating the spilt ones from the seat, then slowly slid into it herself.

Lisa had not drawn breath, but Jane's accident with the peanuts finally brought her verbal assault course on wallpaper to a grinding halt. There was one of those classic silences among the women, during which Frank's voice could still be heard.

Lisa turned her full attention on Jane. "I hear you were on the *Crime Night* program?"

"That's right, I was answering the telephones, I was the one passing the blank sheet of paper backwards and forwards."

Missing the sarcasm in Jane's voice, Lisa ploughed on, "I *am* impressed! I never watch it, it scares me, but I'm paranoid about locking the house. And if a man comes near me when I'm walking Rambo . . ." She laughed. "That's our red setter, I'm not talking about Frank!"

Jane switched off for a moment, gazing into the bottom of her empty glass. When she snapped to again she realized that Lisa hadn't paused once.

"But don't you think, honestly, that a lot of them ask for it?"

"What, ask to be raped?" Jane shook her head and her voice grew loud, "How can anyone *ask* to be raped?"

She jumped to her feet, swaying slightly and glaring as if interrogating Lisa, who shrank back in her seat. "Where do you walk your dog?"

"Well, on Barnes Common . . ."

"Barnes Common is notorious, women have been attacked on Barnes Common!"

Lisa rallied a little. "Yes, I know, but I wouldn't go there late at night!"

"There are gushes, gullies, hidden areas. You could have a knife at your throat, your knickers torn off you, and bang! You're dead. But you weren't asking for it!"

"I—I was really talking about prostitutes . . ."

"What about them? Do you know any? Does Sue know any?" She turned to the men, she had their attention now. "How about you? Can you three tell me, hands on hearts, that you've never been with a tom?"

Lisa whispered to Sue, "What's a tom?"

Tennison snapped, "A tart!"

In the ensuing silence, the telephone rang. Peter said, "It'll be for you, Jane."

She weaved her way to the door, but turned back, blazing, when she heard Peter say, "I'm sorry about that!"

"Don't you ever make apologies for me! We were just having a consev . . . a conservation! She slammed the door.

"Keep her off the building site, Pete," Frank said in a low voice.

"Actually, I'd like an answer to her question," said Lisa.

"I think that went off all right, didn't it?" Jane, creaming her face, was talking to Peter.

"You asking me?"

"No, I was talking to the pot of cold cream! You're going to do the deal, aren't you?"

"Yeah . . . Did you have to bring up all that about tarts?"

"Put a bit of spark into the evening."

"It wasn't your bloody evening!"

"Oh, thanks! I broke my bloody neck to get that dinner on the table!"

"It's always you, Jane! You, you, you! You don't give a sod about anyone else!"

"That's not true!"

"You care about the blokes on your team, your victims, your rapists, your "toms," as you call them, you give all your time to them."

"That's my job!"

"Tonight was for my job, Jane. But no, you've got to put your ten cents' worth in!"

"Ok, I'm sorry . . . sorry if I spoilt the evening!"

The tiredness swept over her like a tidal wave. She had no energy to argue, and went for the easy way out, giving him a smile. "OK? I apologize, but I think I had too much to drink, and they were so boring . . ."

He stared at her, infuriated. Her comment really got to him. "This is business, Jane, do you ever think how boring all your fucking talk is? Ever think about that, ever think how many conversations we've had about this guy George Marlow? You ever consider how fucking boring you get? Do you? I don't know him, I don't want to know about him, but Christ Almighty I hear his name . . ."

"Pete, I've said I'm sorry, OK? Just let it drop."

He was unwilling to let it go, but he shrugged. Jane put her head in her hands and sighed. "Pete, I'm tired out. I'm sorry tonight didn't go as well as you'd planned, but you've got the contract, so why don't we just go to bed?"

The memories of the day swamped her: the smell of the factory, the smell of the two tarts' flat, her feelings, the smells, all muddled and out of control . . . She couldn't stop the tears, she just sat hunched in front of the mirror, crying, crying for the waste, the little tart who had been raped by her stepfather when she was seven, little Jeannie with no one to bury her, who Jane didn't even know, yet she was crying for her and all the other Jeannies who lived and died like that and nobody gave a shit for . . .

Peter squatted down and brushed her hair from her face. "It's all right, love. Like you said, I got the contract. Maybe *I* had a few too many . . . Come on, let's get you to bed."

Jane went to bed, but she didn't sleep for a long time. When she woke she found the kitchen full of the debris of dinner; not a single dish had been washed. She put her coat on, ready to leave for work, and took two aspirin with her coffee.

Peter, his hair standing on end, joined her.

"Pete, I've been thinking over everything. Last night . . ."

With a grin he reached for her, tried to kiss her. She stepped back. "I love you, Pete, I really do, but you're right. It doesn't work, does it? I do put my work first. I don't think I can change, because I'm doing what I always wanted, and to succeed I have to put everything into it. I have to prove myself every day, to every man on that force—and to myself . . ."

She was telling him that they could never lead the sort of life he wanted. It hurt a lot, and he wanted to gather her in his arms, make it all right. But the doorbell rang. They just looked at each other, with so much more to say and no time to say it in.

Peter said quickly, "Don't say anything more now, let's talk it over tonight. Maybe I haven't been easy to live with, maybe if I was more secure . . ."

The doorbell rang again. "You'd better go, Jane."

"I don't know what time I'll be back."

Peter stood for a moment after she'd left, surveying the kitchen, then he lashed out at the stack of dishes on the draining board, sending them crashing into the sink.

Tennison sat silently beside Jones as he drove. It unnerved him. Eventually he said, just to break the silence, "Still no trace of Marlow's car." She didn't react. "Are you OK?" he asked.

"I want that bloody car found!" she snapped.

"Trouble at home? I got all your shopping OK, didn't I?"

"Yeah!"

"I got an earful when I got home. My dinner had set like cement."

"The difference is that you get your dinner cooked for you. At my place, I'm the one who's supposed to cook it." She thought a moment. "Shit's gonna hit the fan this morning, though. You got an aspirin?"

Chief Superintendent Kernan had come in early to review the Marlow case, and for once Tennison had got her oar in first. Now he listened in growing anger as Tennison and Otley raged at each other, but he let them get on with it.

"George Marlow was questioned in nineteen eighty-four about the murder of a prostitute, Jeannie Sharpe. John Shefford, then a DI, was on the investigating team. He was transferred to London because it was discovered that he'd been having a relationshp with the murdered girl!" Tennison stormed. "None of this is in the records. We now know that he was having a sexual relationship with Della Mornay; he must have known he'd identified the wrong girl, but he was prepared to cover that up as well!"

Otley was seething. "Everything you're saying is a pack of lies, and if John Shefford was alive . . ."

"But he's not, he's dead, and you're still covering up for him. *You* requested the Oldham case, *you* wanted to go up there because you knew Shefford was involved . . ."

"That's not true! Della Mornay was a police informer . . ."

"She was also a prostitute, picked up and charged by John Shefford when he was attached to Vice—and what a perfect job for him!"

Tennison's last remark brought Kernan to his feet. "That's enough! Just calm down!"

"Sir, I have been working against time ever since I took over this investigation, at first because of Marlow's release, now because I'm going to be pulled off it. George Marlow is my only suspect, still my suspect for both murders, and now very possibly a third: Jeannie Sharpe."

"I don't know anything about any previous case up north," Otley insisted. "I know some of the men fraternize with the girls on our patch . . ."

"Fraternize! Christ!"

Kernan thumped his desk, really pissed off. He pointed to Otley.

"Come on now, did Shefford think there was a connection between the first murder and the one in, er . . . Oldham?"

"I dunno, but I wanted to check it out. There was no ulterior motive."

"So you know John Shefford had worked in Oldham? Knew he'd been on this—" Kernan thumbed through the file "—this Jeannie Sharpe case?"

Otley was falling apart. He shook his head. "No! I didn't know anything, but when I read the report and saw John's name down . . . Look, I know you knew, we all knew, he was a bit of a lad, so I just reckoned maybe I should check it out. That's all there was to it, nothin' more. If, as ma'am says, he was having a relationship with this tart, I knew nothin' about it."

Tennison couldn't keep quiet. "Just as you knew nothing about his relationship with Della Mornay? Bullshit! You knew, and you've been covering up for him . . ."

Kernan gave her the eye to shut up and keep it shut. "Did you get anything from your trip to Southport, Bill?"

Otley shook his head. "We're still checking, but no."

Kernan nodded, then gave him a hard look. "Well, keep at it. You can go."

Otley hesitated. It was obvious that Kernan wanted him out of the office and wanted Tennison to stay. With an embarrassed cough, he turned to her.

"Maybe we got off to a bad start," he said quietly. "Should have taken a few weeks off after John . . ."

She gave him a rueful nod. "I'll be in the Incident Room," he said, and opened the door.

They waited until he had gone, then Kernan turned to Tennison and asked, "What do you want to do?"

She looked him straight in the eye. "I worked with a good bloke, in Hornchurch. Detective Sergeant Amson."

Finally Kernan nodded. "That's the deal, is it?"

"He's available, could be here in an hour or so. I'm going to drive up to Rochdale to see the woman Marlow attacked there. It would be a good opportunity to fill him in on the investigation."

Kernan nodded again. Knowing she had won, Tennison went on, "Marlow served eighteen months. All the cases were either before or after he was in jail. I want the surveillance put back on him."

"OK. I'll do my best to hold Hicock off."

"Thank you, sir. Detective Sergeant Amson."

"I got it the first time."

At ten Tennison was in the car park, getting some things from her boot, when Otley came up beside her.

"I reckon we got off on the wrong foot. I was just going back to the pub, wondered if you wanted a drink?"

"Has the Super not spoken to you?"

"No, I went out and put a couple under my belt. I didn't know about John's spot of trouble in Oldham . . ."

Tennison said quietly, "Yes, you did. You're off the case, Bill. I'm sorry, you've already been replaced."

Otley seemed to shrink before her eyes. He turned to go and she said to his back, "I want the names of every officer on my team who's taking sexual favors from prostitutes."

He faced her again, but he had no anger left in him. She gave him a small nod and walked towards a car that had just drawn in to the car park. It was driven by the burly new sergeant, Terry Amson. He got out and opened the passenger door for her.

"I owe you a big one. My arse was dropping off in Hornchurch, I was sitting on it so much. How are you dong?

She beamed and punched his arm as she climbed in. "I think I'm doing OK."

As he returned to the driving seat he gave Otley a small wave of acknowledgment. It wasn't returned. Otley's dejected figure was still standing there when they drove away.

9

Terry Amson drove fast and well up the motorway while Tennison put him in the picture on the murders.

"So we have three girls, Della Mornay, Karen Howard and Jeannie Sharpe, who were all strung up, with these clamp marks on their arms. The first two are different, but it's quite a coincidence."

"Maybe he just perfected his technique! Have you tried talking to any of the guys he was banged up with? He's talkative, isn't he?"

"You could dig around while I'm with Miss Gilling, see if you can set something up for when we get back. And have a look at Marlow's statements, you never know what a fresh eye will come up with."

The little terraced cottage that Pauline Gilling shared with her father had a neat, well-cared-for garden. The inside was daintily decorated with Laura Ashley paper and a large collection of little glass animals, giving it a fragile feel which was echoed in Miss Gilling herself.

In her late thirties, she appeared older, with a pleasant but worried face. It took a while for her to unlock the front door, which was festooned with chains and bolts.

She sat on the edge of her chair and recounted the events of that day in a soft voice. It was as though she had learned it by heart; her eyes glazed slightly and she focused somewhere beyond the wall.

"It was the seventh of November, nineteen eighty-eight. At four-thirty in the afternoon . . ."

Tennison prepared herself to work this lady over. Without taking her eyes from Gilling, she settled herself on the sofa and took out a cigarette, nodding encouragingly.

"I was working in a florist's, and it was half-day closing. I don't work there anymore." She was wringing her hands unconsciously. "The shop is called Delphinia's, and the owner's name is Florence Herriot. November the seventh is her birthday. She asked if I would go to the pub with her at lunch-time, for a sherry. I had an appointment at the hairdresser's, so I did not arrive until . . ." She gave a strangled little cough, as if her throat was too tight, and continued, "I arrived at two-thirty-five. I had a glass of sherry and stayed for approximately half an hour. I always come home to get father's lunch, but on early closing day I have my hair set, so I leave a tray for him."

There was that strange little cough again. She was really tense now; her hands continually smoothed her skirt over her knees, which were pressed tightly together. Tennison said nothing, just waited for her to go on.

Her body went totally rigid and she had to force herself to speak. "I—I went up the path, I had my key out. I'd opened the door a few inches when . . . he called my name. 'Pauline! Hallo, Pauline!' I turned round, but I didn't recognize him. He was smiling, and . . . he walked up the path to-wards me, and he said, 'Aren't you going to invite me in for a cup of tea, Pauline?'"

She froze, like a rabbit caught in car headlights. Her mouth was open, but she made no sound. Deliberately, Tennison coughed, and she shook her head as if awakening, then started gabbling. "I said I was sorry, I thought there was some mistake, I didn't know him. He came very close, pushed me into the hallway, got me by the throat, kept pushing me backwards . . . I was so terrified I couldn't scream, I was afraid for my father. I tried to de-fend myself with my handbag, but he grabbed it and hit me with it. The clasp cut my cheek open and broke my front teeth . . ."

After a decent interval, Tennison prompted gently, "And then your father came in?"

"Yes. He was upstairs, I was lying on the floor, and he kept kicking me, then Daddy called out and he ran away. My father is blind, he couldn't see him, couldn't be called to identify him . . ." She was going to cry.

"But you were able to pick George Marlow out of the line-up?"

Gilling swallowed, held back her tears. "Oh, yes. He was clever, though; he had a beard when he attacked me, but he shaved it off before the identity parade. I still recognized him. It was his eyes, I will never for-get his eyes . . . I know, if it hadn't been for my father, George Marlow would have killed me."

Tennison crossed the room and squatted beside Gilling's chair. "Thank you, you did very well, and I'm sorry to have made you go through it all again."

Gilling shrank from her, fearing to be touched, and stood up. Her ner-vousness was beginning to grate on Tennison.

"I go through it all the time, every time the doorbell rings, every strange sound at night . . . I see his face, keep expecting him to come back, to finish . . . I had to leave my job, I can't sleep. He should have been put away for years, but they let him go after eighteen months. I live in terror of him coming back, because he said he would, he said he'd come back!"

Tennison climbed into the patrol car and breathed a sigh of relief. Beside her, Amson was immersed in a file.

"Marlow had a beard at the time of the rape, shaved it off for the line-up! That matches with what the toms said in Oldham, they thought the guy had a beard."

He looked up. "D'you think there's any truth in the story that she gave Marlow the come-on? She's, what, thirty-eight now, and a spinster . . ."

Tennison bridled. "So am I, it doesn't mean I want myself raped, and my front teeth kicked in!"

"Take it easy, it's just that from the description she's a bit of a dog. Marlow, on the other hand, is a goodlooking bloke, like myself."

She replied with a laugh. "Be very careful, Sergeant, or you'll be back rotting in Hornchurch!"

Two men were painting the row of garages on Marlow's council estate. They were making quite a good job of it, considering neither of them had done much in that line before. A few yards away George Marlow was standing, hands in pockets, watching them.

One of the men went to his nearby van for a new tin of paint. He opened it and stirred it with a screwdriver, then wiped the blade on his already paint-covered overalls.

"Excuse me, are you going to be painting the whole block, or just the garages?" Marlow asked.

"Just this lot, far as we know, mate," DC Lillie replied.

"They aren't for residents, you know. Council rents them out to anyone who can afford them. The tenants have to park in the bay over there, known as Radio One . . ." He flashed a grin at Lillie. "Means you had one when you parked it!"

He waited for a response, which didn't come, so he went on, "I had one, but it was nicked."

"What, a radio?"

"My car. Rover Mark III, three-liter automatic. More'n twenty years old, collector's item, you know." He stared down into the tin of paint, then up at the garages.

Rosper joined in. "You leave it out? Bodywork must 'ave rusted up?"

Marlow touched the paint on the nearest garage door, then peered closer. "Had a bit of filler here and there. Suppose some kids nicked it for a joyride, be stripped down by now. Had all my emblems and badges on the front, RAC and AA, owner's club . . . all on a chrome bar at the front." He examined the paint again. "I'm in the paint business, typical of the council . . ." He put a hand out towards Rosper. "Can I just borrow your brush? Like to see how this goes on . . ."

He dipped the brush in the paint and applied a stroke as Rosper and Lillie exchanged glances behind his back. Totally unaware, he said, "You work out, do you?" He glanced round at Rosper. "You look as if you do. What gym do you use?"

He chatted on, painting the door, while they stood and watched.

Late in the afternoon, Tennison and Amson arrived at Brixton Prison to interview convict 56774, Reginald McKinney. While they waited for him to be brought to them, Amson explained that McKinney had shared a cell with Marlow in Durham and had been picked up again a few weeks ago for breaking and entering.

The warder who brought McKinney told them there was a call from the station for them. Tennison asked Amson to take it, then offered the tall, skeletal prisoner a seat.

He was suffering from a migraine, and had come from the hospital ward. One of his eyes watered and his face was twisted in pain. "We'll try and keep this short, Reg. Now, you shared a cell with George Marlow in Durham, that right?"

"That is correct."

His eyes were crossing, it was like putting questions to a demented squirrel. "You told your probation officer that you had met Marlow after your release."

"That is correct."

"And you were living in a halfway hostel in Camberwell then, yes? So where did you meet?"

McKinney looked up as Amson returned. He kept his back to McKinney and leaned over to whisper to Tennison.

"There's a buzz on, looks like another one in Warrington. They'll get back to me when they've finished checking."

Feeling a bit perkier, Tennison turned back to Reg. He said, "I've forgotten what you asked me . . . I've got a migraine."

"Where did you and Marlow meet?"

"Oh, yeah . . . Kilburn. We went for a curry, then he drove me back to my place. Bit of a schlepp, an' I offered to get the tube, but he said it was OK. He wanted to do some work on his motor, in his lock-up."

Tennison was careful not to show the excitement she was feeling. "Lock-up—you mean a garage?"

"I dunno . . ." He stopped a moment and rubbed his head, in obvious agony. "The car was, like, an obsession with 'im."

"He never mentioned where this lock-up was?"

"No . . . I got a terrible headache."

A prison warder put his head round the door. "Urgent call for DCI Tennison."

Tennison took the call. The team were doing a good job; the Warrington murder had checked out, plus another one, in Southport. Both victims had identical marks on their arms.

George Marlow hung around the garages chatting and joking with Rosper and Lillie until dark. They got on well together, and had done a fair bit of painting, but the two DCs were beginning to wonder when he was going to go home—they couldn't paint all night. The floodlights had come on around the estate and were just enough to work by, but it wasn't easy.

"Bit late to be painting, isn't it?" Marlow enquired.

"We're on bonus, mate," Rosper told him. "Never know what's gonna happen with all this council privatization, so we gotta make the cash while we can."

Marlow sympathized with them, then launched into a story about a bet he'd had with someone at the gym where he worked out when they heard sirens coming close.

All three turned to watch the cars drive onto the estate. In the first one were DI Muddyman with DC Jones, behind them Tennison and Amson. They had barely come to a halt when Tennison leaped out and ran to catch up with Muddyman.

As they hurried towards Marlow's flat she gasped, "He's got a lock-up, some kind of garage where he stashes his car. Look for a set of keys, anything that might fit that kind of place. Get the bloody floorboards up if necessary."

"I don't believe this," Marlow was saying with exasperation to Lillie and Rosper as he wiped his hands on a rag. He stood and watched Tennison, Amson and Jones legging it up towards his flat.

"What are they after?" Lillie asked, watching him carefully.

"Me! I'd better get up there, the old lady next door'll have heart failure . . ." He laughed. "Not because of them, but because she's out playing bingo. Means she'll miss all the drama. Ta-ra!"

Moyra was at the door, looking at the search warrant. From the bottom of the steps Marlow called, "Hi, you want me?"

Moyra was very near to tears as she stood in the hall and surveyed the wreckage of her home. The carpets had been rolled back, all loose floorboards had been prised up, the hardboarding around the bath had been removed, the toilet had been taken apart, even the U-bends of the handbasin and the kitchen sink had been disconnected. Every video had been taken out of its jacket, every book taken down from the shelves and shaken, every crevice in every piece of furniture delved into. Tennison and Amson had every key in the place laid out in the lounge and were examining them minutely.

Moyra's self-pity turned to rage, and she screamed, "I don't believe this! I want everything put back as it was, and what you've done to the plumbing I want repaired professionally! You've had all our bloody keys down the nick before, why don't you tell me what you're looking for?"

Tennison gestured to Amson to close the door on Moyra, then turned to Marlow, who was standing in front of the fireplace, hands on his hips. "Why don't you tell us, George? You know what we're looking for."

"I know you've been asking the neighbors. I park my car outside, I don't have a garage."

"But your car isn't always parked outside, George. We know you've got a lock-up."

"When it's not parked here it's because I'm away on business. I drive— correction, I drove—for a living. Instead of all this, why don't you just try and find my car?"

There were thuds and hammering noises from the kitchen, and the sound of crockery being moved. Moyra's screaming voice could be heard telling Muddyman and Jones that the bottom of the percolator didn't come off. She started yelling for George.

Tennison turned to Amson. "Tell them to keep it down out there. George, you've got a lock-up, we know it."

"A lock-up? How many more times do I have to tell you? I park my car at the back of the flats!"

"We have a witness . . ."

"Not that old bat from next door!"

"No, a friend of yours."

"What friend? I don't have one left because of your crowd. Mates I worked with for years turned their backs on me! You got a friend? Great, introduce me!"

"We have a witness who stated that you told him you had a . . ."

"Him? Was it someone I was inside with? Yes? Don't tell me, let me guess. It was Reg McKinney, wasn't it?" He shook his head, laughing. "You must be desperate. Reg McKinney? He's no friend of mine. Stung me for fifty quid when we got out. He's a known nutter. Look at his record, in and out of institutions since he was a kid. He's no friend of mine, I told him to take a hike."

There was a tap on the door and Amson opened up.

"Nothin'," said Muddyman with a shrug, "but we need a plumber."

In a low voice, Marlow told Tennison earnestly, "I don't have a lock-up, I don't have a garage. If I had, maybe my motor wouldn't have been nicked. It's the truth!"

Suddenly anxious to get home to Peter, Tennison decided not to go back to the station to pick up her car, so Terry Amson gave her a lift home. She was very aware of the difference having a genuinely friendly face on her team made to her job. She knew she could talk to Terry and it wouldn't go any further.

Amson was saying, "If he's got his car stashed somewhere between Camberwell and Kilburn, we'll find it."

"If!" She looked at him sideways. "Terry, now you've met him, what do you think?"

"For real? If he's lying, he's one of the best I've ever come across."

"Yeah," she said with a sigh. "Tonight, for the first time, I had doubts." She pointed ahead. "It's the second house along."

When he had stopped the car she turned to him. "What do you think about John Shefford?"

"As a suspect? He was a crack officer, you know."

She said sadly, "He was also in the vicinity when Karen, Della and Jeannie Sharpe were killed. We're going to have to check him out on the two that just came in."

"You know I'm with you on this, Jane, but there's only so far I'm prepared to go. I've got a wife and four kids to support, remember."

"I don't like it any more than you." She put her hand out to open the door. "Just keep it under your hat, but we've got to check it out. So you pull Shefford's record sheets, first thing in the morning, OK? You want to come in for a drink?"

Amson shook his head and Tennison climbed out. "G'night!" she said as he started the engine.

Jane felt for the hall light switch, pressed it down. The flat was quiet; she dumped her briefcase and took off her coat, shouting, "Pete! Pete?"

There was no answer. She opened the kitchen door to find it clean and tidy, nothing out of place. She tried the bedroom; it was just the same.

Sighing, she unbuttoned her shirt and opened the wardrobe. One half of it was empty. She checked the chest of drawers—all Peter's were empty! Turning away, she unzipped her skirt and let it slide to the floor, stepped out of it and walked towards the bathroom.

As she opened the door the phone rang. She let it ring, looking around to see only one toothbrush, one set of towels. The answering machine clicked into action and she waited, listening.

"Jane, it's your mother . . ." Jane saw the white envelope propped against the phone and reached for it. "Didn't you get my message this morning about Pam? Well, in case you didn't, she's had a girl, eight pounds seven ounces, and she's beautiful! She was rushed into St. Stephen's Hospital last night, I'm calling from her room . . ."

Jane picked up the phone as she ripped the envelope open. "Hallo, Mum! I just got home."

Jane drove to the hospital and parked, with the unopened letter from Peter on the seat beside her. She turned the lights off and reached for the white manila envelope with her name hastily scrawled on it.

It contained one sheet of her own notepaper. *Sweetheart*, she read, *I took on board everything you said this morning. I can't quite deal with you, or the pressures of your work, and at the same time get myself sorted out. I am sorry to do it this way, but I think in the long run it will be for the best, for both of us. I still care for you, but I can't see any future in our relationship. Maybe when we've had a few weeks apart we can meet and have a talk. Until then, take care of yourself.*

It was signed simply *Peter*. She laid it face down on the seat and sighed, then realized that there was a postscript on the back.

I'm staying with one of my builders. When I get an address I'll let you know where I am, but if you need me you can reach me at the yard. Then he had put in brackets: (*Not Scotland Yard!*).

Jane opened the door slowly, but remained sitting. Was it always going to be like this? Peter wasn't the first, she'd never been able to keep a relationship going for more than a few months. She flicked her compact open and delved into her bag for a comb, stared at her reflection in the oval mirror for a long time. She looked a wreck, her hair needed washing and the make-up she had dashed on in a hurry that morning had long since disappeared. She studied the lines around her eyes and from her nose to her lips, the deep frown lines between her brows. She fished in her bag and brought out her lipstick, closed the mirror and ran the lipstick around her mouth without looking at it. She was so used to freshening up in a hurry that she didn't need a mirror.

Locking the car, she walked briskly towards the bright hospital entrance. An anxious-looking woman in a wheelchair was holding an unlit cigarette. Jane smiled at her and she gave a conspiratorial grin.

"I don't suppose you've got a match, have you?"

"Yes, love." Jane took a half-used book of matches from her pocket. "You keep them, and mind you don't get cold. It's freezing out."

As Jane headed for the night nurse at reception, she thought to herself, So what if you're going home to an empty flat? You've done that most of your adult life. By the time she reached the desk she had persuaded herself that she preferred it that way.

She gave the nurse a cheerful smile. "I've come to see my sister. I know it's late . . ."

After signing the visitors' book she headed towards the lifts, as directed. The woman in the wheelchair called out, "Thanks for the matches!"

"That's all right, love. Good night, now!"

The corridor was deserted. Jane checked each room, peering through the little windows, until she found the right one. She could see Pam through the glass, holding the new baby, Tony's arm resting lightly around her shoulders. Although it was way past their bedtime her two little boys were there too, spick and span, swarming over the bed and admiring their new little sister.

Watching them, Jane's hand tightened on the door handle, but she found she couldn't turn it. They formed a picture of a family in which she had no place. She turned away and walked slowly back down the corridor.

She headed automatically towards the river, needing quiet, space to think. It was an ordeal to cross the King's Road; she found herself shrinking from the traffic, from the faces passing her in their shiny cars; happy faces, drunken faces, all going somewhere, all with a purpose, with someone . . .

She found herself in Cheyne Walk, beside the water. Tonight the Thames looked like a river of oil, sluggish and smooth, and she could not shake off the feeling that dead and rotting bodies floated just beneath the surface. She had come here to celebrate a new life, but all she could see was death, and pain.

By the time she returned to the hospital, visiting hours were officially over, but she slipped along to the private section without being stopped.

The room was decked with flowers and bowls of fruit, and the baby lay asleep in her cot, but Pam's bed was empty. This time she didn't hesitate, she walked into the room and gazed down at the baby girl, moved the blanket gently away from her face.

Soft footsteps behind her announced Pam's return. Jane looked up, smiling, back in control.

"Hi! Just checking she has all her fingers and toes! She's OK? Bit of a dent in her head, though . . ."

Pam climbed cautiously into bed. "Her skull is still soft, it'll go. If you'd been here earlier you'd have seen Tony and the boys. Mum's staying until I go home."

"I feel a bit cheap—no flowers, no fruit. But I'd just got in from work."

Pam was still in pain. She shifted uncomfortably in the bed.

"Could you just plump up my pillows?" She lowered her voice. "You know we got this on Tony's firm? It's a new scheme, a private patients plan. We can all get private medical attention now . . ."

Jane rearranged her sister's pillows and straightened the sheets, then kissed her sister's cheek. "Well, congratulations! What are you going to call her, Fergie? Eugenie? Beatrice? I mean, now it's all private . . ."

Pam pulled a face. "Well, Mum's actually hinted . . ."

"What? No, you *can't* call her *Edna*!"

They were interrupted by a nurse, who gave Jane a pleasant smile that nonetheless indicated that she shouldn't be there. "It's time for her feed, I'm afraid. Beautiful, isn't she?"

She disappeared with the baby, and Jane prepared herself to leave.

"You can tell this is private: no bells and everybody out!" She kissed Pam's cheek and smiled. "I gotta go, anyway."

"Thanks for coming. Give my love to Peter."

"If I see him I will . . ." She hesitated at the door. "It's all off."

Pam was instantly concerned. "Oh, no! Why?"

Jane shrugged. "You know me."

"Is there someone else? I mean, are you OK?"

"No, there's no one else. I'm . . . It was a mutual decision."

"Well, you know what you're doing. Is the case we saw on television over?"

Jane paused before she answered. Her family's total lack of understanding when it came to her work, to herself, on top of Peter leaving, swamped her, but she managed to keep her smile in place.

"No, I haven't got him—yet!" She gave her sister a little wave. "G'night, God bless the baby."

As she closed the door behind her, only the expression in her eyes betrayed Jane's loneliness. She had made a tremendous effort, forcing herself to come here. Having done her duty, at last she could go home and cry.

10

"What in Christ's name do you think you're playing at?" Kernan demanded.

"We had good reason to search Marlow's flat," she protested. "Bloke he was in jail with said he had a lock-up . . ."

"I'm not talking about Marlow! You've had Sergeant Amson going over Shefford's record sheets."

How the hell had he found out so quickly? She opened her mouth to speak, but Kernan ploughed on, "If you want information regarding one of my ex-officers, then you know bloody well you should have come to me!"

"I think we've got our wires crossed here."

"Don't bullshit me, Jane! Are you so desperate? It's pretty low, just because you can't prove your case, to try shifting the blame to John Shefford!"

"I first mentioned my suspicions to Sergeant Amson last night, and until I have more evidence . . ."

"I'm telling you, back off! If there was one viable piece of evidence against DCI Shefford, you should have brought it to me. And don't harp back to the diary, that's sorted, and Otley's paid for it. Don't try to do my job, Inspector."

She tried again. "We've got two unsolved cases, one in Warrington and one in Southport, both with similar bruising to their upper arms, hands tied with the same sort of knots. George Marlow was in the vicinity when both . . ."

"Are you telling me Shefford was also in the vicinity? Have you got the evidence to start an internal investigation?"

"I don't know if Shefford was ever attached to . . ."

He wouldn't let her finish. "I'm telling you he wasn't, because I've checked!"

"I apologize, but under the circumstances . . ."

"Under the circumstances I am bringing in DCI Hicock! Don't you know what you've done, Jane? You've been running around the country trying to rake up dirt on one of the best officers I ever had! It stinks, and I won't take any more of it."

"Shefford falsified evidence, and is known to have been on close terms with two murdered girls, both prostitutes—Della Mornay and Jeannie Sharpe. Of the two other cases we have uncovered, one was a prostitute . . ."

Kernan strode to the door. "The man is in the graveyard."

"So are they, sir. Re-opening cases as far back as nineteen eighty-four is a slow procedure."

"I've nothing more to say, I'm bringing Hicock in as soon as he can get here. You concentrate on the investigation you were assigned to for as long as you remain on it, is that clear? And if you want some advice, put in for a transfer. I want you off the Marlow case, and I want your report on everything that went down yesterday on my desk by lunchtime, is that clear?"

"Yes, sir!" said Tennison.

Amson came racing up the corridor as she left Kernan's office, waving a sheet of paper.

"We've got another one! Blackburn, 'eighty-seven!"

Tennison hurried to meet him and grabbed the paper, but Amson wouldn't let it go until he'd finished. "It's about one a year, apart from the time Marlow was in jail! Caplan and Haskons are still watching him, and everyone else is mustered in the Incident Room—apart from these three."

Tennison looked puzzled, and he finally handed over the note. "Otley coughed up the names of the blokes who were fooling around with the toms! They're waiting for the Super to call them in now."

"What about Shefford?" she asked urgently.

"He's in the clear, on all the new cases. He may have done a surface job on the Jeannie Sharpe murder, but then he wasn't the DCI on the case, so you can't put it all down to him. And he wasn't around when the others were killed."

"I'm glad," Tennison said. He gave her a disbelieving look and she protested, "I am! Even if it dropped me right in the shit!"

Amson looked around and lowered his voice. "As a matter of interest, did you know that the Chief and Shefford were"—he crossed his fingers—"like that? They played golf every weekend—not at Sunningdale! Chief was Shefford's guv'nor when he was on Vice."

Tennison shook her head and raised her eyes to heaven. "I think I'll leave that one well and truly alone!" she said.

. . .

At least thirty people were crammed into the Incident Room. The air was thick with smoke. Every chair was taken, and the latecomers were sitting on desks or propped against the walls. While they waited some drank coffee and ate sandwiches, but most of them just talked. The din was deafening.

Sergeant Terry Amson was setting up a projector in the center of the room. Tennison was thumbing through her notes while she waited.

She looked up when the door opened. It was DI Burkin and two others, returning from the Super's office. They all looked rather sheepish.

"Sorry, guv, we've been upstairs."

Tennison nodded, well aware that these were the men who had been a bit too familiar with the local prostitutes. She gave them a moment to disperse amongst the others.

Burkin had found a place next to Muddyman, who asked him what was going on.

"Got our knuckles rapped for off-duty leg-overs. She's got eyes in the back of her head, that one! Just a warning this time, so maybe she's not all bad, but rumor has it that Hicock's definitely taking over, no kidding. He's in, she's out."

Tennison stood up. "OK, can I have a bit of hush?"

She waited for the room to grow quiet. Slowly they sorted themselves out, and she was able to start the meeting. She played it to the gallery.

"Right. I've been told that unless we get results very quickly indeed, I'm on traffic . . . Joke! I don't think it's quite that bad, but there will be some changes around here if we don't pull something out of the hat. In case I don't get another opportunity, I'll now say that I appreciate your back-up, and all the hard work . . ."

There were moans and unprintable comments as the word went round. Tennison yelled, "Come on, settle down! Maybe there's something we've missed, something that, if we all think about it, will whack us right between the eyes. OK, Sergeant . . ."

The lights went off, the blinds went down, and Amson ran the mock-up of Karen Howard's last night. They watched her stand-in talking to the builder who had tried to help her, then crossing the road and walking up Ladbroke Grove.

"Oh, boy, we gonna watch you again, guv?" Tennison recognized the voice from the darkness as Rosper's.

Amson summarized all the evidence as they watched. "Karen Howard, our first victim. Her body discovered in Della Mornay's efficiency and mistaken for her."

The film ended, followed by close-up stills of Karen's badly beaten body, then her various appalling injuries. The last frame was of the bruising on her arms.

"OK, take a good look at these marks. Now we have the other victim, Della Mornay, who was killed approximately six weeks before Karen . . ."

The shot of the decomposed body was sickening. The close-ups showed her upper arms and what appeared to be bite marks.

"The foxes had a go at her, and the dog belonging to the man who found her. But look at the arms again: the same marks, almost identical to those found on Karen."

Another body was flashed up on the screen. "Jeannie Sharpe, killed in Oldham in nineteen eighty-four. Again, note the bruising and welts on the upper arms. Fourth victim . . ."

Amson pointed to DI Muddyman and whispered, "You ready?" Muddyman climbed to his feet.

"Another video now, this time of Angela Simpson, whose family sent it to us. She was knifed to death in a public park in nineteen eighty-five. She was a hairdresser, well-liked kid, about to get married. This is her engagement party."

The sweet face of Angela Simpson smiled into camera, showing off her engagement ring, then self-consciously kissing the young man beside her. Her smiling fiancé gave a thumbs-up sign, and Angela turned to the camera, laughing, and put her hands over the lens. Then she loomed very close and kissed the camera.

"During the house-to-house enquiries, George Marlow was interviewed. He had been staying in a bed and breakfast only fifty yards from the gates of the park where she was found. There were no marks on her upper arms, but look at this . . ."

There was a shot of Angela, lying face down, legs apart. Her hands were tied behind her back.

"The rope, the way the hands were tied were just the same as in victims one and two."

There was a slight commotion as a WPC entered and tried to find Tennison in the dark. She delivered a brief message and departed, clocked by the men. Frank Burkin stood up to take DI Muddyman's place.

"The fifth girl"—Burkin waited for the shot to appear on screen—"was Sharon Reid. She was sixteen, still at school, and worked part-time in a local beauty salon . . ."

When he had finished they broke for lunch, and the discussion was continued less formally in the canteen. Reading the menu, DC Lillie was reminded about the old woman, the one found in the chicken run. She had

had similar marks on her arms to the others. He asked Sergeant Amson, who was in the queue behind him.

"Marlow was in the vicinity, that's good enough for me to try and pin it on him." He looked around Lillie to see what the hold-up was. "Come on, Burkin!" he yelled.

Lillie persisted. "But they didn't all have clamp marks . . . Oh, not ruddy Chicken Kiev again! The garlic's a killer!"

Burkin, his plate full, moved away from the counter, and joined Muddyman, who was holding forth about Marlow.

"I've been watching him for weeks now, he's a real friendly bloke, right? He chats to the lads every day. Just because he was in the area, it doesn't mean he's guilty."

Burkin picked up the lurid plastic tomato from the table and squeezed ketchup all over his plate, then stuffed a huge forkful of chips in his mouth. Bits of potato flew everywhere while he talked.

"There must be hundreds of salesmen workin' that area, you could take your pick. You ask me, all that film was about this morning was that we've got more bloody tarts being bumped off"—he paused to burp—"an' no bloody suspects."

The "bing-bong" sounded and a voice requested the presence of DCI Tennison in Administration. The men ignored it and carried on talking about Marlow; everyone who had had contact with him seemed to be convinced that he was a good bloke and therefore not a murderer. Terry Amson arrived and picked up on the conversation.

"He lied about the lock-up, we know that."

"We've only got the word of an old lag on that, it's not proof," Burkin retorted. There was another call over the PA system for Tennison. "Looks like the boss is gonna get the big boys pullin' the rug on her . . . Coffee all round?" He looked at Lillie. "Your turn."

Maureen Havers found Tennison hiding in the locker room, eating a large hamburger.

"Is DCI Hicock a big red-haired bloke? He's in with the Commander and the Super's there too. You're being paged all over the station."

"Am I?" Tennison asked innocently. "Well, they'll just have to find me."

Having successfully evaded her bosses, Tennison returned to the Incident Room to continue the briefing. She pinned photographs of all six of the victims on the notice-board while she waited for everyone to settle down.

"Right! Six victims, no set pattern. They did not, as far as we can ascertain, know each other. They didn't look alike, they belonged to different age groups, different professions. Apart from certain minor similarities they were not all killed in the same manner. The only link between them all is that Marlow was in the area when they were murdered. Did he kill all six? Is there something we've overlooked, another link?"

Muddyman was slumped right down in his chair, totally relaxed. He waved a hand to attract Tennison's attention.

"In the case of Karen, a witness stated that she heard a man call out her name. It was the same with Jeannie. But what about Angela, the little blond one? She was killed in the shrubbery in broad daylight, a good distance from the path, which was her usual route home. So how did she get there? If someone had called out to her . . . And the one who was raped, Gilling, she said he called her name . . ."

"Point taken," said Amson, "but you've got two toms, one hairdresser, a schoolgirl . . . How did he get to know their names, if he knew them?"

Havers had made her way to the front, using her elbows, and was standing by the photographs. She raised her hand, about to say something, but lowered it, not sure of her ground. She moved closer to Tennison and touched her arm.

"Boss, I think . . . It may be off the wall . . ."

"Anything, my love, I'm right up against it. What you got?"

"I did a bit of checking, but it all falls down with Gilling. She was a florist, but there's one link with the others. It was mentioned once . . ."

"To Marlow?"

"No, not him—Moyra Henson."

Tennison could barely hear her against the growing racket in the room. "Come on, lads, keep it down a bit!" she yelled, then turned back to Havers. "Go on."

"When she was brought in for questioning I typed her statement. She put herself down as unemployed . . ."

"Yeah . . . Quiet! Quieten down!"

The noise slowly subsided. Some of the men closed in on Tennison and Havers, realizing something was going on.

Havers coughed nervously. "She was picked up for prostitution, fifteen years ago, according to her record. But on that charge-sheet she's down as a freelance beautician. If she worked when she was traveling around with Marlow, he could have met the girls that way. But Gilling doesn't fit in . . ."

"Good on ya, Maureen!" Tennison gave her a quick hug. "We'll check it out."

Unaware of the tension, Jones walked in carrying an MSS internal fax sheet. "This might be useful, ma'am," he said to Tennison. "I've checked back on Marlow's past addresses. They've been in Maida Vale for three years, and before that they were in Somerstown, not far from St. Pancras.

He's had the Rover for twelve years, so what if he had a lock-up close to his previous flat?"

Rosper had a sudden thought. "Yeah! Those garages we've been painting, Marlow told us he tried to rent one, but the council leases 'em out to the highest bidder. Maybe he kept his old garage because he couldn't get one near by . . ."

The phone rang and DI Muddyman answered it, then covered the mouthpiece. "Guv? You're wanted upstairs, you here or not?"

"No, I'm not! Go and bring that hard-nosed cow in!"

Moyra wasn't happy at being taken down to the station, and she made sure the whole estate knew about it.

"Had a good eyeful?" she screeched at her next-door neighbor as she was led out to the car. "I tell you, they get more mileage out of you lot than a ruddy video . . . *Don't push me!*"

Marlow trailed behind them. "I don't understand, do you want me as well?"

Tennison emerged from the car and held the back door open for Moyra. "Not this time, George."

They left him standing there, still trying to work out what was going on.

Tennison had a quick wash and checked that the Super had left for the day before she emerged with Maureen Havers from the locker room, ready to interview Moyra.

Amson was pacing up and down the corridor outside. "Mrs. Howard is sending some of Karen's latest model photos by courier, shouldn't be long. You all set? Got plenty of cigarettes?"

She took a deep breath and nodded, then followed Amson and Havers along the corridor to room 4-C.

Havers went in first, followed by Amson, who held the door open for Tennison. After a beat, Tennison followed, like a prize fighter.

"I am Detective Chief Inspector Jane Tennison, this is WPC Maureen Havers, and Detective Sergeant Amson. Thank you for agreeing to answer our questions . . ."

"I had an option, did I?" Moyra interrupted.

Amson placed a thick file on the bare table in front of Tennison. She opened it and extracted a statement.

"You were brought into the station on the sixteenth of January this year, is that correct?"

"If you say so!"

"Is this the statement you made on that occasion?" Tennison laid it in front of her.

Moyra glared at it. "Yesss . . ."

"And is this your signature?"

"Of course it bloody is!"

"Thank you. I would like to draw your attention to the front page—here. It states that you are unemployed, is that correct?"

"It says so, doesn't it?"

"So you are unemployed."

"Yes, I'm on the bloody dole. What's that got to do with anything?"

Tennison extracted another document from the file and put it in front of her. "We have this previous statement from you, dating back to nineteen seventy-five. You were charged with soliciting, and stated your profession as beautician."

"Is there a law against it?"

"Did your training include a hairdressing course?"

Moyra was getting rattled. She answered abruptly, "No!"

"So you are not a hairdresser?"

"No, but I once had a Siamese cat."

"So you are a freelance beautician?"

"Yeah, you know, manicures, hands, facials." She peered at Tennison across the table. "You could do with a facial, smoking's very bad for your skin."

"Do you work as a beautician?"

"What do you want to know all this for? You think George is a transvestite now, do you?"

"George Marlow, your common-law husband, is still under suspicion of murder. I need the answers to my questions to help us eliminate him from our enquiries."

"Pull the other one, you're just interested in incriminating him."

"I'd like you to tell me where you were on these dates: March the fifteenth, nineteen eighty-four . . ."

"No ruddy idea, darlin'. Ask me another."

"The second of November nineteen eighty-five. Twenty-third of July, nineteen eighty-six. Ninth of April nineteen eighty-seven."

"I dunno, I'd have to look in me diaries, not that I've got them that far back." She bent down and started fiddling with her shoe.

"They were dates when your common-law husband was traveling in Warrington, Oldham, Burnley, Rochdale . . ."

Moyra looked up. "Oh, in that case I was with him. I always travel with him."

"So on the dates that I have mentioned, you are pretty sure that you were with George, yes?"

"I travel with him, I stay with him."

"Doing freelance work as a beautician?"

"Well, yeah. I do a bit."

"In salons?"

"Yeah, no law against that."

"There is if you've been claiming unemployment benefit and not declaring income, or paying tax on it. There's a law against that."

Moyra actually shrank back in her chair, though her answer was bold enough. "It's nothing, just a bit of cash, you know, pin money."

"How long do you think it would take for me to check out just how much you've been earning?"

"You bastards never give anyone a break."

"I'll give you a break, Moyra. No charges if—*if*—you give us a detailed list of the salons you've worked in, the names of your clients . . ."

As Tennison placed a pen and a sheet of paper in front of Moyra, Amson leaned over and whispered to her. With a nod to Havers, she followed him from the room.

"If this pins any of those cases on Marlow, she's virtually making herself an accessory!"

"What are you suggesting?" Tennison snapped. "Get her lawyer in just when she's co-operating?"

"You're jumping the gun. What we need is a lever, something to push Marlow with. She's his alibi, and so far she's not backed down on that."

Tennison banged the coffee machine with the flat of her hand. "Christ, you're right! An' we need a fucking lever to make this machine work . . ." She looked at her watch. "OK, leave it with me. I'll have one more go." She smiled. "But gently does it!"

Moyra was beginning to look tired. She leaned her head in her hand.

"I've listed the salons, but that doesn't mean to say that I work there regular. Sometimes they don't have any customers for me, and it's mostly manicures."

"What's this Noo-Nail?" Tennison asked, looking over the paper.

"It's American, paint-on nails; your own grow underneath." She held out a hand for Tennison to inspect. "See, they look real, don't they? But that part's false."

Havers, trying to look interested, stifled a yawn. Amson was half-asleep.

"Aah, I see!" Tennison nodded, then asked nonchalantly, "Did you do Miss Pauline Gilling's nails?"

Without a flicker, Moyra replied, "Look, love, I do so many, I don't know all their names."

"Surely you'd remember Pauline Gilling? George was sent down for attacking her . . ." She pushed a photograph across the table.

Moyra refused to look at the photo and snapped, "No, no! An' she lied, she came on to George! She'd been in the pub, she lied . . ."

"What about Della Mornay? Did you do her nails?" She put another photograph on the table.

"No!"

"Take a look, Moyra. Della Mornay."

"I don't know her!"

"No? You stated that George returned home on the night of the thirteenth of January this year at ten-thirty . . ."

Under pressure again, Moyra fought back. "Yes! Look, I know my rights, this isn't on! I've been here for hours, I've answered your questions, now I want a lawyer."

"George's car, the brown Rover, where is it? We know he has a lock-up, Moyra, and we'll find it, it's just a question of time. I'll need to talk to you again." She stood up. "OK, you can go, thank you."

"Is that it? I can go home?"

Tennison nodded and walked to the door, leaving Moyra nonplussed.

It was light before Moyra got home. George made her a cup of coffee and brought it to her in the lounge.

"Bastards are going to get me for fiddling the dole and tax evasion. They know I've been working."

"They kept you all night just for that?"

"There were a few other things."

"What? What did she want to know? Ask about me, did she?"

Moyra stood up and started unbuttoning her blouse. "What do you think?"

She walked out of the room and, after a moment's hesitation, Marlow followed her to the bedroom. She tossed her blouse aside and unzipped her skirt, leaving it where it fell. He picked them up and folded them while she went into the adjoining bathroom and turned on the bath taps.

"What are you following me around for?"

"I just want to know what went on!"

She turned to him, snapping. "They wanted to know about the bloody florist! Kept asking me about her. I've stood by you, George, but so help me if I find you've been lying to me I'll . . ."

She turned and walked out. "Put some Badedas in for me . . ."

He picked up the big yellow bottle and squirted some of the contents into the water, then stood in the doorway, watching her cream her face.

"I've never lied to you, Moyra, you know that." He reached out to touch her but she slapped his hand away, finished wiping her face with a tissue.

"Where's the car, George?"

"It was stolen, I don't know where it is."

She picked up her hairbrush. "It wasn't here, George. You came home that night without it. I remember because your hair was wet, you said it was raining." She turned to him while she brushed her hair, slowly. "Is it in the lock-up? They're going to get you because of that bloody car . . . They can plant evidence, you know, and they're out to get you."

"What did they say?"

"The bath'll run over."

"What did they say?"

"Maybe they've already found it, I dunno. I've got my own problems. They'll get me just for doing a few manicures." She threw the brush down on the dressingtable and stormed into the bathroom. Marlow picked up the brush and began to run it through his hair.

Peter looked around the efficiency. It was clean and close to the building yard. The best thing was the rent, a hundred a week. He had paid the landlady up front for a month. Dumping his suitcase without bothering to unpack, he went straight out again, arriving outside Marianne's just after breakfast. He watched from a distance until Marianne's husband had taken Joey to school, then rang the bell.

Marianne offered her cheek, which he kissed, and coffee, which he accepted. She tidied the breakfast dishes into the dishwasher and sat opposite him at the kitchen table.

"I've moved, so if you need me, here's my new address," he told her.

"Oh, so it didn't work out with the policewoman?"

"No, it didn't."

"I'm sorry."

"Really? Because I won't be able to have Joey to stay? Well, wrong, because he can stay with me for as long as need be."

Marianne unfolded the small note of his address and got up to pin it on the notice-board. He sipped his lukewarm coffee and asked, "How are you?"

"I'm fine. Do you want toast?"

"No. I want to know if this new baby's mine. Is it?"

"What?"

"Come on, don't mess me around. I got the sort of nudge, nudge when you came round, so tell me the truth. Is it mine?"

"Well, of course not, don't be ridiculous!"

"That afternoon, it could have been mine, couldn't it?"

"No, I'm too far gone. I must have been pregnant, or just . . . Look, Pete, that was a stupid mistake, and I don't know why I let it happen. I'm sorry if by going to bed with you that one time I let you think . . ."

"Wait, wait! I don't think anything, I just wanted to know for sure, and now I do, I'll go."

She caught his arm. "I'm sorry, Pete, I know how much I've hurt you, and I'm truly sorry. But it was just something that happened."

"Just something?"

Peter walked to the front door. He felt helpless, inadequate, there was so much more to say but he didn't know how to begin. The sweet smell of her in her dressing-gown, her softness, got in the way of his anger. It always had.

His hand was on the door, about to open it, when he turned back. "I want Joey, every other weekend. I'll start paying maintenance as soon as my business is on its feet."

Marianne nodded, but before she could say anything he had the door open. "Goodbye, then," she said at last.

Peter didn't reply. All the way down the neat gravel path, across the street to his truck, he couldn't even think straight. How had it happened? One day, a wife he adored, a son he doted on, a secure business, a house—albeit with a mortgage . . . He had had so much, and now it was gone. Marianne had a bigger house, a new husband, another baby on the way, and all Peter had was a rented efficiency and a suitcase. Even his business was in bad shape. In fact, no matter how he viewed his life, he was on a downward spiral. He just couldn't understand how it had happened that his best friend, a man he had been at school with, trusted and liked, had taken everything from him.

As he drove off, Marianne watched from an upstairs window. She felt wretched, part morning sickness and part guilt. She was genuinely sorry for him, sorry for leaving him, sorry for everything that had happened. He was such a kind, gentle man. She had never set out to fall in love with someone else, it was just one of those things. It upset her that he had believed the new baby was his, but she hadn't lied.

She patted the curtains back into place and ran herself a bath. While she waited she started making out a list of groceries and Peter was forgotten.

Peter unpacked his belongings and went to a café for a bacon sandwich and a cup of tea. He arrived at work much later than usual and one of his chippies asked if everything was OK.

"Yeah, everything's fine."

"How's the Inspector?"

"That's all in the past."

"Can't say I blame you. That one looked as if she'd nick you if you laid a finger on her!"

Peter laughed loudly, and the chippie pushed the day's mail across the untidy desk. "Looks like a lot of bills to me, guv'nor. Be out back if you need me."

Peter had hardly given Jane a thought since he left. She had been important to him for the time he had been with her, but he knew he wouldn't see her again. There really wasn't any point. If the truth was on the line, there was a side to her that he hated, that masculine, pushy side. She had never been his kind of woman, and he doubted if any man could cope with a woman who loved her career more than anything else. At least he wouldn't have to listen to all the ramifications of who had done what, how and to whom, and what she was going to do about it. He wouldn't have to hear about her "toms," her "lads," or that bloody George Marlow. The next girl would be young, pretty and without prospects, and he'd make sure she could cook, didn't mind ironing shirts and liked kids.

"Boss! Karen's photographs have arrived."

Tennison turned from the washbasin where she was brushing her hair. "Be right with you."

"Everybody's waiting in the Incident Room, and . . . the Super's in there."

Tennison was suddenly not so cheerful. "Shit! OK, I'll be there."

A few moments later she found Superintendent Kernan standing in the middle of the Incident Room among a general hubbub. The moment she entered the room, silence fell.

"Sorry, guv, you wanted to see me?" She felt a flush creeping up her face.

"Just a few moments." He gestured to the door, then said to Amson, "Carry on."

Tennison waited for him at the door and followed him out, hearing Terry Amson saying, "Right, I want everybody to have a look at these new photographs of Karen Howard . . ." She closed the door behind her and faced Kernan.

"This was on my desk when I came in." He handed her a sheet of paper. "They backed you one hundred per cent, refused to have Hicock take over. Did you know about it?"

Every single man had signed the petition. Tennison's eyes brimmed with tears. "No . . . No, I didn't."

"Things have taken a big turn, eh? You're lucky."

"Luck had nothing to do with it, sir. We've worked our butts off."

"Let me have all the new information as soon as possible, and"—he smiled—"good luck!"

He strode away and she opened the door. All the men in the room had their backs to her; they were watching Maureen Havers.

"These shots were taken on the day Karen died," said Havers, pointing to a group of photos on the notice-board. "You can see quite clearly that her nails were short. But these"—she pointed to another group—"these were taken a week before. Look at her hands."

In the second batch Karen's nails were long and red. Sergeant Amson turned to Jones. "Get on it, check with her flatmates, see where she got them done!"

While Jones looked up the number, the others crowded around the photos. Still not one man had turned towards Tennison. Jones picked up the phone and started dialling.

Highly embarrassed, Tennison walked to the center of the room. "I won't harp on, but I want all of you to know that I appreciate you backing me up . . ."

Muddyman hurtled in, shouting, "Suspect's on the move, guv'nor, with his girlfriend! The lads reckon something's going down!"

Jones was through to the flat. "Lady Antonia? This is DC Jones from Southampton Row police station. We need to know if Karen used a beauty parlor or hair salon, and if so do you know if she had . . . excuse me . . ." He beckoned frantically to Havers. "What do you call them?"

"Nail extensions."

Excited, Tennison was getting into top gear. "Right, I reckon this is it, we've got him on the run . . ."

Jones slammed the phone down. "Yes! She went to a place in Floral Street, Covent Garden; had an account there!"

Amson, already on the move, pointed at Jones. "Check it out, Daffy! Take Rosper with you, and keep in radio contact!"

Tennison was champing at the bit. "Let's go! Terry, you're with me!"

She ran out, Amson on her heels. DC Jones grabbed his jacket, a rather smart double-breasted job, and bellowed to Rosper, "Let's go!" But he paused a moment beside Maureen Havers and winked. "Good on ya, Maureen! See ya in the bar tonight."

She watched him leave. "What a bloody prat! Since he got those suede shoes he thinks he's Don Johnson . . ."

It was suddenly quiet, as it always was before the scream went up. Havers looked at the photographs Karen Howard's mother had sent, glossy six-by-ten modeling shots. They had only been interested in her nails, but now she looked at the girl's lovely face. Karen had been a beautiful girl with a freshness to her skin that shone out from the photographs. Her hair was silky, her eyes bright. It was obvious that she had still been an amateur, the poses weren't quite right, but maybe that was what gave her an air of innocence, of childlike vulnerability.

Havers was not the only police officer, male or female, who felt protective towards such victims, as if it was their responsibility to ensure that they could rest in peace. She brushed her hand across the photograph.

"I think we've got him, Karen, love," she whispered. The dead girls stared sightlessly into the empty room: Karen, Della, Jeannie, Angela, Sharon, Ellen, as if they too were waiting to rest.

11

As her patrol car raced through the heavy traffic, Tennison sat next to the driver, listening in on the open channel. Amson was sitting on the edge of the back seat, trying to see where they were going.

DC Oakhill was reporting George Marlow and Moyra Henson's every move direct to them.

"Suspect leaving taxi now, with Henson. Entering Great Portland Street station. They've split up, she's gone down to the trains and he's coming out on the north side, over."

DI Haskons cut in. "I got him! I'm on foot, heading down the Euston Road, outside Capital Radio, repeat, I'm on foot. He's hailed another bloody taxi, over."

"I'll take the woman . . ." Oakhill's voice faded out.

"We'll go straight to Euston, see if we can head him off at the pass," said Tennison.

George Marlow leaned in at the taxi window to speak to the driver, and pointed towards Euston. Then he hopped in the back, but the taxi made a left turn towards Camden Town.

A plain car, driven by DC Caplan, slotted into the traffic behind the cab. His passenger, DI Muddyman, reported, "OK, we're there. Suspect in black cab, heading for Camden Town. No, right, he's turned right, towards Euston again. We've got him, we've got him now, turning right again, back towards the Euston Road, over."

DC Jones rushed out of the Floral Street beauty salon and stuck his head through the car window to talk to DI Burkin.

"They had her down for a full day on the second of January, the day before that modeling job where she had the long nails. But she didn't book a manicure, and they don't do these nails, whatever they're called. One of the assistants, a Dutch chick, says she recommended a woman in the market."

"Shit," Burkin said. "We can't get the car in there. You leg it, and I'll meet you in Southampton Street."

The black taxi weaved its way down a side street and reached the corner of Euston Road. There were two vehicles now between it and Muddyman's unmarked car.

The cab edged into the solid traffic on the Euston Road. Marlow was out of the door on the far side and had disappeared into a junk furniture store before any of them could blink.

"Shit! This is Muddyman. Marlow's out of the cab, taxi is empty, repeat, Marlow again on foot. Biker, come in, biker . . ."

Outside the junk shop the cyclist in the skintight Lycra pedal-pushers slowed down and bent to fiddle with his toe-clips. He spoke softly into his radio.

"He's out, heading along the Euston Road again, on foot, over."

On the opposite corner, Muddyman was out of the car and following, keeping a good distance from Marlow.

Oakhill came close to losing Moyra Henson in the crowded complex of tunnels and staircases at Baker Street, and had to force the doors open to board the southbound Jubilee line train.

He threaded his way through the carriage to stand by the next set of doors. Henson was staring into space; then she turned and studied her reflection in the dark window, and fished in her handbag for a square double-sided mirror. She licked her lips and threaded her fingers through the front of her hair and shook it out, then folded the mirror and zipped it back into her bag.

She was totally unaware of Oakhill watching her, strap-hanging only a few feet away.

Amson was leaning between the front seats with a map in his hand. "He's here, could be heading for Euston or King's Cross, but he's ducking and diving . . ."

"Hold it, Control's coming through." She raised a hand to the earpiece on which she was picking up relayed messages. "He's jumped on a number seventy-three bus. No, he's off it, he's turned in the direction of Battle Bridge Road, behind King's Cross station . . ."

Amson pointed it out on the map. "That's here. Doesn't look like he's going for a train, but there are lock-ups in the railway arches all along here . . ."

"Come on, you bugger, go for the car, get your bloody car!"

A voice said in her ear, "You're out of luck, car five-four-seven. Your man's just gone into a café, he's sitting talking to the owner. It's the taxi stopover . . ."

Tennison pursed her lips and tapped her foot regularly against the transmission tunnel of the car. Her ear was aching because she was so uptight at the possibility of missing a radio call that she kept pressing the earpiece harder into her ear.

"What the fuck d'you think he's doing?"

Amson shrugged. "Could do with a cup of coffee myself." His fingers drummed against the back of her seat. He was shrugging it off, but like everyone else he was right on the edge, waiting, waiting . . .

Among the crowded little stalls selling jeans and T-shirts, DC Jones found a tiny booth containing only a small white-covered table and two chairs. A sign nailed to the top of the wooden frame announced: "Noo-Nails by Experienced and Qualified Beautician."

Annette Frisby, the proprietress, was bending over a client's hand, carefully painting her new nails a violent pink. Jones squashed himself in beside them and showed Annette his identification and a photograph of Karen Howard.

"Have you ever done this girl's nails?"

She squinted at the photo. "I couldn't tell you, I do as many as eight a day . . ."

"Look at her again." He tried to squat down to her level and pointed at the beautiful young face. "She was found murdered, on the fourteenth of January last. Look again, did she ever come to this stall?"

"January? I wouldn't have been here anyway. My friend takes over when I can't do it."

Jones ground his teeth in frustration. "Have you got her name and address?"

The café was too small to contain more than a long bar and a few stools. George Marlow was sitting at the far end, drinking cappuccino.

The only other customer got up and left. Marlow approached the man behind the bar.

"Can I have the keys, Stav?"

Stavros pulled a cardboard box from beneath the bar. "Been away, have you, John? Haven't seen you for a long time."

"Yeah. Mum was taken bad." Marlow held his hand out for the keys. "What's the damage?"

From across the street it wasn't possible to see the object that had been passed to George Marlow, but when he opened his wallet Muddyman could see him counting out ten-pound notes.

Moyra Henson had changed tubes twice, doubling back on herself, then she hurried onto a Central line train. Oakhill was certain that she had no idea he was tailing her.

He was four or five bodies behind her as she went up the escalator and emerged at Oxford Circus. Keeping well back, he radioed in for back-up, fast; Oxford Street was packed with shoppers and Moyra was moving like the clappers. He stayed on her tail in and out of Richard Shops, then across the road to Saxone, back again to another shoe shop, then on up the street to Next.

His back-up arrived; a plain-clothes WPC to take over the close tail, plus a patrol car. The WPC followed Moyra in and out of shops as far as Wardour Street, where she entered a shopping mall. The driver of the patrol car and the uniformed officer took up their positions near the exits. Oakhill kept about fifty yards back from Henson, while the WPC peered into windows and watched Moyra try on shoes from a few feet away.

The patrol car was parked a good distance from the café and Muddyman, directly across the road, kept the radio contact going, informing Tennison that it looked as though the suspect was on the move again.

"Yeah, he's buttoning up his raincoat. Shit! He's sat down again. He's having another bloody coffee!"

Tennison's foot was still tapping and she was chain-smoking, building up a real fug in the car.

A message started coming through from Jones. "Would you believe Moyra Henson sometimes works from this booth in Covent Garden, and she was working here in January. An assistant at the Floral Street Health Club told me she directed Karen here. The woman who runs it can't say if Karen had had her nails done here or not, but she says that when Henson was working here Marlow used to pick her up! Moyra could have done Karen's nails, and if he saw her, knew her name . . ."

DC Jones was standing in the middle of a breakdancing troupe, battling to make himself heard. The steel girders above the stalls distorted the radio waves.

"How long does this Noo-Nail treatment take?" Tennison's voice asked.

"The woman said she can do eight a day, so it must take a while."

"You hear all that?" Tennison asked Amson. He nodded. "That's how he could have known their names! If the treatment takes a while and he was hanging around . . .

Tennison stubbed out her cigarette. They were both beginning to sweat; it was coming down, they could feel it.

"It's the two of them, then!"

"Looks like it," Tennison replied. "Let's pick Moyra up now, and see if the lads back at base have come up with anything from the cross-check. Della and Moyra both came from Manchester originally, it's just their ages, Della was a lot younger. Car five-four-seven to base . . ."

"Looks like she's been lying from day one!"

While Tennison gave the go-ahead for Moyra Henson to be picked up, Muddyman radioed in that Marlow was on the move. Then there was silence, but the crackle of the open channel added to the tension. Everyone was waiting . . .

"He's moving fast now, turning left out of the café, crossing the road. He's stopped, he's on to me, looking over . . ."

Another voice cut in. "I've got him! He's just passed me, walking briskly, crossing the road again. He's heading for the lock-ups, he's walking right along Battle Bridge Road to the lock-ups . . ."

The radio controllers nearly deafened Tennison with their cheering, as if Arsenal had scored a winning goal in the Cup Final. Like the men in the street, they were feeding Marlow's every move to the cars and to the rapidly closing ring of officers in the area. Now they passed on the instructions for the lads to take up their positions . . .

"Yes!" Tennison yelled, and punched Amson's arm. "He's going for the goddamned lock-ups, I knew it, I knew it!"

Amson tapped the driver on the shoulder to warn him to be ready. He started the engine.

Tennison was gabbling. "Everyone keep back, just hold your positions, don't frighten him off . . . Stay put until we get the go . . . Over . . ."

They could only listen, they couldn't move out, couldn't see, in case they tipped Marlow off, as the team moved in. Some were dressed as mechanics, bending over broken-down cars, another pedaled past with a ladder, someone else drove a grocery van, but they were moving in, surrounding Marlow. The tension was explosive . . .

George Marlow strolled casually along the street. He passed two open lock-ups where mechanics were at work. Cars in various stages of repair littered the street.

He reached the corner where a road ran at right angles under the railway lines. He paused, looked around, checking carefully to see if he was being followed.

"Hold your positions, no one move," Tennison instructed. "Let him open up and get inside before you grab him."

Apparently satisfied that he was in the clear, Marlow walked unhurriedly, swinging the keys around his finger as he went. He approached a lock-up that looked as though it hadn't been occupied in years. A small access door was set into one of the huge main doors.

Tennison's tense voice broadcast softly, "I want him to use the keys, everybody wait . . . wait . . ."

After another long look around, Marlow stepped up to the small door and selected a key from the ring.

Muddyman's voice was low, breathy. "Shit, I think this is it, he's going for it. Stand by, suspect has his key in the lock. He's opening up! He's opening up!"

The small door swung open and Marlow raised one leg to step over the high sill as Tennison shrieked, "Go! Go! Go!"

The cars converged into the street, sirens wailing, but before they could get to Marlow the lads emerged from their positions like greyhounds after a hare: Rosper, Caplan, Lillie and Muddyman. They charged across the street and before Marlow could step right inside they had him. Rosper, the first there, grabbed Marlow by the scruff of his neck, almost tearing the raincoat off him as he dragged him from the doorway. Marlow stumbled as his foot caught on the sill, and the next moment his head was cracked back on the edge of the door. They all wanted a go at him—it was part tension, part adrenaline—and they handled him roughly, pinching the skin on his wrists as they handcuffed him.

Muddyman was shouting the caution as Tennison's car screamed up. She was about to get out when she hesitated, to give the boys a chance to spot her and ease up on Marlow. It was in that moment, no more than a few seconds, that she saw another side to her suspect.

He seemed completely unconcerned at being knocked around, arrested. In fact he was unnaturally calm. He looked up with a puzzled frown, first at Rosper, then Lillie. Tennison did not hear what he said, but she could see the expression on his face as if he was angry with himself.

But the lads heard him: "Ahhh . . . the painters." He seemed satisfied that he had recognized them, but there was still a look of irritation on his face. He hadn't suspected them, in fact he had trusted them. He had been foolish, made a mistake. They were not painters.

Moyra Henson emerged from a boutique with a large carrier bag and strolled along the mall, stopping beside the plain-clothes WPC, who was loaded with bags, to look in the next window. Their elbows nearly touched.

She was so intent on the goods in the shop that for a moment she didn't clock the reflection of the uniformed officer speaking into his radio a few feet away. Oakhill moved in and the WPC right next to Moyra dropped her bags and held out her ID.

"Moyra Henson, I am WPC Southill. We would like you to accompany us to the Southampton Row—"

Moyra swung her boutique bag to slap Southill in the face, then went for her, kicking and spitting, screaming that she wanted to be left alone. Her screeching drew everyone's attention: shop assistants rushed out to see what was going on, customers rammed into each other on the escalators, as Moyra's screams echoed throughout the mall. Her face was puce with hysteria.

She seemed to cave in suddenly, her back pressed against the window, hands up.

"I just want to be left alone, ahhhh, please, please leave me alone! Don't touch me! I'll come with you, just don't touch me!"

She started to retrieve her fallen purchases and stuff them into the torn boutique bag. She had hurled her handbag to the floor, spilling cosmetics, wallet, mirror all over the marble floor, and she insisted on picking everything up herself. She was crying now, her mascara running down her face, her hysteria over.

She allowed herself to be led to the waiting patrol car where she sat, sniffing noisily, her nose all red, and stared out of the window. As the car moved off and the siren started up, she seemed to gather her senses, taking a hankie from her bag and blowing her nose. WPC Southill watched closely as she pulled out a perfume atomizer and gave Oakhill the nod to check it.

"It's perfume, Chanel, and it's very expensive. Cost over thirty quid, and I only use it sparingly—I mean, too much and you overdo it. So if you don't mind giving it back? What'd you think I was gonna do, spray it in the driver's eyes and make my escape? Screw you, screw the lot of you, you're all wankers!"

She spent the rest of the journey to the station checking her wallet, counting her money and repacking everything in orderly fashion. But she didn't say anything else; she felt there wasn't any point.

The lock-up was cavernous. Water dripped constantly, forming pools on the floor, and the shape of it amplified the eerie sounds of the trains overhead. The place stank of damp, ancient oil and many other things.

The far end was pitch dark. Near the center of the empty space Tennison could just make out a large, shrouded shape in the gloom. She chose to ignore the little scuttling, splashing noises of the rats.

"Everybody watch where you stand," Tennison ordered, her voice echoing. "Lights, are there any lights?"

Fluorescent lights blinked on slowly, casting a cold blueish light which reflected in the puddles. Tennison advanced, picking her way slowly and carefully until she reached the middle. She lifted the old tarpaulin by one corner, exposing gleaming chrome and gold-brown paintwork.

"Well, we've got the car!" she called briskly, peering inside it. There was no radio between the seats. "I want the Forensic crowd down here ASAP. The less we move or touch, the better."

DS Amson was tiptoeing through the pools of water towards her. She stepped back, knocking into him, and turned to give him an earful when she saw his smile freeze. He was looking past her to the far end of the lock-up. Tennison followed his eyes.

"Oh, my God," she whispered, and pointed. "This is where he did it."

Arrayed on the wall like an exhibit in a black museum were chains, shackles and a hideous collection of sharpened tools.

"How are you going to play it?" Kernan asked Tennison.

She was tense, champing anxiously at the bit. "Henson first, break the alibi. Marlow's brief's on his way in."

"Right, Jane, and . . . well done!"

"Not done yet," she replied, flexing her fingers. "Not yet."

Flanked by Amson and Muddyman, with Havers in her wake, Tennison swept along the corridor to the interview room. Muddyman and Amson entered first, going to opposite sides of the room. Tennison walked straight to the table where Moyra Henson sat smoking, her solicitor beside her. Tennison could feel the change in her; she was afraid.

She addressed the solicitor. "Mr. Shrapnel? This is Detective Inspector Muddyman, Sergeant Amson and WPC Havers." With a nod to Havers to close the door, she sat down and placed some files on the table. "You have been made aware that your client has not been arrested at this stage, but is here of her own free will to answer questions and assist in the investigation into the murders of Karen Howard and Della Mornay."

"Yes, I am aware of the situation, and my client is prepared to assist in any way that will not incriminate her or instigate criminal proceedings against her," the small gray-suited man replied.

For the first time since entering the room, Tennison looked directly at Moyra.

"At twelve forty-five today we gained access to George Arthur Marlow's rented lock-up garage in King's Cross. A brown Rover car, registration number SLB 23L, was discovered on the premises, together with certain incriminating evidence. In your recent statement you claimed that you had no knowledge of the whereabouts of this car, is that true?"

There was no bravado left in her. "I didn't know anything about it, I thought it had been stolen."

"In the same statement you gave George Arthur Marlow an alibi, stating that he returned to the flat you share on the night of the thirteenth of January, nineteen-ninety, at ten-thirty. Is that correct?"

Moyra glanced at her solicitor, then back to Tennison and gave a nod.

"When I interviewed you on that occasion, you were shown pictures of murder victims, do you remember? You stated that you had never met any of the women in the photographs."

Again Moyra nodded and looked to Mr. Shrapnel. Tennison opened one of her files and brought out two photographs.

"On the sixteenth of May, nineteen seventy-one, you and Deirdre Mornay were on trial at Manchester Juvenile court." She laid the photograph of Della on the table. Moyra did not react. "In early January of this year, Karen Howard was a customer at the booth in Covent Garden that you took over from Annette Frisby." Karen's photo was put in front of Moyra. Again she did not react.

Two more photographs; this time of the bodies of the murdered girls.

"Moyra, you are not looking at the photographs. If you don't want to look at Della, then look at Karen. George called out to her, offered her a lift, then took her to King's Cross and tortured her, mutilated her. But first, he hung her on the wall in chains and raped her. Look at it, Moyra, see her hands tied behind her back, the marks on her body . . . *Look at her, Moyra!*"

Shrapnel raised his hands as if to say, "That's enough!"

"Your client, Mr. Shrapnel, stands to be accused as an accessory to murder. Don't you think she should know what that crime involved?"

"My client has co-operated fully—"

Slowly, Moyra put out a hand and picked up the photos.

"Your client, Mr. Shrapnel, has systematically lied to us. Now she has a chance to—" Tennison stopped and watched Moyra's reaction to the photographs; she stared at each one, then covered the one of Karen's body with her hands and closed her eyes.

Shrapnel was saying, "Moyra is George Marlow's common-law wife . . ."

Tennison raised a hand to quieten him as Moyra started to speak to her.

"Would you get the men to leave, just the women stay . . . I won't talk in front of them."

Amson gripped Shrapnel by the elbow and hurried out, followed by Muddyman. In the silence, Moyra sat with her hands over the picture of Karen, looking at Tennison with dead, unemotional eyes.

"I didn't know Della, I didn't even remember her. She was just a kid. But I did her nails, she used to bite them and . . . I didn't know her, it was just that she used to come and have the odd nail replaced, you know, if she'd broken one."

Tennison nodded without speaking. Moyra didn't really want to talk about Della, this was not why she had wanted the men out of the room, there was something else. Moyra tugged at her skirt, darting glances at Tennison, her whole body twisting and turning, her hands picking at her own false nails. She looked at Havers, chewing at her lip, then back to Tennison. Then she leaned forward, her chin in her hand, as if she didn't want anyone else to hear.

"He . . . he did it to me once," she whispered. Tennison leaned closer, but Moyra immediately sat back, coughed and stared at Havers. Tennison waited patiently while Moyra straightened her skirt yet again, twisted her hair. Then she released a deep sigh.

This time she didn't whisper. She faced the wall. "He made this thing, with straps, for here." She touched her arm. "He said it made . . . it made the vagina tight, you know, stretched out, but it hurt me. I didn't like it, I wouldn't do it."

She hung her head, as if the horror was slowly seeping into her brain. She still couldn't face Tennison; her head sank lower and lower until it was nearly resting on her knees.

"I didn't know, I didn't know . . . Oh, God forgive me, I didn't know . . ."

Moyra buried her face in her arms and began to sob.

Amson, Muddyman and Shrapnel were all leaning against the wall of the corridor when Tennison's face appeared in the glass panel. She opened the door.

"George Marlow *was* home by ten-thirty that night, but he went out again at a quarter to eleven. She doesn't know what time he returned."

She stood very erect, head up, eyes blowing. "We've got him," she said quietly.

George Marlow lay in his cell, staring at the ceiling. A uniformed officer outside kept a constant watch through the spyhole.

The key turned in the lock, and Marlow sat up, swinging his feet to the floor as his solicitor, Arnold Upcher, stepped in.

With a glance at his watch, Upcher said, "Five minutes!" to the officer, who remained in the open doorway, Upcher put his briefcase down on the bunk and faced Marlow.

"They are charging you on six counts of murder, George."

Marlow shook his head, sighed, and looked up. "I don't know what's going on, Arnold. On my mother's life, I haven't done anything."

Arc-lights had been brought into the King's Cross lock-up to improve the illumination. White-suited Scenes of Crime men were moving in to start photographing and fingerprinting. The place was strangely quiet; only the constant rumble of the trains and the distant sound of a chained dog barking disturbed the silence.

The Rover had been surrounded by plastic sheeting. One man was kneeling on the plastic, leaning in through the open door, combing the fitted carpets with great care, passing anything he found to an assistant beside him.

DI Burkin and DC Jones were examining a row of old metal lockers.

"Oh, look at this!" exclaimed Burkin, holding up a hideous mask with cut-out eyeholes by his fingertips. He dropped it into a plastic bag.

In the next locker, Jones had found suits, shirts, ties, shoes, all covered in plastic dry-cleaner's bags.

"Even his sneakers, look . . . Neat bastard."

Burkin sniffed. "Jesus, this place smells like an abattoir." He turned to stare at the wall where Marlow's chains and torture instruments hung, his nose wrinkling in disgust.

Two men were crouched near the wall, prodding at a small drain with sticks. Above the drain, where a single tap was fitted, a makeshift shower had been rigged up, with a plastic shampoo spray and a plastic curtain, spotted with black mold and streaked with blood. Beside it a dish contained soap, wire brushes and a plastic nail brush.

"This is caked in blood, we'll need swabs of it all," one of the men was saying. "Ugh, the drain's clogged with it, and this looks like skin . . ." He covered his face. "Jesus, the stench!" he mumbled, retching.

Burkin had found a handbag. He handled it carefully, wearing disposable plastic gloves. Inside was a wallet; he flipped it open.

"It's Karen Howard's!"

More arc-lights came on, bathing the Rover in a bright pool of light. The SOCO was holding a pair of tweezers up and peering at the tiny item they held.

"The carpet's been scrubbed, smells of cleaning fluid, and it's damp. What's this? Looks like a tiny gold screw." He dropped it into the bag his assistant held open for him and something else caught his attention. "Was your girl blond?" he called over to Burkin and Jones as he carefully stashed a single blond hair into a bag.

Burkin was examining a jacket, peering at it through the plastic bag. "I got one of these jackets from his flat, he must have two sets of clothes . . . See his shoes, did you take his shoes from the flat?"

DC Jones wasn't ready for it, couldn't understand how it happened, but one moment he was doing his job, sorting through the gear, and the next he burst into tears. He stood there, unable to control his sobs, almost in surprise.

Burkin put an arm around his shoulder. "Go an' grab a coffee, a few of the others might feel like one, OK?"

"I'm sorry, I'm sorry, I dunno what made me get like this . . ."

Peering into the cabinet again, Burkin replied, "We all go through it, Dave. I think it's just natural, a release . . . Mine's black, no sugar."

Jones threaded his way across the duckboards, mindful of the plastic sheeting. He had to turn back because he couldn't remember if it was four black and six white or the other way round.

The silent shadows of the men loomed on the walls where hideous splashes of blood, and worse, had dried. The greenish glow of the fluorescent lights and the brightness of the arc-lights did nothing to lift the dank darkness, the stench, the horror. This was where that sweet girl was brought; he could only imagine her terror, only imagine it.

DI Burkin had pulled out a thick black wardrobe bag, the kind used by the uppercrust type of dry cleaners. It was strong, would have fitted a full-length evening gown, and it had a zip from one end to the other. It was slightly open at one end and he could see a tangle of blond hair jammed in the teeth. They knew Marlow was strong—this had to be how he had carried his victims undetected, zipped up in the wardrobe bag, hung over his arm . . .

It was not for Burkin to find out, that was down to Forensic, but be wondered. He placed it into a see-through evidence bag, tagged it, then bent to check over Marlow's shoes. They were all neatly wrapped in clingfilm, ready to slip on and walk out, or walk into Della Mornay's efficiency. No wonder they had been unable to find a single item, a single fiber, in her room.

The tape recorder emitted a high-pitched bleep, and Tennison started talking.

"This is a recorded interview. I am Detective Chief Inspector Jane Tennison. Also present are Detective Sergeant Terence Amson and Mr. Arnold Upcher. We are situated in room 5-C at Southampton Row Metropolitan Police Station. The date is Thursday the first of February, nineteen ninety. The time is four forty-five pm."

Tennison nodded to Marlow. "Would you please state your full name, address and date of birth?"

He leaned forward and directed his voice towards the built-in microphone. "George Arthur Marlow, twenty-one High Grove Estate, Maida Vale. Born in Warrington, eleventh September, nineteen fifty-one."

"Do you understand why you have been arrested?"

He gave a half-shrug. "I guess so."

"It is my duty formally to caution you, and warn you that anything you say may be used in evidence. You have been arrested on suspicion of the murders of Karen Howard and Deirdre Mornay. Do you understand?"

"I am not guilty." Marlow turned and looked at Upcher.

"Would you please describe to me the meeting that took place between yourself and Karen Howard on the night of January the thirteenth, nineteen ninety."

"I didn't know her name, I was told her name later," Marlow began. "She approached me. I asked how much she wanted. I drove her to some waste ground and had sex with her. I paid her for sex. I didn't know her, I had never seen or met her before. Then after I dropped her off at the tube station . . ."

"What about the cut on her hand? In a previous statement you said that she, Karen, cut her hand on the car radio which was between the seats." Tennison held up the statement for Upcher to see.

"Yes, that's right."

"The statement was taken on the fifteenth of January, nineteen-ninety. We have since discovered that there is no radio between the front seats of your car."

He didn't seem to register what she had said. He began. "I was at home at ten-thirty . . ."

"So, you arrived home at ten-thirty that night. Could you tell us what time you next left the flat?"

"I didn't, I watched television with my wife."

"You are referring to your common-law wife, Miss Moyra Henson, is that correct?"

"Yes."

"Miss Henson made a statement at three forty-five this afternoon. She states that you actually left the flat again at fifteen minutes to eleven. She cannot recall exactly when you returned, but you returned without your car. She says that your car was not stolen from outside your block of flats."

"She's wrong! My car was nicked, I never went out again."

"You have denied having any previous contact with Karen Howard."

"Yeah, never met her before the night she picked me up . . ."

"Miss Henson has, on occasion, worked at a booth in Covent Garden. She has admitted that she met Karen, and that she gave her a nail treatment. You were there at the time and you spoke to Karen. Is that true?"

"No." Marlow shook his head.

"You have also denied knowing the other victim, Deirdre Mornay, also known as Della. Miss Henson agrees, however, that contrary to her first statement, in which she too denied knowing Miss Mornay, she was in fact lying. I suggest that you are also lying and that you did know Della Mornay."

Marlow sat back in his chair, folded his arms. "I don't believe you play these games. Moyra is scared to death that you are going to arrest her for tax evasion and claiming unemployment benefit. She's terrified of the police since she was picked up on a false charge of prostitution. Well, you don't scare me, I'm innocent." He spoke to Upcher. "I don't have to answer any more questions, do I?"

The team were kicking their heels in the Incident Room. Jones asked generally, "How's the guv'nor? She must be knackered."

Burkin shook his head. "Taking a long time. After what we found in the lock-up, I don't think he'd admit to knowing his own mother right now."

Slumped in chairs, perched on desks, propped against walls, they waited.

Marlow was looking tired. "How many more times do I have to tell you?"

Tennison pressed on. "This morning?" she prompted.

"I told you, I got an anonymous call, I dunno who it was. He says to me that he knows where my car is, he's seen it on the TV program, right? It's been reported stolen, right?"

"What time was the call?"

"Oh, about ten . . . Anyway, he says he knows where the car is, at King's Cross."

"He told you that your car was in a lock-up at King's Cross, yes? Did he give you the keys?" Marlow shrugged, and she went on, "Mr. Marlow, you were seen unlocking the door."

He answered angrily, "Because he said I could get them from a Greek guy in a coffee bar. So I picked up the keys, but I didn't find my car because just as I opened the door the police jumped on me! I don't know why I have to keep repeating myself," he said to Upcher. "I've told them all this a dozen times . . ."

Tennison showed no sign of fatigue or impatience as she asked, "What was the Greek man's name?"

"I dunno, the tip-off just gave me the address of the café." He sighed.

Arnold Upcher shifted his position, checked his watch and glanced at Tennison. He was getting fed up. He looked around; Amson had sat down in the corner.

"Stavros Hulanikis has sub-let the lock-up to a man he knows as John

Smith for eight years. After you collected the keys from him this morning, an officer, Detective Inspector Burkin, took a statement from him. Your Greek friend also does certain items of dry-cleaning and laundry for you, doesn't he?"

Marlow shook his head in disbelief, not bothering to answer. Tennison continued, "Come on, George, how did you get Karen into the efficiency? Where are Della's keys? You know the place was empty, didn't you? You knew, because Della Mornay was already dead."

Marlow leaned towards her. "You are trying to put words into my mouth," he said emphatically. "Well, that's it, I'm not saying another thing." He appealed to Upcher: "Tell her that's enough! I agreed to this interview, I've done nothing but assist them from the word go! I want to go home."

Upcher replied quietly, "That won't be possible, George," then turned to Tennison. "It's almost ten."

Marlow was getting really uptight. He shouted, "I wanna go to the toilet, I wanna have a piss, all right? I have to call my mother, I don't want her reading in the papers that you arrested me again! I want to be the one to tell her—"

"I agree to a fifteen-minute break," Tennison told Upcher. To Marlow she said, "You will not be allowed to see Miss Henson, or make any phone calls until this interview is terminated. I will arrange for Miss Henson to phone your mother . . ."

Marlow pushed his chair back as if to stand up. Amson moved towards him.

"No! They don't get on. I don't want Moyra calling my mother." He sighed with irritation and stood up with his hands on his hips, facing Tennison. "This is a mess, isn't it? Oh, all right, I did it."

Upcher jumped to his feet. Tennison just sat and stared at Marlow, then managed to pull her wits together.

"Could you repeat that? You are still under caution."

Marlow closed his eyes. She could see his long lashes, every line of his handsome face. He licked his top lip, then he opened his eyes. The color seemed even more startling, the pupils were like pin-points. As if watching in slow motion, Tennison felt every tiny movement recorded in her mind.

He tilted his head to the right, then to the left, and smiled. No one in the room moved; they all focused on Marlow, on his strange, eerie smile.

"I said I did it."

There seemed to be nothing else to say. Everyone in the room except George Marlow held their breath, ready to explode, but he seemed totally relaxed. Eventually Tennison breathed out and said, "Please sit down, George."

He slumped into his seat. She watched him closely as she asked, "What exactly did you do?"

He checked them off on his fingers. "Karen, Della, Angela, Sharon, Ellen and . . ." He screwed up his eyes, trying to remember, then snapped his fingers. "That's right, Jeannie . . ."

Only Tennison's eyes reflected the impact of his words. George Arthur Marlow had just casually admitted to killing all six victims.

12

When George Marlow had been led back to his cell, DCI Tennison lit a cigarette and inhaled deeply. The welter of emotions inside her was under rigid control, and she showed none of it to the others in the room.

She had just caught the man she had devoted every ounce of her energy to catching, a man who had caused her the loss of the only lover she had ever really cared about, had deprived her of sleep for days on end, had nearly lost her job and her self-respect. She sat quietly and smoked her cigarette down to the filter, then stubbed it out.

DC Jones, his face flushed, raced into the bar of the local pub. Pushing the other regulars aside, he stopped in the middle of the floor, raised his hands in triumph and yelled, "He's bloody admitted it! All six of them, he's admitted doing the lot!"

The team rose to their feet as a man, although one of them was Maureen Havers. The cheer went up; Jones grabbed Havers and danced her around the floor as everyone congratulated everyone else.

A group of DIs from another team looked on the feverish celebration with interest. When Havers finally sat down again, one of them came over to her, carrying his pint.

"What gives?"

Beaming, Havers replied, "Our guv'nor's just got a suspect to admit to six charges of murder! Biggest case this station's ever had . . ."

DI Caldicott returned to his own table and spoke to his mates. The racket in the bar was so great that no one else could hear what he was saying, but they all turned to stare at Tennison's team and raised their glasses in salute.

• • •

DCI Tennison was facing the Superintendent across his desk. He poured her a large whisky and said, as he handed it to her, "Well, congratulations! The trial'll be a long process, but you go home now and get some sleep, you deserve it."

"Yeah, I need it. It was a long night." She looked and sounded exhausted. Downing the whisky in one, she stood up and made for the door.

The phone rang and the Super picked it up. "Kernan . . . Yes, just a moment." He covered the mouthpiece and spoke to Tennison. "You were right to stick to your guns. Six counts of murder! And the beautician link . . . It was a woman's case, after all!"

He put the phone to his ear again, dismissively, and swiveled round in his chair; it's business as usual. "I'm putting Caldicott on it," he said into the phone. "They're bringing the son in for questioning."

Tennison rose to the bait. "Fifty per cent of murder victims are women, so it looks as if I might have my hands full!" she retorted.

The door slammed behind her before Kernan could swivel round to reply.

"Woman's case, my arse!" Tennison muttered to herself, still seething about Kernan's comment. She spotted Maureen Havers peering at her from the double doors further down the corridor.

"Maureen, any of the lads about?"

Havers replied casually, "Oh, I don't think so, we were all on two till ten. Oh, DCI Jenkins wants the Incident Room cleared, could you pop along before you leave?"

Pursing her lips, Tennison pushed through the other side of the doors and marched towards the Incident Room. Havers hung back and watched her go.

The Incident Room was crammed to bursting, but surprisingly quiet. Every single member of Tennison's team was there. Someone called, "Here she is!" and they all watched expectantly as the door handle turned.

Tennison walked in to cheers, whistles and the sound of popping corks. A huge bunch of flowers was pressed into her hand and Burkin started singing, the others quickly joining in: "Why was she born so beautiful, why was she born at all? She's no bloody use to anyone, she's no bloody good at all!"

"Three cheers for our guv'nor, hip-hip . . ."

"*Hooray . . . !*"

Tennison nearly choked on her champagne, her back was slapped so hard. "You bastards!" she spluttered. "I thought you'd all pissed off! Cheers!"

She bit her lip, but the tears brimmed over. Then out came her great, bellowing laugh and she punched the air. "We did it! We got him!"

Many months later, George Marlow stood in the dock to answer the charges against him. The Clerk of the Court read them out:

"George Arthur Marlow, you stand before this court accused of six indictments of murder. That on the fourteenth of January, nineteen ninety, you did murder Karen Howard, contrary to common law . . ."

Major and Mrs. Howard were holding hands, staring straight ahead, unable to look at George Marlow, to turn their heads just a fraction to see him. He had taken their beloved daughter, he had raped her and mutilated her, and waiting for them to catch him had been the longest time they had ever lived through, a lifetime, Karen's lifetime. There would always be pain, that would never go away, and the confusion. Marlow had destroyed not just their daughter's life, but theirs.

". . . That on the third of December, nineteen eighty-nine you unlawfully took the life of Deirdre Margaret Mornay . . ."

Two prostitutes, friends of Della, leaned forward for a glimpse of her murderer. One of them sat back, afraid of her own feelings. Looking at him, with his handsome face, his fresh, immaculate white shirt, if he was to pick her up she wouldn't be likely to refuse him. They nudged each other and stared at DCI Tennison, who was sitting with the prosecution counsel. Her face was impassive. She gave them an almost imperceptible nod.

"You are also charged that on the fifteenth of March, nineteen eighty-four, you murdered Jeannie Avril Sharpe, that in January nineteen eighty-five you murdered Ellen Harding . . ."

Carol and Linda had traveled down from Oldham. They were sitting in the gallery. Linda leaned forward on her elbows but could only just see the crown of his curly head. Jeannie had wanted to emigrate to Australia, she had wanted . . . But she had never got anything, anyone to help her, love her. Now, maybe, she could rest in peace. Maybe.

Carol twisted a paper hankie in her hands. She could hear him as clear as anything, calling to Jeannie, calling her to come to his car.

In her wheelchair at the end of a row of spectators, Mrs. Marlow sat, as well-groomed as ever. She held her head high, making no effort to wipe away the tears that trickled down her face. Her pale blue eye shadow, her carefully outlined lips and powdery cheeks framed in false chestnut curls, seemed to crumble before George Marlow's eyes. He couldn't look at her, couldn't bear it; she was dying in front of him.

A young man sitting near her was leaning forward in his seat, staring intently at Marlow.

". . . That in July nineteen eighty-six you murdered Angela Simpson . . ."

The young man's face crumpled when he heard Angela's name, and he cried. He tried hard to control himself, but the years between Angela's murder and the arrest of George Marlow had been a nightmare. Five years, five long years of his life under suspicion, always wondering if somehow he could have saved her. Five years of nightmares, but above all the loss of his childhood sweetheart, the only girl he had ever loved.

When George Marlow's eyes flickered towards him he had never known such hatred. He had never believed himself capable of killing, but he could have killed Marlow with his bare hands; kill him, hurt him, make him feel the pain he had inflicted on Angela.

". . . And in October, nineteen eighty-seven you murdered Sharon Felicity Read . . ."

Sharon's father sat stiffly at the back of the gallery in his best suit, starched shirt and bowling club tie. Sharon's mother had died, a year after they received the news; he had lost his wife and daughter because of the same man. Not a day passed without this quiet, respectable man remembering his daughter, his sweetheart, his own darlin' . . .

He wept because she had only just begun to grow into a woman, and he wept because he was haunted by his wife's face when he had told her that their daughter had been found. The arrogance of Marlow didn't anger him, didn't inspire him to revenge; it just left him with an overwhelming sadness, because nothing mended his heart.

Tennison kept her eyes averted from Marlow, her head bowed, but he seemed to draw her attention as if willing to look at him. She stared suddenly as a door opened, throwing a wedge of light onto a dark figure, hunched at the back of the court. It was Moyra, and she had aged twenty years.

"George Arthur Marlow, having heard the charges against you, how do you plead?"

Tennison looked up at him. He was astonishingly handsome; his dark eyes, high cheekbones and glossy hari oozed vitality. She drew a sharp breath because he was looking at her. As their eyes met he seemed to smile, yet his lips did not move. It was just a lightness in his eyes . . . there was no anger, no malice.

"Not guilty, sir," he replied.

PRIME SUSPECT 2

A Face in the Crowd

LYNDA LA PLANTE

For Sally Head

1

The young black man was very good-looking. Tall and lithe, with a fine pair of shoulders, he kept himself in shape with regular workouts. He sat at the square wooden table in the interview room, long supple hands clasped in his lap, his body erect, and his handsome face impassive. His suit was well cut with an immaculate white shirt and a neat, precise knot in his tie. He was very calm, very sure of himself. The remote-control video camera high in one corner recorded all this, as he tilted his head back slightly, looking straight into the eyes of the woman opposite with just a hint of lazy insolence.

She stared back unflinchingly. "I am Detective Chief Inspector Jane Tennison, attached to Southampton Row Police Station. We are in the interview room at Southampton Row. I am interviewing . . ." She leaned her elbows on the table. "Would you please state your full name and date of birth." When the man didn't respond, she patiently tried again in the same quiet, unhurried tone. "Will you please state your full name and date of birth."

"Robert Oswalde. The t'irteenth of August, 1961."

From his appearance you might have expected an educated voice, but it was a strong Jamaican accent, the t's and d's heavily emphasized.

"You are entitled to speak to a solictor at any time," Tennison informed him, "and this legal advice is free."

Oswalde stared back, black man to white woman, the insolence in his dark eyes almost like a blatant sexual challenge.

There was a dumpster half-filled with rubbish outside Number 15 Honey-ford Road, so the police car was parked at an angle, its rear end sticking out into the street. Already, within minutes of its arrival, a small crowd was gathering in the late-afternoon November gloom, peering out from under umbrellas as the drizzle thickened and swirled in the sodium-yellow street-lights. The neighborhood was mainly West Indian, with a sprinkling of Asians, and rumor spread much faster here than it might have done in a white middle-class area. And ever since the Derrick Cameron case a few years ago, any police activity aroused curiosity and suspicion in equal measure; the presence of white cops didn't mean protection for the local community, it invariably spelled trouble.

The front door of Number 15 was wide open, with a uniformed policeman on the top step and his colleague in the hallway talking to the builder. Or trying to hear him, which was difficult with Mr. Viswandha, the house's owner, gabbling away in Urdu on the phone. His wife and their two children stood shivering and bewildered in the foyer, the draft from the front door whipping through the house.

"One of my men found it." The builder jerked a grimy thumb toward the rear. "We're laying new drains. Seems to be wrapped in polyethylene . . ."

The crowd at the garden gate was growing by the minute. Several young black kids had climbed on the wall, trying to peer through the open door. One had propped his bike against the gatepost and was jostling for a position. The murmur and rumble of voices continued under the pattering of rain on the umbrellas and plastic hoods as the drizzle turned into a steady downpour. Then a real buzz rose. Two cars had pulled up, Criminal Investigation Department officers piling out, shouldering their way through the crowd. Rumor and speculation were rife now: the heavy mob didn't show up unless a serious crime had been committed, and by the look of it this was shaping up to be the most serious of all.

As the officers came through, the young boy with the bike piped up, "Have the Pakis murdered someone?"

Detective Inspector Frank Burkin didn't break his stride. "Shut up and move that bike!"

The kid's older brother, wearing a beaded cap with dreadlocks trailing down, wasn't too thrilled with Burkin's attitude. "What makes you think you can talk to him like that?" he burst out angrily. "We live here, man, not you . . . what is it with you?"

Impatiently, DI Tony Muddyman pushed past, leaving Burkin to argue with the youth. Diplomacy never was top priority on Burkin's list, but why the hell did he have to alienate the local community the minute he planted his size elevens on Honeyford Road, he thought. Getting people's backs up was no way to start.

Mr. Viswandha had finished on the phone and met Muddyman as he came through the front door. Eyes glittering, head jerking back and forth, the Indian watched the file of men troop past him down the hall.

"Are you in charge?"

"For the time being, sir," Muddyman nodded.

"Then please . . ." Mr. Viswandha's brown, plump hands paddled the air nervously. "Just take it away."

"We will, sir, as soon as possible—"

"Not as soon as possible." He glanced at his wife hugging the two children to her, a boy of seven and a girl of five. "*Now.* I pay my poll tax."

"I'm afraid it's a suspicious death, sir, and as such, all this has to be done properly." Muddyman beckoned a District Commissioner forward. "Now, will you go with this officer and answer his questions, please."

With a nod to Mrs. Viswandha, Muddyman went on; he always tried to be polite, especially with the ethnics, but why was it that he always felt he had to compensate for Burkin's crass, insensitive behavior? As if the bloody job wasn't hard enough.

"So she consented to sex with you?"

Tennison kept her voice deliberately flat, unemotional. She wanted to feed him just enough rope to hang himself with.

Oswalde gave a lazy grin. "What ya gwan an with? She was beggin' for it, man."

"If she was a willing partner, why did you use violence?" Casually the Chief Inspector fed him a bit more rope. "Why did you hit her?"

"You know these t'ings," said Oswalde with a shrug, "how them happen . . ."

"No, I don't know."

"Some of them white t'ing like it rough." Again the overt sexual insult in his eyes, teasing, taunting. Watching him, Tennison decided to draw the noose tighter. She glanced down at the sheet of paper in front of her.

"But the doctor reports 'severe gripping contusions to the upper arms.'" She glanced up. "Bruises where you'd held her down."

Oswalde looked blank. Turning, he frowned at DCI Thorndike who was sitting to one side, arms folded across his double-breasted lapels, his narrow, pale face and watery eyes just beyond the arc of lamplight. Thorndike dropped his eyes, as though embarrassed by the explicit nature of the interrogation. But Tennison was not in the least put out. It seemed as if nothing could shock her, not even if Oswalde had stripped and done a handstand on the table.

"All right, Robert, let me ask you this." Tennison leaned forward, the curtain of honey-blond hair slanting across her forehead. "How did you know that this girl liked it 'rough'?"

"I knew. The way she looked."

"Well . . . how did she look?" Tennison pressed him.

"She had blond hair." Oswalde stared straight back. "She was wearin' a red blouse . . ."

Tennison had on a red blouse.

"An' she had a tight, tight black skirt . . . like for you."

"I see. So she didn't actually say anything to encourage you?"

Tennison let the silence hang for a moment, and then her voice had a harder edge to it. "But then that's not surprising since you tore her tights off and rammed them down her throat."

Oswalde stiffened. "That's just her word against mine." There was a faint sheen of perspiration on his smooth wide forehead.

"No, it's the doctor's report, the forensic evidence, *and* her word against yours," Tennison corrected him. She pulled the rope a notch tighter. "How many other women have you attacked? How long before you kill someone, Robert?"

Oswalde's handsome face had gotten sullen. Perhaps he could feel the noose tightening around his neck.

By the time Superintendent Mike Kernan arrived at Honeyford Road, the Area Major Incident Team, known as AMIT, based at Southampton Row, was already in action. Kernan had been looking forward to a quiet evening at home, feet up, glass of Famous Grouse, something undemanding on the TV. In fact, already hightailing it in his BMW when the call had come through, he had debated whether to respond or let the AMIT boys get on with it. But he hadn't debated for long; first reports from the scene of the crime suggested that this was more than just a run-of-the-mill case of domestic violence—the cause of most murders. And with his interview coming up, the Super didn't want to be conspicuously absent in what might turn out to be a major homicide investigation. So he turned around at the next intersection and headed back, grimly reconciled to his duty, the TV and the Scotch already a fading memory.

"Heh—policeman! Kernan!"

A small pudgy West Indian woman in a shapeless dark coat tried to grab his sleeve as he pushed his burly frame through the crowd on the slick, wet pavement. Kernan was annoyed—not so much with the woman, whom he recognized as Nola Cameron—but that the area hadn't been cleared and cordoned off. Where were the uniformed men? This could reach the level of public disorder if it wasn't nipped in the bud.

"What's happenin'? Heh, policeman, listen to me! If that's my Simone in there . . ."

Kernan appealed to her. "Nola, you can see I've just arrived. Give me a chance to find out what's happening. We won't be issuing any statements tonight. Now go home." He looked around, raising his voice. "You should all just go home."

"You never tried to find my daughter," Nola accused him passionately, bitterly. "If it's her in that garden . . ."

Halfway up the path, Kernan swung his head around, really angry now. "You people *should go home!*" He went on, gritting his teeth as Nola's wailing voice pursued him. "If that's my Simone . . . you won't be able to stop us getting to her . . ."

Kernan made a beeline for Muddyman, who seemed to be directing operations from the kitchen.

"Get the area cordoned off properly," he snapped. "If it turns out to be Simone Cameron we could have a real problem."

Notepad in hand, his muscular six-foot-three frame looming over her, DI Burkin was interviewing Mrs. Viswandha, while the two kids clutched their mother and peered out with large brown eyes, more curious than apprehensive. Burkin was having problems. She had to spell "Viswandha" for him, and when he asked for her first name, she said, "Sakuntala." Burkin sighed.

DC Jones and Mr. Viswandha were just inside the front room, off the foyer. The constable's glasses had misted up, and he was peering over the top of them, looking like an eager boy scientist, with his fresh-faced looks and wavy, brown hair.

"And the slabs were already in place when you bought the house?"

"Of course."

"You've done no work yourself in the garden? Or had any work done?"

"I'm telling you, no," said Mr. Viswandha through tight lips, his patience wearing thin.

Superintendent Kernan took Muddyman by the arm, leading him to the back door, which overlooked the garden. "Are the forensic boys here?" he asked, satisfied that inquiries with the family were proceeding smoothly.

"Waiting for you, Guv." Tony Muddyman opened the door. Kernan went first down the steps. With the entire garden area as brightly lit as a film set, the steady downpour was like a boiling mist under the arc lamps.

The back garden had been completely paved over when the Viswandhas moved in. But then there was trouble with the drains. A local building firm had been brought in to lay new pipes to connect with the main sewage system which ran along the rear alleyway. Paving slabs had been lifted and digging begun to remove the old pipework. About two feet down, the workmen had uncovered something far more grisly than broken pipes. Their spades had slashed through some polyethylene sheeting, exposing the pale gleam of human bones.

Kernan, raincoat collar turned up, stood at the edge of the makeshift structure of plastic sheeting the forensic people had erected to keep the rain out. There were three or four people down in the shallow trench, so it was difficult to make anything out. Water had seeped down, and the bottom and sides had congealed into sticky, clinging mud. Peter Gold, Forensic's bright new boy, was there, Kernan saw, clad in white overalls and green Wellington boots, down on his knees in the mire. Above him, crouched down on the paving slabs, Richards, the police photographer, was trying for the best position to get a clear shot.

Farther along the trench, buttoned up to the neck in his rain gear, the portly, balding figure of Oscar Bream, Chief Pathologist, was leaning forward, gloved hands gripping his knees. Bream's heavily lidded eyes, as ever, revealed nothing. He had only one expression—inscrutable. Perhaps he really felt nothing, felt no real emotion, just another job of work; or perhaps the years of looking into the pit of horrors of what human beings were capable of doing to their fellow creatures had forced him to adopt this dead-eyed mask as a form of protective camouflage.

Gold was using a small trowel and paintbrush to clear away the mud. "Over here, sir . . . see?"

"Right," Bream grunted, bending lower. "Let's take a look."

Protruding from the wall of the trench, about eighteen inches from the surface, part of a rib cage and pelvis gleamed under the arc lamps. Bream stepped back and gestured to Richards. The camera flashed three times. Bream bent forward, brushing away a smear of mud with his gloved hand. The remains of a human skull stared up, black sockets for eyes, with an expression almost as inscrutable as Oscar Bream's.

"So tell me what happened," Tennison said, "when you sodomized her."

Oswalde was out of his chair. She had him on the run now; she knew it, and he was catching on fast.

"I know what's gwan on . . ." He looked down on Tennison, and then his eyes flicked across to Thorndike, who was trying not to meet his gaze. Oswalde was nodding, dredging up a faint smile. ". . . with little pinktoes here." His accent thickened. "Look 'pon her nuh," he sneered derisively, inviting the other male in the room to join forces against this sly, female conspiracy.

"Sit down please, Robert," Tennison said calmly.

"She love it." Oswalde snapped his fingers. "Cockteaser, ennit? What she say I did to that bitch is just turnin' her on—"

"Sit down please, Robert," Tennison repeated, and under the force of her level stare he slowly sank back into the chair. "The thought of a woman being humiliated doesn't turn me on, Robert. Someone being frightened half to death. But that turns you on, doesn't it?"

Oswalde twitched his broad shoulders in a shrug.

"It must. Why else would you need to force yourself on someone? You're a very attractive man. How tall are you?"

"Six foot four."

Tennison raised one eyebrow. "Really? I'm sure a lot of women do fall for you. But not this one."

"Some women say 'no' when they mean 'yes.'"

Tennison's head snapped up, eyes narrowed. "So she said 'no' to you?"

"I said 'some' women."

"But she said 'no' to you?"

"I got nothin' to say . . ."

"She said 'no' and that's not begging for it. That's not consent."

"Bullshit." Oswalde licked his lips. Getting rattled, he turned again to Thorndike, complaining, "She puttin' words into my mouth."

"She said no—that's rape." Tennison pointed a finger. "Okay, let me ask you this—"

"Good," Thorndike interrupted, standing up. He cleared his throat, running his finger nervously inside his short collar. "Yes, well, that seems a convenient place to stop."

"Oh no—Mr. Thorndike," Tennison protested, "I haven't finished yet."

DCI Thorndike slid back his cuff to reveal his thin freckled wrist and tapped his watch. "Unfortunately we're going to have to since it's well past six." And with that he opened the door and went out.

Tennison brushed a hand through her hair and rolled her eyes towards the ceiling. "Unbelievable," she said through gritted teeth.

Oswalde stared at her, laughter bubbling in his chest. He smothered it with a cough. Tennison just shook her head.

As DCI Thorndike emerged through the door of the prefabricated "interview room," built into one corner of the conference hall, he wondered what the grins and smirks were all about. Over ninety grins and smirks, lurking on the faces of the police officers seated at rows of tables who had been watching the interrogation on the banks of screens. They'd caught Jane Tennison's final words and seen her expression, but he hadn't, so he was never to know.

With his jerky, stiff-legged walk, Thorndike strode to the front of the hall and faced the assembly. This was the second session of a three-day seminar on interviewing techniques: lectures and study groups interspersed with simulated interview situations conducted by senior officers. The hall quieted as Thorndike raised his hand.

"Excellent . . . though I would just sound one word of warning. Some of DCI Tennison's more unconventional questions might get a less-experienced officer into difficulties. Remember," he went on pedantically, "under PACE no attempt may be made to bully or threaten a suspect." This was a reference to the rules and regulations for dealing with detainees as laid down by the Police and Criminal Evidence Act. "Finally, well-done to Detective Sergeant Oswalde for playing his part so convincingly."

There were a few more snide grins at that. Convincing all right, because it seemed like he was damn well enjoying it, a lowly DS coming on strong to a female DCI—one of only four such female senior officers in the country. And although Tennison had a reputation as a ballbreaker, there was hardly a man in the room who didn't fancy her.

She joined Thorndike at the front, shrugging into her tailored, dark jacket. "And finally, *finally,* tomorrow's first session will be on interviewing the victims of rape. I'll see you all at ten o'clock."

As the meeting broke up to the shuffling of papers and the scraping of chairs, Thorndike gave her a patronizing pat on the shoulder, and she returned a brief, tight smile. God, she thought, he's like some prissy, old maiden aunt. It was all theory with him, book learning. If he encountered a real-life villain he'd have been totally clueless; probably have to skim through the PACE manual to find the right questions and in which order to ask them. He wasn't attached to the regular force, but a member of MS15, the Metropolitan body which investigated complaints by the public on matters of police procedure and suspected rule bending—in other words, digging the dirt on his fellow officers.

Going up to her room in the crowded elevator, Tennison glanced behind her to DS Oswalde. "You're too good at that, Detective Sergeant."

"Thank you, ma'am."

"Are you going for a drink later on?"

"Maybe. But I might just have an early night."

The bell pinged for the second floor and the doors slid open.

"Oh, well, might see you," Tennison said, going out. "Good night."

"Quick as you can," Bream urged Richards, standing aside as the photographer took another series of shots. When he was done, the pathologist had another look at the crumbling trench wall. "I'm going to need all the bones if I'm to reassemble the bugger," he told Gold. "So make sure you collect all the earth from around the corpse as well."

Gold was relishing this. It was his first really juicy forensic investigation, and working with Professor Oscar Bream was a bonus. He instructed his helpers with enthusiasm: "We'll put all this in these boxes and take it to the labs for sifting. We're after small bones, cloth fragments, jewellery, coins . . . well, absolutely anything, really."

"The skull's been badly smashed, so collect those pieces with care," Bream cautioned the two assistants.

Standing just inside the plastic canopy, Kernan said gloomily, "Let's hope the rain gets people back inside."

Gold was carefully scooping out dollops of mud and putting them in plastic boxes, his assistants sealing the lids and marking each one to indicate the sequence in which the various fragments were excavated. Gradually, piece by painstaking piece, the corpse was excavated, the larger bones bagged and tagged in black plastic bags.

"Looks like it is a female, Oscar . . ."

"Oh, yes, and what makes you say that, Mr. Gold?"

The young scientist looked up, positively beaming. "It's wearing a bra."

Kernan rubbed his chin and groaned. "Oh, God."

"Don't worry, Mike," said Bream, deadpan as usual. "It could still turn out to be Danny La Rue."

"Yeah, and if it is, Nola Cameron will claim him for a daughter." Kernan had seen enough. He turned to Muddyman, whose brown, curly hair was plastered down, his bald spot plainly visible. "Tony, take over until Tennison gets here."

Muddyman blinked at him. "She's got on that course, isn't she, Guv?"

"Not anymore she's not," Kernan said, trudging back over the muddy paving stones and mounting the steps.

Muddyman huddled deeper into his raincoat. "Oh, great . . ."

The kiss was long and deep, making her senses swirl. He had gorgeous skin, smooth enough for a woman's, but with the hard, sensual feel of solid muscle rippling underneath. Jane drew back, took a breath, and gazed into Bob Oswalde's dark brown eyes. He smiled as her fingers slid from his chest and probed under the terry bathrobe to his shoulder.

"Already?" he teased.

"Mmmm . . ." Wrapped in his arms, she gave him a wicked little grin.

They had dined here, in her room, drunk the bottle of Chateauneuf-du-Pape dry, and then made love. Secretly, she was amazed at how naturally it had come about, without, it seemed, any devious planning or premeditation on either part. She wasn't a promiscuous woman, had had only one brief fling since she broke up with Peter with whom she'd lived for less than six months. The demands and pressures of her job had been the cause of that; taking charge of the Marlow case, her first murder investigation, had consumed every waking moment—and most sleeping ones too. Peter had been understanding, up to a point, though he was going through a rough time himself, trying to get his building firm up and running, and the pair of them found themselves between a rock and a hard place. Something had to give, and something had. The relationship.

While her job still had priority, the attraction, the sexual chemistry between her and Bob Oswalde had been just too great to resist. And she'd thought, Why the hell not? All work and no play makes Jane a dull girl. She wasn't feeling dull and jaded now; her body felt vibrant and alive, and the night was still young.

Taking up his teasing mood, she said archly, "Now what was it you were saying about white women liking it rough?"

The instant the words came out, she knew that it was the wrong thing to say. Bob Oswalde reared back a little, his arms slackening, and she cursed her own clumsiness.

"Hey, that wasn't me," he protested, hurt. "I don't think like that."

"I know—I'm sorry." She kissed his chest and then the side of his neck, snuggling up to him, cozy and warm in the fluffy, white bathrobe, feeling the heat of his body. She had an idea. "Know what I'd like to do now?"

"No, what?" Bob Oswalde said through a crooked half grin.

"Let's drink the entire contents of the minibar."

"Why?"

"Oh, I don't know—I just feel like it." Jane suddenly sat up and grinned at him. Her short, ruffled blond hair and impish grin made her appear like a mischievous tomboy, a startling transformation from her conventional role as the cool, at times obsessive professional policewoman with a daunting reputation.

Bob Oswalde swung his long legs around to sit on the edge of the bed. "Okay, what would you like first?"

Jane clapped her hands. "Champagne!"

"Right."

As he went over to the minibar she flopped full-length on the bed, stretching out her arms luxuriously. She hadn't felt so content and totally relaxed in a long time. She hadn't been looking forward to this three-day conference at all, confined to airless, smoke-filled rooms and conference halls (especially as she was trying to give up the noxious weed!), having her brains picked by male colleagues who, deep down, probably resented being lectured to by a woman. The Super had suggested she "volunteer," which was his unsubtle way of giving a direct order by stealth. Well, the laugh was on him. She was enjoying herself, and at the public's expense to boot.

The phone rang, a soft trilling tone. Bob Oswalde was stripping the foil from a half-bottle of champagne, and Jane said quickly before she answered it, "That's Dame Sybil. Don't make a sound."

But it was Kernan, and Jane sat up straighter, holding her robe close to her neck, as if it made any difference.

"Oh, hello, Guv. About two hours . . . why?" She listened, her eyes serious, nodding her head. "Yeah, right . . . okay. Oh yeah, absolutely. Okay, see you. 'Bye."

She hung up, staring straight ahead at the built-in closet.

"What's wrong?"

"That was my Guv. He wants me back."

"Oh." The champagne dangled in his hand.

"Now."

"What?"

"Yeah." Jane slid off the bed, unfastening her bathrobe, while she hopped around to open the closet door. "He wants me to head a murder inquiry. I'll have to tell Thorndike." She brushed her fingers through her hair. "Damn, and it's my lecture tomorrow too . . ."

"Look, nuts to Thorndike." Oswalde glanced down at the bottle he was holding, then placed it on top of the minibar.

Burrowing in the closet, Jane said over her shoulder, "I'm sorry, Bob, there's nothing I can do about it."

"I know that." The words were neutral enough, though he was looking at her sharply. Jane paused in laying out her blouse and suit on the bed. She glanced up.

"So what's your problem then?"

"What about us?"

"What about us?" she asked, frowning slightly.

"Oh, I see."

Jane spread her hands. "Bob, I'm not saying I don't want to see you again. Okay?"

"Aren't you?"

She watched him in silence as he whipped off his bathrobe and rapidly dressed, eyes downcast, handsome face empty of expression.

Jane sighed. "C'mon, this is hard enough as it is . . ."

"Look, I hear you, okay?" He sat with his back to her, pulling on his socks and shoes. He stated flatly, "The Detective Chief Inspector has received her orders."

"What did you expect?" His attitude was annoying her, and she clenched her fists. "You know that's really unfair. It's not as though the love of your life is walking out on you."

Bob Oswalde snatched his sweater from the back of a chair and dragged it on over his T-shirt. His dark eyes flashed at her. "I just don't like being treated like some black stud."

Hands on hips, Jane said with faint disbelief, "Is that what you think's been going on here?"

"Yes, I do."

"Well, that's in your head."

"Is it?"

She could do without this. It was he who was hung up on racial stereotyping, not her. He was an attractive man, period, and she'd enjoyed tremendously having sex with him, but if he had difficulty accepting it simply for what it was, tough luck.

Jane said, "I think you'd better go."

"Don't worry," Oswalde said, already on the move, "I'm going."

"I hope I can rely on you to be discreet."

With his hand on the doorknob, Oswalde slowly turned his head and gave her a long, hard stare over his shoulder.

"You really are something else, aren't you?" he muttered softly, and with a little shake of the head went out.

Returning to his room after dinner, DCI David Thorndike was fumbling for his key when he heard a door slam, followed by the rapid thump of footsteps. Craning backwards, he spied DS Oswalde, head down, marching along the corridor towards the elevator. He'd come out of the room two doors away from his, Thorndike noted. Well, well, well. Tennison . . . fraternizing with the troops no less.

He turned the key in the lock and slipped into his room as Oswalde, muttering to himself, came up to the elevator. Standing with his ear to the crack in the door, Thorndike heard Oswalde's low, angry "Bitch!" as he punched the button.

Pursing his lips prudishly, DCI Thorndike eased the door shut.

2

Within ten minutes Tennison was fully-dressed, had applied a dab of makeup, run a brush through her hair, packed her bag and was ready to go. She gave herself a final once-over in the dressing table mirror and set off to see Thorndike in his lair. He was the type, she knew very well, who never made life easy, always had to nitpick. But she steeled herself to deal with him as quickly and calmly as possible and get the hell out. She had a job to do.

After she'd broken the news, he paced up and down his room, rubbing the little cluster of blue veins at his temple, shaking his head distractedly. "But I don't know anything about rape victims," he complained, realizing he would have to give the lecture at ten the next morning.

"Then it's time you did. It's attitudes like that that account for the fact that only eight percent of rapes are ever reported." Tennison took a sheaf of papers from her briefcase and held them out. "I'll leave you my notes."

"Well, that would be a help, but . . ." Thorndike dropped the papers on a table, sighing. "It's still bloody annoying."

"What can I do, David?" She was fed up to the back teeth with his prissy, old-womanish whining, but she controlled her temper.

He glanced at her with a pained expression. "Hasn't Mike Kernan got other DCIs available?"

"Yes, but he wants me to head it."

"Why?"

"Maybe he thinks I'm a good detective," Tennison said tightly.

Thorndike nagged on. "But why this specific investigation?"

"The body's been found in Honeyford Road, where the Cameron family still lives. Added to which, it looks like it could be Simone Cameron."

"Politically sensitive, certainly," Thorndike agreed. He gave her a sideways look. "A word of advice. Charges may be brought against the officers involved in the Derrick Cameron case if it goes to the Court of Appeal . . ."

"Quite right too if that boy was framed." She frowned at him. "What are you getting at?"

"I'd be careful if I were you—this may not turn out to be such a prize for you." And then turning away, not meeting her eye, he added, "Obviously you're a liberated and enlightened woman."

"Thank you, David," said Tennison dryly. But she still didn't have a clue what, in his pussy-footing way, he was driving at. Of course it wasn't straightforward police work to him, it was bloody politics, dropping poison into people's ears, watching your back all the time in case there was a knife sticking in it. Tennison hadn't the time nor the patience for all that bullshit; life was too short.

Thorndike saw her to the door. "Don't be too trusting of our Afro-Caribbean friends."

"That's your advice, is it?" She tucked the briefcase under her arm, giving him a quick, formal smile. "Good luck tomorrow."

Thorndike waited by the open door, his weak, watery eyes fixed on her as she entered the elevator. "Oh, and drive carefully if you've been drinking," was his final word of warning.

Going down in the elevator, Tennison cupped her hand to her mouth, trying to smell her own breath. Didn't seem that bad, and besides, she'd only had two glasses of red wine. Old Mother Thorndike must have a keen sense of smell if he'd got a whiff of alcohol fumes from that.

Honeyford Road was quiet again. The crowd had dispersed, returned to their homes, the stretch of pavement outside Number 15 cordoned off with striped tape that had POLICE—NO ENTRY stamped on it in red letters. The rain had eased off, but there was a damp, chill breeze blowing as Tennison drove her car along the street, searching for a place to park. She slowed down, bending sideways to peer through the misted-up passenger window at a lone figure still standing vigil next to the flapping tape. Tennison recognized the short, dumpy woman in the woven cap, the long shapeless coat reaching almost to the ground; she pressed the button to lower the window.

"Nola—go home!"

Nola Cameron shook her head defiantly. "Not if that's my Simone. I won't lose her a second time!" She turned back to stare at the house, chin set stubbornly, feet planted on the wet pavement.

Gold was enjoying himself. He didn't seem to notice, or to mind, that he had been kneeling at the bottom of a cold, slimy trench since early evening, and it was not past ten-thirty. With the arrival of DCI Tennison, the officer appointed to take charge of the case, he had a new and receptive listener on which to vent his expertise. Crouched down on her haunches on the paving stones, muffled inside the hood of her raincoat, Tennison watched intently as the work of excavation went on; the skull and most of the upper part of the skeleton had been removed, and the team was not concentrating on the lower torso. For the moment she was content to listen to Gold give his impromptu lecture.

". . . natural plant fiber such as cotton tends to disintegrate, form part of the diet of the early inhabitants of the corpse. But wool, like hair—they're made of the same stuff—can be remarkably resilient. Now, I've got some pieces of sweater and Professor Bream has quite a lot of hair—"

"If only," Bream said lugubriously, cleaning his spectacles with the end of his tie. It was meant to be a joke, but everyone was too tired and cold and pissed-off to even give a smile.

"With beads in it," Gold continued, so intent that the pathologist's remark hadn't even registered with him.

"Did the Cameron girl wear her hair like this?" Tennison's question was addressed to the assembly at large.

"I'm told she did sometimes," DI Muddyman put it.

Arms clasped around her knees, Tennison rubbed her gloved palms together, already feeling the cold night air creeping into her fingers and toes. "How old do you think she is, Oscar?"

"She hasn't quite finished growing, so still in her teens, I'd say."

"Well, how long do you think it would take for a corpse to get like this?"

"That I can't tell." There was the suggestion of a weary sigh in Bream's voice. Always the same, the murder squad, expecting answers up front to impossible questions. They'd only ever be happy if he could look at the decaying remains of a corpse and give them its name, address, and national insurance number.

Tennison was a terrier, not so easily put off. "Come on, Oscar. Minimum time?"

"Two years? Don't quote me on that."

"So it could be Simone . . ."

"You see, you're doing it already!"

Tennison eased herself up, stamping her feet to get the circulation going. She could have cheerfully murdered for a cigarette, but this was the real testing time, and she was determined to kick the habit. It had scared her badly when her consumption climbed to sixty a day, the dread specter of the big C giving her the cold sweats. Now or never, shit or bust. Quelling the desire, she glanced around to her officers, Muddyman, Lillie, and Jones, their tall figures silhouetted in the glare of the arc lamps.

"When were these garden slabs laid?"

"Before the Viswandhas came here," Jones told her.

"Which was?"

"About eighteen months ago."

"Do we know who they bought the house from?"

"All Mr. Viswandha could tell me was the name of a property developer," Jones said.

"So have these slabs been disturbed since then?"

DC Lillie shook his head. "Not according to the workmen."

Tennison gazed down into the shallow trench, trying to get the chronology straight in her own mind. "So she must have been put there before the slabs were laid, which means our prime suspect has to be whoever was living here when she was buried. We need a definite date of death, Oscar."

Bream gave her his fishy-eyed stare and called out to Lillie, "Is there any of that soup left?"

"Oh—if there is," Tennison said, "can you get some to Nola Cameron, if she's still out there?" She looked at her watch. "The rest of you might as well go home and get some sleep. I'll aim to brief the team at ten in the morning."

"Right, Guv," said Muddyman, not bothering to hide his heartfelt relief. Knowing Tennison, her obsessive tenacity with any case she took on, he'd been afraid she'd keep them there till the wee small hours, standing around watching Bream & Co. digging up the rest of Simone Cameron—if that's who it was. The woman didn't seem to have a home to go to; any private life at all, as far as that went.

The officers dispersed, leaving through the back garden gate. Tennison stayed. She was glad she did, because a few moments later Gold made an important discovery. He beckoned the photographer over to take several close-up shots of the corpse's wrists, behind its back, beneath the pelvis.

Bream craned forward, speaking softly into a small pocket recorder. "Hands tied together at the back with . . ."

Gingerly, Gold pulled something out and held it up.

". . . a leather belt," Bream intoned.

A movement caught Tennison's eye and she turned to see the little Viswandha boy standing on the top step, all agog.

"For God's sake . . . didn't anyone think to get the family moved?" She went up the steps, ushering him ahead of her. "It'll be gone soon," she said reassuringly.

He wasn't a bit frightened, just filled with curiosity. "Is it a real person?"

"Let's get you inside, you'll catch cold. You should be in bed."

"It should have been buried deeper, shouldn't it?" he said with a child's irrefutable logic. "Then it wouldn't have come back."

Mrs. Viswandha was on her way downstairs, clearly distraught after trying to comfort her daughter. She clutched the boy to her, scolding and hugging him at the same time.

"Don't you have family or friends you could go to stay with?" Tennison asked sympathetically.

"My husband won't leave here . . ." She was almost in tears.

"Do you want me to talk to him?"

The woman found a wan smile, nodding gratefully. "Thank you."

Tennison had hoped that the forensic boys might have finished before daybreak, folded their tents and stolen silently away under cover of darkness. But it was not to be. In the gray light of dawn, with gray, haggard faces to match, they trudged along the alleyway carrying a body bag and several large plastic containers. As they came between the tall Victorian houses into Honeyford Road where the dark-blue police van was parked, rear doors open, the pathetic figure of Nola Cameron, shivering, eyes red-rimmed, let out a shrill cry and went stumbling towards them.

"Simone! Simone!"

Standing by her car, Tennison watched the uniformed policeman on duty at the front gate step forward, barring her way. The pitiful cries rang out in the quiet street—"Simone, *Simone!*"—as the body bag was hoisted into the van and the doors slammed shut.

Tennison drove away, averting her eyes from the rearview mirror, from the terrible pain of the grieving mother. If it really was Simone Cameron in that body bag, she knew one thing for sure. All hell was about to break loose.

There wasn't time to return to the apartment. She drove straight to Southampton Row, knowing that Mike Kernan would be hopping about like a cat on broken glass. The cafeteria didn't open till eight-thirty. She had to make do with a styrofoam cup of disgusting machine coffee to wash down three paracetamol, in the hope that she could keep the dull, throbbing headache at bay for a few hours at least. Going without sleep was part of the job, but she was no spring chicken anymore and couldn't handle it as she used to.

Kernan was at his desk, enveloped in a cloud of blue smoke, which wouldn't do his ulcer much good, Tennison thought. With his heavy-lidded eyes and pouchy cheeks, he put her in mind of a grumpy chipmunk with a hangover. He launched right in, telling her about the meeting, that same evening, which couldn't have come at a worst time. "It was all arranged weeks ago. I'm going with the Community Liaison Officer, guy named Patterson. I can't back out now, but it's going to be a nightmare. I want you to be there. Starts at eight."

Kernan sucked in a lungful, pushed his packet of Embassy her way.

"No thanks." Tennison shook her head firmly. "I'm trying to give it up."

"Christ," Kernan muttered, in a state of shock. "Since when?"

"Five days, six hours and . . ." Tennison gazed at the ceiling ". . . 'bout fifteen minutes."

Kernan was so impressed he stubbed out his cigarette and immediately lit another. "The meeting's supposed to be to discuss community policing, but given what's happening just now we're sure to be dragged facedown through the shit about the Cameron family." His heavy brows came together. "And Phelps is coming down tonight, and he's bound to have the media in tow. That man can smell a vote-winner from fifty miles."

"Let's face it, Guv—Nola may be jumping to conclusions but we can't claim to have done well by her family, can we? Not if it turns out that Derrick was framed."

"Yeah, well . . ." Kernan was uncomfortable with the subject. "Let's concentrate on the immediate problem. Is it the Cameron girl or not?"

"I don't know. And I won't find anything out from Oscar Bream till tomorrow at the earliest."

The phone rang and Kernan snatched it up. His secretary informed him that Commander Trayner was on the line. "Right, I'll hold." He looked at Tennison through the wreaths of tobacco smoke. "If we knew one way or another before tonight's meeting, our lives would be a whole lot easier."

Tennison nodded. "I'll see if the forensic boys can shed some light. And I want the rest of the garden dug up in case there are other bodies . . ."

"Jesus, what do you want?" Kernan growled, aghast. "Another Nilsen?" He stiffened slightly as the commander came on. "Sir?" He listened, nodding, his drooping eyes fixed on the desk blotter.

"That's right. I thought she was the very best person for the job. It requires tact and . . . well, I'm sure she'll be able to cope."

Tennison pursed her mouth, giving a little rueful half-smile. The anti-women bias in the Force extended all the way from the ranks right to the upper echelons. Having a female DCI heading a murder inquiry still went against the grain, even though the official line was that there was no sexual discrimination; everyone rose by merit, experience, hard work. Which was a load of crap.

"I will do. 'Bye, sir." Thoughtfully, Kernan hung up. He took a long drag, letting the smoke plume from his nostrils, and stared across the desk with cloudy eyes. "Now how in hell does the commander know what happened on your course already?"

Tennison went very still. "What do you mean?"

"That I brought you back to lead this inquiry?"

She breathed out. For a nasty moment there she had had a dreadful, sinking sensation that her dalliance in the hotel room had spread like wild-fire, sniggers and dirty jokes in the locker rooms . . . *Hey, heard the latest—that bitch Tennison likes her men big, rough, and black!*

"I'll give you one guess," she told Kernan. "And it involves some funny handshakes."

"Thorndike? The same lodge?"

"I'd put money on it," Tennison said, getting up, smoothing her skirt.

"Then you'd better make sure you vindicate my decision," Kernan said, and he wasn't joking.

"I'll do my best, sir," she said crisply, and went out.

The cold water felt good. Leaning over the washbasin in the locker room, Tennison splashed a couple more palmfuls into her face, then dried herself and made a critical inspection in the mirror. Oh God. The Creature from the Black Lagoon. It seemed a world away now, though it was less than twelve hours since she'd been lying in Bob Oswalde's arms in the hotel room, drinking Chateauneuf-du-Pape.

Two clerks came in, chattering away, though Tennison seemed oblivious, intent on repairing the ravages of a night without sleep, giving her hair a vigorous brushing and applying fresh makeup. Usually sparing with perfume when on duty, this morning she put an extra dab on her wrists and behind her ears to perk herself up. Then, shrugging into her tailored jacket and straightening her shoulders, she was ready for the fray.

There was a fog of smoke in the Incident Room, the members of the team lounging around drinking coffee, laying bets on the identity of the collection of bones discovered in the back garden of Honeyford Road.

"Fiver says it's Simone . . ."

"You're on!"

"What odds you offering?"

"I'm starting a book."

"Huh!" said DC Lillie with a scowl. "Last time I ended up seventy-five quid out of pocket . . ."

Tennison came in, calling out to Muddyman as she strode briskly to the desk in front of the long white bulletin board that took up one full wall. "Tony, we need a name. Where we up to in the A to Z?"

"I think it's N, Guv."

"Look up the first N for us then, Tony." She stood at the desk, waiting a moment or two for the chatter to die down. When there was complete silence, Tennison began.

"As some of you will be aware, workmen digging in the back garden of Number fifteen, Honeyford Road, have uncovered skeletonized human remains. The arms had been tied behind the back and the body wrapped in polyethylene, so it's a suspicious death."

Tennison pointed to the photographs of the corpse, which had been processed overnight and pinned up on the board by DC Jones.

"Those of you who've been down there will know that there's a lot of speculation that it could be the body of a local girl who was reported missing two years ago—Simone Cameron. Her mother, Nola, who still lives a few doors away from Number fifteen, is completely convinced it's Simone. We'll get the forensic boys and the pathologist boys to give us an answer to that as soon as possible."

Tennison paused, her eyes raking over the assembled officers, who were all, to a man, paying rapt attention.

"In the meantime, we have to treat Nola Cameron's fears seriously. The unfortunate thing is that the Cameron family have been the focus of attention in that area for some years now. The oldest boy, Derrick, was accused of stabbing a white youth to death. He was sent to prison on the basis of that confession, made here in this station. Now there are doubts about the safety of that conviction."

Dark glances were exchanged between the men. Tennison raised her voice to cut short the rumbling murmurs.

"A campaign led by Jonathan Phelps—Labour's candidate in the by-election—to have Derrick's case brought before the Court of Appeal is gaining a lot of support from all sorts of people. So . . . there's a lot of anger and bitterness, and resentment against the police. It looks like we can rule out the present owners, so our first priority is to locate all former occupants of Number fifteen. Let's get down there straightaway and see what information we can gather."

There was a general movement. Climbing to his feet, DI Burkin glanced around, a grin on his handsome, slightly battered face, the result of several bouts in the boxing ring, which made him the current holder of the south Thames Metropolitan title. "Passports at the ready, lads . . ."

"Frank, you know that's out of order," Tennison snapped, wiping away his grin. "Have you been listening to anything I've said?"

Silence fell. Tennison's gaze swept around the room, her face stony. "I don't want the Camerons—and that means aunts, uncles, all of them—interviewed at all. As far as the other residents go, remember this: if we go in there expecting aggro, start leaning on people, we'll get it. So it's easy does it." She came around the desk, raising an eyebrow and softening her tone to take the sting out of her rebuke. "You're all graduates of the Rank Charm School, right? I want a list of all former residents of the Honeyford Road area over the last ten years."

Groans and muttered oaths. That kind of follow-up meant days of futile legwork, endless hours tramping the streets, knocking on doors, and getting blank stares and shaken heads. In short, a lot of hard work for minimal return.

"I've asked DS Haskons to be office manager." Tennison looked toward Muddyman, leafing through a dog-eared copy of the A to Z directory. "Tony—a name for this operation."

"The first N is Nadine Street, Guv."

"Very nice. So it's Operation Nadine then."

Somebody snapped his fingers and started to sing an old Buddy Holly number "Nadine, Honey, Is That You?" and the others took it up, joining in the chorus.

Already halfway to the door, Tennison rapped out, "Right, let's go . . . Jonesy!"

While the team got on with the house-to-house, Tennison, with DC Jones trailing in her wake, went down two flights to the Forensic Science labs, situated in an annex at the rear of the station. Two white-coated technicians were scooping mud from the plastic containers, mixing it with water into a thin soup, and sieving it. Any resulting fragments, even the tiniest specks, were placed on sheets of white blotter for Gold to examine later.

Gold looked a bit pale and drawn, but his enthusiasm was undimmed, and so was his industry. He'd separated the various items of clothing and artifacts found with the body and lined them up in shallow trays on the bench. He went along, detailing his finds to Tennison, while Jones took notes.

"I'll get all this stuff bagged for you as soon as possible if you want Mrs. Cameron to look at it." Gold lifted some woven material with a rubber-gloved hand. "The sweater remains—pretty color, don't you think?" He moved along. "Bra, pants, labels, some studs from her Levi's, Adidas sneakers, and so on. Not very helpful, I'm afraid . . ."

One of his assistants came up, holding a small fragment in stainless steel tweezers. Gold squinted at it. "Looks like a piece of skull. Get it sent over to Oscar Bream."

He gestured Tennison forward to another bench. Here, laid out on separate sheets of blotter, were a number of smaller, tarnished items. They didn't look like much to Tennison, though Gold seemed quite pleased. "But we have found several coins! The most recent of which is 1986."

Tennison frowned at him. "So?"

"Have you got any change in your pocket?"

Jones fished out a handful and Gold plucked out a five-pence piece, which he held up with a conjurer's flourish. "There. 1991. Which proves that you were walking around above ground until at least that year."

"Thank God for that," Jones muttered, pulling a face for Tennison's benefit behind the young scientist's back.

Gold was holding up a scabby piece of coiled leather, covered in green mildew. Evidently his prize specimen, from the way he was beaming. "Perhaps most promising so far—the belt that secured her hands behind her back. Distinctive buckle."

Distinctive, Tennison thought, but not all that rare, having seen the design before: a Red Indian chief with full-feathered headdress, in profile, cast in silvery metal that was now dulled and pitted.

"Could have belonged to her, I suppose," Gold conjectured.

Tennison nodded slowly, tugging her earlobe. "Or the killer," she said.

As the front door opened, Ken Lillie switched on his best smile, showing his warrant card to the middle-aged black woman in a floral print pinafore and fluffy pink slippers.

"Good morning, madam. DC Lillie, local C.I.D. We're investigating a suspicious death in the—"

He jerked his head around, distracted by one hell of a commotion coming from two doors along. He could hear a man's voice, yelling, and then a woman's, screaming blue murder. "Excuse me . . ." Lillie muttered, retreating fast down the path. He caught sight of Frank Burkin dragging a black teenager through the garden gate into the street. Behind the pair, a woman in a brightly patterned head scarf—the boy's mother, Lillie judged—was beating her fists at Burkin's broad back, screaming at him to leave the lad alone.

People from neighboring houses were running into the street, shouting and shaking their fists as Burkin wrestled the black kid into the back of the Ford Sierra. Lillie ran up, waving both hands in an attempt to placate what had already the makings of an ugly mob. As he reached the spot, the Sierra's doors slammed and the car sped off with a squeal of tires, leaving Lillie to confront a sea of angry black faces and the distraught mother, tears streaming down her cheeks.

Tennison sent DC Jones off to get her a mug of decent coffee instead of the pig swill from the machine, and returned to the Incident Room to help Haskons collate whatever information was to be had. She was suffering the symptoms of nicotine withdrawal acutely, and desperately trying to concentrate while ignoring the craving itch at the back of her throat.

"What have we got on the property developer?" she asked, leaning over Haskon's shoulder.

"Has since gone bankrupt and disappeared off the face of the earth, boss . . ."

Mike Kernan pushed open the swing door and stuck his head in. "Jane. A word."

Tennison glanced around. "I'll be there in a minute."

"My office," Kernan barked. "Now."

Tennison exchanged a look with Haskons, tugged her jacket straight, and went through the door, catching it on the second swing. Haskons's doom-laden voice floated after her. "Kernan the Barbarian . . ."

Cigarette in hand, the Super was pacing his office, shoulders hunched, thunderclouds gathering overhead. He said, "Burkin has just arrested a young black lad for possession."

Tennison leaned against the door, eyes closed. "Oh God."

Kernan jabbed the air. "He's doing his bloody house-to-house, there's the smell of pot, and he barges in. Pulls the lad out by the scruff of the neck."

"I don't believe it . . ."

"So now we've got bricks thrown into the garden of Number fifteen and a reception full of people bleating on about infringement of civil liberties and police harassment." He kicked his desk. "And with this bloody meeting tonight—I just don't believe it!"

"Do you want me to remove Burkin from this inquiry?" asked Tennison quietly. She didn't know what else to suggest.

Kernan shook his head and gave her a sideways glance. "We can't do that, Jane." He took a drag. "I'm up for promotion."

There was a slight pause as it sank in. "Promotion?"

"Chief Super." Kernan cleared his throat. He'd kept this under wraps till now, hadn't intended to tell anyone, least of all DCI Jane Tennison. "Right now I can't afford to do my dirty washing in public," he went on, a bit pathetically, she thought. "My interview will be a nightmare if this keeps up."

Tennison let a moment pass. The sly bastard wouldn't have breathed a word if this mess with Burkin hadn't happened. She stepped forward and said in a quiet, controlled voice, "I hope you'll be recommending me for your post."

"Oh do you?" Kernan said darkly, glowering at her from under his brows. "Well, don't take too much for granted." More finger jabbing, as if he were trying to bore a hole through galvanized steel. "Now make sure this boy is cautioned and released and tear bloody Burkin up for arse paper!"

Seething and trying not to show it, Tennison marched straight to her office and told her secretary, WPC Havers, to have DI Burkin report to her *pronto*. She wasn't sure who she was most pissed-off with—Burkin for antagonizing the local community and trying to wreck the murder inquiry before it had even got off the ground, or Mike Kernan and his devious little schemes to get shunted up the ladder without telling her. Bloody typical, and she was fed up with it! As the senior AMIT officer under his command, she was naturally next in line for his position, and what's more she deserved it. She'd paid her dues, eighteen months at the Reading Rape Centre, five years with the Flying Squad, and to top it all, cracking the Marlow serial killer case when the rest of the team had been flapping around like headless chickens. She was damn sure that if Kernan's most senior officer had been male, Kernan would have been grooming him for stardom, bringing him along, even putting in a good word for him with the "board," the panel of senior Metropolitan officers who decided these matters. But of course she was a stupid, weak woman, with half a brain, hysterical with PMS once a month, and what's more a dire threat to the macho image that even today prevailed throughout the police force. God, it made her feel like weeping, but she wouldn't, and didn't.

So she was in a fine mood for Burkin, when he appeared, and she faced him standing, even though he was a clear twelve inches taller, his bruiser's mug showing not a trace of doubt or remorse.

"Look, he was blatant, Guv. Almost blowing the smoke in my face, as if to say, go on, nick me."

"That's not the point. At the moment, what with the Cameron case—"

Burkin rudely interrupted. "Derrick Cameron was a criminal and he deserves to be locked up."

"Frank . . ." Tennison said, holding on to her temper, but Burkin barged on, as set in his ways as quick-drying concrete.

"So we had to lean on him a little to get a confession—so what?"

Tennison bristled. "So what? So our reputation goes down the toilet again!"

"What reputation?" Burkin's mouth twisted in a scathing sneer. "They bloody hate us. Well—I'll tell you something, I ain't so keen on them. As far as I'm concerned, one less on the streets is no loss."

"You're making a fool of yourself, Frank."

"Look," Burkin said stolidly, "if they don't want to be part of our country they should go home."

Tennison stared up at him, her eyes glacial. "That's enough, Frank. Just shut it."

Burkin's mouth tightened. He was near the edge and he knew it. It chafed him raw that he had to stand here, like a snotty-nosed kid in the headmaster's study, taking all this crap from a bitch with a dried-up crack. Give him half a chance, he'd soon straighten her out, give her what she was short of, wipe that holier-than-fucking-thou expression off her face. Make her into a real woman instead of this Miss-Prim-Little-Bossy-Boots act she tried to put on. Underneath she was like all the rest. A good, juicy fuck from a real man would fix her up.

"If I hear an outburst like that from you again, it'll be a disciplinary matter."

"Yeah, then perhaps you better take me off the case," Burkin said, looking straight past her to the opposite wall.

"You won't be off the case, Frank, you'll be off the Force." Tennison's voice was lethal. "If you think setting someone up because they're black is okay, then you shouldn't be a cop at all. Simple as that."

The intercom buzzed. Tennison reached over to press the button, and Maureen Havers announced that Nola Cameron was in reception, waiting to see her. Tennison said she'd be right there, and turned back to Burkin, shaking her head.

"Jesus, this is a murder investigation, Frank. A young girl ends up buried in someone's backyard like the family cat? Her skull smashed to pieces? What difference does it make what color her skin used to be?" She said with quiet finality, "I want the boy cautioned and released and then get back to work."

Without a word, Burkin turned and left the office.

3

Nola Cameron was a pathetic sight, still wearing the woven cap and shapeless coat of the previous night. Tennison escorted her into the interview room, holding her arm. "This way, Nola, my love . . ."

The clothing and other items were laid out on a table; stained with mud and partially decayed, they were sad mementos of a young life that had been brutally cut short, stopped in its tracks before it had time to flower into womanhood.

Tennison said gently, "Now, Nola, I want you to look at these things and tell me if you recognize any of them as having belonged to Simone." She kept her eyes on the woman's face, watching her closely as Nola Cameron fingered the sweater, then touched the other scraps of clothing. Almost at once she was nodding, a haunted expression straining her features.

"Yes." She swallowed hard. "These are her things."

"Nola, please, look carefully, take your time."

"These are all her things," Nola Cameron insisted, nodding again, blinking back her tears.

"We found this belt buried with her." Tennison showed her the large silver buckle in the shape of the Red Indian's head. "Do you recognize that?"

"Yes, yes," Nola Cameron said, hardly glancing at it. "That is her belt. She always wore this belt."

"I see." Tennison slipped off her wristwatch and laid it next to the Adidas sneakers. "And what about this watch?"

"That is hers." Nola Cameron started sobbing, head bowed, rocking back and forth. "I bought her this watch."

Tennison wrapped her arm around the shaking shoulders. "Nola, would you like a cup of tea? Do you want to sit down?"

"No, thank you."

Tennison led her to the door. "The experts will be able to give us a lot more information soon. Your dentist has provided Simone's dental records and we can compare those against those of the girl we found. That will tell us for sure." She hesitated. "And so until then—these things are all we have to go on. Are you sure you recognize them?"

"Oh, yes," Nola Cameron whispered. "Yes."

"I see, all right. Well, thank you very much."

Thoughtfully, Tennison watched as the bowed figure shuffled off across the reception area. Then with a sigh she picked up her watch, slipped it back on, and returned to the Incident Room.

DC Jones was standing at the board. While most of the desk-bound team worked in shirtsleeves, Jones prided himself on keeping up appearances, jacket on, necktie neatly knotted; with his glasses firmly on his nose, he looked like an earnest insurance salesman about to make a pitch. He held up a sheaf of typewritten sheets, claiming her attention.

"Report in from Gold, boss. He reckons Nadine was infested by maggots. Bluebottles."

"So?"

"Bluebottles won't lay their eggs underground."

Arms folded, Tennison studied the 10 × 8 glossy photographs pinned to the board, the whole grisly sequence as the corpse was disinterred.

"So that means she was above ground for a while before she was buried?"

Jones nodded eagerly. "At least a few hours. The other thing is that she must have been killed in the summer, 'cos that's when bluebottles are active."

"And Simone was missing in February." Tennison subsided into a chair, rubbing her eyes, feeling suddenly very weary. "Which means I go into tonight's meeting none-the-bloody-wiser."

The community center was packed to overflowing. There would have been a reasonable turnout anyway, but with the Derrick Cameron case back in the headlines, and now the discovery of the body in Honeyford Road, the local, mainly black residents had turned out in force. Community policing had always been a contentious issue, and here was a golden opportunity for them to air their grievances and put the senior police officers on the spot.

Tennison and Kernan arrived together, to be met by Don Patterson, who was to chair the meeting, a young West Indian casually dressed in T-shirt, jeans, and leather sandals. He led them through the crowd milling around the entrance, skirting the television crew and knot of reporters clamoring for Jonathan Phelps to make a statement. Phelps, of mixed-West

Indian and Asian parentage, was a tall, balding, well-dressed man, rather good-looking in a severe way, keenly-intelligent and a forceful presence. He had been educated at the London School of Economics, where he himself now lectured, and had been selected as Labour's candidate in the forthcoming by-election. Tonight's meeting was a gift on a silver platter, and he was making the most of the media exposure to pursue his political ambitions.

Tennison couldn't quite see him through the crowd of newsmen and photographers, but she could hear him all right: the firm, resonant voice, the incisive delivery, confidence in every phrase.

". . . my concern is that Derrick Cameron's case reaches the Court of Appeal—and that someone who has been wrongly imprisoned for six years is released. The Police and Criminal Evidence Act brought in stricter safeguards for the interrogating of suspects, but that was not much help to Derrick Cameron, who along with an increasing number of individuals"—here a pause for emphasis, while his voice took on a dry, mocking tone—"apparently wanted to confess to the police in the car on the way to the station."

The media lapped it up. Passing inside, Tennison and Kernan exchanged gloomy looks. This was going to be as bad—worse perhaps—than they had feared. Phelps had set the tone and the agenda for the evening with his opening remarks, and any hope of a cool, reasonable discussion had flown out the window. And that's how it turned out. Seated up on the platform with Phelps and Patterson, and Tennison beside him, Kernan was fighting a losing battle from the start, struggling to make himself heard above the rowdy, packed hall, constantly interrupted in mid-sentence by people leaping up, not so much to ask questions as to hurl abuse.

The TV crew had set up at the back of the hall, the photographers crouching in the center aisle, getting lovely close-ups of Kernan's mounting frustration, and then swiveling to take in the crowd's angry reactions.

"If that means a no-go area," Kernan was saying, palms raised, "if that means a no-go area . . ."

"With respect," Phelps chimed in.

". . . I can make no such assurances. I am unable"—Kernan valiantly tried again, almost drowned out by the racket from the floor—"I am unable to give any such assurances."

"The idea is not to create no-go areas," Phelps said, responding to the point but directly addressing the audience and the cameras. "Quite the reverse. We've heard from your Community Liaison Officer—who is of course a white police officer . . ."

Kernan was stung. "Surely that's a racist remark."

Ignoring him, Phelps steamrollered on. ". . . heard about sensitive policing, so-called community policing. Yet once again local people are being treated as second-class citizens."

A chorus of cheers at this, waving fists, the bottled-up antagonism and anger of the black crowd as potent as an invisible, yet deadly nerve gas.

It was obvious what Phelps was referring to, and for the first time Tennison spoke up, determined to get her two cents in before Phelps turned the meeting into a one-man election address. "If you are talking about the investigation that I am heading—"

"I am!"

"Then I believe it's being carried out in a—"

"In a hostile and intimidatory manner—exactly." Phelps was nodding, and almost smiling, happy to have scored another point. "With violent arrests being made by your officers . . . though of course, no charges were brought."

It would be so easy, too easy, to get into a slanging match with Phelps, but that would have been catastrophic. He held all the aces. The best she could do was to remain calm, state the facts as best she could, and trust that there were enough reasonable people out there to give her a fair hearing.

"One of my officers was provoked into making what in retrospect was seen as a hasty action . . ." The hall erupted in a storm of derisive laughter and catcalls. Tennison waited for the din to die down.

"Look—the most important thing is that we have a murderer who has been walking free for six years. We have to find that person. To do that we need the support and cooperation of this community. Now, I and two of my colleagues are going to stay behind afterward to see if you can help to give us some crucial information. For example, who lived at Number fifteen before the Viswandhas."

"We know, we know that . . ." Midway down the hall, Nola Cameron was on her feet, waving her arms, appealing to those around her. "He left at the same time as Simone was missing. What was his name? Someone here will remember . . ."

Before anyone could, however, Don Patterson had what he thought was a more pressing question. "I'd like to ask Mr. Kernan about the heavy police presence in the Honeyford Road area at the moment . . ."

About to reply, Kernan was cut short by a young guy in the audience, who leaped up, face livid, dreadlocks swinging, pointing an accusing finger. "I wanna ask him how he's got the nerve to come here at all!" he shouted, "when Derrick Cameron's locked up for somethin' he didn't do!"

Kernan held up his hands. "Obviously, I am unable to discuss the details of that case . . . but I should have thought my mere presence here this evening is an indication of good faith."

Howls of laughter at that. More people were climbing to their feet, gesticulating, screaming their heads off, and the whole thing was fast sinking to the level of farce. Tight-lipped, Kernan glanced aside at Tennison, shaking his head as if to say, What was the use?

Phelps waited for a slight lull and seized the opportunity.

"The justifiable anger and unhappiness at what has happened to Derrick Cameron cannot be so easily dismissed by a police officer who was stationed at Southampton Row."

"I'm not dismissing anything," said Kernan heatedly. "I'm just trying . . . I'm just . . ."

"When the boy," Phelps went on, "supposedly confessed. Because—just let me finish—the Cameron case focuses on a fundamental question: *Is it possible to expect justice in this country if you are a person of color?*"

Excluding Kernan and Tennison on the platform and DCs Rosper and Lillie at the back of the hall, the verdict was unanimous.

Afterwards, pencils sharpened, notepads at the ready, Rosper and Lillie manned two desks in the entrance hall. They felt like a couple of lepers. The crowd had streamed out, most not bothering to give them a second glance, one or two openly sniggering and dropping heavy hints about the officers' parentage.

Lillie was doodling clock faces when the man in the leather hat plunked himself down in the seat opposite and leaned his elbows on the desk. He was chewing the stub of an unlit cigar, and seemed to have a sunny disposition, judging by his permanent grin that revealed two gold front teeth.

"I don't like the police," he began cheerfully.

Lillie nodded. "Thank you."

"But I'll tell you this, you should talk to the guy that Nola mentioned." He removed the cigar stub, leaving the glinting grin intact. "White guy about fifty. Worked as a builder."

Lillie dutifully jotted this down. "Can you tell me his name, sir?"

"We argued about parkin' space, you know. Then in the mornin' all my car is covered in brake fluid."

"I see."

"Don't worry, I got me own back."

Lillie waited. "Go on, then, tell me."

The man in the leather hat started wheezing. "I pissed in his petrol tank." He let out a bellow of laughter, thumping the desk.

Lillie smiled, still waiting.

The man chewed on the dead stub, eyes roaming about. "Dave Hardy? Harley? Somethin' like that. You talk to him."

Lillie wrote it down.

When Tennison returned from seeing Kernan off, the haul was meager. Lillie gave her what little information he had, though Rosper thought he might have gotten a lead.

"Word is that a family lived in Number seventeen called Allen. One or two people reckon they might have owned Number fifteen as well." He tore off the sheet and handed it to her. "Point is, Esme Allen still runs a West Indian take-out nearby."

Tennison looked at the address he'd jotted down, then at her watch. She was starting to see double. "Give it another half an hour here, then call it a day."

As far as she was concerned, DCI Jane Tennison was about to call it a day, a night, and a day.

She let herself into the empty apartment and trailed through to the bedroom, carrying the small suitcase she'd had with her on the course. Dumping it on a chair, she switched on the bedside lamp, kicked off her shoes, and lay down on top of the pink duvet, fully-clothed. The instant her eyelids closed she was fast asleep, arms by her sides, snoring softly.

The hand-lettered sign in the window read "Esme's Take-Away Fast Food." The cafe was in the middle of a row of small shops which served the local West Indian community, cardboard boxes and wooden trays of exotic foodstuffs—breadfruit, mooli, okra, and yams—laid out on the pavement.

Tennison lingered outside the open door. It was a few minutes after nine-thirty, the sky hazy overhead with the sun doing its best to break through. She was warm inside her Burberry raincoat, beginning to wish she'd put on something lighter, though it had looked like rain when she left the apartment. Her hair, hastily dried after a shower while she wolfed down two pieces of toast, was still damp at the roots.

Inside the cafe, behind the high counter, Esme Allen was chatting with a middle-aged woman with silvery hair coiled into a neat bun. Esme was a tall, graceful black woman, somewhere in her early forties, Tennison judged, noting the faint traces of gray in her curly, cropped hair. She wore a long plastic apron over a red sweater, the elegant curve of her neck accented by a pair of dangling earrings that swung as she chattered away.

"Me small son study for his school exam, you know, an' me daughter Sarah, she study law at the university."

Tennison stepped inside. "Mrs. Allen?"

". . . I tell you, them think the world is at them feet. They'll never have to scrub floors or take out rubbish!"

The silvery-haired woman nodded. "Let's hope them don't come down to earth with a bump, ennit?"

"Mrs. Allen? Mrs. Esme Allen?"

Esme Allen turned to her with a bright smile. "Yes, dear?"

"I'm Jane Tennison. I'm a police officer."

The smile faltered and her large brown eyes clouded over. "It's not bad news? Don't tell me someone's been hurt . . . Sarah? Not Tony?"

"No, no, it's nothing like that," Tennison said promptly, shaking her head. "I'm making some inquiries, that's all."

"Oh, my Lord, you gave me such a fright," Esme Allen breathed, clutching the sweater above her heart. She patted her chest, regaining her composure. "Is it about that poor Cameron girl?"

"In a way." Tennison glanced round. The cafe was quite small, with just two tables for those customers who wanted to eat their food on the premises. "Is there somewhere more private we could talk?"

The silvery-haired woman, a friend, it seemed, as well as a customer, put her shopping bag down and made a shooing motion. "You take the lady through to the back. I'll look after the shop."

Esme Allen raised the counter flap and Tennison followed her into a narrow, cramped room with a single window, part office, part storeroom, shelves to the ceiling stacked with provisions. The air was pungent with the mingled odors of herbs and spices. Esme indicated a canvas-backed folding chair and invited Tennison to sit down. She herself took the chair next to the desk, pushing aside a bundle of invoices to rest her elbow. She smiled attentively, lacing together her long, slender fingers.

"Mrs. Allen, I understand in the 1980s you and your husband owned Number fifteen, Honeyford Road."

"Yes, that's right."

"While you lived at Number seventeen with your family."

"Yes."

Without a pause, Tennison said, "I'm sorry to have to tell you that a body has been found buried in the back garden of Number fifteen."

Esme Allen sat back, her strong white teeth biting her lower lip. "My God . . . you think he killed poor Simone?" she asked in a small, shocked voice.

"We just want to eliminate him from our inquiries," Tennison replied, giving the standard line. If Esme Allen had been friendly with the occupant of Number 15, then it was possible that she might wish to protect him, or throw the police off the scent. "What was his name, Esme?"

"David Harvey." No hesitation. Straight out with it.

Tennison nodded. "Right." She unscrewed the cap off her gold pen and wrote down the name on her notepad. She glanced up. "Do you know where he is now?"

"No." Esme shook her head, blinking as she tried to think. "My husband Vernon might know, but . . . well, we tried not to have anything to do with the man. I would never let my daughter Sarah go near that house. We all knew what he was like. Particularly with young girls."

Tennison leaned forward slightly but said nothing.

"He wasn't always like that, but after his wife died . . . I thought they were a lovely couple, but after she'd gone . . ." Esme lowered her voice. "Drinking and cursing and, you know, carrying on . . ."

Tennison put her fountain pen away and slipped the notepad into her pocket. "I'd like to speak to your husband if it's possible—in fact to the whole family." She got up to leave. "As soon as possible, please."

"This evening," Esme said, ushering Tennison through to the shop. "We'll all be there this evening."

"Fine. Thank you."

Tennison went directly to a phone booth and got through to Muddyman in the Incident Room.

"It's Harvey, not Harley or Hardy—Harvey. H-A-R-V-E-Y. So we've got to start again. I'm off to see Oscar Bream. 'Bye."

"It makes a pleasant change, not being up to the armpits in someone's viscera," Bream said, opening the door to the Path Lab. He went in first, his considerable bulk swathed in a green plastic apron, rubber gloves up to the elbows. Two of his assistants were at work, assembling and measuring the skeleton on a table in the center of the lab. His senior assistant, Paul, was busy at another bench, reconstructing the smashed skull, piece by piece. It was largely complete, except for a jagged hole towards the back on the right-hand side, and he was fiddling with several fragments, puzzling how they might fit into the bone jigsaw.

Bream gestured towards the skeleton. "Though I must admit this girlie is sorely taxing my memory of my student anatomy classes," he admitted to Tennison. "You know there are two hundred and six named bones of the body? Twenty-six to each foot alone. Luckily, most of those were still inside her shoes."

"Fascinating, Oscar. But is it Simone Cameron?"

Bream had planted himself in front of the skeleton, arms folded across the green plastic apron. "Absolutely not."

Tennison, coming around to join him, stopped dead in her tracks, mouth dropping open. "What?"

"As I said before, like Simone, in her teens—sixteen to seventeen. But taller—Simone was five seven, this girl is five eight, five nine." He bent his head, peering at Tennison over the top of his glasses. "At the moment it looks as if she was all there, no mutilation. Good head of hair . . ."

And there it was, in a shallow tray, like a discarded wig, plaited and beaded. Bream moved over to the skull, which was raised up on a plinth, the beams of a spotlight shining eerily through the empty eye sockets. "Luckily, Paul here likes jigsaws." He examined a fragment and handed it to his assistant, muttering, "Could be a bit of the zygomatic arch."

Tennison was still grappling with this new revelation. It was always unwise to jump to conclusions without any sort of proof, but it was easily done; and Simone's disappearance and the discovery of the body had seemed a neat fit. Too neat, as it now turned out. But she had to be absolutely certain that Bream himself was certain.

"You're sure it's not Simone?"

"Yeah." He wandered over to the lightbox and stuck up x-rays of two skulls, side by side. One was Simone Cameron's, taken from her medical records, the other Nadine's. Bream turned to her. "Do you want me to point out the differences?"

"Not particularly, no."

"Well, what else?" Bream mused, scratching his chin with his gloved finger. He looked across at the skeleton. "Fractured her wrist when she was younger . . . playing ball? Perhaps she fell off her bike? That's for you to discover."

Tennison sighed. "Don't rub it in. Can you tell me if she was black or white?"

"No."

"*Shit*. I've been going up a dead-end street."

Bream was trying to be helpful. He had a good deal of respect for Jane Tennison, considered her a fine police officer with a keen intellect and an intuitive grasp of the many complex strands that went to make up a homicide inquiry. And to top it all, he rather liked her. Not an opinion he would have extended to quite a few chief inspectors of his acquaintance. He said, "Well, we've got a man here who does all kinds of jiggery-pokery with the skull to ascertain ethnic origins. Better still, a medical artist who could make you a clay head, at a price."

"Is he good?"

"He's our very own Auguste Rodin," Bream said, a glimmer of a smile lurking behind his usual deadpan facade.

"Yeah, but is he good?"

"*Naturellement.*"

"That's expensive, right?"

Bream nodded, looking down on her over his glasses. "Do you want a word with Mike Kernan?"

Tennison nibbled her lip. Then she decided. "No, screw it. Let's just do it."

"Okay."

"So how long before I can pick it up?"

"Three weeks."

"Fine," Tennison said, moving back to watch Paul engaged in his painstaking assembly of the skull. "I'll pick it up in three days."

"I'll have a word with him." Bream stood at her shoulder. "Perhaps if you were prepared to model in the nude . . . ?"

"That's sexual harassment."

Bream slowly blinked, his expression sanguine. "What isn't these days?"

Tennison folded her arms, stroking her chin as she gazed at the skull in the bright cone of light. "How did she die, Oscar?"

"I've no idea," Bream confessed. "Her skull could've been smashed after death. For all I know she could've been buried alive."

The Incident Room was buzzing with activity when Tennison walked in. Almost all the team was here, shirtsleeves rolled up, plowing through all the Harveys in the telephone directories. It was tedious and frustrating, having to redial when the line was busy, or waiting with drumming fingers for a phone that was never answered. When they did get through to someone, the routine was always the same.

"David Harvey? I'm a police officer carrying out routine inquiries. I wonder if you can help me. Can you tell me whether you were ever domiciled at Number fifteen, Honeyford Road?"

The same routine, and up to now, the same response. Tick the name off and start again. What the hell, Rosper thought, tapping out the next number. It was better than digging up gas mains for a living.

Tennison draped her raincoat over the back of a chair and tucked her blouse into her straight, black skirt. Covering her mouth, she belched softly, still digesting the egg and cottage cheese sandwich she'd eaten driving back in the car, washed down with a carton of orange juice. She did a quick scan of the board, checking if anything new had been pinned up.

"Got anything for me?"

"Nothing so far, boss," Haskons said, glancing up, keeping his finger on the number he was about to dial. "But we have got some more stuff that's been dug up in the garden of Number fifteen. Jonesey's getting it from Gold."

"Let's hope it's good." Standing at the desk, Tennison raised her voice. "Right, listen up. I've just come back from Oscar Bream at the Path Labs. It's definitely not Simone Cameron." A wave of disgruntled mutters and sighs went through the room; dark looks were exchanged. As well as an unidentified murderer, they now had an unidentified victim too.

"So we need to operate on two fronts," Tennison went on. "Find David Harvey and identify Nadine. It's a bottle of Scotch for David Harvey."

The team went back to work. Tennison busied herself with the duty roster wondering if she needed to ask the Super for more manpower. Then she remembered the clay model head she'd requested, without first clearing it with him, and decided to let it hang for the time being.

Jones arrived with the new material from Forensic. Tennison shoved the papers aside to make space on the desk.

"They found a plastic bag buried as well, ma'am, and Gold has linked it to the girl. Contained this."

Tennison stared down at the roll of heavily-woven cloth, dark browns and greens with threads of gold. Next to it Jones had placed two large chunky bracelets, hand-carved with an intricate design.

"The cloth is West African," Jones said, consulting his notebook. "Several yards of it, in fact. And these ivory bracelets are Nigerian."

Tennison picked them up, turning them round and round. She was surprised at their weight. She slipped one onto her own wrist. Worn smooth through long use, its internal circumference was large enough to slide up to her elbow.

"Yoruba amulets," Jones informed her, "supposed to ward off evil spirits. Obviously didn't work for our Nadine. Apparently they're very old and very valuable."

Tennison was shaking her head and frowning at the two bracelets she held in her hands. As if speaking to herself, she murmured under her breath, "Who was this girl?"

4

Many of the houses on the quiet, tree-lined road were detached, others substantial semi-detached properties of the thirties period. It was clear that the Allens had gone up in the world. Esme's cafe must be a little gold mine, Tennison thought, parking the Orion alongside a low stone wall bordered by neatly-trimmed shrubbery. She made a mental note, and walked up the driveway, briefcase in hand.

Lights glowed behind a vestibule door of stained glass. She rang the bell, and in a few moments a boy of about nine appeared, very smart in a white shirt and school tie, shorts with knife-edge creases in them, polished black shoes.

Tennison smiled. "Can I see your mummy, please?"

"Yes. Please wait here," said the boy politely, and turned back indoors. She heard him call, "Mum, someone to see you," and then Esme Allen came through, smiling, holding the door wider.

"Hello, it's Jane Tennison."

"Yes, come in."

The living room was warm and cosy, with a beige carpet and furniture upholstered in burgundy with embroidered backs. Wall lights with red tasseled shades and thick velvet curtains made for a restful atmosphere. Tennison had interrupted a dressmaking session. On the coffee table stood a pretty child of three, with pigtails, being fitted for a bridesmaid's dress. The hem of the pale yellow satin dress had been partly pinned. The little girl's chubby black fists dreamily smoothed the material as she waited patiently for it to be finished.

A young man in a gray sweater and jeans, early twenties, Tennison guessed, and rather good-looking, was sitting on the edge of the sofa, hands between his knees, rubbing his palms together. He gave her a brief sidelong glance as she came in, then looked away shyly. Still smiling, the elegant, graceful Esme introduced them.

"This is my son Tony. And this is his daughter, Cleo. Say hello, Cleo."

"Hello," Cleo said, dimples in her cheeks.

"Tony and his girlfriend are doing the decent thing—at long last," Esme confided, casting a look at Tennison under her eyelashes. She spoke educated, standard English; no trace of the heavy West Indian patois she'd used in the shop that morning. "Their daughter is to be a bridesmaid. Lord, how times have changed! You wanted to see my husband?"

"Yes, please."

Esme sat the little girl on the edge of the coffee table and went out. Tennison took the armchair opposite the sofa and placed her briefcase flat on her knees. There was a momentary, awkward silence, filled with the ticking of a gilt carriage clock on the mantelpiece.

Tennison said, "So when's the happy day, Tony?"

Nervously, Tony cleared his throat. "Ummm . . ." He gazed off at something in the corner of the room.

"Do you like my dress?" Cleo asked, plucking at it, her legs in white ankle socks swinging under the table.

"Yes, I do. I think it's lovely—oh, Tony, just a minute."

Tennison put her hand up as he half-rose, about to leave. He sank back again.

Tennison opened her briefcase and handed him a typewritten sheet. "Could you have a look at this, please? That's a description of the dead girl. Do you remember seeing anyone like her in the Honeyford Road area in the mid-eighties? She may have been at school with you."

"I'm a Bride's Maid," Cleo said importantly, pronouncing it very clearly as two distinct words.

"You are, aren't you?" Tennison agreed, touching the satiny material and smiling.

"Have you ever been a Bride's Maid?"

"Do you know, I have. But never the bride."

Tony held out the sheet of paper. "No," he said shortly, and got up again to leave as Esme came in. She swung the child up. "Come along, baby. Say bye-bye."

Cleo waved her fingers at Tennison, mouthing, "Bye-bye."

"Bye."

In the doorway, Vernon Allen stood aside to let Tony pass. "Wedding boy," he said jovially, adding a chuckle, his voice a deep rumbling bass. He turned then, a big bear of a man casually dressed in a check shirt and loose-buttoned cardigan, and looked keenly at Tennison through horn-rimmed glasses. "Chief Inspector . . . what can I do for you?"

In the tiny storage room upstairs that Vernon Allen used as an office, Tennison sat at the desk, flicking through the pile of old rent books dating back ten years. Everything was neatly filled in: tenants, dates, amounts. It all seemed kosher.

She screwed the cap back on her pen. "But you have no idea where David Aloysius Harvey lives now?"

"I'm afraid not."

Tennison sat back in the swivel chair, tilting her head to look at him. In the light of the desk lamp her blond hair shimmered like a fuzzy golden halo. Her first instinct, which she put great faith in, was that Vernon Allen was a decent, trustworthy man. He'd answered her questions simply and directly, speaking slowly in his deep, rumbling voice. At all times his eyes met hers, slightly magnified through the lenses of his spectacles. She'd have laid bets he was as kosher as the rent books, but she had to probe deeper.

"So you bought the property in 1981, right?"

"Yes."

"And Harvey moved in shortly after?"

Vernon Allen nodded. "With his wife. After she died he let things go."

"And you sold the property in . . ." Tennison checked her notes ". . . '89, with Mr. Harvey as a resident tenant?" Vernon Allen's nod confirmed this. "Did that lead to much bad feeling between you and Mr. Harvey?"

"Some. Not much." He wagged his head from side to side, the light catching the flecks of gray in his thick hair. "The problem we had was that he was very erratic in paying the rent. Sometimes he seemed to have money; sometimes not."

"Mmm," Tennison said, as if mulling this over, and then she said quickly, "I presume you have a set of keys to the property?"

"Yes."

"Mr. Allen, did you do anything to the garden while you were the owner of the property?"

"No. Harvey laid the slabs. I didn't want him to, but he did very much as he pleased really."

"When were those slabs laid?"

"I'd say 1986. 1987 . . . ?"

The door was ajar a couple of inches. There was a movement outside on the landing, the creaking of a floorboard.

"Because, you know," Tennison went on, "it's almost certain that the body was buried before the slabs went down."

"Yes, I can see that," Vernon Allen said.

"Mr. Allen, how is it you could afford two properties on your pay?"

He didn't seem surprised at this change of tack, or even mildly annoyed by the question.

"Esme's cafe has always done well." He shrugged his broad shoulders in the rumpled cardigan. "To tell you the truth, it was her money that paid for the second mortgage."

"And your son's at private school?" Tennison said, having jotted down in her mental file the blue-and-green striped tie the polite schoolboy had been wearing.

At that moment the door was pushed roughly open and a tall, willowy girl barged in, an exact younger version of Esme Allen, hair cropped very short with tiny-plaited dreadlocks trailing over her ears. Attractive and vivacious, with large flashing eyes, the effect was spoiled somewhat by the way she was twisting her mouth.

"When will you ever learn, Pop? Black people aren't supposed to own businesses, houses, get an education . . ."

She regarded Tennison with open hostility.

"This is my daughter, Sarah," Vernon Allen said, standing up. "There's no need to be rude," he gently rebuked her.

"I agree," Sarah snapped.

Tennison rose, glancing down at the notebook in her hand. "Sarah . . . you're the law student. And you're twenty. So in the summer of, say, 1986, you would have been . . . let me see . . ."

There was a slight pause.

"Fourteen. Mathematics not your strong point?" the girl said sarcastically.

Tennison was unabashed. "Not particularly, no." She smiled. Sarah's rudeness didn't upset her one bit, but it embarrassed Vernon Allen.

"It's my son David who's the wizard at math," he said, trying to lighten up the atmosphere.

Tennison took the description of Nadine from her briefcase and handed it to the girl. "Do you recall seeing anyone like that in the vicinity of Honeyford Road?"

Sarah hardly glanced at it. "Yes, of course, Simone Cameron," she said curtly.

"It's not Simone. We're quite sure about that," Tennison stated evenly. "Would you look at the description, please."

Sarah blinked rapidly, obviously taken aback. Then the icy, scathing tone returned, this time with a touch of venom.

"Well, then, if it's not Simone, you'll need to be a bit more specific, won't you? That's if you can be bothered!"

"And would that mean . . ."

Sarah interrupted, "The police aren't exactly noted for their enthusiasm in solving cases when the victim is black, are they?" Again the sneering twist to her mouth, her contemptuous summing up of all police officers, be they male or female.

Tennison raised her eyebrows. "Was she black? It doesn't say so here." Taking back the description, she gave Sarah a cool, level stare. "Maybe it's you who's jumping to conclusions."

Tony was in the hallway with Cleo in his arms when Vernon Allen showed Tennison to the front door. Tennison smiled at the little girl and asked, "When's the happy day, Tony?"

He looked down at the carpet, throat working, too shy or too tongue-tied to give a coherent reply. Sarah had followed them downstairs. She came into the hallway, transformed into a beautiful young woman by a beaming smile as she looked fondly at her brother and his daughter, and Tennison noticed that she gripped Tony's hand and squeezed it reassuringly.

"Two weeks away now," Sarah said, and even her voice was different, warm and affectionate, when speaking of Tony.

"Well, I'll see you again before that," Tennison said, nodding to Vernon Allen as he held the door open for her. "Thanks for your help. Good-bye."

It was late when she returned to Southampton Row. The cleaners didn't start their assault on the disaster area of the Incident Room till the early hours. Everyone had gone, except for DS Haskons, who was tidying up his desk, getting ready for home. He looked frazzled after the long day, shirt collar wrinkled, tie undone, wavy, brown hair tousled from continually brushing his fingers through it.

"Got anything on David Harvey?" Tennison asked, dumping her briefcase on the desk.

"Not yet, Guv," Haskons said wearily. He wondered what Tennison did in her spare time. Traffic duty at Hyde Park Corner? "We've tried the electoral rolls, NHS, DHSS, taxes." He gestured at the piles of directories. "I've just finished working my way through the phone book . . ."

"You know," Tennison said, her brain still ticking over after twelve straight hours on the job, "Vernon Allen said Harvey was erratic in paying his rent. Have we checked out the credit reference agencies?"

Haskons mumbled that they hadn't. Tossing her raincoat aside and pushing up her sleeves, Tennison got down to it. She pulled a chair up to the computer terminal, and slipped a Nicorette lozenge into her mouth while she studied the code manual. Haskons leaned over, watching as Tennison keyed in the letters "SVR." The computer clicked and whirred, and in a second or two the "CREDIT REFERENCE AGENCIES" program flashed up to the VDU screen.

Tennison carefully typed, "DAVID ALOYSIUS HARVEY, 15 HONEYFORD ROAD, LONDON N1." A few more clicks followed while the computer carried out its search. Then up came:

"CREDIT REF: DAH/18329

DATE: 12 2 86

SUM: £5000 × 60 FIN."

Tennison leaned forward, rubbing her hands. "Yes . . ."

The next line appeared.

"FORWARD 3 10 90—136 DWYFOR HOUSE, LLOYD GEORGE ESTATE, LONDON SW8."

Tennison snapped her fingers for a pen. Haskons handed her his ballpoint. She noted down the details, then keyed in a new code, and the computer responded.

"LOAN REPAYMENTS TAKEN OVER BY MRS. EILEEN REYNOLDS, 6 6 90."

"Well done, boss," Haskons murmured admiringly. You had to hand it to the woman. Like a bloody terrier with a bone.

Tennison was scribbling on the pad. "Do you fancy a drink?" she asked, the Nicorette bulging in her cheek.

Haskons hesitated. "I should get home really . . ."

Tennison glanced around. "Yes, right—the twins." She gave him a grin and a quick nod. "Off you go."

"'Night," Haskons said, on his way out.

"'Night, Richard."

The door swung shut, rocking to and fro on its hinges. The room was silent, except for the low hum of the computer. Alone, crouched over the keyboard, in a world of her own, Tennison clenched both fists and stared at the screen in triumph.

"Got you . . . got you!"

Muddyman drove along Wandsworth Road, heading for Clapham. Beside him, Tennison was doing her best to control her impatience. They were twenty minutes behind schedule, caused mainly by a traffic tie-up on Waterloo Bridge. The day couldn't be far off, Tennison fantasized, when they'd switch from cars to helicopters; given the paralysis of central London, it would soon be the only way of getting around.

The Lloyd George Estate was situated to the northeast of Clapham Common. It was easy to find, four twenty-story concrete towers sticking up into the overcast sky, some of the balconies festooned with washing. Muddyman drove into the parking lot of Dwyfor House and found a space.

As he switched off the engine, Tennison hung up the handset in its cradle, having received a message from Lillie back at base.

She said, "They've done the tests on Nadine's skull. Seems she was of mixed race, West Indian and English."

"That would explain the Nigerian bracelets," Muddyman said.

Tennison climbed out and stared up at the tower block. "Right." she muttered, a gleam in her eye. "Let's see what David Harvey can tell us."

The elevator was out of order. Harvey lived in Flat 136, on the thirteenth floor. They began to climb the concrete stairs, trying to ignore the unidentifiable odor that permeated the place; the nearest Tennison could come to it was a mixture of greasy cooking, stale underwear, and dead cat. She inhaled Givenchy Mirage from her silk scarf, and plowed steadily onward and upward. Muddyman lit up, pausing on the half-landings for a swift drag.

Tennison said, "You know, you ought to give up cigarettes. Make you feel a whole lot better."

Leaning against a wall, taking a breather, Muddyman gave her a fishy-eyed stare. "There's nothing worse than a born-again nonsmoker," he growled.

Tennison hadn't formed any preconceived idea of what David Harvey would be like, but even so she was taken aback by the appearance of the man when he opened the door of 136. It was a small miracle that he'd made it to the door at all. A slight, stooped figure in a grimy striped shirt and threadbare cardigan, he had a pale, rinsed-out face and bleary blue eyes, a ragged gray mustache adding to his mournful, hang-dog look. Just standing there, he seemed to be fighting for every breath, and Tennison could hear his chest whistling and wheezing. The hand holding the edge of the door was thin and veined, visibly trembling.

"Mr. David Harvey?"

"Yes."

"We're police officers. We'd like to have a few words with you."

Harvey didn't seem surprised; but then he didn't seem anything. It was as though he'd lost interest in the business of living, or it had given up on him.

As he led them inside, Tennison glanced at Muddyman. He met her look, registering the same faint sense of shock she felt. They hadn't expected to be interviewing a semi-invalid.

Harvey shuffled across to an armchair, trousers hanging baggily at the seat, and using both arms, lowered himself into it. There was a lit cigarette in the ashtray, and Harvey picked it up and stuck it in the corner of his mouth, the smoke trailing past his eyes.

The flat was neat if spartan. There was the bare minimum of furniture: armchair, sofa, a couple of straight-backed chairs against the wall, a coffee table with circular heat rings and cigarette burns. Next to the window, the best piece of furniture in the room—a glass-fronted bureau—had arranged along the top a collection of framed photographs. A gas fire with an imitation coal-effect hissed in the grate. Above it, in the center of the mantel, a luridly-colored picture of the Virgin Mary gazed into eternity.

Tennison explained the purpose of their visit, sitting opposite Harvey on the sofa, while Muddyman stood near the window, open notebook in hand. She showed him the description of Nadine, which he read without expression or comment, squinting his eyes through the smoke. Now and then he had to remove the cigarette in order to cough. Something else Tennison hadn't expected was his pronounced Glaswegian accent. With his wheezing breath it made some of his answers hard to catch, and it took her a while to get accustomed to it. She was taking it very gently. Harvey was a seriously sick man, no question of that. And the way he was lighting one cigarette from the stub of the last one, it would be unwise of him to take out a subscription to a book club.

Having established that he had lived at Number 15, Honeyford Road, Tennison was anxious to broach the main subject. But she was still soft-pedaling, keeping her tone casual and low-key as she asked him, "So why did you move away, Mr. Harvey?"

"I had my first heart attack. When I got out of hospital, I came here to be closer to Eileen—my sister. I didna' want to live there anyway, not after the wife died. I only stayed on because that big darkie wanted me out so badly . . ." He narrowed his bleary eyes and looked around with an expression of loathing, the first real emotion he'd shown. "I should never have moved to this dump though. I'm a bloody prisoner. Elevator's always on the blink, the place full of junkies and pimps . . ."

He broke off to have another puff and a cough. Tennison waited for him to wipe his mouth with a bunched-up tissue. She was about to continue her questioning when Harvey pointed a quivering finger at one of the photographs on the sideboard.

"That's her. The wife. She was the gardener. Lovely garden when she was alive."

Muddyman picked it up in its gilt frame to show Tennison a rather muddy black-and-white image of a plump, pleasant-looking woman in a floral print dress, sitting in a deck chair and smiling at the camera.

Harvey gave a wheezing sigh. "I tried to keep it going after, but . . . d'ye know? In the end I paved it over. I can tell you exactly when as well."

He dragged himself out of the chair and shuffled over to the sideboard and rummaged in the left-hand drawer, pushing aside bundles of old bills, leaflets, and junk mail. Muddyman caught Tennison's eye, and she could tell by his slight frown that he was struggling to get a handle on David

Harvey, but thus far the jury was out. She felt the same, bemused and disconcerted by the man.

"I hired some stone-cutting equipment . . . Ah!" Harvey found what he was searching for. "There ye go. The last week of August," he said, peering closely at a faded, creased invoice. On his slow, stooping creep back to the armchair he handed it to Tennison. "I did all the digging during that week. Took up the grass, leveled it all off. I suppose I'd laid about half the slabs by the Saturday. I went down to Eileen's first thing Sunday morning. Stayed till Monday."

"And Eileen lives locally?" Tennison asked.

"She does now, but in those days she lived in Margate," Harvey replied, puffing a new cigarette into life. "Anyway, when I got back Monday I finished laying the rest. Cemented them in."

Tennison slowly nodded. "So the only time the house was left unattended was . . . that must have been Sunday the thirty-first of August?"

"That's right."

"Did you notice anything unusual when you got back?"

Harvey scratched his chin with long, dirt-rimmed nails, his fingers brown with nicotine. "Unusual . . . ?"

"No signs that anyone had been digging in the garden? No extra earth anywhere?"

"No."

Tennison allowed a small silence to gather. Hands clasped on her knees, she tilted her head a fraction, raising one eyebrow. "I must say, Mr. Harvey, if someone asked me what I was doing the last weekend in August in 1986 I don't think I'd be able to remember. How is it that you can recollect so clearly?"

Without hesitation, Harvey said drably, "Because my wife died on that day the year before."

"Oh, I see . . ."

"Eileen asked me down to stay with her—you know, so I'd not be on my own." The front door opened and they heard someone enter. Harvey jerked his head. "That'll be my lunch." He took a drag and went on, "I spend that weekend with her every year. Don't know how I'd manage without her. She always sends my food over."

Tennison looked towards the door. "Perhaps I can ask her a few questions while she's here . . . ?"

"Oh, no, that's not her," Harvey said, and with an effort craned around in his chair as a young man carrying a tray covered with a clean white tea towel came in. "This is my nephew Jason."

Jason paused in the doorway, pale blue eyes under fair lashes flicking from one to the other. "What's going on?" he asked sharply.

"We're police officers," Muddyman said. He picked up the typewritten sheet from the coffee table and dangled it in Harvey's face. "You're sure you don't recognize the girl from this description?"

Jason flushed, getting angry. "What do you want with my uncle?" he demanded, hands gripping the tray tightly. He wore faded jeans and sneakers, a dark Windbreaker over a white T-shirt, which he filled quite impressively. His blond hair was cut short and neatly brushed, though he favored long sideburns.

In reply to Muddyman's question, Harvey said in a tired, undisturbed tone, "Quite sure." To his nephew he murmured, "I'll tell you in a minute."

Jason was glaring at Muddyman with ill-concealed distaste. "You know he's very ill?"

"It's fine, don't worry," Harvey said, waving a trembling hand placatingly. "I'm fine . . ."

"No, you're not! What's this about?"

"Your uncle will tell you later, Jason," Tennison said, fastening her briefcase and getting up. "Thank you very much, Mr. Harvey. We'll see ourselves out."

"Have a good meal," Muddyman said, and followed Tennison, Jason's stare burning holes in his back.

On the landing below, lighting up, Muddyman said, "Lying bastard. Trotting out his alibi like a speech he'd learned by heart." He flung the match into the piss-stained corner.

"Yeah, right . . ."

"And he wasn't shuffling about like that six years ago! If he could lay those slabs he could smash a young girl's skull."

"Well, we'd better get a move on," Tennison said, giving him a hard, sidelong look. "Before David Aloysius Harvey dies on us."

Superintendent Kernan pushed the swing door of the Incident Room and held it open for the tall, handsome, broad-shouldered figure who came after him. He looked around the busy room and approached Haskons at the duty desk. "Where's DCI Tennison?"

"Following up a lead, Guv."

The bustle ceased as Kernan called out, "Can I have your attention please." Heads turned. Kernan held out his hand. "This is DS Bob Oswalde. Bob's joining us from West Lane to assist on Operation Nadine."

There were one or two puzzled, uncertain looks exchanged; this was the first they'd heard about drafting in new manpower. Never one to waste time on formalities, Kernan waved to them to get on with it, then beckoned Oswalde over. "DS Haskons here is the office manager. He'll fill in."

"Hello Bob."

Oswalde returned the nod. "Richard."

"You two know each other?" Kernan said.

"I used to be at West End Lane," Haskons said.

"Of course you were. Good." Job done, Kernan departed.

Haskons was as puzzled as some of the others. He said, "Tennison didn't mention that you were joining us."

Oswalde turned from sizing up the situation, seeing if there was anyone else he recognized. He looked down on Haskons's mere six feet from his six-feet-four. "She doesn't know," he said.

5

A hospital porter pointed the way to the medical artist's studio. Tennison walked along the echoing, white-tiled corridor and found the door with a piece of white card taped to it, "STUDIO" scrawled on the card in green felt-tip. It looked to her like a shoestring operation; this guy had better be good for the money they were shelling out.

Upon entering, Tennison saw that it wasn't a studio at all, but more a medical science laboratory. There were human organs immersed in fluid in giant test tubes, which she didn't examine too closely in case they turned out to be real. A tall young man in a black polo-necked sweater and a gray apron was working on the far side of the room, next to a wide-slanting window to gain the maximum natural daylight. Tennison threaded through the exhibits, keeping her eyes to the front. She'd seen real human beings in gruesome conditions, and the sight of blood didn't bother her, but these mummified floating bits of internal plumbing gave her the creeps.

"I'm DCI Tennison. I think you're making a clay head for us?"

It was the clay head he was actually working on. He stood back, wiping brown clay onto his apron, allowing her to get a good look.

"It may not look like much at the moment, but I have high hopes." He had a drawling, dreamlike voice, as if he spent much of his time on another plane of existence. Probably did, Tennison thought.

She moved closer. A plaster cast had been taken of Nadine's skull into which he had hammered dozens of steel pins. These formed the scaffolding for the features he was building up in clay. At the moment the underlying structure could be seen, exposed muscles and ligatures, and the effect was macabre, a face stripped down to its component parts.

"She had the most beautiful skull I've ever seen," the young man said.

"Really?"

"Yes. See this . . ." He used a stainless steel scalpel as a pointer. "The orbicularis oris. The muscle originates on the maxilla and mandible, near the midline, on the eminences due to the incisor and canine teeth. Its fibers surround the oral aperture. Function—closing of the mouth and pursing of lips. You see, I'm a scientist," he added, giving her his shy, dreamy smile. "Otherwise I'd have said it's the muscle that allows you to kiss someone."

"When will she be ready?"

"By the end of the week."

As office manager, Haskons was doing a bit of reorganizing—much to Ken Lillie's displeasure, because he was the one being reorganized.

"But why?" Lillie asked, his arms piled up with document files.

"I'm moving you."

"Why me?"

"Bob needs a desk."

"No, no, that's not an answer . . . why me?"

Haskons plunked a cardboard box of miscellaneous stuff on top of the pile, so that Lillie had to raise his head to peer over it.

"Because you're only ever at your desk to drink coffee."

"Yeah," Lillie agreed vehemently. "Normally I'm out there making sure the streets are safe to walk."

Hoots of derision from all corners of the room. Catcalls and shouts of "SuperLillie Strikes Again," and "Batman and Lillie."

Oswalde was studying the photographs of Nadine on the big bulletin board, keeping well out of it. He was edgy enough as it was, nervously watching the door for Tennison's arrival. Kernan had arranged his transfer without consulting her, which put Oswalde in a spot he knew he shouldn't be in. Especially after what had occurred at the conference. Had he been paranoid, Oswalde reflected, he might have suspected that Kernan had deliberately thrown the two of them together, part of a gleeful, devious plot so he could sit back and watch the pair of them squirm.

No, Kernan would never stoop to that. Would he?

Oswalde had other eyes on him. Burkin was slumped in his chair, long legs splayed out, chewing a matchstick. He muttered to Rosper at the next desk, "It's bad enough having to police the buggers, let alone work with them."

"You're only saying that 'cos he's taller than you," Rosper quipped, always the easygoing one.

Burkin was stung. "No he ain't."

The door swung open and Tennison breezed in, raincoat flapping around her. Halfway to her desk she caught sight of Oswalde and stopped dead in her tracks. Oswalde was attempting the impossible, hoping not to draw attention to them both by not looking at her, at the same time trying to convey to her by some mysterious telepathic process that he was as blameless as she was, just another innocent pawn in the game.

"Tony. Can I have a word, please?"

Tennison turned about-face and went out.

Muddyman left his desk and went into the corridor, where he found her pacing up and down, hands deep in her raincoat pockets.

"Guv?"

"What's Bob Oswalde doing here?"

"You know him?"

"Answer the question, Tony."

"He's part of the team. Kernan brought him in."

"Thank you."

With that she marched off to Kernan's office, leaving Muddyman standing there, wondering what the fuck this was all about.

Kernan was dictating letters to a clerk when Tennison walked in. He seemed very pleased with himself about something, leaning back with a smug grin on his pouchy, pockmarked face. Tennison's mind was racing ten to the dozen. It was all a jumble; she wasn't sure which emotion came first, nor which one to trust. She knew she had to be careful how she handled this.

"Jane?" Kernan said, which showed he was in a good mood, because normally he would have said with a sigh, *Well, what is it?*

"I want a word with you, Guv. Now."

"Thank you, Sharon."

Immediately after the WPC had gone and the door had closed, Tennison said, "Why did you co-opt someone onto my team without telling me?" She was holding herself in check, her voice reasonably calm, her temper under control—for the moment.

Kernan lit a cigarette. "It seemed to me that a black officer would be a—how can I put it?—a useful addition."

"Why didn't you consult with me?"

"Actually, I consulted the Community Liaison Officer, who thought it was an excellent idea." Kernan gestured with the cigarette. "A black face prominent in this inquiry. An antidote to the Burkins of this world. You're saying you can't use an extra man?"

"No."

"Well, what are you saying?"

"You've called in this officer as backup," Tennison said questioningly, making sure she understood, "because he's black?"

Now Kernan did sigh, and rolled his eyes a little. "Jane, I'm not looking for a political argument . . ."

"It would have been different if he'd been part of the team from the beginning, but now every time I ask him to do something, it's open to misinterpretation."

Kernan gazed blankly up at her. "I don't understand."

Tennison came nearer the desk, her hands clutching the air. "It smacks of tokenism. It's political maneuvering."

Kernan didn't want to listen to this claptrap, and didn't see why he should. But Tennison had pumped herself up and wasn't about to stop. She said heatedly, "You should have asked me first. Pulling rank just undermines me."

It was Kernan's turn to get annoyed. "I wasn't pulling rank. I was trying to help you out . . ."

"Oh, bollocks," Tennison said. Then added, "Sir."

What could he do with the bloody woman? Against all the odds she'd made it to Chief Inspector of the Metropolitan Force, in charge of a murder squad—which was what she'd always wanted—and still she wasn't happy. He never had this problem with his male colleagues. If only she wasn't so good at her job, he'd have dumped her double-quick. On yer bike, sunshine.

Kernan rubbed his eyelids with his fingertips, feeling the ulcer start to nag. "You can't work with the man?" he asked finally, doing his level best to get to the root of her objection.

"Yes, I can work with him."

"Because all my sources reckon he's a good officer."

"I'm sure he is."

Kernan spread his hands, appealing to her. "Then what have you got against him?"

"Nothing," Tennison said, tight-lipped. "Well . . ." She gave a halfshrug. "We didn't hit it off particularly well on the course, but . . ."

"I don't want you to marry the man, for Chrissake!" Kernan practically shouted, squashing his cigarette in the overflowing ashtray.

Tennison's tangle of emotions nearly got the better of her. She almost blurted out the real reason why she objected to Bob Oswalde joining the squad—how could she possibly work with a man she was strongly attracted to, who had been her lover? It would set up all kinds of impossible conflicts, make normal, everyday working relations a knife-edge balancing act. And what if it came out? She'd become a laughingstock. Her credibility would pop like a toy balloon, her reputation plummet to zilch, lower than a snake's belly.

But in the end, sanity prevailed. She didn't make a fool of herself, and she didn't blurt anything out. She simply stated, as forcefully as she could, that she didn't want him on the team.

Kernan's patience had been worn to a fine point, and finally it snapped. "He's on the team already. I've made my decision and I'm not going back on it. Get the man briefed and put him to work. We'll review the situation at the end of the week. I'll be watching the progress of this case very carefully from now on."

Tennison left the office.

Ten minutes later, on the pretext of officially welcoming DS Oswalde to Southampton Row, Tennison summoned him to her office. She was still pent up and dying for a smoke. She stood in front of her desk, arms folded, looking up at him, accusation in her eyes.

"Are you expecting me to believe this is a complete coincidence?"

Oswalde regarded her placidly. "I don't know about coincidence—how many black detectives did he have to choose from? What I'm saying is that it had nothing to do with me. You know me well enough to know I wouldn't ask to be the token black on your team."

He seemed quite sanguine about it.

Tennison said sharply, "Just don't think that what happened on the course gives you any special privileges."

"I don't."

"And don't you dare tell anyone."

"Jane, please . . . what do you take me for?"

"And don't call me Jane."

Oswalde wore a pained expression. "Look, give me some credit. What happened, happened. It's gone, long since forgotten about. Let's not give it another thought . . ."

"Yes. Right." Tennison waved her hand, dismissing him. "Go back to the Incident Room. I'll be along in a minute."

When he'd gone she stared at the door for a long moment, then stuck a Nicorette in her mouth and chewed the hell out of it.

All the team was there, assembled for the four o'clock briefing. There was an odd, strained atmosphere, Tennison snapping out instructions, and the men uneasy. They guessed it had something to do with Kernan and Oswalde, but beyond that they were completely in the dark.

Tennison stood in front of the board, her eyes raking over them. "We could have the clay head by tomorrow with any luck. By the end of the week at the latest. After talking to Harvey, our best bet is to concentrate on Sunday, August the thirty-first, 1986."

"Has Harvey got an alibi?" Burkin asked.

Tennison nodded. "His sister, Eileen. I'm going to talk to her soon. We need a name. We need to build up Nadine's life story, then we might be able to connect her to Harvey."

"I've been wading through these statements," Haskons said, sitting on the edge of his desk and indicating a pile of papers. "One or two people talk about a young girl staying in the basement of Number fifteen."

"Really?" Tennison said.

"Conflicting reports, but it could have been eighty-six."

"Brilliant. I'd like to make a start on missing persons. Bob, perhaps you could handle that."

Oswalde straightened up, his face stiffening, and then gave an abrupt nod. Some of the others exchanged looks. "Mispers" wasn't normally a job for a Detective Sergeant, especially one as experienced as Oswalde.

"Tony, can you go and see if you can have a word with Harvey's doctor, make sure he's not just a bloody good actor."

"If he is, he should win an Oscar," Muddyman said.

"Right. That's all for now."

As she went out, Burkin turned to Haskons with a grin, muttering, "Glad to see the boss is keeping our colored friend in his place." Haskons didn't agree, and he was less than happy with Tennison's duty allocation. He followed and caught up with her in the corridor.

"Guv . . . can I put someone else on Mispers?"

"Why?"

"With respect, ma'am, it's ridiculous having a man of his experience . . ."

"No." Tennison was already striding off. "He might pick up on something a more junior man might miss. Don't call me ma'am."

Haskons watched her go, shaking his head. Of all the crap excuses . . .

Eileen Reynolds was a younger, much tougher version of her brother David Harvey. A hard-bitten Glaswegian woman with a shrewd, sharp-nosed face under a silvery cap of bleached hair, she sat in Tennison's office wearing a powder blue coat and a tartan scarf that clashed badly with everything. Her son Jason sat meekly by her side, as if cowed by her domineering presence.

Tennison was trying to establish the pattern of Harvey's visits to his sister, and whether he had been there on the weekend in question.

"I'm sure, of course I'm sure! Every year since his Jeanie died. He wouldn't have left till the Monday morning." Eileen Reynolds suddenly bent forward, her work-worn hands clutching the shiny black handbag in her lap. "What you lot've got to remember is that he's a sick man. You shouldn't be hounding him."

"Mum." Jason tugged at her sleeve. He seemed embarrassed. "They've got their job to do."

"He's waiting for an operation you know? You'll be the bloody death of him . . ."

"We're not hounding him, Mrs. Reynolds. We're trying to eliminate him from our inquiries."

Leaning forward again, beady eyes glittering, the woman said hoarsely, "You wouldn't be hounding him like this if he was a black man."

"Mum . . . !"

"Mrs. Reynolds," Tennison said patiently, "I've questioned your brother once, that's all. Which is not surprising given that the body of a young girl was found buried in his garden."

Eileen Reynolds snorted. "Well, that's a lot of rubbish. Simone Cameron this, Simone Cameron that. Was it Simone?"

"No."

"Exactly. It's my brother you should be concerned about. He's the one that's dying."

"Is that all for now?" Jason asked, standing up.

"Yes. Thank you very much for coming."

"Come on, Mum . . ."

"Don't pull me about!" At the door she turned her sharp, angry face towards Tennison for a parting shot. "He's at the hospital tomorrow thanks to you."

"Come on," Jason said, steering her out into the corridor.

Tennison went to the door and indicated to a passing WPC that she should see them to reception. With his arm around the back of the powder blue coat, Jason guided his mother after the WPC, the dutiful, attentive son.

Tennison looked at her watch, debated for a moment, and grabbed her coat from the hook. If she hurried she'd just be in time to catch Vernon Allen before he left his office.

He wasn't as friendly and cooperative this time. Perhaps it was because he was in his management role, sitting at a mahogany desk, his broad frame inside a well-cut suit and matching waistcoat. Or perhaps he was just fed up with Tennison retreading the same questions he thought he'd already answered.

Aware that he was fretting, impatient to get away, Tennison said, "Just one last thing, Vernon. You said that you and Mr. Harvey fell out because he wouldn't move."

"Yes."

"Nothing else?"

"What? No."

"But didn't he sublet the basement? To a girl?"

"That had nothing to do with me."

"What had nothing to do with you?"

"Whatever she was doing."

"What was she doing?"

"Look—I don't know. It was none of my business."

Vernon Allen sniffed and turned his head away, gazing through the venetian blinds at the London skyline in the gathering dusk. Far below, the rush-hour traffic was clogging up the Euston underpass.

"It was if she was a prostitute, Vernon," Tennison said.

"Why?"

"Because as the landlord you could have been charged with running a brothel."

He was offended. "How dare you use the word 'brothel.'"

"What word would you use?"

He looked at her through his heavy, dark-framed glasses, a hint of uncertainty there, as if he wasn't sure of his ground anymore. With a weary motion he pressed the palm of his hand to his forehead, and said, "I was at work all hours, Esme was too. A neighbor told us men were calling there. I spoke to Harvey right away but I had no proof. Then suddenly the . . . the girl . . . seemed to have gone."

Tennison leaned forward. "But did you see her?"

Vernon Allen gave a barely perceptible nod. "Yes."

"Was it the girl whose remains we've found? Is that why you won't cooperate?"

"Listen. My family is very upset." He was making a great effort to speak slowly, holding his emotions in check. "It's an important time for us. A wedding should be a time of joy. I have cooperated with you in every way so far . . ."

"Then please answer the question. Did she answer the description I've given you?"

"No." He stared straight back. "She was a white girl."

"Not just light-skinned?"

"No. White."

Tennison leaned back, pressing her lips together. "Can you describe her, please?"

Vernon Allen thought for a moment. "Small, perhaps five foot two. A tiny thing, really. Blond hair—bleached, I would say." Tennison nodded, making notes. "Young, but not the girl you described."

Tennison looked up from her pad. "Did you have sexual relations with this girl?"

She saw in his eyes how disturbed he was by this question.

"I did not," Vernon Allen replied gravely.

"What was the relationship between Harvey and this girl?"

"God knows. I wouldn't put anything past that man."

"And when did all this happen, Vernon?"

He stared down at the desk, evading Tennison's gaze, but she was quite content to wait. He cleared his throat and swallowed, and reluctantly admitted, "It could have been the summer you're talking about."

Tennison replaced the cap on her pen and screwed it tight.

The medical artist had promised it by the end of the week, and the next day, shortly after three in the afternoon, he delivered the goods.

On her way back from the ladies' room, Tennison nipped up to Kernan's office and invited him to come along to the Incident Room and take a gander at it. She thought it was the least she could do, seeing as how Kernan had been burdened with finding the money from his budget to pay for it.

"The Viswandhas' lawyer has been bending my ear," Kernan grumbled to her as they walked along the corridor. "He tells me Forensic are still there, poking around inside the house, lifting carpets, floorboards, the lot."

"So?"

"Let's get out of there as soon as possible."

"Yes, of course."

Kernan pushed open the door of the Incident Room, waving her to go first, and said with a distinct lack of enthusiasm, "Let's see it then."

There was an air of expectancy. All the team had gathered for the grand unveiling. Richards, the police photographer, had set up his tripod and lights. Tennison nodded to Haskons, who stepped forward and whisked off the cloth. There was a moment's stunned silence, and then a kind of collective gasp. The medical artist had been too modest, Tennison thought. He was as much artist as he was scientist, without doubt.

Modeled in brown clay, the head was astonishingly lifelike. The girl was young and very beautiful, rather proud-looking, with braided hair swept back from a wide forehead. The artist had caught exactly the mixed-race cast of her features, high cheekbones had a generous mouth, and it reminded Tennison strongly of the sculpted head of an ancient goddess.

Everyone, even the hardened longtime pros who thought they'd seen everything, were impressed . . .

Everyone except Kernan, cynical old bugger, who was seeing a hole in his budget rather than an expertly crafted clay head.

His only comment was a surly, "Very nice," and then the swing door was wafting the air as he disappeared through it.

Richards was popping off photographs, moving his camera around to cover all the angles. Tennison turned to the men.

"Right . . . I want these photographs to appear everywhere they can, local and national press. From now on you'll show them to anyone who might be able to help. Let's get the Allens in to see this . . ." She gestured towards the head. "Vernon Allen has confirmed that there was a hooker working from the basement of Number fifteen that summer. From his description it wasn't Nadine but it's possible that Nadine was a tom as well . . . perhaps Harvey was a small-time pimp? Harvey is at the hospital all day tomorrow," she added, "so I won't be able to see him till the evening to tackle him about it."

"She doesn't look like a prostitute," DC Lillie said.

"Start asking around anyway." Tennison moved to the board. "Vernon Allen has accounted for his family's whereabouts on the thirty-first. For the last ten years there's been a Reggae Sunsplash concert in Honeyford Park on the last Sunday in August. Vernon says Esme was at that concert—she's there every year running a stall selling West Indian food."

The men were silent, paying close attention. Glancing down at her notes now and then to refresh her memory, Tennison continued.

"Apparently Tony, the son, attended the concert, which is an all-day affair—ten to ten. Vernon says he spent the day at home with Sarah and David. Tony returned at about nine P.M. to look after his brother and sister so Vernon could go to work. I've checked Vernon's work record. He did a double shift through Sunday night and late into Monday. By the time Esme had packed up, returned things to the cafe and got back home, it was about ten-forty-five P.M. She says by then all three children were asleep in bed. Obviously, wherever possible, I'd like these accounts verified."

She looked around, and was about to call the briefing over when Oswalde, leaning back nonchalantly against a desk, arms folded, said casually, "Perhaps that's the link between Nadine and Honeyford Road."

"What?"

"The Reggae Sunsplash."

Tennison's eyes narrowed. "Go on."

"Harvey could have met her there, or Tony Allen. Perhaps the victim's bag of African cloth was a costume of some sort. She might even have been performing at the concert."

Nobody said anything. Oswalde's first contribution, after being on the team less than twenty-four hours, was a good one, and everybody knew it.

Tennison looked away from him, tapping her fingers on the desk. "It's an interesting thought. Worth following up. Frank, Gary, I'd like you to visit the Sunsplash organizers first thing tomorrow—see if they can point you toward any bands using back up singers or musicians in African dress."

Oswalde slowly unfolded his arms. He couldn't believe this. He'd just single-handedly come up with a promising lead and she'd tossed the juicy bone to someone else. Knowing what he must be feeling, the rest of the team couldn't meet his dark, angry eyes. Something was going down here, but they were damned if they knew what it was.

"Anything else?" said Tennison briskly. "Right. That's it for now." She strode out.

Oswalde went after her. He caught up with her in the corridor and made her stop. "Why are you doing this to me?" he demanded, his voice low and furious.

"What?"

"Treating me like the office boy?"

"I don't know what you're talking about," Tennison said, braving it out. Her eyes shifted away; people were passing, and it was a bit public for this exchange.

"Why didn't you send me to see the concert organizers?"

"You're busy already," Tennison said, another convenient crap excuse. "Besides, I thought that you didn't want to be given special tasks because of the color of your skin."

"I don't," Oswalde said curtly. "I want to be given a task commensurate with my abilities and experience."

He was right to be pissed-off, and right to make this request, they both knew it. Tennison was anxious to end this public confrontation lest tongues started to wag. She said, "I want you to carry on overseeing Mispers . . ." Oswalde was about to protest, and she cut him short. "But I'd also like you to arrange for the Allens to see the clay head. Watch their reactions."

"Thank you," Oswalde said stiffly, and went back to work.

While he was still sore at Tennison, Oswalde was glad to be more centrally involved in the investigation; combing through the endless Missing Persons files on the computer was brain-numbing, soul-destroying work. He'd done his stint at it as a young DC, and had thought those days were behind him.

He contacted the Allens and arranged for Vernon and Esme, and their son Tony, to come into Southampton Row to view the clay head. He went down to reception to meet them, and before taking them through to the interview room, explained to the three of them what was involved. They were being asked to say if they recognized the girl, and if possible, to identify her.

As they filed in, Oswalde kept a close eye on them, noting their reactions at the first sight of the head on the small wooden plinth. They studied it in silence. Oswalde glanced at Vernon Allen, who shook his head.

"Are you sure, Vernon?"

"Absolutely."

"Esme?"

"Yes?" Her brows were drawn forward, gazing at the head with a harrowed expression. "No, dear. I'd remember if I had." She let out a pitiful sigh. "What a beautiful child . . ."

There was a strange gasping, choking sound. Oswalde swung around to find Tony Allen on the verge of collapse. The boy was shuddering violently and clutching his throat, the awful noises issuing from his quivering mouth. He seemed unable to properly draw a breath.

"Tony—what's wrong?" Oswalde said, alarmed.

Esme took charge. "Come, Tony, sit down." She led the boy to a chair and sat beside him, her arm around his shoulders. "Now don't make a fuss, you're all right," his mother comforted him. "It's very hot in here. He suffers from asthma," she explained to Oswalde.

"I see."

Oswalde watched him. He seemed calmer now, though there was a mist of sweat on his forehead. He kept staring at the clay head, then down at the floor, and then back again, as if the sight mesmerized him.

"Have you seen her before, Tony?"

"No." He gulped air. "I've never seen her."

"You're certain?"

"I'm certain," Tony Allen said.

6

"He's our prime suspect and he's dying. I'm not going to sit back and watch."
"I don't know why you're so bothered," Muddyman panted. "Just another runaway, another dead prostitute . . ."

Tennison halted on the ninth floor of Dwyfor House and turned to him, her chest heaving. "You don't mean that."

"I do if it means climbing these poxy stairs again," Muddyman said, staring up with deep loathing.

"She's someone's daughter, Tony."

"Yeah, yeah, yeah . . ." Muddyman set off again. He said bitterly, "Anything we get from the old sod will be thrown out of court anyway. 'He didn't know what he was saying,'" Muddyman mimicked a light brown voice. "'Oppressive conduct by the police . . .'"

If when they'd seen him the previous time Harvey was on his last legs, he was at death's door now. He looked even more haggard, and kept swallowing tablets—ten different shapes, sizes, and colors—as if they were candy. Tennison, seated opposite him on the sofa, treated him as gently as she knew how. She spread the photographs of Nadine on the coffee table and gave him plenty of time to mull them over. Finally, chest wheezing and rattling, he shook his head.

"No, I've never seen her before. I did let the basement room that summer, I admit it. There's nothing wrong with that." He fixed Tennison with his rheumy eyes. "The big darkie complained about everything I did. He just wanted me out."

"Why did you let the room, David? Did you know the girl already?"

"No, I'd never seen her before. It seemed such a big house for just me and I needed the money. I put a card in the newsagent's window."

"What was her name?" Muddyman asked, leaning against the back of the sofa.

"Tracey? Sharon? I don't remember," Harvey said wearily.

"How long did she stay?" Tennison asked.

"Couple of months."

"What months?"

"June, July . . ."

"Not August?"

"No, she'd gone by then."

"Did you know that she was a prostitute?" Muddyman said, his tone nowhere near as gentle as Tennison's.

"No."

"Could she have been friends with that girl?" Tennison indicated the photographs.

"It's possible."

"Could she have had a set of keys to the flat?"

Harvey's narrow shoulders twitched. "Possible I suppose . . ."

"Could she and some friends have used the flat that Sunday you were at your sister's?" Tennison pressed him.

"How should I know?" His eyes were upon her, but unfocused, as if he couldn't quite make her out. "As you say, I wasn't there . . ."

His shoulders started heaving as he went into a coughing fit. Muddyman hesitated when Tennison pointed to the kitchen, but then went off and came back with a glass of water, which Harvey gulped down with four more assorted pills.

"Just one last thing, David." Tennison smiled at him encouragingly. "Could we have a photograph of you, please?"

Harvey wiped his mouth. Beads of water clung to the ragged fringes of his mustache. "Why?"

"It'll help us eliminate you from our inquiries."

"Will I get it back?"

"Of course." Tennison watched him on his snail's progress to the glass-fronted bureau. "One from the mid-eighties if you've got it."

Harvey took a tattered, red album from the drawer and leafed through it. Tennison went over to stand beside him. She picked up one of the framed photographs, a moody sunset over a gray, restless ocean, which to her inexpert eye looked to be of a professional quality.

"Are you the photographer?" Muddyman asked, taking an interest.

"No. My nephew Jason."

"They're very good," Tennison said, putting it back.

"Here." Harvey gave her a snapshot of himself, a darker-haired, stronger-looking Harvey with a brown mustache. "Younger and fitter, eh?" he said with a wan smile.

"Thank you. I'll get this copied and get it back to you as soon as possible." She put it in her briefcase along with her notebook and snapped the catches.

They went through into the tiny hallway. Harvey leaned on the jamb of the living room door, resting. Tennison reached out to release the Yale lock when she noticed the front door key hanging down from the mailbox on a piece of string. "I'd remove that if I were you, David. Not very safe."

"It's so someone can get in if I collapse." Harvey stated it matter-of-factly; no self-pitying appeal for sympathy.

Tennison gave him a look over her shoulder as she went out. "Even so."

As they were going down the stairs, Muddyman said mockingly, "You'd make a wonderful Crime Prevention Officer."

"Oh yeah?" Tennison drawled, punching him.

DS Oswalde lingered by the frozen food cabinets, not even bothering to put up a thin pretense that he was wondering what to buy. The supermarket wasn't all that busy at this late hour, and Oswalde had an uninterrupted view along the aisles of Tony Allen, neat and dapper in his short dark-blue coat and polka-dotted bow tie, the plastic badge on his left lapel engraved in black letters: "A. ALLEN. TRAINEE MANAGER."

Tony was aware of the scrutiny. Oswalde had made sure of that. The more rattled the young man became, the better he liked it. Esme Allen had called it an asthma attack. A load of old baloney. Tony had been scared shitless the minute he laid eyes on Nadine's clay head. He'd recognized her instantly, of that Oswalde hadn't the slightest doubt.

Oswalde stalked him around the store for another ten minutes, watching him openly, noting with satisfaction the jerky body language, the fumbling with the clipboard when he tried to make an entry. At last, deciding that Tony had stewed long enough, Oswalde moved in. He cornered him next to cooked meats and stuck the description, the one Vernon Allen had given of the girl living in the basement, under his nose.

"Your father remembers her," Oswalde said, looking down on Tony, a good eight or nine inches shorter. "Bleached blonde, slim, about five-foot-two . . ."

"Well, I don't." Tony dodged around him and strode off.

"Do you like reggae, Tony?" Oswalde asked, matching stride for stride.

"What?"

"I do. Reggae, soul, jazz. Do you like jazz?"

Tony whirled around. "What are you talking about?"

"I'm just talkin', man." Oswalde shrugged, all sweetness and light.

"Well don't, just leave me alone . . ."

"All right, Tony," Oswalde said with a glimmer of a smile, "don't jump the rails."

Tony started off, turned back, his face twitching. "I don't remember any girl," he said, grinding it between his teeth.

Oswalde stood watching him stump off. Nearly done, but not quite. Tony Allen needed to stew just a little while longer.

"This'll do," Tennison said, and Muddyman pulled over at the corner of Glasshouse Street and Brewer Street. She tucked her briefcase under her arm and opened the door. "I'll get a cab home."

Muddyman raised his hand. "'Night, Guv. Hope you get something."

Tennison strolled along through Soho, past the strip joints with their garish neon signs and life-size color photographs of semi-naked women contorting themselves to entice the johns downstairs. Separating the strip clubs were shadowy booths peddling racks of soft porn, and at the back, behind a curtain of fluttering plastic streamers, the hard Swedish and German stuff wrapped in cellophane. There was plenty of business about, and groups of working girls in miniskirts and fishnet stockings, clustered around the concrete lampposts, their faces anemic in the harsh sodium glare, black slashes for mouths.

Tennison glanced across the street. A tall girl with a mass of dark hair piled on top of her head, wearing a lime-green shortie plastic raincoat, registered who it was, and gave a nod. Tennison strolled on. She stopped in a darkened doorway, waiting for Rachel, and hadn't been there more than a few seconds when a man approached and leaned towards her. She smelled whisky on his breath.

"Oh, I wouldn't if I were you," Tennison said, and the man moved on, bewildered. A minute later Rachel appeared, and Tennison gave her a smile. "You look like you could use something to eat, darling."

In the cafe on the corner they sat at a plastic-topped table while Rachel did justice to a hot salt beef sandwich and Tennison sipped an espresso.

"If he's a pimp, I've never seen him before," Rachel said, handing back the snapshot of David Harvey. She took another bite of her sandwich. "I'll ask around about the bleached blonde, but it's not much to go on."

"You're telling me," Tennison said with feeling.

Rachel chewed while she had another think. "Maybe she was one of those that tried it for five minutes and decided it was no kind of life. One of the sensible ones," she said, the corner of her mouth curling up in a bleak, sardonic smile. "I suppose someone might remember, since most of the girls who worked that area are black."

Tennison held up the picture of Nadine.

"Look. This is the likeness of the dead girl . . ."

Rachel bent forward to peer at the clay head, staring sightlessly into the camera. She pulled away with a little shudder. "Spooky. No." She shook her head of tousled curls. "Never seen her before either."

Tennison folded a twenty-pound note and slipped it under Rachel's saucer. "Do your best, darling," she said with a smile, and got up to leave.

"I always do," Rachel said.

"Ask around. I must go . . .'bye."

Jane poured herself a treble of neat Bushmills and on her way back to the sofa pressed the playback button on the answering machine. She kicked off her shoes and curled up on the sofa, closing her eyes and resting her head on the cushions. She felt bone-weary, yet her brain was ticking like an unexploded bomb. She couldn't turn off her thoughts, they crowded in, swamping everything. When she was working on a case, she gave it every ounce of her concentration and emotional energy. No wonder Peter hadn't been able to stick it out. Would any man? If it wasn't an empty-headed bimbo they wanted, it was a wife and homemaker, and she didn't fit either category.

The machine clicked on. It was her mother.

Jane, remember, this Friday is Emma's first birthday, so don't forget to send a card, will you?

Emma was her sister Pam's little girl. Pam was happily married to Tony, a company accountant, with three children, the perfect nuclear family. While Jane was the black sheep of her own family, the mad, obsessive career woman doing a job no woman should do—or so Jane's mother thought. She had learned to live with, if not fully accept, her family's total lack of understanding about the kind of work she did; it never ceased to puzzle them why she didn't find herself a steady guy and settle down, have a couple of kids before it was too late, forget all this career nonsense.

"I haven't forgotten, Mum . . ." Eyes closed, both hands around the glass, she took a sip of whisky.

. . . if you're in before ten-thirty you can telephone me. Daddy sends his love.

There was a click, a hissing pause, followed by the next message.

Mike Kernan at nine thirty-five. I was hoping for an update, Jane. Any results from your clay head? A slight hesitation then, throat-clearing. *Er . . . it's my interview tomorrow and they're, um, bound to ask me about Operation Nadine. Particularly whether my DCI's come in on budget. Anyway, ring me tonight if you can—or drop by my office first thing.*

Jane stretched out and took another sip, feeling the Bushmills burn a molten path all the way down. She had no intention of calling a living soul.

Tennison was at the station bright and early the next morning. After dumping her coat and briefcase in her office, she went to the Incident Room and checked on the duty roster for the day. It was a few minutes after nine-thirty when she hurried along to Kernan's office and found him primping in front of the mirror, getting ready for his interview.

She reported, "We've spoken to the Sunsplash concert organizers. They've given us the names of the bands using backup singers. We're talking to them now."

"Tread carefully there, Jane. We're under the microscope." Kernan adjusted the knot in his silk tie, glancing at her in the mirror. "How's Oswalde getting on?"

"Fine."

He turned and caught her smiling. "What?" Tennison edged up his breast pocket handkerchief a fraction and smoothed it flat. "How do I look?" he asked anxiously.

"Like a Chief Superintendent."

"Good," Kernan said, and she could almost see his chest swell.

As she entered the Incident Room, DC Jones called her over.

"Guv!" He was elated, his eyes bright behind his rimless glasses. "I thought you'd like to know—Forensic have found a fragment of our girl's tooth between the floorboards of the front room of Number fifteen . . ."

Tennison punched the air with her fist. "Yes!"

News was coming in thick and fast. Next it was Oswalde's turn. He came over waving a page of computer printout, the result of all those hours crouched over the VDU screen.

"I think I might've found her."

"Yeah?" Tennison barely glanced at him, her tone neutral.

"Joanne Fagunwa, mixed parentage, became missing in early eighty-five from Birmingham."

"Is there a photograph?"

"Yes, well, I suppose that's with the file in Birmingham."

Tennison nodded brusquely. "Let's get it faxed through. If it looks promising, then go . . ."

Oswalde looked incredulous. "To Birmingham?"

"Yes." She turned away. "Richard, have we checked when Mrs. Harvey died?"

"August eighty-five, wasn't it?" Haskons said.

"Let's check."

"Course."

Muddyman put his head in and said to Tennison, "Let's go."

She was gone, leaving Oswalde with the computer printout in his hand and an expression of pent-up frustration on his face.

"Nice one, Bob," Haskons said sincerely, a small token in lieu of Tennison's lukewarm appreciation for his efforts. Oswalde went back to his desk; he was getting more than a bit pissed-off with being given the brush-off. As if he were here on sufferance, not really part of the team at all. Well. We'd see about that.

DI Burkin didn't like what he saw, and he took no great pains to disguise the fact. The recording studio was in a prefabricated building, provided by the council, two streets away from Honeyford Road. A sheer criminal waste of poll tax, in Burkin's view, most of which had been coughed up by white people to give these jungle bunnies somewhere to hang out all day, amusing themselves at the taxpayers' expense.

In respect to his seniority, Rosper let Burkin carry out the questioning, though he was uncomfortable about it.

There was a recording session in progress. Through the large glass panel they could see, but couldn't hear, a group of musicians banging away at guitars and drums, with three guys in the brass section. The band they were interviewing had played at the Sunsplash festival, but they were none too cooperative; mainly, Rosper suspected, because of the hostile vibes coming off Burkin like a bad smell.

One of them, the bass player, lounging back in an old armchair with the stuffing spilling out, was more interested in the recording session than the photographs of Nadine Burkin was showing him. He gave them a cursory glance. "Don't know nothin' about it . . ."

"Do you wanna look at them, sir, before you answer?" Burkin said, making the "sir" sound like he was having a tooth extracted without anesthetic.

The bassman plucked one out, looked, flipped it back. "I tell you I don't know her."

Burkin's lips thinned. "Okay. I'm going to ask you one more time. Will you please look at the photograph before you answer—"

The drummer, a thin, wiry fellow wearing a Bob Marley T-shirt and a black velvet Zari hat, interrupted. "You can't make a man look at a photograph if he doesn't want to."

"Oh, can't I?" Burkin bared his teeth in a nasty grin. "I can arrest him for obstructing police inquiries . . ."

Rosper put his hand over his eyes.

The drummer said, "He wasn't even in the band then!"

Burkin's eyes flashed. He opened his mouth, and Rosper said quickly, "Can I have a word, Frank? Guv?"

"Let me have a look," the drummer said, reaching out.

"Your battyman wants a word with you, Frank," the bassman said to Burkin, pinching his nose, but keeping a straight face.

Rosper handed the sheaf of photographs to the drummer and got Burkin outside before he exploded. They stood on the piece of waste ground adjacent to the studio. Burkin was physically shaking.

"What did he call you?"

"I dunno," Rosper muttered.

"Yes you do . . ." Burkin couldn't get over it, being referred to as having a "battyman," West Indian slang for homosexual. His face was livid. "I'm going to arrest him . . ."

Rosper sighed. He wasn't sure how to handle this. He thought Burkin was making a prize dickhead of himself. He said, "That'll be a big help . . . look, perhaps the Guv gave you this lead to see if you could manage to talk to a black guy without arresting him."

Burkin flexed his broad shoulders, breathing hard, but it had given him something to think about. He calmed down.

"And listen," Rosper said, "I think the drummer might know something. Can I go back and have a word with him on my own?"

"Go on then." Burkin lit up and walked towards the car. "You're wasting your time."

"Where's Dirty Harry?" the drummer asked when Rosper returned.

"Eh?"

"Your partner."

"Clint Eastwood, ennit?" the bassman said.

"Oh yeah," Rosper said, catching on. He scratched the back of his head. "Sorry about that."

They regarded him with amusement.

"Do you like reggae?" the drummer said.

"Yeah, solid guy," Rosper said, thrilled to be speaking their language.

They all laughed, even more amused.

"Then peruse these at your leisure," the drummer said.

Rosper accepted the four videos, nodding enthusiastically, and gave them the thumbs-up. "Wicked."

When he got back to the car, Burkin was slumped in the passenger seat, sullenly blowing smoke rings. Rosper slid behind the wheel, proudly showing the indifferent Burkin the fruits of his labors.

"Videos from eighty-six. Apparently two bands used girl backup singers," he said, well-pleased with himself, his pug-nosed face split in a broad grin. "Do I have what it takes or do I have what it takes?"

Staring through the windshield, Burkin blew another smoke ring.

• • •

Tennison chose her words carefully. "I'm not saying you killed her, David, but I am saying she was killed in your house."

The same vague expression came into Harvey's eyes as if he wasn't really seeing her. He opened his mouth wide, closed it, and opened it again, wide; he looked to be doing an impression of a goldfish. Then he leaned to his right and kept on leaning.

"Are you all right, sir?" Muddyman said.

Stupid question. The man was hanging over the arm of the chair, doing his goldfish act.

"Shit." Tennison was on her feet. "Call an ambulance. Quick."

Before she could get to him, Harvey was struggling to stand up, one hand clawing the air. He made a lunge forward and fell across the coffee table, upsetting it and sending the ashtray, cigarettes, and other bits and pieces flying. He lay on his side, face white as a sheet, staring sightlessly at the coal effect gas fire.

Muddyman was through to the emergency services, requesting an ambulance. It took nine minutes to arrive, which wasn't bad for central London, and Harvey was still alive when the paramedics got him downstairs and into the ambulance.

Tennison and Muddyman watched them close the doors and drive off. They would follow in their own car. As the ambulance pulled out of Lloyd George Estate, siren wailing, Tennison said grimly, "We could lose this one if Harvey croaks."

Muddyman thought, That's all she cares about. All the cold-blooded bitch really fucking cares about.

Oswalde drove up the M1 to Birmingham. It was a relief to get away from Southampton Row, out of London in fact, if only for a few hours.

Mrs. Fagunwa lived on the southern outskirts of the city, not many miles distant from Stratford-upon-Avon. It was a well-heeled, white, middle-class area with neat hedges and well-tended gardens. Some of the houses had double garages.

Oswalde had made an appointment, and Mrs. Fagunwa was expecting him. Just like the neighborhood, she was white and rather genteel, younger-looking than her forty-seven years, with thick black hair parted in the middle; she still possessed the good bone structure and fine complexion that must have made her something of a beauty as a young woman.

She led him through the parquet-floored hallway, polished like an ice rink, into a large, comfortably furnished sitting room which had patio doors looking out onto a lawn and flowerbeds. From the records Oswalde knew that she was a widow, and there was a stillness to the house, an un-lived-in feeling, that told him she had no companion and lived here alone.

She had been married to a Nigerian businessman, and there was a large framed photograph of him on top of the bookcase, along with several more of a dark-skinned girl, showing her at every stage from cheeky pigtailed toddler up to vivaciously attractive teenager.

Oswalde felt a flutter in his chest. Instantly, he hadn't the slightest doubt. The resemblance to the clay head was as close as it could be. Part of him was elated—*they'd found Nadine!*—but then he had to prepare himself for what he knew was not going to be a pleasant duty. He started gently.

"May I show you these photographs?"

"Yes . . ."

They were of the carved ivory bracelets, and she nodded as she looked at them. "Do you recognize these amulets, Mrs. Fagunwa?"

"Yes. They belonged to my husband's family. He gave them to Joanne."

"Then I'm sorry to tell you that they were found with the remains of a young girl. May I show you a picture of a clay head that we've had made."

Oswalde waited while she studied it. Her dark eyes in her pale face remained expressionless. He said quietly, "Does that look like your daughter?"

She nodded. "Oh yes. It's very like her. How clever."

"I'm sorry," Oswalde said. This was horrible, he felt like he had a knife in his guts.

Mrs. Fagunwa gazed at him. "How did she die?"

"We're not certain, but the circumstances are suspicious."

"Don't tell me she suffered." And now there was a shadow of pain in her dark eyes, and her voice was husky. "Please don't tell me that."

Riding in the car seemed to have loosened her tongue; it was like watching a dam slowly crumbling, the unstoppable surge of water pouring out. Oswalde drove back down the M1; Mrs. Fagunwa, now she'd started, unable to stop.

". . . her father died that year, you see. I still don't know why she left home. She had everything. She even had her own pony, she had everything . . ."

"Did Joanne ever have any accidents as a child?"

"Oh, no, the usual cuts and bruises, you know." Then she bethought herself. "Oh, yes—once she did. She broke her wrist. She fell off her bike."

Mrs. Fagunwa looked across at him. For him to have asked that specific question meant that he knew, that he was certain. She refused to make herself believe it, but it did no good. She knew now that it was her daughter that had been found, but she couldn't bring herself to ask.

Swallowing hard, she plunged on. "Well, anyway, then she rejected it all. She started having things woven in her hair. You know, beads and things. Her hair isn't even black really, more a dark brown, with threads of gold in it. She was almost blond when she was little. Her skin looks more tanned than anything else. She was such a pretty little girl—we have so many photographs. I keep meaning to sort them out."

She made a sound in her throat and her voice stuck. Oswalde gripped the wheel tightly, doing seventy-five in the center lane. Driving was about the best he could manage at the moment.

Mrs. Fagunwa took a deep breath, rallying herself.

"I don't think the local police treated her disappearance seriously. Just another young girl leaving home, going to London. Loads of them do that, don't they? I saw a documentary. It's not just Joanne . . ."

Oswalde saw a sign for a service area, one mile ahead. His throat was parched and aching, and besides he needed to call base.

"She always thought the best of people. Perhaps we protected her too much. I don't know. Do you have children?"

"No, I don't. Would you like a cup of coffee?"

"Oh, that would be lovely." Mrs. Fagunwa smiled at him. Oswalde signaled and pulled over to the inside lane. "Perhaps if ours hadn't been a mixed marriage. Do you think that could have been the problem? Made her run off like that?"

Hands behind his head, Rosper leaned back in his chair, watching the videos on the TV in a corner of the Incident Room. He was enjoying himself, tapping his foot to the reggae beat. The band was on a makeshift stage out in the street, bathed in sunshine, a real carnival atmosphere. Many of the performers wore colorful African costumes, as did the crowd, packed close to the stage, clapping their hands above their heads. Rosper hummed along and tapped his foot.

Haskons came over and leaned on his shoulder. "How's it going, Gary?"

Rosper looked up with a beaming grin. "I'm having a shanking good time, Skip."

"Are you indeed."

The incessant reggae beat was getting on people's nerves; some of them complained, so Rosper turned the sound low, but kept his eyes glued to the screen as one band followed another, studying the faces of the backup singers and the women in the crowd. His perseverance paid off. Leaping to his feet, he peered closely at the screen, and just at that moment the camera obligingly moved in on one of three girl backup singers to the left of the stage.

"Yes," Rosper breathed, and then louder, "Yes. Yes!"

It was she, no mistake, dressed in African costume, happily smiling in the sunshine, swaying and clapping, having one hell of a good time. So full of vibrant energy and youthful joy, her whole life ahead of her, a life that had less than twenty-four hours to run its course.

Standing in the busy hospital corridor, Tennison held one hand flat to her ear while she tried to concentrate on what Haskons was telling her over the phone. He was having to shout too, trying to be heard over the babble of noise as the men clustered around the TV. Not helped by the thumping reggae beat, which Rosper had turned back up.

"That's right," Haskons was saying. "And Bob Oswalde called in. He's got a positive ID. Joanne . . . Fagunwa?" Not sure of the pronunciation. "He's bringing Mum in now." He shouted away from the phone, "Look, turn it down, please."

"Brilliant," Tennison said. "All right, thanks, Richard."

She hung up and joined Muddyman, who was using his powers of persuasion on the Chinese female doctor, Dr. Lim, in the hope that they would be allowed in to see David Harvey. He wasn't having much success.

"He's a very ill man, you've seen that for yourself," Dr. Lim said. "You've also seen how he has great difficulty breathing when lying flat. He needs complete rest."

Tennison laid it on the line. "Dr. Lim. We have reason to believe that Mr. Harvey was involved in the murder of a seventeen-year-old girl. Now, I don't mind what conditions you make, but we have to talk to the man."

Dr. Lim didn't say anything, because the discussion was at an end; the look in the eyes of the Chief Inspector told her that.

Mrs. Fagunwa was turning over Joanne's things in interview room C3 off reception. She was bearing up well, Oswalde thought. Not a tear, not a quiver, just quietly picking things up—muddy Levi's jeans, wrinkled Adidas sneakers—until she came to the blue sweater, and her hand shook as she held it up.

"This I recognize. My one and only attempt at knitting . . ."

She crumpled it in her hand, head bowed low over the table, her shoulders heaving. Oswalde did what he could to comfort her, uttering some soothing platitudes, his arm around her.

"Why her?" Mrs. Fagunwa moaned, tears dripping off the end of her nose. "Why her . . . ?"

When she had dried her eyes, Oswalde asked if she would like a cup of tea in the cafeteria, but she said no, she'd prefer to start back. He walked her out to the car he had ordered, waiting in the parking lot.

Mrs. Fagunwa faced him. She had regained her composure, though her chin kept quivering. She said, "Thank you for your kindness. Do you think you'll find out how it happened? You know . . . find the person who did it?"

"I'm sure we will," Oswalde replied, and this wasn't a platitude.

"I wonder, this may seem . . ." She hesitated. "Could I buy the clay head when your inquiries are over? It's just . . . does that seem strange?" she asked anxiously, as if seeking his approval.

"No. I'll find out for you."

"Only there's nothing else is there?" Mrs. Fagunwa plucked at a loose thread on her scarf, her eyes a million light-years away. "Nothing to remind me of my baby."

Harvey was sleeping, breathing through his mouth. Tennison sat by the bed, back straight, hands clasped in her lap, watching him sleep and breathe, her eyes never leaving his face.

7

After seeing Mrs. Fagunwa off, Oswalde went back up to the Incident Room and sat at his desk. It was twenty past four. He should have been famished, having missed lunch, existing since breakfast on cups of coffee and a chocolate bar, but he wasn't hungry. It was the hours spent with the dead girl's mother, he reckoned, and seeing her grief, that had killed his appetite. Not good. After nearly nine years on the Force he ought to be able to shut his own emotions away, not get personally involved. You had to be cold and dispassionate or you couldn't do the job. Doctors and nurses and paramedics and firemen had to handle it, deal unflinchingly with things that would have turned most people's stomachs, and then go home and sleep nights. He wished he could do it too, learn the trick. Cultivate a heart like a swinging brick, as one of the tutors in training college was fond of saying.

Get your brain back on the case, Oswalde advised himself, that was the best way. He looked around. "Did the Allens have keys to Harvey's place?" he asked of no one in particular. "I suppose they must have. Where did Tony Allen go to school?"

Lillie chucked a file over. Oswalde spent a few minutes going through it until Rosper wandered over and interrupted him.

"Have you seen this?" Rosper asked, parking himself on the corner of the desk. He was holding a video tape.

"Is that the tape of Joanne?"

"You should watch it, Bob." Rosper made a flicking motion with his tongue. "I think I'm in love."

Haskons had sent over a PC to relieve her. He came in and removed his helmet, holding it under his arm.

Tennison stood up and stretched. She bent over to peer closely at Harvey, his face lined and gray in the shaded light above the bed. He was out for the count, asleep or unconscious, it was hard to tell. She put on her coat, tucked in her scarf, and picked up her briefcase.

"Call me if he comes around."

"I will."

Mr. Dugdale taught history, which possibly explained why he had such a good memory for dates. He wasn't bad on names either, and had no problem whatsoever with Tony Allen, as soon as Oswalde mentioned him.

"I was his adviser of year. I remember it very well." They were walking towards Dugdale's office, the corridor deserted except for a cleaner with a bucket and squeegee mop. Oswalde had turned up on the off chance that some of the teachers might have stayed behind to mark papers or something, and had struck lucky.

"He was a bright lad, had done very well in school, good results, going on to A levels, sights set on college." Dugdale shook his head of shaggy, graying hair, depositing more flakes of dandruff on the collar of his tweed jacket. "Then when he came back in September he'd changed. He was surly, introverted, a loner."

They arrived at his office and Dugdale went straight to the filing cabinet and started delving. Oswalde looked at the timetables pinned to the bulletin board, at the silver trophies gathering dust on the shelf next to the wilting potted plant, but he was taking in every word.

"I spoke to him, the headmistress spoke to him. I got Dad up here. Nothing seemed to work." Dugdale slipped on his glasses and opened the buff folder. "There, you see . . . September eighty-six. I'm usually right. Educational psychologist's report. Help yourself."

Oswalde scanned through it and made a few notes while Dugdale fussed around.

"I see Tony played in a band . . ."

"Did he? I didn't know that. We did our best but there was really no point in him staying on. The only person he seemed to relate to was his Sarah. He was gone by Christmas. I see him in the supermarket from time to time," Dugdale said absently, polishing his glasses with the end of his tie. "Waste really, he was a bright lad."

Tennison was on her knees, scrubbing the bathtub, when the intercom buzzer sounded. She dried her hands on her loose cotton top and went to answer it, frowning as she lifted the receiver from its wall cradle. She hadn't a clue who it could be; she wasn't expecting anyone.

"Hello?"

"Jane?"

A man's voice, deep and resonant, one she couldn't put a name to. "Who's this?" she asked guardedly.

"Bob Oswalde."

She leaned her outstretched arm against the door frame, wondering what the hell was going on, and more specifically just what game he thought he was playing.

"Jane . . . ? Look, I know this is a bit, er, unexpected . . . but I really do need to talk to you."

"Well, can't it wait? I'm waiting for a call from the hospital."

"No."

Sighing, she pressed the button to release the street door and dropped the receiver back in its cradle. She started towards the living room, only just realizing in the nick of time that she was practically on display, wearing only the loose top with nothing underneath. She nipped back into the bathroom and pulled on a floppy sweater, then walked through the living room, brushing her fingers through her hair.

Oswalde knocked and she opened the door. He was carrying a video tape. She said crisply, "This'd better be good," already walking off, leaving him to close the door.

She stood with her arms folded, watching him insert the video into the machine and turn on the set. He sat down on the sofa, still in his raincoat, and operated the remote. The image flickered and steadied: a reggae group blowing up a storm, a host of black faces smiling in the sunshine, women swaying to and fro in their multicolored robes and turbans.

Tennison knelt on the carpet in front of the TV, chin propped on her fist. "I've seen this," she told him in a voice flat as a pancake.

Oswalde suddenly leaned forward and touched the screen, indicating a tiny figure on the far right. "There."

"Your finger, very interesting."

"There's a better shot in a moment," he said, on the defensive, hurt by her flippancy. The camera cut to a close-up of the bass player. Oswalde pressed the pause button and jabbed at the screen. "There!"

Squinting, Tennison slowly leaned forward. "Is that Tony Allen?"

Oswalde gave a grim smile. "Tony Allen. He's concealed the fact that he was playing at the Sunsplash concert and evidently knew Joanne."

"Jesus!"

"The Allens had keys to the house. I've been to the school—"

"Yes. Okay." Tennison cut him short with a raised hand. She sat back on her heels. "Let's think this through. Just because he was on the bandstand with her doesn't mean—" Her beeper went off. "Shit, this could be it." She dived for her shoulder bag, found the beeper and killed it. "I'm waiting for

Harvey to come around," she told him, already reaching for the phone and dialing.

Oswalde discovered he'd been sitting on a plate of half-eaten congealed food. He removed it, mouth curling in distaste. "What's this?"

"Last night's dinner—one of those frozen chili con carne things."

"What have you got for tonight?"

Snapping her fingers impatiently, waiting for the connection to be made, she glanced over at him. "One of those frozen chili con carne things . . . DCI Tennison," she said into the phone.

Oswalde draped his raincoat over the back of the sofa, picked up the disgusting plate between outstretched fingertips, and wandered off with it. Tennison was momentarily distracted.

"Where d'you think you're going?" Then she was nodding, talking fast. "Right. Did she leave a number? A pay phone?" She scribbled it down. "Okay . . . right . . . thanks." She hung up and started to redial. Oswalde had disappeared. "It's not the hospital," she called out to him. "It's an informer of mine trying to get through to me."

"Right . . ." Oswalde's voice floated in from the kitchen.

"What are you up to?" she wondered aloud. "Rachel? It's me, Jane Tennison, darling. What've you got for me, darling?"

When she came through into the kitchen there was water on the boil, a package of pasta waiting to go in. Bob Oswalde had raided her meager shelves and come up with canned tomatoes, a can of tuna, one onion, and a few dried herbs, the last in the jar. He'd found a clean pan and had made a start on the sauce. Shirtsleeves rolled up, he was standing at the countertop, expertly chopping garlic and crushing it into a saucer.

Tennison leaned in the doorway, watching him. "What the hell do you think you're doing?"

Oswalde wiped his hands and opened the refrigerator door. He rooted inside and picked something up. "What's this?" he asked, holding up what appeared to be a moldy brown tennis ball.

"It's lettuce," Tennison said. "Well, it was once."

Oswalde chucked it in the trash, tut-tutting. "You need to eat some decent food. What was the call about? Anything interesting?"

"No, not really," she said, deciding to humor him, and besides, the smell was making her ravenous. "Apparently it seems the girl that was at Number fifteen sacked it in afterward and went legit. No one seems to know where she is now, but they're all sure she's not on the game."

"Right," Oswalde said, busy now forking tuna into a bowl. "I took a look at Tony's school record. Everything was fine until 1986. When Tony came back from the summer vacation, he was a different person." He glanced around at her, eyebrows raised. "Educational psychologist's report talks of depression, anxiety attacks, low self-esteem."

Tennison studied him for a moment, lips pursed. "What is it with you?"

"What?" Oswalde said, blinking.

"What are you trying to prove?"

He emptied the tomatoes and stirred them in with a wooden spoon. "Do you have any tomato puree?"

"No."

"How can I work in these conditions?" he complained to the cupboard door, his brow furrowed.

"It's as if you're taking some kind of test all the time . . ."

"You should know," he retorted, and that made her stand up straight. "I watched you on the course. You know they're all lined up, wanting to see you fall flat on your face. Thorndike, all the Senior Shits. You always want to be the best, come out on top."

This was straight from the shoulder, and Tennison wasn't sure she liked it. She certainly wasn't used to be spoken to so directly, least of all by a subordinate.

"I'm the same as you," Oswalde went on imperturbably. He tasted the sauce, added black pepper. "Which is why—when I calmed down and thought about it—I understood why you'd been treating me like the office boy."

He was one cool customer, had it all down.

"And why you've gone off and done a number on your own?" Tennison accused him sharply. He had the gall to laugh—a confident, unforced laugh at that. "I mean it, Bob. You are a member of a team," she reminded him.

"Am I?" Oswalde said, instantly serious, his stern dark eyes coming around to meet hers.

"Well," Tennison said, wishing to high heaven he wasn't such a big, broad-shouldered, handsome bastard. "From now on you are."

"Okay," Oswalde said, back to his cheery self. He tipped the pasta into the boiling water and ladled the tuna into the sauce. "I don't suppose you've got anything to drink?"

That she had, and she went off to open a bottle of Bulgarian red.

Tennison was confused, and annoyed with herself for letting him get the upper hand. Was Bob Oswalde taking liberties or just trying to be friendly? She knew she was paying the penalty for that one hour of passion in the hotel room. The demarcation lines had been blurred; no other officer under her command would have waltzed into her flat and made himself at home by cooking dinner, without so much as a by-your-leave. Damn Kernan for drafting him onto her team! It was all his bloody fault! But she was as angry with herself for getting herself into this pickle in the first place. Being ruled by her libido instead of her brain. Cunthead.

They ate off the coffee table in the living room. Tasting freshly prepared food and drinking three glasses of wine worked a minor miracle. It took the sting out of her anger and made her almost mellow. It even crossed her mind to wonder what might happen later, and instantly slammed the door shut on *that* speculation. Hadn't she made enough of a fool of herself already, for Chrissakes?

They didn't talk about work until the end of the meal, when Oswalde again brought up the subject of Tony Allen. He seemed to have almost a personal vendetta against the boy. Tennison was wary, not wanting to rush their fences. Oswalde couldn't see why. The fact that he'd known Joanne Fagunwa was sufficient in itself to have him picked up.

Tennison drained her glass and set it down. "Not yet."

"The boy was involved in that murder," Oswalde insisted. "I'm sure of it . . ."

"We have no evidence of that."

"You didn't see his response to the clay head," Oswalde told her bluntly.

"All we know is that he was on the same bandstand as Joanne—"

"So he's been lying."

"—and we'll question him about that at the right time."

"What does that mean?" asked Oswalde rudely, his face becoming stiff and surly. He detested all this fooling around. Get in there and get it done with.

"It means not yet." Tennison's voice was firm. Three glasses of wine didn't make her a pushover. She held up a finger. "I can crack Harvey. He holds the key—except the bastard might croak on us any minute. I'll talk to Tony when we've got more on him."

"More?" Oswalde was both pained and puzzled. "I thought you'd really go for this."

"Look, Bob, I don't want to argue about it." In other words, the Chief Inspector was saying, subject closed.

Oswalde got the message, or thought he did. He stared across at Jane Tennison, a muscle twitching in his cheek. "But the real point," he said stonily, "is that I shouldn't have come here, should I?"

"No, you shouldn't have—we said that in the hotel room. But that's not the point, actually. Look, all I'm trying to say is . . ."

"Don't bother."

Ten seconds later he was gone, raincoat over his shoulder, door slammed. Tennison piled the dirty dishes in the sink and went to bed.

• • •

The Incident Room was quiet when she arrived the next morning, shortly after eight twenty. She went to her office to catch up on some paperwork before the rush started.

WPC Havers eventually turned up, looking a bit worse for wear, and Tennison sent her off to the cafeteria to get a coffee and bring one back for her. She was sipping this and fighting the desperate urge for a cigarette when word came from the hospital. Tennison slurped the rest of her coffee, spilt some on her best chiffon blouse, and made the air blue and Maureen Havers's ears turn red as she grabbed her coat from the coatrack and hurried out.

"Hello, Guv," she greeted Kernan, who was about to enter his office, and kept on going.

"Yes, it went very well since you ask."

Tennison halted. "Sorry?"

"My interview."

"Oh good . . . right . . ."

"Any news on Harvey?"

"He's regained consciousness. I'm going down there to see him right now."

Kernan nodded, gave her a look. "Well, gently does it, Jane."

"Yes, I . . ."

"Get him everything he wants—lawyers, nurses, doctors, geisha girls—anything. Just so long as his lawyer can't say you got a statement from him unfairly."

Tennison tightened her belt, knuckles showing white. "Of course." What did he think her intention was—throttle the truth out of a dying man?

Lillie emerged from the Incident Room, looking for her. "Excuse me, Guv. Apparently Harvey's wife died in October eighty-five. Not August."

"So his sister's been telling fibs."

"So it would seem."

"Well, let's see what Harvey's got to say about that."

Lillie went off, and Tennison was about to leave, when Kernan said, apropos of nothing, "By-election today."

Then she twigged it. Jonathan Phelps, Labour's firebrand, was up for election. There was a chance, a slim chance, that he might get in, and if he did there could be one or two repercussions. Phelps was riding on the ticket of community policing in black areas, on newsworthy items such as the case of Derrick Cameron. And now Tennison was investigating a murder in the Honeyford Road area involving a girl of black-white parentage. A highly-sensitive, highly-potent mixture. Like most policemen, Kernan was a staunch Tory, and the last thing he desired was to give the opposition the ammunition to fire a broadside.

With a ghost of a smile, Tennison said, "Well, why aren't you wearing your blue rosette?"

It wasn't a joke to Kernan; it was deadly serious.

"Senior policemen are politicians first and foremost, Jane. Remember that if you're up for Super."

It was bad enough that he believed it, Tennison thought, even worse to realize that he was right.

The teenager in the black leather jacket, baseball cap worn back to front, stood at the counter of Esme's cafe, dithering. He pointed to a large bowl of mashed yams with cinnamon and nutmeg, topped with grated orange rind.

"How much is that?"

"One seventy-five," Esme said.

"How much?" the boy said, goggling.

Esme switched her attention to the tall, good-looking man waiting patiently to be served. From her bright smile and cheerful, "Yes, dear?" Oswalde knew that she hadn't recognized him.

"Let me have a medium fried chicken, rice, and peas."

While she dished it up, the boy in the baseball cap continued moaning. He obviously had a sweet tooth, because he next pointed to a portion of plantain fritters, fried in butter and apple sauce. "How much is that?"

"Seventy-five pee."

"You're jokin', man . . . yeah, all right, then."

Esme served him and he slouched off, the flaps of his sneakers protruding like white tongues. She handed Oswalde his meal in a polystyrene tray and gave him change from a fiver. Oswalde ate it at the counter, watching Esme ice a large cake; Tony's wedding cake, Oswalde thought, the wedding a week from Saturday.

"How is it?" Esme asked him.

"Very good. It's been a long time."

"Your mother doesn't cook for you?"

"No."

She flashed him her bright smile. "Then you come to Esme's. I'll cook for you."

Oswalde moved along the counter, nearer to where she was working. "You don't recognize me, Esme?" She straightened up, frowning, a slight shake of the head. "I'm a police officer. I'm investigating the murder of Joanne Fagunwa. That was her name, Esme. The girl who was buried in Harvey's garden . . ."

Esme stared at him, surprise and shock mingled on her face. But she was in for an even bigger shock when Oswalde said softly, "Did you know that she was a member of Tony's band? That she was with Tony on the day she died?"

"No," Esme said in a whisper. No longer smiling, her eyes were scared now.

Oswalde pushed the chicken aside, leaning his elbows on the counter. "Are you sure Tony was there that night when you arrived home?"

"Yes. I'm sure."

"He couldn't have been with Joanne?"

"No."

Oswalde was convinced she was telling the truth—as much of the truth as she knew, anyway. He said, "Why did you think he changed so much that summer, Esme? He's never been the same since, has he? What happened to change him like that?"

She didn't answer, though from her expression Oswalde knew he had scored a bull's-eye.

Muddyman was waiting for her outside Harvey's room. "Are we in?" Tennison asked tersely.

"Dr. Lim is still a bit jumpy, but yeah, I think so."

At that moment Dr. Lim arrived. As they were about to enter, she held up a cautioning hand. "I don't want him upset. Any extra pressure on his heart could be fatal."

No more fatal than what happened to Joanne Fagunwa, Tennison reckoned, though she merely nodded, following the small, round-shouldered doctor inside.

Harvey's breathing filled the room. He was looking up at the ceiling with his dull, bleary eyes. Tennison eased the chair up to the bed and leaned over, her mouth close to his ear. She held his hand.

"Don't you think it'd be a good idea to talk to me, David?" she said very softly. "Get it off your chest?"

Harvey's tongue came out to lick his dry lips. He stared straight up, his voice a horrible croak. "What . . . ?"

"David, we know that Joanne—that was her name—we found that Joanne was killed in your home. A fragment of her tooth was found inside the house."

Harvey swallowed. "Doesn't mean I killed her," he gasped.

Tennison went on steadily, "Your wife didn't die in August, did she, David? Jeanie died in October 1985. What's the point of lying, David? Carrying all that guilt?" From the corner of her eye she saw a blur of white coat as Dr. Lim, concerned for her patient, moved nearer, but Tennison kept on.

"You're a very ill man. If you do tell me, nothing will happen to you—it'll never come to that. We'll be able to clear all this up and . . ." She paused. "Most important of all, you'll feel so much better."

Harvey closed his eyes and then opened them again, as if he might be thinking about it. Tennison waited, the hoarse, ragged breathing loud in her ears, the smell of it foul in her nostrils.

Oswalde stalked his prey, biding his time until Tony Allen had moved on from chatting to one of the checkout girls, and then he closed in behind him, reaching inside his jacket pocket for the color photograph of Joanne Fagunwa.

"Hello, Tony."

Tony Allen jumped. "Sorry?"

"You don't remember me? Detective Sergeant Oswalde. I was just doing a bit of shopping." Tony Allen retreated a pace as Oswalde loomed over him. "While I'm here, perhaps you could have a look at this. Recognize her?"

Tony barely glanced at the photograph. "Why don't you people leave me alone?" he said, a tremor in his voice.

"Because you're telling us lies. You knew Joanne."

"No . . ."

"You were both at the Sunsplash together. Better than that," Oswalde said, quiet and lethal, "you played in the same band."

Tony's mouth dropped open. He wasn't expecting that. Another bull's-eye.

"Remember her African costume . . . her bracelets?"

"I don't know what you're talking about."

"Oh, yes, you do."

"I don't." Tony backed into a freezer cabinet. "*I don't.*"

Oswalde watched him scoot off. There was no need to pursue him. Tony Allen wasn't going anywhere.

"I'm a Catholic, too, David, and it's been a long time since my last confession, but one thing I do remember is that feeling of relief. That weight being lifted off your shoulders." Harvey's drab eyes stared up, and Tennison wasn't sure how much of this was getting through. But she kept at it, soft and remorseless.

"I think we all want to have faith in something, don't we? We'd like to think we can repent and it'll be all right . . . if only we could turn the clock back, make it all right. You're dying, David. Best get it off your chest. Tell me what happened, David. No more lies. It's too late for lies."

Harvey blinked, and tears ran down from the corners of his eyes into his gray hair. Tennison leaned nearer, stroking his hand, her voice like velvet.

"You can talk to me . . ."

"Can I?" Harvey croaked.

"Of course you can. You can have a doctor present, a lawyer, your sister, Jason, anyone."

Harvey's chin quivered. He said huskily, "You know, I'm only fifty-five years old. It's a fucking joke."

"I'm sure the doctors will do all they can," Tennison said.

"I'm so frightened," Harvey said. His face suddenly crumpled, and he wept.

The streetlights were just flickering into life as Tony Allen came out of the supermarket and walked to his car. He unlocked the door and was about to climb in when he noticed a tall figure leaning against the hood of a black Ford Sierra three cars away.

"Yo, Tony," Oswalde greeted him. "All right?"

Fists bunched, Tony stormed around his car and went up to him. "What's wrong with you? Why're you doing this to me?"

Oswalde spread his hands, eyebrows raised. "Hey, doin' what, man? I've been shopping, that's all . . ."

"Leave me alone," Tony ground out, his eyes bulging furiously. *"Just leave me alone!"*

Oswalde grinned at him. Tony swung around and marched back to his car. In his haste and rage he nearly smashed into the car behind by going into reverse, then shot out across the parking lot and into the street. All the way home he kept glancing in his rearview mirror, and every time he looked the black Sierra was there, openly, blatantly, following him.

Tony gripped the wheel so tightly his arms ached. Over and over, almost choking on the words, he kept repeating, "Leave me alone, leave me alone, leave me alone . . ."

Tennison and Muddyman were having a quiet confab outside Harvey's room when his nephew arrived. The young, fair-haired man came up to them, slightly out of breath, and asked straight out, "How is he?"

"He's a little better," Tennison replied, aware that she was being economical with the truth. Looking into the pale blue eyes, and seeing in them a family resemblance, she said quietly, "Jason, your uncle wants to talk to me."

"Yeah, so I was told."

"And he's asked for you to be there."

Jason nodded. "Right."

"But I would just ask for you to remain quiet, not to interrupt while I'm talking to him."

"Right," Jason said again, as if mentally preparing himself for an ordeal, which indeed it would be.

Tennison glanced at Muddyman and gave a slight nod. He opened the door and the three of them went in.

Oswalde rang the bell of the second-floor flat. From within he heard the murmur of voices, and a moment later the door was opened by Esta, Tony's wife-to-be. She glared up at him, chewing her lip.

"Is Tony in?"

Before she could answer, Tony appeared in the narrow hallway. He grabbed the edge of the door. "You know I am, you followed me home."

"Can I come in, Tony?"

"No, you can't."

"I'd like to ask you a few questions," Oswalde said.

"You heard him, he said no," Esta snapped.

Tony pointed a finger, which was quivering with pent-up rage. He said hoarsely, "I don't have to answer your questions."

"Who told you that?" Oswalde said. His face wore a twisted grin. "Sarah the Law Student?"

Cleo, dressed in her pajamas, holding a teddy bear by its ears, was standing in the living room doorway. Esta waved to her distractedly. "Go back inside, love . . ."

Pumping himself up, convinced he was in the right, Tony was jabbing his finger in Oswalde's chest. "She says you either arrest me or stop harassing me."

That did it. If Oswalde's mind hadn't been made up already, that made it up for him. He lunged forward and grabbed Tony's arm, dragging him through the door onto the landing. "Tony Allen, I am arresting you for the murder of Joanne Fagunwa."

"No!" Esta shouted. But she was too late. Oswalde had Tony in an armlock and was frog-marching him to the stairs.

"You can't . . ." Esta wailed. "Where are you . . ."

Bent double, Tony yelled back, "Esta, phone my dad . . . phone my dad!"

Oswalde bundled him down the stairs. Seeing her father snatched away in front of her eyes, Cleo had burst into tears; but the child's crying didn't deter DS Oswalde, who knew what had to be done, and did it.

Harvey had been miked up. Tennison sat close to the bed, leaning over, while Muddyman kept an eye on the tape recorder's winking red light. Jason stood behind Muddyman, his face and cap of blond hair a shadowy blur.

"Do you wish to consult an attorney or have an attorney present during the interview?"

"No." The lost, bleary eyes stared up at the ceiling. "Water."

Tennison poured water into a glass and helped him to a couple of sips. Her entire job, it seemed, consisted of waiting, and she waited now, very patiently, for Harvey to compose himself.

Custody Sergeant Calder and an Asian PC were having one hell of a struggle, trying to get Tony Allen from the charge room into the cells. The boy was close to hysteria, his eyes wide and terrified in his sweating face. He was babbling, "No, don't lock me up, don't lock me up, please don't lock me up . . ."

Eventually, after much straining and heaving, they managed to get him inside cell 7 and slammed the door. Calder walked back to the charge room, wiping his bald head, and tugging his uniform straight. He was an experienced officer and he didn't like the look of it; the kid was half-demented, and even now his moaning voice echoed down the corridor, pleading, "Let me out . . . don't leave me alone, please . . . please let me out!"

Calder entered the charge room, shaking his head worriedly. "I'd better get the doctor to take a look at him. I don't think he's fit to be detained."

Oswalde thought this was overdoing it. "He's all right," he said dismissively. "Just let him stew for a bit . . ."

"Look, I'm the Custody Sergeant," Calder blazed at him. "Don't try to tell me my job. Right?"

Oswalde gave him a look. Then he shrugged and went out. Calder reached for the phone but he didn't pick it up. He stood there for a moment, undecided, cracking his knuckles, and then barked, "Yes?" at the Asian PC, who was holding out a docket to be signed. Calder scrawled his signature, which reminded him he had a mountain of paperwork to process.

He made a noise that was half snort, half sigh. That's all they were these days, a legion of bloody pencil pushers.

When he was ready, she began:

"You do not have to say anything unless you wish to do so, but what you say may be given in evidence. Do you understand, David?"

"Yes." His breathing rasped in his throat. Slowly he turned his head on the pillow and looked straight at her.

8

Tennison had to steel herself not to show repugnance as his breath wafted over her. It seemed to her she had been sitting by his bedside for an eternity, breathing in the foul miasma of death. She herself felt soiled by it, as if it had entered her pores, and she had to use every ounce of willpower to repress the shudder at the touch of his cold, damp hand.

Her face betrayed none of this. And her voice stayed quiet and calm, almost soothing.

"All right, David . . . let me take you back to what you said originally. That you were with your sister in Margate on Sunday and Monday, and not at Honeyford Road."

"Lies," Harvey said drably. "I didn't stay the night. I came back Sunday. Sunday afternoon. Not Monday like I said."

"So—did you ask Eileen to provide you with an alibi?"

Harvey shook his head weakly. "No. She knows nothing of this . . ."

Tennison frowned. "But she must, David, because she confirmed your story. She said that weekend was the anniversary of your wife's death. It wasn't. She said you spent it with her. You didn't."

"I don't want my sister dragged into this," Harvey insisted, his voice thickening. He was staring at Tennison, blinking rapidly.

"I'm afraid she already is, David . . ."

"Leave her out of it." Suddenly angry, he levered himself up on one elbow, the effort making him gasp. His eyes were wild, rolling. "I'll tell you nothing if you drag her into it!"

Tennison put her hand on his shoulder, and he slowly subsided, flecks of spittle on his mustache. He lay flat, his chest heaving. The vehemence of his reaction puzzled her. She had seen real fear in his eyes . . . but fear of what? Involving his sister? His emotion had been too fierce and panic-stricken for that alone, Tennison thought. Unless he was trying to shield Eileen, divert suspicion from her possible complicity in what had taken place that weekend.

Harvey went on, almost in a drone, as if talking to himself. "I hated it down there anyway. Godforsaken cold bastard of a place. Thought I might as well go home—do something useful, get some work done in the garden . . ."

"So what time did you get back to London?" Tennison asked.

"About five. I did some more work, then I went inside. I was watching the TV in the front room when I saw her."

Tennison leaned forward, her eyes narrowing a fraction. "Who did you see, David?"

"I saw the girl. Joanne." Harvey stared into the shadows, as if seeing her now. "She was standing at a bus stop. Waiting for a bus that didn't run on a Sunday."

"What time was this?"

"'Bout half past eight, nine. It was just getting dark. I watched her . . ." His voice took on a dreamy, faraway tone. "She stood with one leg behind the other, sort of swinging herself. I thought I'd better tell her. I went out to her. I told her the bus didn't run. I said she should phone for a taxi. Told her she could use my phone.

He paused, his dry lips parted. "She came into the house," he said in his drab, dreamy voice, and then, as if the recollection had exhausted him, he closed his eyes.

DI Burkin wasn't at all happy about this. Calder, the Custody Sergeant, had already voiced his doubts to him, and Burkin could see why. The kid was practically gibbering with fear. Sweat was trickling from the roots of his short black hair, making his face a shiny, petrified mask. Oswalde didn't seem to notice—or if he did, didn't appear to care.

Arms folded, Burkin leaned against the wall of the interview room, watching with hooded eyes as Oswalde set up the tape recorder. He didn't know what grounds Oswalde had for arresting Tony Allen, but they'd better be bloody good, or there'd be hell to pay.

Oswalde placed the mike on the table in front of Tony Allen, who stared at it like a rabbit hypnotized by a snake. Oswalde stretched out and pressed the record button. Still standing, he began: "This interview is being tape recorded. I am Detective Sergeant Robert Oswalde, attached to Southampton Row. The other officer present is . . ."

"Detective Inspector Frank Burkin," Burkin said.

Oswalde sat down opposite Tony Allen. "You are?"

Nothing. Not a flicker. The young man looked to be in some sort of trance. Oswalde leaned his elbows on the table and laced his fingers together. "State your full name and date of birth."

Tony's lips moved. In a mumble that was almost inaudible, he said, "Anthony Allen. Fifth of May . . ."

"Louder for the tape, please."

The command galvanized Tony into life. His head came up, eyes bulging, and he started gabbling like somebody on speed, *"Anthony Allen. Anthony Allen. Fifth of May. Nineteen sixty-nine. Nineteen sixty . . ."*

Burkin gloomily rolled his eyes towards the ceiling. A jungle bunny off his trolley; that's all they fucking needed.

Vernon Allen and his wife had been in the waiting room over an hour. Esme was frantic, out of her mind with worry, and it was all he could do to pacify her. The call from Esta, telling them that Tony had been arrested, had left them both shocked and scared. Vernon kept telling himself that it was a mistake, it would soon be straightened out, but as the minutes dragged by and they were told nothing, a hollow feeling of sick apprehension rose up inside, nearly choking him. But he had to keep a grip, not let it show, otherwise Esme would go completely to pieces.

She was back on her feet again, unable to sit still for more than a minute. The Asian PC behind the reception desk could only shrug and offer a bland, "I'm sorry," as Esme leaned against the counter, fists clenched, her eyes large and moist.

"We must be allowed to see our son!" she demanded for the umpteenth time.

"The officer in charge will be out to see you shortly, madam."

Esme turned away, shaking her head, not knowing where to put herself. In a small, lost voice she said faintly, "I don't believe this is happening . . ."

"Well it is," Vernon said. He sighed and gave a weary gesture. "Now come and sit down."

"The officer won't be long," the PC assured them.

Esme slumped down on the bench beside her husband. What was happening to her boy, her Tony? Why wouldn't they let them see him? What were they doing to him in there?

"I tried to touch her," Harvey said, his voice harsh and rasping. "Touch her tits."

He returned Tennison's calm gaze with a challenging stare, as if hoping she might be offended by his crudity. But he was disappointed; she wasn't.

"Do you remember what she was wearing, David?" Tennison asked in the same quiet, even tone.

"No."

"Was she wearing a bra?"

"I don't think so, no," Harvey said after a slight hesitation.

Tennison paused a moment to consider this before asking, "Then what happened?"

Harvey turned his head away. Under the shaded light on the wall above the bed his lined face and sunken cheeks had the appearance of a death's-head. "I hit her," he said.

He was going to break him; it was just a matter of going at him, unrelentingly, until he tripped himself up. But it wasn't quite working out that way. The more Oswalde pressed him, the angrier and more defiant Tony became. Burkin was surprised by the guy's guts. He'd have laid odds that Tony Allen was the type to crumple as soon as the heat was turned on. It gave him a sly sense of amusement to watch Oswalde banging away and getting nowhere fast. Teach the cocky bastard a lesson.

"What did I just say?" Tony threw up his hands. ". . . I admit it, I admit I knew her!"

"She was your girlfriend, Tony," Oswalde repeated for the third time, making it sound like a statement of established fact.

"No, she wasn't. I told you. She was going out with the lead singer. I asked her out but she said no—"

Oswalde pounced. "So how come she ended up back at Honeyford Road with you?"

Tony closed his eyes and rested his forehead in the palm of his hand. He sighed and said wearily, "I had some tapes there she wanted. Songs for her to learn." He looked up at the man sitting opposite him, as taut and intense as a coiled spring. "She came in after my dad went to work. Stayed for an hour or so, that's all."

"And then you took her into Harvey's house."

"No."

"Because you knew he was away for the weekend. Used your father's keys and went next door with her." More statements of fact, according to Oswalde. "What happened then, Tony?"

Tony Allen shook his head. He went on shaking it as he said, slowly and distinctly, "I—didn't—kill—her."

Oswalde knew in his bones that the boy was lying through his teeth, but Burkin wasn't so sure.

"I tied her up. Hands behind her back."

"What with?"

"I don't remember. I gagged her. Had sex with her. Afterwards I left her lying there."

"Where was this?"

Harvey frowned. "What do you mean?"

"Which room were you in?"

"The kitchen." His eyelids flickered. "A belt. I tied her with my belt . . ."

Without moving her head, Tennison turned her eyes to meet Muddyman's. He was leaning forward, elbows on his knees, a frown of concentration on his face. Behind him, in the darkened corner of the room, Jason was nothing more than a vague blur, his black T-shirt and dark Windbreaker merging into the background. Tennison turned her attention back to Harvey, to the drab, droning voice.

". . . I left her lying there. Went and watched the TV. I don't know why. It was like a dream. As if it hadn't happened."

Tennison pursed her lips, remained silent.

Tony twisted his lips in disgust. "What kind of a brother are you?" he demanded contemptuously. "To say things like that to me?"

"I'm not your brother, I'm a police officer," Oswalde said stolidly. The guy was trying to play the black power card, and he wasn't having any. Burkin would just love that, all dem black folks jess one big happy family crap. Well stuff that.

With utter loathing in his voice, Tony practically spat in his face, "Because you want to be white! You hate your black brothers and sisters. You're *black!*"

Oswalde was getting more irritated by the second. But he wasn't going to be drawn down that road. No chance. To show how calm he was, unaffected by Tony's outburst, he studied his fingernails and asked casually, "Why did you give up playing the bass after that concert, Tony?"

"You're a sellout, you wouldn't understand."

"Try me."

Tony's whole face seemed to be moving, as if he was trying to say something he didn't know how to express. There was a strange light in his eyes. Then it burst out of him in a flood.

"Bass notes are the pulse, they come up at you through the soles of your feet . . . they sound inside you, here. They beat with your heart. From beneath. A heartbeat. From beneath the earth." He was like a mechanical doll, the words jerking out of him. His eyes suddenly focused on Oswalde, his voice filled with scathing contempt. "You see, you don't understand. I couldn't play anymore . . . how could I play anymore?" Head straining forward, he yelled in Oswalde's impassive face, "*Why ask questions when you don't understand?*"

Burkin was staring at Tony, fascinated. Maybe Oswalde didn't understand, but he sure did; the kid was a loony tune. End of story.

The feel of the clammy hand clutching hers made Tennison feel nauseous. She swallowed hard, telling herself it would soon be over. Harvey was tiring fast, his voice becoming weaker, the gasping pauses more prolonged; but she nearly had it all now, down on tape, in his own words. The repulsion she felt was a small price to pay.

". . . she must have choked on the gag. There was vomit all around her mouth, her nose . . . I didn't mean to kill her."

The door opened and a nurse came in bearing a small tray. Standing at the foot of the bed, she said quietly. "I must give Mr. Harvey his medication."

Tennison nodded. She indicated to Muddyman and Jason that they should leave, then turned back to Harvey.

"I'll be back soon, David." For the benefit of the tape, she said, "I am concluding this interview. The time is eight-ten."

Muddyman was standing with Jason in the corridor. The young man's hands hung limply by his sides, and the ordeal he was going through showed plainly on his face.

Tennison squeezed his shoulder. "I'm sorry, this must be awful for you."

Jason was staring at the floor, ashen to the lips. "I've known him all my life," he said in a stunned whisper. "And I don't . . . I don't know him at all."

"Will you be all right to go back in?" Tennison asked gently, and received a brief nod.

Muddyman stirred himself. "I'll get us a coffee," he said, and went off to find a machine.

Tennison felt soiled and grubby. What she really wanted was a hot cleansing shower and a large brandy. Wash away the stink from her body and deaden the memory of that gaunt, wasted face gasping out its last confession.

"If I had buried her," Tony Allen told Oswalde, his eyes dangerously bright, "I'd have buried her so deep you'd never have found her again. She'd never have come back . . ."

"Has she come back?" Oswalde asked, watching him closely.

Tony gave a pitying half-smile, the smile of someone trying to communicate an ultimate truth to an ignoramus. "She's inside you," he hissed. "I can see her looking at me. Looking at me through your eyes. Reaching out to me." He tapped his chest. "I'm her friend. She wants to get away from you. You're a coffin. You suffocate her. *You're her coffin.* Your eyes are little windows. I can see inside you. Through your eyes. See Joanne. She hates you . . ."

He wiped his mouth with the back of his hand. When it came away he was grinning at Oswalde with a strange mixture of triumph and the deepest loathing.

Harvey seemed to have regained a little strength. The pill, or injection—whatever it was—had brought him back into the world, banished for a short while the shades closing in around him.

Tennison pressed on, anxious to get it over and done with. "What did you do with Joanne's body?"

"I kept it in the cupboard under the stairs. Till the following night. I dug a hole. I put the earth in bags. I had a lot of plastic sheeting. I wrapped her in the sheeting." His voice broke. He stared sightlessly upwards. "Buried her."

Muddyman leaned forward into Tennison's eye line, stroking his chin. She nodded slowly. Harvey was coming out with crucial details—the belt, the plastic sheeting—that hadn't been released to the media. Harvey couldn't possibly have known about them unless he was personally involved with the disposal of Joanne's body. It was the kind of clinching evidence they required to make the case stand up in court.

She was about to ask a further question when Harvey suddenly, and with great effort, raised himself up. His eyes probed the darkness, his slack mouth working desperately.

"I'm sorry, Jason, I'm sorry you have to hear all this. I just needed you to be here . . ." Exhausted, he fell back, and Tennison waited for calm.

"Did you bury anything else with her, David?"

"Yes."

"What?"

"A plastic bag."

That hadn't been mentioned in the press either.

"What did it contain?"

Tennison had to crane forward to catch his mumbled. "I don't know," and it seemed to her that, having confessed to the murder, he was losing interest in the more mundane details of the crime.

Again she glanced towards Muddyman, who was looking like the cat that got the cream. Harvey was a goner, in more senses than one. He'd given them chapter and bloody verse on the whole sordid saga, committed it to tape, with three witnesses in attendance. Game, set, and match.

Harvey continued to mumble. Tennison strained to hear, hoping the tape was picking it up.

". . . I banged the earth flat. Laid the rest of the slabs, cemented them in. There was a smell. The darkie next door complained. I told him it was . . . the drains . . ."

His eyes closed.

The wheezing breath fluttered from his lips, emphasizing the silence.

Tennison straightened her shoulders, sat back in her chair. "Thank you, David," she said, and indicated to Muddyman that he could turn off the machine. Thank God that was over. Her flesh crawled at the memory of his clammy grip.

They went out into the corridor. Muddyman sealed the tape and asked Jason to countersign and date it. The young man did so, the pen shaking in his hand. He was still deathly pale, and looked sick to his stomach.

"Would you like a car to take you home?" Tennison asked, concerned about him.

"It's all right, thanks." He raised his head and took a deep breath. "I'd rather walk."

They watched him trail off down the corridor, looking lost and aimless, but he turned the corner heading for reception, so that seemed okay. Muddyman stuffed the tape in his raincoat pocket and turned to Tennison with a fat grin.

"Well done! Nailed the bastard's balls to the floor."

"You think so?"

Muddyman lit up and hungrily sucked in smoke. "Know so."

Tennison nodded, as if in agreement. She'd have given a month's pay for Muddyman's complete, unwavering certainty, but she couldn't make it jell. Something nagged at her. Some of the details Harvey had spilled she kept returning to, worrying at like a loose tooth.

But it had been a long, grueling pig of a day and she was exhausted. And somehow depressed on top of it. All her mind could focus on right this minute were the hot shower and the large brandy.

As they went down the stairs to the parking lot, Tennison said dully, "God, hospitals depress me."

Having finally got someone to babysit for her, Esta flew down to Southampton Row and barged into the waiting room. "Have you seen him?" she asked them, huddled there on the bench. *"Have you seen him?"*

Esme shook her head tearfully. "They won't . . . let me see my boy," she wailed. "My Tony . . ."

Esta stormed up to the counter. She banged on it with both fists. Through the glass panel she could see two or three uniformed officers sitting at desks in the back room. Beating on the counter, she yelled at them, "I want to see somebody now! I want to see the person in charge! Come here—where is he!"

Vernon waved to her. "They say somebody is just coming."

Esta banged again, harder, louder.

"Come and sit down," Vernon pleaded. "Take it easy . . ."

Esta ignored him. She had no intention of taking it easy.

Tony was leaning his elbows on the table, his head in his hands. His voice was muffled.

"I'm a black bastard. I deserve all I get . . . I'm a black bastard, I deserve all I get . . ."

Standing opposite him, Oswalde thumped the table. "Tony, just stop it, man!"

"I'm a black bastard, I deserve all I get . . . I'm a black bastard, I deserve all I get . . ."

"Tony, stop it! Just stop it, man . . ."

"That's enough," Burkin said curtly. He strode to the door. "Can I have a word with you, Sergeant Oswalde?"

"In a minute."

"Now, Sergeant Oswalde!" Burkin went out.

Oswalde looked at his watch. "I'm concluding this interview at eleven-twenty-five P.M." He switched off the machine and followed Burkin out.

Tony's hands came away from his face and clenched into fists.

"No, don't leave me alone! *Don't leave me alone in here!*"

In the corridor Burkin faced Oswalde. He had to raise his voice to be heard above Tony Allen's terrified, near-hysterical cries.

"What's all this about?"

"What?" Oswalde said. He was an inch or two taller than DI Burkin, and he stared into his eyes, knowing the man for the racist he was.

Burkin held up a warning finger. "I don't know what's going on between you two . . ."

"What do you mean?"

"What do I mean?" Burkin's eyes bulged. He jerked his thumb at the pitiful, wavering sobs coming from the room—"*Don't leave me alone . . . please don't leave me alone, please . . .*"

"He's off his head!"

Oswalde looked down his nose at Burkin with narrowed eyes. "That's your considered psychological opinion, is it?" he sneered.

"You're one arrogant bastard, do you know that?"

Oswalde dropped his voice to a low growl. "Don't look at me like that, Frank. You've been wanting to have a go at me ever since I arrived at this poxy station." He squared up, flexing his shoulders. "Well, go on then," he challenged.

Eyeball to eyeball, the two men glowered at one another. Both well over six feet tall, both strongly built, both fired up with mutual hatred:

Burkin the area boxing champion, Oswalde top of his class in unarmed combat, they could have knocked seven kinds of shit out of one another. Both of them on a hair trigger, ready and raring to have a go.

"What the hell's going on?" Alerted by Tony's racket, Custody Sergeant Calder bustled into the corridor from the charge room, on his way to investigate.

"Butt out, Mike," Oswalde said, tight lipped.

Calder sized up the situation and acted at once to defuse it. He pushed the two men apart. "I'm in charge of this area. Prisoners are my responsibility, right?"

Burkin turned his fury on him. "So where's his lawyer?" he demanded.

"He said he didn't want one."

"Look," Burkin exploded, pointing his finger. "That boy's climbing the fucking walls in there! Has he been seen by the doc?"

"Not yet," Calder said defensively. He cleared his throat. "It's all under control . . ."

Burkin shot a fierce look at Oswalde. He said disparagingly, "The arresting officer hasn't even got credible evidence."

Calder was nettled. "Look, don't tell me my job—"

"How do you know, anyway?" Oswalde said, glaring at Burkin.

"You've got nothing from him that would stick in court. He should go back into the cells until the boss has been informed."

Calder tried to peer past them to the half-open door. "Have you left him alone in there?"

Oswalde was really riled up now. He knew what Burkin's game was, and he told him straight. "Hands off, Frank, this is my kill. You're just pissed off because the token black is going to have this case signed, sealed, and on the guv'nor's desk by morning!"

Burkin said quietly, "Bollocks you are." And went striding off down the corridor to phone Tennison.

Oswalde returned to the interview room and slammed the door.

Calder, gnawing his thumbnail, was left standing. Knowing he should have done as Burkin said and called the doc. He'd better do it. Right now.

Tennison, freshly-showered and talced, wearing silk pajamas, was on her way to bed when the phone rang. Passing by the little table, through sheer force of habit, she reached out to answer it. Her hand hovered, and then the answering machine clicked on. That's what answering machines were for, she reminded herself. For when you were out or too bloody tired or not in the mood to answer it. Score two out of three.

A voice was burbling. She turned the sound right down, switched off the lamp, and went through into the bedroom, shutting the door firmly behind her.

Whatever anger, whatever defiance, had been in Tony, it had left him as swiftly as the air leaves a punctured balloon. He sat with head bowed, shoulders hunched, his hands resting limply in his lap. Tears rolled down his cheeks. He made hardly any sound, just sat there weeping softly. Behind him, Oswalde paced, turned about, paced again, turned about. Burkin had got through to him, right to the quick. He'd nearly lost his temper, blown it completely. When above everything else he prided himself on his control, on not giving in to provocation. *That* close, and saved by the bell—or rather by Calder.

Oswalde saw it all too clearly. Burkin couldn't stomach an outside officer—a black one at that—coming in and solving the case and taking the credit. That's what this was about. That's why he'd blown a fuse. Well, sunshine, you were going to have to like it or lump it, Oswalde thought with grim satisfaction. He alone had collared Tony Allen and he intended to sweat it out of him. He didn't care if it took all night. From the minute he saw Tony's reaction to the clay head, he knew the boy was implicated in the girl's murder. All he had to do now was prove it.

Oswalde gripped the back of the chair and leaned over him.

"This is a waste of time. You're just wasting my time. Come on, Tony. You're as guilty as hell. I've known it from the first time I saw you." He dug his fingers into Tony's hunched shoulder and hauled him back. "Your guilty secret is written all over your face."

Tony nodded feebly, his cheeks wet with tears. "I'm guilty . . ."

Oswalde quickly moved around and bent down, his face close to the boy's. "Then tell me what happened that night."

"We're all guilty . . ." Tony opened his mouth wide, fighting for breath. He clutched his throat. "I'm choking . . ."

"No, you're not."

"I'm choking," he gasped, clawing at his open-necked shirt with both hands.

"No, you're *not*," Oswalde barked at him. He turned away, fists clenching with frustration as Tony's face crumpled, tears squeezing out from under his eyelids. This was bloody hopeless. They'd been here for hours and he was getting nowhere. He had to make the boy crack. *Had* to.

He shook his head in disgust. "All you've done is cry like a baby. Well, I'm sick of listening to you. You're pathetic. A bloody mummy's boy. Come on." Oswalde waggled his thumb. "You're going back in the cells."

"No . . . I can't breathe in there," Tony pleaded, gazing up at Oswalde with his pitiful, tear-streaked face. "Don't please . . ."

He half-rose out of the chair, tugging at Oswalde's sleeve. Oswalde shook him off. "Fuck you. You tell me how Joanne met her death or you go back in the bin and you *sweat*."

Tony's head wobbled. "No . . . no . . ."

Enough was enough. Oswalde turned away. He didn't see the change come over Tony's face. The eyes go suddenly wide and mad. The lips draw back in a snarl of rage. Tony leapt out of the chair. He went for Oswalde's throat, charging into him so that Oswalde was sent crashing against the wall. He was a head taller than Tony and over forty pounds heavier, but what a moment ago had been a pathetic cringing wreck was now transformed into a raving maniac with blood lust in his eyes, attempting to throttle the life out of him.

Winded, Oswalde struggled to get a grip on the boy's wrists. He grabbed hold of the left, pivoted on one foot, and wrenched Tony's arm halfway up his back. He caught the other one and pinned both Tony's hands behind his back and slammed him head first against the wall.

Calder was yelling, "Number seven, right in, right in!" as the five officers ran with Tony Allen spread-eagled horizontally between them along the corridor and into the cell block. He was kicking and screaming bloody murder. They got him inside, facedown on the floor, arms pinioned behind him, ankles trapped under two heavy boots.

"Out!" Calder yelled. "Out! Out!"

He was the last to leave, heaving the door shut and turning the key. Tony was up on his feet, battering the steel door with his fists. His terrified screams pierced the air. Calder wiped his face and blew out a sigh. That bloody racket was enough to wake the dead. He slid back the bolt and dropped the metal trap, peering in through the bars at the sweating black face and crazy rolling eyes.

"I'll leave the flap open—all right!"

Tony's screams sank to a whimpering moan. Calder turned away. Thank Christ for that. He jerked his head around at a drunken voice shouting from the cell next door. It was the drunk they'd picked up on disorderly conduct charges. "Fascist pigs!" the slurred voice raved on. "Fucking police brutality! Kicking the shit out of innocent victims!"

Calder banged on the door, told him to shut it, and went off to find Burkin. He was in the corridor outside the charge room, waiting by the wall phone for Tennison to return his call.

"Tony Allen is back in his cell," Calder reported. Burkin nodded, looking decidedly uneasy. He moved aside as Calder unhooked the phone, fretting, "What's happened to that doctor? I'll give him another call."

"Right." Burkin moodily watched him dial. "Are Mr. and Mrs. Allen still in reception?" he asked.

"They won't budge." Calder gave him a look. "You should have gone hours ago." He nodded back towards the cells. "Let the guy sleep it off. Tennison can deal with it in the morning."

Burkin was about to say something, and gave it up as a bad job. He slouched off. Calder listened to the ringing tone, shifting impatiently from foot to foot. "Come on . . . come on . . . !"

Oswalde took the elevator up to the cafeteria. It was almost empty at this late hour, a few small groups dotted about, officers taking a break during night patrols. He didn't know any of the faces, and he was glad about that; he wanted to be alone. In the far corner a TV was burbling to itself, the sound turned low.

Oswalde carried his black coffee to an empty table and sat down. His official duty shift had finished three hours ago. He should have been home in bed now, getting a reasonably early night, because he was due on again at eight-thirty the next morning. He was in a curious mood, couldn't unwind. He felt tired and yet jumpy and keyed up at the same time; his mind was racing, and he knew he was keeping alert on nervous energy alone.

The late-night news roundup was showing voters coming out of a polling station. It was the by-election, Oswalde remembered. Though not much interested, he switched his mind over to what the announcer was saying. Anything to sidetrack his thoughts away from Tony Allen's wild, staring eyes and slobbering mouth.

". . . pollsters keeping a record at the door suggest that Conservative Ken Bagnall may have held his seat but with a greatly reduced majority. There were angry scenes earlier when members of the Free Derrick Cameron Campaign clashed with Bagnall, who is a self-confessed supporter of capital punishment. Labour's candidate, Jonathan Phelps, has issued a statement . . ."

Whatever the statement was, Oswalde never learned. Somebody got up to switch channels, and boxing took its place. Oswalde sipped his coffee and watched with dull eyes as two black middleweights slugged it out.

Three floors below, in cell Number 7, Tony Allen had stripped down to his boxer shorts. He was standing at the door, staring out through the square grille. Slowly and very methodically he was tearing his shirt into strips. In the cell next door the drunk was snoring off his skinful. The two prisoners in adjoining cells were sleeping more quietly. Tony stared out, tearing at the cloth, and he didn't stop until the shirt had been ripped apart.

9

Calder looked up at the wall clock. He took a last drag, stubbed his cigarette in the ashtray and heaved himself up from the desk. On his way out he lifted the heavy bunch of keys from the hook and walked along the corridor, humming under his breath.

Sliding back the greased bolt, he lowered the flap and took a peek at the old guy in Number 5. Sleeping it off. Chances were they'd let him go in the morning with a caution. Silly old bugger, taking a piss in the street. Calder checked on the drunk in 6. A disgusting spectacle of matted hair, earrings, and tattoos. The smell of booze and stale sweat coming through the grille made Calder step back, waving the air. He slammed it shut, operated the bolt.

The next flap was open, as Calder had left it. He took a pace forward and then froze. Something was very wrong. A rope of white cloth was looped around one of the bars, hanging down inside. Calder's heart dropped into his bowels. Whatever the worst was, he feared it had happened. Breathing hard, he jammed his head against the bars and squinted down. At first he saw only a heap of clothing, a pair of brown shoes. He strained farther, his heart trip-hammering in his chest, and made out the top of Tony's head, a few inches below the open flap.

"*Shit!*" Calder dived for the panic button and the alarm bell drilled through the cell block. "Dave, John," he bellowed, "get here quick!"

Back at the cell door, he fumbled for the right key, cursing through gritted teeth. Boots pounded along the corridor. Suddenly there were four or five uniformed bodies crowding around the cell door as Calder turned the key in the lock. The door was pulled open, dragging Tony's body with it, bare legs splayed out. It was very ingenious and very simple. He'd made a rope out of the torn strips of his shirt, looped it around the bars, and hung himself from a sitting position. His bloodshot eyes bulged out, his tongue lolled between blue lips. Calder had seen his share of dead people, and he was looking at one now.

"Get me a knife," he said, and kneeling down, took the clasp knife and cut through the rope of knotted shirt strips. The others grabbed Tony's body as it slumped forward, a dead weight, and laid it on the floor of the cell. Calder stood up, his hands shaking, a mist of sweat on his bald head.

"Oh, Jesus Christ Almighty!" Oswalde arrived, pushing through the men crowding in the doorway. He dropped to his knees at Tony's side. He cupped the boy's slack jaw in his hand, bringing the head back, preparing to give mouth-to-mouth. "Get a mask."

Calder shook his head weakly. "It's too late . . ."

"*Now.*"

"Mask!" Calder snapped.

Oswalde was leaning over, both hands spread flat on Tony's chest, using his weight to massage his heart. A hand thrust a resuscitation mask at him. Making sure the bloated tongue was clear, Oswalde fitted the mask over Tony's mouth. He filled his lungs and blew into the plastic mouthpiece. It whooshed back at him, forced out under the pressure of the surrounding air. He did it again, and again, and he was still doing it, watched in silence by the men in the doorway, when Burkin shouldered his way through.

He glanced at Calder, who shook his head. Then he watched Oswalde straighten up and thump Tony's chest with the heels of his palms, do a silent count, and thump it again. Everyone knew it was hopeless, a lost cause, everyone but him.

Burkin had seen enough. He said gently, "Bob, it's no good . . ."

Oswalde thumped, did a silent count, thumped.

"It's no good, Bob . . ."

Thump, count, thump.

Burkin couldn't stand it. He leaped in, pulling Oswalde away. "Listen to me. *Look at me!*"

Oswalde went stiff. He stopped counting. He felt Burkin's firm grip on his shoulder and heard Burkin's voice, quiet, in his ear.

"The boy's dead . . . he's dead."

Oswalde slowly sat back on his heels, his arms flopping to his sides. Tony lay on the floor of the cell, the mask around his mouth, staring sightlessly up. Silence. Nobody said anything. There was nothing to say.

Tennison switched on the bedside lamp. Blinking painfully against the light, she reached for the ringing phone, a wave of blond hair falling over her eyes. "Oh shit," she mumbled, and then into the receiver, "Yes?" and listened with her eyes half-shut to Burkin's voice. "Can't it wait till morning?"

Burkin told her it couldn't and told her why.

Tennison said faintly, "What was he doing in the cells?" Burkin told her. "Jesus Christ. I'm on my way."

She hung up, but for a minute she didn't move. The horror of what Burkin had told her was still sinking in. It still hadn't fully sunk in as she padded through into the living room. She switched on the lamp and pressed the playback button on the answering machine. Burkin's message to her earlier that evening came on. She turned up the volume and his voice filled the room.

"Ma'm, it's DI Burkin. I'm a bit worried . . . well, not exactly worried, but, well . . . the thing is, Oswalde's arrested Tony Allen on suspicion of murder. He's got him in the interview room now, and, well, the kid's climbing the walls. I mean freaking out, and I'm . . . worried. Could you call me back?"

The line clicked off. Supporting herself on the table's edge, Tennison stared into space. This wasn't happening. It wasn't real. She'd wake up in a minute. It had to be a dream. A fucking nightmare.

Superintendent Kernan had been hauled out of a rugby club bash. Wearing his blazer and club tie, wreathed in whisky fumes, he arrived at Southampton Row and stumped inside with the ferocious look of a drunken man sobering up fast to an ugly reality.

Calder, puffing on a surreptitious cigarette behind the duty desk, was the first to get Kernan's glowering stare as he marched through like a thundercloud. Calder gazed hopelessly at the ceiling, as if seeking divine deliverance or a swift and painless death.

The thundercloud passed on through the station.

Oswalde was sitting in one of the interview rooms, trying to compose himself, when the door was shoved open and Kernan glared in at him. Then the door was slammed shut, leaving Oswalde alone like a penitent monk in a cell, with only purgatory to look forward to.

Kernan moved on. The Allens were still in reception, patiently waiting for news of their son, but Kernan couldn't bring himself to face them. Going up in the elevator to his office, exhaling Johnnie Walker Black Label, he had only one thing in mind. The mirage of Chief Superintendent Kernan fading farther and farther away in the distance. By God, he'd have someone's balls for this. And if Tennison was in any way to blame, he'd have her balls too.

The police photographer had just finished taking shots when Tennison entered the cell block. She had taken some time, and a few pains, to make herself smart and presentable, even at this ungodly hour. Freshly made-up, wearing a dark red suit with a flared jacket, she came in and took a long look at Tony Allen's body on the floor of cell Number 7. The resuscitation mask had been removed. The boy's face still bore the expression of frozen terror that had been his last emotion. Tennison turned away. Through tight lips she said to Burkin, "Cover him up, Frank."

She stood aside as two uniformed officers escorted the drunk from the cells. They were hustling him along, trying to prevent him getting even a glance of what had happened in the cell next door. The drunk knew though—or had guessed from all the commotion—and nobody was going to shut him up.

"You've killed him, you bastards!" he started shouting, straining his unshaven face around to get a look. He kept it up, his angry voice floating back as they dragged him out into the corridor, "You bastards have killed him, you bastards . . ."

Tennison brushed a hand through her hair. "Oh brilliant," she said.

Ten yards away from his office, Tennison could plainly hear Kernan's bellowing voice giving somebody a raking over. She came up to the door, wincing a little. She felt sorry for whoever was on the receiving end, whether they deserved it or not.

"It's just not good enough, not bloody good enough!" Kernan raged. "The prisoner is your sole responsibility!"

It was Calder, the Custody Sergeant, Tennison realized. She listened to the quiet, abject mumble of his reply, which was cut short by Kernan's "Don't tell me—put it in your report! Now!"

Calder emerged, looking white and shaken, and walked straight past without acknowledging her. He was close to tears. Tennison went in. She was glad she'd put a dab of perfume on because the office reeked of whisky. Kernan's tie was loose and his shirt collar was crumpled. He looked a bit of a mess, his eyes more heavily-lidded than usual, and his hands were none too steady as he lit a cigarette.

"Well, that's my promotion down the toilet," was how he greeted her, blowing out smoke in a disgruntled sigh.

Tennison was shocked. "A boy's lying dead in the cells and you're worried about your promotion?" she said, not bothering to hide her disapproval.

"Just don't start, all right?" Kernan said, flapping his hand. He gave her a baleful look. "The Custody Sergeant told me Burkin was trying to call you, worried by what Oswalde was up to . . ."

The knives were out already, Tennison thought. But she wasn't about to be dumped on from a great height. She said with venom, "Burkin's supposed to be a Detective Inspector, not a limp dick. He should have straightened it out. Calder should have straightened it out." And to think that two minutes ago she'd felt sorry for the man!

"But they bloody didn't, did they?" Kernan said, a veiled accusation in his voice.

Tennison paced in front of the desk, clenching her fists. "Christ Almighty, do I have to do everything myself?"

Kernan said wearily, "All right, all right . . ."

"I mean, what's Burkin being paid to do? For Christ's sake—"

"All right! I hear you."

Tennison ceased pacing but she was still fuming. If Kernan wanted a scapegoat, he could damn well look elsewhere. She glared at him and he shifted his eyes. He said, "How did it go with Harvey?"

"He confessed to murder."

"Thank Christ for that," Kernan said, relieved.

No point in hanging back; she was an experienced officer, paid to exercise her judgment. She said evenly, "But I've got my doubts about it . . ."

"What?" Kernan goggled at her. "We're being handed it gift-wrapped and you have your doubts?"

"Yes, I do. And I have good reason." Tennison appealed to him, "Look, Guv, right now I need to know what went on in that interview room. I mean—what made Tony kill himself, for chrissake . . . ?"

Kernan stubbed out his cigarette and stood up. "All hell's gonna break loose when this gets out," he said gloomily. "Riots, the lot."

"Oh, don't be ridiculous," Tennison said shortly.

Kernan slowly turned his head and gave her a hard stare. "You remember who you're talking to."

Now it was Tennison's turn to look away. She lifted her chin and said stiffly, "I'll listen to those interviews and report back as soon as I can. Sir."

"You do that."

The cigarette was still smoldering in the ashtray. What with that and the whisky fumes, the place smelled like a saloon bar. "By the way," Tennison said, "you know Tony's mum and dad are still in reception, don't you?"

"Well, they can't be told." Kernan rubbed the side of his face and stifled a yawn. "Not until we've got things arranged."

"*What?*" Tennison said, aghast.

"Send them home. Tell them tomorrow." It was starting, he could feel it now, a beaut of a headache working its way up from the back of his neck to the base of his skull. Terrific. "For their own sakes it'll be better to be told in the morning," he said.

"We can't do that."

"Yes, we can," Kernan said irritably.

Tennison blinked rapidly. "How would we explain that in court? It'd reek of a cover-up . . . besides, think of the way they'd feel."

"I've made my decision."

"Yes, and it's a bad one."

"Well, that's what I'm paid for!" Kernan snapped at her. His patience, threadbare at the best of times, was wearing dangerously thin. When he was in this frame of mind he sometimes blurted out things better left unsaid. And the icing on the cake was that his headache had just shifted up into second gear.

But the bloody woman wouldn't let it rest. She said tartly, "You're paid to make bad decisions, are you?"

To stop himself from landing one on her, Kernan went over to the little bar and picked up the whisky bottle. "You know what I mean," he growled under his breath.

Tennison watched him pour, at least three fingers' worth. She said quietly, "Mike, how much have you had to drink?"

Kernan shot a fierce glance over his shoulder. "Now you bloody watch it," he warned her, mottled patches appearing in his cheeks. "None of this would have happened if you'd kept Oswalde on a tighter rein . . ."

That was rich, and Tennison flared up. "You brought him in, not me," she reminded the superintendent. "I didn't ask for him. He's a loner, a one-man-band, he's not my type."

"That's not what I've heard."

There was dead silence. Tennison wasn't sure he'd said what she'd heard, and then with a sickly feeling she knew that he had. She controlled the sudden panic fluttering in her chest and said coolly, "I beg your pardon?"

"Nothing," Kernan said. He took a gulp.

"No," Tennison said, and her cool tone now had icicles hanging from it. "You explain that comment."

Kernan came back to the desk, swirling his whisky. "I'm merely suggesting that you might have let your personal feelings for him cloud your judgment."

"My personal feelings?" Tennison said carefully, and regretted saying it before the words were out of her mouth. She was right to, because Kernan put his glass down, and placing both hands flat on the desk, leaned towards her, looking her squarely in the face.

"Do I have to spell it out for you?" He paused. "You had an affair on that course! There. Now. I didn't want to mention it. But . . ." He shrugged and picked up his glass.

Tennison stared him out. "Nothing happened on that course," she said, her face stiff as a wooden mask.

"You will bloody argue, won't you?" Kernan closed his eyes, unutterably weary and pissed-off with the woman.

"You've been misinformed . . ."

"I hope so," Kernan said with a small sigh. "For your sake."

Tennison left the room. She needed to go to the lavatory, quick.

Downstairs, on the main floor, Tennison stopped a WPC in the corridor. "Show Mr. and Mrs. Allen up to my office, will you, please? Not a word about what's happened, understood?"

"Yes, ma'am."

"Thank you."

Oswalde came through the swing doors, on his way to the elevator, summoned by Kernan. Tennison glanced around, making sure the corridor was deserted. "Bob . . ."

He stared past her with dull eyes. "Look, I'm sorry, I can't talk about it right now," he muttered. "I've got to see Kernan."

From the set of his mouth she could tell he was holding himself as tight as a coiled spring. But she couldn't let him step into the lion's den without warning him. As he moved to go around her, she said, "Kernan knows about us at the course."

Oswalde halted. Now he did look at her, his handsome face creasing in a bewildered frown. "I don't know what . . ." he started to mumble.

"Listen." Tennison cut him short. She was holding judgment on whether she ought to be absolutely furious or not. She said, "If you've been bragging about laying the Guv'nor . . ."

"What do you take me for?" Oswalde was plainly hurt by this. "Do you think I'd say anything? You think I'd . . ." He swallowed and looked away.

Tennison kneaded her palms anxiously. "Well, all I can think about right now is I've got to tell that boy's parents that their son is dead."

"And that boy is dead because of me . . ." Oswalde choked on the words. He was very near the edge. He said emptily, "Do you really think it matters that Kernan knows about us . . ."

Tennison's look was stony. "Yes, it matters," she said, and turned on her heel, leaving him to face Kernan's music.

The Allens were sitting in her office. Tennison would rather have walked barefoot on white-hot coals than go through with this, but that was the price she paid for being in charge of a murder investigation: the shitty end of the stick.

Ever the gentleman, Vernon Allen rose to his feet as she came in. "About time, Chief Inspector. We've been waiting out there for an eternity." Even so, he sounded more reproachful than angry, blinking at her through his horn-rimmed spectacles. The man had the patience of a saint, Tennison thought; she quailed at the duty before her, almost turned and fled.

"Please . . . can you give my son this?"

Esme had risen and was holding out a thick wool sweater, neatly folded. Tennison accepted it. She didn't know what else to do.

Esme wore a strained smile, her eyes large and moist. "Esta said he didn't even have time to get a coat. I hate to think of him spending the night in a cell. I don't want him to catch cold . . ."

Tennison placed the sweater on the corner of the desk, next to Vernon's hat. She held out her hand. "Please sit down. I have some bad news for you."

"I just want my son!" Esme blurted out plaintively. Vernon patted her shoulder. The three of them were still standing. Tennison went around the desk, turned and faced them. "Esme—Esme, please sit down."

She waited then, hands clasped in front of her, until they were seated. She raised her eyes and looked at them. "I'm afraid that after Tony was returned to his cell, after questioning, he took his own life."

Vernon leaned forward slightly. He seemed puzzled. "Is he hurt?"

Tennison said quietly, "Vernon, your son is dead. I'm very sorry."

The Allens just sat and looked at her with blank expressions. Was any of this getting through? "Do you understand?" she asked them. She hesitated, then said wretchedly, "I'm so sorry . . ."

Vernon had removed his glasses. In slow motion he reached out and put them on top of his hat. He looked up at Tennison, shaking his head almost imperceptibly. "How?"

"He used strips of his own clothes to . . ."

Esme came up out of her chair. Her eyes gleamed. Spitting and scratching, she launched herself at Tennison, screeching at the top of her voice, "You killed him! You killed my boy! You killed him! You killed him! You killed him . . . !"

Making no attempt to retaliate, defending herself as best she could by holding up her arms, Tennison retreated into a corner. She felt the bony fists and sharp nails striking at her head and face. There was a panic button under her desk. She could have tried to get to it and summon help, but she didn't. She huddled in the corner, arms crossed to ward off the blows Esme was raining down on her with berserk, mindless rage.

"You killed him, killed my boy, killed him, you killed him . . ."

When finally Vernon managed to pull her off, Esme turned her fury on him, lashing out in a frenzy and pounding her fists into his chest. Vernon held her shoulders, taking the blows, letting her punch herself out. Esme sagged against him, sobbing into his chest, and the sight of this pitiful, distraught woman took from Tennison a lot of willpower to hold on to herself.

She felt so helpless in the face of this naked human pain and misery that she felt like sobbing too.

Vernon's arms were wrapped around his wife, holding and comforting her; without their support she would have collapsed.

Over her head, and calling upon some deep reserve of calmness and dignity, he said to Tennison, "How did it happen?"

"He hanged himself."

"When?" It seemed very important. "I mean when exactly?"

Tennison pushed back her tangled hair. Her left cheek was stinging, and she touched it lightly with her fingertips, feeling a bruise starting to form. "Between midnight and twelve-thirty," she said.

Vernon stared at her, his wife huddled against him; muffled, broken sobs shuddered out of her. It was all Tennison could manage not to look away. "While we were waiting in reception?" Vernon said.

"Yes."

Vernon closed his eyes, his throat working above his collar and tie. He opened his eyes, and a spasm passed over his face. He said huskily, "Lady. May you rot in hell for that."

With a stiff, jerky movement he turned away, and half carrying her, steered his wife to the door. Tennison came forward, holding his hat and glasses. He slipped the glasses into his overcoat pocket and took his hat. "Thank you," he said politely.

Tennison stood in the doorway watching as they wandered off aimlessly, two lost souls numb with anguish.

"Where are they going?" Burkin asked, appearing at Tennison's side.

"I don't think they know. Arrange a car for them," she said. "I think Mrs. Allen may well need to see a doctor. Probably they both do."

Burkin nodded, about to do her bidding, when he noticed her face. "Are you okay, Guv?"

"Right away, please, Frank."

Burkin went after them, leading them out.

Tennison leaned weakly in the doorway for a moment. She felt nauseated, as though she'd been kicked in the stomach. She went back into her office.

Kernan had taken off his jacket and shoes and was lying on the leather sofa in his office, listening on the phone to Commander Trayner. He'd crunched three aspirin and swilled the mush down with neat whisky. He shaded his eyes, waiting for it to take effect, as he half-watched the television picture, the sound turned low. The by-election count was still going on. It was going to be a close one.

At one time, Kernan reflected, in the dim and distant past, he'd been a copper on the beat. A real policeman. Doing real police work. Now he was trapped and tangled up in bleeding internal politics and PR and career moves, like a fly in a sticky web. On top of which he had a murder investigation that threatened to go off the rails, a dead black boy in the cells, and a rowdy DCI who'd been caught fucking a junior officer. He shut his eyes, and through the dull pounding in his head, tried to concentrate on what the commander was saying.

"Has the family been informed? Good . . ."

Immaculate in a dark-blue suit, pale cream shirt, and polka-dot tie, Trayner stood in the hallway, keeping one eye on the TV in the living room. He'd invited the Thorndikes around to dinner, and they were sitting with his wife Dorothy, lingering over brandies and Harrods' mint crisp wafers, while they watched the election result.

"What about MS15?" Trayner asked. "Well, get onto them right away." He passed a pink, plump hand over his smooth glossy hair, graying at the temples. "David Thorndike should lead the investigation, which is good news for us," he said glibly.

At the mention of his name, Thorndike swivelled around in his chair, sharp nose in the air, all ears. Trayner winked and favored him with a conspiratorial smirk.

"Absolutely." Trayner was nodding, agreeing with Kernan. "A complete bastard—but a complete bastard who is the most likely candidate to take over from you if you get the move upstairs." He added silkily, "And that will surely depend on how you handle this business from now on . . ."

Dorothy had turned the sound up, and Trayner said, "One moment," leaning towards the living room door as the party official stepped up to the microphone.

"Kenneth Trevor Bagnall, Conservative . . . thirteen thousand, one hundred and thirty-seven."

"Not enough," Trayner muttered tersely, shaking his head.

"Jonathan Phelps, Labour . . . sixteen thousand, four hundred . . ."

The rest was drowned in a storm of cheering from the Labour supporters in the hall. Phelps, smiling broadly, had both fists raised in the air. Trayner turned his back on it.

"Did you hear that?" he said into the phone. "It's in David's best interests to stop Southampton Row being dragged through the mire. Keep me informed."

He hung up. Thorndike came through, buttoning his jacket. "Well, we'd better be going." The two men looked at one another. Things might work out after all. The MS15 investigation, with Thorndike in charge, couldn't have come at a more opportune moment, everything considered. If nothing else, it would cast a cloud over Tennison's promotion prospects. And if Thorndike could perform a damage limitation exercise on the Met's reputation, impressing the powers-that-be, he'd come out of it smelling of roses.

Trayner patted him on the shoulder, and Thorndike responded with his thin-lipped watery smile. "Looks like I've got an early start in the morning," he said.

"I'm a black bastard, I deserve all I get, I'm a black bastard, I deserve all I get . . ."

"Stop that!"

Tennison sat at her desk, her elbow on the blotter, her head propped in one hand. She tapped the ash off her cigarette and put it to her lips. She inhaled deeply and breathed out, the smoke pluming from her nostrils. The tape reel slowly turned, semaphoring plastic gleams under the lamplight with each revolution.

"I'm a black bastard, I deserve all I get, I'm a black bastard, I deserve all I get . . ."

"Tony, just stop it, man!"

Tennison closed her eyes and took another long drag.

This was worse than she had feared. Much worse. What in heaven's name had possessed Oswalde? Why had he allowed it to go on? Pushing and pressuring the boy when it was obvious that he was stricken with hysterical panic, teetering on the edge of a complete nervous breakdown? What the hell was he trying to prove? That black coppers were superior to white ones? Or that he had nothing to learn from the Gestapo?

The procedures laid down under PACE were quite explicit, and this interview was a case-book study on how to disregard every one of them. Whoever was appointed from MS15 was going to have a field day.

"That's enough. Can I have a word with you, Sergeant Oswalde." Burkin's voice.

"In a minute."

"Now, Sergeant Oswalde!"

Tennison mashed her cigarette next to the five stubs and switched off the tape.

10

Tennison had the nine A.M. briefing put back to nine-fifteen. First she wanted Burkin in, and she told DS Haskons to send him along as soon as he arrived. He came in, pale and hollow-eyed, a shaving nick on his chin, and stayed standing and silent while she tore into him. The second time in under two weeks; it was getting to be a bad habit.

"I'm not talking about Oswalde's part in this," Tennison stormed at him. She stayed on her feet, pacing, because if she sat down she'd have had the cigarette packet out. "You and Mike Calder had the authority to stop those interviews. Instead, you let them continue—no, better still, you let Oswalde interview the boy on his own while you sat by the telephone waiting for me to do your job for you—"

She broke away to answer the door. It was Haskons.

"Ready when you are, Guv."

"Right." She closed the door and walked around Burkin to the desk. He was looking carefully at nothing in particular, as long as it wasn't her. She didn't care what he was feeling, or what he thought of her; this was a professional matter; she was expected to do her job, and she expected him to do his.

"The rank of inspector is supposed to mean something, Frank. It carries responsibility. It's supposed to denote a certain authority." She stared up at him, hands clasped at her waist. "You won't make excuses. You'll face the music like a man. That'll be all."

Burkin turned and left the office.

He went directly to the Incident Room, where Muddyman was perched on the corner of a desk, sipping coffee from a styrofoam cup. The other members of the team were lounging about, and Muddyman was saying, "I don't understand it—we're at Harvey's bedside getting a confession and meanwhile Oswalde's off chasing Tony. It doesn't make sense."

"His ass is grass," said Rosper, the jive slang specialist, with a shrug.

Haskons was more sympathetic. "It's a dreadful thing to have happened. You carry that around with you for the rest of your life," he said.

Still smarting from his encounter with Tennison, Burkin didn't see why anyone else should be let off the hook. "The spade should be suspended. I mean, why was he brought here in the first place?"

"You know why," Muddyman said.

"To talk to his people," Jones said.

"Yeah . . . and now one of them's dead and it's down to him," Burkin growled. He looked around the circle of faces, aware that not all of them were convinced. "Look, I'm not exaggerating or nothing," he told them stridently. "That boy was really weird, I mean climbing the walls, screaming and shouting, like mental or something. And believe me, I tried to tell him . . ."

"Yeah, course you did, Frank," Haskons said, nodding, as if Burkin was insisting that Santa Claus really did exist.

The discussion dried up as Oswalde entered the room. No one greeted or looked at him, and he didn't seem to care either way, going straight to his desk and sitting down. He was a stranger in a strange land, no use seeking sympathy or comradeship around here.

A moment later Tennison arrived. The men gathered around. The mood wasn't one of sweetness and light.

"Morning everyone." Her gaze swept over them—Burkin, Muddyman, Lillie, Rosper, Haskons, Jones—and last of all Oswalde, who was standing on the edge of the circle.

"I expect you've all heard about the events of last night. Just to clarify. Tony Allen hanged himself in cell Number seven—using strips of his own clothes. I informed his parents shortly afterwards. Now, obviously we can expect some adverse publicity. I'm told we can also expect an internal inquiry led by DCI Thorndike to begin almost immediately."

There were dark looks and a few suppressed groans. Those who knew Thorndike didn't like him. Those that didn't know him were well aware of his reputation as a cold-blooded bastard, a career policeman who'd never collared so much as a shoplifter.

"Needless to say, I regret what has happened, but Operation Nadine continues . . ."

Lillie raised a hand. "But surely, ma'am, if Harvey's confessed—I mean, that's it, isn't it?"

"Quite frankly, I'm not convinced by David Harvey's version of events."

This was news to Muddyman. He said, "Admittedly, there are some inconsistencies, Guv . . ."

"Inconsistencies?" Tennison raised an eyebrow. "He said she wasn't wearing a bra. She was. He said he put a gag on her—there was no trace of a gag."

"He could have removed it," Muddyman pointed out. "It could have rotted away."

"Yes, it could have," Tennison conceded. With the possible exception of Oswalde, she was aware that she was in a minority of one. The rest of the team agreed with Muddyman: the case was signed, sealed, and as good as delivered. She went on, "Harvey said he killed her in the kitchen, but the fragment of tooth was found in the front room."

Muddyman had an answer for that too. "Perhaps there was violence in the front room—he said he hit her—before the murder took place. Perhaps he moved the body after . . ." He spread his hands. "I mean, he did say he hit her."

"'Perhaps.'" Tennison said doubtfully. "'Perhaps' won't stand up in court. I'm not sure the confession of a dying man will stand up in court either."

"He knew her hands had been tied with a belt."

"Yes—and he said 'my' belt." That was something that had nagged at her. Tennison appealed to them. "Does the belt we found look like something Harvey might wear?"

Muddyman patiently went through it, counting off on his fingers. "She was wrapped in polyethylene sheeting. And there was a plastic bag buried with her. And he said the body remained above ground—which ties up the maggots and that . . . none of those details were mentioned in the press!"

By now most of the team was nodding. It was an open-and-shut case. The evidence was overwhelming, whatever inconsistencies there might be. Murder was a sloppy business, not a scientific theorem.

"Look," Tennison granted them, "I'm as certain as you are that Harvey was involved. Most probably in the disposal of the body. But I'm not sure he killed her. We need to go over Harvey's statement with a fine-tooth comb. We need to examine what Tony Allen said—"

"You won't get much there, Guv," Burkin interrupted. "I know, I was there."

"You may have been there," Oswalde said derisively. "You obviously weren't listening."

". . . Sir."

Oswalde glowered at him. "Sir."

"Frank," Tennison said with a touch of asperity, "don't you think it's a bit late to be pulling rank?" She faced them. "Now listen. We messed up. Very badly. Which means we've got to work twice as hard from now on.

Why, if he wasn't involved in the actual murder of Joanne, would Harvey involve himself in the burial of the body? Can we connect Tony Allen with David Harvey? A connection strong enough for Harvey to confess to a murder he didn't commit."

She gave each and every one of them a hard searching look.

"I want to go back to Eileen Reynolds. I want evidence. I want corroboration. I want to solve the case."

And with that, ignoring their muttered grumbles, she dismissed them.

Thorndike got out of the Rover, briefcase in hand, and waited while his driver locked the car. Together they strode briskly to the main entrance of Southampton Row. One of Esme Allen's customers, the middle-aged woman with silvery hair, was in the act of placing a small bunch of flowers on the steps. She straightened up, tears streaming down her face, and turned to go. The two MS15 officers exchanged a look and went inside.

"DCI Thorndike, DS Posner to see Superintendent Kernan," Thorndike informed the young PC behind the duty desk. "We're expected."

The PC pressed the buzzer, releasing the glass-paneled door reinforced with steel mesh, and they passed inside.

Barely three hours' sleep made Tennison edgy and fractious; and what she didn't need right now was Thorndike's oily, unctuous presence and smarmy twitterings. God, how she despised the man. Closer acquaintance had only increased her dislike. Sitting opposite him in the interview room, watching him fuss with his papers, she really had to control herself, fight the impulse to burst out and tell him what an officious prick she thought him.

"Southampton Row's reputation precedes it, Jane," he said, sighing and shaking his head. He gave her a frank, accusing look. "If you come in the front, you're likely to go out the back with blood on your face."

"Is this on the record, David?" Tennison asked politely.

"Of course not," Thorndike said, smiling his tepid smile. "We're just talking . . ."

"Good," Tennison said. "Because that's bullshit." With satisfaction she saw his smile drain away. "If it was ever true, it's not anymore. I've never seen excessive force used in this station. Oswalde's certainly not like that."

"What with the Cameron case . . ."

She could see his game. He was trying to dredge up the past, the Derrick Cameron saga recently revived by Phelps, and use it as smear tactics. But she wasn't about to let it happen.

"Look," she told him, "you're here to investigate a death in custody."

"I know why I'm here, Jane."

"Well then, let's concentrate on the case in hand."

"I intend to, don't worry." He was flustered, and started fussing through the documents spread out in front of him. He had thin, bony hands that gave her the creeps. "I think it's important for you to know I take this job seriously," he said, putting on the stern voice of authority. "I'm not prepared to do a whitewash."

"No one's asking you to."

"It's my belief that when one of the foot soldiers messes up it comes down to the officer in charge."

"I accept that."

"I don't know . . ." Thorndike gave her his fishy-eyed stare. "Perhaps you let your personal feelings cloud your judgment."

Tennison went cold. The same words, or very close, to the ones Mike Kernan had used. Suddenly she understood. What an idiot that it had taken her till now to realize that it was Thorndike who had done the blabbing. This was the slimy toad who had spread the rumors about her and Oswalde.

"I beg your pardon?" she said frostily.

"It'll keep." His eyes slid down to his papers. "Can you ask the Custody Sergeant . . ." He pretended to search for the name.

"Mike Calder."

". . . yes, to step into my office, please?"

"One more thing, David." Tennison was simmering. With a great effort she kept her voice level and cool. "If I'm to be interviewed I'd like to speak to an officer senior in rank to me."

Thorndike looked up. He said blandly, "Well, that may not be possible."

Well, Tennison thought, it had better not be *you*, or you can go screw yourself.

There was a chill drizzle just starting to fall as Tennison drove into the hospital parking lot. It was a few minutes after midday, and she had arranged to be there when Vernon Allen came to make the formal identification of his son. Although not strictly necessary, she felt an obligation, as a gesture of regret and condolence, to put in an appearance on behalf of the police authority. She was deeply sorry for what had happened, and felt it was the least she could do.

She locked the Sierra, and was about to start for the main entrance when Sarah Allen came through the rows of parked cars. She must have driven her father to the hospital, and was waiting for him in her car when she spotted Tennison. She made a beeline across the lot, her attractive face twisted in a terrible grimace, her large brown eyes wild with hate and loathing.

"How could you have him arrested for murder? If it wasn't for you, none of this would have happened!"

Tennison stepped back a pace, afraid for a moment that the distraught girl was going to attack her. She tried to console her, but Sarah went on in a hoarse, broken voice. "Tony wouldn't hurt anyone, let alone tie them up, rape them . . ."

"Wait a minute . . . Sarah . . ."

"What's his daughter going to do now?"

Tennison had gone still. It had hit her what Sarah had just said.

"How did you know that she was tied up?" she asked. She tried to grab Sarah's arm, hoping to calm her. "How did you know she was raped?"

Sarah wrenched herself away. "That's another life you've ruined," she almost snarled.

Tennison still wanted an answer. "Who told you that?" she demanded.

"He was going to be married this weekend . . ." Sarah broke down, sobbing. Tennison reached out, and the girl backed away. "Just leave us alone!" She turned her tear-stained face away and did a staggering run back to her car.

When Tennison got there, she had locked herself inside. Tennison tapped on the window. "Who told you that she was tied up?"

But she soon saw that it was useless. Sarah was gripping the wheel with both hands, her head resting between them, her shoulders heaving as she wept uncontrollably. For the time being, at any rate, the question would have to remain unanswered.

The door opened and the mortuary attendant stood there. "Would you like to come this way, sir?"

Vernon Allen rose heavily from the bench and followed him through. Tennison was sitting in the corridor outside. She stood up as Vernon passed, but said nothing and made no move as he went through the white door into the mortuary itself. She sat down again.

Tony Allen was lying on a metal table, covered to the waist by a sheet. His eyes were closed, and but for the puckered purplish circle round his neck, he might have been asleep. Vernon gazed down at him. His eyes were dry. A tiny muscle jumped at the corner of his mouth. Very slowly, he bent forward and kissed his son on the lips.

Tennison stood up as Vernon emerged from the mortuary. He walked past her, looking straight ahead, his face empty of all expression, and went outside into the gray drizzle sweeping down from a dark sky.

When Tennison rang his office she was told that the super was having lunch in the cafeteria. She went up in the elevator, and having no appetite, got herself a cup of black coffee and carried it across to his table. She might grab a sandwich later on, if she felt like it.

Kernan was finishing off apple crumble and custard, watching the lunchtime news. She told him about her visit to the mortuary, and of what Sarah had said. He licked his spoon and held it up to quiet her as a photograph of Tony Allen appeared on the screen.

The announcer was saying, "Tony Allen, who was to have been married this weekend, leaves a fiancée and a three-year-old daughter . . ."

Kernan dropped his spoon in the bowl and wiped his mouth on a paper napkin. "You can't pull Sarah Allen in. Not with all this going on."

He gestured at the television, which was showing "all this," in the person of Jonathan Phelps. Together they watched the newly elected Labour MP being interviewed outside the House of Commons.

". . . today should have been a day of celebration for me and my supporters. Instead, it has turned into a wake as another black man dies in police custody."

Turning away, Tennison leaned towards Kernan. "I just want to talk to her off the premises," she said reasonably.

It wasn't reason enough. Kernan shook his head. "Too soon. Go back to Harvey."

"He can't talk at the moment. I don't know whether he'll be able to again."

"Well, then, see where other lines of inquiry lead you. We'll review the situation in a few days." He crumpled the napkin and tossed it down, giving Tennison a critical scrutiny. Her makeup couldn't disguise the lines of tiredness at the corners of her mouth and the slight puffiness under her eyes. "Go home and get some sleep, Jane."

"Yeah . . ."

"And leave Sarah Allen out of it," Kernan ordered. "For the moment."

He departed, leaving Tennison gazing listlessly at the TV screen, where Phelps was saying, "With all due respect, a system where police officers investigate their fellow officers cannot be sufficiently objective. All too often a blanket of silence falls on the case . . ."

A shape moved behind the panes of colored glass in the vestibule; the light came on and Tennison saw that it was Vernon Allen. He opened the inner door and peered out, trying to see who had rung the bell.

Tennison tapped on the glass panel at the outer door and pressed her face closer. "Vernon, I have to speak to Sarah . . ."

He flinched, as if someone had spat in his face. "How dare you come here! How dare you . . ."

"Vernon, it's really important that I speak to Sarah."

"Haven't you done enough damage?" He was trembling, the outrage in his voice strained and pitiful. "Just leave us alone—"

"But I have to speak to Sarah!" Tennison insisted. She tapped again, urgently, seeing him about to close the door.

"My wife is . . ." Vernon Allen choked, overcome at the thought of Esme's grief. The huge man seemed to be physically shrinking. He bowed his head in anguish. "My wife . . ."

Sarah appeared beside him. "Go inside, Pop. Let me handle this. Go on."

He shambled off. Sarah stepped forward, tight-lipped, and stared coldly at Tennison through the glass panel, making no move to open the door. Tennison knew she had only a few seconds. She said quickly, "Sarah, were you there that night?"

"I don't know what you're talking about."

"—or has Jason Reynolds spoken to you?"

"I don't know any Jason Reynolds," Sarah snapped. "Now leave us alone! I'm closing the door—"

"Sarah, please," Tennison said, "for Tony's sake—"

"I'm closing the door."

She did. The light went out. And that was that.

At first Tennison couldn't figure out what the screeching noise was, or where it was coming from.

Nearly ten-thirty, the station was quiet, and she was on the point of leaving when she heard it. Puzzled, she walked down the empty corridor and pushed through the doors into the Incident Room. All alone, Oswalde was crouched in a chair in front of the TV, the remote control in his hand. The screeching was speeded-up reggae as he fast-forwarded the tape of the Sunsplash concert. He paused it, leaning forward with a fixed, obsessive stare, his eyes glued to Joanne and Tony on the stage.

Tennison moved quietly toward him, frowning to herself. He pressed the rewind and played the same sequence over again, and she could see the tension in the hunched shoulders and the hand gripping the remote.

"Bob," Tennison said, making an effort to sound casual. "Give yourself a break."

Oswalde flicked a glance at her and went back to the screen. "You can talk."

She watched him for a moment longer, then unslung her shoulder bag. She found her Filofax, and scribbled something on a slip of paper and handed it to him. "Call this number. It's a friend of mine. She helped someone who was at Broadwater Farm. She's good."

"A shrink . . . ?" Oswalde was bitterly amused.

"Sort of," Tennison said. "Listen, there's no shame in that. Other people make mistakes at work and the firm loses a few grand. We make a mistake and someone loses their life." It was an argument she used on herself, whenever she screwed up or was feeling depressed.

Oswalde had zapped back and was studying the same sequence all over again, just as intensely as before. Tennison hitched her bag onto her shoulder and turned to go. He was a big boy, and she wasn't a wet nurse. She stopped as a thought occurred to her.

"Did Mrs. Fagunwa recognize that belt?"

"No."

Tennison nodded, on her way to the door. "Go home, Bob," she said, and went out.

The house where Eileen Reynolds lived was a stone's throw from the tower blocks of the Lloyd George Estate. In fact, Tennison thought, as she knocked on the door, if you threw a stone from Harvey's balcony it would break one of his sister's windows.

Eileen opened the door, her arms filled with sheets and pillow slips ready for the wash.

Tennison smiled. "Hello, Eileen."

Eileen didn't return the smile. In the clear light of day her face had a hard, pinched look, that of a woman who had lived through a few trials and tribulations in her time, and survived to tell the tale. Her short, bleached hair was showing brown and gray at the roots.

"I've been expecting you," she said, and went inside, leaving Tennison to shut the door.

"I wasn't lying. He was there with me that weekend. He came down a lot in those days. He had a trailer there. Sometimes he'd stay with me, sometimes at the van." Eileen stuffed the last of the washing in the machine, straightened up wearily, and banged the door to with her knee.

Tennison said, "So why did you say it was the anniversary of his wife's death?"

"Makes no difference." Eileen folded her arms and gave a contemptuous shrug. "I've spoken to a lawyer and he tells me that confession is not worth the paper it's written on. It was 'obtained under duress,'" she enunciated, her Scottish accent coming to the fore. "And if my brother did it, why has that blackie killed himself?"

"Did you know Tony Allen?" Tennison asked, quietly curious.

"No, I seen it on the TV." Eileen leaned forward, thrusting her face, eyes screwed tight, at Tennison. "Because he did it—that's why!"

"Then why did your brother confess?"

She had a sharp-tongued Glaswegian answer to everything. "To get you lot off his back."

"Eileen, you're not helping your brother by lying . . ."

"I'm not *lying!*"

Tennison leaned against the sink, watching as Eileen heaved a basket of clean washing onto the kitchen table. She was a small, almost scrawny woman, yet tough as old boots, and Tennison wouldn't have fancied her own chances in a scrap, even with the tricks she'd learned from the Met's karate instructors.

She said, "You don't have to stop loving him, you don't have to stop supporting him. But you do have to stop lying for him."

"You know something?" Eileen swung around, blazing. "You're a pious cow! I've done everything for that bloody man since he's been ill. I work my fingers to the bone to support him . . ."

"I know." Tennison nodded. "That's what I'm saying. I know you support him. I know that must be a struggle. Like taking on that loan—"

"You all think you know everything!"

"—for him. Five grand's a lot of money." She paused. "How could you afford to do that, Eileen?"

"My son helps out." She glared across the kitchen. "All right?"

Tennison reflected. "What does Jason do for a living?"

"You leave that boy out of this!"

"It's a simple question," Tennison said placidly.

Eileen sniffed. "He has a sort of . . . photography business."

"What does that mean?"

"In the summer he works on the beach. I don't really know. I don't pry like you do," she said with something like a sneer.

"You mean he's a beach photographer?" Tennison said, and a tiny surge of excitement, like electricity, ran through her. She didn't quite know why, but then something clicked in her brain.

Eileen was busy sorting out the stuff that needed ironing. "Yeah—he used to keep a bloody monkey here at one time, okay?"

Tennison left her car parked at the end of the street and walked along the flagged pathway that led to the flats. She entered Dwyfor House and began to climb the smelly staircase. She wanted to have another look around Harvey's flat, and in particular at the photographs on the glass-fronted bureau. The ones taken by Jason Reynolds, professional photographer.

On the thirteenth floor, in flat Number 136, Jason Reynolds was on his knees, searching in the cupboard under the sink. He found what he was after, a black plastic bag, and padded through into the living room. The place was in a bit of a shambles, coffee table on its side, ashtray and loose cigarettes spilled over the floor, nothing tidied up since they'd carted his uncle off to the hospital.

He shook the bag open and went around the sofa to the bureau. He reached for the nearest framed photograph and suddenly went still. He tilted his head, listening. There was someone outside the front door. Silently he skirted the sofa and crept into the hallway, his sneakers making no sound. Somebody was fumbling with the mailbox flap. Fingers poked through and fished for the string, and started to pull it up, the key attached to the end. Jason watched as the key was drawn through the mailbox.

He looked around, instantly in a sweat. As the key went into the lock he dashed sideways into the kitchen and closed the door a bare crack, putting his eye to it. He held his breath, white-faced and tense, and through the crack saw Tennison pass along the hallway to the living room. He felt sure she must hear his heart.

Tennison moved slowly around the sofa to the bureau. Along with Muddyman she'd merely glanced at the photographs in their cheap Woolworth's frames. Now she examined each in turn closely. The one she had looked at before, of Harvey and his wife. The sunset over the sea. Harvey and Eileen together. A smaller print of Eileen on her own. And one of Harvey and Jason, in a back garden, smiling, Harvey's arm around his nephew's shoulder. Tennison touched the glass. Her finger traced Jason's check shirt down to the Indian Chief's head on the belt looped through his jeans.

The surge of electricity was now a jolt, stiffening her spine.

She turned her head, feeling a cool waft of air on her cheek. Putting the photograph back, she went through into the hallway. The front door was open. Had she closed it? She was positive she had. She looked out onto the landing. She listened for a moment, heard nothing, and went back inside, making sure the door was locked.

In the living room she took the photograph down, turned it over, and flicked up the plastic tabs, intending to take just the print itself. As the cardboard backing came away, Tennison froze. Concealed there, behind the print, were half a dozen polaroids. She spread them out on the back of the frame, her mouth dry, struggling a little to catch her breath. They were of Joanne Fagunwa and Sarah Allen, fully clothed yet posing rather suggestively, their hands squeezing their breasts. They looked to be in a kitchen. And there was a close-up of Joanne and Sarah, giggling into the camera, with Tony Allen between them, pulling a funny face.

Tennison shut her eyes. This was it. What they'd been seeking all along. The link—Joanne—Sarah—Tony—and whoever had taken the polaroids. All together. And whoever had taken the polaroids was the wearer of the Indian Chief's head belt.

She went to the phone and dialed Southampton Row, and asked for DS Oswalde. When he came on the line she said, "Bob, it's Jane. I'm at Harvey's. I've found something interesting."

11

Oswalde was sitting on the sofa, hands laced together, the Polaroids spread out on the coffee table in front of him. He nodded slowly. "So Tony was involved . . ."

"Yes."

As if a string had snapped, Oswalde's head dropped forward. "Thank Christ for that." He sucked in a huge, relieved breath, then sat forward, staring hard. "Isn't that Sarah?"

"Yes," Tennison said. She leaned over, pointing. "And even better . . . recognize that?"

Oswalde studied the photograph of Harvey and Jason in the garden. He looked up at her, his expression clearing. "It's the belt . . ."

Tennison's eyes gleamed. "We've got him, Bob—I want him picked up and I want this place turned over," she said, gesturing around the flat, fingers snapping.

"Have you got a search warrant?"

"I'll worry about that."

Forty-five minutes and two phone calls later the flat was in the throes of a minor invasion. A systematic search brought up piles of soft porn magazines and two shoe boxes filled with original prints and Polaroids: Jason's private collection, that no doubt he'd stored here to keep from his mother's prying eyes, Tennison thought. She sorted through it with Lillie.

Some of the early, amateurish stuff was fairly innocuous—pouting adolescent girls pretending to be page three models, quite a few in school uniforms. But there were other, later shots that Tennison found sickening and repugnant. Naked girls bound and gagged, fear in their eyes; real or faked, Tennison couldn't tell. Some showing groups of two or three, using various implements on themselves. And a number of them featured the kid himself. Jason the porno star, taking the leading role in his own production. These had been taken with remote-control shutter release. The wire could be seen, trailing from his hand to the camera, as he pumped away, face contorted, veins standing out. The girls didn't look to be enjoying it.

The more professional the photograph, it seemed, the more extreme the poses and situations became, as if Jason was trying to keep pace with his growing technical expertise by dredging up ever more outlandish fantasies from the depths of his sordid imagination.

Lillie held up a magazine cover of an over-blessed blonde and the original, matching color print from Jason's private hoard. "Quite the little photographer," he muttered sourly.

Tennison pushed the pile away with disgust, having seen more than plenty. "Get on to Vice. See if you can find out who publishes this muck." She called out to Oswalde, "Bob, get someone down to Harvey's bedside. Make sure I'm informed as soon as he can utter a sound."

She stood up, feeling soiled and grubby and faintly nauseated. Turning away from the piles of magazines and heaps of photographs, she said between gritted teeth, "We've got to find this little shit."

She thought, with a flutter of panic: Before he does to some poor innocent girl what he did to Joanne Fagunwa.

Haskons had used his discretion. He'd weeded out the more explicit material and pinned up on the bulletin board only those shots that might have been deemed fit for mixed company. Even so, some of the sequences, while starting innocently enough, ended up as blatantly pornographic.

"Seems as though Jason prefers amateur models," Tennison said, moving along them with Muddyman, who himself dabbled in amateur photography, on a more modest scale.

"Yeah, well, he doesn't have to pay them, does he?" Muddyman pointed them out. "The Polaroids are early photographs. The later ones are much better quality, thirty-five mil. Quite professional."

"Would he develop them himself?"

Muddyman smoothed back the hair over his bald spot. "I think black and white's pretty easy. You need more sophisticated equipment for color."

Tennison pinched her nose, thinking. "I suppose he could have a studio or something . . . it's worth checking with any of those places that specialize in developing shady photos. They might have an address, a contact number even."

Muddyman nodded and went off, back into the fray. The Incident Room was buzzing. Rosper, aided by WPC Havers, was working the computer terminal. Burkin and Oswalde had document files a foot deep on their desks, heads down, plowing through. The other members of the team were on the phones, chasing down even the most tenuous lead. DC Jones came through the desks, looking faintly flushed, eyes blinking behind his spectacles. He held an open folder.

"You were right, ma'am—Jason Reynolds attended the same school as Tony Allen. They were in the same year. When Eileen moved to Margate, to be near one of her boyfriends, Jason stayed on in London, living mainly at Number Fifteen . . ."

"Oh, right!" Tennison breathed.

"Their class president reckons they weren't friends though. He says Jason was a troublemaker—bit of a jack-the-lad." Jones added doubtfully, "I suppose if they were neighbors they might have hung out together, but they sound very different."

"Which brings us back to Sarah." Tennison smacked her knuckles into her palm, fretting, frustrated. "Who Kernan has ruled out-of-bounds."

"Boss . . . ?" Haskons beckoned, and went back to frowning at two photographs on the board. They were earlier shots of an attractive blond teenager, in bra and black fishnets, gazing over her shoulder with an invitation in her dark eyes.

"This is a bit out of left field, but I think I recognize her."

"Go on."

"I don't know." Haskons was distinctly uneasy. He cleared his throat. "I've been looking at them for ages."

"Richard . . ." Tennison said warningly, her eyes like gimlets.

"No, I mean, Camilla's really happy there," Haskons said feebly.

Tennison was stumped. Camilla was his eldest girl, six years old. "What's Camilla got to do with it?"

Haskons stared at the photos, worrying his thumbnail. "I think it's her teacher," he said.

Miriam Todd, in charge of the third grade at St. John's Primary, was attractive enough, and dark eyed, but she wasn't blond. She had shoulder-length black hair and was about twenty-two, Tennison guessed. Supposing the pinups of the girl in bra and fishnets to have been taken five, six years ago, Miriam would then have been in her mid-teens. Near enough the right age.

Perched on tiny chairs, they sat in the sunny classroom during the lunchtime break, the cheerful clamor of kids in the playground an odd and unsettling backdrop to the purpose of Tennison's visit.

She took the two photographs of the blond girl Haskons thought he recognized from her bag and showed them to Miriam.

"Tell me if you recognize this person."

"No, I've never seen them before, Inspector."

But her nostrils betrayed her. They had flared, just a fraction, enough for Tennison to notice the sharp intake of breath Miriam was trying to disguise. She tried a different tack.

"What about this girl?"

Miriam looked at the full color studio portrait of Joanne that her mother had supplied, happy and smiling, sparking with life.

Miriam shook her head slowly. "No. She's beautiful . . ."

"No, Miriam," Tennison said bluntly. "She was beautiful. Her remains were found buried in the garden of Number Fifteen, Honeyford Road. Her hands had been tied behind her back with a belt. The belt belonged to Jason Reynolds. Do you recognize this man?" She held up the picture of Harvey and Jason together, and Miriam blanched. "Do you want to look at these photographs again?"

"No need." Miriam's voice was barely audible. She avoided Tennison's direct gaze.

"Tell me what you know about the photographer."

"Jason Reynolds." Miriam sat up straighter and moistened her lips. "I met him in the summer of . . . eighty-six. At that time I was still at school, still living with my parents in Margate. He was taking photographs on the beach. You know, a seaside photographer. He was charming, funny . . ." She took a breath and plunged on, "As you know, I let him take photographs of me. For a while he made me feel attractive, the center of attention. I stripped and posed, I dressed up and posed. Whatever he asked for, really. I wanted to get away from home. My mother was ill."

She looked down at her hands, twisting in her lap. Tennison waited.

"He said . . . he said his uncle had an flat I could rent, that he'd look after me. I came with him to London. To Honeyford Road . . ."

There was a noise in the corridor as the children trooped in from the playground. They bunched in the doorway, one or two spilling into the classroom. Tennison put the photographs away in her bag.

"Can you wait outside, please," Miriam called to them. "Just line up quietly." They went out. She turned back, brushing a few strands of hair from her pale forehead. "I lived in the basement flat there for two months."

"June and July?"

"Yes."

"Did you work as a prostitute, Miriam?"

She colored a little. "No, not really. Jason tried to get me to go with various friends he brought around, but . . ." She shrugged. "Well, none of us really knew what we were doing."

Tennison looked into the dark eyes with their fringe of black lashes. Sick shit that he was, Tennison thought, Jason Reynolds must have something going for him, some form of mesmerizing power, to have snared, among many others, such an attractive teenager as Miriam Todd must have been six years ago. She said, "Did you have sex with his uncle? David Harvey?"

"Sometimes," Miriam admitted. "When I couldn't pay the rent."

"Do you recognize either of these men?" Tennison showed her pictures of Vernon and Tony Allen. "Did you have sex with either of them?"

"No."

"Where were those photographs of you taken?"

"At the flat."

"And in Margate?"

"His uncle had a trailer."

"Can you tell me where that was exactly?"

Tennison felt herself tense up, willing Miriam to provide a name, a location, but she was shaking her head. "I can't remember the name of the site. It was somewhere out of town."

"Right. Well." Tennison stood up. She fastened her shoulder bag. "Thank you very much."

"That's it?" Miriam said, staring up.

"Yes. Thank you," Tennison said, and departed.

It was too late for a cafeteria lunch, and she couldn't face another sandwich, so once back in the hectic Incident Room she smoked a cigarette to fend off the hunger pangs. Her consumption was gradually creeping up again. To hell with it, no good worrying: she'd try stamping out the filthy weed once this case was finished.

"Boss—have you seen this?" She glanced around at Lillie, who was unpinning one of the photographs.

"What?"

He brought it over and laid it on the desk: a young girl ogling the camera, hands cupping her breasts. The room was tiny and cluttered, a bunk bed and a small window visible in the shot. It looked like the interior of a trailer. Lillie pointed to a calendar behind the girl's right shoulder, taped to the end of the bunk bed.

"That's a 1992 calendar," he said.

It was, Tennison saw, peering at it closely. "So he could still be using the trailer. Try all the sites in the Margate area." She stubbed out her cigarette and stood up. "I want Eileen Reynolds arrested," she informed everybody. "Bring her in, put her in an interview room and let her stew. Perhaps that might bring Jason out from under his stone."

Muddyman called to Rosper, "Check all the campsites in the Margate area—Jonesy, give him a hand."

There was a bustle and excitement in the room, as well as a fog of cigarette smoke. Now they had something positive to go on. They had a real live prime suspect and they were going after him.

Lillie opened the plastic bag and took out the belt with the Indian Chief's head buckle. He passed it to Tennison, who held it in her spread hands for Eileen Reynolds to see.

Eileen had been sitting in the interview room for half an hour or more, with only a WPC for company. She'd drunk two cups of machine coffee, smoked three cigarettes, and she was looking sullen. Tennison didn't expect her to cooperate, but that didn't matter. The woman seated opposite her, she was convinced, was the mother of a murderer, so she was in no mood to be gentle or pull any punches.

"This is the belt, Eileen, that was used to tie Joanne's hands behind her back."

"I've never seen it before." Eileen dismissed it with hardly a glance. From an envelope Tennison took the photograph of Harvey and Jason. She saw Eileen register that the buckle on Jason's belt was identical. But all it brought was an indifferent shrug. "Lots of belts that look like that."

"Really. I think it's quite distinctive." Tennison took out the polaroids and placed them, one by one, in a row, on the table. She said, "The dead girl, Joanne Fagunwa. Joanne and Tony. Joanne and Sarah."

Eileen stuck her head forward. "So why isn't it Mrs.-fucking-Allen sitting here?" she snarled. "Go and arrest her. Arrest Sarah."

Tennison said quietly, "Because it's my belief that Jason took those photographs."

"You have no proof of that."

"They were found in your brother's flat, Eileen."

"I don't know anything about that," Eileen said shortly. Her sallow cheeks were flushed. She was putting up a stone wall, but it was crumbling at the foundations. In her eyes Tennison could see the fearful uncertainty, and thought: she's going to crack.

But she was not about to spare Eileen's feelings; she intended carrying on the way she had started. Coolly, as if dealing a hand of cards, she placed a set of the later, harder, more explicit shots in the middle of the table.

"That's your son, Eileen. Your son the pornographer. Would you look at them, please?" Eileen deliberately stared off. "Look at them, please. You won't look at them. All right," Tennison said, her back straight, her clasped hands resting on the table, "I'll describe them to you. The first shows a girl, she's about fourteen, I would say. Your son's penis is inserted in the girl's anus. Her face shows pain . . . and fear."

"Stop it . . . !" Eileen's whole body was straining forward, her mouth an ugly twisted shape. "You sick bastard bitch!"

"It's not me in the photographs, Eileen," Tennison went smoothly on, "I didn't take them. Your son Jason did that." She glanced down. "The next, a different girl, slightly older perhaps . . ."

There was no need to go on.

Eileen rocked forward, covering her face, her head shaking to and fro. A strangled sob escaped from her. She was breaking into pieces. Tennison looked at her, unmoved. She said, "Tell me where Jason is."

"I don't know . . ." Eileen looked up, spittle dribbling down her chin, her eyes tortured. "We should never have come south. God . . . I did my best . . ." Tears rolled down her face. "He's no son of mine. He's . . . he's . . . he's some sort of . . ."

"Tell me where Jason is," Tennison repeated.

"I don't know," Eileen said in a pathetic high-pitched voice, almost like a little girl's. Tennison believed her.

"Where's your brother's trailer, Eileen?"

"As far as I know he . . . he sold it." She was sobbing, fighting for breath. "To help pay off the loan."

Tennison replaced the photographs in the folder. With it tucked under her arm she left the room, not looking back. All the way down the corridor she could hear Eileen's racking sobs. She wondered if Joanne Fagunwa had sobbed like that, just before Jason Reynolds bashed her brains in.

Vernon Allen was sitting at the table in the living room, newspapers spread out in front of him. Unusually for a man who took pride in his appearance, he was unshaven and disheveled, almost scruffy. He wore his shapeless cardigan, his shirt collar was undone, and his felt hat was shoved to the back of his head. Rather mechanically he was cutting out articles and photographs, placing them in a neat pile. The room was in semi-darkness, the flickering blue light from the TV set and a small lamp in the corner providing the only illumination.

Vernon snipped away, added the clipping to the pile and reached for another newspaper. He looked up as a shadow fell across the table. Sarah was standing in the doorway. She was barefoot, a terry robe wrapped around her.

"How is she?" he asked. His voice sounded dull, as if he didn't care one way or the other; he did care, deeply, but he was wrung out of all emotion, hollow inside.

"Sleeping."

"I don't like her taking drugs."

"It's better than having her crying all night." Sarah came in and sat on the arm of an armchair. She looked in silence at the clippings and mangled newspapers. "Pop, why are you doing that?" she asked quietly.

"They're about Anthony."

"I know that. I just don't see how it helps."

"Well," Vernon said wistfully, "if it helps me, then surely there's nothing wrong."

"You know I'll be going back to college right after the inquest," Sarah said.

"Of course." The scissors snipped. "Is there someone who can take notes for you, so you don't fall behind?"

"Yes." She sighed; as if it mattered at a time like this. "Yes, don't worry."

"Sarah, did Tony ever talk to you about . . . about that night?"

"No." Sarah got up. She folded her arms tightly across her chest, hands underneath her armpits. "My bath'll be running over."

Vernon became still, the scissors poised in his hand. His son was on TV. His Tony. It was the local news, and there was a small picture of him in the corner of the screen, above the announcer's left shoulder.

". . . twenty-two-year-old Anthony Allen, who is at the center of an internal police inquiry into the running of that station. Detective Superintendent Mike Kernan today issued the following statement, after the news was announced that the coroner's inquest into the death would start tomorrow."

Sarah couldn't stand it anymore. She had to leave him, unable to bear the glazed, obsessive expression on her father's face. The picture switched to Kernan outside Southampton Row.

"I'm very pleased that the inquest opening tomorrow comes so promptly after this tragic event. I am confident that the verdict will fully vindicate the police . . ."

In the darkened, flickering room Vernon stared at the screen, his cheeks wet with tears. He didn't realize he had any left to shed.

The train rattled past, briefly illuminating the figure crouched beside the track. As soon as it had disappeared around the curve, Jason skipped nimbly over the tracks and went down the opposite embankment. He stopped halfway, partially concealed behind some bushes, almost level with the bedroom window of the house that backed onto the railroad. The light was on and the curtains hadn't been drawn.

Sarah Allen entered the bedroom. She was wrapped in a large bath towel, a smaller towel around her head. She took down a suit that was hanging from the closet door and removed the plastic cover; the suit had just been dry cleaned. She held it up to the light for inspection, and hung it back on the closet door.

Jason unzipped his Windbreaker. He reached inside for the Pentax Z10 that was slung around his neck. The camera had three-speed power zoom with auto-focus and automatic wind/rewind. He clicked it on and checked the LCD display for battery level. Then he was ready.

Sarah unwrapped the large bath towel and let it fall. No need to draw the curtains, when the rear of the house wasn't overlooked. She removed the towel from around her head and began to dry her hair.

Grinning, Jason put his eye to the viewfinder and pressed the shutter.

The death of Tony Allen in police custody was a hot story, and the press and TV were there in force, milling about on the steps of the Coroner's Court. Jonathan Phelps never missed an opportunity, and he was keen to make an early statement, announcing that he personally had secured the services of a top attorney, Mrs. Elizabeth Duhra, to represent the Allen family.

It was just as well he got in quick. The arrival of Tony's fiancée Esta with their daughter Cleo stole his thunder. This was the shot the media wanted, and they closed in, jostling and elbowing each other aside as she stepped out of the cab with Cleo in her arms. Esta pushed through and struggled up the steps, a barrage of flashes dazzling her and frightening the little girl. Gratefully she accepted the help of an usher, who came to her rescue and led her inside, from pandemonium to relative peace and calm. And the ordeal hadn't yet begun.

Oswalde sat with Burkin and Calder on the witnesses' bench. To his left he could see Tennison, talking quietly with Superintendent Kernan. Oswalde's eyes swept around the packed court, then he bowed his head and stared at the floor. He couldn't look at the Allen family. Vernon's arm was clasped around his wife's shoulder; she looked to be in a state of shock. Not even crying, just blank-eyed, drugged to the point where she hardly knew what was going on or whether it was actually happening.

Sarah was sitting with Esta, Cleo between them. Sarah was staring at Oswalde, and even though he kept his eyes on the floor, he could feel the force of her emotion, like a wave of hatred sweeping over him. No mercy there, and it didn't surprise him, when he had none for himself.

The coroner was anxious to get the proceedings started. He waited while the court official called for silence, and then began by addressing the jury. His voice was brisk, neutral, cleansed of all nuance or feeling.

"No one is on trial. We are not investigating a crime, but a death. It is our job—yours and mine—to decide how Anthony Allen came to die in police custody. One word of warning. You may be asked to study some distressing photographs taken both at the time of the young man's death and at the autopsy. I consider the viewing of these pictures to be vital as an aid to reaching your decision. We will begin today by hearing from the pathologist, Professor Bream."

Bream was on the stand less than ten minutes. He stated the cause of death, from asphyxiation, and answered one or two questions from the coroner. Custody Sergeant Calder was then called to the stand. He swore the oath, and knew he was in for a tough time immediately when Mrs. Duhra started questioning him. She was a slim, elegant, dark-haired woman with high cheekbones and quick, intelligent eyes; a member of a prominent Anglo-Indian family, most of whom were in the legal profession.

Calder wasn't sure that she was deliberately playing to the largely black public gallery, but she didn't seem to mind their occasional shouts and angry interruptions.

"It must have taken a great deal of force, and determination, to strangle himself in such a manner." Mrs. Duhra tilted her head a fraction, inviting his agreement. "Wouldn't you say?"

As procedure demanded, and as he had been taught, Calder directed his replies to the coroner.

"I don't know about that."

"Professor Bream thought so. He thought Tony Allen may have taken rather a long time to die." She glanced down at some papers, and looked up again. "You did make your checks every fifteen minutes, didn't you?"

Calder gazed straight in front of him, the globed lights reflecting on his bald head. "Thirty minutes, sir."

"Oh yes . . ." Mrs. Duhra nodded. Her lips thinned. "Because it's checks every fifteen minutes for prisoners at risk. And, of course, you'd decided that Tony Allen wasn't at risk, hadn't you?"

"Mrs. Duhra," the coroner mildly rebuked her. She was making assumptions about Calder's judgment at the time without any supporting testimony to that effect.

"Why was the flap left open?" Mrs. Duhra asked.

"Because the prisoner requested it to be left open, sir."

"Why?"

"To let in some fresh air."

"Because he couldn't breathe . . . because he was claustrophobic?"

"I don't know about that, sir."

"No, I don't suppose you do," Mrs. Duhra said, though her tone implied that any person with half a brain ought to have known. "If, as you say, he refused the offer of a lawyer—"

"He did, sir." Calder wanted that on the record.

"—why did you not make sure that some responsible adult was with him? His father, for example, who was in reception almost the whole time?"

"Because there was no need."

Mrs. Duhra frowned, giving him a quizzical look that was more for the benefit of the jury. "But his mental health was of concern to you, was it not?"

"No, sir," Calder said stolidly. "It was not."

This reply seemed to puzzle Mrs. Duhra even more. She consulted her papers. "But as we can see from the custody record, you called a doctor at nine-fifteen P.M." She glanced up, waiting.

"Yes," Calder admitted. He'd forgotten about procedure, addressing his reply directly to her.

"So you must have been concerned," Mrs. Duhra went on, logically proving her point. "But he didn't arrive, did he? Until after one A.M. Didn't you think to call another doctor?"

Calder's mind went blank. He said in a rush, "I was busy."

Mrs. Duhra let the silence work for her. She said, all the more effective for her quiet tone, "A boy loses his life because you were busy?"

The coroner leaned forward. "Please, Mrs. Duhra . . ."

"Doctor or no doctor, you had it in your power to send Tony Allen to the hospital. With hindsight would you not agree that you made a series of ill-judged—not to say fatal—decisions?"

The court waited. Calder finally nodded. "Yes. I made mistakes, I admit it . . ."

In the hubbub that followed, while the court official called for silence, Kernan muttered to himself, "For God's sake, don't cry about it, man!"

The call came a few minutes after eight P.M. Tennison was in the kitchen, preparing her evening meal. This entailed removing the dinner-for-one (complete meal with two vegetables) from the freezer and nuking it in the microwave. She unhooked the wall phone. "Tennison."

"It's Muddyman. I'm at the hospital. David Harvey died at seven-thirty this evening."

"God . . ." She sagged against the door frame. "This investigation is turning into a graveyard."

"How did it go today?"

"Dreadful."

"Oh, well, tomorrow's another day."

She said good-bye and hung up. The microwave pinged. She took out the shallow tray, peeled back the cover, and contemplated the dinner-for-one. There were a couple of muddy shapes swimming in a sea of streaky orange-brown sauce. A dog couldn't live off this, she thought, reaching down a plate and rooting in the drawer for a knife and fork.

12

"Would you say that the interview was carried out in accordance with PACE regulations?" Mrs. Duhra asked.

"Yes, ma'am."

"You made no attempt to bully or pressurize Tony Allen?"

"No, ma'am."

"Sergeant Oswalde, do you hold a Higher National Diploma in Psychology?"

"Yes, ma'am."

"Passed with Distinction?"

"Yes, ma'am."

The door at the rear of the court opened and a uniformed figure slipped in. Kernan hadn't noticed, but Tennison had. She nudged him, and they both stared in dismay as Commander Trayner slid into a seat. What the hell was the top brass doing here? Come to decide which heads were to roll?

Oswalde was standing up well to the questioning. He was keeping his answers short and to the point, not laying himself open to misinterpretation. He was an imposing figure on the witness stand, very tall and very handsome, with a natural quiet dignity. He was immaculately turned out, in a well-cut dark suit, his shirt a crisp dazzling white against his dark skin.

"It is my intention to call an expert witness in a moment," Mrs. Duhra continued. "A professor of forensic psychology. But before I do so, I'd like to read you some of Tony Allen's last recorded words—before you had him returned to his cell—and ask for your assessment."

Oswalde's face was a closed book. This was the part he'd been dreading, and he had to keep telling himself to stay cool, don't give her an opening, keep it short and sweet.

Mrs. Duhra began reading from the transcript, holding it up in her left hand so that her face was visible to the jury and her voice carried across the crowded courtroom.

"Tony: 'I'm choking.'

You: 'No you're not.'

Tony: 'I'm choking. I can't breathe.'

You: 'There's nothing wrong with you.'

Tony: 'I'm dirt. I'm dirt in everyone's mouth. Choking them. My life is dirt.'

You: 'This is pointless. I'm putting you back in the cells.'

Tony: 'My life's a cell. I'm trapped. So much earth, and mud. Earth to earth. Dust to dust.'"

Mrs. Duhra put the transcript down. She folded her arms and looked at Oswalde, tilting her head in that characteristic, faintly mocking way of hers. "In the cold light of day, Sergeant, how would you assess Tony's mental state?"

"From that I'd say he was hysterical."

"Obsessed with death?"

"Yes."

"In despair?"

Oswalde hesitated. "Yes."

"Suffering from claustrophobia?" Mrs. Duhra said, her eyes narrowing as she scrutinized his impassive face, searching for a chink of weakness, of doubt, she could exploit.

"Possibly," Oswalde said, realizing that she was trying to drive him into a corner, and refusing to be driven.

He could feel the eyes of the entire court upon him. The coroner on his high bench was leaning on one elbow, his chin cupped in his hand. In the well of the court, the Allen family, seated in a row, were as if carved from stone. Vernon Allen's large hands were clasped tightly to his chest, in an attitude of prayer. Beside him, Esme gazed dully into space. Sarah's eyes were filled with a cold, implacable hatred.

Mrs. Duhra's voice went on, quietly, lethally, "Yet you had him returned to his cell. His ten-foot-by-six-foot cell. You had an exemplary record, Sergeant. Could it be, that in some subtle way, you were being tougher . . . harder . . . on this black suspect because you too are black?"

There were murmurs and a few muffled shouts from the public gallery. Somebody yelled angrily, "Coconut!"

"I'm afraid your question is too subtle for me," Oswalde said evenly.

Mrs. Duhra permitted herself a tiny smile. His reply, however cleverly evasive, hardly mattered. She had made her point. She said, "Turning then to the attack that Tony is alleged to have made on your person . . ."

"Do you intend to question Sergeant Oswalde for much longer, Mrs. Duhra?" the coroner asked.

"Well, that rather depends on his replies, sir," Mrs. Duhra said.

"Then I should like to adjourn for the day. The court will resume at ten tomorrow morning." He gathered his papers together. The court official's voice rang out, "All rise!"

There was a small but vociferous group of antiracist demonstrators on the steps outside, waving placards and chanting slogans. As she came out with Kernan, and they crossed the road together, Tennison heard shouts of "Bounty bar" and "coconut," being directed at Oswalde, who pushed his way through, grim-faced.

Kernan unlocked the door of his car. He looked to be in a foul temper. "What the bloody hell was the commander doing there?" he asked angrily.

Tennison, walking on to her own car, turned around. "Mike—the verdict has to be suicide," she reassured him. "Any other is unthinkable."

Kernan scowled. "Meanwhile my station is portrayed by Duhra as a hotbed of racism and brutality. Well, I can kiss my promotion good-bye. Thanks to two black bastards . . ."

Tennison stared at him, genuinely shocked. "I beg your pardon!"

"Well . . . you know what I mean," Kernan muttered, giving her a shifty look.

"No. I don't."

"Oh, for God's sake . . ." he said wearily, and with a heavy sigh he got in the car and slammed the door.

For once, Tennison was having a relaxing evening at home. There was paperwork in her briefcase, waiting to be looked at, but she thought, to hell with it. She wasn't in the mood to settle down to anything. The inquest was preoccupying her mind. Until it was over and done with, the verdict in, she couldn't fully focus her concentration.

After a long soothing shower she put on pajamas and her luxurious Chinese silk dressing gown, a special present to herself. She wasn't the kind of woman to pamper herself, but just occasionally she felt the need to splurge on something extravagant, and damn the expense.

She wasn't expecting anyone, least of all Bob Oswalde. She let him in, wondering if this was a wise thing to do, but the instant she saw the despondent look on his face, her heart went out to him. He was wearing a long overcoat, and underneath it the dark, conservative suit he had worn in court. He was polite and apologetic, but tightly bottled up, she could tell from the way he stood in the center of the room, glancing around with jerky, distracted movements, kneading his palms together.

"I'm sorry just to show up like this. I had to talk to someone."

She gave him a searching, quizzical look. "Someone?"

He looked at her, biting his lip. "You."

She indicated the armchair, and he sat down, elbows on his knees, staring at the carpet. "I just don't know what happened to me that night. When she read that stuff back to me today, it was"—he swallowed, his brows knitting together—"so obvious that Tony Allen was at risk, and that I'd been bullying him. Why . . . ?"

His face was stricken. He looked to be in pain. She went to the bar tray on the small ornate table and poured two good measures of Glenlivet, carried them back and gave him his.

Oswalde held the glass, not drinking. "Perhaps they're right," he said after an age. "Perhaps I am a coconut."

Tennison sat down on the sofa, smoothing her dressing gown over her knee. "Yes, I heard them shouting that. What does that mean?"

"Coconut. A Bounty bar. Brown on the outside, white on the inside." His voice was bitter.

"I should have thought it was a bit more complex than that, Bob."

He raised his head. "Do you think I was responsible for his death?"

He looked so forlorn that she had to resist the urge to go to him and put her arms around him and comfort him. Instead, she said firmly, and truthfully, "No, I don't. But it's what you think that matters."

The pain in his eyes was mingled with fear. He said huskily, "I think I as good as killed him." Abruptly, he put the glass down on the carpet and stood up. "I've got to go."

Tennison stood up. "You can stay if you want."

"No. I'd better go."

She saw him out, and walked with him along the hall to the street door. On the step, hugging herself against the chill, Tennison said, "Call me if you need to talk."

"Thanks."

Feeling somehow that she had let him down, not helped him at all, she reached up and, pulling his head forward, kissed him lightly on the lips. "Take care."

She watched him walk off down the dark street, shoulders hunched, his overcoat flapping around his long legs. In the shadow of a tree, directly opposite, Jason kept his finger on the button, thinking he might as well use up all thirty-six frames because he was going to get the film processed first thing in the morning anyway.

"And at eleven twenty P.M. you interrupted Sergeant Oswalde and asked to have a word with him." Mrs. Duhra looked up from the notes she was consulting to DI Frank Burkin in the witness box. "Because you were concerned about the way Sergeant Oswalde was conducting the interview?"

"No, ma'am."

"You weren't concerned for Tony Allen's safety or well-being?" Mrs. Duhra asked, a suggestion of surprise, incredulity even, creeping into her voice.

"No, ma'am."

"Then why the need for 'a word'?"

"I thought a particular line of questioning was proving fruitless," Burkin said in a steady monotone, as if he'd rehearsed his reply, which of course he had. "I wanted to suggest another approach to Sergeant Oswalde."

"I see." Mrs. Duhra glanced towards the jury, making clear her total skepticism of that, and turned once more to Burkin. "So *nothing* in Tony Allen's behavior gave you cause for concern?"

Burkin's face was immobile, his eyes opaque. "No. Nothing at all, ma'am. What happened was a complete surprise to me. And a shock."

The transformation, Tennison thought, was truly incredible. Not a trace of the tattoos, the earrings, the matted hair, and the five-day growth of beard. In their place, standing there in the witness box, a presentable young man with a short haircut, wearing a neat dark suit, pale green shirt, and navy-blue tie. The former drunk had been smartened up so that he wouldn't have known who it was if he passed himself in the street.

Mrs. Duhra had a friendly witness, and she treated him accordingly.

"Mr. Peters, you were in the cell next door to Tony Allen on the night he died . . ."

"Yes, miss."

Polite too, Tennison thought. Such a well-mannered boy wouldn't dream of screaming Fucking Fascist Bastard Pigs.

"Did you see or hear anything that is relevant to this inquest?"

The reformed crusty wormed his finger inside his collar, tugging his top button open. "I saw the body. They didn't want me to. They were trying to move me but I saw it lying on the cell floor."

"I see. Anything else?"

"Yes, miss. I heard the prisoner sobbing. Trying to tell the police he couldn't breathe. I heard some policemen kicking at his cell door, shouting at him, telling him to shut up. Then I heard him threaten them."

He paused there, as if, a cynic might have supposed, he had been told to, and Mrs. Duhra picked it up.

"Threaten them? What exactly did he threaten them with?"

"Killing himself. If they didn't let him out of the cell he . . ."

His words were drowned in the commotion from the public gallery. The court official was on his feet, calling for quiet, and the noise subsided.

"He threatened to kill himself," Mrs. Duhra said. "Go on."

"I heard a police officer—I'm not sure which one—shouting at him."

"What did the police officer shout?"

Probably enjoying this part, the crusty said in a loud voice, "'Go on, then, nigger, hang yourself.'" The public gallery burst into an uproar. People were standing and waving their fists. Through it all, the crusty went on, "They were all shouting, 'Do it. Do it. Do it.'"

"Quiet!" The court official was back on his feet. "*Quiet!*"

It subsided again, but this time an angry rumbling murmur continued, like distant yet ominous thunder. Sarah Allen had half-risen to her feet, her father pulling at her arm. Her head on one side, Esme was weeping silently, huge tears trickling down her face.

The coroner became impatient, having to wait several moments until he could be heard.

"Sydney Peters, can you tell the members of the jury how you came to be occupying the cell next to Anthony Allen on the night he died?"

"I had been arrested, sir," said the crusty meekly. "For being drunk, sir."

"Mr. Peters, is it true that you are a member of Narcotics Anonymous?"

"Yes, sir."

"Perhaps you could tell the members of the jury why that is."

The crusty blinked, and gave the jury an ingratiating smile. "Because, ladies and gentlemen, I used to be addicted to various narcotic substances."

"Thank you, Mr. Peters," the coroner said icily.

The coroner's heavy-handed attempt to discredit her witness brought a fleeting sardonic smile to Mrs. Duhra's face. His testimony had been heard, that's what mattered, and what had been said couldn't be unsaid.

Tennison, in her bra and slip, was rooting in the closet for a clean blouse when the phone rang at twenty past eight the following morning. She flopped down on the bed and reached out to answer it. She listened and then said sharply, "Who is this? And why should I want to read that rag?"

Jason was in a phone booth on the shore. It was a gorgeous day down here, a clear blue sky above, the sun sparkling on the waves and making dazzling white triangles of the sails of the yachts setting out for a morning sail around the bay.

He said silkily, "I think you'll find something in it to amuse you. Now promise me you'll buy it."

"Who is this?"

Jason hung up. He didn't really want to, because he liked the sound of her voice, but it could have been dangerous, staying on the line. She had a sexy voice. She was sexy-looking too. Nice figure, big tits. As a rule he liked them young, the younger the better, because they were innocent and impressionable. But he would have made an exception in her case. Give her a few drinks, get her down to bra and panties, load up the Pentax and shoot off a roll. And after that, well, who knows? Could be her lucky day, a bit of throbbing young meat. They said the older ones really appreciated a good, strong hammering.

Jason came out of the phone booth onto the sunny promenade. He was breathing quite heavily and his erection was chafing inside the tight crotch of his jeans.

He set off at an amble, his black T-shirt under his open Windbreaker damply clinging to him, and went looking for amusement, diversion, thrills.

Sarah Allen was on her way to the kitchen when she heard the mail drop through the mailbox. Upstairs, her nine-year-old brother David was complaining that he couldn't find his shoes and that Miss Hoggard would make him stay behind if he was late again. From the bathroom, muffled by the sound of running water, came the bass rumble of Vernon's reply.

Sarah leafed through the bills and advertising junk to see if there was anything for her. There was. She ripped open the large manila envelope and took out a sheaf of ten-by-eight glossy photographs. At first, and rather stupidly, it only registered that they were of a young and slender naked black woman, a towel wrapped around her head. Then she gasped when she realized it was she. Staring in horror and total disbelief, she looked at the grainy images of herself in the privacy of her own bedroom, taken with a powerful zoom lens.

There was some writing on the back of one of them. In such a state of shock, Sarah had to read it twice before the words sank in. Her legs turned to water. Trembling and sick with fear, she stuffed the photographs back into the envelope and pushed it under her sweater as Esme came downstairs.

Gorgeously sunny at the seaside it might have been, but in London it was pissing down. Tennison came out of the newsagent's and made a dash to her car through the downpour. She slid behind the wheel, shaking cold rainwater from her hair. She unfolded the tabloid newspaper and quickly turned the pages. She didn't have to look very far. There it was, spread across page five, bold headline that smacked her between the eyes. "TOP COP'S DARK SECRET."

Underneath it, three muddy photographs that nevertheless clearly identified the two figures kissing on a doorstep as Bob Oswalde and herself; and as if that weren't bad enough, she was in pajamas and that bloody Chinese silk dressing gown.

Tennison slumped back in the seat. The inside of her head was like a snowstorm, thoughts swirling around. It took her a couple of minutes to get a grip, steady herself. When she had, she knew what she had to do. There was a phone booth on the corner. She ran to it and called Mike Kernan at home, hoping to catch him before he left. Thank God he hadn't. He listened to her, but didn't seem to get the full drift of it right off.

Boiling with rage and frustration, Tennison explained angrily, "It's a threat. From Jason—he's the photographer." She nodded vigorously, showering raindrops everywhere. "Yes, of course I'm going to court! I wouldn't give them the satisfaction. Someone needs to warn Oswalde . . ."

At that moment Oswalde was sitting in a cafe, down a side street nearly opposite the Coroner's Court, polishing off bacon and eggs. He was just finishing his coffee when Burkin strode in, a snide, knowing grin on his face. He was loving this; about time that stuck-up, holier-than-thou bitch got what was coming to her.

Hardly stopping on his way to the counter, he rudely waved a folded newspaper in Oswalde's face and slapped it on the table.

"What—?"

"Page five."

"What?" Oswalde said again.

"Fried egg, bacon, and beans, two of toast, cuppa tea with, please, love." Burkin brought his tea to the table and squeezed in next to Oswalde. "Page five." He said with a smirk, "That explains it—why the boss was so keen to take your side when Tony killed himself."

Oswalde had found the item. He read the headline and stared blankly at the picture, too shell-shocked to feel anything.

Burkin stirred his tea. "So tell me, is she good? Does she do tricks?" He leered at Oswalde, gave him a sly nudge. "I bet she likes it on top, doesn't she?"

Oswalde stood up fast, in the process catching Burkin's elbow and upsetting his cup. Hot tea spilled into Burkin's lap, and he stood up fast too, grinding out, "*Shit!*" When he looked up, tight-lipped, the door was swinging shut behind Oswalde's departure.

It was the final day of the inquest, and there was an air of nervous expectation as the court quickly filled up. Tennison took her seat next to Kernan, who gave her a fishy-eyed stare; by now he'd seen the tabloid splash, another nail in the coffin of his promotion prospects. He didn't know that he could ever forgive her for this, and he wasn't sure that he wanted to.

Both of them watched the Allen family filing in. Tennison wasn't keen on catching their eye, because up until today it had been plain, unadulterated anger and hatred directed at the benches occupied by the police, especially from Sarah. Now Sarah was looking directly at her with an expression Tennison couldn't fathom. Almost as if she sympathized, or at least understood, what Tennison must be going through after the seedy revelations in that morning's paper. It was baffling. Sarah should be reveling in her discomfiture—positively gloating over it—Tennison thought, and yet she wasn't, and wondered why.

Everyone rose as the coroner entered, and settled down again. The public gallery was packed with black faces. Total silence fell like a shroud as the coroner began his summing up.

"Ladies and gentlemen of the jury. The time has come for you to withdraw and consider your verdict. But before you do I should like to offer you some advice. There are a number of possible verdicts, but I think under the circumstances you should focus your attention on just three."

He paused and stated them, separately and distinctly, so that there should be no confusion.

"Unlawful killing. Misadventure. Suicide."

There were murmurs from the public gallery. Three possible verdicts, but only one would satisfy them, and convince them that justice had been done.

During the recess, while the jury was out, Tennison went for a smoke in the white-tiled basement which served as a waiting room. She sat apart from all the others, needing to be alone. Besides, the Allen family was down there, surrounded by friends and well-wishers from the public gallery. Therefore it came as a surprise when Sarah came up, and after a slight hesitation, sat down beside her.

She looked at Tennison with the same sort of understanding as when she had entered the courtroom, as if they shared some secret sorrow.

"I'm sorry about that tabloid shit."

"So am I," Tennison said with feeling, puffing on her cigarette.

"I received these this morning." Sarah glanced around, and shielding it with her body, took a brown envelope from her bag and handed it over. "From the same source, I'd say. No—look at them in private," she said quickly, as Tennison lifted the flap. Then she got up and returned to sit with her family.

In the ladies' lavatory Tennison took the photographs from the envelope and looked at them. Jason's handiwork, no question. He and his phallic zoom lens, poking it where it wasn't wanted.

Now she knew why Sarah's attitude towards her had changed so dramatically. They were sisters in this, two female victims of the same ugly, sick masculine mind.

She read the message scrawled in green felt-tip.

"DON'T EVEN THINK OF TALKING TO THAT FUCK TENNISON. I'M WATCHING YOU."

Tennison felt her fury mounting to white-heat. Not because of what he had written about her, she didn't waste a second worrying about that. It was his sheer egotistical arrogance that incensed her. The swaggering bully who'll stoop to the lowest, meanest, most cowardly tricks and thinks he can get away with it. Up to and including rape, buggery, and murder.

God, she was going to nail that little shit if it was the last thing she did.

The court official waited for complete silence. "And have you reached a verdict?" he asked.

The jury foreman rose to his feet. "We have. The verdict is suicide."

The crowd of reporters, photographers, and TV crews was in danger of becoming a riot, fighting to get near Vernon and Esme Allen as they came down the steps of the courthouse. Esme was weeping openly, in the protective circle of her husband's arm as he shouldered his way through to the waiting cab. Behind them, spilling through the doors, came their friends and supporters from the public gallery, still angry, still booing at the verdict. The antiracist demonstrators joined in. Chants of "coconut" and "Bounty bar" went up as Oswalde appeared. He struggled down the steps, being jostled and pushed on all sides.

Tennison and Kernan were largely ignored. They managed to slip through as the media pack surged after the family, wanting shots of Esta and the little girl, who were being helped by Sarah.

Vernon was doing his best to get Esme into the cab. She was hysterical, swaying and shaking her head like somebody drunk. "He wouldn't kill himself, never," she wailed. "He had no reason. He was to be married this weekend . . ."

The photographers closed in, flashes going off.

"He loved his daughter, his family, he was always a happy boy . . . he would never kill himself!"

Sarah, handing Cleo into Esta's arms in the cab parked farther along the street, straightened up and looked through the crowd to where Tennison was standing. The eyes of the two women locked and held. Both of them knew that Esme, the grieving mother, was deluding herself. Far from being a happy boy, Tony had been eaten away inside by some dreadful knowledge, a secret he carried with him to the grave.

Watching Sarah climb into the cab, Tennison wondered how much of that secret she shared with her brother. How much both of them really knew about the cause and circumstances of Joanne Fagunwa's brutal murder.

Tennison drove down Chancery Lane, turned left onto Fleet Street, heading for Ludgate Circus. She'd decided that the station could do without her for a couple of hours. It was just after midday; she'd take an extended lunch break and maybe stock up with frozen dinners at Sainsbury's.

The rain was still drumming down as she waited for the lights at the intersection with Shoe Lane. Gazing through the windshield, her eyes drifted down to the envelope Sarah had given her, lying on top of the dashboard behind the steering wheel. Tennison leaned forward, frowning. There was a postmark. Of course there was a postmark, cretin, if the bloody thing had been posted! She snatched it up. The postmark said "CLACTON" with yesterday's date.

Instead of turning right, Tennison swung into the left-hand lane, getting a few looks for her pains, gave them the finger in return, and drove up Farrington Street, back towards Southampton Row.

She barged into the Incident Room, unwinding her long scarf, already halfway out of her raincoat. Copies of the offending tabloid were swiftly stowed away. She didn't show that she noticed, and if she noticed she didn't care.

"Richard."

"Yes, boss."

"Start again with the trailer parks. Start with Clacton and any others that come within the postal district. And then work out along the Essex coast from there. Fast, please."

Haskons jumped to it, organizing the team to begin the search.

Jason had been studying her for a good five minutes before he made his move. She was wearing an anorak over a white blouse and a pleated gray skirt, white ankle socks, and Adidas sneakers. Cutting school, he could spot 'em a mile off. Feeding her lunch money into a slot machine. This was the fourth one she'd tried in the shore arcade, and at this rate she'd be out of cash in no time flat.

He circled around, closing in. Fourteen, he guessed, maybe just turned fifteen. Ripe as a peach waiting to be plucked. Firm pair of titties sprouting under that starched blouse. Nice arse on it too. He liked a nice tight arse.

He breezed up, and leaning nonchalantly against the machine she was working, started reading aloud from the tabloid he was holding, spread open at the page three pinup.

"'Lovely Donna, from Clacton. Thirty-six, twenty-two, thirty-four.' It's you, innit?"

"What?" the girl said, chewing gum. She had small, very white teeth and a soft downy complexion. Her long dark hair was pulled back in a severe, straggling bunch, but it couldn't hide how pretty she was.

"In the paper." Jason swiveled around to show her the picture of the girl arching her back and bending over slightly so that her breasts hung down, nipples teased erect. "You're Donna."

The girl shot him a glance from under her eyelashes. "Dirty creek," she said, but she was laughing when she said it.

13

Young David answered the telephone. "Hold on, please," he said, polite as ever, and called out, "Sarah—phone."

Sarah came through from the kitchen, wiping her hands on a tea towel. She glanced up the stairs, to where the sound of her mother's racking sobs was rending the air. She had been crying like that, almost without pause, for the past hour. Vernon had had to call the doctor in, and they were upstairs with Esme now.

"Who is it?" Sarah asked, taking the phone.

"I don't know." David went off into the kitchen.

"Hello?" It was Tennison. Sarah went stiff. She shook her head, watching furtively as her father and their G.P. came down the stairs. She said in a low voice, "It's not a good time to call . . ."

Vernon came into the hallway. "Thank you, doctor. Perhaps she'll sleep now." He opened the vestibule door to show the doctor out.

"Hang on a sec." Sarah carried the phone into the living room and pushed the door to with her foot. "Okay."

Tennison sounded serious and urgent. "We can't let him get away with this, Sarah, He can't turn us into his victims as well."

Sarah looked up at the ceiling. Her mother's sobs were like hacksaw blades, slicing through her brain. She didn't know how much longer she could stand it. She looked wildly around the room, as if seeking some means of escape, and then made up her mind. "All right. But off the record. I'm not giving evidence. Tomorrow . . ."

"No, tonight," Tennison said. "Please."

Sarah shut her eyes tight and breathed in. "All right. I can probably make it around seven."

"Thank you. 'Bye."

Sarah replaced the receiver. Her hands were sweating and she was trembling all over. Above her head, Esme's broken sobbing went on, and on, and on.

The Incident Room was a cacophony of voices and jangling telephones. Each man on the team had been given a segment of the Essex coast, from Burnham-on-Crouch to Harwich, checking out every trailer park in a wide radius of Clacton. At her desk, Tennison watched over the bustle and babble of activity, chewing on a Nicorette and anxiously waiting for the first sign of a positive lead.

It was Gary Rosper who struck lucky. He banged the phone down and was up on his feet, eyes alight, scurrying across the room to Tennison, waving his notepad. "The Shangri-friggin'-la, Walton-on-the Naze."

"Where the hell's that?" Tennison frowned.

"Christ knows." Rosper didn't.

"Richard," Muddyman called out to Haskons, who was already unfolding a large-scale map. "Walton-on-the-Naze."

Everyone gathered around. Muddyman pointed it out, nine miles north of Clacton, right on the tip of a peninsula of tiny scattered islands, creeks, and mud flats.

"How long will it take to get there?" Tennison asked.

"This time of day, about three and a half hours," Muddyman said.

"I want Oswalde to go," Tennison said. She ignored the looks that were being bandied about, and went on crisply. "Inform the local police. Tell them to sit tight until he gets there."

"Why Oswalde?" Muddyman wanted to know, voicing the question none of the others dared ask.

"Because I say so."

No arguing with that. Haskons went to phone Oswalde at home, telling him to put his skates on. After three days in a stuffy courtroom a day at the seaside would make a welcome change.

With a professional eye, Jason delved through the rack of frilly slips, cami tops, and lacy French panties. He selected a cute little number in peach, pleated sides and a see-through lace panel at the front. A crafty, calculating look in his pale blue eyes, he stepped over to the changing cubicle and swept aside the plastic curtain.

"Oi," Sandra said. Down to her bra and panties, she turned away, covering up. He'd been right. Well-blessed up top. This was going to be fun.

"There you go, Sandy." Jason grinned. "Try them on."

She took the pleated French panties and gave him a long stare as he lingered by the open curtain. "Go on then."

Jason pursed his lips and blew her a wet kiss before turning away. His chest felt tight, his breath catching in his throat.

It took Oswalde a shade over three hours to reach the campsite at Walton-on-the-Naze. Three officers from the local Essex C.I.D. were waiting for him in the site manager's office. Taking charge, he told them to stay put until he'd had the chance to size up the situation, and escorted by the manager, he walked down the sloping gravel path through row upon row of trailers to the one pointed out to him as belonging to Jason Reynolds. There was a cool breeze whipping in off the sea, and Oswalde was glad he'd put on a thick-knitted polo-neck sweater and his leather jacket.

The site was on two levels. Jason's trailer, painted yellow with shiny metal strips along its sides, was on the upper level; below it, another thirty or forty trailers were grouped in an area bordering the sand dunes, and beyond them the ground sloped sharply down to the beach, a wide expanse of flat wet sand that was deserted as far as the eye could see.

This being off-season, there was no one about. Any movement, Oswalde realized with satisfaction, would be immediately spotted. He looked at his watch. It was a few minutes after six, and the light was already fading. He spoke on his mobile phone to the officers in the manager's office at the entrance to the site.

"Yeah, come through . . . one of you stay in the office and keep an eye out. The other two join me at the van, okay?"

Oswalde had a quick look around, then walked up the little concrete pathway to the door. All the windows, he noted, were masked off with black curtain material. He tried the door, and glanced around at the manager, a dumpy, bald-headed man with tufts of gray hair sticking out over his ears.

The manager shrugged. "I haven't got a key."

Oswalde went to work. In two minutes he had the door open. Inside, it was pitch black. He felt for a switch, and the interior was bathed in red light. The entire trailer had been converted into a dark room, fitted out with processing and developing equipment, an enlarger, print trimmer, everything.

"Bloody hell," the manager muttered, gawking inside.

"Can you wait outside, please?" Oswalde pulled the door to and poked about. Strips of film hung down on wooden pegs. There was a cork board with dozens of girlie shots pinned to it, mostly black and white, a few in color. Three large wire trays held stacks and stacks of prints. On top was one of Sarah Allen, taken through her bedroom window. Oswalde's mouth tightened as his eye fell on some photographs of him and Tennison, kissing on her doorstep. He stuffed them inside his jacket and zipped it up.

A few minutes later the two Essex C.I.D. officers arrived. They looked at him expectantly, their faces ruddy in the dim red light.

"We'll just have to sit tight till he shows up," Oswalde said.

Tennison did her best to make Sarah relax. The girl was so tightly wound up that at first she just sat in Tennison's office, her back rigid, hands locked together in her lap. The station was quiet after the busy day, most of the team having gone home, so there were no interruptions. Tennison bided her time. She didn't ask any questions, content to let Sarah say what she felt like saying, no pressure, no hassles.

Of course, all her immediate thoughts were centered on Tony. They had been very close; the pain she felt at his death was like a raw wound, her grief for him nakedly displayed on her face.

Eventually, in a small, very hushed voice, she began to unburden herself, recalling how depressed Tony had become.

"I think when it was really bad he heard voices. I know he dreamed of Joanne, night after night. Always the same dream . . . that she'd been buried alive. He could hear these muffled screams." Sarah's large dark eyes clouded over. She clenched her jaw, fighting back the tears. "He couldn't bear to be alone. Confined spaces petrified him. If only I'd been around I could have explained . . . but Mum and Pop just wouldn't believe there was anything wrong with him."

She stared miserably into space, overcome with guilt that she'd let her brother down, been away at college when he needed her.

Tennison allowed a small silence to gather. She said gently, "Sarah, you could still help by giving us a statement about what happened."

". . . he never had a girlfriend," Sarah went on, not listening, following the track of her own thoughts. "No one was more surprised than me when Esta came onto the scene. I don't suppose that would have lasted if she hadn't become pregnant."

Tennison knew that Sarah was circling around and around it, steeling herself to make the plunge and reveal the truth. But it was no good here, in the privacy of this office. It had to be a statement, freely given, committed to tape. Without it, all this was leading nowhere.

She leaned forward, gaining Sarah's attention by the force of her gaze. "Please, Sarah . . ."

Sarah turned her head away, and Tennison's spirits sank. But then, looking resolutely away, tears standing in her eyes, Sarah gave a tiny, almost imperceptible nod. Tennison let her breath go.

As she sat down at the restaurant table, Sandra's breasts swelled above the low-cut neckline of the black velvet dress. The dress had a cutaway panel at the back too, revealing that she wasn't wearing a bra. With her dark lush hair brushed out and cascading over her shoulders, her eyes made-up with dusk-gray eye shadow and Virgin Rose lip gloss emphasizing her full lips, she could easily have passed for eighteen. Jason was very pleased with himself. He could certainly pick 'em.

Sandra was flushed and excited, already a bit tipsy on the two drinks she'd had in the pub. Jason ordered a pint of lager for himself and a Martini and lemonade for her. It was early in the evening and the place was quiet, not more than a dozen diners all told, mostly couples.

"Can we have some of them popadoms?" Sandra asked, wriggling in her chair.

Jason smirked at her naïveté. "This is a Chinese restaurant, Sandy."

"I know," she said sulkily, coloring.

"I'll order for us." He patted her hand. "Don't worry your pretty little head."

When the food came she didn't know how to use chopsticks, and had to eat it with a fork. Jason got another round of drinks, even though Sandra protested she'd had enough. Her eyes were glassy, and she got the giggles. Every time Jason whispered in her ear, usually some crude sexual innuendo, she shrieked with laughter. Some of the other diners were becoming irritated. At a nearby table a man muttered to his companion that it was a disgrace, they shouldn't allow that type in the restaurant in the first place.

Jason was up on his feet, neck pumping, fists bunched. He strode across and stuck his head in the man's face.

"What you say? My type? What's 'my type,' eh? Eh?" White-faced with rage, he grabbed a plateful of food and chucked it in the man's lap. "You fuck." He gripped the edge of the table and tipped the whole thing over.

Two waiters rushed over and started yammering away in Chinese. Jason angrily brushed them off. He marched back to his table, threw down some money, and jerked his thumb at Sandra. "C'mon darlin'."

Sandra rose to her feet, a little nervous smile hovering on her lips. She'd never seen anyone change so quickly, so suddenly. He was like a different person. A shiver ran down her spine, but she did as she was told, and meekly followed him out.

In the darkened trailer, Oswalde and the two local C.I.D. officers waited. They'd made themselves as comfortable as possible in the cramped space, Oswalde taking the bench couch under the window, the other two sitting on cushions on the floor. From time to time all three looked hopefully at the mobile phone, standing upright on the sink unit. Their man in the site manager's office would give them advance word the minute Jason drove in. Then they'd be ready for him as he stepped through the door.

Oswalde smothered a yawn. Join the police for a life of thrills and excitement. They forgot to mention the endless hours of boredom while you waited for something to happen.

The embossed plastic sign in the center of the door read: TAPED INTERVIEW ROOM.

Sarah paused on the threshold as Tennison pushed the door open and bade her enter. She said tremulously, "Was this the room Tony was interviewed in?"

Tennison shook her head. "No, love." She touched Sarah's arm reassuringly. "No."

Sarah went in. Tennison followed and closed the door.

Jason's arm was hooked around Sandra's waist, leading her to his Cavalier hatchback at the curb. The giggles were back. She staggered tipsily in her high heels and nearly tripped, and he had to hoist her up. His hand slid down to squeeze her buttocks. Lovely firm body on it, not an ounce of flab. That's why he preferred them young; those old fucks with their arses hanging out turned his stomach. He bet this tart would go at top speed, a regular rattlesnake.

He unlocked the passenger door and got her safely installed. He had a hard-on like a tent pole, couldn't wait to see her stripped off and get stuck in. He had some whisky back at the van, just in case she needed loosening up, a bit of Dutch courage. He went around to his side, chest tight, grinning into the night air. He was going to give her a lot more than whisky and Dutch courage.

Sarah had taken off her coat and scarf. She hadn't bothered to change before she left home; wearing a simple dark dress and loose knitted cardigan, she sat opposite Tennison, her feet together, hands resting in her lap. Even in her fraught condition there was a noble dignity about her, Tennison decided. She held herself proudly, shoulders back, and it was only in her large liquid eyes that the terrible anguish and pain she was struggling with showed itself.

Tennison started the tape. Without any prompting, Sarah began to speak in a level, controlled voice, quiet yet distinct, recalling the events of the last day of August 1986.

"I was at home with Pop until Tony got back. That was just before nine, as arranged. As soon as Pop had gone, Tony said he had to go out for a while. Of course he wasn't supposed to, so we started arguing. I watched him go back out to a girl who was waiting for him. Joanne. Tony must have got Pop's keys from somewhere, because they went next door . . ."

"Into Harvey's house?" Tennison said, clarifying it for the record.

"Yes. Joanne was looking for a flat to rent and Tony told her about Harvey's basement. How his father owned it and all that. I followed them and watched. They went into the bedroom together. They kissed, lay on the bed together. I watched for a while. It made me feel odd. But I was fourteen, and curious, I suppose."

She stared past Tennison, a slight glaze over her eyes, reliving the memory.

"Then I saw Jason come in. Tony didn't know he was staying there . . ."

The Cavalier hatchback turned in at the gate and bumped over the rutted track past the site manager's office. It passed within a few feet of an open window, through which a storm of cheering erupted as Paul Merson headed in the equalizer against Liverpool. Leaning forward in his chair, the C.I.D. man punched the air and grinned across at the manager. Show those bleeding natives how it's done. He took another bite of his corned beef and pickle sandwich, and settled back with eager anticipation in the comfy armchair.

Outside, the red taillights grew faint, and finally disappeared from view as the gravel track dipped down.

"I went around to the front door and rang the bell. Jason answered. He invited me in. I had quite a crush on Jason at the time . . ." Sarah's eyes rolled towards Tennison, the thought of it filling her with horror. She moistened her lips. "Tony was pissed off to see me but I wouldn't go. Tony and Joanne were dancing together. Jason was watching them, encouraging them, telling them to kiss . . ."

Randy and raring to go, Jason gave Sandra a sloppy wet kiss as they staggered up the concrete pathway together. Her giggles now weren't altogether convincing. The cold night air had sharpened her senses, cut through the alcoholic haze swirling inside her head. He had bought her fancy new clothes and underwear, wined and dined her, and she wasn't fool enough not to know that he expected something in return. She wasn't at all sure that she wanted to give it.

But it was too late; she was here, at his trailer, and she didn't know how to get out of it.

Jason fished out his keys. Cuddling her, he turned the key in the lock, yanked the door open, and pushed her inside, into the pitch blackness.

". . . Jason found a Polaroid camera. It must have belonged to Harvey. Jason took photographs. We were drinking Harvey's booze, getting quite drunk."

Sandra stood blinking as the light came on. Sidling past her, Jason slapped her neat little bottom in the black velvet dress. "Make yourself at home."

He went to a cupboard, hunting for the bottle of White Horse. "This is my studio . . . I got me darkroom in another van," he told her.

Swaying a little, Sandra gazed around. She was feeling a bit queasy, and it wasn't only the drinks and the Chinese food. The walls were covered from floor to ceiling with pictures of naked girls. There was a camera set up on a tripod and a battery of lights. And there was a couch, draped in a satin sheet. Suddenly she realized she was trembling all over. A horrible cold crawling sensation was seeping up from the pit of her stomach.

She jumped as he turned to her, clutching a bottle and two glasses. His fair eyebrows were raised, and there was a devilish gleam in his pale blue eyes.

Oswalde closed his eyes. He wasn't tired, didn't feel at all sleepy, but it was a strain just sitting there, staring into black nothingness, the minutes dragging painfully by. His nostrils twitched. Somebody had let one off, silent and deadly. Great. He lay back on the couch, trying to think of something pleasant to pass the time, but it wasn't easy with that reek pervading the air.

"Then Jason started making suggestions."

"What kind of suggestions?" Tennison asked when Sarah paused.

"That we should undress. Encouraging Tony to touch Joanne. I could see Jason was getting turned on by it . . . we were all turned on in a way," she admitted. "He ran out of film after about ten pictures but he wouldn't stop. He became more serious. More insistent."

Sandra took another sip of whisky, just to keep him quiet. He was going on and on at her, so she did. She hoped it might make her feel better, but it didn't. The room was spinning. She sat down heavily on the couch, and then he was beside her, his breath on her cheek, his hand creeping over her breast. She tried to push him away. Somehow she didn't have the strength. The room was whirling around and her head felt hot. And all the time he was whispering, whispering in her ear in a sly, silky voice. She couldn't make sense of the words but she knew what he wanted her to do. She knew from the way his hand was kneading her breasts and tugging at the black velvet dress. And his soft voice whispering in her ear.

"When Joanne wouldn't pose topless he started pulling at her clothes."

Tennison sat quite still, not interrupting or asking questions, allowing Sarah to tell her story. Her voice had taken on a mechanical, almost dreamlike quality. As if she were describing a film that was unrolling inside her head. A horror film from which she couldn't avert her eyes, had to see it through to its grisly end.

"She tried to stop him. It wasn't funny anymore. He was pulling at her clothes. Joanne was scared. Tony tried to stop him. But Jason got really angry. Angrier than I've ever seen anyone. He went completely wild. He punched Joanne in the face. Her mouth was bleeding . . ."

Sarah's own mouth twisted into an ugly shape. Her eyes went wide and bright with fear, watching the film unroll. A spasm shook her entire body, held rigid and bolt upright in the chair. The real horror was about to begin. She forced herself to carry on.

". . . he broke a bottle. I really believed he'd use it. He made Tony tie some tights, they were my tights"—she faltered, her throat working—"around Joanne's mouth. Jason took off his belt and tied Joanne's hands behind her back."

He'd gotten her dress off at last. She was sitting on the silken-draped couch, shivering in her low-cut bra, staring up at him with fearful eyes as he undid the buckle and slowly slid the belt through the loops of his jeans. He felt he was in a state of fever. The blood was pounding in his temples. He breathed in a deep lungful to steady himself, to take the quaver out of his voice and make it sound natural as he said casually, "Don't be afraid . . ."

Sandra stared up at him, hugging herself. It made her breasts swell over the lacy top. He could see right down her cleavage. Beautiful. Firm young titties. He was going to have the time of his life with this lovely piece of cunt; shaft the arse off it, literally.

"Nothing to worry about, eh?" he said soothingly. "It's the johns. They love a bit of bondage." He coiled the belt in his hands. "I won't tie you too tight. It's all acting really . . ."

"I don't like it," Sandra whimpered, her mouth trembling.

"Course you do," Jason grinned, uncoiling the belt.

"I don't . . ."

"He raped her there in front of us," Sarah said, the pain of that dreadful night frozen in her eyes. "He held the broken bottle over her face. And we did nothing. We stood and watched. Joanne was choking on the gag. And we stood and watched."

She shuddered.

He had her just how he wanted her. Facedown on the couch, hands behind her back, the belt wrapped around her wrists and pulled tight so that it cut into her flesh. Sandra cried out then, in agony, as Jason thrust down with all his strength, forcing rear entry. She felt she was being ripped apart.

Getting into his stroke, Jason pumped away. Sandra's head bounced on the couch under the impact of his incessant pounding. She felt suffocated. She couldn't see. Her tangled hair was in her eyes and stuck to her forehead. Her cheeks were mottled and blotchy from the hot tears rolling down. She gasped as he went in, deeper. The pain was searing, tearing at her inside. She tried to scream but her head was being rammed into the couch, and what came out sounded like the muffled, terrified squeals of a whipped animal.

Jason kept at it, grunting with every thrust. Sweat from his chest sprinkled her back. His cap of blond hair was saturated. In his left hand he held the remote control. Every few seconds he pressed the button. The shutter clicked. The camera whirred to a new frame. He pounded away and pressed the button. The shutter clicked. He'd been careful in his advance preparation, made sure there was a new roll in. Five down, just thirty-one to go.

"When it was all over he went . . . suddenly quiet. He warned us that we were guilty too. That he had the photographs to prove it. He let us leave. We didn't know what to do. We went home. We went to our rooms. When Mum got back we pretended to be asleep in bed. The dreadful thing was that we just left Joanne there. We weren't even sure whether she was dead or not . . .

"The following night I heard noises in the next door garden. When I looked out my window I saw Jason and Harvey digging. They were putting the earth into sacks and Jason was taking them off somewhere to dump. I guessed why, but . . . but I couldn't look after that." Her voice sank to a choking whisper. "My nightmare was the sound of those shovels. The following morning I told Tony. We took an oath together never to tell a soul. The next time I made myself look from my bedroom window all the slabs were in place. Not a sign that anything had happened. Sometimes I could almost believe it hadn't . . . until she was dug up again."

Sarah's face collapsed. She was moaning and sobbing, tears dripping off her chin and splashing onto her bare arms. She was shaking her head, helpless and bereft. "It was an awful secret we carried around with us . . ."

She covered her face and her body slumped forward until she was bent almost double, great racking sobs shuddering through her.

"Oh, God, what am I going to do . . . without him? Without Tony . . . ?"

Tennison went quickly around the desk and knelt down beside her chair. She put both arms around Sarah and held her.

14

With a groan, Oswalde rocked himself forward and swung his feet to the floor. He wriggled his toes inside his Reeboks and arched his back, stretching. He must have been sitting in that same semi-crouched position for over an hour, and had possibly, without realizing it, dozed off. His buttocks tingled as the circulation got going.

Light was filtering through the curtains. From the floor of the caravan came a bass-baritone duet of snores; both C.I.D. men were well away in the land of nod.

Oswalde twitched the curtain aside and looked out at a new day. Over the sea, the sky was a clear tranquil blue, as if it had been washed clean overnight. It was very early, not yet six-thirty. Oswalde stared dismally out, wondering what the fuck had happened to Jason Reynolds. Had he got wind of them? Or just been delayed somewhere and would show up later? The thought of having to spend all day cooped up in here with the phantom farter made Oswalde profoundly depressed.

He went outside and gratefully sucked in some of the chill morning air. He'd better give Tennison a call, he thought, rolling his head around to loosen up his cramped neck muscles. She'd want to be brought up to date on what was happening, or rather *not* happening.

Oswalde's head stopped in mid-roll. Below him, on the lower level, a Cavalier hatchback was parked outside one of the trailers. It hadn't been there last night. How the hell had it got onto the site without the man at the gate noticing it?

Thoughtfully, Oswalde zipped up his jacket. Stepping lightly, he moved down the grassy slope and skirted around to approach the trailer end on, because he could see a curtain was drawn across the large picture window, blanking out the view. Arms spread to keep his balance, he tiptoed over the grass and pressed his face close to the glass, hoping there might be a chink in the curtains. No luck. He moved around to the door, pausing at another window, but that too was curtained off.

Oswalde edged up to the door and gripped the handle. In one swift smooth movement he had it open and was ducking through the doorway, eyes narrowed as he peered into the gloomy interior.

Lying on the bed of crumpled satin, Sandra's eyes rounded with terror as the tall, athletic black man burst in. She was wearing a school uniform—blouse, gray pleated skirt, white ankle socks—and was manacled and chained up for a Jason special: schoolgirl bondage. Oswalde moved towards her. Sandra pressed back into a corner and screamed, loud and piercing, and kept on screaming even when he raised both hands in an effort to calm and reassure her.

"It's all right, I'm a police officer! I'm a police officer!"

Oswalde knelt down, trying to make the girl understand that it was okay, she was safe now. Behind him, Jason crept through the narrow doorway from the kitchen area. He was gripping the empty Scotch bottle by the neck. His lips drew back in a silent snarl. His pale blue eyes with their fringe of blond lashes were wide and murderous. He swung the bottle and brought it down on the back of Oswalde's head. Oswalde went sprawling, a cascade of stars and flashing sparks filling his universe. He pushed himself back up onto his knees, groggily shaking his head. It took another ten seconds to stagger to his feet. When he looked round, squinting painfully towards the door, Jason had gone.

Oswalde stumbled outside. He touched the back of his neck. Blood was trickling down through the roots of his hair. He staggered forward a few paces, shaking his head to clear it, and looked wildly around. The bastard couldn't have got far. Then he spotted the blob of blond hair, just disappearing through the waving tufts of coarse grass that grew along the edge of the sand dunes. He was heading for the beach.

Oswalde went after him. Elbows pumping like pistons, he ran towards the broken lip of the cliff top, where it crumbled and fell away to the flat open expanse of wet sand. The blond head vanished as Jason hurtled down the steep sandy slope. Oswalde ran through the coarse grass, feeling it whipping against his legs. He reached the same spot and plunged down, arms cartwheeling as he sought to maintain his balance. He landed with a jarring thud on the hard wet sand and then he was sprinting, long legs at full stretch, the running figure in his sights, the blond head wobbling as Jason started to tire.

Got you, you bastard!

Gaining on him with every stride, Oswalde rapidly closed the distance between them. He could hear Jason's labored breathing as he reached the shallows of the retreating tide. Jason splashed through them, staggering and sending up curtains of flying spray. He was just recovering when Oswalde launched himself. He hit Jason like an express train. Down they both went into the water. Oswalde got an iron grip on Jason's wrist and twisted his arm halfway up his back. With his other hand he grabbed Jason by the scruff of the neck, forcing his head down into the water.

Jason came up, coughing and spluttering. He twisted around, a face filled with hate. "Coon, black bastard, jungle bunny, nigger . . ."

Oswalde rammed him under.

Jason came up again, spewing seawater, snarling, "Rastus, sambo, fucking wog!"

Oswalde rammed him under.

Jason came up again, coughing and gasping. "That's right, you fucking coon, kill me as well!"

Oswalde could have done it, easily, there and then, he knew it. And there was nothing in the world he'd have liked better than to drown the little shit. Rid the world of that perverted scum.

Instead, with an icy, purposeful deliberation, Oswalde gave him handcuffs and slapped them on. Fighting for breath, Oswalde gave him the full caution, as per the book. "Jason Reynolds, I'm arresting you on suspicion of the murder of Joanne Fagunwa . . ."

The two C.I.D. men splashed through the shallows. Oswalde continued: "You do not have to say anything, but if you do it may be given in evidence."

Jason raised his head and spat in Oswalde's face. Hauled to his feet by the C.I.D. men, he was dragged away, still screaming, "Coon, nigger, wog, fucking black bastard . . . !"

Oswalde sat in the water. He closed his eyes. He could feel the warmth of the early sun on his face. It felt very good.

Tennison was waiting in the rear yard of Southampton Row when Jason arrived. She wanted the satisfaction of seeing for herself the little shit being brought in and formally charged. Handcuffed and pinioned between two officers, Jason was led inside. As he passed Tennison, he thrust his blond head towards her, leering into her face.

"Thanks for the show the other night. Just your scene, eh? Nice bit of beef . . . nice black tubesteak up your stank!"

Then he was bundled through, snorting and sniggering to himself. Tennison turned away. She'd seen what she wanted to see. She didn't believe in the death penalty, but she was always open to persuasion.

• • •

The morning was damp and misty. Oswalde came along the neat gravel path, dressed for a funeral he hadn't attended; that had been yesterday, only he knew that his presence wouldn't have been welcomed, that it would have upset the Allen family.

Tony's grave was smothered in wreaths and flowers wrapped in cellophane. Oswalde carried a small bunch of flowers, but there was no card attached. He stood for a moment, looking at the headstone, then laid the flowers at the foot of the grave.

Suddenly overcome with emotion, he crouched down and bowed his head. Jane had said he wasn't to blame. She had said that when other people made a mistake, it was only money involved. When the police made a mistake, sometimes a human life was put in jeopardy. And sometimes a human life was lost. He had tried to believe her, to convince himself that she was right, but it had a hollow ring, and the pain refused to go away. He would carry it with him for the rest of his life, a corrosive acid eating away at his soul.

He stood up and walked slowly back through the headstones to the gravel path, a tall dark figure that was gradually swallowed up in the morning mist.

Commander Trayner and DCI Thorndike were drinking sherry with Kernan in his office. There was an air of subdued yet distinct jubilation. Kernan detested sherry, but the occasion seemed to demand it, so he clinked glasses and forced the stuff down, hiding his grimace.

Thorndike was at his most overbearingly pompous. His voice was a pedantic drone, the corner of his thin mouth curling up in a tiny smug smile.

"This is not official, you understand, but under the circumstances it seems appropriate to give you a little preview. My recommendation is that disciplinary papers are served on Calder, DI Burkin, and DS Oswalde. I am critical of the way the station was run." He cast a glance at Kernan, who blinked and took another sip of the disgusting muck. "Procedures need to be tightened up," Thorndike went on primly. "Too many canteen cowboys. But I find no one to blame for the death of Tony Allen."

Kernan breathed a heartfelt sigh of relief.

Commander Trayner was nodding, well-pleased. "Clearly, David, you're the right man to sort this station out." He turned to Kernan, smiling. "And of course, congratulations to you too, Mike. Nailing Jason Reynolds and getting the move upstairs. I shall have to give you the name of my tailor. He's particularly adroit at disguising any tendency towards the middle-age spread . . ."

"Thank you, sir." Kernan refilled the commander's glass. "Do you intend to do anything about the press story, sir?"

Trayner considered a moment, and then shook his head. "Let it blow over. Oswalde is back at West End Lane."

"Yes, sir," Kernan said, again relieved. He said reflectively, "Besides, Tennison is a bloody good detective."

"Perhaps," Commander Trayner said, acknowledging the fact in rather a grudging tone. "But one who has displayed a considerable lack of judgment . . . I think you know what I mean?"

The debriefing in the Incident Room was also a subdued affair. The team had done its job well, had every reason to feel proud, but the death of Tony Allen in police custody cast a long, gloomy shadow.

Tennison had assembled all her detectives who had worked on the case; all but one. Bob Oswalde was absent, and she felt an obscure pang of guilt that he wasn't here today, even if the mood was far from celebratory. He deserved better than to have been sent packing, back to his old post, without so much as a word, some small gesture from the super. But that was Mike Kernan for you. More damn interested in his reputation, his bloody promotion prospects.

Despite what she feeling, she put on a bright face.

"I don't think there's any doubt that Jason Reynolds is going away for a very long time. The CPS has informed me that they are not going to press charges against anyone else."

The men exchanged looks. There was some justice after all. It would have been unnecessarily cruel for the Crown Prosecution Service to have implicated Sarah Allen in the murder.

"Now I don't know about the rest of you," Tennison said, clapping her hands lightly, "but I'm off to the pub—where I'd very much like to buy each and every one of you a large drink . . ."

"That won't be necessary, Jane."

Everyone turned. Commander Trayner had entered. There were a few puzzled frowns as Kernan and Thorndike followed him in. Not the usual thing for all the top brass to put in an appearance, even at the successful conclusion to a case.

Trayner said, with a faint smile, "Perhaps I can take this opportunity to make an announcement. Mr. Kernan here, will—from now on—be known to you all as 'Chief Superintendent' Kernan . . ."

Mock groans from the men, a few caustic cheers, and a scattering of applause. Kernan scowled self-consciously.

"I'm also very pleased to be able to introduce his successor here at Southampton Row. 'Superintendent' Thorndike."

A solitary cough from somewhere emphasized the deafening silence.

The men were looking anywhere but at Tennison. As Kernan's senior detective, she should rightfully have been next in line for his job.

Tennison felt the blood draining away from her face. It would have been the same if Trayner, instead of mentioning Thorndike's name, had walked up and punched her in the stomach. She stared across the room at Mike Kernan, who quickly shifted his gaze elsewhere. She didn't feel angry, not yet; she just felt numb.

Thorndike stepped forward, rubbing his palms together. "Thank you, Commander. I realize I may have made a few enemies carrying out the investigation on behalf of MS15." He gave a little cough, accompanied by a watery apology for a smile. "The best thing is to clear the air straightaway. If anyone thinks that's going to be a problem for them—get in the way of the smooth running of the station—then they should apply for a transfer immediately. Now, since we're all about to go off duty, and just to prove I have a lighter side, I've arranged for us to have a drink to mark the occasion."

Most of the team brightened up considerably as two uniformed PCs came in carrying several six-packs of Tennants Export and a case of Budweiser. The formal atmosphere vanished, and within moments there was the buzz of conversation and bursts of laughter, as the men drank. Thorndike mingled, even accepting a can, which he sipped as if it were a glass of sherry. Somebody offered Tennison a drink, which she refused. She was standing slightly apart, very pale, holding herself erect as if the effort cost her a great deal of willpower. She pushed her way through, and approached Kernan.

"So I didn't even merit an interview," she said stiffly.

Kernan squirmed a little. "Jane . . ."

But she'd already moved on to Thorndike. She said, politely and formally, "May I have a word with you, sir?"

"Official or unofficial?" Thorndike said.

"Official."

Kernan tried to intervene, his expression pained. "Jane, it can wait, surely . . ."

"No, it can't wait."

Thorndike looked at her, flat-eyed. "You'd better come to my office."

Thorndike sat behind the desk, occupying what had been Mike Kernan's chair and was now his. He'd already acquired the approved manner of pressing his fingertips together and pursing his lips while he waited for Tennison, standing in front of the desk, to speak.

She said quietly, "You'll have my formal request for a transfer first thing in the morning."

"Very well," Thorndike said, without a pause or the slightest hesitation. He sat, unmoving, and gazed at her.

Tennison stood. She didn't know what she was waiting for, unless it was perhaps some small expression of regret at her decision. Even of sadness at her departure. Or that she might like to sleep on it. Or to say that all her hard work at Southampton Row had been much appreciated. Or to say what a good officer she was and that they'd miss her. Or simply to say thanks, and good luck.

In the event she received nothing.

Fuck all.

She turned and went out.

Tennison went straight to her office, put her coat on and collected her briefcase. They were still carousing in the Incident Room when she walked past, a lot of raucous laughter and a babble of animated chatter. Always a good feeling when a case was over. Relax, loosen up, let it all hang out.

Tennison turned right at the end of the corridor. She walked on through reception, down the steps, and into the street.

PRIME SUSPECT 3

Silent Victims

LYNDA LA PLANTE

*I would like to acknowledge the talent of the writer Trevor Hoyle,
without whom this book could not have been published.*

1

The color slide of a naked female corpse flashed up on the screen. The girl was about seventeen, with long blond hair trailing over her white shoulders. She had once been very pretty. The projector clicked and the screen was filled with a close-up of the girl's head. The ligature, a piece of fencing wire, bit deeply into the soft flesh of her neck. Her once pretty blue eyes were swollen, blood filled, bulging blindly toward the sky. Her tongue protruded like a fat purple worm.

The audience in the darkened lecture hall didn't stir. Trained not to display emotion and hardened by experience, the homicide officers, police medical teams, and Pathology scientists sat in silent rows, enduring the grisly peep show. Hardened or not, experienced or otherwise, some stomachs churned. A few of the younger men felt faint, nauseous, or both. The voice of the lecturer didn't help. Jake Hunter went remorselessly on, the catalogue of human depravity and perversion made even more chilling by his educated Boston drawl.

"So far, apart from a recent case in the United States, known serial killers have all been male, almost all white, often unusually intelligent or extremely cunning. Most victims are female, usually young women, whose death—as you see here—is frequently accompanied by violent sexual assault. Invariably there is evidence of torture and mutilation. A number of cases have involved homosexuals."

Another slide flashed up. A full-face close-up of a swarthy, dark-haired, unshaven man with piercing, crazed eyes separated by a bony blade of nose. His thin, veined neck was cut off by a nine-digit mug-shot ident code.

"Richard Trenton Chase, the Sacramento 'Vampire Killer,'" Hunter went on. "Arrested for seven murders." The slide changed. "Note his own handwriting, taken from a scrawled message left at the scene of one of his crimes. *Catch Me Before I Kill More, I Cannot Control Myself.*"

Hunter turned to the audience. He was of medium height, with an athletic build that filled out his expensively tailored tweed suit. Under it he wore a button-down cream shirt with a striped silk tie. If the suit marked out his fashion sense as transatlantic, the brown cowhide boots with stirrup trim were strictly Dallas by way of Fifth Avenue.

Hunter went on, "Later, I'll come back to the clues the handwriting gave as an insight to the killer's personality."

He hadn't spotted Tennison. She'd arrived late, quite deliberately, and was standing by the door, her short hair a honey-blond blur in the flickering darkness. It rather amused her, Jake not knowing she was there, although they had already met twice during his lecture tour of England. Observing him secretly in the reflected glow of the screen gave her a tiny flutter of excitement, part nerves, part sexual danger.

His short brown hair was a little more flecked with gray, especially noticeable at the neatly trimmed sideburns, yet the bastard was still as ruggedly handsome as ever. His eyebrows were sun bleached, standing out against his tanned, craggy features. Had she aged as attractively? She still got her share of looks on the street, workmen whistled at her from scaffolding, but inside she sometimes felt like the Wicked Witch of the West. That was the job. A woman in a man's world. Required, *expected*, to handle the daily dish of crap and not flinch.

So she wasn't surprised, as she'd noticed on entering, to be the only woman present. She'd been the only female Detective Chief Inspector in the Murder Squad, at her previous posting at Southampton Row. About to move to Vice on the northern perimeter of Soho, Jane Tennison had no doubt that she'd be the senior female officer there by several light-years.

"Mass murder is the quintessential American crime," Hunter told his attentive audience. "Virtually unheard of a century ago, it has now become almost an epidemic. We are coming through a phase where males in the thirty-to-fifty age group are more brutal, more violent, than ever before. I have no doubt that these mass murders have a contagious element . . ."

They were listening silently not out of politeness or boredom, but because Jake Hunter spoke with the authority of hard-won experience. He had lived through it, been there on the front line. As a consultant to the New York Police Pathology and Forensic Research Unit, he was one of the world's top-ranked experts in the field; not only had he studied in depth the theoretical and historical background, he had witnessed the terrible bloody fact firsthand. He had been at the forefront in pioneering the technique of psychological profiling, now used by police forces in the United States and Europe. His books had become standard texts for the training of homicide officers, and were also required reading for students and academics specializing in criminal psychology.

In recent years he'd turned to fiction, producing three best-selling novels, two of which were under option to Hollywood studios. His latest book, however—and the reason he was here, lecturing to colleges and promoting it to a wider public—was nonfiction, a distillation of his many years' experience as a leading criminologist in the country that had patent rights on the concept of serial murder.

Another slide flashed up.

"George Henard executed"—Hunter repeated the word in his soft drawl—"*executed* twenty-three people, aiming point-blank volleys to their heads before turning the . . ."

He stopped short, seeing Tennison, and paused, eyes blinking. Tennison gave him a warm, slightly mischievous smile.

". . . before turning the nine-millimeter semiautomatic gun against his right temple for one final shot. What we cannot believe," Hunter said, winding up to his chilling conclusion, "is that the world is full of people with the potential to do this."

Someone had done something singularly unpleasant to little Connie. He was a slender, pale, waiflike creature with loose, curly red hair that in sunlight was imbued with a golden sheen. He was lying on a sagging sofa in the flat of a drag queen named Vernon—or Vera—Reynolds who at that precise moment, 9:35 P.M., was floating in a mauve spotlight dressed as Marlene Dietrich singing "Falling in Love Again" in a husky, tremulous baritone.

Connie tried to raise himself. His luminous dark brown eyes were muzzy. The cloud of auburn hair tumbled over his white forehead, but his beauty was marred by the dark stain of dried blood, like a slug's trail on his smooth cheek, where it had oozed down from the sticky gash on his right temple.

Again he tried to get up, failed, fell back. There was a racing blue edge of flame on the carpet. It touched the sofa and climbed the wrinkled cover. The flames turned to orange, their bright reflection twinkling in Vera's spangled and sequined gowns on the rack in the rear alcove.

The peacock feathers on another gown wafted in the updraft as the fire took hold. Half the room was ablaze, engulfing the sofa and the young boy so quickly that it sucked all the air from his lungs, leaving his scream stillborn in his raw throat.

The rack of gowns caught fire. Feathers and charred bits of chiffon wafted upward in a writhing cloud of smoke. The curtains went up. The paintwork on the frame of the closed window bubbled and peeled off. The entire living room and cluttered tiny kitchen of Vera Reynolds's shabby little flat were now ablaze.

With the sound and fury of a small but powerful bomb, the window blasted out into the night. The explosion shattered the peace of the six redbrick blocks of the flats. Burning debris showered down into the paved courtyard three floors below, setting alight a line of washing.

Already, from somewhere across the city, came the wail of an ambulance siren.

He'd find that bastard! Jimmy Jackson swung the old midnight-blue Merc into a side street near the canal, the headlights making oily smears on the wet cobblestones. He gripped the wheel tightly, his scarred, pockmarked face thrust forward, his slitted eyes hot and mad, peering through the cracked windshield. His thick, fleshy lips were drawn back against his teeth. Where the fuck was the little turd! Sure bet that Fletcher was down here with the dregs, another homeless, snotty-nosed kid living in a cardboard box with winos, dossers, and sewer rats for neighbors.

Jackson spotted a movement. He snarled a grin and stamped on the big brake pedal. Next second the door was flung open and he was out and running, tall and mean in a studded leather jacket and torn jeans, knee-length biker boots ringing on the greasy pavement.

The terrified kid had taken off, heading for the iron bridge over the canal. But each of Jackson's thumping strides was equal to three of Fletcher's. He caught up with him by the edge of the canal that had the carcasses of bed frames, bikes, and supermarket carts sticking up from its putrid surface. Reaching out a clawed hand, Jackson grabbed the kid by the hair and yanked him to a skidding halt; the act of doing it, the thrill of power, gave him something close to sensual pleasure.

The kid was babbling with abject terror. Jackson stooped over from his lean yet muscular six foot height and smacked him in the teeth. He hit him again with both barrels, left fist, right fist, to forehead and jaw. The kid squirmed on the ground, one grimy hand with bitten nails forlornly held up to ward off more punishment.

Jackson raised his fist.

"Dunno . . . dunno where he is!" Fletcher screamed through his bloody mouth. "I dunno where he is—I swear!"

Jackson took a pace to one side and kicked him in the groin. The steel toe cap went in with a satisfying solid *thunk*. He pushed his spiky mop of hair back with both hands. The kid might not know after all, but then again he might. Jackson needed a bit more convincing. He reached down for him.

Fletcher screamed, "No, please . . . I dunno, I swear! Please don't, don't . . . PLEASE DON'T HURT ME!"

• • •

Small groups of people in nightclothes were standing on the balconies watching the fire crews at work. Some of the crowd had babies and toddlers in their arms. Hoses from three tenders snaked up the brick walls and over the concrete balconies to the third-floor flat. The fire was out, just a plume of dirty gray smoke eddying from the blackened, blasted-out window and wafting away on a northerly breeze.

A patrol car, siren off but with lights flashing, sped into the courtyard from the main road and stopped with a squeal of brakes, rocking on its suspension. Two uniformed officers, bulky, square framed, leapt out and ran toward the stairway. A slighter figure, round shouldered and rather hunched, wearing a shapeless raincoat that should have been given to Oxfam years ago, climbed out and shambled after them. He paused to look up to the window. The bright flare of arc lamps, set up by the fire crews, illuminated the balcony like a film set. Detective Sergeant Bill Otley sniffed and pinched his beaked nose. The call on the closed police band had reported at least one body. Not strictly his line, but Otley was in the habit of poking his nose in where it didn't belong.

Taking his time, as he always did, Otley went up the bleak stairwell. On the third-floor landing, pools of water everywhere, he glanced around, sharp eyes in his narrow, intense face missing very little. He appeared intense, Otley, when he was reading the *Mirror*'s sports page or watching the weatherman on TV. As if he was suspicious of everybody and everything, seeking out the guilt, the real motive, behind life's innocent facade. Life wasn't all that innocent, he knew damn well; everybody was guilty of something.

"Some of the tenants want to know if it's safe to return to their flats," said a voice from within.

"Keep everybody clear," the fire chief replied. "We're checking the flats immediately above and below . . ."

The ambulance attendants were bringing out the body. Just the one. Otley stood a couple of feet inside the tiny hallway watching as they lifted it onto a stretcher and covered it with plastic sheeting. Curious position. The heat of the fire had petrified the charred, spindly black bones into what must have been the corpse's physical attitude at the moment of death. Arms stuck out like rigid sticks. Legs bent, feet curled underneath. The skull was a shapeless knob of sticky tar.

Otley pressed himself to the wall to let them pass.

"Anybody got an I.D. on it?"

"You jokin'?" one of the ambulance attendants said, maneuvering the stretcher through the front door. "Can't even tell if it's male or female yet!"

Otley grinned. He let them go and stuck his head into the living room.

The arc lamps made stark shadows of the firemen and the two uniformed officers rooting about in the wreckage.

The fire chief gestured. "Can somebody get duckboards on the balcony landing?"

Otley retreated through the hallway. As he went out he heard one of the uniformed officers say, "The flat belongs to a Vernon Reynolds. Lived alone. Aged somewhere between late twenties and early thirties . . ."

Otley pinched the hooked tip of his nose and descended into the gloom of the stairwell.

"I thought it might be nice to eat in the room tonight," Jake Hunter said. He was lounging in the passenger seat, one arm draped casually along the back of Tennison's seat as she drove him to Duke's Hotel just off St. James's Street where his publisher had booked him a suite. A cheroot dangled from his lips. He had the expansive air of an actor winding down after a performance. But then he always felt easy in the company of Jane Tennison. She felt easy with him too, though sometimes she wondered why the hell she should.

It had been ten years since his last trip over here. That was when they first met, and when they had their affair that became a long-term relationship. Long term in the sense of the seven months and fourteen days they had lived together in Jane's Chiswick flat. As a Detective Sergeant with the Lambeth Met, she had attended a course at the Bramshill Officer Training College where Jake was visiting lecturer. She was unattached, and so was he. Drinks in the bar one evening plus an almost instantaneous mutual attraction had led, naturally and inevitably, to their becoming lovers. At thirty-four years of age she was no starry-eyed innocent virgin. Jake, two years older, had been married in his twenties; his wife had died in a car crash before they had celebrated their first anniversary. But when they embarked on their affair, neither of them had realized what they were getting into. And when they did, it was too late to do anything about it.

Sooner or later, however, an awkward fact had to be faced. Jake was due to return to the States, to take up his consultative post with the New York Police Pathology and Forensic Research Unit. Jane was in line for promotion to Detective Inspector—something she had been fighting tooth and nail for—and had the chance of taking charge at the Reading Rape Centre. There was no middle way, for either of them. They were both committed to their careers, and both deeply in love. Impossible to reconcile the two. Jake had gone home, Jane had got her promotion and moved to Reading.

Since then, nothing much. Postcards, a few telephone calls, one birthday card—from her, carefully worded, to his office. End of story, until three weeks ago, when the flame had been rekindled.

Tennison was aware of his scrutiny, gentle, rather amused, and concentrated all the more on her driving.

"I thought it went really well tonight," Jake said. Not bragging, just a simple statement of fact. "Better than last Tuesday. It felt more relaxed, don't you think?"

"Oh, you always impress me," Tennison said, with just a touch of mockery, though it was true, he always did. "How long will you be away?"

"Two weeks." His publisher had fixed up nine speaking engagements and double that number of signing sessions from Brighton to Edinburgh; a punishing schedule. "You are coming with me?"

Tennison hesitated. Then she gave a firm shake of the head. "I've been meaning to tell you. I'm starting this new job . . ."

"Aahhh . . ." Jake blew smoke at the windshield, nodding sagely. He might have expected this. In fact he had. "Are we still going back to the hotel?" he asked, keeping his voice neutral.

"Yes," Tennison said evenly, without a pause. "Just for a drink."

Mike Chow, the senior pathologist, and his three assistants in their long green plastic aprons and white Wellington boots prepared the corpse for the autopsy. Lying on the stainless steel table, the body had been straightened to a more natural position. The blackened sticks of arms rested straight by its sides, the legs had been uncurled from their defensive fetal crouch.

"Okay," Mike Chow said, poking at the charred scraps of fabric with a steel spatula, "we'll get the clothes cut off and see what's left."

A police photographer moved around the table, taking flash shots from every angle. One of the assistants began to snip away, delicately stripping off the burnt clothing with his gloved fingers.

The pathologist leaned over, taking a close look at the corpse's head. A few singed strands of reddish-auburn hair could be seen still clinging to the gray knob of skull. Impossible to tell, though, whether it was male or female.

Mike Chow picked up his clipboard, flicked over a page. He blinked through his glasses. "Could be a . . ." A frown clouded his face as he turned to stare at the body. "Vera stroke Vernon Reynolds. What's that supposed to mean?"

They'd eaten a late supper, suprisingly good by hotel standards, in Jake's suite. A bottle of vintage Chateau-neuf-du-Pape to go with it, and two large brandies with their coffees. Jake was sprawled on the bed, vest undone, his tie pulled loose from his unbuttoned collar. He still wore his fancy cowhide boots, which far from detracting from it, added to his aura of total well-being.

Tennison stood at the small table next to the window, leafing through one of the twenty copies of Jake's book stacked on it. There was a bookstore display unit with a blowup of the dust jacket and several glossy photographs of Jake at his most seriously thoughtful. One of these took up the whole back cover of the book Tennison was holding.

She read the blurb inside the jacket and glanced up, smiling.

"You've taken four years off your age!"

Jake lazily swung his legs down and got up, flexing his shoulders. He wasn't abashed. "Serial killers are big business." His voice was a little slurred at the edges as he made a flippant gesture toward the pile of books. "Help yourself. Well, they were big business—last year! I think I missed the gravy train." He gave her a look from under his sun-bleached eyebrows. "Story of my life."

"Can I?" Tennison asked, holding up the book.

"One? Just one?" Jake came across and picked up a pen. "Take one, you get eight complimentary copies," he threatened, waggling the pen.

Tennison rested her arm on his shoulder as he leaned over to write. She smiled as she read the dedication. Very personal, but not so intimate—or incriminating—that she couldn't proudly show it off to a close friend or two. She gave him a hug.

"Thank you."

Jake took her hand in both of his. "Why don't you come with me?" The wine and brandy may have gone to his head, but she knew he was serious, not just fooling around.

"I don't want to get hurt again," Tennison said quietly.

"Again? That doesn't make sense."

She swallowed. "Jake, there wasn't anyone else before . . . you know." Ten years on, the memory hadn't faded, though she had exorcised the pain, or so she thought. "Just it was going too fast. It was such a big decision."

"Then why didn't you talk it through with me?"

"Because if I had, you would have made the decision for me."

He raised an eyebrow, watching her intently. "Would that have been so bad?"

"There's no point in discussing it now," Tennison said, withdrawing her hand. She turned away.

"There might not be for you, but there is for me. I wanted to marry you. I wanted to have kids with you, you know that." His voice rock steady now, befuddlement swept away. "Don't you think I deserved more than a kiss-off phone call . . . 'I'm sorry, Jake, it's not going to work.'" He gave a slow, sad shake of the head. "You never gave it a chance."

Tennison spun around. She said in a tone of sharp accusation, "I didn't know you wouldn't come back."

"What did you expect me to do? Come running after you?" He spread his hands helplessly. "You said it was over, then you hung up on me. Now you're doing the same thing. What are you so afraid of?"

"This is a bit ridiculous." Tennison clenched her fists impotently. If only she'd acted sensibly, like the mature woman she was, and stayed well away. If only she didn't still fancy him like crazy. "It was all a long time ago, and it isn't the same now." If only! "I shouldn't have started seeing you again . . ."

"So why did you come tonight?" Jake asked softly.

"Maybe I just couldn't stay away from you," she said, avoiding his eyes.

"Just stay tonight," Jake said, softer still. "Then I'll go on my tour, you go . . ." He gestured.

"Vice. I'm heading a Vice Squad." Tennison was looking anywhere but at Jake, yet she was keenly aware of his approach. Her stomach muscles were knotted with tension. His fingers gently touched her shoulder, turned her toward him. Slowly he put his arms around her and drew her close. His warmth, his nearness, the musky odor of his after-shave mingled with tobacco smoke, took her breath away. She made no attempt to resist.

"I mustn't," she said, her gray-green eyes looking up directly into his. He touched her cheek. "I mustn't."

2

Already, before 9:30 A.M., Commander Chiswick had twice tried to get through to Superintendent Halliday, and no joy. This had better be third time lucky. Tall but rather stooped, with receding gray hair, Chiswick stood at the window of his ninth floor office at New Scotland Yard, phone in hand, gazing out across Victoria Embankment toward the Thames, barely a ripple on its sluggish, iron-gray surface. A mass of low dark cloud threatened the rain that the morning's forecast had said was imminent.

He straightened up and his eyes flicked into hard focus as Halliday, finally, came on the line.

"It's public." Chiswick's tone was clipped. "John Kennington's formal resignation accepted due to ill health. That's it. No option, so I've heard—case dismissed." He listened, breathing heavily with irritation. "I've only just been told. I'll see you there, why not? We'll have to go, otherwise it'll look suspicious . . ."

He glanced sharply over his shoulder as his personal assistant tapped at the door and came in, a sheaf of opened mail in her hand.

"Good," Chiswick said impatiently into the phone. "I'd better be on my way over to you now. Your new DCI should be there any minute."

He banged the receiver down and headed for the door. His assistant held up the mail, but he walked on, ignoring her. His gruff voice floated back as he went out.

"Call my wife. I have a dinner tonight. Ask her to send over my dinner suit."

His assistant opened her mouth to remind him of something, but too late, he was gone.

• • •

When he'd worked with the Murder Squad at Southampton Row station, Bill Otley was known to everyone as "Skipper." The name traveled with him when he transferred to Vice at the Soho Division on Broadwick Street. One of the longest-serving officers on the Metropolitan Force, yet still a lowly sergeant, his personal problems, his bolshie attitude, but even more his solitary drinking had held him back. His wife Ellen had died of cancer of the stomach eight years earlier. They'd always wanted children, never been able to have them. His marriage had been very happy, and since her death it seemed as though all warmth and light and joy had been wrung out of Skipper Bill Otley. He lived alone in a small terraced house in the East End, shunning emotional entanglements. The job, and nothing but the job, held him together, gave some meaning to what was otherwise a pointless existence. Without it he wouldn't have thought twice about sticking his head in the gas oven.

Now and then the notion still occasionally beckoned, like a smiling seductress, usually when the moon was full or Chelsea had lost at home.

Leaning back in his swivel chair, a styrofoam cup of coffee with two sugars on the desk by his elbow, Otley jerked his leg, giving the metal wastebasket a kick that clanged like a gong. Everybody looked around. The full complement of Vice Squad officers was here, ten of them male, and five women. The WPCs acted as administrative support staff, as was usual in the chauvinist dinosaur of an institution that was the British police force.

"We supposed to sit here all morning?" Otley demanded with a sneer. The team was gathered to be formally introduced to their new DCI, Jane Tennison. Five minutes to ten and no Tennison. Otley was pissed-off, so of course he had to let everyone know it.

Inspector Larry Hall walked by, cuffed Otley on the back of the head. Hall had a round, smooth-skinned face and large soft brown eyes, and to offset this babyish appearance he went in for sharp suits and snazzy ties, a different tie every day it seemed. He was also prematurely balding, so what hair he had was cropped close to the scalp to minimize the contrast.

He addressed the room. "Right, everybody, I suggest we give it another five"—ignoring Otley's scowl—"and get on with the day's schedule. We need an I.D. on the body found in the burned-out flat last night."

"Voluptuous Vera rents it." Otley gave Hall a snide grin. "But it wasn't her. It was a kid aged between seventeen and twenty."

"Working overtime, are we?" Hall ribbed him. But it wasn't overtime to Otley, as everybody knew. He was on the case day and night; probably dreamt about the job too.

"I wouldn't say she's overeager to get started," Otley came back, always having the last word. Turning the knife in Tennison gave him special satisfaction. He'd never liked the ball-breaking bitch when they'd worked together on the Marlow murder case at Southampton Row, and nothing had changed, he was bloody certain of that.

He finished his coffee at a gulp, and instead of hanging around waiting like the other prats, scooted off to the morgue, a couple of blocks and ten minutes' brisk walk away, north of Oxford Street.

Mike Chow was in the sluice room, removing his mask and gloves. He dropped the soot-blackened gloves in the incinerator and was filling the bowl with hot water when Otley put his head around the door.

"What you got on the barbecued lad?"

"I'll have to do more tests, but he had a nasty crack over his skull." The pathologist looked over the top of his rimless spectacles. "Legs and one arm third-degree burns, heat lacerations, rest of the body done to a crisp."

Otley tilted his head, indicating he'd like to take a gander. Nodding, Mike Chow wiped his hands on a towel and led him through into the lab. He pulled on a fresh pair of gloves.

"We've got an elevated carboxyhemoglobin—blood pink owing to high level of same."

Otley peered at the remains of the skull on a metal tray on the lab bench. He then took a long look at the illuminated skull and dental X rays in the light box on the wall. Glancing over his shoulder, mouth pulled down at the corners, he gave Mike Chow his famous impression of a sardonic, world-weary hound dog. "Bloody hell . . . looks like someone took a hatchet to him!"

Shit and corruption! First day in her new posting and she was over an hour late. After spending the night at the hotel she hadn't arrived back at her flat till nearly ten. She'd freshened up, grabbed her briefcase, and battled with the traffic. Even the Commander had beaten her to it. He was waiting to show her around, make the introductions, though fortunately he seemed too preoccupied with something else to show any displeasure.

Tennison tried to keep pace with Chiswick as he strode along the main corridor, shrugging out of her raincoat and trying not to get her feet caught up in her briefcase.

"Bomb scare, so all the traffic was diverted, and then my battery ran low, so I . . ." It sounded pathetic and she knew it. "Sorry I'm late."

Chiswick didn't appear to be even listening. He pointed to a pair of double doors with frosted panes, not breaking his stride. He seemed to be in one hell of a hurry. "That's the Squad section office. You have a good hard-working team assigned to you."

Tennison nodded breathlessly.

He turned a handle, pushed open a door to what Tennison first took to be the cleaners' broom closet. Bare wooden desk, one metal-frame chair, dusty bookshelves, three filing cabinets, a small plastic vase with a wilting flower.

"If you want to settle yourself in . . ." Chiswick was already moving back out, leaving her standing there on the carpetless floor. "I'll see if Superintendent Halliday has made arrangements. He's right next door." The Commander pointed to the wall, painted a mixture of old mustard and nicotine.

He went out and closed the door.

Tennison dumped her briefcase on the desk, sending up a cloud of dust. There was an odor she couldn't identify. Dead cat maybe. A rickety blind covered the window. She raised it, hoping for some light and space. It rattled up and she stared out at a blank brick wall.

She turned and said, "Come in," at a tap on the door. There was a scuffling sound. With a sigh, Tennison went to the door and opened it to find a red-faced uniformed policewoman weighed under a stack of files and ring binders. Tennison stood aside and watched as the pudgy, rather plain girl with short dark hair staggered in and deposited the files on the desk, sending up more dust.

"You are?"

"WPC Hastings. Norma. I was instructed to bring these to you."

No "ma'am." Were things that casual around here, or just plain slack?

Tennison folded her arms. Take it slow and easy, don't jump the gun. "Do you have a listing of all the officers on the squad?"

Sweating and flustered, WPC Hastings frowned. "Didn't you get one this morning?" She had large, square teeth with a gap in the middle.

"I've just got here," Tennison said, breathing evenly, trying not to get irritated, though she already was. "If you could do that straightaway, and arrange for everyone to gather in the main office."

"Most of them are out." Norma shrugged. "Would you like a coffee?"

"No, just the list," Tennison said patiently.

The girl went off. Tennison gazed around at the four walls. This had to be a joke. This wasn't April 1st, was it? She looked through the files, then tried the top drawer of the desk. It came out four inches and stuck. She tried the next one down and that stuck after only two. She kicked it shut, making her big toe sting, and the air blue. What kind of stinking shit-hole was this?

Superintendent Halliday was a neat, fastidious-looking man with short fair hair and pale blue eyes fringed by blond lashes. Not puny, exactly—he was nearly six feet tall with bony shoulders that stretched the fabric of his dark gray suit—but not all that robust either, according to Tennison's first impression. From the moment she entered his large, spacious, nicely decorated corner office (right next door to her rabbit hutch!) he kept glancing at the gold Rolex on his freckled wrist. She hadn't expected the welcome mat, but at least he might have shown her the courtesy due a high-ranking officer who was about to take over the Vice Squad. Damn well would have too, Tennison reckoned, if only she'd been a man.

"I want you to give Operation Contract your fullest and immediate attention. I know it'll be a new area for you, but I am confident your past experience will be an added bonus."

All the feeling of a talking clock, Tennison thought. As if he'd rehearsed it in his sleep. She had no idea what Operation Contract was. She thought about asking, and then decided not to give him a stick to beat her with by displaying her ignorance. She nodded to seem willing.

Halliday tapped the desk with manicured fingers. "It is imperative we get results—and fast. There's been enough time wasted." He shot his cuff and glanced at his watch yet again.

"As yet I have not had time to familiarize myself with any of the cases . . ." Tennison was distracted as WPC Hastings entered without knocking. Halliday showed no signs of noticing her presence. Norma draped a black evening suit in a cleaner's bag over the back of a chair and went out.

". . . the cases I will be taking over. But, er—Operation Contract I will make my priority."

Halliday stood up. "Good." He stuck his hand out. Tennison shook it. "The team will fill you in on our progress to date." Another swift glance at the Rolex. "I was expecting you earlier."

Small wonder he could remember who she was, Tennison thought, leaving his office.

Sergeant Otley flicked the sugar cube into the saucer. He did it twice more, leaning his head on his hand, elbow on the table. Observing him with heavy-lidded, soulful eyes, hands twisting nervously in her lap, Vera arched her neck, her Adam's apple rippling like a trapped creature. Inspector Hall stood with casually folded arms near the door of the interview room. He was interested, and secretly amused, to see how the Skipper would handle Vernon stroke Vera Reynolds. There was the vexed question of gender, for a start.

"I told you . . . I did the show and then went out for a bite to eat with some friends." The reply was half-whispered, yet it wasn't a lisping, camp voice.

Offstage, Vera wasn't dragged up like some transvestite queen. There was no secret about who and what she was, but she chose to dress plainly and conservatively, favoring a simple blouse in dusky pink, a straight dark skirt, and leather sling-back shoes with low square heels. A few rings and a string of purple beads were the only bits and pieces of jewelry. Under her wig and makeup, in fact, Vera had rather a strong face, Hall reckoned, with good bones; though the mouth, shapely and sensitive, was a dead giveaway.

Otley flicked the sugar cube. "And you don't know who was in your flat?" he inquired in his usual drab tone.

Vera gave a little shake of the head.

Hall put his hands on the back of Otley's chair and leaned over. "Vernon," he said, not unkindly, "if I go out and leave somebody kippin' in my place, I wouldn't be stupid enough to say I don't know them. I mean, that is stupid, isn't it?"

Vera threw up her hands, the knuckles red where she'd been kneading them. She swallowed hard, the Adam's apple doing a double gyration. "It could have been any number of people—you see, it was well known I leave a key on top of the front door . . ."

Otley made a sound, a kind of muffled snort. He sighed and shook his head, crumbling the sugar cube between his long hard nails.

"About seventeen years old?" Hall said. "Reddish blond hair . . . ring any bells?"

Vera bit her lip, staring down at the table. Then a tight, rapid shake of the head. She was steeling herself for the next question when she was saved by Norma's face at the small glass panel in the door. She tapped and stuck her head in.

"Fire team would like Mr. Reynolds as soon as possible. There's sandwiches and coffee served in the Squad Room. Can you get everybody mustered, same as this morning, for twelve-thirty sharp." Norma waggled her dark unplucked eyebrows at them. "She's here."

While Inspector Hall escorted Vera Reynolds out and put her in the charge of two uniformed men, Otley followed Norma along the corridor to Tennison's office, which at the moment was minus Tennison. The Skipper peered in, an evil grin on his face, watching Norma in the dim, dusty cubbyhole trying valiantly to wrench open one of the desk drawers. Norma looked up, perspiring.

"She won't like this," Otley gloated, rubbing his hands.

"She's not here, Sarge. Nor should you be," Norma said pointedly.

Otley cackled.

Tennison capped her fountain pen with a decisive click and stood up. She tugged her suit jacket straight at the front and came around the desk to face them. The Squad Room stilled. Not very tall, under five feet five, her honey-blond hair cut in a swath across her forehead, she seemed rather out of place in a room of hulking men; all but one of the women police officers were taller, even if they didn't have her rounded, sensual figure.

The tension in the hot, crowded room was almost palpable. Tennison certainly wasn't relaxed, and neither were they. A new Detective Chief Inspector heading Vice might spell all kinds of trouble, and already she had two strikes against her. Her reputation as a tenacious round-the-clock obsessive who worked her team to the bone, and the fact that she was female. Even the WPCs were wary of that.

Fingers laced together at her waist, feet braced apart, Tennison let the silence gather for a moment. She wanted control from the start, and was determined to have it.

"So . . . please accept my apologies. Not got off on a very good footing on my first day." Small smile. Let them know you can afford it. "I will obviously need everybody's cooperation, and I would also appreciate it if . . ."

She caught a movement as Hall slithered in. He gave her a weak, apologetic smile and she returned a curt nod. He grabbed a sandwich from the cafeteria tray and it was halfway to his mouth when Tennison said:

"It's Inspector Lawrence Hall, yes?" He nodded, mouth open, sandwich unbitten. "Well, let's you and me start off on the right footing, shall we? If I ask everyone to be at a place at a certain time, and only unless you have a good excuse . . ."

"I'm sorry," Hall interrupted, "but I had to arrange for Reynolds to be taken over to the Fire unit. I was waiting—"

"Is Sergeant Otley with Reynolds?" Tennison asked sharply.

Hall hesitated. "Yes," he lied. "You know about the fire, do you?"

Tennison nodded, slowly folding her arms. "Why is this fire and the boy of such interest to you, or this department? I know Vernon Reynolds. I know what he is, but that isn't against the law."

"Well—one—it was on our patch. And in the area we have been targeting, Euston and St. Pancras, on Operation Contract. The dead boy was possibly a rent boy." Hall glanced toward the door, wishing Otley would show up. "Vernon was probably taking a few quid for letting them use his place."

"Has he admitted that?"

Hall shifted uneasily under her gaze. Where the fuck was Otley? "No, ma'am . . . well, he's not likely to, is he? He's saying he doesn't even know who was in there."

Tennison scented that matters were spinning beyond her control. Nip it in the bud. No mavericks on *her* team. She said briskly, "I'd like a full report on this fire business and then I will tell you whether or not this department wishes to continue with the investigation. Our priority is Operation Contract."

Hall stared at his feet. The other officers, munching sandwiches and slurping coffee, exchanged looks. First morning in and she was throwing her weight around. This was going to be a load of fun, they didn't think.

With a curt nod of her head, Tennison indicated that work should continue. The officers turned back to their desks, to their mounds of paperwork, reaching for phones. They were all aware of her scrutiny: new regime, new boss, and they were being required to pass muster.

Tennison beckoned to one of the WPCs standing in a small group next to the wall-length filing section. She came over, a tall, striking girl with frank, open features and friendly blue eyes.

"What's your name?"

"Kathy."

"Can you give me a brief rundown on the operation?"

WPC Kathy Trent led her over to the large board. "I've been trying to question as many of the kids as possible." She smiled diffidently, eager to help.

Tennison watched closely as Kathy took her through it. She still hadn't got a handle on this Operation Contract thing. The board was crammed with information. Under "TOMS"—police slang for female and male prostitutes—a long list of names and locations: Waterloo Street, Golden Fleece, Earls Court, Euston Station, Stars & Stripes. Farther along, headed "OPERATION CONTRACT," photographs of young boys, some of them no older than eleven or twelve, with video stills of supermarket checkouts, tube station platforms, mainline station concourses. More typed lists of targeted locations—cafes, coffee shops, street markets, soup kitchens, cardboard cities—spotted in different colors. Tapes led from these to a huge map of central London with corresponding colored pins. A duty rota of officers on surveillance was marked up in black felt-tip, with dates, times, and frequency, all cross-referenced to file number such-and-such. At first sight it seemed to be an efficient and comprehensive operation, well planned, rigorously executed.

"Most of the older rent boys are carrying pagers, portable phones, so our team—four of us, ma'am—concentrate on the younger ones skiving around Soho." Kathy pointed to a sheet marked up in colored felt-tip, a blizzard of asterisks, arrows, code numbers. "We staked out the Golden Fleece, Euston Station, Earls Court . . ."

Tennison nodded, content for now to listen and learn, get some kind of grip on it.

"Our problem is that when the kids are actually *out* on the street, they've already accepted the lifestyle." Kathy didn't sound sad, simply resigned to reality.

Over by the door, behind Tennison's back, Sergeant Otley sneaked in, made a rapid gesture to Hall. The Inspector scuttled over.

"You've been with Reynolds and the Fire team," Hall said under his breath, tapping his nose.

"I haven't." Otley grinned. "I've been up at Records and we got . . ."

He pulled Hall behind the half-open door as Tennison glanced their way.

". . . boy is Colin Jenkins, known as Connie."

Otley punched Hall's arm. He then made a show of arriving for the first time, all innocent, to be met face-to-face by Tennison, who'd marched smartly over.

"Sorry I'm late, ma'am," said Otley with a straight face. "But I've been seein' if I can get your drawers loosened."

Everybody heard but nobody laughed.

Tennison stood with her back to the window. On the other side of the desk piled high with three-inch thick files, Otley waited, sardonic grin absent for the moment. He'd had to deal with this slit-arsed bitch before, and knew what to expect.

The room was still in an almighty mess, though WPC Hastings had managed to find her a desk lamp that worked and two more straight-backed chairs with the varnish worn through to bare wood. For the moment, Tennison had more important preoccupations.

"Right, Sergeant, I am not prepared to take any crap from you, or stand by and let you stir it up. So let's clear the air." Tennison jerked her head, eyes hard as flint. "Sit down."

"Judging by the state of the rest of your office I don't think I should risk it!" Otley pulled a chair forward and sat down, an uncertain half smile hovering on his face. "Joke!"

"If you don't want to work with me, I can get you transferred."

Otley studied his thumbnail. "I was out of line at Southampton Row, but, that said"—he shrugged—"I know you did a good job."

"Thank you," Tennison said, her sarcasm like a saw's edge.

Her last case with the Murder Squad had been a racial and political minefield. Teenage half-caste girl dug up in the back garden of a West Indian area seething with antagonism against the police. Despite this, Tennison had stuck to the job like a terrier with a bone. Tracked down and collared a young white bloke with a sickening, sadistic streak who liked taking photographs while buggering his schoolgirl victims.

Otley was looking anywhere but at Tennison as she moved a stack of files from her chair and sat down. She stared at him a long moment, letting him sweat a little, and then flipped open the green cover of a file. She tapped the report.

"I have a lot of catching up to do, so, come on . . . are you going to help me or not?"

"I got an I.D. on the boy in the fire at Reynolds's place," Otley volunteered. He took a folded sheet from the pocket of his crumpled suit. "He was a runaway, fifteen years old. Colin, known as Connie, Jenkins. All the state-run homes have their kids' teeth checked on a regular basis and filed on record—"

"What's this boy got to do with Operation Contract?" Tennison asked bluntly.

There were connections here she couldn't make. Otley and Hall seemed to be running some cowboy operation of their own. Plus there was an undercurrent in the department; she'd sensed it right away. Not unease exactly, more a kind of apathy. Lack of motivation. She had to get to the bottom line of all this before the whole bloody mess swamped her.

She strode along with Otley to the Squad Room and up to the board.

"It was supposed to be a slow start to a massive big cleanup." He swept out his hand. "All the areas targeted were those specifically used by rent boys." A glance at her under his brows. "It's Halliday's obsession."

"Yes . . . And?"

"That's what it is—cleanup operation."

"So what's the big deal? Why has it been taking so long?"

"Because it's a bloody cock-up—if you'll excuse the pun!" Otley said with some heat. "The Guv'nor before you got dumped. Somebody had to take the blame."

Tennison saw a chink of light. The entire room, while ostensibly working, was taking in every word. Kathy and Norma were sitting at their VDUs, staring at the green screens. Otley was about to go on, checked himself, and looked toward Inspector Hall. Hall came up and the two men swapped some kind of coded message.

Hall turned to Tennison, keeping his voice low.

"Ma'am, a few of us think the same way. There was a leak, word got out. No gamblers, no boys on the streets." His tone turned bitter. "We spent weeks getting ready for a big swoop, all hush-hush . . . came out empty-handed. Surveillance trucks, uniformed and plainclothes officers—it was a fiasco. It had to be a leak but Chiswick and Halliday keep on pushing it."

Tennison looked at Otley standing a few feet away, head sunk on his shoulders, flipping through the pages of a report that just happened to be on the desk.

Under the force of her gaze he raised his eyes. "I'd say, now, the buck stops with you."

She knew that. It was the sly curl of his lip she didn't like.

3

"So we stop, and old John looks at this unattended vehicle, he looks at me, we're both wet behind the ears, and I said, 'What do you think?' There it was, parked without lights in the middle of this copse on a housing estate in Cardiff . . ."

Chief Superintendent Kernan paused, smiling down at the man seated next to him at the top table, the "old John" in question. Kennington, receding silver hair brushed back, distinguished, with a supercilious air, returned the smile. He puffed on his cigar, smiling and nodding at the great and the good gathered for his farewell dinner in the banqueting room of the Cafe Royal. Every senior-ranking policeman on the Metropolitan force was here. These were colleagues he had worked with, served under, commanded during the nearly forty years of his rise to very near the top of the heap.

Several judges were in attendance, not one under sixty-five. Barristers who'd defended against him, prosecuted with him. Pathologists, forensic scientists, doctors, one or two people from the Home Office, a junior Minister, and a sprinkling of sober-faced top brass from the security services whose names and photographs never appeared in the newspapers.

Kernan took a sip of brandy before continuing. In spite of his apparent joviality, the puffy, pasty face with its mournful hangdog look seemed painfully at odds with his black tie, starched shirt, and black dinner suit. Leaning forward, hands splayed on the white tablecloth, he spoke into the microphone.

"So we drive across the copse. Midway across we get bogged down in the mud. So we get out and radio for assistance."

Grins and nods from the rows of tables stretching down the long elegant room, chandeliers reflecting in the gilt-framed mirrors. Everyone relished a good cock-up story.

". . . a Panda was just passing, so they followed us across the copse—and they got bogged down about ten feet away from us. Next came a Land Rover. They got as far as our patrol car. So there we all were . . . and John says, maybe we should check out this abandoned vehicle. So we wade across this bloody bog, and find a note pinned to the windshield. 'GONE FOR HELP. STUCK IN THE MUD.'"

Thumps on the tables. Flushed faces guffawing. Everybody having one hell of a good time, getting better by the minute so long as the free booze kept flowing.

Three seats down from Mike Kernan at the microphone, Commander Chiswick took advantage of the laughter to mumble into his companion's ear, "Sweep it under the carpet job. Now I've been warned to keep it there . . ." He met the other's wide-eyed gaze, nodding meaningfully.

Kernan had consumed three large brandies while on his feet, and his speech was getting slurred. He now poured another treble, ready for the finale. "So I would like to propose my toast, and to give my very good wishes for a happy, productive retirement—to John Kennington. Gentlemen! Please raise your glasses!"

There was a gulping silence while everyone drank, and then a loud buzz of animated chatter, ribald comment, and hee-hawing laughter. Plump hands beckoned urgently to the waitresses, beavering around in their short black dresses and white pinafores. The speeches were only halfway through, a powerful incentive to get three sheets into the wind by the shortest possible route.

Kernan stood back from the microphone. He then remembered and swayed forward, bending over to speak into it. His voice boomed like a station announcer's, bringing winces and bared teeth.

"Gentlemen . . . please may I ask your attention for Commander Trayner."

Kernan shook hands and slapped backs on his unsteady return to his seat next to Superintendent Thorndike. He flopped down, belching, grinning at everyone for no other reason than he was half-pissed. Thorndike pursed his lips. He didn't approve of such behavior in a senior officer. He didn't actually approve of Kernan full stop, even though it was Kernan who had wangled him the post of Super at Southampton Row. It should have gone to Kernan's next in line, his senior detective Jane Tennison, but Kernan, a founding member chauvinist pig, wasn't going to stand for that. So prissy boots Thorndike got promotion and ball-breaker Tennison got dumped.

At the microphone, Trayner was burbling on about more good old days with good old John Kennington. This time it was Manchester, not Cardiff, from where Trayner had some very happy memories, and some not so great ones. ". . . and John here brings a Tom into the station. He was writing up a charge sheet, listing drunk and disorderly, abusive language, and—as the lady in question was stark bollock naked at the time . . ."

Kernan leaned in Thorndike's direction. His eyes were gone and his breath enveloped Thorndike like a toxic cloud.

"Why don't we just give him his watch, eh, and piss off home? Eh?" He guzzled some more brandy. "Unless there's a cabaret—eh? Is there a cabaret?" He squinted at Thorndike, whose thin wrists stuck out of his starched cuffs like celery sticks. Prim and proper, he was like somebody's bleeding maiden aunt, Kernan thought sourly. Never had really took to the man, but then Mike Kernan didn't take to the human race in general.

"You not drinking?" he asked suspiciously. He reached for the brandy bottle and poured Thorndike a whopper. "Bill Otley's with the same squad, did you know that? With Tennison—Vice Squad!"

Kernan laughed loudly, coinciding with the general laughter at something Commander Trayner had said. He pushed the glass across.

"Have a drink! This is going to be a long night!"

Thorndike hesitated, but finally took a sip. Keep on his good side. Never know when you might need him.

". . . if you think I was pissed," Trayner was saying, building up to the punchline, "wait until you see what's inside the greenhouse!"

Not having a clue what the story was about, Kernan banged the table, joining in the laughter and applauding like a maniac, bellowing, "More! . . . More! More!"

Edward Parker-Jones tilted the boy's head to the light and examined his face. Bruising around the forehead and left cheekbone. A diagonal gash extending from his ear down to his jawline. His lower lip was split and had dried into a crusty scab.

"What am I going to do with you, Martin?" Parker-Jones sighed. "Look at you! Have you eaten today? You haven't, have you?" He ruffled the boy's hair. "Do you want some soup? Cup of tea?"

Martin Fletcher twitched his thin shoulders in a shrug. He was reluctant to even open his mouth. The beating he'd taken from Jimmy Jackson the night before, down by the canal, had scared him to quivering silence, his gut churning as if he were riding a roller coaster, jumping at shadows. He'd spent the rest of the night curled up in a shop doorway, whimpering. Today he'd wandered the streets, a forlorn lost figure in a grimy windbreaker and jeans ripped open at the knees, his toes sticking through his sneakers.

The recreation and advice centre run by Parker-Jones was the only refuge he could think of. It was an oasis of warmth and comfort—a hot drink and a bite to eat—before slinking back to the streets for the night. But it wasn't safe even here. That bullying swine Jackson sometimes showed his ugly, pockmarked face, on the prowl for some poor kid who owed him money, or a favor, or who Jackson just might want to beat the shit out of for the sheer fun of it.

Parker-Jones put his arm around Martin's shoulder and led him through the reception area, where a few lads were idling the time away gazing listlessly over the notice board. Jobs, hostel accommodation, personal messages, dubious offers of help by phone.

"Go and sit down and I'll get Ron to bring you something in."

He had a deep, resonant voice that went with his neat appearance and confident personality. A tall man, broad in the chest, late thirties, Parker-Jones carried himself as someone of authority: an organizer, intelligent and decisive. His black hair, parted in the middle, flopped over his ears when he was in a hurry, giving him a rakish look that was somewhat at odds with his image of a solid rock in a shifting world.

"Did you call home?" he asked Martin. "You promised me you would at least call your mother. Do you want me to do it? Martin?"

Martin shook his head and wandered off into the TV lounge. Broken-down armchairs and two old sofas were grouped around the set, and there was a shelf of dog-eared paperbacks, some jigsaws, and board games. The walls were a sickly purple, with green woodwork. It was empty at this hour; between seven and eight was usually quiet, which was why Martin had dared take the risk.

On the way back to his office, Parker-Jones called out to a scruffy black kid with a hearing aid, wearing a back-to-front baseball cap, "Ron, get some hot soup for Martin Fletcher, would you?"

The black kid dropped the duster and metal wastebasket he was carrying and went over to the alcove where a copper urn with a brass tap bubbled and spat, steam jetting out of the top.

Otley came down the narrow wooden stairway from the street, the shoulders of his raincoat stained dark with drizzle. The advice centre was on his beat. It was situated just off Brewer Street in Soho, at the bottom of a cobbled alley that during the day was crowded with market traders, selling everything from fruit and veg to lampshades, toilet paper, and bootleg records and tapes. The doorway was directly opposite the neon-lit entrance to a strip club. Farther along, a couple of shops stayed open until past midnight, catering to the soft porn magazine and video trade.

Otley knew about the hard Swedish and German stuff in their back rooms, for selected clients only, but he let it ride. The perverts had to go somewhere. Better they got their jollies that way than molesting the young and vulnerable.

"Bit quiet tonight, isn't it?" Otley said.

The three boys loitering at the notice board looked him up and down with sullen eyes. No one spoke. Hands in his raincoat pockets, Otley glanced around at the peeling mustard-colored walls with posters tacked up for rock concerts long gone. The carpet was a dank green, greasy and black with the tread of many feet. The wall opposite the reception counter was bare brick, steam pipes near the ceiling, huge Victorian radiators jutting out into the passage. To the left was the games room, which had a pool table and a football table with wooden players; to the right, past the office door, the fluted glass panels of the TV room. Otley thought he saw a rippling shadow move inside.

He said casually, "Any of you know Colin Jenkins? Nicknamed Connie?"

The door marked "E PARKER-JONES—PRIVATE" opened, and Parker-Jones came out. He spotted Otley at once and marched straight over.

"What do you want?" Dark eyes under thick black eyebrows staring hard. "If you are looking for a specific person, why don't you ask me?"

Otley remained unruffled. He'd been stared at before.

"You know a lad called Colin Jenkins?"

"Yes. Red-haired, about your height. Nicknamed Connie."

Otley nodded slowly. "Used Vera Reynolds's place. I need to ask some of the boys about him." Parker-Jones was about to say something, but Otley went on in a monotone, "He's dead. He was on the game, wasn't he?"

"Are you telling me or asking me?" Parker-Jones drew himself up to his full height. "Is this official? I've already discussed this with an Inspector . . ." He frowned and snapped his fingers. "Inspector Hall. I really don't understand why you and your associates persist in coming in here . . ."

His indignation was wasted on Otley, who had strolled off in the general direction of the television lounge. Ron came from the corner alcove with a plastic cup of soup. Parker-Jones took it from him and hurried past Otley into the lounge, still complaining in his fruity, rather portentous voice.

"You people make my job and the social services work exceptionally difficult. I attempt to get these boys off the street, give them a place they can come to—and I am continually harassed, as are the boys."

He held out the cup of soup. A tousled head poked up from behind an armchair. A nail-bitten hand reached out.

"They are not in my care, they come here of their own free will. They come here because this is one of the few places they *can* come to." He sounded righteously outraged, as if he had been accused of something, his reputation besmirched.

Otley stood in the doorway watching as Martin Fletcher took the soup in both hands. The boy looked up at Parker-Jones, his bruised and battered face breaking into a wan smile. Parker-Jones ruffled his hair and smiled back, the steadfast rock in an ugly, shifting world.

Tennison pushed through the glass double doors into the corridor leading to the Pullman lounge at Euston Station. She checked her appearance in a small hand-mirror, flicking her hair into place with her fingertips. The stewardess behind the glass door pressed the entry release buzzer. Tennison entered the thickly carpeted room, the din of the station below hushed behind triple glazing and velvet drapes. She looked around nervously. The stewardess held out her hand, presumably for a first-class ticket.

"I'm just meeting someone here." Tennison returned the stewardess's smile with a small embarrassed one of her own. "I don't have a—"

"It's okay, she's with me."

Jake Hunter threaded his way through the deep comfortable armchairs grouped around low tables. The lounge was almost empty. The stewardess dimpled at his smile, and he led Tennison across to his table. She put her briefcase by the chair and unbuttoned her raincoat.

"I've never been in here before. Mind you, I don't usually travel first class. Thank you," she said, as Jake helped her off with her coat. She hadn't dressed to please him, though the dark red linen jacket and charcoal gray pencil skirt made her feel slim and attractive, and she was glad she wore it.

They sat down. Jake drew his armchair closer.

"I've got about an hour before my train, but I just wanted to—"

Tennison interrupted, speaking in a rush. She was still flustered. "I'm glad you called. I wanted to talk to you. There's a case I'm working on."

Jake caught her arm as she reached for her briefcase.

"I don't want to talk about any work, Jane. I just didn't think we, or I . . . could walk away without, without . . ."

He sighed and sat back, rubbing his chin, as the stewardess appeared beside them with the drinks menu.

"Whisky and soda, please," Tennison said, ignoring the card. She watched the stewardess go, and then took a good look around. "I'm very impressed. I didn't know this was even here."

Jake leaned forward and took her hand. She thought of pulling away, but didn't. He had to have his say, and she couldn't stop him. Did she want to? Good question. If only she knew herself.

"Jane, we've got to talk, because, I . . ." She realized he was nervous too. It was a struggle to get the words out. "Jane, I'm married and I have four kids. . . ."

"I know," Tennison said calmly. "It's on the flyleaf of your book."

"Yeah!" Jake sounded almost angry. He leaned closer, his voice low and urgent. "But what isn't is the way I feel about you. What I've always felt about you."

"No, but you wrote that in the front of the book."

"Can you just be serious, just for a second, for chrissakes!"

"There's no point." She repeated quietly, "There's no point."

"Then why did you come?" Jake asked stiffly.

"I just wanted to ask you your opinion about something I'm working on." Tennison glanced away from him. His eyes were like lasers on her cheek.

"I don't believe you."

The stewardess placed Tennison's drink in front her, along with a napkin and dish of peanuts. Jake took the bill and nodded his thanks.

Silence then, while Tennison stared at her untouched drink. She said, "I knew you were married. I shouldn't have stayed."

"Why did you?"

"Because . . ." She gave a tiny vexed shake of her head. "Because you wanted me to. Don't—" She held up her hand as he tried to speak. "I wanted to, Jake. I wanted to be with you."

It was hell to handle, and the only way she knew how was to make light of it, kill the feeling with fake humor.

"I've always been a glutton for punishment, maybe that's why I'm so good at my job. I've got that, you've got a family—perhaps we've both got what we wanted. If I haven't, then I've no one else to blame but myself."

Jake sighed miserably. "What a mess."

"No, it isn't," Tennison said briskly, "because we'll do what we agreed. We won't see each other again. You'll get on the train, and in the meantime . . ." She reached down for her briefcase.

Jake turned his face away from her, but she could see his throat working. "I love you," he said, hardly moving his lips, and took her hand, holding it tightly.

"Yes, I know," Tennison said softly.

Jake let go of her hand. He took a huge breath and turned back to look at her. "So . . . what's this case you're working on?"

Larry Hall looked up from the computer as he heard the door swing. Otley was standing there, hair plastered to his forehead, hand on the shoulder of a puny kid with terrified eyes in a face that had been through the mangle.

"I want an interview room and somebody to take a statement."

It was 7:43 by the clock on the wall of the Squad Room. Hall frowned. "You're not down for tonight, are you?"

A couple of officers were working a few desks away. Otley lowered his voice. "This lad knows something, but he's scared." He nodded toward the corridor. "Come in with me?"

Hall took his jacket from the back of the chair and slipped into it, automatically adjusting the knot in his tie. He looked at Martin Fletcher, then tugged the lobe of his ear. "Hey, Bill, how old is he?"

"I think your boy was already dead," Jake said, studying the pages of the autopsy report spread out on the table. There were some grisly morgue photographs that Tennison had shown him and quickly tucked back into her briefcase. She leaned forward, her clasped hands resting on her knees.

Jake indicated a paragraph. "Says here that the fluid taken from the blisters showed no sign of vital reaction."

Concentrating hard, Tennison tried to put the pieces together. "So, if the fire wasn't accidental, he was murdered? . . . Is that what you're saying?"

Muted chimes rang out. *The train on platform thirteen is the eight P.M. Pullman Express to Liverpool, calling at Watford, Crewe . . .*

"What does 'pugilistic attitude' mean?" Tennison asked, fretting.

"Arms held out, legs flexed." Jake thought for a moment. "It's caused by the coagulation of the muscles on the flexor surface of the limbs . . . so the body could look as if it was in a sitting-up position." He raised his eyebrows. "Jane? I'll be back in London next week, and maybe—"

"No, we agreed, no more meetings." Tennison shuffled the pages together and closed the file. "That's your train." She put the file in her briefcase and snapped the locks. "Don't call me again, please."

Jake picked up his bag. He dropped it and fished in his pocket for change. Tennison got up and took the bill from his hand. "I'll get this. You'd better go."

He looked down at her gravely and put his hand on her shoulder. She did what she promised herself she wouldn't, but she couldn't help it. She took his hand and pressed her lips to it.

She could still taste him when he'd gone, turned abruptly and walked out, while she stood staring at nothing. She sat down for a moment and then went to the window. He was striding across the concourse to platform 13. Suddenly he stopped, turned quite slowly, and stared up, his fair eyebrows standing out against his tanned face.

Tennison saw him move on and watched his tall figure until it was lost to sight, beyond the barrier. She came away from the window. The stewardess was clearing the table.

"Ah . . . I'd like another whisky and soda." Tennison felt as if her insides had been scoured raw. She managed a smile. "If that's okay."

"For he's a jolly good fe-ellow, for he's a jolly good fe-ellow, for he's a jolly good fe-el-low! And so say all of us!"

Mike Kernan wasn't singing. He was staring, bleary-eyed, watching them sing their stupid heads off. Chiswick. Trayner. Halliday. All the rest at the top table, up on their hind legs, bellowing away. And John Kennington, slightly flushed, holding the velvet presentation box, that haughty smirk on his lips.

In Kernan's book, Kennington wasn't a jolly good fellow at all. Far from it. Did he have a tale to tell, if only he felt like telling it. . . .

"I'm out of here." Kernan pushed his chair back. He tried to stand and fell back. "Can't take any more of this crap." He leaned over, almost in the lap of Thorndike, who gazed at him with naked disapproval. "Somebody should ask him to start the cabaret," Kernan said, nodding, wagging his finger. "I saw him at the Bowery Roof Club . . ."

Thorndike's attention sharpened. "The Bowery what?"

Kernan had made it to his feet, swaying. He tapped his nose. "Keep this out of it . . . but you see that iron-haired bloke, Judge Syers, top table? Ask him if he can get you a membership. 'Iron' being the"—he belched—"operative word. G'night." He staggered off.

Iron? Thorndike pursed his lips. What did that mean?

The singing had finished. A slow applause started as Kennington stepped forward to the microphone, holding the velvet box in one hand and a gold pocket watch in the other. He raised an eyebrow, beaming down at them.

"Gentlemen . . ." He waited for the applause to die away. "Gentlemen, tonight is a sad, very sad occasion for me, but you have made it a night I will never forget."

They were on their feet, applauding, none more vigorously than the iron-haired judge. Thorndike never missed an opportunity. He'd wheedled his way nearly to the top of the greasy pole, currying favor, playing the smiling sycophant, but there was some distance to go.

He took advantage of the applause to sidle around, finding himself very conveniently at the judge's elbow. "Excuse me . . . it's Judge Syers, isn't it?"

Judge Syers turned and stared at him, cold probing eyes under bristling gray brows.

"We met at a lodge dinner," Thorndike lied smoothly.

Judge Syers seemed to think this not impossible. He gave an almost imperceptible nod of his iron-gray head. "What's your name?"

• • •

388 | *Lynda La Plante*

Cutting through the smoke, the mauve spotlight picked out the face of Marlene Dietrich. Huge dark eyes, a gash of red for the sultry mouth. Thin arcs of eyebrows against an alabaster forehead. Silvery blond hair framing high cheekbones and the rouged hollows beneath. The spotlight widened to reveal her tight, skin-toned dress, figure-hugging from neckline to her ankles. Sequins gave off glittering sparks so that she seemed to shimmer like a cloud of dazzling light.

"Falling in love again, never wanted to
What am I to do?
I can't help it . . ."

Vera swayed hypnotically on the small stage against a backdrop of silver satin drapes. Her arms floated like pale slender reeds, nails sharp as talons, teardrops of blood. Her low throaty voice caressed the words like a hand stroking fur, inviting, suggesting, seducing.

Below the stage, small lamps in the shape of tulips glowed on the gold lamé tablecloths. The close-packed faces were blurs in the dim light. Some were focused on the stage; Vera Reynolds was a hot act, one of the most popular with the members. Other faces—older, lined, jaded, belonging to men in muted, well-cut business suits—were constantly on the move, eyes roaming the darkness, searching for that special someone.

Half past midnight. The Bowery Roof Top Club was reaching its peak.

Thorndike followed Judge Syers out of the elevator into the small lobby on the ninth floor. A handsome young man with a thin mustache that curved down to a pointed beard, his sleek ponytail looped into a bun, sat behind the reception desk. He was checking names and numbers on a screen. Through the doors, Thorndike heard a husky voice singing, "Falling in love again, never wanted to . . ."

He was secretly thrilled. He'd never before entered such an exclusive establishment. The place reeked of power and privilege, even if the decor wasn't to his taste. In fact it was rather vulgar, in an expensive way, Thorndike decided. Heavy tapestries of silver and gold adorned the walls. Pillars of vine leaves in wrought iron, painted gold, supported tubs of exuberant foliage. Large mirrors framed in gilt reflected the heated exotic splendor. Thorndike didn't quite know what to make of it all; he'd certainly never seen anything like it.

He stared, blinked, and pursed his thin lips in a prudish pout. That marble statuette—good God! A full-size male nude, the anatomical detail leaving nothing to the imagination. He quickly averted his gaze.

"Member and one guest," the receptionist said, pushing the book forward. Judge Syers stood aside as Thorndike signed.

The act was just finishing. They came through into the bar, and Thorndike got a glimpse of a blond head bowing low, arms gracefully extended, acknowledging the applause. The air was thick with smoke and heavy with perfume. The little flutter of apprehension he felt became stronger as he gazed around. What struck him most forcibly was the height of the women. Many of them were over six feet tall in their spiked heels. Gorgeous, slender creatures in sparkling evening gowns, exquisitely made up, with manes of wavy hair cascading over their shoulders, silver blond, molten red, raven black. Their dresses were cut away in the most revealing places, except there was nothing to reveal. In fact, Thorndike decided, goggling, they looked like women and they moved like women, only more so. His apprehension escalated into dry-mouthed panic.

There were boys too, some of whom looked no older than sixteen. Their hair was slicked back, glistening with gel. They wore black leather jackets over white T-shirts, with tight jeans fashionably faded at the knees and crotch.

The bar was crowded with respectable city types, middle-aged and older, in close conversation with the willowy, preening creatures and the young boys. Thorndike seemed to recognize a face here and there, and blanched at the thought that if he knew them, they might know him.

He followed Judge Syers down the four steps from the bar area to the tables clustered around the stage. The judge knew practically everyone, the way he was nodding and smiling. Then Thorndike spotted the look-alike Marlene Dietrich on the far side of the room. She pushed through the crowd toward them, silvery-blond hair gleaming in the smoky light. She came straight up to Judge Syers, a head taller, placed her hand on his arm, and leaned over to whisper in his ear.

Thorndike backed away. He looked around, eyes swiveling, panic rising in his chest. A tall graceful creature with flowing red hair, sharp painted nails, and a low-cut gown revealing a chest as flat as an ironing board winked at him.

Thorndike stumbled up the steps and fled.

"It was an accident," Vera Reynolds said in a low, frightened voice. Her grip tightened on the judge's arm. "A terrible accident."

She glanced nervously over her shoulder. He was there in the bar, as usual. He was looking straight at her. Vera shuddered. She couldn't make a move without Jackson knowing about it.

Judge Syers was reaching for his wallet. "I'm sorry. If there is anything I can—"

"No." Vera held up the palms of both hands, whitened by constant applications of lemon juice. "No, I don't want money," she protested. She half-turned. "I'd better go and change."

Judge Syers watched her threading through the crowd. He went up into the bar. He nodded to one or two people, and gradually worked his way around the intimately chattering groups. A tall elegant man with snowwhite hair, leaning on a cane, was deep in conversation with a paunchy balding man of similar age, late sixties. Frampton was a Member of Parliament, and in common with most MPs he liked the sound of his own voice. Those within ten feet had to like it too, given no choice.

"It is a bloody outrage!" Frampton's watery eyes bulged. His nose had been broken in a public school boxing match, and the years of booze had covered it with a maze of tiny broken blood vessels. "They are saying that the leak sent four times the permitted amount of radioactive dust into the atmosphere. Claims by the government that this could not harm people or the food chain are simply a cover-up!" He thumped his cane. "I fully intend to raise the matter in the House."

Kilmartin sipped his drink, nodding.

"Greenpeace campaigners have been targeting the place for years," Frampton went on heatedly. "To state that a Chernobyl-style disaster could not happen here is rubbish!"

Smiling to himself, Judge Syers moved to the bar. He ordered a gin and tonic, then indicated Frampton and Kilmartin with a nod of his head. The barman set about fixing the drinks.

Farther along the bar, a cigarette hanging from his mouth, Jackson squinted through the smoke at the judge. His biker gear had been replaced by a hip-length leather jacket, designer jeans, and Reebok sneakers. As Judge Syers turned, Jackson lazily looked away.

The music started up as another act came on. This time it was a Bette Midler look-alike in army uniform, burning red hair, six-inch silver heels, a high bust like two melons under a blanket, blasting out "Boys from the Backroom."

"If one of the biggest nuclear reprocessors for nuclear warheads in the world can have a leak, no matter how small, it means their security and safety rules must be monitored more closely . . ."

"You're in good voice as usual," Judge Syers said. "Are you well?"

"Terrible," Frampton boomed. He waggled his stick. "I've got ruddy gout. First time out in weeks."

They shook hands. The barman placed their drinks down. Judge Syers lit a cigar and puffed it into life. The three men raised their glasses. "Cheers!"

Judge Syers watched Bette Midler strutting her stuff for a moment. He stared into his drink. "Colin Jenkins is dead." Frampton frowned over his brandy glass, rather puzzled. "I think he called himself Connie," the judge said quietly. He looked at Frampton. "We should talk . . ."

The three men moved off, Frampton limping, toward a curtained doorway leading to the members' private bar.

Jackson watched them go, cold as a snake. He turned then, his fleshy lips curving in a dead smile as Vera Reynolds moved slowly up the steps and came to stand beside him.

4

Piece by piece, the Fire team had reconstructed the sitting room of Vera Reynolds's flat. The charred furniture had been replaced in its exact position, according to the drawings made by the team and the fire brigade immediately after the blaze had been put out. Sections of fabric from the burnt-out sofa had been salvaged and draped over its blackened frame; the scorched covering still bore the clear outline of Connie's body.

A cool breeze blew in through the glassless window frame, weak beams of morning sunshine showing the ravages of the fire in every grimy detail.

"The paraffin heater was found here." Ted Drury, heading the Fire team, squatted on his haunches, pointing to the white plastic tape in the shape of a cross on the sodden, ashy carpet. "Right by the settee. Not—as described by the owner-occupant—on the far wall."

A second cross of red tape marked the location of the heater, as stipulated by Vera. His colleague, also attired in waterproofs and green Wellington boots, took notes. A Polaroid camera was slung around his neck.

"Cold that night, so the boy lies down . . ." Drury pointed. "Maybe has moved the fire closer, from there to here."

"No, it was found with the ridges facing away from the settee." His colleague laid the smoke-blackened paraffin heater on its side, demonstrating. "If he had moved it to get warm by, the heater would have been the other way around."

They both turned as footsteps scuffled through the debris in the hallway. Vera Reynolds stood in the doorway. She stared around, ashen-faced, her lower lip trembling. Her friend Red was with her, a mop of curly dyed red hair bright as a flaming beacon, long legs, and a firm little rump in tight blue jeans. They carried black plastic rubbish sacks filled with pots and pans and other kitchen utensils.

Vera gave a tiny squeal and reached down.

"Please don't touch anything in the room," Drury warned her.

"It's my photograph album," Vera said, anguished. It lay open on the carpet next to the sofa, its edges buckled and scorched.

Red put her arm around Vera's shoulders, hugging her.

"Don't look—just don't even look. You're insured. Keep on saying to yourself, 'I am insured.'"

Vera gazed at the rack in the alcove where all her lovely, beautiful, gorgeous evening gowns had been, fighting back the tears. Red led her out. "You'll have to have every carpet replaced. The water's done more damage than the fire!"

The two fire officers looked at each other. Odd to think that pansies had the same feelings as normal folk.

Tennison called the first briefing for 9:30 A.M. Except for two or three officers who were out checking statements, the entire Vice Squad, Soho Division, was assembled in the Squad Room. After the tension of the previous day, the atmosphere was markedly more relaxed. People lounged around drinking coffee, wisecracks were bandied about, snatches of laughter, general good humor. Tennison thought she might even get to like working here.

"Is there anyone on the squad who has had any past dealings with Colin Jenkins?"

Kathy passed over a sheaf of reports that she'd winnowed out concerning boys of Connie's age.

"He might have been picked up a few months back, maybe more. We rounded up a lot. I can't find the report on him, but I'm sure that a Jenkins—I think it was a Bruce Jenkins—was interviewed with a probation officer, as he was underage."

"What's this advice centre?" Tennison asked, leafing through. A whiff of cigarette smoke floated by, and she had to battle against the temptation. Did the urge never, ever let up?

"One of the places we targeted," DI Hall said. "I've already been there. The guy that runs it—"

Otley chimed in. "Mr. Parker-Jones. States he hadn't seen our Connie for months." And if you believe that, his tone said, I'm a dead ringer for Richard Gere.

"Has it been confirmed yet whether the fire was arson or accidental?"

Hall shook his head. "Don't know. Fire team are still working on it."

Everyone straightened up a little, took their feet off desks, as Superintendent Halliday walked in. "Want to run over a few things," he said brusquely. Tennison nodded. She was on her way, following him out, when she heard Kathy saying to Hall, "Guv, there was an emergency call placed at nine-fifteen, night of the fire. Caller did not leave his name."

"What emergency call?" asked Hall.

Tennison paused at the door.

"Somebody called an ambulance."

"An ambulance?" Hall frowned. "For Reynolds's address? Get the emergency services to send over the recording."

Tennison hurried along the corridor, catching up with Halliday as he passed her open door. Norma was laboring mightily, logging the stacks of files and placing them on the shelves. Soon it might start to resemble an office.

Halliday turned to Tennison, rubbing his forehead. He looked distinctly green around the gills.

He said, "Last night a lad called Martin Fletcher was brought in— Otley will explain the circumstances—but the last thing we need is any aggro from Social Services about questioning underage kids without legal advisors." He shot her a warning look, then his face creased with pain. "Christ, I've got a headache . . ."

Kennington's farewell bash was taking its toll. Serves you bloody well right, Tennison thought with satisfaction.

"I'd like you to set up meetings with the British Transport police, get to know all the centres and halfway homes in our area. I'd like us to try for another swoop on those areas we've targeted."

"Sir, this boy in the fire, Colin Jenkins," Tennison said as Halliday walked on to his office and opened the door. "According to the team he was on the game!"

"Well, he isn't anymore, so he's one less to worry about." Clutching his head, Halliday went in and slammed the door.

Norma looked up as Tennison came smartly in, heels rapping. She didn't need smoke signals to know that a storm was brewing. Tennison sent her off to get Martin Fletcher's file, and when she returned her boss was pacing the small space between the desk and window. Still pacing, Tennison quickly scanned through the file, and then snatched up the phone. Norma kept her head down, literally, sorting out the files.

"DCI Tennison. Extension seven-eight, please." While she waited, fingers drumming, she spotted some Post-It memo slips stuck to the blotter and attracted Norma's attention.

"There were three messages. The Fire team, Forensic department, and someone called Jessica Smithy. She's a journalist. Said she is doing a piece on rent boys—"

"What paper is she from?" Before Norma could answer, Tennison said into the phone, "Would you please ask Sergeant Otley and Inspector Hall to . . ."

There was no need, as Otley tapped on the door and stuck his head in. Tennison banged the phone down. Hall followed the sergeant in.

"That's it, Norma," Tennison said. "Out, thank you." She waited until the door had closed and came around the desk, brandishing the file.

"What the hell do you think you're playing at—*no!* Don't interrupt!" Otley shut his mouth as Tennison glared at him. "Last night, according to the roster, *you* were not even on duty—but last night the pair of you interviewed a Martin Fletcher, correct?" She opened the file, glancing down at the yellow slip paper-clipped to the top sheet. "When later interviewed by his probation officer, a Miss Margaret Speel, she noted that this same Martin Fletcher had extensive bruising to his face, arms, and upper neck . . ."

"Wait, wait," Otley said, shaking his head rapidly. "We brought him in like that!"

"*Don't* interrupt me, Bill." Tennison's eyes blazed. "This same proba-tion officer has subsequently filed a complaint against this department—which, in case you two had not bloody noticed, *I am head of!*" Her voice sank to a dangerous whisper. "Martin Fletcher, you idiots, is fourteen years old!"

Otley swore under his breath and flopped down into a chair, a hand covering his eyes. Hall stayed on his feet, goggling.

"Oh, man—he swore under caution he was seventeen. He said he was seventeen . . ."

"And as such he should have been allocated a lawyer, a probation offi-cer, or an appropriate adult," Tennison went on relentlessly. She tossed the file on the desk and folded her arms. "So, which one of you wants to start?"

Otley looked up at Hall, who coughed and as a nervous reflex smoothed down his tie, a garish swirl of reds, pinks, and purples.

He said, "There's a known heavy, beats up on the young kids. Jackson, James—"

"So? Get to the point."

"He picks up the young kids, the really young ones, in and around central London—Euston, Charing Cross—"

"I know the stations. Go on."

Hall blinked his large baby-brown eyes. "Martin Fletcher was one of his boys."

Otley's fists were clenched on his knees. With a great effort he kept his voice under tight control. "Reason I brought Martin in was because I reck-oned he might help us get a handle on Connie, why he was in that flat."

"We just wanted to talk to him about Colin Jenkins," Hall added. "Then he starts to tell us about Jackson."

"The bastard plucks 'em off the station," Otley said, "takes them out, gives them food, offers a place to stay—that's it, he's got them." His mouth twisted in his long, haggard face. "Keeps them locked up. Not just boys, it's very young—only the very young—girls as well. He drugs them, keeps them dependent."

Thoughtfully, Tennison went back around the desk. She leaned her knuckles on the edge.

"Did Martin Fletcher tell you all this? Or is it past history?"

"We've sort of known about the scams," Hall said, "but we can't get any of the kids to name Jackson—he was one of our main targets. We don't know where he holds the kids, but Fletcher, he admitted—"

"Just hang on a second." Tennison's narrowed eyes flicked between them. "What do you mean, 'holds the kids'? Kidnaps them?"

"No, they go with him willingly," Otley said. His voice had a raw, ugly edge to it. "And then once he's got them—that's it. We're talking about kids as young as twelve and thirteen . . ."

"None of the kids will talk. We've had him hauled in on numerous occasions, we've even got as far as getting charges compiled against him, but the statements are always withdrawn, the kids are terrified of him, they won't go against him. So when Martin tells us Jackson beat him up because he wanted to know where Connie was, we reckoned we got something." Hall gestured irritably toward the desk. "Have you read my report?"

Tennison straightened up. "Yes!" She flipped open the buff cover, and began to read out loud.

"SGT. OTLEY: 'Where does he stay? Do you know his address?'
FLETCHER: 'No, sir.'
SGT. OTLEY: 'Did he beat up on you, Martin?'
FLETCHER: 'Yes, sir, he did.'
SGT. OTLEY: 'Why did he do that, Martin?'
FLETCHER: 'I don't know.'
SGT. OTLEY: 'Did you know Connie?'
FLETCHER: 'No.'
SGT. OTLEY: 'Come on, Martin, he was murdered.'
FLETCHER: 'No, sir!'"

Tennison brought her fist down on the page, glaring across the desk at them. "We do not as yet have any proof that Colin Jenkins *was* murdered."

Hall took the file, turned it around and thumbed over a couple of pages. He looked up. "Excuse me, Guv . . ."

"Help yourself," Tennison said curtly.

Hall read out loud:

"INSP. HALL: 'Tell me about Colin Jenkins.'

FLETCHER: 'I don't know him.'

INSP. HALL: 'I think you are lying.'

FLETCHER: 'I'm not, I didn't know where he was, that's why Jackson done it to me. . . .'"

Hall looked at Tennison. "Jackson beat up Martin Fletcher on the same night Colin—Connie—died." He read on.

"INSP. HALL: 'What time did Jackson beat you up?'

FLETCHER: 'Eight to nine-ish.'"

Hall closed the file and stepped back. During the silence Otley stared at nothing and Tennison tapped her thumbnail against her bottom teeth. "Have you got a realistic time for when the fire started?"

"Yes," Otley said, getting up. "About nine-thirty." He yanked his crumpled jacket straight at the back. "Jackson could have done it! Even if he didn't, this could be what we need to get him off the streets so we can get the kids to talk." He stared hard at Tennison. She thought some more and then gave a swift nod.

"Okay. You get hold of the probation officer and Martin Fletcher, and bring Jackson in for questioning . . . just helping inquiries," she added quietly, staring him out. In other words, no more bloody cock-ups that would leave her holding the shitty end of the stick.

Tennison wanted to see for herself. Statements, autopsy reports, tapes, photographs told one version of events. They might be true and accurate, but they were one-dimensional, open to interpretation. Nothing like being there, seeing it, smelling it, touching it.

She took Otley along with her to Vera Reynolds's flat. The Fire team was still there, sifting through what remained of Vera's most treasured possessions. A plastic sheet had been taped over the window to keep out the draft. Even so it was cold, the air acrid with the lingering smell of smoke that seemed to enter every pore, making Tennison's eyes sting.

"Body was found here, on the settee." Drury showed her, his gloved hand tracing the outline of Connie's body on the singed fabric. "This is, or was, a paraffin oil heater, and the seat of the fire."

He pointed to the white cross on the carpet.

Tennison crouched down for a closer look, lifting the tail of her beige Burberry raincoat to prevent it getting soiled. "Was it an accident?"

"No." He was very definite. No pussy-footing around. The man knew his business, and his confidence gave her a lift. "The heater was pushed or kicked forward. And there are signs that paraffin had been distributed around the room, probably from a canister of fuel that we found by the door."

"So somebody started the fire," Otley murmured, stroking his jaw.

Tennison leaned over to inspect the covering with its ghostly imprint of Connie's last few seconds alive. No longer just a poor dead lad, she thought; now he was the subject of a possible murder inquiry.

"If you stand by the fireplace, for example, and say you trip . . ." Drury acted it out for them. "There's an armchair, a footstool, a coffee table, but none would indicate the victim had fallen. Coming from the opposite direction . . . if he had, say, fallen against the heater, then he wouldn't have been lying that way around. His head would be at this end."

Tennison pictured it in her mind. It was as important to know what hadn't happened as what actually had. She thanked him with a smile and stepped onto the duckboards leading outside. In the Sierra Sapphire, heading for the morgue, she asked Otley if anything had been found in the flat that might be a possible weapon.

Otley sat in the passenger seat, not wearing his seat belt as she'd asked him to. "Yes, taken to the labs," he said, rhyming them off. "A heavy glass ashtray, a pan, a walking stick handle, er . . ."

"Any prints on them?" Otley shook his head. "What about Vera Reynolds? She in the clear?"

"Time of the fire he was on the catwalk in a tranny club." Otley looked across at her. "He still insists he didn't know the boy. You want to talk to him?"

"I suppose so." Tennison sighed, gnawing her lip. "But if Connie was killed, it won't be down to us to sort it." Seeing her murder inquiry vanishing over the horizon, she said, "We won't get a look in."

Like a kid who's had an ice cream snatched from under her nose, Otley thought. It should have made him feel gleeful, her disappointment, but somehow it didn't.

"DCI Tennison's gone walkabout," Halliday said darkly to Commander Chiswick. "Nobody knows where she is."

Chiswick closed the door and tossed the report onto Halliday's desk. "It's just official, the fire—it wasn't accidental."

"Well, in that case it's nothing to do with us, is it!" A smile broke over

Halliday's pallid features. Maybe now he could shake this blasted hangover. He sat back, relieved. "Thank God!"

"Make sure she understands that this is the Vice Squad," Chiswick told him stolidly, spelling it out. "Any other crimes are forwarded to the correct departments."

"We might have a bit of a problem. The boy was earmarked in Operation Contract, could be a tie-in, but I'll have a word . . ."

"You'd better," Commander Chiswick said, his face stern. "I don't want her—us—to have anything to do with this murder, so reallocate the investigation." He wagged his finger. "And tell her, Jack, she has no option."

Chiswick went out, leaving Halliday delicately massaging his temples with his fingertips.

They arrived at the morgue a few minutes before two-thirty, and were about to enter the laboratory when Tennison received a call on her mobile. She waved Otley on and listened to Norma relaying her messages.

"Right. Okay. Did he leave a number?" Tennison couldn't get to her notebook fast enough, so she wrote the number on her hand. "Anything else?" She listened impatiently. "Again? Just tell her I am unavailable, or put her onto the press officer."

She zapped the aerial back and strode into the white-tiled laboratory. Otley was standing with Craig, a scientist with the Forensic team, before a large, oblong lab bench with a white plastic worktop. Pieces of burnt remnants from the boy's leather jacket, trousers, boots, and underwear were pegged out and separately tagged. There were some loose change, covered in sticky human soot, and sections of what had been a leather wallet, calcified in the heat so that it crumbled to the touch.

"Just official, the fire wasn't accidental," Tennison informed Otley. "What's all this?" she asked, sticking her nose in and watching Craig poking with a glass rod at a hard wad of blackened paper that was crumbling to grayish ash.

"Money. Or the remains of it. We've still got some under the microscope, but it's quite a lot."

"Like about how much?"

Craig was squinting at it through horn-rimmed glasses, wrinkling his hairy nostrils. "At least five hundred, could be more." Using the glass rod as a pointer, he took them through the display. "The clothes, all good expensive items. Quality footwear. We've got a label from his leather coat, it was Armani. . . ."

He moved on, and Tennison said in a quiet aside to Otley, "Martin Fletcher didn't say anything about money, did he? You think this is what Jackson was after?"

Otley shrugged. Money hadn't even been mentioned."

Farther along the bench, Craig was pointing to some crinkled bits of glossy paper. "These are sections of phtographs, all beyond salvaging, but they were stuffed inside his jacket. And these scraps of paper, all charred, I'm afraid. Possibly letters . . . hard to tell."

"This is it?" Tennison said, surveying the worktop.

"Yes, this is all that's left of him," Craig said.

On their way out, Tennison said quietly to Otley, "Get Vera brought in again."

Inspector Larry Hall and WPC Kathy Trent were cruising Euston Station in reverse, so to speak. They weren't looking to be picked up, they were planning to do the picking up—when they found him. To a casual observer they would have appeared just like any other young couple waiting to meet someone. Hall wore his dark navy car coat over his double-breasted blazer, and Kathy had on a loose, deep purple trenchcoat and black suede ankle boots.

Already they'd walked the full length of the concourse at least a dozen times. As each train arrived and the passengers surged up the ramp from the platform, they stood midstream, scanning the wave upon wave of faces rolling toward them.

At ten minutes to three, with Hall starting to fret that they were wasting their time, he got a call. He inclined his head, listening intently, and then spoke into the small transceiver inside his turned-up collar. "Is it him? Sure? Okay, we're on our way."

He set off, Kathy walking briskly beside him. "Jackson's hanging around platform seven." He held out his hand, and Kathy slapped it. "You owe me a fiver!" Hall said, grinning. "I said Euston, you said Charing Cross!"

The Liverpool train had just pulled in. Jackson was sitting on the metal barrier at the top of the ramp, eating a burger. He looked quite relaxed, waiting, it seemed, like several others, for the arrival of a friend. His eyes roamed over the passengers: businessmen, families, older people with their luggage on a cart, but he wasn't interested in any of them. Then he spotted a young boy, fourteen, perhaps fifteen, scruffily dressed, carrying a cheap suitcase tied up with string. Jackson tossed the burger away and slid down. Wiping his mouth, he watched the boy coming up the ramp. He sidled to his left, getting into position to intercept the boy as if by chance.

Hall and Kathy, and a third plainclothes officer, moved in slowly, threading their way through the stream of passengers.

"Hi, how you doin'?" Jackson was all smiles, a friendly face in a strange, hostile environment. "Do I know you?" The boy gave a little nervous smile, shaking his head. "You from Liverpool? You know Steve Wallis?" Jackson patted his shoulder reassuringly. "I'm not the law, just waitin' for a friend. You got somebody meetin' you? First time in the Smoke?" Jackson stuck a cigarette in his mouth and offered one to the boy. "Hey, man, you want a drag?"

As the boy reached to accept it, Hall stepped between them, nose to nose with Jackson. Jackson fell back a pace. He half-turned, nearly colliding with the third officer standing right behind him. Hall muttered a few words in Jackson's ear.

Her arm around his shoulder, Kathy said to the boy, "Have you got somebody meeting you, love?"

The boy shook his head. He looked past Kathy and got a glimpse of the two officers walking off with Jackson between them, merging into the crowd.

Otley came into the interview room with a tray of canteen teas in proper cups and saucers. He slid it onto the desk between Tennison and Vera Reynolds. Norma was sitting next to the wall, plump black-stockinged legs crossed, taking notes. She looked bored to tears.

"Vera's admitted that she knew Colin."

"Connie," Vera corrected Tennison. Her head was bowed, her long pale hands with the manicured nails clasped tightly in the lap of her leather skirt. She wore a loose halter-neck knitted top, colored bangles on her bare arms. "He didn't like his name, sometimes he called himself Bruce."

Tennison made a note on her pad.

"Bit butch for his kind, isn't it?" Otley said, standing with legs apart, sipping his tea.

Vera turned her face to the wall.

Tennison's patience was running short, but she summoned up some more. "Vera, the sooner this is all sorted out, the sooner you can leave."

"On the other hand, if you killed your little feathered friend," Otley said, "then you'll be caged up—with no makeup bag in sight."

Tennison looked at Vera over the rim of her cup. She glanced up at Otley, who rolled his eyes. They waited.

"If it's proved to be arson . . ." Vera's voice was croaky; her eyes red-rimmed. "I mean, if somebody did it, does that mean I won't get the insurance?" Her brow puckered as if she were about to cry. "Oh, God . . . all my costumes. I don't know what I'm going to do."

"Never mind your costumes, Vera, what about Connie?" Otley's patience was running shorter than Tennison's. "Who do you think set light to him?"

"I don't know." Staring at the desktop, fingers plucking at the baggy sleeve of her knitted top.

DI Hall tapped on the door and looked in. Otley went over, and Hall whispered to him, "I've got Jackson and the probation officer waiting to see . . ." He nodded at Tennison. "And Martin Fletcher's being brought in."

Tennison was making one last try. "Vera, if you are protecting someone, then you had better tell me. You have already lied to us, wasted our time . . ." She looked across at Hall. "Five minutes." Then back to Vera. "Why did you lie about Connie?"

Norma looked at Hall, cross-eyed. She tapped her watch, blowing out her cheeks. He grinned and went out. Tennison leaned her elbows on the desk, waiting. Otley stood holding his cup and saucer, waiting. He glanced impatiently at his watch. Vera took a long time lighting a cigarette. She blew out a great gust of smoke, then, as an afterthought, hesitantly offered the packet.

"I've given up," Tennison said.

"I've tried, I've had the patches." Vera smiled weakly. "I've got patches for hormones, nicotine—my arse looks like an old pub table. I even tried the chewing gum. How did you give up?"

"With great difficulty."

Norma's mouth sagged open as she watched the pair of them. She looked at Otley, who gave her a snide wink.

Tennison pushed the loaded ashtray across. "You had better help me, Vera, I am losing my patience. Why did you lie?"

"I wasn't lying—about knowing him. Nobody really knew him. He was very gentle, very beautiful. He wanted to be a model. A professional model," Vera insisted, making sure Tennison understood the difference. "He used to answer the ads . . ."

Tennison glanced up sharply and glared at Otley as his sigh exploded in the quiet room. She rapped her knuckles on the desk. "What about James Jackson, Vera?"

Vera drew deeply on her cigarette. "He's an animal, should be caged."

"Did Connie have someone looking after him? Say Jackson?"

"You mean like a pimp? No, the older boys don't have them, really. Not like the Toms."

The *bing-bong* of the chimes came over the wall speaker. "Sergeant Otley to main reception please."

He looked to Tennison, and at her nod left the room.

"I would help you, you know that," Vera said slowly, as if, with tremendous effort, she was forcing the words out of herself. "I always have in the past. You're . . . you're not like the others, and I've always appreciated the way you speak to me—" She broke off to suck in a lungful of smoke. "But—I can't help. Maybe . . ."

Tennison counted silently to five. "Maybe what?"

"He used the advice centre, for letters, I know that." She stubbed out the cigarette. "Edward Parker-Jones runs it."

Tennison's hand reached toward Vera's, but instead of touching it she picked up the ashtray and tipped it into the wastebasket. Abruptly, she stood up. "Norma, will you show Vera the way out." She tore the sheet from her notepad. "And check out this. Give it to Kathy."

Tennison went into the corridor, leaving the door open. She stood there, grinding her teeth. She was annoyed with Vera and bloody angry with herself. She found it difficult to concentrate, and her insides were jumpy. Was she coming down with flu or what? She wasn't in top form, and knew it.

Otley strode up. She faced him wearily.

"Martin Fletcher's now in reception, and the probation officer's with him. I think you need to have words with Martin, and before Jackson."

Tennison nodded abstractedly, trying to get her train of thought back on the tracks. Vera appeared, clicking her handbag shut, followed by Norma, who pointed along the corridor. "Down the staircase and right . . ."

Kathy hurried through the double doors from the opposite direction. "Guv, there's a couple of messages—that reporter again, Jessica Smithy. I've told her to contact the press office but she's really pushy, insists she wants to talk to you. So does Superintendent Halliday, and there's . . ."

She was interrupted by the loitering Otley, who'd gone beyond fed up to plain pissed off. "Guv? How do you want to work it?"

Tennison waved Kathy away. "Leave them on my desk," she said sharply, tiredness nagging at her. Kathy looked hurt, but Tennison couldn't be bothered. "I'll talk to Martin first," she answered Otley.

Having set off for the stairs, Vera was back, clutching her bag, in a distressed state.

"You are going the wrong way, Vera," Tennison said with the forebearance of a saint. "The main exit is back down the corridor."

"I wanted to talk to you!" Vera burst out, on the edge of panic hysteria. "You see, if it gets out that it was me who told you . . ."

"You didn't tell me anything, Vera," Tennison said, tight-lipped.

Vera suddenly flinched. Her eyes grew large and round. Terrified, she stared past Tennison to where Jackson was being escorted toward them by Inspector Hall and a uniformed officer. Backing away, Vera whispered hoarsely, "Don't you let this go, don't stop. Please, don't let this go, you dig deep, don't let it go . . ."

Jackson had seen her, and Vera saw that he had. She kept on backing away, and then turned and scurried off. She looked back, once, at Tennison, naked fear in her eyes, and vanished down the staircase.

Otley stood aside as Jackson was taken into the interview room. He waited by the door, watching Tennison dithering in the corridor.

"Where's Martin Fletcher?" she asked irritably.

"Room D oh six," Otley said, and when she dithered some more, he said loudly, as if she were deaf or stupid, "It's the one next to the coffee machine!"

Tennison took three paces and stopped. *"Where's the bloody coffee machine?"* she said through gritted teeth, but the door had closed.

Halliday came through the double doors. He went past at a clip, not breaking his stride. "Colin Jenkins. Can you get me the full case records to date?"

"Yes, sir," Tennison said. "Where's the coffee machine?"

"Make sure you get everything to me ASAP. That's firsthand, Chief Inspector," Halliday said over his shoulder. "I don't want anything sprung on me. That understood? I'll be in my office . . ." He disappeared around a corner, his voice floating back, "Downstairs on your right."

Stumping down the stairs, Tennison made a silent screaming face.

5

Martin Fletcher's bruised face had matured over the past twenty-four hours. The blow on his forehead had ripened into a huge purple swelling. His cut lip was an angry puffy red. The gash on his cheek had crusted over, weeping yellowish pus. A plug of bloodstained cotton was stuck up his left nostril.

Head sunk between his shoulders, he sat in the interview room, smoking, continually flicking at the filter tip with a gnawed-down thumbnail. The ashtray had overflowed onto the tabletop. Nearby, the unwinking red light of the tape recorder glowed like a tiny ruby.

A uniformed officer stood by the door. Next to Martin sat his probation officer, Margaret Speel. She was in her early thirties, neat and unfussy in a light gray suit, with an oval small-boned face and frizzy black hair cut in severe bangs just above her eyes. She leaned toward him, bowing her head to be on a level with his.

"You understand the question, Martin? Now, we're all getting tired, we've all been here a long time . . ."

Tennison looked up from the report in front of her. It was after six in the evening, it had been a hectic yet frustrating day, and under the harsh strip lighting she knew that she must have looked like a worn-out old hag. She certainly felt like one. She tried again.

"Martin, last night you talked to Sergeant Otley and Inspector Hall, and you told them that the man who attacked you—"

"No! That was words put in me mouth." Martin sniffed loudly. "I never told nobody nuffink—and that is the Gawd's truth."

Tennison plowed on. "You also said that the man's name was Jackson and that he specifically asked you if you knew where Colin Jenkins was—"

Again Martin jumped in. "No—I never said that—never." He took a swift drag, his fingers trembling, showering ash everywhere. "What happened was . . . you know that escalator top of King's Cross station? I was comin' down, me coat got caught like, and I fell forward." He ducked down to demonstrate. "I hit me head on the stairs, and then, when I got up, I fell over again and hit me nose. Nobody hit me." He stared at her, one eye swollen and bloodshot.

"So you lied to the police officers who questioned you?" Tennison said quietly.

"Yeah, I suppose so." He grew bolder. "Yeah, I lied 'cos . . .'cos I'm underage—I mean, they really scared me like, and . . ."

"Martin, did you know Colin?"

He glanced sideways at Margaret Speel and then took another deep swift drag, a single plume of smoke issuing through one nostril.

"Yeah, not like—well, red-haired bloke, wasn't he? Quentin House, he was there wiv me, now he's burnt like a crisp!" Due to his cut lip his grin was lopsided, showing the black gap of two missing front teeth. "That's a joke goin' round—Quentin Crisp, famous poofter . . ."

"Have you ever had sex with a man?"

"Me? Nah!"

"What about a blow job? Ever been paid for doing that?"

Martin shrugged. "Few times, when I'm broke like, but I'm not into that. I got other means of employment." He was sounding cocky now, starting to brag.

"Such as?"

"Breakin' and enterin', nickin' cars, radios. Beggin'—do a bit of that." He smirked. "Sell my life story to the newspapers."

Tennison looked at Margaret Speel, whose expression remained exactly the same: in fact hardly any expression at all, apart from a slight cynical twist of the mouth, that must be part of the job description, Tennison thought.

Martin was laughing. "I can nick a motor, go for a joyride, an' you lot can't do nuffink!"

Tennison snapped her notebook shut.

"You listen to me, Martin. You think you can play games with us, lie to us, and it's all a joke. Well, it isn't. Colin Jenkins has no one to claim his body, no one to bury him." Tennison stood up. Martin wouldn't look at her. "Nobody cares about Colin Jenkins but us."

Absolutely seething, Tennison went up the stairs and strode along the corridor, muttering to herself, "I have just about had enough of this bloody place—kids can run riot over us without—"

Otley was leaning against the wall outside interview room D.03 having a smoke. He eased himself into his usual round-shouldered slouch as Tennison stormed up.

"—Is Jackson in here?" she snapped, jerking her thumb.

"He denies knowing Martin Fletcher," Otley said.

"And Martin Fletcher denied his entire statement! Can we hold Jackson on attempting to pick up that boy at the station?" Otley shook his head. "So we've got nothing on him . . . ! No prints from Vera's flat?" Otley shook his head. "Nothing off the possible weapon?"

"Nope, nothin'," Otley said, still shaking his head.

For just an instant Tennison seemed to deflate before his eyes. Then she rallied, straightened up, took a deep breath, brushed a hand through her hair, and jabbed her finger at the door. Otley pushed it open.

She had expected Jackson to be a nasty piece of work and she wasn't disappointed. What she hadn't expected was his overweening confidence bordering on insolence. He was sprawled back in the chair as if he owned the place, long legs splayed out, leather jacket undone, blowing smoke rings into the thick blue haze that filled the room. Cigarette stubs floated in the cups of cold coffee on the table. He couldn't be bothered to look up as she entered, heavy-lidded eyes in the long, pockmarked face glazed with boredom, scruffy mop of hair sticking up in spikes. He leaned back, blowing another lazy smoke ring.

"Open the window," Tennison rapped out to Hall. "Shut the door," she told Otley. Jackson sniggered. Bossy bitch.

She whipped around on him. "And you, take that smile off your face! Because I am going to book you and send you away, Jackson, for a very long time."

Jackson looked at Hall as if to say, *Where the fuck did you dig this twat up from?* He looked at Tennison and then dropped his eyes to the Marlboro packet he was turning slowly over and over. He said in a calm, controlled voice, "What am I supposed to have done?"

"One—you were caught approaching a juvenile. Two—attempted murder of another juvenile, Martin Fletcher, and three—that you did on the night of the seventeenth murder Colin Jenkins."

Jackson stubbed out his cigarette and rose to his feet wearing a pained, crooked smile.

"SIT DOWN!!"

Sighing, he dropped into his seat. Still amused, he watched the manic Tennison dragging out the vacant chair with a clatter, picking up the laden ashtray and banging it into the wastebasket. She threw it down on the table, turning to Hall. "You've read him his rights?" Then to Otley, "Sergeant, has he given you his contact number for his brief yet?"

She sat down opposite him, scanning his statement sheet, cheeks slightly flushed. "What's your address?"

"Flat four, Addison Lane Estate, my mother's place . . ."

"And your full name is James Paul Jackson, yes?"

"Yes, that's my name." He turned the packet over slowly, as if it were a tricky, delicate operation.

Tennison went down the sheet. "Unemployed . . . arrested . . ." Hardly audible, she read on. "No charges, no charges, no charges . . . you are very well known to the Vice Squad, aren't you?" She closed the report. "You've been very lucky until now," she said, smiling, the boss congratulating a promising recruit before dumping on him from a great height. "Because obviously we couldn't formally charge you until we had interviewed Martin Fletcher."

The smile vanished. Hard-eyed now, she let the silence hang.

Jackson looked at Hall, then at Tennison. He opened the packet and eased out a cigarette. Slow and deliberate, with a steady hand, he picked up his lighter. The phone rang. Hall reached for it and had a whispered conversation.

"I never touched Colin Jenkins," Jackson said, sucking the smoke deep. "I wasn't even there. I wasn't at Vernon Reynolds's flat full stop." He sighed, shaking his head, still very full of himself. "End of questions."

"But you admit that you attacked Martin Fletcher on the night of the seventeenth—"

"I was at the advice centre," Jackson stated calmly, flicking ash. "Ask Mr. Parker-Jones, he saw me there. There was also a kid called Alan Thorpe, and I got three or four more witnesses to prove I was there." Again the heavy sigh, glancing around the room. "This is ridiculous, waste of time."

"Why did you want to find Colin?"

"I never found him. I admit though, I was looking for him. Martin must have told you that. I was looking for Connie, but—I—never—found—him."

"Advice centre," Tennison said, making a note. "Why were you looking for Colin Jenkins?"

Jackson closed his eyes momentarily and opened them the barest slit, staring straight at her. "He owed me some money."

"How much?"

"Couple of hundred."

"Couple of hundred?" Tennison said, eyebrows raised. "But you are unemployed! That's a lot of money."

"Yes, that's why I wanted it back." Jackson rubbed his unshaven chin and leaned forward. "Look, I'll be honest with you." He cleared his throat, big confession coming up. "Sometimes I . . . do the odd trick, I mean work is really hard to come by, you know? And my mum, she gets behind with the rent . . . so, I blow a few blokes, an' I don't like it when some kid nicks my dough."

Tennison laced her fingers together and stayed silent. She wasn't going to waste an ounce of breath on this kind of bull. She heard another of Otley's long-suffering sighs. Hall leaned over and murmured that the Super wanted to see her in his office.

"I'm not going to lie about Martin," Jackson said, waving his cigarette about carelessly. "I guess I just lost my temper. You tellin' me he's gonna press charges? Martin? No way." He was staring at her, tugging his earlobe, as if he was trying to figure something out. "Like you said, it was a lot of money. . . ."

Tennison said nothing. He sounded brash and cocksure, right enough, but she sensed that underneath the swaggering bravado he was getting rattled. Good. Get him rattled some more.

"I'm not sayin' anything until I got a brief. Because you . . ." Finger jabbing, fleshy lips twisting. "You're not listening to what I'm sayin'."

Very businesslike, Tennison collected her things together and stood up. She said to Inspector Hall, "I think Mr. Jackson should be taken to the cells until we have, as he has requested, contacted his brief, and we have verified his alibi for the night in question."

"Right, let's go through your witnesses," Otley said. "Names, Jackson."

Tennison went out. Hall looked to Otley, patting his tie. She was sailing bloody close to the wind. She'd nearly charged him with murder without a shred of real evidence.

Jackson was making a brutal job of stubbing his cigarette in the ashtray. He glared up at Otley. "What's her name?"

"One dead rent boy, Chief Inspector, is not going to bring the entire department to a standstill, is that understood?"

Halliday stood with his hands stuffed in his pockets, looking out onto a darkening Broadwick Street. It was the vacant hour, lost in no-man's-land between the exodus of the office workers and the first stirrings of Soho nightlife.

Tennison was taken aback. "I wasn't aware of any standstill—

"Just let me finish, please." Halliday swung around, an abrupt movement that betrayed his edginess. Usually neat to the point of fastidiousness, his tie was slightly askew and his short fair hair was ruffled as though he'd been combing his fingers through it. He placed his pale, freckled hands on the back of his swivel chair. "As Colin Jenkins's death is now a homicide, I suggest we hand it over—"

"But we have . . ."

"—to the correct department."

"But we have a strong suspect in custody," Tennison protested. "And far from any standstill, we are making progress. The reason I am interested in Jackson is because of the direct link to Operation Contract."

The Superintendent released a small sigh. "Go on."

"Jackson's well known to Vice, and has in actual fact been questioned on numerous occasions. If he did murder Colin Jenkins, I think it will act as a strong lever for more information." She hesitated, knuckles tapping her palm. "There's also an advice centre that keeps cropping up, run by a man called Edward Parker-Jones."

"Operation Contract at no time initiated an investigation into Edward Parker-Jones . . ."

"I wasn't contemplating any investigation into Mr. Parker-Jones. But he is my suspect's alibi, and the longer we have Jackson locked up, the easier it'll be to question the kids." Tennison was furious with herself that she sounded to be pleading, and didn't know why the hell she should have to. "Look, you did say that my priority was Operation Contract . . ."

"All right," Halliday conceded. He rubbed his forehead and swung the chair around to sit in it. "Just keep me informed if there are any new developments."

Tennison nodded and left the office. Halliday sat down, drumming his fingers. He stared at the closed door for a moment, picked up the phone and started to dial.

As Tennison closed the door to Halliday's office, Kathy came up.

"Guv, have you got a second? You asked me to check back if Colin Jenkins had been brought in. Well, he was—but he used the name Bruce Jenkins, charged with soliciting."

"So who did the interview?"

"Sergeant Otley. But it was almost a year ago, and he was underage, so a probation officer took over from our department. I've traced her," Kathy said, "but she's not much help. She's sending the report in."

"You remember anything about him?" Tennison asked.

Kathy shook her head glumly. "No, sorry . . ."

She went off, leaving Tennison gazing dully at the dark green wall opposite. She felt totally drained. Her brain had seized up, and she felt unable to connect one coherent thought to another. She started to drag herself back to her office next door when she heard Halliday talking on the phone, his voice faint but distinct.

". . . how can I tell her to back off something if it has a direct link to the bloody job she was brought in to do?"

Tennison looked up and down the corridor and leaned in.

"If she isn't suspicious now, she would be if I pulled her off it," Halliday said, sounding exasperated. After a pause he went on, "She knows nothing, because I'm sure of it. We'll just make damned sure it stays that way."

The receiver went down and rapid footsteps thudded on the carpet. Tennison made it to her door just as Halliday's door opened. She nipped in and gently pushed the door to with her fingertips, seeing him pass by through the crack. She clicked the door shut.

Otley had been on the bevvy the night before. His gaunt face was grayer and even more deeply lined than usual, eyes like piss-holes in snow. Nonetheless he was enjoying himself. He kept sneaking wicked little grins at Hall, whose return smile was rather lukewarm.

It was the 9:30 A.M. briefing in the Squad Room, and the entire team—with the exception of DCI Tennison and WPC Kathy Trent—was assembled, paying close attention to Commander Chiswick. Halliday was there, the Colin Jenkins autopsy report and forensic lab reports on the desk in front of him. There was also a new face. Otley recognized him as Detective Inspector Brian Dalton—dark, tanned, with sleepy brown eyes that had the women turning somersaults, Otley reckoned. A real handsome bastard.

So Otley's delight was twofold. Chiswick was holding court while Tennison was conspicuous by her absence (maybe she hadn't even been *told*!) and new people were being drafted in, probably without her knowledge. At any rate, *something* was going down, Otley gloated, and the old cow would hit the freaking roof when she found out.

"The deceased, Colin Jenkins, was, according to the Path. reports, unconscious when the fire took hold." Chiswick had a pedantic, monotone delivery, better suited to reading the weather forecast. "This is verified by the low amount of smoke inhalation, indicating very shallow breathing. But his death was due to carbon monoxide poisoning, therefore we are treating the case as murder . . ."

Otley folded his arms, hugging himself, as Tennison came in, followed by Kathy. Halliday nodded a greeting to Tennison, who went to stand beside him.

". . . as it is clear from the fire reports that the fire was not accidental, but an act of arson. We all have a backlog of cases," the Commander said, looking toward Tennison. He didn't nod or smile, he just looked. He faced the front.

". . . and my own feelings concerning the murder and its obvious complexities are that we keep it inhouse. So I'd like this case brought to a conclusion as fast as possible, and have requested backup to assist Detective Chief Inspector Tennison's inquiry from C.I.D. AMIT area seven-stroke-eight."

AMIT 7/8 was the Area Major Incident Team, based at New Scotland Yard, which covered the Soho, Piccadilly Circus, and Leicester Square beat.

"Thank you," Chiswick said, and a buzz of chatter started up.

Otley nudged DI Hall. They both watched, Otley with undisguised glee, as Tennison stalked out, face like a storm cloud.

She was halfway along the corridor when Chiswick and Halliday appeared behind her, following on at an even pace. When she was a reasonable distance from the Squad Room, Tennison halted and turned, facing squarely up to Halliday.

"I do not, at this stage, need any assistance. I already have a strong suspect."

"James Jackson," Halliday muttered to Chiswick, "earmarked in Operation Contract."

"I would also appreciate it," Tennison said crisply, getting it off her chest, "if I were to be informed before the squad of any further decisions connected to the Colin Jenkins investigation."

DI Dalton ambled up, tall, dark, and handsome, with an engaging grin. Otley's head poked through the Squad Room doors, wearing a devilish smirk, relishing every moment.

"Ah, I'm sorry, Jane, I didn't have time this morning to introduce you." Halliday extended his hand. "This is one of your new team, DI Brian Dalton. Brian, this is Chief Inspector Jane Tennison."

"Good morning," Tennison said without so much as a glance at him, and went into her office.

She busied herself for an hour with a mound of paperwork. The mind-numbing chore brought her anger down from white heat to a dull smoldering red. Why in heaven's name she hadn't developed an ulcer was one of the unsolved mysteries of the age. Or had a nervous breakdown. But she was saving that for her three-week vacation.

Norma kept her supplied with coffee, and at eleven o'clock DI Hall came to her office with the tape sent over from the ambulance emergency service. All such calls were taped and kept for a period of months. They listened to it several times, straining to hear through the whining distortion and crackling electronics; also there was music and pinging noises in the background, which didn't help.

"I want to report an accident. It's flat five. I need an ambulance. I want to report an accident. It's flat five. I need an ambulance . . ."

"Call logged at nine-fifteen P.M.," Hall said.

Tennison rewound the tape. "Recognize the voice? It's not Vernon, is it?"

Hall shrugged. It could have been King Kong.

As they were replaying it, Brian Dalton knocked and came in, and leaned against the wall, supported by an outstretched arm, one ankle crossed over the other, studying his fingernails.

"Didn't leave his name?" he said, when it was finished.

"Of course!" Hall said, beaming brightly. "We're just replaying this because we like the sound of his voice!"

Tennison started the tape again. She turned it off when Otley put his head around the door. "Jackson is now with his brief, Guv!" He pushed the door open, holding his wrist up, pointing at his watch.

Tennison went into the corridor, nodding at Otley to come with her. Dalton followed. Tennison gave a sweet smile. "Just stay put a minute," she said, and firmly pulled the door shut on him.

She moved a small distance along the corridor, then leaned against the wall, head bowed, inspecting the worn carpet. Hated that color, even when it was new. Sort of snot-green.

"Bit overqualified, isn't he?" Otley said, jerking his head.

Tennison's head came up fast. "You interviewed Colin, alias Bruce, Jenkins. What happened, Bill? Did it slip your mind?" He blinked a couple of times, and Tennison really tore into him. "Here am I trying to get a handle on the boy, and you, you—*interviewed him!*"

Otley looked at the ceiling. A cord of muscle twitched in his hollow cheek. Here we go again. Ball-Breakers Inc.

He said, "I had a two-minute conversation with him, just after I first came here. I didn't remember it until Kath told me . . ."

"And? Is that it? Was he intelligent? Was he dumb? Was he cheeky? Where was he picked up? Was he caught in the act? What was he doing? I presume you did question him. He was soliciting, wasn't he?"

It was Otley's turn to inspect the carpet. "He was just . . . very young, quiet." Small shrug. "Very quiet."

"Take Dalton with you. I want Martin Fletcher brought back in." Tennison's face was stony. "I presume you can remember who he is."

She walked off and Otley trudged back to get Dalton and do the bitch's bidding.

With his brief present—Mr. Arthur, a short squat little man with a sweaty bald head, wearing a threadbare suit and scuffed brown suede shoes—Jackson seemed more inclined to talk. The cockiness was still there, the indolent sprawling posture, the sneering fleshy lips, the chain-smoking. You can't touch me, I'm fireproof: he might have carried it around with him as a neon advertising sign.

Tennison and Hall listened, not interrupting, getting as much down on tape as was possible in the time. Time was the problem.

". . . and there was another kid, Kenny Lloyd, he was there. And—oh yeah, Driscoll. Dunno his first name. Disco Driscoll, and Alan Thorpe, Billy Matthews, they was with me, from . . ." He sucked on the Marlboro, held the smoke in, let it explode through his nostrils. "'Bout half eight on-ward, at the advice centre." He wagged his head, lips pursed. "Played some pool, watched TV . . . I told you this, I told you about even Mr. Parker-Jones being there."

"Well, we will check out these witnesses, but until then you will remain in custody," Tennison said officiously. A fair and honest copper playing it by the book.

Mr. Arthur was agitated. His false teeth weren't a perfect fit, and his speech was accompanied by constant clicking and a spray on the sibilant consonants. "But my client has clearly stated to you that on the evening in question he has not one, but *five* witnesses, and you were given their names last night!"

Tennison said primly, "Mr. Arthur, until we are satisfied that these witnesses can verify that Mr. Jackson was where he said he was . . ."

She looked up at Otley, who had just entered the room and was beck-oning to her. She went over to him while Mr. Arthur's querulous clicking voice kept on complaining.

"What about these other charges? I mean, you have held my client for nearly twenty-four hours. If there are other charges to be leveled at my cli-ent, then we have a right to know exactly what they are."

Otley said quietly in Tennison's ear, "Nobody can trace Martin Fletcher. He was in the Bullring last night, Waterloo underpass this morning."

"The probation officer, Margaret Speel, doesn't she know where he is?" Otley shook his head. Tennison ground her teeth. This bloody investigation was falling apart at the seams. She poked her finger into Otley's chest. "Then you'd better get out and find him! Find every one of Jackson's alibis and wheel them in. All of them!"

She turned back to Jackson, who was lighting a cigarette from the stub of the last one. Cocky little prick. "Take him back to the cells," she said to Hall.

Jackson grinned at her. He said to his brief, "How long can they hold me here?"

"What time did you bring my client in?" Mr. Arthur asked Hall, almost bouncing up and down in the chair. "The exact time, Inspector . . . ?"

Tennison glanced back from the door, then made a swift silent exit.

She went directly to the Squad Room. One of the team was writing up the names of Jackson's alibi witnesses in black felt-tip on the board: ALAN THORPE. BILLY MATTHEWS. ?? DRISCOLL. KENNY LLOYD.

Kathy was showing Norma some holiday snaps. "Not got any work on, girls?" Tennison asked.

Kathy hesitated, then passed one over for Tennison to see. "They're my kids." She exchanged a quick guarded glance with Norma; neither of them had worked under a female DCI before—hardly surprising when they were rarer than duck's teeth—and they weren't sure how to take Tennison.

"I was just saying that after each one I've got to start all over again."

"What do you mean?"

"Maternity leave," Kathy said. "Back I come and everyone's changed over. I'm shuttled here and there."

"Your decision though, isn't it?" Tennison said, flicking through the snaps. Two blond-haired toddlers paddling in the sea, the younger one only just past the baby stage.

Kathy bridled. "No way—I don't know where I'm going to be sent."

"No, I meant it's your decision to have kids. Norma, do you have any?"

Norma shook her head. "No, but I'm not married either."

Tennison handed back the photographs. "That probation officer for Colin Jenkins, she send over anything?"

Kathy went across to her desk. Norma pointed behind her to the board, a typed list of Colin Jenkins's clothing and possessions.

"He had to have somebody shellin' out. His gear, the Armani jacket, designer jeans. Then there's the money—five hundred quid."

"Traced to a children's home," Kathy said, coming back with a wallet-type cardboard folder. "They've sent a few photographs, just small black-and-white jobs." She laid them out and glanced through the résumé she'd compiled. "No family. Taken into care aged three. His mother OD'd a year later, and he was moved from one—two—three homes, a foster home, and then back again." She held up the sheet. "That's about it."

Tennison looked at the smudgy photographs, which showed Connie standing in various groups, children's homes and schools, aged from six to roughly thirteen. A good-looking kid, but terribly solemn in all of them. Small wonder, Tennison thought. What a miserable existence . . .

She glanced around as the Squad Room doors swung open, and got a shock. She stared uncomprehendingly at Haskons and Lillie, standing there large as life: two detectives who'd served under her at Southampton Row.

Tennison stood up. "What are you doing here?"

Haskons tossed his raincoat down and gave an elaborate shrug. "You tell us. Thorndike said you needed some backup—so, well, he sent you the cream."

DC Lillie, the taller, thinner of the two, more easy-going and laid-back than DS Haskons, merely shook his head.

Tennison came around the desk. She wasn't annoyed, she was totally pissed off. This was getting beyond a fucking joke. She jerked her head for them to follow. "You'd better come into my office."

They went out. As the doors swung shut, Kathy gave Norma a dig with her elbow. "Catch the little snide line about it being my decision? Who does she think she is!"

Tennison opened the door to her office and ushered the pair inside ahead of her. "I'll be with you in a minute."

She closed the door, not quite slamming it, though she felt like doing so, and stood glowering toward Halliday's office.

"Inspector Tennison?"

She turned, feeling like the place was suddenly teeming with strange new faces. He trotted toward her, slightly out of breath, looking a bit flustered, holding a scrap of paper. "I'm from Rossington station. DI Ray Hebdon. I was told by Superintendent Halliday to"—he checked the paper—"report to you."

Tennison made a sweeping gesture, indicating her office. "Please, be my guest." Hebdon went in.

Tennison rapped on Halliday's door. There was a brief pause before he answered, during which she ran both hands through her hair, her simmering temper coming nicely to the boil. She went in, marched up to his desk, and came straight out with it.

"First the male model Dalton. Now it's DS Haskons, DC Lillie, and a pink-faced nervous type from Rossington station. Could I have an explanation?"

Halliday was partly bent over, peeling a hard-boiled egg and dropping the shell in the wastebasket. A plastic lunch box contained three more hard-boiled eggs. He leaned back in his chair, holding up the peeled egg. "They sit like lead in the gut."

"Don't I have a say in the matter? Any choice?"

"Chief Inspector, you have three extra men. Use them."

"Correction, I have four! Dalton."

"I know how many, Chief Inspector," Halliday said testily. "You wanted to retain the murder inquiry, didn't you?" He bit the top off the egg.

Tennison went to the door. She cast him a dark look under her brows. "Any more due? Or is this it? They have a few spare dog handlers at Hammersmith!"

Halliday laughed, mouth full of egg. He tapped another on the desk and peeled it, tossing the shell fragments into the wastebasket.

Tennison left the office, hoping he damn well choked on it.

6

Otley had nothing personal against Dalton—he hardly knew the bloke—but there was something about the young detective inspector (not a day over thirty-five, Otley judged) that irritated him. Not his good looks: Otley had no personal vanity whatsoever. It was more Dalton's impulsiveness. He did everything at the gallop, instead of taking his time and sizing up a situation. And he had no streetwise sense, not a scrap. That's what got to Otley, the fact that the bloke was deskbound for most of his working life, far removed from the seedy pubs and afternoon drinking clubs that were part of Otley's daily round.

That was it. Otley had placed him. An eager-beaver Boy Scout dressed up as a police inspector.

They parked the car and set off on a tour of the Bullring and the Waterloo underpass. This area, south of the river, between the Royal Festival Hall and the National Theatre, was notorious for the hundreds if not thousands of people who inhabited its concrete walkways, its brick viaducts near Waterloo Station, dossing down in cardboard boxes, huddling near the heating vents, constructing little shelters out of bits of timber and plastic sheeting. Dossers, winos, junkies, bag ladies, the physically sick and the mentally ill, kids on the run from home and institutionalized care, and on the game: the hopeless and dispossessed and forgotten, the new London poor of 1993.

It wasn't Otley's patch, though he knew the area and its floating population of misfits well. Trouble was, a lot of them knew him, so it was difficult to wander about incognito. And in broad daylight, two o'clock in the afternoon, there weren't any shadows to skulk around in, creep up on them unawares.

They walked through the Bullring, a huge concrete bowel wrapped around by a network of roads heading north across Waterloo Bridge and south to the Elephant and Castle. The noise was horrendous, the continuous streams of traffic shattering past overhead. Dalton spied a group of kids in a concrete cubbyhole behind one of the massive arching supports. They were crouched in a circle on the filthy, rubbish-covered ground, empty spray cans, squeezed-out tubes of glue, and broken syringes and needles everywhere.

"We're looking for a kid nicknamed Disco Driscoll—" Dalton made a grab as they scattered, and collared one. "Hey—I'm talking to you!" The boy was squirming. Dalton wrenched the aerosol can from his grimy hand. "What's this?"

"Makin' a model airplane, mate!"

Dalton tried to swipe him as he ran off, and missed. Otley looked away, hiding a grin.

The squalid brick viaducts of the Waterloo underpass housed a community of down-and-outs, living in patched-up shelters tacked to the walls. Groups of them sat around campfires on the pavements, passing the bottle, and mingled with the smoke was the sharp reek of meths and cleaning fluid. It was gloomier here, under the arches, and the two detectives were able to approach without being observed. Otley touched Dalton's arm, making him slow down, and said in a low voice, "Kid with the lager cans, that's Kenny Lloyd. What I suggest we do . . ."

He was about to suggest they split up and circle in, one head on and one behind, blocking the kids' retreat, but he never got the chance. Dalton was off and away. He ran fast, charging along the greasy pavement, but the group Kenny was in, their instinct for self-preservation honed on the streets, saw him coming and were off in a flash, just dark blurs disappearing into the gloom.

Otley sighed and shook his head. Where had they dug up this dickhead from?

Ten minutes later they were sitting in the outdoor cafeteria of the National Film Theatre, overlooking the river. There was a cool breeze and some ragged cloud overhead, but Otley was enjoying a cup of coffee and a sticky iced bun in the fitful sunshine. He broke off a piece and tossed it to a seagull. At once more seagulls started to swoop down.

Dalton didn't approve. "You shouldn't encourage them—shit all over you." Otley tossed another chunk. Dalton turned away in disgust. There was a poster in the Film Theatre window for Andrzej Wajda's *Man of Iron*. "Good movie that, have you seen it?" Dalton asked.

Otley's eyes were elsewhere. He was watching three ragged kids picking up leftover scraps from the tables. One boy in particular, hustling cigarettes from the patrons, looked familiar. Otley watched him for several minutes, a skinny, pathetic-looking specimen in a torn T-shirt, filthy jeans, and cheap sneakers, bare ankles caked with dirt. His thin, ravaged face was marked and bruised, his mouth erupting in open cold sores.

"Just going for a leak, okay?"

Dalton paid no attention as Otley rose and casually threaded his way through the tables. He came up by the boy's shoulder as he was rummaging inside a trash bin and said softly, "Hello, son . . ."

The boy looked up, pale puffy eyelids and a pair of dark purple bags. "It's twenty quid, down the toilets."

Otley placed his hand on the boy's bony shoulder. "You just blew more than you bargained for—I'm a police officer."

"Okay, so I'll make it ten."

"Hey! Watch it!" Otley was smiling. "I just want to ask you a few questions . . ."

Warily, the boy took a step backward. His eyes flicked past Otley to where Dalton was heading toward them through the tables.

"It's about that fire," Otley said, taking out a fiver. "Heard about it? You know Colin Jenkins? Connie?"

Dalton came up and the boy took off. He barged through the tables, turning chairs over behind him, and leapt the wooden barrier surrounding the eating area, skinny elbows pumping as he hared off along the concrete embankment. Dalton was after him like a shot. Kicking the chairs aside and leaping the barrier, his long legs gained on the boy with every stride.

Otley took his time, going out through the swingbar gate and following after them at his own pace. He saw Dalton reach out and grab the boy by the nape of the neck, they both skidded and went down, the boy punching and kicking wildly. Dalton gripped him by the hair, his other hand under the boy's chin, and the boy sank his teeth into Dalton's hand. Dalton cursed and belted him hard, hauled him to his feet and belted him again.

"That's enough," Otley said, walking up. "Back off him . . ."

Dalton gave him another crack before stepping back, sucking his hand. "Little bastard bit me!"

The boy wiped his bloody nose on his arm, eyes rolling in his pinched face, frightened to death. "I dunno nuffink, I swear to God, I dunno anyfink . . ."

Joe Public strolling by and taking an interest in all of this made Otley jumpy. He moved close to the boy, keeping his voice low.

"I haven't asked you anything yet. Let's start with your name."

"Billy," the boy said, his chin quivering. "Billy Matthews."

The three new members of the squad were in Tennison's office, jackets draped over the backs of their chairs, bringing themselves up to speed on the investigation. Neither Haskons nor Lillie was too enthusiastic about the case; why they were here at all was something of a mystery.

"I dunno why we're going to all this bleedin' trouble—nasty little queen," Lillie complained. "We got an address for him, for Colin?"

"He's not got a permanent one," Haskons replied.

"He must have lived somewhere! What about a recent photograph?"

"These are from a children's home," Ray Hebdon said, spreading them out. "Few years old, black and white." He glanced down the report. "Not much else."

Haskons picked up a photograph of Connie, aged about nine, in school uniform, unsmiling. He stared at it and blew out a disgruntled sigh, his broad face with its fleshy nose and heavy jaw set in a lugubrious scowl. "Was he claiming the dole? Any benefits?"

"No, nothing from the DSS," Lillie said.

Haskons folded his arms and stared through the window at the brick wall. The phone rang and Hebdon answered it. "No, she's not. Can I take a message?" He found a pencil and a memo pad. "Jessica Smithy. What? Yes, I'll tell her."

Haskons yawned. "Any vice charges? I mean, he was on the game, wasn't he?"

"Too young to bring charges," Lillie said. "In 1988 he was picked up, shipped back." He studied the school photograph. "I don't understand, you know . . . what makes a poofter want to screw this scrawny, sickly-lookin' kid?"

"Make our job a damned sight easier if we had a recent photo," Haskon said with a long-suffering tone.

Lillie tossed over the morgue photograph of Connie's head, a knob of blackened bone, the face burnt off. "Here you go!" he said, laughing.

Tennison and Hall came down the stairs into the advice centre. The only sign of life was the black kid with the hearing aid, Ron, mopping the floor near the contacts board. Tennison had a quick gander around, peering into the empty TV lounge. Hall wandered over to the corkboard crisscrossed with tape, colored cards with job notices stuck in it.

"It's usually quiet around now," Hall said as Tennison joined him. "Kids don't drift in until early evening."

Tennison turned to Ron, mechanically mopping. "Is Mr. Parker-Jones here?" At his nod, she said, "Could you get him for me?"

Ron knocked on the office door, opened it an inch or two and looked inside. Tennison reached past him, and with the flat of her hand pushed the door open. "Is he in there?"

The desk lamp was on but the office was empty. Everything was neat and tidy, books on the shelves carefully arranged, wire trays on the desk containing invoices and letters.

"Could you see if he's anywhere in the building? I'll wait in here for him." She showed Ron her I.D. "It's important."

Ron went off, and Tennison gave a nod to Hall, who was at the contacts board, searching through them, jotting down names and phone numbers. He returned her nod and went back to the board, keeping one eye on the stairs as a couple of kids came down.

Tennison went in and pushed the door partway closed.

She went over to the two filing cabinets and tried one of the drawers. Locked. She looked around. On the wall above a thriving rubber plant was a row of impressive framed certificates, elaborately scrolled text and fancy borders. Mallory Advice Center, Maryland. Chicago University Child Therapy Unit. New York Speech and Sign Language Institute. A dozen or so letters trailed after the name "Edward Parker-Jones."

She moved around the desk. There was a stack of stamped and sealed envelopes. She flicked through them, checking the addresses. She leafed through the loose memos and the notepad, glanced at the yellow stickers on the blotter. She bent to try the desk drawers when the door was pushed open and Hall made a quick gesture.

Tennison was standing by the bookshelves when Parker-Jones breezed in. His presence immediately filled the small office. It wouldn't have surprised her to learn he was an honorary Southern colonel as well, judging by the framed credentials.

"Can I help you?" He didn't smile but his deep modulated voice was pleasant enough.

"I am Detective Chief Inspector Jane Tennison," she said, holding up her I.D. "You must be . . ."

"Edward Parker-Jones. Could I see it?" He pointed to her I.D. "Thank you," he said, handing it back. "Well? How can I help you, Chief Inspector Tennison?"

He moved around the desk, rubbing his hands, which gave Tennison the opportunity to exchange a look with Hall. He went out and closed the door, leaving Tennison alone with Parker-Jones, and giving him the chance to sniff around.

Tennison started with a smile. "I've come about the investigation into Colin Jenkins's death. Could you tell me where you were on the night of the seventeenth of this month?"

"I was here. I was here from six-thirty until at least twelve."

Tennison's eyes widened a fraction. Neat answer, very pat. "Do you have any witnesses who can—"

"Exactly how many do you require?" asked Parker-Jones, completely at ease, relaxed and confident. "I can make out a list."

"I am interested in the hour between eight-thirty and nine-thirty," Tennison said.

After a small sigh, Parker-Jones reeled them off. "Alan Thorpe, Donald Driscoll, Kenny Lloyd, one or two other lads . . ."

An identical list, the same familiar names.

"Do you know a James Jackson?"

"Yes." Parker-Jones nodded. "Strangely enough, he was here that evening."

"You have a very good memory," Tennison complimented him, turning on the charm.

Edward Parker-Jones didn't succumb that easily. "Not really. But it is my job to help the social services by keeping some kind of record of the youngsters who come and go here." He suddenly remembered, or gave a convincing performance of doing so. "Ah—oh, yes . . . Billy Matthews." He took a desk diary from the drawer and turned to the relevant date. "Billy Matthews. He was here also."

Tennison watched as he wrote out the list of names, using a gold-nibbed fountain pen. He had strong hands, dark hair sprouting from his crisp shirt cuffs to his knuckles, and wore a chunky gold ring with an amber stone on the little finger of his left hand. He was rather good-looking in a louche way, with dark deep-set eyes, his black hair swept back over his ears.

Parker-Jones passed the list to her. He sat down; there was another chair, but Tennison preferred to stay on her feet.

". . . yes, Billy Matthews, I arranged for him to see a doctor. He was found in the toilets here." Parker-Jones tightened his lips, shaking his head. "He's a tragic case. He's only fourteen, full-blown AIDS. One of the reasons I remember that evening specifically is that Jackson was in a particularly aggressive mood. He'd been trying to find a boy earlier in the day. Martin Fletcher."

"Why was he looking for him?"

"I really don't know," he said with a slight frown, and checked the diary again. "Martin wasn't here on the seventeenth but he turned up the following day. In fact . . . a Sergeant Otley spoke to him recently."

"You said Jackson had been here in the day, so what time did he return in the evening?"

Parker-Jones seemed rather amused. "Is Jackson a suspect?" he asked, one eyebrow raised. "Is that what this is all about?" He found her silence just as amusing. "It was an accidental death, surely? That building's a fire trap, all those old blocks are."

"I'm sorry, but could you . . ." Tennison cleared her throat. "Could you please answer the question? What time did James Jackson return here?"

"Around half eight, or thereabouts. He stayed for about two hours."

"Two hours!" Tennison mulled this over. She slipped her shoulder bag on. "Thank you very much, Mr. Parker-Jones. You know Reynolds's flat?" she asked, going to the door. She turned. "Just that you mentioned it was a fire hazard, so you must have been there . . . ?"

Rising to his six feet two Parker-Jones said without a flicker of hesitation, "Of course, Vera is well known by everybody around here. She—he leaves the front door key for friends to pop in. I have always had a good relationship with the Vice Squad," he said evenly. "You must be new—correct?"

Tennison smiled thinly. "Yes, and I really appreciate your help."

"Most of the kids that come here are wretched—abused, unloved, and friendless. But they do at least come here, and we can maintain contact." He moved around the desk toward her. "These children are prey for the perverted. If my centre was to be closed down it would be very sad. . . ."

"I am sure you are doing a very good and worthwhile job, Mr. Parker-Jones. But I am also trying to do mine." They faced each other in silence for a moment, and then Tennison said, "I noticed you have an impressive list of credentials."

"Thank you." He was standing close to her. She could smell his after-shave. Violets. She recognized it as Fahrenheit by Christian Dior.

"Just one more thing," Tennison said. "Do you keep a record of photographs?"

"Of the boys that come here?" At her nod, he said, "Good heavens no, be far too expensive."

"Not even casual snapshots of, say, a Christmas party? Colin, or Connie as he was called, was a frequent visitor here, wasn't he?"

"Yes, he was, but not recently. In fact I haven't seen him for about three months."

An answer to everything. What with that and his meticulous memory, this was one hell of a cool customer. Tennison pressed him further.

"You have no idea where he was living? Or if he lived with anyone?"

"I'm afraid not. He did leave messages on the notice board, and I think he received letters a few times, but not for quite a while. If you leave it with me I'll ask around and get back to you."

Tennison smiled perfunctorily and opened the door. Edward Parker-Jones put out his meaty, hairy hand to shake hers. It was left in midair as she turned and left the office.

• • •

In the car, while Hall drove, she studied the list in Parker-Jones's beautiful rounded handwriting. Of course it had to be perfect. Mr. Bleedin' Hearts Wonderful.

"He's given me virtually the same names as Jackson—we'll have to release him." She smacked her head back against the headrest. "Shit! Banged up, at least he couldn't scare anyone from talking to us. And they can't find Martin Fletcher now. . . ."

Hall said, "I've made a list of all the jobs and contacts off the centre's notice board. A lot of 'Young Male Models' required. Reads like a Toms' telephone kiosk."

Tennison perked up a bit. "That ties in with something Vera said, that Connie wanted to be a model. Good . . . good . . ."

She leaned across and gazed at him admiringly. "And may I say you are wearing a very positive tie this evening, Inspector!"

Hall's chubby face beamed and he actually blushed.

DI Dalton took the tape from his pocket and handed it to Superintendent Halliday. He then stood fidgeting as Halliday walked back around his desk. The room was warm, though Dalton was uncomfortable with more than mere heat. He didn't know why they'd picked him for this. Skulking hole-in-the-corner stuff was never his style.

"Tennison's got the murder inquiry partly because it'd be more trouble to stop her," Halliday said. He looked directly into Dalton's eyes. "But it is the murder and only the murder we want investigated."

Dalton shrugged, shuffling his feet. "There's nothing else, nothing I've heard. Jackson is still the prime suspect. . . ."

"We want Jackson charged," Halliday said, and lowering his voice for emphasis: "What we do not want is the investigation broadened. Understand?"

Dalton nodded and started to leave. Halliday said, "Better go and let the nurse have a look at that."

Dalton glanced at his hand, wrapped in a handkerchief. Vicious little bastard. He nodded again and went out.

At 5:30 P.M. Tennison fronted the update briefing in the Squad Room. The purpose of this was to acquaint all the team with the day's developments, to coordinate the various activities, and to delegate fresh lines of inquiry. As she spoke, Hall was at the board behind her, writing up the names of Parker-Jones's alibis. It didn't need pointing out to anyone that these tallied exactly with Jackson's witnesses.

Norma took notes, jotting down questions and queries from the floor as well as Tennison's spiel.

"We will stick to the weekly rota as arranged, because we now have"—Tennison gestured to the officers drafted in from AMIT—"DC Lillie, DS Haskons, and DI Hebdon, and DI Dalton handling the murder investigation."

The others were present, but no Dalton, Tennison noticed.

"That said, when we have further information for Operation Contract . . ." A moaning chorus joined in on the word "Contract."

"Cut it out, you know Superintendent Halliday is making it a . . ." Everyone joined in. *"Priority."*

With a smile, Tennison turned to Hall. "Okay, can you farm out all the contact numbers you got from the centre? Keep up the links between each investigation."

The team went back to work. Ray Hebdon pushed through. "Excuse me, Guv, there was a message from some woman Smithy, from a newspaper. I put her name and number . . ." His jaw dropped as Dalton walked in. "I don't believe it!"

A smiling Dalton came up to Hebdon and Tennison. "Hey! How are you?" His right hand still wrapped in the handkerchief, he held out his left, which Hebdon gripped. "We were at Hornchurch together," Dalton told Tennison. "My God, how long is it? You still playing for the rugby team?"

"Nah, did my knee in, tendons, had to have an op. Bit off track for you, isn't it? I thought you were with Scotland Yard."

"Yeah, I was . . . but I got transferred here."

Tennison had clocked the "Scotland Yard," and she also clocked Dalton's evasive look when he said it. He followed her as she moved to the desk.

"We've traced three, all said they were at the advice centre all evening and Jackson was there. We've not traced Alan Thorpe, but we've got a list of hangouts."

"Pass them over to Larry, he's just farming out work for tomorrow," Tennison said. "And those on tonight can have a search for Martin Fletcher. I want him back in!"

"What's this? What you doin' here?" Otley had entered and was gaping with surprise at Haskons and Lillie. He went over, grinning fit to bust, and cuffed Haskons. "He got Fairy of the Week at Southampton Row," he informed the room. "Five times on the trot!"

Haskons squared up to him, ducking and weaving. "Watch it, you old poofter." He jerked his thumb. "Ray Hebdon—Bill Otley, the Skipper!"

The two men nodded. Otley turned his head to watch Tennison leaving the room. He pinched his nose, giving them all a look. As the door swung to, he said, "Jackson was released 'bout fifteen minutes ago . . . does she know?"

Hall called them to attention.

"Okay, we're trying to find anyone with a recent photo of Colin Jenkins, any known contacts, and where he's been living. Clubs, coffee bars, known hangouts for the rent boys. Who's taking what?"

From the door, Otley yelled, "As from today we will be awarding the Fairy of the Week award!"

Kathy yelled back, "Yeah—and we'll award the Prick of the Week. Apparently you're not eligible, as you've been one ever since you arrived."

Lots of raspberries, honks, and hooting laughter.

Otley gave a universal V-sign and disappeared.

Twenty minutes later, having written up his report, Otley took it along to Tennison's office where she was looking over a large-scale street map pinned to the wall. He dropped the report on her desk.

"The advice centre and Vera's flat." Tennison pointed to each, ringed in red, where she'd just marked them.

"I timed it," Otley said, perching on the edge of the desk. "You could make it there and back in ten minutes."

The door was open, and Dalton came in, a bandage on his hand. He stood listening, his tanned face impassive.

"So Jackson could easily have done it." Tennison glanced over her shoulder at Otley. "But five alibis say he didn't."

"I reckon we could break down those kids' statements if we had Jackson behind bars. They'd all say he was visiting the Queen Mother if he told them to. He's got to them, it's obvious."

"It's obvious with Martin Fletcher. I want him brought back in." She went around the desk, biting the end of the felt-tip pen. "Parker-Jones . . . he's Jackson's strongest alibi. Dig around a bit, but on the QT. . . ." She gave him a look.

"He's squeaky clean," Otley told her. "I think your predecessor had a nose around but came up with nothin'."

"Oh, he did, did he?" Tennison was frowning and shaking her head. "Could be just a personal reaction—and there was something about his voice." She rooted underneath some files, then opened a drawer and searched inside. "Shit! Where the hell is the tape?" She looked at Otley. "Did you take a tape from here?"

"No. Is it in the machine?" Otley reached over and pressed the Eject button. Empty. He was conscious that Tennison was staring hard at him, plainly disbelieving.

She straightened up, sighing, and glanced at her watch. "Don't waste time looking for it now. We'll call it quits for tonight, get an early start in the morning."

Dalton gave a nod to them both and went out, closing the door. Otley still waited, watching Tennison opening, searching, and banging shut every drawer in her desk. Finally she stood up.

"You didn't take it, did you, Bill?"

"What? The tape?" He shook his head. "No, why would I do that?"

Tennison suddenly looked weary. She slumped back in the chair, rubbing her forehead. "Getting paranoid. It'll be here somewhere."

There was a reason for Otley's lingering presence. Out it came, a touch of asperity in his tone.

"Guv, can you get Dalton off my back? I can't work with him. I could have got a lot more out of those kids—one bit him this afternoon. I nearly did myself," Otley said darkly.

He was a bastard, Otley, and a chauvinist pig to boot, but she trusted his instincts, because they so often chimed with her own.

"What do you make of him?" she asked.

"Not a lot. Don't know why he's on board, do you?"

Tennison shook her head. With a grunted "G'night," Otley left her alone. She got up, arching her back, and stood with hands on hips looking over her desk. She lifted the reports and files and checked everywhere. She peered down the side of the desk and underneath her chair.

She sat down again, and looked at her watch. Yawning, she picked up the phone and dialed. As she waited she drew Otley's report toward her and started reading.

"Hello . . . Dr. Gordon's receptionist, please." She waited, reading. "It's Jane Tennison. I'm sorry, but I'm running a bit late. I've got an appointment at six-thirty." She listened, nodding. "Great, see you then."

She dropped the phone down and moved slowly around the desk, the report in her hand, still reading. She stopped dead and stared. She read it again, the bit that had frozen her to the spot.

"Oh, shit . . . !"

Moving fast, she went into the corridor. To the left, outside the Squad Room doors, Commander Chiswick was having a quiet word with Dalton, whose back was toward her, and as Tennison strode quickly up, Chiswick lightly tapped Dalton on the arm, shutting him up.

"Evening, sir," Tennison greeted the Commander. She turned to Dalton and indicated her office. "Before you go . . ."

When Dalton came in, a moment or two later, she was leaning against the desk. He'd barely crossed the threshold before Tennison said, "Has anyone looked at that hand?"

"It's nothing," Dalton said, bending his wrist to show her. "I put a bandage over it."

"I'm sorry, there's no easy way to tell you this." Tennison reached behind her for Otley's report and held it up. "Billy Matthews has full-blown AIDS. I think you should get to a hospital."

Dalton frowned at her, blinking rapidly. "The bloody little bastard," he burst out hoarsely. "I had to have a shower when we got back. I'll go and see the nurse." He hadn't quite grasped it, Tennison could see. "The little shit!"

"I'm sorry . . ."

Dalton went very quiet, staring at his hand. Only now was he realizing the full implications, his tan fading as the blood drained from his face. He looked scared now, dead scared.

"He bit me, he broke the skin, he . . . bit me." He swallowed and looked at Tennison, his voice quavering. "Jesus Christ. I was bleeding . . ."

"Go to the hospital, you'll need a tetanus injection for starters."

Dalton didn't move. He simply stared at her, mouth hanging open, looking about ten years old.

"Would you like someone to go with you? Do you want me to take you?"

"No, no, it's okay . . ." He turned away, holding the wrist of his injured hand. "I've got my own car . . . er . . . thank you."

He went out and turned right, heading for the stairs.

Tennison emerged from behind the screen, buttoning up her blouse. She took her suit jacket from the back of the chair and shrugged into it. Seated at the leather-topped desk in his white coat, Dr. Gordon was making an entry in her medical file, having already prepared the sample stickers for the lab tests. The glass slides in their plastic containers were by his elbow.

"Can I ask—if somebody has full-blown AIDS and bites somebody else, actually draws blood, how dangerous is it?"

Dr. Gordon was the same age as Tennison, if not younger, though this had never bothered her. He had a friendly, amiable disposition, which was more important. He looked at her over his silver-framed glasses.

"Very. It's not the fact that the AIDS carrier has drawn blood, but if his blood then makes contact with the open wound . . . human bite is extremely dangerous, contains more bacteria than a dog bite. Full-blown AIDS?" He put his pen down, laced his fingers when he saw how intently she was listening to him.

"Often their gums bleed, it's really dependent on how far advanced the AIDS carrier is, but bleeding gums, mouth sores . . ."

"How soon can it be diagnosed?"

He tilted his head slightly. "It's not you, is it?"

"No, it's not me." Tennison sat down, smoothing her blouse inside the shoulders of her jacket. "I'm fine. Well—a bit ratty, but I put that down to my periods being a bit erratic."

"Well, it could be the onset of the menopause. We'll get these samples over to the lab, but until I get the results I won't prescribe anything." Dr. Gordon leaned forward, regarding her soberly. "Your friend should be tested for antibodies immediately, but that will only prove he or she doesn't have it already. I'm afraid it'll take three to six months to zero convert and they should have HIV tests every four to six weeks for the next six months."

"So it'll be six months before he knows?"

"Afraid so. That's how long it will take to show a positive infection." He held up a cautioning finger. "However, full-blown AIDS can take anywhere up to eight to ten years to develop."

"Thank you very much," Tennison said, getting up. "Do you have any leaflets I could take?"

While he found her some she thoughtfully put on her raincoat and collected her briefcase. She turned to him.

"You mind if I say something? 'Onset of menopause' may not mean much to you, but it does to a woman. It means a lot."

Dr. Gordon paused, watching her, waiting.

Briefcase clasped in her hands, Tennison was studying her shoes. "I'm not married, maybe never will be, so it doesn't make all that much difference to me—but I am only forty-four, and . . ." She shook her head rapidly, shoulders slumping. "Oh, forget it!"

"Be a couple of days," Dr. Gordon said kindly, handing her the leaflets. "I'll call you."

"Thank you," Tennison said, stuffing them in her pocket. "And thank you for fitting me in. I'm sorry I was late."

As she got to the door her bleeper sounded. She fished it out and pressed a button. "Can I use your phone?"

7

In the softening gloom of early dusk the unkempt graves and slanting headstones of St. Margaret's Crypt flashed red and yellow in the lights of the patrol car and ambulance parked outside the rusting iron gates. Two uniformed officers were cordoning off the area inside the churchyard with yellow marking ribbons: POLICE LINE—DO NOT CROSS. Arc lamps had been set up. The sudden harsh glare as they were switched on transformed the crypt into a ghastly gothic world of drunken shadows and crumbling statues, broken glass glittering in the long grass.

A motley collection of human detritus watched with befuddled curiosity. Some were crouched on the low broken-down wall, others slumped on the pavement, wrapped in blankets with layers of newspaper inside. Empty wine and cider bottles filled the gutters. Situated between the Bullring and the underpass of Waterloo Bridge, the derelict churchyard was home to a nighttime population of summer residents; the winter months were far too cold for sleeping on gravestones, even topped up with Thunderbird wine and two liters of Woodpecker.

Otley was talking to the police photographer when he saw Tennison's Sierra nosing along the narrow cobbled street. She stopped some distance away, leaving room for the ambulance, and wound her window down. Otley went across and leaned in.

"Body was discovered about an hour ago. There's a doctor checking him over now."

Tennison followed him, stepping over the heaps of rubbish and broken bottles. As they approached the gates a hand reached out, grabbing at her coat, and a slurred voice said, "Givvus a quid fer a cup o' tea. . . ."

Tennison stopped one of the policemen. "For chrissakes, clear them out of here!" she snapped. "Get rid of them!"

Lifting the yellow tape for her to bend under, Otley gave a half smile. "Can't get rid of them, Guv. Each tombstone's an allocated lodging." He pointed. "He's over there, by the angel. Some bloody guardian!"

He remained at the tape, watching Tennison moving through the headstones toward a huge white praying angel with a shattered wing, marble eyes raised sightlessly to heaven. Then, with his sardonic grin, Otley went out through the gates and along the street in the direction of Waterloo Bridge.

The doctor had been kneeling on a plastic sheet while he carried out his examination. He stood up, clicked his small black leather bag shut, and moved aside. Tennison peered down. In death, Martin Fletcher looked even pathetically younger and frailer than he had in life—short, brutish and nasty as that had been.

He lay on his back on the pitted tombstone, one leg bent under the other, his arms open wide. His head was tilted to one side, puffy eyelids closed in his chalk-white face, a string of saliva and vomit hanging from his half-open mouth. By his outstretched hand were two cans of lighter fluid and a two-liter plastic bottle of Woodpecker cider, empty.

I never told nobody nuffink and that is the Gawd's truth . . .

Tennison had seen all she wanted to. She turned away, thinking that Martin Fletcher must have told somebody something, or he wouldn't have ended up a cold lump of meat on a stone slab, fourteen years of life washed down the drain.

Otley stood at the chest-high wooden counter of the sandwich trailer not a stone's throw from the iron trelliswork of Waterloo Bridge. It was dark now, the patch of waste ground near the trailer dimly illuminated by a sulky fire in an oil drum. A dozen or so kids sat around it, one of them holding a thin shivering mongrel on a piece of string. Cans of beer were being passed around. Somebody had his nose inside a brown paper bag, breathing heavily, then coughing and spluttering as he passed it on.

"You want ketchup? Mustard? Onions . . . ?"

The stallholder held Otley's hamburger in his palm. He pushed a large white mug toward Otley's elbow. "Sugar in the tea? Milk? Top or not?"

"No top, mate," Otley said, reaching into his pocket for change. "An' I'll have the rest, but easy on the ketchup, heavy on the mustard." He plonked a pound coin and fifty-pence piece down and turned to the boy beside him. Alan Thorpe was a fresh-faced kid with jug ears and straight blond hair hacked off in ragged bangs. Otley guessed he was about thirteen.

"Who else was there that night then?"

Together they strolled, Otley munching his hamburger and sipping his mug of tea, toward the group around the fire. On the far side of the trailer, in the vast shadow cast by the bridge, Tennison slowly drew up. She wound her window down. From this distance she couldn't hear, but she could see everything that was going on. Otley saying something that made the blond kid laugh, and Otley laughing too. Otley bending down to feed the dog some hamburger. Otley talking to the blond kid, paying close attention to what he said. And then Otley glancing up and seeing her car, the word "Shit" as discernible on his lips as if she'd heard him mutter it.

He came across, chewing the last of the hamburger, wiping his fingers on his hankerchief. He gestured.

"Come midnight they're around this place like flies. Does a hell of a trade."

"The boy that bit Dalton, Billy. Turns out he's got AIDS."

Otley stared. "Jesus Christ. How's Dalton?"

"We don't know yet," Tennison said bleakly. "It's tough."

"Yeah, it's tough for Billy too," Otley said, and she was surprised by the bitterness in his voice. He leaned on the open window and nodded toward the group. "That was Jackson's third witness, blond boy with the dog, Alan Thorpe." He belched and covered his mouth with the back of his hand. "Says he was too pissed to remember who was at the centre the night Connie died, so that's one alibi that's no good."

"You want a ride home?" Tennison asked him.

Otley hesitated, half shook his head, then changed his mind. As they drove off, the midnight blue Merc with the rusty patches that had been parked under the bridge with its lights off ghosted forward. Jackson slid out from behind the wheel. He stood running his thumb over the rings on his hand, wearing a long, beat-up leather coat that nearly reached his ankles. Pursing his fleshy lips, he gave a low whistle. The kids around the fire turned to look. Jackson whistled again. The dog was released and trotted over to him, trailing its bit of string.

Jackson knelt down, rubbing the dog's head. He looked up, smiling.

"Alan, come here a sec."

When nobody moved, Jackson stood up.

"ALAN!" The smile wiped from his face, he pointed. "You! Come here. Don't mess with me, get over here."

The group of kids shrank away as Alan Thorpe stood up and shuffled across the loose gravel. He was shuffling too slowly, and Jackson made an angry beckoning gesture.

"What was all that about?" Jackson asked softly as Alan came up. And reaching out, Alan shying away a little, Jackson ruffled the boy's hair.

"He wanted to know about Connie," Alan said, barely audible.

Jackson opened the passenger door. "Get in, Alan. We're goin' for a little ride."

"Okay." Alan moved forward. "What about me mates, can they come too . . ."

Jackson grabbed him by the back of the neck and flung him inside. He smiled. "Just you an' me, Alan."

Alan suddenly grinned back, eyes impish in his soft childish face. "Got a punter for me, 'ave yer?"

Jackson slammed the door.

Tennison turned off Holloway Road into the little street of neat terraced houses, each with its own few square feet of scrubby garden. Otley lived three doors from the bottom end, where the viaduct of the London to Birmingham mainline blocked off the street.

She didn't expect him to invite her in for a coffee, and he didn't. She wouldn't have accepted anyway. They were reluctant colleagues, not bosom friends. He was strangely on edge. He opened the door but stayed in the car, one leg out. He looked back at her. In the streetlight his eyes were black pits, unfathomable, perhaps unknowable. She didn't know him.

"Your real bastards are the ones that use them," Otley said. "Can't get to them though, can you?" Grinning at her, teeth clenched. "Especially if they got friends in high places. Dig deep enough an' you come up against concrete . . . know what I mean . . ."

He was out fast then, slamming the door, through the squeaking gate, up the little path, not looking back. As if he'd said more than he should, shown too much of how he really felt.

Tennison drove home, too tired to bother to understand what he had been getting at. A large Bushmills and bed, that was all she wanted. Another day over, thank God.

At 9 A.M. it started all over again. The Squad Room was a cacophony of ringing phones, shouted questions, some foul language, and twenty conversations going on all at once. Updates from the night-duty staff were being passed around. Halliday was at the big notice board with Norma, who was taking him through the various lines of inquiry that were under way. Tennison had one ear to everything that was happening while she listened to Kathy. She felt to be in better shape today, her attention keener, adrenaline buzzing with the noise and activity. Down one day, on a high the next, it was puzzling.

"I've been checking out the cards from the advice centre. One of the so-called photographers was busted a few years ago, so he was quite helpful." Tennison nodded to show she was listening. Kathy went on, "He's mostly porn and girly pics, but he put me onto a Mark Lewis . . ." She passed over a note of the address. "He specializes in male 'beauty' style pictures. I called his number but got short shrift. I think it'd be better for one of the men to have a go. If Connie was trying to be a model he could have used him."

"Thanks, Kathy." Tennison gave her a smile and a brisk nod. Halliday was now talking to Ray Hebdon, so Norma was free. "Any messages?" Tennison called to her.

Hall had gathered some of them together for a pep talk. "I just want a quick word, okay? Can you keep dealing with as much of that backlog as possible, and those in court today—Please Give Times! Availability!" Lurking smiles as he adjusted the knot in his immaculate tie, lemon and gray diagonal stripes with embroidered fleur-de-lis.

"Right, I want to give you all a serious warning. I know it's been said before, but I'm saying it again—and I'll keep on saying it. Some of these youngsters have full-blown AIDS. They know it! You know it—keep it in your minds. Please, I know you are all aware of the risks, but heed the warnings and the instructions you've all had concerning any form of confrontation. Biting is just as dangerous as one of them stabbing you with a hypodermic needle. . . ."

Tennison was at the board, Norma at her elbow reading out the messages. The names of Jackson's witnesses were ringed and ticked, a line in red through Martin Fletcher's name. Billy Matthews had a tick and two question marks.

"Oh, and Jessica from the newspaper, she's the most persistent woman I have ever known!" Norma said, concluding her summary. "She says if you don't have the time to return her calls, she will come in and see you at a convenient time." The stocky girl shook her head, exasperated. "But she refuses to tell me what she wants."

Farther along, Haskons and Lillie were taking notes from the update bulletin board. Tennison said, "Next time she rings, tell her that unless she tells you what is so important . . ." She frowned up at the board. "The Jackson alibis . . . Alan Thorpe was drunk, why the query on Billy Matthews?"

"He doesn't remember where he was that night. We need to question him again—he might remember!" The inference being that if Norma could have ten minutes alone with him, he damn well would.

Tennison returned to her desk. Otley breezed in and came straight up. He seemed to regard the morning briefing as optional, she thought crossly. Went his own sweet way. But as usual he hadn't been idle.

"Martin Fletcher virtually drowned in his own vomit. His blood alcohol was so high, it could have been bottled! Plus other substances." He gripped the edge of the desk in both hands, leaning at an angle. His polyester tie, the knot askew, hung down limp and wrinkled. His suit looked as if it had been slept in. "He'd been sniffing from a gas lighter canister. They said if you'd put a match to him he'd have combusted!"

Superintendent Halliday was standing at the doors, gesturing. Tennison craned her head around Otley to see that she was being summoned. She gave Otley a look, and with a sigh followed Halliday out. Now what?

"So, where are the cream?" Otley drawled, punching Hall on the shoulder. He raised his voice. "That scruff Haskons and Co.?"

Haskons nudged Lillie, and the pair of them turned from the board with wide grins.

Hall said, "Their team's checking into a mini-cab firm that's a cover for a hire-a-cab and a Tom-thrown-in. New place just opened, Kings Cross."

"Inventive," Otley remarked with a sly wink. "But who drives?"

"You released Jackson? That means his alibis pan out?"

"We're still checking, still trying to retrace all the boys, take them through their statements again," Tennison told him. All this was up on the board, so why the grilling? There was a hidden agenda here, though she was blowed if she could even hazard a guess.

Tennison spread her hands. "I didn't have enough to hold Jackson. Pity, because I think the kids are scared of him, covering up for him."

Halliday leaned back in his chair. "So Jackson is still the prime suspect?" Tennison nodded. "And Parker-Jones? You went to see him?"

Again, that note of criticism, censure even, in his voice. It nettled her. "Yes, is there any reason I shouldn't have gone to interview him?"

"No," Halliday said curtly. "Was the interview satisfactory?"

"He was very cooperative—"

She was interrupted. "Do you think it will be necessary to see him again?"

Tennison put her head forward, frowning. "I don't understand—are you telling me not to interview my main suspect's alibi again?"

"I saw the case board, you've *three* boys that gave Jackson an alibi." He added flatly, "So stay off Parker-Jones."

Tennison straightened her spine, getting riled up now. "Am I in charge of this investigation or not?"

"No. I am. So now I am telling you, back off him and stay off him. You are diverting and wasting time. If Jackson is your man, then get him. Concentrate on Jackson and wrap this case up."

She knew better than to argue. He was laying down the law, and he had the clout to back it up. This wasn't the moment to have a flaming row. Besides, she had a hidden agenda of her own.

• • •

From the reception area Tennison could see over the low partition to where Margaret Speel was talking to a woman with dyed blond hair and a sallow complexion, in her late twenties. The probation office was a dismal, depressing place. The carpet was worn thin and the furniture was scratched and shabby. An attempt had been made to brighten things up with posters, and one corner had been turned into a children's playpen, a few cheap plastic toys scattered around, a little slide decorated with Mickey Mouse stickers. Somehow all this made everything seem even more pathetic. It reminded Tennison of an older woman trying to camouflage the ravages of time with daubs of garish makeup and youthful clothes.

The receptionist was on the phone. She had been on the phone ever since Tennison arrived, nearly ten minutes earlier. Tennison looked at her watch and tried to attract Margaret Speel's attention.

"Did you look for the signs?" The probation officer's voice carried over the partition, mingled in with conversations from other parts of the room. "I told you what to expect—if his speech is slurred, eyes red-rimmed. Has he got a persistent cough? Yes? Did you smell it on his breath . . . ?" She glanced up, raising her hand. "Just a minute, Mrs. Line."

She came around with her brisk walk, dark and petite, attractive in a pert, almost elfish way. Large thin gold loops dangled from her small white ears. "Is it Martin Fletcher again?" She gestured to some seats with hideous green plastic coverings.

"No, he's dead," Tennison said, sitting down. "He was found last night, drug abuse."

Margaret Speel sank down beside her. "Oh, no . . ."

Tennison got the impression that the probation officer wasn't all that surprised. She waited a moment, then got straight on with it.

"Do you know a Billy Matthews?" Margaret Speel nodded. "Is there any way you can get him off the streets?"

"What do you mean, 'get him off the streets'?" Margaret Speel said, testily repeating the phrase.

"He has full-blown AIDS."

Margaret Speel looked plaintively to the ceiling and back at Tennison, twitching her mouth. "And just where do you suggest I put him?" She swept her hand out, as if Billy Matthews might possibly doss down on the threadbare carpet. "Oh, really! You know of one boy with fullblown AIDS, and you want him off the streets. Well—where do I put him? With the rest? Do you know where they all are? How many there are?"

Tennison shook her head, smarting at her own blithe assumption, her own crass ignorance. The probation service had to deal with dozens, scores, perhaps hundreds. She only touched the tip of the iceberg. She got up and started to leave.

"I suggest you contact Edward Parker-Jones, he runs the advice centre." Margaret Speel was trying to be helpful, but her voice remained brusque. These people waltzed in, knowing nothing, and expected miracles. She was sick to death of it. "If Billy's there, then I can try and do something for him."

Tennison nodded slowly. "What do you think of Edward Parker-Jones?"

She wasn't expecting such a simple question to produce such a reaction. Margaret Speel's eyes blazed fiercely.

"He should be given a medal! It costs one thousand five hundred a week to keep really young offenders in an institution, and more staff than—"

"Did you ever come into contact with a Colin Jenkins—Connie?"

"No." Her mouth snapped shut.

"Do you know a James Jackson?"

"I know of him but I have never had any professional dealings with him."

Pick the bones out of that.

Tennison thanked her politely, but Margaret Speel was already striding off, and the Detective Chief Inspector imagined she could see steam coming out of her ears.

Mark Lewis's studio was off the Whitechapel Road, down a maze of streets behind the sooty redbrick Victorian edifice of the London Hospital. It was on the first floor above a Chinese take-away, and something of the exotic oriental influence had seeped upstairs to the photographer's studio, which also housed his office and darkroom.

Lewis minced rather than walked. An ex-dancer, he moved lithely and fast as lightning around the black-draped studio. Haskons and Lillie got dizzy just watching him zoom about the place—setting up his camera, arranging the lights just so, explaining to his model—a young black guy with an oiled gleaming torso, posing on a white pedestal—precisely what he was after with expressively floating gestures and a snapping of the fingers. But he was a professional, and good at his work, with a real feeling for it. There was also a steely quality to him, a certain watchfulness in his brown eyes, a thinning of the soft mouth, as if hinting that what you see is not all you get.

He said he could give them ten minutes. He took them along a narrow passage into his office, the darkroom in one corner behind a plywood partition. It was a large room with a skylight, two of the walls covered in silk hangings with oriental motifs. There were paper Chinese lanterns, glass wind chimes floating in the still air, and brass gongs of different sizes. And under a miniature spotlight, a display of Buddhas, fiery dragons, and mythical Eastern gods.

Next to the darkroom were several large cupboards, a row of filing cabinets, and a desk with a leather, gold-embossed appointments diary.

It all seemed legit. To Lillie, Mark Lewis was exactly as he appeared to be—a poofter photographer with curled hair that was remarkably dark and lustrous, given his age, on the downward slope of forty.

"Red curly hair, about five seven, slim build. His nickname was Connie, real name Jenkins," Haskons said.

He and Lillie were sitting on the couch. Mark Lewis had too much nervous energy to stay in one spot for long. He was continually on the move, a figure of medium height dressed in a black shirt, open at the neck, and tight-fitting black trousers, black socks, black moccasins.

Haskons produced a photograph. "This was taken when he was about nine. We're just trying to trace people that knew him, may have known where he lived."

"No need firing names at me. I don't remember names—faces yes, I never forget a face. Now I am very busy, but if you can give an idea of the time he came to me, then you can look at all the portfolios—"

He leaned over from the waist to squint at the photograph. "No. Don't know him."

"Some time last year maybe?" Lillie ventured hopefully.

Lewis went to the office alcove and returned, thudding down three huge albums onto the mosaic coffee table. Spinning around, he was off to the filing cabinets, plucking out brown folders bulging with glossy prints.

"Don't you keep a record of clients?" Haskons asked. "Dates of the sessions?"

"Some don't like to use their real name. I am strictly cash up front and cash on delivery—and I pay VAT and taxes," Lewis said, giving them a direct look. "I run this as a legitimate business."

He dropped the folders on the coffee table, and was spinning off somewhere else. They couldn't keep track of him.

Haskons exchanged glances with Lillie. As detective sergeant, Richard Haskons was the senior of the two, but they had operated together as a team for so long that the question of rank never interfered in their working relationship. They both turned to watch Lewis.

". . . I just take the photographs. If it's for publication, then I charge so and so. If it's for a private collector, then it's between myself and the client." He swished aside a black curtain masking off the darkroom. "I print up all the negs, I do everything myself. I am, my dears, a one-man show. I had an assistant once," he confided, "but—Trouble, with a big T." He smiled briefly. "I'll be in the darkroom." He went inside and drew the curtain.

The two detectives took an album each, turning the pages.

At full throttle, Shirley Bassey suddenly shattered the peace and quiet, belting out, "The minute you walked in the joint, I could see you were a man of distinction . . ."

DC Lillie nearly fell off the couch. Haskons was singing along at the top of his voice—

"Hey, Big Spender . . . spend a little time with me."

After the far-from-veiled warning from Halliday, Tennison was on her mettle. It was the cock-handed way he had gone about it that riled her. Telling her to lay off Parker-Jones was as good as waving a red flag at a bull. The man had as much sublety as a sledgehammer.

She called DI Hall into her office. She didn't know whether Hall was Halliday's man or not, but she intended to find out.

"If it wasn't Jackson—if I've been going in the wrong direction—then I need another suspect, another motive. And it was just something you said that I'm a bit confused about . . ."

Arms folded, Tennison leaned against the desk, studying her shoes. Speaking slowly, as if thinking out loud, she went on, "If I remember correctly, you said the advice centre had been targeted before I came on board . . . did that include Parker-Jones himself?"

"Not the man. It was more his boys. It's where they all congregate, one of the first places for the really young kids."

Tennison's "Mmmm," was noncommittal. "And was it sort of inferred you all stay clear of him?"

Hall fiddled with the knot in his tie. He wasn't very comfortable, kept adjusting his position in the chair.

Tennison looked at him. "Larry, if I have to initiate a full-scale swoop—that's kids, Toms, pimps, punters—close down clubs, coffee bars, centres—and I am under pressure to get it under way, and . . ." She bent down to his eye level. ". . . Parker-Jones's name keeps on cropping up."

"Yeah, but—" Hall's poor tie was getting some stick today. At this rate it would end up as bad as Otley's. "But we never found anything . . . look, I know this is off the record, okay? The Chief Inspector before you was warned off. Parker-Jones is a very influential man, got friends in high places, and we sort of backed off him."

Tennison pointed to the wall. "And this came from the Guv'nor?"

Hall nodded, chewing his lip.

"Okay, okay . . . and then Operation Contract got the green light for the big cleanup."

"Well, you know what happened—we knew it—waste of time." Hall was stumbling over his words. "Chief Inspector Lyall was out, I think he's in Manchester now. I honestly don't think there's anything subversive going on, but . . ."

"But? There was a leak?" When he didn't answer, Tennison got up and paced the office. "Come on, I've checked the charge sheets, nothing subversive? Somebody must have tipped off the punters, never mind the clubs!"

"Off the record, I think we got close to someone with heavy-duty contacts," Hall admitted, looking at her properly for the first time.

Tennison stopped pacing. "You got a suspicion?" She brushed a hand through her hair, a faint smile on her lips. "No? Not even a possible?"

"If I had I'd tell you, honestly." His babyish round features put her in mind of an eager-to-please Boy Scout. He wasn't Halliday's man, she was convinced: too transparent. She believed him.

"What about you?" he asked her.

Tennison laughed. "If I had, Larry, I wouldn't be trying to wheedle it out of you. Okay, you can go, and thanks."

The Squad Room was unusually quiet. Some of the team had gone to the canteen for an early lunch, others were out chasing down leads. An impatient Otley was standing behind Norma, leaning over her as she spoke into the phone.

"Good morning, can I speak to Chief Inspector David Lyall? It's personal, could you say a Sergeant Bill Otley, Vice Squad, Soho . . . yes, I'll hold, thank you."

Two desks along, Kathy was just finishing another call. "Okay, yes, I've got that. I'll pass it on." She put the phone down and called out, "Sarge?"

Otley went over.

"Sarge!" Norma yelled. "I've got him coming on the line now . . ."

Otley scuttled back and grabbed the phone off her. "Go and help Kathy." He turned his back on her and cupped his hand over the mouthpiece. "Dave? Listen, mate, I need a favor. Remember when you were here you thought you got something on a bloke—"

"Sarge." Norma was back. "Kath's just got a call, tip-off from one of the street photographers. He reckons the guy we may be looking for is a Mark Lewis. Where's your lads, Sarge?"

"Just one second, Dave . . ." Otley turned furiously, jabbing his finger. "Bloody check the board—go on!" He cupped the phone, opened his mouth to speak, but didn't. He looked up again. "Mark Lewis? Hang on a second, I think our boys are there now. Check it out."

Leaving him to his call, Norma went over to the board. Kathy joined her. "Who's he talking to?"

Norma tapped her nose. "Chief Inspector here before Tennison . . ."

Kathy scanned the board, then pointed. "Mark Lewis. They're seeing him this morning." Her finger moved along, and she was suddenly excited. "Guv! This Mark Lewis, the photographer we got a tip-off about—he's on the list from the advice centre."

Otley covered the phone and whipped around.

"Well, bloody contact them!" He muttered into the phone, "Dave, sorry about this . . . okay, yeah, can you fax me what you sniffed out?" He looked up wearily. "Hang on."

Hall was standing there, arms folded, looking peeved.

Otley held the receiver against his chest. "Well, what was your little private conflab about?"

"Cut it out, Sarge, that's my phone," Hall said, holding out his hand. "Is it for me?"

"No, it's personal." Otley jerked his head. "Just check over Kath, she's had a tip-off." Hall sniffed loudly and went around the desk to the board. Otley crouched. "Dave? As a favor, mate. We're sniffin' around Parker-Jones again, yeah . . ."

8

"There is nothing like a dame . . . Nothing in the world. There is nothing you can name that is anything like a dame!"

Shirley Bassey had been replaced by the soundtrack of *South Pacific*, and Haskons sang lustily along. He and Lillie were working their way through the albums. There were hundreds of photographs, mostly black and white, all of them featuring gorgeous young men and svelte pretty boys in various states of undress. The shots of couples were suggestive certainly, but not strictly pornographic.

"Some great-lookin' fellas, they must all work out like crazy," Lillie said. "Here, look at this one."

"Yeah, yeah . . . ." Leafing through the album, Haskons couldn't be bothered; he'd seen enough naked male flesh to last him a lifetime. Even the show tunes were beginning to bore him. "I've had worse taken on me holidays."

"What, kissin' blokes?" Lillie sniggered.

"Piss off! I mean in swimmin' trunks." Haskons flipped over a page, scowling. "This is a waste of time. I got some that go back to the seventies. I dunno what we're doing here, why we're here . . ." He threw out his hands. "If he did a bit of modelin', so what? What we lookin' for?"

His bleeper sounded. He reached inside his jacket to kill it, and looked around the room.

"You see a phone?"

"Mr. Lewis? Can I use your phone!"

Mark Lewis cocked his head. He half-turned from the processing bench. In his left hand he held a thick bundle of ten-by-eight glossy prints, color and black and white. With his right hand he was feeding them, one by one, into a bath of acid. They fizzed and buckled, turned brown and sank to the bottom in a gray-brown slimy sludge.

He leaned toward the black curtain.

"Be my guest! I can't come out, I'm working on some negs. Phone's on the shelf in the passage."

He stayed there until he heard Haskons move away, then quickly turned back to the bench and carried on methodically feeding the prints into the acid bath.

When Haskons returned he found Lillie examining the lock on one of the large cupboards. Haskons called out, "Thanks, Mr. Lewis!" and said in Lillie's ear, "That was Kathy. Tip-off. If there was anyone doing the real heavy stuff, then this is our man. . . ."

Lillie had taken out a bunch of keys. He selected one and slid it into the lock. It clicked open.

"Hey, watch it!" Haskons whispered. "We've no search warrant."

From top to bottom the cupboard was filled with videotapes. Lillie pulled one out and looked at the label.

"He's messing us about. Never said anythin' about this lot." He showed Haskons the label. "'Adam and Adam.' That's original."

Haskons went over to the darkroom.

"Mr. Lewis, we need to talk to you a minute."

He pushed the curtain aside and peered in. Mark Lewis's startled face craned around over his shoulder. He shifted across, attempting to shield what he was doing. Haskons went in and shoved him out of the way. He saw the photograph Lewis had just dropped into the bath and reached for it.

"No! Don't!" Lewis anxiously paddled the air like an hysterical schoolgirl. "It's acid, it'll burn your hand off!"

Lillie appeared, in time to see Haskons lifting the print out of the bath with a steel ruler. Crinkling and turning brown, the image was still discernible. A naked, beautiful boy with curly red hair.

They lay on Tennison's desk, a dozen or more of the large color photographs of Connie in various artistic poses that Mark Lewis hadn't had a chance to dispose of. Otley picked one out at random. It happened to be of Connie bending over, firm round buttocks presented to the camera like two peaches.

Tennison leaned against the windowsill, pushing her cuticles back with the clip of her fountain pen. She said thoughtfully, "Parker-Jones is regarded as the Mother Teresa of Soho . . . and he's Jackson's alibi." She scratched her nose with the fountain pen clip. "There's something that doesn't quite sit right. If Jackson was looking for Connie because he owed him money, why—if we presume he found Connie—why didn't he take it?"

Otley shook his head and tossed the photograph down. There was a tap at the door and Haskons looked in. "Mark Lewis is in interview room D oh two. We're getting a video room set up, view Connie's tapes."

Tennison nodded to indicate she'd be right along. She followed Otley to the door. The phone rang. "You go ahead," she told him, and reached for the phone. "Chief Inspector Tennison's office."

It was Dr. Gordon's receptionist. Tennison listened, frowning. "Is this bad news? Is it the tests?"

She moved around the desk to sit down. She closed her eyes, listening. "Yes, yes . . . I'll come in. Thank you."

She put the phone down and sat silently for a moment, rubbing the back of her hand. Snapping awake, she opened the top drawer and took out her diary. Underneath it was the cassette tape she'd hunted high and low for. She took it out and turned it over.

Kathy came in. "You wanted DCI Lyall's contact number. He's in Manchester." She put the paper down. "I think the Sarge . . ." She paused. Tennison was thumbing through the pages of the diary, chewing her lip. "You okay?"

Tennison banged the diary shut. "Kathy, you didn't put this tape in my drawer, did you? It's the ambulance call-out tape."

"No." Kathy turned to go.

"You don't have a cigarette, do you?" Tennison said.

"No, I'm sorry, I don't smoke," Kathy said, leaving.

The diary and the tape lay side by side on the desk. Tennison stared at them, pulling distractedly at the neckline of her blouse. She tossed the diary back into the drawer and slammed it shut.

DS Richard Haskons and DI Ray Hebdon were in Taped Interview Room D.02 with Mark Lewis. As the arresting officer, Haskons was having first crack. Hebdon stood watching, arms folded, his tie pulled loosely away from his collar. The atmosphere was close in the small room, and he imagined he could smell Mark Lewis sweating. Or maybe it wasn't his imagination; the photographer was highly agitated, twisting a handkerchief in his heavily veined hands, the nails neatly manicured and coated in clear varnish.

"Go on," Haskons prompted.

"I last saw him about four, perhaps five days before the fire. He wanted some photographs—not the explicit ones, just some head and shoulders . . ."

"And?"

"He never showed up." Lewis looked his age now, deep lines etched into his forehead, the skin rough and open-pored on his sagging cheeks. His confident, finger-snapping breeziness had been utterly punctured. His tongue flicked out to wet his lips. "Look, I was only destroying them because I know he's dead and I just didn't want to be involved."

The door opened and Tennison walked in. She'd run a comb through her hair, freshened her makeup, and was, outwardly at least, calm and composed.

"DCI Tennison has just entered the room," Haskons said into the microphone. Tennison mouthed *Thank you.* Haskons continued. "Did he say what he wanted the photographs for?"

"I assumed Connie was maybe trying to do some legit modeling work. He . . . well, he was a very good-looking boy. Quite a star."

"When he came to you on the other occasions, when these"—Haskons tapped the three or four photographs on the table between them—"these were taken, did he commission them himself or did somebody else?"

"Those," Lewis said, blinking down at them, "well, he paid for them. I suppose he was going to try for work on spec."

"Did you ever see Connie with anybody else?"

"You mean apart from the other models?"

"Yes. Did you ever see Connie with anybody?"

"No," Lewis said, hardly moving his lips.

Haskons pressed him. "So he always came to the studio alone?"

"Yes, apart from the other people in the session. He was always alone."

Haskons looked at Tennison, standing alongside Hebdon. She gave the slightest of nods. It wasn't necessary now to imagine Mark Lewis sweating, it was plainly visible, his dark curly hair clinging damply to his forehead. The handkerchief resembled a length of twisted, grimy rope.

"What about the videos?" Tennison asked, closing the other claw in a pincer attack. "We know what business you are in, Mr. Lewis, we know about the videos. Now, was Connie ever seen with anyone else when he came to your studio? I'm not talking about the models—did anyone ever *bring* him to your studio?"

"No, he was always by himself." Lewis looked up, his eyes shifting from face to face, an abject appeal. "He was very beautiful, very special, very professional. It was just business—"

"Mr. Lewis." Tennison wasn't moved by any kind of appeal. "We know you made videos with underage boys." Meaning, we can throw the book at you any time we like. "So did you ever see Connie with anyone?"

"Somebody was with him, once," Lewis mumbled. He cleared his throat. "No idea who it was, but he paid for the film. Sat watching . . . I'm going back at least a year, eighteen months."

"How much did this film cost?" Haskons asked.

Lewis wiped his neck with the grimy rope. "Two thousand." He swallowed. "Pounds."

"Describe him," Hebdon cut in sharply.

"Who?"

Hebdon leaned over the desk. "The man with Connie. Describe him. How old for starters?"

"Oh!" Mark Lewis made a vague, fluttery gesture. "Well, be about late fifties, maybe older. Tall, gray-haired, gray . . . he was all sort of gray, really, pinstriped suit, smart, had a briefcase . . ."

"How did he pay? Check or cash?"

"Cash." Lewis nodded emphatically. "He had the cash in the briefcase."

Tennison bent down to have a quiet word in Haskons's ear. He leaned to one side and whispered back, "He waived his right . . ."

"So he's made his call, yes?" Tennison murmured, and was assured by Haskons's nod. Mark Lewis watched them with glazed, slightly moist eyes. He visibly jumped when Hebdon said, "Did he take part in the video? This gray-haired man?"

"Well . . . not physically."

"What's that supposed to mean?" Haskons said beligerently.

Lewis stammered, "He s-said what he wanted, t-told me what he wanted Connie to do."

"Have we got the video?" Haskons asked him.

"Oh, no—that one never even had a copy made. He took it out of the camera. All the others we made came after. Connie got a bit of a taste for it."

It was the first direct answer he'd given that Tennison actually believed. Everything else had had to be, quite literally, sweated out of him. She said, "You got an address for Connie? A phone number?" Mark Lewis shook his head. *"No?"* Tennison said icily, pointing at the tape recorder. "Would you please answer the question?"

"No, I don't know where he lives," Lewis said meekly.

"Lived, Mr. Lewis. Connie is dead. How did you contact him when he was alive?"

Lewis stared dumbly at the table, squeezing the wet rag of a handkerchief. The door was pushed open, and Otley beckoned to Tennison. She went over and had a whispered conversation.

With a tight, icy smile, Haskons said, "We've a stack of your films starring Connie, and you want us to believe you had no way of contacting him?"

". . . search warrant . . ."

Lewis stared glassily past Haskons's shoulder, having caught Otley's words. He saw Tennison nod to Otley, who disappeared. She came back in and shut the door of the humid, claustrophobic room as Hebdon leaned over the desk, putting his face close to Lewis's.

"Mark, you're getting in deeper. You've just admitted you filmed Connie eighteen months ago. He was still a minor."

"I—I didn't know how old he was. He told me he was eighteen!"

Tennison barked at him, "Mr. Lewis, how did you contact Connie?"

Dalton tapped and came in. He wanted a word. With a sigh Tennison followed him into the corridor.

"I think you should have a look at it, it's just a home video."

"Of Connie?" Dalton nodded. "Okay, we'll take a break in ten minutes." She looked into his eyes. "How you feeling?"

Dalton shrugged it off, waggling his hand with the bandage on it. "I'm fine, no problem."

She watched him walk off down the corridor. No question about it, he wasn't fine, far from it, and maybe there was one hell of a problem. She went back in. Lewis was hoarse and ragged, squirming in the chair, his collar, his shirtfront, drenched with sweat.

"I'd leave a message and he'd call me . . . I never knew where he lived, I swear."

He hadn't much resistance left. It was a token effort. Tennison knew they had just about squeezed him dry. But not quite.

"So, if I, for example, saw one of your films, and wanted to contact somebody in it . . . I'd get in touch with you?"

"Yes."

"Then what?"

"I'd go around to the advice centre and stick up a note for him."

"Advice centre, which advice centre?"

"One in Soho, near some old flats."

"Did you get paid for carrying these messages back and forth?"

Rather late in the day, Mark Lewis decided this was an affront. "No. No, I did not get paid."

"You just did it as an act of kindness?" Hebdon said, with only the faintest sarcasm.

"Yes."

Tennison opened the small top window, and then opened the larger one. The fresh clean air was delicious. "Do you know Edward Parker-Jones?" she asked, breathing deeply and turning to him.

"He runs the advice centre." Lewis nodded. "But I don't know him. He wouldn't approve, you know . . ." His eyebrows, as suspiciously dark as his hair, went up and down. "Very straight."

Tennison took a pace nearer and asked quietly, "Why do you think Colin Jenkins was murdered?"

"I don't know."

Tennison let the silence hang for a moment. She didn't believe him, and she didn't not believe him. For the time being, the jury was still out.

She moved up close to the table, standing very straight, looking down on him.

"Mr. Lewis, you were read your rights, and you said that you did not require any legal representation. You were also granted permission to make a phone call, which you did. I now have to inform you that a warrant has been requested for a search to be carried out at your premises, and you will be held in custody until formal charges are presented."

She tapped Haskons on the shoulder, who rose, tugging his jacket straight, and together they left the room. Mark Lewis was slumped in the chair, gray-faced, wrung-out, looking sixty-five if he looked a day.

Striding along the corridor toward the viewing room, Tennison stabbed the air. "We want bank statements, address books, phone numbers, fax numbers. We want names of his clients. We want tax payments, VAT payments—we'll throw the lot at that seedy, revolting pervert and do his place over tonight."

Haskons strode along with her, keeping pace, just. He'd seen her in this mood before, when they'd worked together on a murder case. She was like a woman possessed. She bloody well was possessed, Haskons thought, by whatever demon it was that drove her.

The room was full, the reflected light from the screen showing up the thick wreathes of smoke hanging near the ceiling. The men were enjoying it, laughing uproariously and shouting out lewd remarks. There were high-pitched squeals, effeminate ooohs and aaahhs, as they mimicked the participants in the cheap, tawdry drama that had been shot by shaky hand-held camera in Super VHS PornoScope.

Boys' night out, Tennison thought sourly, standing in the doorway. All they were short of was a bar, and later on a blond striptease act with forty-four inch tits. Superintendent Halliday was there, she saw, sitting near the front. From this angle she couldn't tell if he was laughing too, or even enjoying it. All in the line of duty.

Some of the men noted her presence, but it didn't inhibit them. Probably gave the whole thing an extra charge, that snooty bitch with the cast-iron drawers watching this filth.

But Tennison wasn't shocked by the images, nor even disgusted. She was simply, and very deeply, saddened by them. That boys and young men should do this to make money was enormously dispiriting; that others should pay to see it, and get pleasure out of watching it, was even worse.

She herself felt grubby and demeaned at witnessing this joyless, miserable, pathetic shadow play.

She signaled to Dalton. A general moan went up as he stopped the VCR and a snowstorm filled the screen. The fluorescent lights flickered on. Tennison moved to the front.

"Could just the officers directly concerned in the Colin Jenkins inquiry please remain. Everyone else . . . show's over."

Chairs scraped as the men filed out. Halliday, staying where he was, crooked a finger. Tennison ground her teeth, hoping it didn't show. She looked attentive.

"I'd keep a record of all these tapes," Halliday said gravely. He looked at her from under his brows. "Don't want any to go walkabout."

Tennison's sober expression matched his. She leaned closer and said confidentially, "I'd like you to listen to the Mark Lewis interview."

Halliday nearly smiled and immediately stood up, pleased that his new DCI was inviting a second opinion.

Tennison watched him leave, metaphorically dusting her hands. That's got rid of him.

The team settled down to watch the Connie video. "What we watchin' then?" asked Haskons as Dalton started the machine and stepped back beside Tennison's chair.

"*Gone With the Wind,* what d'you think, pratt," came Otley's reply.

They all waited as the screen jumped and buzzed. Tennison looked up and said quietly, "You know, Brian, if you need to talk, there's always me, or there's a very good counselor."

Dalton didn't move, though it seemed, Tennison acutely sensed, as if he was withdrawing tightly into himself. Both his hands were clenched, the bandage on his right hand vivid against the bloodless skin. A muscle twitched in his cheek. He stared straight ahead at the screen, fragmented pictures starting to form.

Tennison turned away as the film proper began.

A desolate, windswept children's playground. Pools of water on the cindery ground. A row of swings, some with broken seats, creaking to and fro on rusted chains. The shaky camera panned to the left, picking up a slight, red-haired figure in a padded red-and-black baseball jacket and sand-colored chinos. The wind ruffled his curly hair as he sat down on one of the swings and gently rocked. The camera moved in close until the boy's face filled the screen. He had a sweet shy smile. Fringed by long auburn lashes, his brown eyes sparkled. He had a fair complexion and skin soft as a girl's. He giggled, biting his lower red lip with small white teeth.

"Hi! My name is Connie. I am fourteen years old, and . . ."

Again the infectious giggle.

"I'm sorry, I'll start again." He straightened his face. "Hi! My name is Connie . . ."

He couldn't keep it up. He covered his mouth. "This is stupid." He pointed off camera. "It's Billy's fault, he keeps on pulling faces at me!"

A cross-eyed Billy appeared, features contorted in a dreadful grimace. It was too much. Connie had broken up, hanging onto the swing, helplessly wagging his head from side to side. Someone's hand whisked Billy out of sight, but it was past saving, Connie had had it.

"Get Billy Matthews brought in," Tennison said quietly, face set.

The video went off and then started again as they tried for another take. This time a straight-faced Connie, his eyes still moist from laughing, gave it his best shot.

"Hello. My name is Connie"—the same shy, sweet smile filled the screen—"and I'm fourteen years old . . ."

Otley and Hebdon had St. Margaret's Crypt, Haskons and Lillie the Bullring, WPCs Kathy Trent and Norma Hastings the underpass next to Waterloo Bridge.

It was a fine night, with a pleasantly mild breeze blowing off the river. The waxing quarter-moon rose up behind the distant towers of Canary Wharf, a dusty orange-red scimitar seen through the haze of the capital.

The chances of finding Billy Matthews were slim. Just one punk kid among the hundreds sleeping out on the streets, dossing down in shop doorways, huddled on the concrete walkways and beneath the brick archways on the South Bank.

Norma hated it. To the drunks and dossers, she and Kathy were two respectable, well-dressed young women, and as such fair game. They got the lot, and had to endure it. The obscene invitations and suggestions, the grimy faces jeering at them from the shadows, the beggars and buskers accosting them at every corner. Down by Cardboard City, at the tea wagon run by two middle-aged women, they came across a gang of kids with a skinny dog on a bit of string. The kids took off as they approached them, scattering in all directions. One of the boys stumbled, and Kathy managed to get near him, a fresh-faced lad with ragged blond bangs, his face showing signs of a recent beating.

"Do you know Billy Matthews? Have you seen him?"

Fear in his eyes, Alan Thorpe picked himself up and stumbled off past the cardboard and wood shacks lining the viaduct walls, ducking out of sight in the labyrinth of shantytown.

Kathy looked hopelessly at Norma. They both felt like giving up. Drunken voices sang, argued and swore in the darkness. On a tinny, crackling radio, Frank Sinatra boasted that he'd done it his way. A busker with an out-of-tune guitar sang "She said, Son, this is the road to hell," while a reel-ing drunk clutching a bottle of Thunderbird yelled out in a hoarse voice that boomed and echoed under the viaduct, "Oh, when the saints . . . Oh, when the saints . . . Oh, when the saints go marchin' in . . ."

Keeping close together, Kathy and Norma moved along the slimy, lit-tered pavements. A head was thrust out on a scrawny neck, its front teeth missing. "Hello, girls! This way to the National Theatre, have yer tickets ready—pul-ease!" He cackled with insane merriment.

Norma evaded his clutching hand, and bustled on quickly, shudder-ing. She touched Kathy's arm, having had enough, about to retreat from this underworld of the damned—to hell with Billy Matthews—and there he was, lying against the wall, wrapped in a filthy sack. He was in a terrible state. They weren't even sure, at first, if he was alive or dead.

Kathy felt for his pulse. "Radio in for an ambulance! Norma!"

Norma came back to herself, fumbling for her radio. She was sick to her stomach. Along the pavement, the busker with the broken guitar was singing her song.

"This ain't no upwardly mobile freeway—
Oh no, this is the road to hell."

Jessica Smithy didn't give the Sierra Sapphire time to stop before she was out from behind the wheel of the black BMW, switching on the tiny micro-cassette recorder and holding it concealed in her gloved hand. Carl, her photographer, was a few paces behind as she crossed the quiet tree-lined street, thumbing the auto flash on the Pentax slung around his neck.

Jessica reckoned she deserved this break. She had waited over an hour, since 9:45, listening to *The World Tonight* on Radio 4 and the first five min-utes of *Book at Bedtime*. At last she had been rewarded. She flicked the long tail of her Hermès scarf over her shoulder and patted her knitted ski hat down onto her razor-trimmed, slick-backed hair. Tall and athletically slen-der, she had a sharp, fine-boned face and quick, darting hazel eyes. Intelli-gent and tenacious, she never let a good story escape her grasp, and she scented that this one was high-yield plutonium.

"Excuse me, Inspector Tennison? Are you Detective Chief Inspector Tennison?"

Tennison locked the door of her car. She turned warily, eyeing the woman and the bearded man with the camera with deep suspicion.

"I'm Jessica Smithy. I have tried to contact you, I wondered if you could spare me a few minutes . . . ?"

Evidently, Tennison couldn't. Briefcase in hand, she marched around the back of the car to the pavement. They pursued her.

"Can you give me an update on Colin Jenkins?"

Tennison pushed open the wrought-iron gate. Without turning, she said, "There was a formal press conference yesterday. I have no further comment." She banged the gate shut and went up the short path to her front door.

"But is his death still being treated as suspicious or accidental?"

Jessica Smithy hovered at the gate as Tennison let herself in.

"Are you heading the investigation?"

The door was firmly closed.

"Shit." Jessica Smithy kicked the gate viciously and switched off the recorder.

At 10:35 P.M. Billy Matthews was being rushed along a corridor toward the emergency resuscitation section. The red blanket was up to his chin. Eyes closed, a dribble of blood-streaked saliva trailing from his open mouth, his pale peaked face was drenched in sweat. His hands clutched the edge of the blanket, as a child seeks to cuddle up warm in the comfort and security of a favorite fluffy toy.

Trotting alongside, the nurse leaned over him anxiously. Billy opened his eyes, blinking away sweat.

"I'm okay." He smiled up at her. "I'm okay. I'm okay."

9

That bloody woman again! Did she never give up?

Tennison had unlocked the door of her car, tossed her briefcase inside, mentally preparing herself to do battle with the early morning gridlock, and there she was—climbing out of a black BMW across the street next to the park railings. The bearded guy with the camera was with her.

"Chief Inspector Tennison!"

Did the damn woman never sleep? Even before Tennison could get in and zoom off, she was hurrying across, the heels of her high brown leather boots clicking, coat flapping around her.

The photographer nipped in and a flashlight went off.

"Hey—what is this?" Tennison demanded angrily. "What's he taking pictures of me for?"

Jessica Smithy wafted her hand. "Go back in the car, Carl." She gave Tennison a warm friendly smile, all sweetness and light. "I'm sorry, but I just need to talk to you." She held up a press card, a passport-size photograph sealed in plastic. Tennison's eyes took this in, and also the pocket recorder partly concealed in Jessica Smithy's other hand.

"Is that on?"

"You're not interested, are you?" Jessica Smithy's face hardened, the smile evaporating like morning mist. "Why? Because he was homeless? A rent boy? Doesn't he warrant a full investigation?" She was holding up the recorder, quite blatantly. "You are the officer who brought George Marlow to trial—"

"Is that on?" Tennison repeated, getting riled.

"I'm writing an article on the boy that died in the fire, Colin Jenkins. You see, I met him a couple of times, and my editors really want pictures . . . he promised me an exclusive."

"I'm sorry, we have no pictures of him," Tennison said, clipped and precise. She was looking at Jessica Smithy with renewed interest.

"They must have taken some when they found him, surely?"

"How often did you meet him?"

"Just a couple of times. I have been very willing to come in to discuss my entire interaction—"

"An exclusive?" Tennison interrupted. Jessica Smithy frowned; the interrogator had suddenly become the interrogated. "You mean Colin Jenkins was selling his story, yes?" She pointed. "Is that tape on?"

"He was prepared to name his clients, including a high-ranking police officer," Jessica Smithy admitted.

Tennison jerked back, bumping into the side of the car. A spasm tautened her stomach muscles. "Did you record your interview with Colin Jenkins?" she asked, pointing at the recorder.

"Yes, and I'm willing to let you hear the tapes, but I want an exclusive interview with you."

Tennison had a nasty streak. Jessica Smithy got the brunt of it.

"I want to interview *you*, Miss Smithy." She thrust her wrist out, glared at her watch. "You be at my office—with the tapes—at nine o'clock. That's official."

Jessica Smithy smiled, holding up her hands. "Hey, I'll be there! I've been trying hard enough to get to you . . ."

Tennison slid behind the wheel.

"Thank you very much, Chief Inspector!"

Tennison said frostily, "It's Detective Chief Inspector, Miss Smithy," and slammed the door on her.

DI Ray Hebdon pushed through the black curtain, blinking in the light. "Nothing in the darkroom." His expression sagged dejectedly at the sight of the thick albums, several piles of them, on the coffee table. "We got to go through every one of them?" he asked Brian Dalton.

"'Fraid so." Dalton's mouth twisted in his tanned face. "Sickens me. I don't understand it—I mean, there's thousands of them . . ."

"Of what?" Hebdon hoisted one, riffled through the pages.

"Poofters," said Dalton, with repugnance.

Hebdon kept turning the pages, saying nothing.

The caretaker shuffled in from the passage leading to the studio. Tufts of white hair sprouted from under a greasy flat cap and his baggy cardigan almost reached his knees. The unlit stub of a cigarette was welded permanently into the corner of his mouth.

"You goin' to be much longer? Only I wanna go out. I do the place next door. You want the keys?"

"Need you to stay, sorry," Dalton said, though he didn't sound it.

"Only the uvver blokes 'ad 'em." The caretaker sniffed. "Larst night."

Hebdon frowned at him. "Somebody was here last night?"

"Yers . . ." The caretaker nodded, waving his hands around in circles. "Took a whole load of stuff out. Police."

Hebdon pushed past him to the phone.

Vera's friend with the tight firm buttocks, Red, stood in the sitting room of Mark Lewis's flat, smoking a cigarette in an ebony holder. He wore a silk kimono with purple dragons and fluffy high-heeled silver slippers. His eyebrows had been shaved off and redrawn with an artist's flourish, and his lips were glossed a pale pink.

Head back, he blew a graceful plume of smoke into the perfumed air, watching Haskons rooting through the drawers of the gilt escritoire. From the bedroom came the sound of closet doors being opened and banged shut as Lillie conducted a thorough search.

"If I'd known I was having so many visitors I'd have waxed my legs," Red mused, addressing no one in particular.

He swanned across to the long low Habitat sofa and dinked the cigarette in the frosted lead crystal ashtray. He sat down, crossed his smooth bare legs, and with a little sigh began filing his nails.

"You could help us," Haskons said accusingly. Not yet eight-fifteen in the morning, and already he was frazzled, frustrated, and thoroughly pissed off. "Where's his diary? His address book?" Red shrugged, shaping his thumbnail to a point. "What about his tax forms? VAT forms?"

"I don't know, unless they took it all," Red said placidly.

Haskons straightened up, flushed. "Who?"

"They said they were police, and that Mark was being held in custody. I mean"—his painted eyebrows rose in two perfect arcs—"there's not a lot you can say to that. Nobody even asked me about him, you know." He gave a little plaintive sigh. ". . . Connie, he was a sweet kid. Not all the time—he was quite an operator—but then, he had the equipment."

Haskons raised his hand to Lillie, who had appeared from the bedroom, telling him to keep quiet.

"Connie . . ." Red said pensively, propping his chin on two fingers. "He wanted to be a film star. There's a lot of famous stars that pay out to keep their past secret. That's life. Whatever you do catches up on you." He gazed down sadly at his feet. "Tasteless slippers, aren't they?"

The day hadn't started well, and by nine o'clock Tennison was in Halliday's office, spitting mad. Commander Chiswick was there, his portly bulk framed in the window, neat as a bank manager in his blue and white striped shirt and pinstripe suit. Halliday, across the desk from Tennison, was in one of his twitchy moods. But he was determined not to be bulldozed by this harridan.

"Both Mark Lewis's flat and studio cleaned out!" Tennison stormed. "And supposedly by police officers."

"I'll look into it," Halliday said.

"I hope you will, because it stinks."

"I said I will look into it. But we have to abide by the rules," Halliday insisted, "we have to get the warrants issued."

Tennison rapped her knuckles on his desk. "There isn't a single piece of paper with his name left on it, let alone any of his clients' names. What's going on?"

Beneath the level of the desk, Halliday's fingers dug deep into the leather armrests. His pale blue eyes bored into hers. "Chief Inspector, check your transcripts of Mark Lewis's interview. He was allowed to make a phone call. Maybe he arranged for someone to clear his place out, and it had nothing to do with delays in issuing bloody search warrants!"

"Don't go casting aspersions around—or they'll come down on your head," Chiswick boomed, his fleshy jowls quivering with indignation. "We are just as keen to get a result as you are!"

Tennison half-raised her hand in a gesture of apology. She was so fired up, she'd overstepped the mark. What with missing tapes, not-so-subtle warnings, and officers she didn't altogether trust, it was easy to get paranoid around here. Or was she simply paranoid about being paranoid?

Chiswick loomed over her. "May I remind you that you inferred that an arrest would be imminent!" He had her on the defensive and was taking full advantage of it. "How much longer do you require four extra officers to assist your inquiries?"

That was rich, Tennison fumed inwardly, when she'd made no such request for extra manpower in the first place. It had been foisted upon her. However, she let it ride.

"I can't put a time on it. You've seen those videos, there're kids in them . . ." Tennison looked from one to the other. "I got a breakthrough today, from a journalist. I've not interviewed her yet, but she met the victim, taped Colin Jenkins for an exclusive. He was selling his story, and prepared to name his clients." She checked the time. "In fact she should be here now."

Silence. Both men seemed taken slightly off guard by this. Chiswick cleared his throat loudly.

"What's the journalist's name?"

"Jessica Smithy."

He rubbed the side of his face, then gave a curt nod, indicating that she was free to go. Tennison went.

Halliday waited. He jumped up. "Don't cast aspersions! Coming down on whose head?"

Chiswick rounded on him. "Who's idea was it to bring her here! We've got a bloody loose cannon now, and we're both going to be in a compromising position if it gets out."

"I warned her off, all right?" Halliday said, low and angry. He pushed his chair aside and stalked over to the window, massaging the back of his neck. "But now there's this journalist . . . we can't tell her to back off."

"I know what she said," Chiswick snapped. He took a breath, trying to calm down and think straight. "So give her twenty-four hours. If she's not charged Jackson, she's off the case. Get Dalton on this journalist woman."

Halliday stared at him for a moment. He returned to his desk, twitching, and picked up the phone and asked for the Squad Room.

There were three butts in the ashtray, ringed with lipstick. Jessica Smithy added a fourth, grinding it down with a vengeance. She looked at her watch, yet again, and let her arms flop down on the table.

"Am I going to be kept waiting much longer? She asked me to be here by nine o'clock. It's already—"

"Chief Inspector Tennison is caught up right now," DI Hall said, "but as soon as she's free . . ."

He went back to gazing out of the window, at the tiny patch of blue sky he could just see between the buildings opposite, daydreaming about Lanzarote. Three weeks to go. Roll on.

Tennison switched on the tape recorder and sat down. She gestured to a chair, but instead Otley perched himself on the corner of her desk. She noticed he hadn't shaved this morning, and it crossed her mind that he might be drinking again.

Clicks, mike noises, rustlings, and then Jessica Smithy's voice came out of the twin speakers.

"I'm going to put this on—is that okay? Only I don't have shorthand. This always makes my life easier."

Cups and saucers rattling, Muzak playing, background noise of traffic. Cafe? Restaurant? Wine bar?

"Is there any other place I can contact you? I called the advice centre . . ."

"I told you not to do that! I said I would contact *you!*"

Tennison looked at Otley, who nodded. Connie.

"We got to first agree on what you will pay me."

"I can't say we will pay you this or that amount of thousands, without first having at least a bit of information."

"I'll take it elsewhere. . . ."

Tennison tightened her lips in annoyance as Dalton and Haskons came in. She jabbed the STOP button and glared at Dalton. "You're late. We've got tapes of Colin Jenkins." On her feet now, she jerked her thumb to Halliday's wall, and lowered her voice. "This is to stay with us until I say otherwise. This woman said that Connie was selling his story—that he was going to name a high-ranking police officer."

Deliberately not looking at Dalton when she said this, nevertheless she saw his reaction to it in the droop of his eyelids, the slight stiffening of his jaw.

Tennison went on, "And two, a Member of Parliament." She gave each of them a searching look. "If a name comes up it stays with us, understood? Because we could be opening up a big can of worms, and we will need hard evidence to back it up."

The three officers pulled their chairs forward as Tennison restarted the tape.

Dalton was leaning forward, wearing a frown of concentration. "Sorry I'm late, but when did this come up? Who brought this in?"

Tennison shushed him. Dalton dropped his head, staring down at his injured hand, now heavily bandaged and secured with tape.

The Muzak and traffic noises seemed worse than before. They had to strain to distinguish the voices from the irritating background clutter.

"Just telling me that you have important names isn't good enough. I mean, what if this is all a lie? Just to get money out of my paper?"

"I told you I had names—very important people, high up people. An MP, a police officer, a . . ."

The three men flicked glances at one another.

"I have to go to my editor, Connie. I have to sell him the story too, you know."

"I want big money." Tennison recalled the sweet, shy smile in the video. But this was the hard-faced Connie, the calculating hustler out for everything he could get. ". . . Because if they found out I was doing this, then they'd kill me. There's a guy called Jimmy Jackson, he's real crazy."

Tennison clenched her fist, looking around triumphantly. Bingo—first name! She craned forward with the others.

"I want at least twenty thousand quid . . ."

The rest was drowned out in scuffling footsteps, a door opening, the sound of traffic suddenly swelling.

Impatiently, Tennison looked at her watch. From her desk drawer she took out a small Panasonic tape recorder, slipped it into the pocket of her dark-blue jacket, and stood up.

"Get the dialogue transcribed and see if the tech boys can clear off the background noise," she instructed Haskons. "We want names, and as fast as possible."

She gave Otley the nod to follow her outside. In the corridor she paced, turned, paced again, on a real high. At last they were getting somewhere. It was the best buzz she ever got, when the pieces started coming together. Beat an orgasm hollow.

She stabbed her finger in Otley's chest. "Get someone to keep tabs on Jackson. If he knew about those tapes, he wasn't looking for Connie because of any money."

Otley went off at the double. Dalton came out. "I had to go back in for the blood tests," he said with an apologetic shrug, and tapped his bandaged hand.

Tennison faced him. "Yes, I know, and I'm sorry. I didn't mean to sound off at you in there." She turned to go.

"I'll get the results this week. In the meantime I just have to wait," Dalton continued as she walked off. ". . . Can I sit in on the Jessica Smithy interview?"

Tennison paused and looked back at him. Her name hadn't been mentioned in there, and yet Dalton knew. He'd asked who brought the tape in, and all the time he knew that too.

What she knew was that somebody was playing silly buggers, for sure. She nodded. Dalton trailed after her.

"I had two meetings with him. We met once on the tenth in Mr. Dickies at Covent Garden, and on the fourteenth in the Karaoke K bar."

"How did he first contact you?"

"He called the office."

"But how did he know to get to you, specifically?"

"Maybe he reads my column."

"So—if I called your office at the paper and said I had a hot story, you would drop everything and meet me in the middle of Covent Garden?"

"You get to have a feel for a story, intuition."

"And you had a feel for this one?"

"I just don't understand your attitude." Jessica Smithy puffed on her cigarette, eyes rolling at the ceiling. She said tartly, "Unless you don't want an investigation into Colin Jenkins's death."

"I'm not sure what you mean," Tennison said, though she had a pretty good idea.

"But then—if what Connie told me is true, it would make sense."

"What exactly did he tell you?"

"That one of his clients is a high-ranking officer within the Metropolitan Police Force."

"He told you that?"

"Yes. That is why I wanted to talk to you. Being a woman . . . if there was a cover-up." Jessica Smithy stared hard at Dalton, his crime being that he was the only male present, and possibly a pederast into the bargain.

"You had two sessions only with Connie, correct? Just two, and both of them taped?"

Jessica Smithy blew a gust of smoke out in a long sigh. *"Yes!"*

"Did you make any further tapes?"

"No, I did not," she stated, enunciating each word separately.

Haskons came in and leaned over to whisper in Tennison's ear. She listened, nodding, and scribbled on a notepad, tore it off and passed it to him. He went out. Watching every detail of this interaction with her restless, darting eyes, Jessica Smithy smoked furiously. Her long pale cheeks were hollowed as she sucked in, held it, suddenly let go.

Tennison wafted the air. "Have you tried the patches?"

"What?"

"To give up smoking." Jessica Smithy flicked ash, ignoring her. "You had only two meetings with Colin Jenkins . . ." She carried on ignoring her. "And on both these occasions you recorded the entire conversation between you and Colin Jenkins?"

"Yes." Token answer, bored to tears.

Tennison plowed steadily, resolutely on. "You said that Colin Jenkins first contacted you directly at your office. How did you get in touch with him the second time?"

"I left a message for him at an advice centre. In fact I even went there, it's the one in Soho, and I knew it was a big hangout—"

"What date?" Tennison cut in.

"—for rent boys. It would have been the twelfth of this month at three-fifteen P.M., not A.M."

"When you went to the advice centre did you interview any other boy?"

"This is bloody umbelievable," Jessica Smithy snorted, stubbing out her cigarette in a cloud of ash. "No, I did not. I didn't interview anybody."

"Did you speak to anybody?"

"Edward Parker-Jones. He runs the centre."

"What did you tell him?"

"I didn't *tell* him anything." She dusted her fingertips. "I just asked if he knew where I could contact Colin Jenkins."

"Did he know who you were?"

"Look, I'm a journalist, okay, and I have to sometimes . . ." She spread her hands.

"Lie?"

Jessica Smithy's lips came together primly. "No. He presumed I was a social worker and he was very helpful. But somebody must have told him who I was, and he asked me to leave, in fact he got quite abusive. If I'd wanted to interview any of the kids there he wouldn't have let me."

"So Mr. Parker-Jones knew you, a journalist, were looking for Colin Jenkins?"

"*YES!*" Jessica Smithy might have been trying to get through to an imbecile. "So now what?" She leaned forward eagerly, eyes alight. "Is he a suspect?"

Tennison was distracted by movement in the small square window of the door. Haskons was talking to someone, and a moment later she saw Halliday's baby blues peering inquisitively in. Hell and damnation. She might have known he'd be lurking about, nose twitching, quick as a shit-house rat.

"Why aren't you trying to find out which MP or which police officer used him?" Jessica Smithy said angrily. "Maybe even killed him! He was murdered, wasn't he?"

Tennison regarded her calmly. "Who else did you speak to at the centre? Another boy maybe?"

"I've told you," Jessica Smithy said wearily. "I didn't speak to anyone, because Parker-Jones wouldn't allow me to. He asked me to leave . . ."

Haskons was beckoning. He pushed open the door as Tennison went across. They stood together in the doorway, having a murmured conversation. Glaring at them, Jessica Smithy rose, snatching at her shoulder bag, slinging it on. Tennison leaned in.

"Please remain seated, Miss Smithy."

Jessica Smithy sat down again, drumming her fingers on the table. She opened the cigarette packet, found it empty, and crushed it and tossed it away. Tennison came in and collected her things. Haskons sat down in Tennison's vacated chair.

Thinking she was free to leave, Jessica Smithy got up again, and to her intense annoyance was waved down again. She sat there fuming, fists clenched on the table.

"One more thing," Tennison said. "How much did you pay Colin Jenkins for the tapes?"

"I didn't," Jessica Smithy replied, a shade too quickly. "That's why I was looking for him. I'd been given some money by my editor."

"How much?"

She hesitated. "Few hundred. But I don't see that is of any concern of yours."

"Few hundred?" Jessica Smithy nodded, and then nearly jumped out of her skin when Tennison thrust her head forward and barked, "Exactly how much, Miss Smithy? How much were you going to give Colin Jenkins, Miss Smithy? I can call your editor."

"Five hundred . . ."

Tennison leaned nearer, intimidatingly close. Her voice sank to a lethal whisper. "Did you meet Colin Jenkins and give him the five hundred pounds?"

"I—" She nearly blurted something, and checked herself. "No, I did not."

Tennison looked her straight in the eye. Jessica Smithy turned away. First time she'd been caught out. Tennison knew it, and so did Jessica Smithy.

Haskons said formally, "We will, Miss Smithy, be retaining the tapes you made of your two meetings with Colin Jenkins, as evidence. You will be asked to sign a legal document which bars you, and your paper, from using any information—"

Jessica Smithy tried to interrupt.

"—appertaining to the said tapes."

Jessica Smithy was wild eyed and furious. "What? This is crazy! You can't stop me from printing."

Tennison opened the door. "We just did," she said, going out.

"You tell her—" Jessica Smithy pointed a trembling finger after Tennison, turning her furious face to Haskons and Dalton. "When my story gets out, she won't want it in any scrapbook!"

Otley was outside, propped up in his usual indolent slouch, hands stuffed in his pockets. He nodded toward the interview room.

"Anything?"

"Yes." Tennison indicated they should move on, and they walked along together. "Parker-Jones knew Jessica Smithy was a journalist, knew she was looking for Connie." Tennison threw a backward glance. "She's also lying. I think she met Connie. She had five hundred quid, same amount found on his body. I think she paid Connie."

"Maybe I should run a check on Parker-Jones's credentials," Otley suggested.

"I already have. Mallory, Chicago University don't exist, and the rest are a load of cobblers." She gave Otley a big smile. "I'm getting closer, we've got a motive!"

"For Jackson?" Dalton said, right behind her.

Tennison looked around quickly, not realizing he had been following. She nodded. "Until I get back, keep the pressure on breaking those kids' alibis," she told the two of them.

"You want me to come with you?" Dalton asked.

"What, to my doctor's?" Tennison grinned and set off. She halted. "Oh, one more thing. Halliday wants the transcripts of the Smithy tapes." She narrowed her eyes at Otley. "But nobody gets them before me, understood?"

And then she was striding off, a jaunty spring in her step.

Dr. Gordon said, "I'll make an appointment for you to have a laboratory sensitive test, and then we'll get the beta sub-unit hormone measured." He completed the note in her medical records and looked up and smiled. "All very advanced technology now!"

"But are you positive?" Tennison said, fastening the top button of her blouse.

"I think so," Dr. Gordon said, smiling. "You're pregnant—just!"

Tennison needed the edge of the desk to support herself. She gulped hard. She couldn't believe it. This wasn't happening. Things like this never happened to her. Then she realized they did, and had, and she started to smile.

10

One hour later, Tennison was back in the thick of it.

On the return journey she did something she'd never done before. She bought a pound of seedless white grapes and ate them at one go, sitting in her car in the underground carpark of the Soho police station. It didn't occur to her till afterward that she'd always associated grapes with illness and convalescence. But she wasn't ill—she was pregnant! She knew of the hormone cocktail her glands were even at this moment manufacturing, and of the cravings it gave rise to. But so soon? Was her body trying to tell her something? Or was her mind so shell-shocked that it had flipped a circuit and caused her to wolf down a pound of grapes in secret—some kind of bizarre Freudian ritual? Puzzling.

She went directly to the Squad Room, where Haskons gave her the first news, which wasn't good. They'd drawn a blank on the Jessica Smithy tapes. Haskons had listened to the cleaned-up version over headphones and no further names were mentioned.

Tennison felt frustrated. She had really believed, hoped, that this was going to be the breakthrough. It was one step forward, two steps back. As per bloody usual with police work.

She was with Dalton at the board, getting an update on Operation Contract, when Otley arrived. He didn't come over, but instead gave her a private look. Get over here and don't bring Dalton.

"This just came through." Otley was holding a thick bunch of faxes. He moved around so that his back was to the board. "I've been doing a bit of digging after a tip-off . . . 1979. A Mr. Edward Parker was accused of molesting a boy in his care when he ran the Harrow Home for kids, Manchester. Case dismissed for lack of evidence." Otley plucked out another sheet. "Anthony Field. 1983. Indecent assault on a minor. Case dismissed.

Same Mr. Edward Parker again, this time running the Calloway Centre in Cardiff, another home for kids." Next sheet. "Jason Baldwyn . . ."

Tennison held up her hand. She glanced around. "Are you saying what I think you are, that this Parker . . ."

Otley nodded, pinching his nostrils. "Could be Parker-Jones. I've got the addresses of both kids. I can be up in Manchester and back by tonight."

"Manchester?"

"Cross over to Cardiff—be nice to have something on Parker-Jones, and if I can get some dirt on him . . . !" His eyes gleamed.

"I'll do it," Tennison said. "I'll go."

"What? You go?" Otley was choked. "I'd have thought you'd want to be here."

"No, it'll give me a chance to talk to Dalton." Tennison was already moving off, oblivious to Otley's glare. She called the room to attention. "Can I have a word!"

She waited at the board for the team to gather around.

"I don't bloody believe it," Otley said bitterly, as Hebdon and Lillie joined him. "I do all the leg work and she gets the day away."

"Okay, quiet down. I didn't have time this morning to have a briefing, so let's do it now, and crack on. I want us to keep on those kids. Jackson only needed ten minutes from that centre to Vernon Reynolds's flat." She looked to Kathy. "Have we got a tail on him?"

"No, we haven't found him yet."

"Brilliant." Tennison smacked her fist into her palm. "Go back to his hunting ground, the stations, that's where you picked him up the last time." Somebody was mumbling, but she carried on. "We want to break down these alibis. We now have a strong motive for Connie's murder . . ." Her eyes raked over them. "And we all know it isn't robbery."

Slouched against his desk, head bowed, Otley was muttering to DI Hall, "I checked out his credentials. Now I got not one but two possible child abuse cases against him."

Hall frowned, not a clue what the Skipper was nattering on about. But Tennison, senses like needles, had caught some of it.

"What was that, Bill?"

Otley scratched his armpit, eyes shifting away. He shrugged. "I was just saying, pity we got nothin' off the Smithy tapes."

"They're useless," Haskons broke in. "Connie never named anyone! Apart from Jackson, just some clubs where he met his clients."

"No addresses yet," Lillie said, reading from a sheet of paper, "but clubs are: Bowery Roof, Lola's, Judy's, and somethin' that sounded like 'Puddles.'"

"'Poodles,'" Ray Hebdon said. "It's called Poodles. The last two are gay bars, but the Bowery Roof Top is pretty exclusive. Lots of drag acts, transexuals, transvestites, but most members are homosexuals—city types, professionals, not the usual low-life punters."

Grinning broadly, Lillie gave him a dig. "You're pretty well informed, aren't you? I've only just got 'em."

"I'm a member," Hebdon said quietly.

Lillie's loud laugh faltered and dwindled into the general dead silence of the room.

Tennison said, "Ray, are you joking? Because it isn't funny."

Hebdon didn't seem to think so either. "I know it isn't," he said, his face quite serious, composed. "That's why I thought it was about time I came clean." He spread his arms, eyes wide and frank, and looked around. "I'm gay!"

Tennison sipped her coffee. She put the cup down, shaking her head, more in sorrow than in anger. "You took your time in telling us! It's your private business, Ray, but considering the—"

"I'll leave," Hebdon said.

"Let me finish, will you?" Tennison leaned her elbows on the desk. She was trying to assimilate this revelation. She also had a vague, as yet unformed notion that something positive might come of it. "What I was going to say was that it was a pity you didn't have the confidence to tell us sooner."

"Chief Inspector, I have never hidden what I am. Most of us don't go with underage kids."

"I know."

"I feel as repulsed as anyone on the team," Hebdon said with feeling, "but I do know the gay scene. I only proferred the information because it might be of some use."

Tennison nodded. It had never crossed her mind that he might be gay, but now that she knew he was, she thought she could detect certain telltale signs. He grew his dark, rather unkempt hair long, over his collar. He seemed edgy at times, and was prone to blinking nervously. He didn't mince, yet he was light on his feet, his movements quick and alert . . .

All this was bullshit of course, and well she knew it. These weren't telltale signs at all, merely her fanciful imagination. Label anyone gay, and you'd soon invent the evidence to support it. Ray Hebdon's characteristics were those of a human being, nothing more, nothing less.

Put that aside and forget it. Down to business.

"So, which one of these clubs would be likely to be used by, say—"

"Judges, MPs, barristers, solicitors, lawyers . . . top brass?"

"Police officers!"

"The Bowery," Hebdon said at once.

"You well known at the Bowery?"

"No. It's very expensive. I've only been twice." He pointed his finger at her. "But I do know one thing . . . asking questions with that lot in tow!" He jerked his head to indicate the rest of the team. "One, they'd never get past the door. Two, word would leak, you'd never get to the top bracket, let alone get them to talk to you."

"What about access to their membership lists?"

"No way. Most of them use false names, or coded names, even though what they're doing is perfectly legal. But if they are going with underage kids, it ups the ante even further on cloaking their identity. I mean, they'll really have to protect themselves. So who they are would be very hush-hush. One hint of a leak and they'd close ranks." Hebdon's sober expression suddenly cracked in a smile. "Unless we get the lads dragged up—get in that way—nobody pays any attention to them."

Tennison smiled with him. "I'd pay money to see that!"

Superintendent Halliday came in, wanting a private word. He had the Jessica Smithy transcripts in his hand. Hebdon got up to leave.

"Go and get some lunch," Tennison said, and glanced at her watch. "If you see Inspector Dalton, tell him to get his skates on, we've got a train to catch."

He went out and Halliday closed the door. He waved the transcripts, looking like the cat that ate the cream. "Only one name off the Smithy tapes, but it's your man. It's Jackson."

"Yes, I know. Lets you off the hook then, doesn't it?" Tennison said glibly. She saw Halliday flush, and got in quick. "Just a joke . . ."

Halliday sat down, adjusting the knife-edge crease in his trousers, trying to appear mollified when actually he wasn't. Damn woman was too clever for her own good. A loose cannon, Chiswick had called her. More like a loose bloody tank battalion.

Tennison was anxious to have her say before he did.

"This might not be the right time, Jack, but it has to be obvious to you that this case is opening up and treading right on Operation Contract's heels. It is my honest opinion that we should cut our losses . . . Concentrate solely on the murder investigation." She met his stare with a laser beam of her own. "Because the information I am getting goes much deeper than a cleanup of the street kids." She spelt it out. "I think Connie was murdered to silence him, because he was about to name the men involved in a pedophile circle."

"And you think Parker-Jones is involved?" Halliday said after a moment, probing.

Tennison tried to shrug this off. "He is being very cooperative and very helpful," she said carefully. It sounded weak to her, but she hoped it convinced him. "I don't have a shred of evidence to link him to any pedophile circle, but the advice centre, along with a number of other venues—"

"What about Jackson?" Halliday insisted. He had the feeling he was being bamboozled, and he wanted to keep it neat and simple.

"I still think he killed Colin Jenkins, but . . ."

"But?" Halliday said sharply.

Tennison dropped her eyes. "Nothing."

"You'd better reel in Jackson then." He wasn't asking, he was telling. He went to the door. "You've a very impressive career. Don't blow it. Charge Jackson, bury everything else."

When he'd gone she sat thinking for a while. Why was her career in danger of being ruined if she didn't nail Jackson, and what else lay buried at the bottom of this crock of shit? She could have cheerfully murdered for a cigarette.

Haskons unzipped his pants and breathed out a sigh of relief. He looked at Otley, two stalls along. "You've not said anything, Bill. What d'you think?"

"About him being an iron? Doesn't worry me." Otley gazed with hooded eyes at the ceramic wall. "Iron" was Cockney rhyming slang: iron hoof = poof. "We had one at Southampton Row, he didn't last long."

He zipped up and turned away. Ray Hebdon was standing by the wash basins. Otley walked straight past, ignoring him, and went out. Haskons finished, and made a studious effort at looking everywhere but at Hebdon. He fastened his jacket, giving a little furtive smile, and went to the door. "See you in the pub . . ."

Hebdon washed his hands and wiped his face with his wet hands. In the mirror he saw Dalton come in.

"Is it true?"

Impatiently, Hebdon propped both arms against the basin. "What, that I'm gay?"

He sighed heavily and went to dry his face on the towel.

"I just don't believe in this day and age, everybody making such a big deal of it." He returned to the mirror, and started combing his hair. Dalton hadn't moved. His face bore a sullen expression.

"What you looking at me like that for?" Hebdon asked.

"I just don't understand. I thought I knew you."

"You do," Hebdon said.

"Why?" Dalton was angry and mystified. "Ray . . . why?"

"Why? Are you asking me why I'm gay? Because that's the way I am. I've always been."

"Queer?" Dalton said, blinking painfully as if recovering from a kick in the stomach.

Hebdon rammed his comb into his top pocket. "Yes! Queer, poofter, woofter, screamer, screecher—yes, they're all me. I'm gay, I don't apologize for it, I just don't feel I need to broadcast it—for obvious reasons." He raised his hands, clenching and unclenching his fists helplessly. "Look at you! The other two will come out with infantile, puerile cracks from now on . . ."

"I don't believe it," Dalton said, squinting at him. "Do you live with a bloke?"

"Do you?"

Dalton exploded. "Of course I bloody don't!"

"What difference does it make? My private life is just that. I don't poke my nose into yours, what gives you the right to . . ."

Dalton grabbed him by the lapels and shook him.

"Because I work with you!"

Hebdon dragged himself free. He pulled his jacket straight, breathing hard. "I was gay when we first met, did I start touching you up? Propositioning you? Did I? I respect you, why don't you fucking respect me? Now back off!"

He stormed to the door, but then stopped. When he turned he was still white in the face, but he was smiling.

"I was a great rugby player, what I got away with in the scrum . . ." He held up his hands. "Just joking! Look, Brian, I know you are probably going through it, I'm referring to the bite, okay? I just want you to know that if you need to talk to someone, a lot of my friends have been tested and—"

"Piss off."

Dalton barged past him. Left alone, Hebdon stared at his own reflection, and the look on his face was transformed as the bravado crumbled.

15:00. Manchester Piccadilly. Platform 6.

Tennison and Dalton ran across the concourse of Euston Station and reached the barrier of Platform 6 just as the train was pulling out.

"Shit!" Tennison stood there, panting and fuming. She'd never been able to figure out how British Rail got their trains to leave dead on time and arrive late.

"What time is the next one?"

"An hour's wait," Dalton said, looking at the timetable.

"Okay, go and ask the station master if we can use the Pullman lounge. Might as well wait in comfort."

"What's that?"

Tennison said with tart irritation, "It's the lounge for first-class ticket holders. Go on, I'll meet you there."

On the main concourse she glanced up at the indicator board to make sure of the next train. 16:00. Manchester Piccadilly. Platform 5. No chance of missing that one.

Passing behind her, not twenty feet away, Jimmy Jackson was carrying a plastic holdall belonging to a young girl of about twelve years of age. She had pale blond hair, pulled back into a ponytail, and the healthy look and ruddy cheeks of someone brought up in the country. She seemed nervous and lost, gazing around at the milling crowds, her first time in the big city.

"So where you from?" Jackson asked, a broad friendly grin plastered across his face.

"Near Manchester."

Jackson was hugely surprised. "Well, there's a coincidence!"

Tennison hoisted her briefcase and turned, heading toward the Pullman lounge.

"You from there?" the girl asked him.

"No, but I was waiting for a mate, he must have missed the train." Jackson pointed to the sign: Passenger Car Park. "You want a lift?"

The girl hesitated for a second, and then she nodded.

Reaching the glass-fronted entrance to the Pullman lounge, Tennison dumped her briefcase and looked around for Dalton. She couldn't see him, but then she froze. She stood on tiptoe. Jackson and a girl. Walking toward the steps leading down to the underground car park. Lugging her briefcase, Tennison weaved in and out through the crowd, fumbling for her portable phone. Jackson and the girl were turning the corner at the bottom of the steps as she reached the top. She set off down.

Returning from the station master's office, Dalton got the barest glimpse of Tennison's blond head as she disappeared down the steps. He legged it after her.

The girl was giggling at Jackson's chat-up line, Tennison saw, which must be good, whatever it was. She watched from a distance, peeking around a concrete pillar, and saw him take out a bunch of keys and approach a car. He looked up, and Tennison slid out of sight. She couldn't see Dalton, who was scuttling between the parked cars, ducking and diving to get a look at the number plate.

Tennison cupped her hand around the mouthpiece. "It's a dark blue Mercedes, old four-door saloon. I'll get you the number . . . but is there a car in the area? Suspect is James Jackson. Do not apprehend, just tail to destination."

Dalton returned, panting slightly, and eased in beside her. He had the number written on the back of his hand. Tennison passed him the phone. "I told them to look for him at the station exit."

Over the speakers, booming in waves through the concrete cavern, came an announcement.

"THE TRAIN ON PLATFORM FIVE IS THE MANCHESTER PULLMAN EXPRESS. WE ARE SORRY TO INFORM YOU THAT THERE WILL BE NO BUFFET CAR FACILITIES ON THE FOUR O'CLOCK TRAIN TO MANCHESTER DUE TO STAFF SHORTAGES. BRITISH RAIL APOLOGIZE FOR ANY INCONVENIENCE . . ."

At the wheel, Hall kept a sharp lookout on his side of the street while Otley did the same on his. They were somewhere north of Euston—Camden Town, Chalk Farm—Hall wasn't sure where exactly; he was lost in the maze of streets. He pulled into the curb and stopped behind a rusting Skoda with both rear tires flat to the ground. The dark blue Mercedes was parked on the opposite side of the street. Otley pushed his nose up to the windshield to get a good look at the house.

It was four stories with cracked and peeling stucco showing red brick underneath. The windows that weren't boarded up were swathed in thick dark curtains. The entrance porch was supported by one stone pillar, the other a crumbling stump. On the surviving one, the numerals "22" could just be made out in faded black paint.

Hall reached for the radio handset. "See if we can get more info on the house."

A light went on in one of the third-floor windows, visible through a chink in the curtains. "He's still in there," Otley said.

Hall was patched through. "Kathy? You got anything on the Langley house yet?"

Seated at the computer in the Squad Room, the phone cradled in her shoulder, Kathy was scrolling through column after column of names and addresses.

"Getting nothing from the polling lists . . ."

"Come on, come on," Hall's impatient voice said in her ear.

"I'm going as fast as I can. I'll call, soon as I have anything."

She hung up and kept searching. Norma came in with two plastic cups of coffee. She put one in front of Kathy and sat down at her own desk. "Where's her Ladyship today?"

"Up north—doing what, I do not know!" Kathy took a sip and grimaced at the taste. "But she took Dalton with her."

"Did he get cleared—his hand?" Norma said, shaking her head and tutting loudly. She smacked herself on the forehead. "Shit—Billy Matthews. Guv wants him requestioned about the Connie video." She found the number and dialed. "It's all very well her saying arrest him, but he had four court appearances last year alone. They didn't want to take him, you know, said he'd only just been in a few days before—"

She broke off. "Charing Cross Hospital, emergency ward." She waited for the connection. "What was that nurse's name at the hospital?" she asked Kathy.

"Mary Steadman." Kathy blinked her eyes at the screen. "Shit, I still got nothing on this Jackson address. It isn't listed under the name Jackson." She went down the lists, mumbling, "Twenty-two, Langley Road . . . Islington, Kentish Town, Camden . . ."

Norma got through to Mary Steadman. "This is WPC Norma Hastings. I brought in a Billy Matthews . . . yes."

Kathy let out a whoop. "Got it—property owned by an Edward Jones. Two sitting tenants. First floor, Maureen Fuller, and basement, Abdul unpronounceable. It's flatlets." Beaming, she reached for the phone.

Norma banged the phone down. She looked sick.

"Billy Matthews discharged himself an hour after we left him there!"

At six-twenty that evening Tennison was sitting in the back of a patrol car outside a pebble-dashed late-Victorian house with bay windows in one of the posher areas of Salford, trying without much success to get through to DI Hall on her portable. She'd had him once, and then he'd gone, lost in a blizzard of static.

She wound the window down and spoke to the uniformed driver, standing on the pavement. "Is there any way I can get my batteries recharged?"

The PC stared at her.

"For my portable phone, officer. What did you think I was referring to? A vibrator?"

Inspector Dalton was speaking to Mrs. Field on the doorstep, a white-haired woman in her sixties, casually yet smartly dressed in a cardigan and pleated skirt, a single string of pearls around her neck, several gold rings on her fingers. She smiled diffidently and shook her head. Dalton came down the garden path and put his head in the window.

"Ma'am?"

"Just a minute," Tennison said shortly, hearing Hall's scratchy voice coming from Mars. No food on the train, nothing to drink, and no bloody batteries. "Hello? Can you hear me? Hello? Ruddy phone." She gave it a shake. "Hello . . . ? Listen, you can gain entry even on the suspicion that a minor is being held there."

Face screwed up, she was straining to hear.

"*I'm* reporting it, okay? She's already been with him for more than four hours. God only knows what's happened to her . . . *Hello?*"

Dead and gone. She pushed the aerial in.

"Er, his mother's home," Dalton said, nodding to the white-haired woman, "but she said he was working late . . . can we come back?"

The door hit Dalton's leg as Tennison thrust it open.

"Sorry, and no we can't come back," she said, getting out.

As soon as they stepped inside the front door it was clear that Anthony Field's mother was very houseproud. The smell of furniture polish was like incense. The living room was obsessively neat, not a speck of dust anywhere, and bedecked with shining brass ornaments. It was almost a sacrilege to walk upon the thick Axminster carpet.

"Would you like a cup of tea?" Mrs. Field had a rather refined voice, and Tennison suspected she was the kind of woman who thought herself a cut above her neighbors, even if she wasn't.

Tennison nodded and smiled. "That would be really nice."

As Mrs. Field went out there was a creak from the room above. Tennison folded her raincoat and placed it on a chair, not wishing to wreck the symmetry. She sat down and crossed her legs. Another creak from above. She looked up at the ceiling.

"Come on down, Anthony. There's a good boy . . ."

Dalton's eyebrows shot up. "Is he in?" Tennison nodded. "How do you know?"

"Because I saw him at the window."

A few minutes later Mrs. Field returned with a tray of tea things, which she set down on a low table that had a nest of smaller tables underneath. She fussed about, sorting out cups and saucers. "It isn't about the bank, is it? Only Anthony is sure to be made assistant manager."

Just then, the would-be assistant manager himself breezed in. He was a tall, lithe young man, clean-cut and good-looking, in a V-neck lemon sweater and natty bow tie. Not as affected as his mother, he spoke fast, running thoughts and sentences into each other.

"Sorry to keep you waiting, but I only just got in. Is the kettle on, Ma? Well, when it whistles I'll hear it—don't miss your program."

His mother patted his arm, gave him an adoring smile, and went out.

"Sorry, I got cold feet as you were late," Anthony said brightly, standing in front of the gas fire, briskly rubbing his hands. He grinned boyishly. "I didn't expect you to arrive in a patrol car, bit embarrassing . . ." He darted to the door as the kettle whistled.

"Excuse me."

Dalton's gaze shifted sideways to Tennison. He said out of the corner of his mouth, "Another one, isn't he? Gay?"

Tennison looked away, expressionless.

• • •

Jackson stood halfway down the staircase, one hand gripping the banister, the other pressed flat against the wall, barring their way. Otley and Hall stared up at him from the second-floor landing.

The entire place reeked as if ten tomcats had saturated the threadbare carpets. Black plastic bags, ripped open, spilled rubbish and putrefied food over the floor.

Otley put one foot on the bottom step. "We don't need a warrant, we have reason to believe you are holding a minor. You were seen leaving Euston Station accompanied."

The anemic glow from the bare dusty bulb made a yellowy snarling mask of Jackson's face.

"Bullshit. I know my rights. Now—piss off." He aimed his finger at Otley, right between the eyes. "You got no warrant. You are on private property, and I have a right as a citizen to defend my property!"

Hall moved along the murky passage and knocked on a door. He tried the handle. Locks, bolts, and catches were undone, and a frail elderly woman peered around the edge, gray hair trailing over her bleary eyes.

"Are you Mrs. Maureen Fuller?"

Jackson let out a cackle. "Hey, is that the juvenile I'm supposed to have prisoner?" he jeered at them.

Otley moved up another step. He shouted to the floor above.

"HELLO? IS THERE ANYONE UP THERE? THIS IS THE PO-LICE."

Jackson came down, fist raised. Otley ducked under his arm and scrambled up the stairs. As Jackson turned to grab at him, Hall went up fast, grappling with him, and got an elbow in the teeth. Stunned, he fell back against the banister. Jackson dragged him down to the landing, twisted his elbow behind him in an arm lock, and butted Hall's head into the wall. He yelled up at Otley.

"You want me to break his arm? Now get the fuck out of here!"

Otley started to come down, very slowly. "Jimmy, this is crazy . . . we just want to see the girl. Just let us see she's okay."

A shadowy figure appeared on the landing above.

"She's up here," Vera Reynolds said.

Jackson's eyes glittered. His fleshy lips drew back against his teeth. "You're dead, Vera," he said, icy calm. Savagely, he swung Hall around and pushed him into the banister post and charged down the stairs, his thudding boots making the house shake.

Anthony had made the tea. Tennison and Dalton drank, both watching the slender young man standing at the glass-fronted bureau full of china figurines and cut glass knickknacks. He picked up a black-and-white photograph in a gilt frame from several on top of the bureau and showed them.

"This was my dad, my little sister. They were killed in a car crash when I was five. After that, Mother . . ." He looked to the closed door. "She had a mental breakdown. That's why I was sent to the home."

He spoke without any emotion whatsoever.

Tennison said carefully, "Can you tell me about the court case, Anthony? I know how difficult it is."

"Really?" He stared at the photograph.

"I need to know about the man who ran the home, Anthony. You see, I believe that the man who assaulted you is still . . ."

She hesitated, trying to choose her words.

"At it?" Anthony said. He replaced the photograph and turned toward them, drawing in a deep breath. "His name was Edward Parker, and my case never even got to court."

11

Otley sat on the edge of the narrow bed, his hand resting gently on the shaking mound under the smelly gray blanket. There were three other beds crammed into the small back room. A teddy bear with only one arm, the stuffing sprouting out, lay on one of them. Otley got another blanket and pressed it around Billy Matthews's shivering little body. The boy was burning up with fever. His wet face was buried in the grimy pillow, spiky hair sticking up over the blanket.

"I'm okay, I'm okay, I'm okay . . ." It went on and on, a meaningless dirge. He whimpered suddenly—"Don't leave me on me own. Please . . . please."

"Billy?" Otley said, patting the blanket. "Billy? I'll stay with you."

Hall appeared in the doorway. "I called an ambulance. The other kids are being taken in now." He looked along the passage. "And Vera asked if she can go."

Billy's hand crept out and fastened tightly around Otley's fingers. His head came up, eyes drugged and filled with a vacant terror. He wouldn't let go of Otley. "Don't leave me . . ."

Vera came in. She looked dowdy and defeated. There was a deadness in her eyes, as if nothing mattered anymore and never would again.

"I'm doing the club tonight, can I go? Doin' the cabaret."

She looked at Billy, hanging onto Otley like grim death, and slowly shook her head. "You won't get any sense out of him, he'd tell you anything just to stay here." In a flat, weary voice she started to sing, "'Life is a cabaret, my friend . . . come to the cabaret.'"

"I'm okay, I'm okay," Billy said, staring at nothing. "Everythin' okay."

Vera sighed drably. "No, you're not, Billy, love. You're not okay at all. Can I go?" she asked Otley, who nodded.

Vera went along the passage and down the stairs, high heels clacking.

Otley put his arm around the shaking mound of gray blanket, hugging it. He turned his head to Hall. "Where's the bloody ambulance?"

"They said there was about a fifteen minute delay."

"I'm okay, I'm okay," Billy insisted in a voice so thin it was barely a mouse's squeak. "I'm okay."

It took twenty-five, not fifteen, minutes for the ambulance to arrive. They put Billy Matthews inside and off it went, lights flashing. Otley walked over to Hall, who was leaning against the hood of their car. It was growing dark, and there were spits of rain in the air.

"I'm just going for a walk," Otley said. He patted Hall on the shoulder and carried on walking.

"Jackson's car's gone."

"He won't get far." Otley turned on the pavement. "Vera's at the Bowery Club, isn't she?" His eyes were narrowed slits in his craggy, gaunt face. "Get somebody watching the place."

Hall watched him amble off in his unmistakable round-shouldered slouch, hands stuffed in his raincoat pockets. Was he going to get pissed out of his skull? He'd shown no emotion over Billy Matthews, but Hall wouldn't have been surprised if the Skipper got ratarsed.

"It hurt, and I screamed, but he put his hand over my mouth. I bit him once, really bit his hand, but it didn't make any difference. I was very small for my age, and he had a special name for me. He said that when he used that special name it was a code, that was when he wanted me to go to his room."

Sitting very straight in the armchair, feet together, knees pressed tight, Anthony Field recounted his experience at the children's home. His tone never varied, never betrayed any feeling; it was a nightmare, permanently fixed in his head, endlessly repeating itself, that had numbed him into this mechanical retelling. He was pale, however, and his long thin fingers were never still.

Tennison prompted him after a moment's painful silence.

"How long did this abuse go on for? Before you told anyone?"

"Three years. There was no one to tell." Anthony's dark-lashed eyes were downcast. He had shapely dark eyebrows, his brown hair brushed and neatly parted in the approved bank employee manner.

"He always said that if I told anyone, I would have to eat my own feces. I got a letter from my mother, she said she was much better, so I ran away." He blinked once or twice at the carpet. "I went to the police station, they called in a probation officer. A woman. I had to tell her . . . it was very embarrassing."

Tennison again waited. "How old were you then?"

"Eight, nearly nine. They took my statements, and then a plainclothes police officer came in to question me."

His hands clasped, released, clasped, released. He was leaning forward slightly, his body hunching tighter and tighter.

Tennison waited. Smoothing her knees, she said quietly, "I really appreciate you telling me this, Anthony." And quieter still, "Can you go on?" When he nodded, she said, "Thank you very much."

Anthony breathed in a long quivery breath.

"This police officer. I never even knew his name. He asked me if I knew what happened to boys that—that—" His hands were jerking, writhing in his lap. "That tell lies. I said I was not telling lies." His voice went abruptly harsh. "*Well-he-said-We-will-soon-know.* And he undid my pants. And he did it to me. He said that if I told anyone I would go to prison." Anthony stared at the carpet, his face drained of all color. "Hard to tell what would be worse, eating your own shit or going to prison."

"This police officer penetrated you?" Tennison said. He nodded, head bowed. "At the station?" He nodded. "Was anyone present?"

Anthony shook his head. He shuddered. He was close to breaking. Tennison was calculating how much more he could take, and praying to God she hadn't underestimated.

"So I said I was—that I had been telling lies. Case dismissed. And they sent me back to the home. I was there for another two years. Then mother collected me."

"After you left, you didn't tell anyone?"

Anthony straightened up and looked at her. He shook his head.

"Can I ask you why not?"

"My aunt told me that mother was still in a very nervous state, so how could I tell her? I love my mother very much. I always felt that if I upset her in any way, I ran the risk of being sent back. So I never told anyone, and . . ." He gave a listless shrug. "I just got on with my life."

"I am sorry to make you remember, Anthony," Tennison said, feeling the pain with him. But he looked at her as if she'd said something incredibly stupid. He stood up, and almost imperceptibly he thrust out his hip in a tiny flick of campness. *I know what I am, and I don't care that you know it too.*

"Oh, I never did forget, Inspector," he said softly.

Tennison took in Dalton's expression, which was looking distinctly uncomfortable. She said in a quiet yet urgent tone, "Anthony, I sincerely believe the man responsible for the assaults against you is also—"

"I am not interested in what you believe, I am only concerned with my life and career." Fists clenched by his sides, the controlled icy anger came spitting out of him. "Whatever happens to him is no longer my concern. I refuse to let him destroy my life."

"But you'll let him destroy others?"

"No—*you* let him." The room was suddenly filled with his awful glacial rage, for years bottled up inside, festering.

". . . I don't care about anyone else. If there was a court case, *if*—then I would be forced to relive what that bastard did to me! I would be on trial. My private life now would be made public—I don't want that—I only agreed to see you on the condition you didn't want me to go to court. I won't testify, you can't make me, I'm all right now, I'm all right now . . ." His face crumpled and a strangulated sob came from his chest. "Or I was, I was, before you came, so go away, just go away."

He closed his eyes, his dark brows very vivid against his white face, fists clenched with the knuckles showing through. "Leave me alone . . . please."

Red delved into the rack of evening gowns in the bedroom closet. He lifted one off on its hanger, and lips pursed, head tilted, gave it a critical, searching scrutiny. With a tiny vexed shake of the head he put it back, and chose another. This was fractionally more demure, in midnight blue lace, its upper half studded with diamantes, split up one side as far as the knee. With an approving smile he laid it out on the bed.

He opened a drawer and took out a corset.

Dressed in a silk kimono, Detective Constable Lillie sat before the dressing-table mirror, gazing with interest at the beautiful and expert job Red had done on him. Powdered and rouged, with lipstick, blue eye shadow and false eyelashes, his cheeks seductively shadowed, he was mesmerized by his own gorgeous appearance. He wore a short silvery blond wig, a few artful strands teased over his forehead. He couldn't get over the transformation. It was bloody amazing.

Detective Sergeant Haskons, also made up, was struggling into the corset Red had found for him. His wig, a rich glowing auburn swept up to masses of curls, was on a stand on the dressing table. Red had chosen the midnight blue lacy job for him, while Lillie's was a full-length shimmering lamé dress in puce, set off by a huge flouncy ostrich feather boa in blush pink.

Ray Hebdon stood at the door, observing all this, trying mightily and just failing to hide the glimmer of a smile.

Corset on, Haskons was perspiring as he bent down to try on different pairs of shoes. His square, chunky jaw still showed a trace of blue shaving line even after Red had plastered on dark base and powdered it over four or five times. He was complaining bitterly, already regretting the whole daft episode.

"I still haven't found a pair to fit—or ones that I can even walk in!"

"Cuban will be the easiest. These"—Red pointed down at his own blue satin stilettos, rolling his eyes—"Killers. It's not just the high heels, but the pointed toes." Flawlessly made up, he was done up to the nines in a tight, flesh-colored, sequined evening dress, two long ropes of purple beads hanging down, and matching purple globes dangling from his ears.

"You know it's way after ten," Hebdon said.

"Oh, don't fuss." Red fluttered his hands in a shooing gesture. "Nothing starts until midnight anyway."

Haskons squeezed his toes into a pair of spangled turquoise slippers with square heels and stamped his feet into them.

"My wife's never going to believe this. I told her I was off duty, then I had to tell her I was on; now, after midnight?" He blew out his glossy red lips in annoyance. "It's Friday night!"

Lillie draped the feather boa over his shoulders and preened at himself in the mirror. "You remember that film, *Some Like it Hot*? Jack Lemmon and—"

"Tony Curtis," Red snapped. "It was dreadful! Silly walks—they'd never have got away with it. Anyone could see they weren't female."

Lillie thought this was being pedantic. "That wasn't the point though, was it? It was a comedy."

"Well, for some, dear, being in drag is the only time they feel right," Red told him tartly, smoothing his hands over his hips. He cast a sidelong look at himself in the mirror. "And they very rarely fancy anyone but themselves—it's not funny at all." He arched an eyebrow at Hebdon. "Is it?"

"I wouldn't know," Hebdon said stiffly, and jerked away into the sitting room.

Haskons, feeling as though he had a couple of hairy spiders glued to his eyelids, caught Lillie's warning expression in the dressing-table mirror. Like treading on thin ice, they silently agreed. You had to be careful what you said to people of this persuasion. Touchy, touchy.

The patrol car drove up the corkscrew ramp to the main entrance of the Piccadilly Hotel in the center of Manchester. The plateglass doors whispered open and Tennison and Dalton trudged wearily into the lobby. It was gone 10:30 and they were both thoroughly knackered.

"Do you want to have some dinner?" Dalton asked.

"Thanks, but no, I'll order room service." Tennison summoned up a fleeting smile. "Sorry I've been a bit snappy . . . better when I've had a large whisky and soda."

Dalton looked at his watch. "I'll go and find an all-night chemist. Do you need anything?"

"Oh—toothbrush, toothpaste. Thanks."

She watched him walk back across the lobby and through the doors, and then she asked for her key. She was dead on her feet, yet there remained things to be done. A policewoman's lot is not a happy one, Tennison thought sourly.

Otley sat alone in the viewing room. He had the remote control in one hand, a can of Red Stripe in the other, watching the videotapes of Connie that had been seized from Mark Lewis's studio. A half-eaten ham and pickle sandwich was on the arm of the chair. At this late hour the station was quiet. A vacuum cleaner could be heard from the Squad Room down the corridor, whining in the lower register as it practiced its scales. From somewhere in the vicinity of Regent Street, a police siren wailed off into the distance.

Otley had a house, but not a home, to go back to. If he was there now he'd have been sitting in an armchair, can of beer in hand, watching some old crackly movie on TV, the remains of an Indian take-away in a polystyrene tray at his feet. Same difference. Except here he had a reason and a purpose, or anyway the illusion of having them.

The video was very amateurish. Wobbly camera work, hollow soundtrack, pathetic acting. It was set in a school classroom, half a dozen boys in ties and blazers at old wooden desks, a schoolmaster in mortarboard and gown, wielding a cane. He didn't look like a schoolmaster, more like a barrister, Otley reckoned, or maybe a senior politician. He had snow-white hair and bulging watery eyes with heavy bags, a slightly misshapen nose that looked as if it had been broken when he was a young man, its bulbous end reddened by threadlike blood vessels.

The "schoolmaster" whacked the desk with the cane. "Any boy who disobeys me will be severely punished!" Booming fruity voice, the vowels of the privileged public school class.

Otley zapped back and reran the sequence. Connie was in the front row, looking very innocent in his school blazer and striped tie, his mop of red curls cascading over his forehead. Behind him, and partly hidden, was Billy Matthews. Alan Thorpe, with the ragged blond bangs, was sitting farther back.

"Any boy who disobeys me will be severely punished!"

Otley pressed a button, holding the picture in freeze-frame. He rolled it on, held it on Connie's face. Rolled it on and held it. Billy Matthews. Rolled it on and held it as each of the boys' faces came in view.

There was a quick tread in the corridor and DI Hall poked his head in. "Skipper . . . Billy Matthews."

Otley looked at him in silence. "Is he dead?"

Hall came in, shaking his cropped head. "He's got a bronchial infection. He's back at Charing Cross Hospital where the nurse—real old battle-ax—pointed out they would not or could not take responsibility for him as he persistently discharged himself. Once on the seventeenth, again last night, and . . .'"

Otley gave a snide smile. Hall frowned. "Did you hear what I said?"

On the screen, the "schoolmaster" was standing in front of Connie, hand held out, demanding his homework. Otley's face had the ghost of a smile as he watched it.

He said softly, "Seventeenth? Night Connie died? Right?" He nodded slowly. "Discharged? Discharged himself? What time? So he couldn't have been at the advice centre, yes?" He stuck his thumb up, pointed his index finger at Hall. "Yes! Lovely . . . Edward Parker-Jones was very specific about our Billy."

Otley freeze-framed the picture and pointed. "Alan Thorpe! He was too drunk to remember—so we got to find those other two lads and Jackson's screwed!" He bounced up, clapping his hands. "Fancy a hamburger?"

Hall pulled a long-suffering face. "Hey, come on, Skip. You know what time it is? I came off hours ago . . ."

Otley was bending down, changing the tape. He said cheerfully, "On yer bike, then. See you tomorrow!"

Hall went. Tomorrow was less than an hour away. He speculated idly whether the Skipper curled up in the chair or bedded down on the carpet.

Tennison sat with Detective Chief Inspector David Lyall in the grill room of the Piccadilly Hotel. The excellent dinner they had just consumed was on Tennison's expenses, so Lyall hadn't stinted himself. He didn't stint himself on anything, so far as Tennison could see: prodigious drinker, heavy smoker, and he'd gobbled up the mints that came with the coffee as if frightened they'd melt in front of his eyes.

He was rather handsome in a seedy way, with a fine head of graying hair, but of distinctly disheveled appearance. His dark gray suit was speckled with cigarette ash, his tie pulled loose, shoes scuffed and unpolished, and his fingernails were a disgrace. Tennison wouldn't have cared if he had B.O. and farted like a brontosaurus providing he came up with some answers.

She took a document file from her briefcase. It contained the faxes Otley had dug up on the two boys in the children's homes, Anthony Field and Jason Baldwyn.

"I suggested to Halliday this morning that Operation Contract should be quietly put to bed. You worked on it for six months, didn't you?"

Lyall lit up, nodding through the smoke. "I worked for six months, doing surveillance on all the areas we targeted, right. On the night earmarked for the big swoop, we got no more—less than on a usual busy Friday night."

He had a phlegmy smoker's voice, and she thought she could hear his chest wheezing. Lyall drained his glass of wine. He made a face, but went on to refill it to the rim.

"Don't like the vino . . ." He took a deep slurp and wiped his mouth on the back of his hand. "Anyway, three clubs were empty, apart from the hostesses. Course there was a leak, where the fuck, excuse me, where it came from, inside or out, I honestly can't tell you, and I was"—he elbowed the air—"out faster than a greyhound." He looked moodily at his wine. "I prefer a Scotch."

"Did you target Parker-Jones personally?" Tennison asked.

Lyall chewed on his cigarette, gulping in smoke. He found something on the tablecloth to interest him. "Why do you ask that?"

Tennison tapped the file. "I know it was you sent the faxes to Otley about this case up here and one in Cardiff." She watched him closely.

"Look, I'm going to be honest with you." Tennison automatically took that to mean he was going to lie through his teeth, but DCI Lyall surprised her by reaching into his battered briefcase and putting a thick file down on top of hers. His gruff voice dropped to a growling mutter.

"I photocopied these before I left, just more or less to protect myself, if there was any shit . . ." He gave a half shrug. "Sorry, but I didn't want to shoulder the entire blame, right? There's some kind of cover-up—now, I don't know who it's connected to, and to be honest I don't want to know." He sucked hungrily on his cigarette. "Dig into these. I think it goes way back maybe before me. Halliday's a bit of a puppet." His streaky gray eyebrows went up. "Chiswick pulls the strings."

It only rubber-stamped what she already knew. The warning signs were all over the Soho Vice Division, big as billboards for anyone with eyes to see. "So there is a cover-up," Tennison said, leaning in.

Lyall looked over his shoulder. The fact that the restaurant was almost empty didn't encourage him to say any more. Tennison thought of an inducement that might. She signed the bill, and ten minutes later she was handing him a miniature bottle of Whyte & McKay from the mini bar in her room. Seated in one of the low leather chairs next to the teak table, Lyall accepted it with undisguised relish.

"Ah, that's more like it, ta." He poured the entire contents into his glass. Tennison sat down with her own glass of Scotch, tempered with a little soda. Lyall took a healthy sip and smacked his lips, watching her over his glass.

"I've heard very good things about you. That you're not scared into backing off anything. Well, I am." He wasn't shamed by the admission; a small shrug and that was all. "They'll be demoting lots of us in our rank, and I happen to know there's a Superintendent vacancy coming up. So, you take this." He nodded to the file. "I'm sorry, but I'm lookin' out for my future. This Sheehy inquiry's gonna put the flutter around." He drank, and stared into his glass. "Only ones safe will be those with thirty years' experience. I don't fancy being demoted. Worked hard enough for the DCI rank as it is."

The hard drinking and general scruffiness didn't mean that he wasn't a good copper, Tennison thought. Her gut feeling told her that he was a good 'un. Plus, he wouldn't have been shunted up north if he was a gutless pushover or plain incompetent.

Lyall's head whipped around as someone knocked. Tennison went to the door and opened it. Dalton held out a small plastic bag with a chemist's logo on it.

"One toothbrush, paste—and I thought you might need this." He shook the bag. "It's makeup remover."

"Oh, very thoughtful. How much do I owe you?"

She stepped back to get her purse, pushing the door wider.

"Receipts are in the bag. It's the type my girlfriend uses," Dalton said, pointing to it. He looked up and saw Lyall. "The remover . . ."

Tennison gestured as Lyall rose to his feet. "This is Detective Chief Inspector David Lyall. This is Detective Inspector Brian Dalton."

The two men acknowledged one another from a distance. Tennison counted out change and handed it over. "Your room okay?" She smiled, holding up the bag. "Thanks for this!"

Dalton hovered in the doorway, waiting to be invited in. "Room's fine . . . er . . ." He raised his hand in a little wave. "Nice to meet you."

There was no use waiting, because Tennison closed the door on him. She didn't see Dalton's blink of surprise, though Lyall did. On her return she tossed the bag of toiletries onto the bed. "I didn't expect to stay overnight." She sat down, hands laced around her knees, leaning forward. "There was a leak, wasn't there?"

Lyall's answer was a cool, rather ironic smile.

"How did you get on with Bill Otley?" Tennison asked.

"Good man, one of the old school, hard worker." Lyall drained his glass and set it down. "He tell you that?"

"Yes."

Lyall took out a cigarette. He offered the packet. "You smoke?"

Tennison shook her head, which turned before she knew it into a nod. She took one and accepted a light. Lyall's faint ironic smile was still in place. "I reckon I've done my favor." He tapped the file and got up, holding out his hand. "So, good luck to you."

They shook hands, and Tennison walked him to the door.

"Where, just as a matter of interest, is the vacancy?"

Lyall chuckled throatily. "Want in on the fast track, do you? I'd get your skates on." He prodded her gently on the shoulder. "Area AMIT, one of the eight. Everybody can't go up, but I'm gonna give it my best shot. Good night, love."

Eight Area Major Incident Teams in the London Metropolitan region, but which one? Lyall wasn't saying.

Clutching his battered briefcase under his arm, trailing smoke, he went off. Tennison slipped the chain onto the door. She stood there thoughtfully for a moment, and then went to the phone by the bed and dialed room service.

"Room forty-five. Could I have a pot of coffee and . . . do you have cigarettes?"

She went over to the table and picked up the thick file, holding it in both hands. From experience she knew there was about four hours' solid reading here. She hung her suit jacket over the back of a chair, switched on the free-standing domed lamp, settled herself, and dived in.

The doorman wore a red plush uniform with gold braid epaulettes. Behind him stood two heavyweight characters in white dinner jackets, arms folded in the regulation manner, guarding the elevator entrance to the Bowery Roof Top Club. Looking like a million counterfeit dollars, Red sashayed toward them across the marble-floored lobby, hips swiveling, the purple globes swinging from his ears like miniature golf balls. Haskons and Lillie followed, accompanied by Ray Hebdon, who appeared insignificant and nondescript in his dark suit alongside their plumage and finery.

As one of the Bowery's artistes, Red got the royal treatment. The doorman thumbed the button, the bronze-colored doors slid open, and a moment later the four of them were on their way up to the top floor.

Red adjusted his wig in the smoked glass mirror wall of the elevator. "Well, that part was easy," he breathed in a quivery sigh. He dabbed his shiny nose with a tissue. "Now it's the third degree—I must be out of my mind, I'm sweating."

Inside his tight corset, so was Haskons. He stared at himself in the mirror. All that he recognized were his eyes, gazing back at him in a kind of stricken glazed terror. Completing his midnight-blue ensemble, he wore long satin gloves up to the elbow, with large flashing rings on his gloved fingers. A dinky gold shoulder bag with thin gold straps dangled at his waist. His feet were killing him.

Lillie's face was lost in fluttering ostrich feathers. The rest of him was a shimmering vision in puce lamé, a V-split up the back of the dress almost to his panty line. His short blond wig kept slipping over one eye, and it was the devil's own job trying to tug it straight, the false red nails getting snagged and entangled. Also, he was dying for a piss. He suddenly wondered how, with these bloody pointed nails, he was going to manage that simple act. He might do himself a serious mischief.

"It doesn't stop on any of the other floors," Red said, pointing to the indicator panel.

"I know," Hebdon said, giving him a surly look.

Haskons had already had second thoughts. He was on about his fourth or fifth. "Red—if we want to leave, is this the only way?"

But Red was more preoccupied with the appearance of his two protégés, inspecting them critically, a pat here, a tweak there.

"Well," he observed crisply, an eyebrow raised, "I doubt if you'll pull anything, but that said, I think it's a good job."

"How do we work it then?" Haskons asked, dry-mouthed.

"I won't be on until about twelve-thirty. Then I have another show—at Lola's, two o'clock." He wagged a finger. "But I will need the wigs back, so I've left the main front door key under the old scraper thing . . ."

"Don't you have a spare set?"

"No, I'm not a permanent fixture," Red said tetchily. "But I'm working on it." He groomed himself in the mirror with little fluttery movements, and moistened his lips. "I'm also really nervous. Why I said I'd do this . . ." He shook his head at himself. "Names—what are you calling yourselves? And voices, don't put anything on . . . we don't . . ."

"What you calling yourself?" Haskons asked Lillie.

Red pointed to Haskons. "You be Karen. You . . ." He frowned at Lillie. "Jackie'll do. Remember, this is my life. This gets out, and it won't be worth living. Don't fiddle with the wigs."

The doors opened. Red straightened up, head high, shoulders back.

"Here we go, eyes and teeth, luvvies."

Queenlike, he sailed out into the foyer, Karen and Jackie traipsing behind like two dowager duchesses.

Tennison's resolve had been busted wide open. She was halfway through her second pack already, the room a blue mist of smoke, the ashtray spilling over onto the table. Two silver coffeepots, one empty, one half full but nearly cold, were on the tray with two dirty cups.

Crouched over, a cigarette sticking out of her mouth, she was frowning with concentration as she listened to Connie's voice on the headphones. These were the conversations Jessica Smithy had taped, which Tennison had heard a dozen times before. But in light of the information supplied by DCI Lyall she was hoping desperately to make new connections, ferret out some tiny fact that until now had seemed obscure or unimportant or both.

". . . no, I mean top brass—there's judges, barristers, Members of Parliament." The innocent little voice that had the impervious quality of a six-inch steel nail driven through it. "I know them all, but I'm not stupid, Miss Smithy. I need some guarantee."

Tennison flipped back over several pages of scrawled notes. She searched on the table among the scattered photocopies. Checking, cross-referencing, matching Connie's assertions with the file that Lyall had hoarded and kept locked away as his own insurance. It was here somewhere, she was convinced, in these tapes and documents. The clean, clear, direct line that connected Connie and Vera Reynolds and Mark Lewis and Jimmy Jackson and Edward Parker-Jones and . . . and who else? *Who else?*

Tennison lit a fresh cigarette from the stub of the old one. She leaned forward, eyes shut, listening to that young-innocent-old-cynical voice.

"I got the names of high brass, Miss Smithy, they're all in it. Young boys, kids . . . they only want really young kids."

12

"**B**rian! Have you missed me?"

Arms held wide, fingertips all aquiver, Red floated across the foyer to the handsome receptionist with the slicked-back ponytail and Vandyke beard, gelled to a glistening point.

Red posed before him, one hip thrust out. "Now, I've got one member, this youngster . . ." He indicated Hebdon with a graceful wave of the hand. "And two from Hampstead Garden Suburb." He giggled and fluttered his eyelashes coquettishly. "No, we're old friends . . . is it okay?"

Brian wasn't too sure. He was giving Haskons and Lillie a close, gimlet-eyed examination.

To divert attention, Red was practically doing his stage act right there in the foyer. Twirling around, high-pitched to the point of hysteria, he squealed to Hebdon, "Show your member, darling." He leaned forward over the desk, trying to cover his jangling nerves with a breathily confidential whisper.

"Now, I know this is naughty, but these are very old friends of mine. And, Brian, daahhhling, we've only got one member!" He rolled his eyes theatrically under azure lids. "Oh, I'm so tired of that gag."

"Members sign," Brian said, handing the pen to Hebdon. He stared hard at Haskons and Lillie, who were hanging back, attempting to merge into the wallpaper. "Are they for the cabaret?"

Red let out a little trill of amusement. "No, dear, but they just want to learn from me! Don't they all? You remember that bitch that came up with me a few months ago—she's only ripped off my act!"

Brian checked Hebdon's signature against his membership file on the computer screen. He gestured the party to go through, but he still needed some convincing about Karen and Jackie. His eyes never left them. "There's no table free, not until after one, but there's a booth, far side."

Red linked arms with Haskons, sweeping him on, and ushered Lillie quickly forward. "Booth will be fine, we're not staying long, just until my act's over . . ."

He pushed the two of them on ahead, toward a doorway swathed in red velvet, and leaned back to Brian.

"Anybody in I should know about? Film producers? Casting agents? I need exposure." Brian shook his head. "Back room busy?" asked Red, but Brian's attention had switched to some new arrivals emerging from the elevator.

Haskons and Lillie stood just inside the red velvet curtain. The club was dark and smoky, and Haskons was having trouble with his false eyelashes. He had to keep looking down, about three feet in front of him, to see where he was treading as Red led them past the crowded tables and up a short flight of steps to a small balcony on the left-hand side of the stage, which at the moment was empty. The cabaret was due to start in a few minutes.

Haskons was half blind, but Lillie was taking it all in. The clientele was certainly an exotic mixture. The bar area, to the rear of the club, was favored by groups of elderly, distinguished men, most in lounge suits, but a few in evening dress. Ostensibly chatting with their cronies, Lillie could see them casting glances to the tables in front of the stage. This was the unofficial "stage show," where the young boys sat with their companions and the transvestites congregated, drinking champagne and shrieking with laughter. The butch boys wore white T-shirts and leathers, one or two in Marlon Brando leather caps. The more overtly gay were elegantly dressed in velvet jackets and frilly shirts, long shiny hair draping their shoulders in the style of Lord Alfred Douglas, Oscar Wilde's bosom chum.

The transvestites and transexuals were fabulous creatures. Lillie felt dowdy by comparison. All, without exception, were tall and willowy, with masses of either blond or red hair tumbling down. They wore glittery evening gowns slashed low to reveal shaved chests and the sensuous slant of their backs, curving to tiny waists and slender, nonwomanly hips. The makeup of each one was in itself a work of art. Lillie, contrary to what he had expected, was fascinated rather than repulsed. It wasn't in the least a threatening experience, just endlessly engrossing.

Having got them seated, Red went off on a circular tour, flitting like a vivacious gadfly from one group to another. Vera Reynolds had seen Red come in with the others. Furiously, she tried to attract Red's attention. What the hell was the stupid bitch playing at? The management weren't thick. They'd have a blue fit when they found out—as they soon would—that the fuzz was around. And not only would the management find out; that was the least of it. Vera's blood ran cold when she thought of the consequences of what the crazy queen had done, bringing them in here.

It was Vera's spot any moment now, and she only had time for a quick, explosive word in Red's startled ear as she headed backstage to prepare for her act.

Hebdon brought drinks to the table. Luridly colored cocktails in long-stemmed glasses. Haskons had all but given up trying to peer into the gloomy depths of the club. "I can hardly see myself, never mind clock any faces," he complained morosely. The blue shadow on his square jaw was even more evident now. He had the horrible feeling that the straps in his corset had gone. Would this fucking living nightmare never end?

Finger extended, Lillie took a dainty sip of his drink. "How much did these set you back?"

"A lot—buy a bottle for the price of one," Hebdon replied. "Knock 'em back, you both look like you need something . . ." He turned his head. "Here's Red now."

Red leaned over the table, his eyes hot and agitated. Vera's word in his ear had got him seriously rattled. "I've not much time before I'm on, so let's make it snappy." Haskons and Lillie started to rise.

"One at a time," Red hissed. He cast a nervous glance to the private members' bar behind the curtained door. "I don't know if I can get you in the back bar, it's jammed in there. Maybe you can work it yourself."

Haskons and Lillie stared miserably after him as he went off. Left to their own devices, their chances of getting in there were zilch.

Two spotlights stabbed through the smoke, and there was a spattering of applause as the compere came on, a comically stocky figure in a leather bomber jacket and leather pants cut off to reveal fat, hairy calves. He grabbed the mike off its stand.

"It's cabaret time! And we have a great favorite, a truly beautiful, talented act. Please welcome—Vera Reynolds!"

Taped music started up. A twenties-style dance orchestra with muted cornets and plunkety percussion. Vera's tall, lithe figure glided on, clad in a high-necked flesh-colored costume speckled with sequins, the spotlight making a dazzling halo of her platinum-blond wig. Her red-tipped fingers caressed the microphone suggestively.

"I wanna be loved by you, just you, and nobody else but you . . ."

The breathy voice was uncanny, the luscious pouting lips a perfect replica. It was Marilyn to the life.

Thinking of Jack Lemmon and Tony Curtis, alias Karen and Jackie, Haskons kicked Lillie under the table. "Well, we got the whole cast now!"

"I wanna be loved by you alone . . . boo-boo-bee-doo . . ."

Down by Waterloo Bridge, Otley was on his own private one-man patrol. He'd had no luck in the Bullring, drawn a blank at St. Margaret's Crypt. At the hamburger stall, in the shadow of the iron trelliswork, he caught up with Alan Thorpe. The boy was sullen and uncooperative. Otley didn't blame him. These kids lived on a knife edge. As young as fourteen and fifteen, they had to fend for themselves, keep body and soul together, survive in a hostile, uncaring environment.

"I just want to buy you somethin' to eat. Have a talk, Alan."

Otley put his hand on the boy's shoulder, as much to reassure him as restrain him.

"Leave me alone!" Alan squirmed away. He pointed to his right eye, puffy and shiny purple. "I got this 'cos I talked to you before!"

"Nasty," Otley said. "So who did that to you, then?"

"It's always questions wiv you, innit?"

"You want a hamburger or not?"

Alan jerked his thumb to the group around the smoldering fire. "What about me mates?"

"You hungry?" Otley called to them. He put a tenner on the counter.

Alan Thorpe stared down at the cindery ground. He said bitterly, "Jackson done me, Sarge. Okay?"

Vera came storming into the dressing room. She tore off her wig and flung it down among the pots of cream, tubes of glue, foams and sprays. "Are you crazy? Why?" She thumped Red in the chest, hard. "Why did you do it?"

"Because they asked me to!"

"Well, I'm out of here—and if you'd got any sense you'd leave too."

"But you've got another spot—"

"You do it!" Vera was throwing her makeup into her vanity case.

"But I haven't done my own yet!" Red protested.

"They stick out like a sore thumb," Vera snorted, grabbing her wigs off their stands and ramming them into plastic bags.

"They don't . . ." Red said uncertainly.

"*Yes they do!*" Vera turned on him in fury, arm outstretched, pointing. "They're asking everybody bloody questions! That's why I clocked them." Her lips thinned. Her eyes were large and fearful. "You don't know, you just don't know . . ."

Red lowered his voice to a husky whisper. "About Connie—yes, I know, that's why they're here. I wanted to help. I thought you cared. Somebody killed him, you know it, I know it." He was on the verge of tears. "Well, you might be able to stomach what goes on . . ."

"*Me?!*" Vera shrieked. "You live with that slime-bag, Mark Lewis, not me! I have never been involved in it all, I've never wanted to know." She wrenched her outdoor coat off the hanger and dragged it on over her dress.

Red gripped her arm. "But you are involved, aren't you?" His tone was low and venomous. "You lied to me. I covered up for you. But this other stuff with the kids and Jackson . . ." He shook his head in disgust.

Vera pulled her arm free, struggling into her coat. "I am shacking up at his place because I got nowhere else." The mask slipped, and behind it was a trembling, abject creature terrified half out of her wits. "He won't leave me alone until this all blows over, and now you've gone and got the cops in here." Vera said hoarsely, "He'll think I done it—not you—me!"

The door was pushed open and Brian, the receptionist, came in. Vera slammed her vanity case shut, picked up her wig box, and barged past him into the corridor. Brian yelled after her.

"You've got another spot, Vera!"

"I'll do it." Red was sitting at the dressing table, shoulders slumped, toying with a hairbrush.

Brian leaned on the back of the chair, looking at Red in the mirror. "Those two queens—I've just had a complaint. They'll have to go."

Red sighed heavily and started powdering his face. "Oh, all right, I'll come clean. I don't know them. They latched onto me at Lola's club, gave me a few quid to get them in." He met Brian's accusing stare in the mirror. "It's the truth, I swear before God! Now can I have some privacy—my tits need readjusting!"

A chill wind with a flurry of drizzle hit Vera in the face as she stepped into the street. She blinked, looked quickly up and down, and set off at a trot. The blue Mercedes ghosted around the corner behind her, with just its sidelights on. Vera started to run, hampered by the small cases she was carrying. The Mercedes speeded up, Jackson's head sticking out of the window.

"Hey! YOU! Vera!"

Vera kept running. The Mercedes came alongside and mounted the pavement. Its brakes squealed, and Jackson was out, pinning her against the wall, his hand gripping her by the throat.

"I've bloody protected you, slag, and you . . ." He gave her a stinging slap with the flat of his hand. "You bring the filth to the house!" He slapped her again, back of the hand. She felt his ring snag her cheek. "Why did you do that, Vera?" Jackson snarled, fingers digging into her throat, forcing her head up.

"*It wasn't me.* I swear before God, Jimmy, it wasn't me." Vera was gasping and choking, spittle running down her chin. "I wouldn't, would I, I wouldn't . . ."

Jackson eased back, releasing his grip. "What?"

Vera massaged her throat, trying to calm him, talk him down.

"I need you, why would I tip off the law about you?"

"Who is it to do with, then, Vera?" He gathered the front of her coat in his bunched fist and drew her closer. "Is it Red? How much does he know?" He shook her. "Where's Red? Eh? *Eh?*"

It came out in a gabble. "I dunno, she's not on tonight, she had a cold. She's stayin' at Mark Lewis's." Vera let out a long quivering moan. "It's the truth, Jimmy, honestly . . . that's how she knows everything."

Jackson looked back along the street. A taxi was standing outside the wrought iron, glass-domed entrance to the club. Two figures came out, tripping across the pavement in their high heels, hurrying to avoid the thickening rain. One of them wore a red wig. They climbed in.

Jackson let go of Vera. She dodged past him, staggering in a blind panic, banging into the wall.

Half-stunned, she heard the car door slam. Jackson drove off the pavement and did a U-turn, blue exhaust fumes billowing up. Vera leaned her head against the wall, watching his taillights disappear, feeling the trickle of blood on her cheek.

Otley had gone the whole hog and taken the lot of them to a greasy spoon diner two blocks along from Waterloo Station. Leading the ragged-arsed, snot-nosed, filthy, stinking tribe in, he felt like Fagin, devious mastermind of London's poor dispossessed youngsters, the forgotten underclass.

Alan Thorpe he knew well, most of the others he knew by sight. He made it his business to put names to faces. Tennison might have muscled in on his graft in uncovering the kids in Manchester and Cardiff, but Otley was confident that there was more than one way of skinning a cat. This sorry, scurvy bunch held the key. Otley was about to turn it.

He bought burgers and fries all around, with plenty of Cokes, milk shakes, and tea to wash them down. They occupied two tables, set at right angles, in a corner next to the steamy window. He told them to keep the noise down, but with food inside them, fags lit, they were a rowdy, foul-mouthed lot. More than once, Otley saw the manageress casting a disapproving look to their corner. But with their bellies full, he'd got them relaxed, got them talking, and the last thing he wanted was to start throwing his weight around by showing his I.D. So he held tight, hoping there wouldn't be trouble.

Otley reared back, hands raised defensively, as another kid sidled in and sat down.

"Hey, what is this! Think I'm made of money, do you?" The kid's two grimy fists rested on the scratched Formica table. "S'okay—here!" Otley tossed a fiver. "Get what you want, and a cuppa for me."

The kid, whose name was Frankie, scurried off to the counter like a starving rat.

Alan Thorpe went on with his tale. "So how it works—he, Jackson, picks yer up from the station, right?" He squinted up at Otley with his one good eye. "Wiv me? An' that 'ouse—one you was at—he takes us there, like, an' he—"

"He never done me!" Disco Driscoll boasted, tapping his chest. He looked about twelve but was possibly fourteen, a half-caste kid in a torn green baseball jacket. Filthy matted hair hanging over his eyes, mouth smeared with ketchup. "I got me own gaff!"

"No, you 'aven't, yer fuckin' liar!" Thorpe shot back.

Otley half-covered his face, looking over his hand at the other customers. It was after one in the morning, but it was still pretty busy, with overspill trade from the station.

"I'm not," Driscoll said, pulling a face. He turned to Otley, and said fiercely, as if it was a matter of real pride, "He done 'em all, but he ain't done me, he done 'em all." He gave a defiant nod.

A pug-nosed boy named Gary Rutter said, "He keeps yer there, like, gives yer stuff. He gives yer gear, so, like, yer don't mind stayin'—know what I mean?"

Frankie returned from the counter with a cheeseburger and fries, a raspberry milk shake for himself and tea for Otley, slopped over into the thick saucer. He plonked the change down onto the greasy table, strewn with mashed chips and ketchup.

"The woman behind the counter said you can't take the cup out, and that you're a pervert!" he chortled, giving Otley a gap-toothed grin.

"Know what that means, do you?" Otley asked Frankie.

"Him? He don't know nuffink," Alan Thorpe said derisively.

A middle-aged man and woman got up from a nearby table and went out, muttering darkly and shaking their heads. Otley huddled over the table, keeping his voice low.

"Did you all know Connie?"

"Nah, we don't know him—pervert!" Alan Thorpe jeered.

Otley cuffed him lightly on the back of the head. "You know what pervert is—I've seen you in a film with Connie . . ."

Alan Thorpe went a mottled pink as the table erupted with raucous laughter. Hooting loudly, the lads started throwing chips at him.

"He's a pervert, he's a pervert!" Frankie chanted.

Incensed, Alan Thorpe reached over and belted Frankie on the side of the head. It was getting out of hand. Otley waved his arms.

"Come-on-now! Cut it out, or we'll be thrown out."

Alan Thorpe wasn't through. He swung another punch at Frankie, then grabbed a fork and tried to stab him with it.

Otley pushed him down, fingers splayed against the bony chest, and slumped back into his own seat. "What am I?" he asked wearily. "The pied piper?"

Lillie turned the key in the front door and let himself into the gloomy passageway leading up to Mark Lewis's flat. He passed the key back to Haskons, who slid it into its hiding place under the outdoor rubber mat.

Across the street, Jackson drew up, and killed the lights. He saw the shadowy figure in the dress and red wig stooping to replace the key. So Red was sick, was he? Too ill to do his act. That bitch Vera had lied again. It was all fucking lies.

In the dim streetlight he watched the figure straighten up and totter inside, lifting the hem of his dress. The door closed. Jackson patted the pocket of his leather coat, just to reassure himself. A light went on in the flat above. Jackson lifted the handle and the door clicked open.

The manageress had the phone in her hand. She peered around from the kitchen doorway, keeping a beady disapproving eye on the gang in the corner. Ten of them now, not including the bloke, flocking in like wasps around a honey pot. She set her jaw and started to dial.

Fag in his mouth, Alan Thorpe was on a boasting streak. Not yet fifteen, he was a forty-a-day lad, when he had the money.

"I done arson, robbery, indecent assault and . . ." He frowned into space. "Can't remember the other, I got four though," he bragged.

Otley needled him. "Not as many as Connie."

"Connie? Huh! All he ever done was dirty old men."

"That wasn't what I heard."

"When he lived at Jackson's he went out more'n any of us," Alan Thorpe confided, looking up through his fair lashes. "He liked it."

"That's true, that's true," Disco Driscoll said. Probably high on lighter fuel or something, Otley suspected, which accounted for his slurred, rapid speech. "That's true—he went for whole weekends, didn't he?"

"Yeah! That film I did was nuffink!" Alan Thorpe stubbed out his cigarette on a paper plate and stuck it upright in the sugar bowl. "I just got me arse tanned—me dad gimme worse. Connie was doin' the nobs."

The heads around the table nodded. Connie had been chosen for better things, moved in higher circles. Several of them—Thorpe, Disco Driscoll, Kenny Lloyd, Gary Rutter, Frankie Smith—at one time or another had served time at Jackson's place, observed Connie's comings and goings. None of them liked him, stuck-up little poofter.

Disco Driscoll fixed blurred eyes on Otley. "He wasn't like us, different you know, always sniffin' around, lookin' for fresh meat, I reckon he got a back hander. . . ." He tilted his matted head, seeking Otley's ear. "You know Billy OK Matthews? Well, when he first came up, he was, what . . . ?" He looked to Alan Thorpe. "Ten? Yeah, he'd be about ten. His mother's bloke raped him, so he's a bit—you know." Driscoll screwed his finger into his head. "Connie nabbed Billy fast, didn't he?" he said, gazing blearily at the others.

"You think Connie was paid for finding young kids then?" Otley said casually. Inside, he felt the opposite of casual. His nose twitched. He could almost smell it, he was that close. He'd got their confidence, and they were spilling the lot, only they didn't know it. To them it was just shop talk.

Alan Thorpe nodded, lighting another cigarette. He sucked in the smoke like a seasoned professional, which was what he was. "Yeah, for the films like . . ."

"Who was the bloke in the mortarboard?"

"The what?" Kenny Lloyd said, sniffing up a greenish candle drip from the end of his nose.

"The gown," Otley said, plucking at the lapels of his raincoat. "He had a cane."

Kenny despised them, and his pale young face showed it, mouth twisted. "He's a pervert, they're all perverts. Big posh 'ouses, lotta dough—dirty bastards!"

Otley's heart was trip-hammering. He kept his eyes hooded as he looked around at them, shaking his head disbelievingly, grinning his snide skeptical grin.

"You scruffy buggers were never taken to posh houses—who you kiddin'?"

Haskons knelt on the mat, leaning into the bath, soaping his face and hair. The shower curtain hung down, obscuring his upper body. The red wig was balanced on the edge of the washbasin, a bedraggled ferret of a thing after Haskons had sweated into it all night. He still wore his dress, open down the back, the half undone corset straining at its straps.

He groped for the shower head on its flexible stem. The water was too hot. Blindly, he spun the taps, adjusting the mixture. The water hissed out and gurgled down the drain, covering the creak of the door as Jackson came in sideways, bringing his hand out of his pocket, the click as the knife sprang open also lost in the hissing and gurgling, and in Haskons's grunt as he bowed his head into the bath.

Slowly, Jackson reached out to the plastic curtain. Drag it down over the bitch. Wrap it around her and in with the knife, clean and neat and quick. His fingers gripped the edge of the curtain. The plastic rings clinked and jostled on the rod.

Haskons raised his head, soapy water running down his face. "Can you untie the ruddy corset strings! I can't get it off . . ."

He heard the plastic rings clash and ping as Jackson tore the curtain off the rod. Blinking wildly, trying to clear the soap from his eyes, Haskons saw the gleaming blade. He twisted his body, half leaning into the bath, his feet churning at the mat as he tried desperately to get out of this exposed and vulnerable position. From the corner of his eye he saw the blade swoop. Tensing his body against the impact, he swung out his right arm in a helpless reflex action, and in the next instant had the breath knocked from his body as Lillie hurled himself at Jackson. Tangled together, the three of them crashed to the tiled floor between the bath and the washbasin.

Lillie had hold of Jackson's knife arm, but he wouldn't let go. Haskons struggled to get up, feet slithering. He grabbed out for support, hitting the shower head, which spun around, spraying water everywhere.

Lillie got a handful of Jackson's hair and held him still while he punched him in the face, really laying into him. Jackson bucked and squirmed, boots flying. Lillie hit him again. "Drop it!" A boot whacked into Lillie's ribs, making him gasp. "Get the bastard's legs!" he yelled at Haskons.

Together they pinned Jackson to the floor, Haskons hanging on to his legs. Jackson tore his head free from Lillie's grasp and butted him in the face, making blood spurt. This made Lillie mad. He cracked Jackson across the mouth. He dug his thumbs into Jackson's wrist, jerked it viciously, and the knife went skittering away. This time he got two handfuls of hair and banged Jackson's head against the tiled floor. Then for good measure smacked it sideways into the washbasin pedestal. This seemed to work, so he did it again, twice more.

"That's enough," Haskons panted in his ear. Lillie did it again.

"HEY—THAT'S ENOUGH! Get off him!"

"It's my blood," Lillie said. He was trembling all over. He still had Jackson's spiked greasy hair entwined in his white-knuckled fists. "And I'm not gettin' off him," he snarled. "Tie his legs."

Otley wasn't altogether surprised when, behind Disco Driscoll's tousled head, he saw the red and blue stripe of a Panda car sliding in, its blue light casting a ghostly aura through the steamy window.

They all trooped out, Otley leading the way, and stood on the wet pavement, the lads jostling one another and sniggering. The two uniformed PCs were from south of the river; they didn't know Otley, and he didn't know them. He took one of them aside and produced his I.D. The other policeman, barely out of his teens himself, kept watch on the motley bunch of giggling boys.

Alan Thorpe grinned up at him insolently, nodding toward Otley. "He's a copper, you stupid git!" The lads hooted, loving it.

The young policeman made a grab at him.

"Leave him alone, he's with me," Otley said, coming over.

"See, what did I tell you?" Thorpe chortled, and gave the young PC the finger.

Otley beckoned. Alan Thorpe and Kenny Lloyd followed him a few paces. "You two want a ride around in a Panda? Take me to that posh house? Yeah?" He slid his hand inside his jacket. "Tenner in it—what d'you say?"

The two lads exchanged looks. Thorpe nodded. "Okay."

They had only a hazy idea of where the house was—"Somewhere just off the Heath," according to Kenny. With the two uniformed officers in front, Otley and the boys crammed in the back, they drove up through Highgate and circled the northeast fringe of Hampstead Heath. Up here, the large detached houses stood safe and secure behind tall hedges and wrought-iron fences. The red ruby eye of a burglar alarm glowed from each one. When they'd covered Cranley Gardens, Muswell Hill, and Aylmer Road north of the golf course, Otley was growing impatient. "Now, come on, this is the fifth road. Is it here or not?"

The Panda car turned into a secluded tree-lined avenue, and Alan Thorpe sat forward and pointed. "That's the one—'as it got a big double front door with stone animals? Connie said they was lions."

The house was set back behind a thick hedge of trimmed conifers. It had a steeply gabled roof and white-leaded windows. The house itself was in darkness, but the frosted globe of a security light shone down on the gravel driveway.

The older of the two policemen got out to take a look. He peered in through the gates, saw the studded double doors and the two lions flanking it, and nodded back to the car.

Otley grinned and ruffled Alan Thorpe's hair. "Good boy . . . remember any more?"

The policeman came back and leaned in the window. He was shaking his head. "I think the lad is pulling your leg, Sarge! This is Assistant Deputy Commissioner Kennington's home."

Otley slowly sat back, staring out, pinching his nose.

13

Tennison had phoned ahead and there was a car waiting to meet her and Dalton at Cardiff Station. The driver was a young WPC, Bronwen Webb, who'd dug Jason Baldwyn's file out of Records. Tennison skimmed through it while they drove to the estate.

It was a dismal day, an unbroken sheet of murky cloud scudding in from the Severn Estuary. What with the late night and the early call at six-thirty, Tennison wasn't feeling her best. Her first sight of the estate did nothing to lighten her mood. It was a huge gray barracklike place, ten-story tower blocks with balconies and drafty walkways. Some humorist had named the bleak crescents after trees: Sycamore, Birch, Cedar, Oak. Much of it was boarded up, graffiti everywhere, gutters choked with uncollected rubbish. Wrecked cars rested on their axles, leaking pools of oil. Tennison gazed out on the depressing scene, feeling more depressed by the minute. Welcome to the armpit of the universe.

The car stopped outside a tower block, and she sat there for a minute, summoning up the resolve to move. Dalton was reading the file, quizzing Bronwen about Jason.

"You say he's known to the locals?"

Bronwen unfastened her seat belt and half-turned, leaning on her elbow. "He's more than known—he spends more time in the cells than out!" There was only a trace of the singsong Welsh accent. She gave a little resigned shrug. "He's a nice enough bloke when he's sober, but he's a nightmare when he's not. Been had up for assault, petty crimes. Has a lot of marital troubles—she's always calling us in, but then withdraws the charges."

Bronwen's eyes widened, as if to say, *What can you do?*

She got out and went to open the rear door just as Tennison's phone beeped. Bronwen stood with Dalton on the crumbling pavement while Tennison spoke to Halliday. The driver's window was open an inch, and Dalton tried to listen in, none too successfully, except it was apparent that the Super was giving her one hell of an earful.

Tennison was nodding, trying to get a word in edgeways.

"I can't really do anything about it from here, Guv . . ." More nodding as she looked out at the estate. "Yes. Well, as I just said, I can't do anything right now, hopefully by twelve, yes . . ."

She finished the call and zapped the aerial back in with a vengeance. She got her briefcase and pushed the door slightly open with her foot. She looked at Dalton. He didn't get the coded message, and it was Bronwen who jumped to it, sweeping the door wide for the Detective Chief Inspector to get out.

Belatedly, Dalton tried to assist. Tennison buttoned her raincoat and glowered around. Dalton looked at her expectantly.

"The bad news is not worth discussing, Haskons and Lillie got themselves dragged up." Dalton's jaw dropped. "*Don't* even ask. But the good news is, they brought in Jackson, and this time we can hold," she said with grim satisfaction.

"You serious, they got dragged up?" Dalton said with the glimmering of a smile.

Tennison was not amused. "I said I don't want to talk about it. But we've also another alibi down. Driscoll this time!" She seemed more ferocious than triumphant. "He's admitted he lied because Jackson threatened to beat him up." She turned to Bronwen, waiting patiently. "Thank you. It's number—what?"

"Sixty-three." Bronwen pointed up to the third-floor balcony. It was reached by a concrete walkway that zigzagged several times, so you had to walk five times the distance to get where you were going.

"Do you want me to come up with you?" Bronwen asked. "It's a bit of a warren in there."

"No, thanks. Judging by the look of the place, you'd best stay with the car." She gave a nod, squared her shoulders, and set off with Dalton up the ramp. "Jackson physically assaulted Lillie and Haskons, and Larry Hall, all in one night." She stumped upward, eyes fixed straight in front of her. "Just let that oily little brief try for bail . . . !"

Dalton didn't know what effect Tennison had on suspects, but in this kind of storming mood she scared the shit out of him.

The girl who let them in—not more than eighteen—had a baby in a shirt but no diaper balanced on her hip, and she was about seven months pregnant with the next one. She had a hollow-cheeked wasted look and lackluster eyes. She led them through the tiny hallway, where they had to squeeze past a pram, into the living room. It was oppressively hot, with the close dank smell that comes from clothes drying in a sealed room. The source was woolen baby clothes steaming gently on a wooden frame in front of a gas fire that was going full blast. Fluffy toys and plastic building bricks were strewn everywhere, along with empty beer cans and dirty cups and plates, strategically located to make it odds on that you'd step onto or into something. The few sticks of furniture looked like the remnants of a car trunk sale on a bad day.

Jason came in from the kitchen. He was tall and very thin, with straggling hippie-length hair, and to Tennison's consternation he was exceptionally good-looking. Over ragged blue jeans he wore a striped pajama top. The buttons were missing, showing his ribs and flat, fish-white belly. He was barefoot, the nails long and curved, grime between his toes.

"She's no need to be in on this."

"Not unless you want her to be," Tennison agreed.

Jason jerked his head. "Go on."

The girl went out with the baby. Jason heeled the door shut.

"I'm Jane Tennison, and this is Brian Dalton. Can we sit down?"

"Sure. Sorry about the mess." He pushed both hands up into his hair and flung his head back.

Tennison sat down in the lumpy armchair, shifting to avoid the spring. Dalton chose a hard-backed chair, well away from the fire. Jason semireclined on the arm of the settee, one knee pulled up to his chin. "You want tea or . . . ?"

"No, thanks," Tennison said politely. That was the second surprise. He had a lazy, low-pitched voice, easy to listen to. What had she been expecting? she asked herself. Grunts and slobbering growls? She glanced at Dalton, making sure he was taking notes, and smiled at Jason. "So, where do you want to begin?" He was studying his thumbnail. "You're from Liverpool originally, aren't you? How old were you when you went into the home?"

"Which one?"

"The home run by Mr. Edward Parker."

"Ten." Jason flicked away something he'd found under his thumbnail. "I was sent there from a foster home. I got into a bit of thieving, so they got shot of me."

"Would you be prepared to act as a witness for the prosecution?"

"Sure." Jason twitched his thin shoulders in a listless shrug.

"Would you tell me when the sexual abuse started?"

His eyes flicked toward her, and quickly away. He had thick, dark lashes any woman would have been proud of. And any woman would have fallen for the full-lipped mouth with a slightly sullen droop to it.

"Second or third day I was there, Parker just called me into his office and that was it . . . started then. And you couldn't say anything, or do anything about it—like he was a law unto himself. And it wasn't just me, he was having us all. He'd give you a certain amount of fags, like five say, for a blow job. Always knew when one of the kids had gone the whole way with him, they were flush with fags. Have you got one, by the way?"

Tennison reached into her briefcase. "I have, as a matter of fact. Here, keep the packet, I've given up."

Jason uncoiled from the arm of the settee and knelt down to get a light from the gas fire. Tennison rummaged for matches, but he was already lit up. He stayed where he was, long legs stretched out on the tatty hearth rug. The pose was overtly sexual, the pajama top falling open, the tight jeans displaying the bulge at his crotch. It made Tennison unsure whether he was behaving naturally, unself-consciously, or trying it on, deriving some secret amusement from the situation. He was a very disconcerting young man.

"I'm grateful that you're being so frank with us," Tennison said. The heat of the closed room was making her perspire, and she was sorry she hadn't taken off her raincoat when she came in. Now didn't seem the right time.

"No other way to be, really, is there?" he said, dribbling tiny puffs of smoke from his mouth.

"What made you report him?"

"He shortchanged me on some fags, so I thought—screw him. So I went to the probation officer. Stupid bitch, I think she fancied him—he used to get it off with women, too. Anyway," Jason said in a long sigh, "she went on and on at me, did I know what I was saying, what it meant? I said, 'Oh yeah, you know what it fuckin' means to me?' I said, 'If you don't do something, I'll go to the cops.'"

"And how old were you?"

"Twelve or thirteen."

"And did you go to the cops?"

"Yeah . . ." Jason rolled onto his stomach, flicking ash onto the carpet. "Well, he wouldn't leave me alone, and she wasn't doing anything about it. So I went to the police station, made a statement, and then—sort of everybody run around, like, asking me all these questions. Then a doctor examined me, and . . ." He dragged deeply, letting the smoke trickle out. "Oh, yeah. This copper. He gets me into his office."

"And?" Tennison leaned forward. "What happened then, Jason?"

"He said that if I said I was lying, that he would make sure I had it cushy—you know, money, cigarettes. Things like that. And that they'd move me—somewhere nice."

He shook his hair back and looked up at her. He had beautiful eyes, but their expression was opaque, a deadness deep down.

"Do you remember this police officer's name?" Tennison asked quietly. "Was he wearing a uniform?"

"Nah! He was a friend of Parker's. They worked it between them." His tone was dismissive. That's how the world operated. Those with power and influence dumped on the great unwashed below. Fact of life. "So they sent me back," he went on, and laughed without humor. "They never got around to moving me, and I became a very heavy smoker."

Jason took a last drag and stubbed out the cigarette on the tiled hearth. He sat up and favored Tennison with a sunny, beaming smile.

"That's it."

Tennison nodded. "Do you remember the name of the doctor? The one that examined you?"

"Be no help if I did. He died of cancer, nice guy. Think his name was something Ellis."

Dalton made a note.

Tennison said, "Was it all the boys, Jason? Or specifically the very young ones?"

"The little 'uns, he liked the little ones."

"Do you have a job?"

"Nope. No qualifications. A five-year-old kid reads better than me. I do odd jobs around the place, fix up cars." He smiled in a simple, childlike way. "I get drunk, and sometimes I get angry."

"And then you get into trouble?" Tennison hesitated. "Have you ever told somebody about your past, Jason?"

"There's no point." Again the offhand dismissal. "I just have to live with it."

Tennison fastened her briefcase and sat with it across her knees, her hands gripping the sides. She said softly, "I will do everything possible to put this man away. I promise you."

Jason stared at her, as if she might possibly mean it, and then he laughed harshly. "You haven't even got him, have you?"

She couldn't find it in her heart to lie to him. She shook her head, and Jason laughed again, harsh and angry.

He led them out, past the pram in the hallway, and stood on the concrete balcony in his bare feet. A short flight of steps led down to the walkway, littered with broken bottles and crushed beer cans. The breeze ruffled Jason's pajama top. A change had come over him. He followed after them, speaking in a mechanical monotone, telling them a tale, his breathing rapid.

"One night at the home we was watching a documentary, Nazi thing. This guy ran a concentration camp, you know what they are?"

Tennison and Dalton had paused to listen. They both nodded.

Jason leaned back, his shoulder blades pressed against the concrete wall. "Yeah, well, this guy was called the 'Angel of Death,' right? And after the war, he escaped, right? He was never hanged, nobody arrested him, nobody brought him to trial . . ." He gave a peculiar croaking giggle. "Just like Parker. He did me for eight years, he did every boy in his care. You know what we used to call him? We called him 'The Keeper of Souls.'" He grinned down at them.

Tennison put her hand out. "Go back up the stairs, Jason. There's glass on the stairs, you'll hurt yourself . . ."

Jason's fingers tore at the pajama top. He ripped it off and flung it down the stairs. "You want to see what the 'Keeper' did to me?"

He staggered down the steps toward Tennison. Dalton tensed, about to dive up, thinking he was about to attack her. But Jason turned around, showing the pale scars on his skinny back. Tennison touched his shoulder, and moved her hand gently down the hard ridges of puckered flesh. "I will make him pay, Jason, I promise you . . ."

Jason slowly turned, and Tennison could barely tolerate the terrible desolate anguish in his eyes. The buried pain, the torment of those years, was even worse than the horrible scars. His lips trembled, but he couldn't speak. He bowed his head and nodded mutely, his hair hanging down over his bare white shoulders.

Tennison went down. Hunched inside, her throat dry and tight, she heard his agonized whisper, swirled by the breeze down the concrete stairwell. *"Keeper of Souls . . . Keeper of Souls."*

Bronwen stood by the car, the rear door open. "We'll only just make your train."

Drained of all energy, Tennison tossed her briefcase inside. She turned, holding the door, taking one last look back at the godforsaken place. She clutched her throat. Jason was balanced on the edge of the balcony. His arms were spread wide, exposing his ribcage, the narrow chest. He swayed forward.

"Jason! No!" Tennison's cry was shrill, almost a screech. *"NO!"*

He fell, a pale blur, turning over in the air, and they heard his body hit the ground, a soft moist sound, hidden behind a concrete parapet. Dalton raced forward across the scrubby patch of mud and scrambled over the wall. Tennison, in her heeled boots, struggled up the slope. She gripped the wall and craned to see over. Dalton was kneeling by the crumpled body, feeling for his pulse. He lifted the eyelids, searching for a reflex. Very gently he cupped Jason's head in his hands, and looked toward Tennison.

Badly hurt, but he wasn't dead, Tennison knew that, because the boy was weeping. She could see the tears streaming down his cheeks from his closed eyes.

She closed her own eyes and rested her forehead against the rough gray concrete. Tears smarted her eyes, but she wouldn't cry. She refused to cry. She held on to the emotion, hoarding it, needing it like a fix, feeding her the strength for what she had to do.

Tennison sat at one of the three computer consoles in the Records Department of Cardiff Police Station. It was 12:35 P.M., and the train had long gone. Bronwen stood with arms folded, looking over her shoulder. Tennison scrolled the list of addresses up the screen. She took a mouthful of lukewarm coffee and made a *Yuck!* face. She jotted an address down and held up the pad.

"Is there any way you can do a cross-check on this for me?" Bronwen hesitated, rubbing her palms. "It's lunchtime. Come on, see what you can do."

Bronwen took the sheet and went out, almost colliding with Dalton. Tennison looked up anxiously.

"He'll live. Broken leg and hip bone." Dalton shrugged out of his raincoat, giving Tennison a straight look to reassure her. "He's okay."

"You've been a long time."

"Yeah, he . . . he wanted me with him." Dalton cleared his throat. "He was crying, kept on saying he was sorry . . . sorry for crying." Dalton gave a wan smile. He was still badly shaken. "His wife and kid, I sent a cab for them."

"There's another train at two twenty-five," Tennison said, glancing at her watch. Already she was back studying the screen, concentrating.

"Jason and Anthony, it's too much of a coincidence." She chewed her lip. "If Edward Parker-Jones moved on, maybe so did the same police officer."

She was watching the screen, but even so she could feel Dalton's unease. She'd let him go his own sweet way, allowed him into her confidence. Sooner or later he would have to pay for the privilege. She judged the time was ripe.

"Any developments on Jackson?" Dalton asked. He blinked several times when she looked at him. "You said he'd been picked up. . . ."

"No. What about you? Have you heard from the hospital yet?"

Involuntarily he touched his bandaged hand. "No, not yet," he said stiffly. "Still waiting."

"How long does it take?"

"Don't know."

There was a silence. Tennison sat back in her chair and gave him a cool level stare. Dalton fidgeted, then shoved his hands in his pockets in a weak show of indifference.

Yes, the time was definitely ripe.

"Why don't you tell me what a high flyer like you is doing attached to this investigation?"

"What do you mean?" Dalton blustered.

"You're from the Fraud Squad, university educated, you're hand-in-glove with Chiswick, you report back to him." Tennison swept her arms wide. "For God's sake, when are you going to come clean! You're my mate, come on!"

Dalton stared at the floor, no doubt hoping a yawning chasm would appear and swallow him up. He wagged his head back and forth. "I have to report back to Commander Chiswick if—only *if*—your investigation crosses another investigation."

Tennison waited.

"Yes? And? Come on, now you've started." Tennison's eyes bored into his, whenever he had the nerve to meet them. "You have to report back to Chiswick. About what exactly?"

Dalton was a deeply unhappy man. His usual tan was looking none too healthy. "It's about the blackmail of an Assistant Deputy Chief Commissioner. He was or had been on enforced leave for eight months. Six months previous to the blackmail threats."

Tennison stared at him. She snapped her teeth together. "I don't believe this."

"One of the most senior officers ever to be subjected to disciplinary procedures. The matter was passed to the Home Office from Scotland Yard . . ."

"So who the hell is it?"

Dalton jumped as if her bark had bitten him. "Assistant Deputy Commissioner John Kennington." It only just crept out.

"What was going on before the blackmail? Eight months is a long time. It must have been something big."

"His possible connection to a pedophile ring," Dalton said.

Tennison rested her forehead on her hand, shaking her head to and fro. She was thinking that she must have porridge for brains. Not even an inkling until now. And it was so obvious—all the incestuous spying and rumors and heavy hints. Where had she been *living*? Disneyland?

Bronwen came in. She was smiling.

"Margaret Speel. She's now based in—"

"London!" Tennison said, jumping up. "Thank you very much!"

"Kennington vehemently denied all the allegations of wrongdoing, which also included bribery and handing out favors, and he cooperated in a full inquiry. My department was brought in, we examined every log book, letter, document in his entire career file. We checked his associates outside the police—receipts, hotel bills, airline tickets."

Tennison and Dalton sat on a bench seat, platform 4, waiting for the London train. The rain had held off, but there was a nasty gusting wind, shuffling the cigarette packets and candy wrappers at their feet, piling them in corners.

Unable to stomach British Rail coffee, Tennison was drinking hot chocolate from a plastic cup. She was still getting to grips with what Dalton had told her. She felt numbed by it, the double-dealing and duplicity going on all around while she was busting a gut, doing her level best to conduct an honest, professional investigation. Her anger, like the other violent emotions, was seething under the surface.

"And at the end of this big investigation, what was the outcome?"

"One and a half million quid later we were no farther in proving otherwise." Elbows on his knees, Dalton was leaning forward, smoothing down the tape on his bandaged hand where the edge had come unstuck. "And no evidence that he was involved in any perverted sexual activity."

Tennison frowned to herself. Something here that didn't make sense. As yet she couldn't quite put her finger on it.

"Kennington was reinstated, but moved to a different department," Dalton continued. "The entire investigation made everyone really jumpy, especially if it ever got leaked to the press."

"Well, of course," Tennison said caustically, "and they put a lid on it." Put a lid on her, too.

"But it all opened up again." Dalton peered at her from under his brows. "About six months ago, of his own volition, Kennington . . ."

"Admitted it?"

Dalton shook his head. "No, this time he was being blackmailed. He wanted to press charges. But I suppose under pressure he withdrew. He resigned. No case was ever brought."

Tennison's anger bubbled up dangerously. "And who was doing the blackmailing?"

"I don't know. I was off the case by then." He caught the full impact of her flat disbelieving stare, and insisted, "I really don't know. But I would say, whoever it was, must have some connection with your investigation, otherwise why would they have brought me in?"

"Are you expecting me to believe that Kennington was prepared to bring charges of being blackmailed but never named who was doing it to him?"

"If he did, I was never told . . ."

Tennison decided she couldn't stomach British Rail hot chocolate either. She got up and chucked the half-filled cup into the basket. She paced up and down, scarf whipping in the chill gusts. She stopped in front of Dalton.

"Did Edward Parker-Jones's name ever come up? Was there any connection proved between him and Kennington?"

"The Fraud Squad discovered there had been several charitable donations from Kennington to Parker-Jones." Dalton held up his hand to forestall Tennison's fierce nod. "But they were all legal, all documented. The advice centre was only one of a number of organizations Kennington donated monies to. They found nothing incriminating."

The smell of all this was positively reeking now.

"Could that be why Chiswick wants me to back off Parker-Jones?" Dalton made a vague gesture. Tennison pressed him. "There has to be some reason unless . . . was it Parker-Jones doing the blackmail?"

"No way. As I said, he was checked out."

"Who do *you* think it was? Oh, come on, you must suspect somebody," Tennison said, losing patience.

Dalton looked up at her. "It could be Jackson."

"Yes, there's always Jackson." Tennison paced, pushing her wind-ruffled hair back from her forehead. "Let me try this on you." She was trying it on herself as much as on Dalton. "Kennington had been investigated and came up smelling of roses. He must have been very confident, but then he's forced to resign. Connie was selling his story to Jessica Smithy, right? Claiming that he was prepared to name names—one a high-ranking police officer. What if it was Kennington? Connie was just a rent boy, swat him like a fly. He was just a kid, no parents, nobody to even identify his body."

Tennison stood in front of Dalton, pushing her hair back, staring down at him. Dalton was intent on his hand, pressing the tape flat with his thumbnail.

The minute Superintendent Halliday walked into the Squad Room, Otley picked up the warning signal. He was in one of his twitchy moods. He kept squirming his neck inside his collar and rubbing his throat as if undergoing slow strangulation. Most of the Vice team were there, busy at their desks. Ray Hebdon looked to Larry Hall, who in turn glanced at Haskons and Lillie. Norma stopped typing.

The room quieted. Halliday tapped his watch. It was late in the afternoon, going on for five.

"Is there anyone in this building who can tell me where Detective Chief Inspector Tennison is?"

"She's on her way from Cardiff, boss, expecting her any moment," Otley called out.

Halliday nodded, lips tight. He turned to leave, and turned back, seething. He pointed at Haskons and Lillie, available targets to vent his spleen on.

"And you two, as far as I am concerned, have behaved in what can only be described as an utterly farcical manner—one which would, if ever it were made public—put not only myself but also this entire department in jeopardy."

Lillie colored up, while Haskons looked defiant. Otley turned away to hide a grin.

Commander Chiswick pushed open the door and said to Halliday, "In your office," and went out.

"Just tell me—what in God's name possessed you to do it?"

"But we brought Jackson in, sir!" Haskons protested, rising to his feet. "He is still the main suspect for the murder of Colin Jenkins."

The door opened again, and Chiswick's stern face appeared.

"Sorry, I'll be right with you," Halliday said. He strode to the door, rubbing the back of his neck. He whipped around. "DS Haskons, DC Lillie—you will return to Southampton Row as from tomorrow evening. DI Ray Hebdon will leave today. That's all."

He pushed at the door, and something caught his eye. A doll was pinned to the notice board, golden curls and a frilly pink dress with pink satin slippers. The block printing above it read: "DI HEBDON. FAIRY OF THE WEEK."

Halliday's nostrils twitched. "Get this crap down!" He slammed out.

The door squeaked to a stop, and in the silence everyone looked at one another. Otley leaned against the desk, hands in his pockets.

"Just a passing thought, but does anybody have any idea where she is?" He nodded to the clock. "She should have left Cardiff hours ago!"

14

On arrival in London, Tennison deliberately hadn't reported in. She'd sent Dalton off to pick up a car while she took a cab to the Islington Probation Department, with instructions for him to meet her there. It was after five o'clock, and she was afraid that Margaret Speel might have gone, but she hadn't. She was writing up reports in a tiny cluttered office that had a look of impermanence about it, as if she were in the process of moving in or moving out, Tennison couldn't decide which.

However temporary her office, Margaret Speel's sarcastic manner was firmly in place, exactly as before. There was something about the cynical slant of her mouth that was extremely irritating. In her petite bouncy way, she reminded Tennison of a chirpy strutting sparrow with an attitude problem: however smart you think you are, I know I'm smarter.

"Now what can I do for you, Chief Inspector?" she said world-wearily, gesturing to a chair. Her mouth slanted. "You want any more boys off the streets?"

Tennison sat down. She placed her briefcase on the faded carpet and sat up straight. She was all through with taking crap, especially from a cheeky sparrow with an irritating smirk.

"You were at one time working in Cardiff, yes?"

Margaret Speel rocked back in the chair. She recovered quickly. "Yes, and Liverpool. And I've also worked in Birmingham."

"Was Edward Parker-Jones also working in Liverpool and Birmingham?"

"No."

"Well, we can be thankful for that, can't we?" Margaret Speel's eyes narrowed under her dark bangs; she was a mite uncertain now, getting edgy. Tennison kept up the barrage. "Do you know Anthony Field?"

A hard glare, and a frown.

"No? What about Jason Baldwyn? He was a resident at—"

"Yes," Margaret Speel interrupted. "Yes, I remember Jason."

"Do you have a relationship with Edward Parker-Jones?"

"I don't think that is any of your business," Margaret Speel said in a quiet, outraged voice.

"But it is. It is very much my business." Tennison leaned toward her. She stared her full in the face. "Jason tried to kill himself this afternoon, right in front of me, Margaret. He's prepared to make a statement that when he was in the care of Parker-Jones he was sexually abused, for a period of six years. You were at that time his probation officer!"

Margaret Speel's hand jerked to her throat. Her fingers plucked at a necklace of jade beads. Her pale neck was taut and strained.

"You were Jason's probation officer, weren't you? Jason Baldwyn's probation officer."

"Yes, yes I was," Margaret Speel said in a barely audible whisper.

"Do you have anything to say about these allegations? Were you aware of them when you were working in Cardiff?"

Margaret Speel was struggling to take this in. Her chirpy sarcasm was gone, shocked out of her. She made a valiant, desperate effort that only came out sounding weak. "Jason was always telling lies, he was a compulsive liar—"

"Ten-year-old boy, Margaret, and you refused to believe him, and he had six more years of abuse," Tennison went on relentlessly.

"This isn't true!" She shook her head, almost in pain. "This is terrible . . . if I had believed, for one moment . . ."

"Believe it, Margaret. What do you know about Connie? Colin Jenkins—Margaret?"

"I was telling you the truth! I swear I didn't even come here until eighteen months ago. Edward contacted me. He even tried to renew our relationship. . . ." Her head dropped. Tennison let her stew. She believed that Margaret Speel was genuinely distraught, she even felt sorry for her, but Tennison's bottled anger fueled a passion to cut straight to the rotten heart of this, to ruthlessly expose it to the light, no matter who got hurt along the way.

"Are you sure?" Margaret Speel asked, feebly grasping at straws. "You know, these young boys make up stories, and I remember Jason—"

"Margaret—do you also remember if a doctor examined Jason Baldwyn?"

"Yes, of course he was examined."

"Margaret, do you recall a police officer? Someone who would have known Parker-Jones in Cardiff?"

"Do you mean John Kennington?"

Tennison's face remained calm, she didn't so much as move a muscle. She felt as if she had been struck by a lightning bolt. With scarcely a pause she said blithely, "It could possibly be John Kennington. Do you recall what rank, or if he was uniformed or plainclothes?"

"Er, yes, um . . ." Confused, still in a state of shock, Margaret Speel rubbed her forehead. "I think he was—Superintendent. I never saw him in a uniform. He lives in London now."

As if it was of minor interest, Tennison said casually, "Do you happen to know if John Kennington and Parker-Jones are still in touch? Still friendly?"

"Yes, yes I think so."

Tennison thanked her and left. On her way out she heard Margaret Speel sobbing at her desk. She didn't like the woman, though she did pity her.

Tennison sat in the driver's seat outside the steeply gabled house with white-leaded windows, a dense windbreak of conifers shielding it from the road. Dalton, very subdued, sat woodenly beside her. Tennison clicked the door open and looked across at him. He knew what she was about to do, and what the consequences were, and both of them knew where it put him. Between a rock and a hard place. Anyway, his decision, she thought. He was a big boy now and she certainly was no wet nurse.

"You can stay in the car if you want!" Tennison said bluntly.

Dalton clenched his jaw, bit the bullet, and reached for the door handle.

A middle-aged housekeeper with a foreign accent showed them into the large L-shaped drawing room. French windows gave a restful evening view of a flagged patio with stone urns of flowers, and beyond a stone balustrade a lawn sloped down to a grove of beech trees.

A grandfather clock, genuine antique to Tennison's inexpert eye, ticked solemnly in the corner, emphasizing the silence. There was a baby grand on a small platform, a Chopin étude on the music stand. Two long wing-backed sofas covered in rose silks faced each other across a coffee table that was bigger than the kitchen table in Tennison's flat. The fireplace was white lacquered wood inlaid with gold leaf, and displayed on the mantel were family photographs in ornate silver frames. Tennison went over for a closer look.

"Well, he didn't buy this on wages," was her considered opinion, after giving the room the once-over. "This place must be worth a packet."

"It happens to be my wife's."

John Kennington stood in the doorway. He came in, tall and distinguished, with silvery hair brushed back from a high tanned forehead. As a young man he must have been stunningly handsome. Even dressed in a buttoned fawn cardigan and dark green corduroys, with soft leather loafers, he gave the appearance of fine taste and casual elegance. He was totally at ease, charming, and rather patronizing.

Tennison had never met him before. She'd seen him from afar, once, at a grand reception for a delegation of European police chiefs. At the moment she was a bit unnerved, both by him and the surroundings, but she was damned if she was going to show it.

She said formally, "I am Detective Chief Inspector Jane Tennison, and this is Detective Inspector Brian Dalton."

Kennington didn't invite them to sit. He looked from one to the other, and negligently scratched an eyebrow.

"What seems to be the problem?"

"I am making inquiries into the death of a young boy, Colin Jenkins. Do you know him?"

Kennington shook his head. He strolled over to the fireplace.

Tennison turned to keep facing him. "Do you know a James Jackson?"

"No."

"Do you know an Anthony Field, sir?"

"No."

"A Jason Baldwyn?"

"No."

"Do you know Edward Parker-Jones?"

Kennington hesitated before shaking his head. "No, I can't say that I do." The grandfather clock ticked on in the brief silence.

"You were at one time stationed in Manchester," Tennison said, "and previous to that, Cardiff, is that correct?"

"Yes."

"Did you at any time meet a Miss Margaret Speel?" She watched him closely. "A probation officer?"

Kennington shook his head again, this time more abruptly. "I'm sorry, I don't recall the name."

He was good at stonewalling, and this could have gone on all night. Tennison didn't have time to waste.

"Your recent resignation, sir—you were about to initiate charges which due to your retirement—"

"What exactly is this inquiry about, Chief Inspector?"

His tone had sharpened. He no longer held the rank of Assistant Deputy Commissioner, but he retained the gravitas of past authority, the prestige of office that demanded a certain respect.

"I should be most grateful if you would answer the questions, sir," Tennison persisted, refusing to be bullied or patronized.

"I have no inclination to answer anything else, and I would appreciate it if you left my house." He made a brusque gesture of dismissal. Dalton shuffled his feet. He looked to Tennison, a mute agonized plea in his eyes.

"Colin Jenkins also used the name Connie," Tennison said, standing up straight. "Do you recall ever meeting him? He was fifteen years old, about my height, with pale red hair. He was, sir, a practicing homosexual . . ."

Mottled spots of red had appeared in Kennington's cheeks. He was nearly a foot taller than Tennison, and he came forward, using it to intimidate her.

"I'd like you both to leave. Now."

Dalton was already halfway to the door. He wanted to physically drag Tennison with him, but the woman hadn't budged. She stood her ground, gesturing to the silver frames on the mantel.

"It was just that I noticed . . . you have a number of photographs of young—"

"They are my sons," Kennington said, his outrage giving his voice a harsh rasp. "Please leave my house NOW!" He stood over her, trembling, fists clenching and unclenching.

"Was Colin Jenkins blackmailing you? Was Parker-Jones attempting to put pressure on you? Which one of them was blackmailing you? Were you aware Colin was selling his story to the newspapers?"

Kennington raised his fist as if he might strike her. He dropped it as an attractive, middle-aged woman came briskly in, her streakily gray hair cut short in a young style that actually suited her. She passed Dalton and looked around, smiling vaguely.

"Oh! I'm sorry . . ." She looked to her husband. "John?"

Tennison stepped forward, holding out her hand. "Mrs. Kennington, I am—"

Kennington grasped her by the elbow and started pushing her. Tennison pulled her arm free and stood back, holding up both hands.

"Please!" She smoothed her sleeve straight. "Mrs. Kennington, your husband was just answering some questions. I am investigating the death of a young rent boy, fifteen years old, and I'm—"

Mrs. Kennington's eyes widened in alarm as her husband bodily propelled Tennison across the room. Leaning forward, face carved out of stone, he thrust her ahead of him into the hallway, and kept on going.

"His name was Colin Jenkins, you may have read about it . . ."

Tennison's fading voice was interrupted by the sound of the front door being swung violently open on its hinges.

Dalton and Mrs. Kennington looked at one another. It was hard to know who was the more shocked. Dalton gathered his wits and quickly went out.

Standing at the coffee table, Mrs. Kennington reached down, and without looking took a cigarette from a black ebony box. The front door slammed shut. She held the cigarette between her fingers and slowly and deliberately crumpled it, her face frozen in a white mask.

Dalton beside her, Tennison drove into the yard at the rear of Southampton Row Police Station. This was her old division, before being shunted sideways to Soho Vice. Her old boss, Chief Superintendent Kernan, was crossing the yard to his car. Genuinely, or by design—hard to tell—he happened not to see her. She rolled the window down and stuck her head out.

"Buy you a drink?"

Rather reluctantly, he came over. "Sorry, I'm late as it is." His pouchy cheeks and heavy jowls always reminded her of a disgruntled chipmunk. She couldn't once recall him looking happy, except when he was pissed. He nodded to Dalton. "Nothing wrong, is there?"

"What do you know about John Kennington?" Tennison asked.

Kernan sighed and stared off somewhere. He didn't hold with women having senior positions in the force, and that applied to Tennison in spades. She was a real ball-breaker. He bent down to the window.

"He just got the golden handshake. Why?"

"Is he homosexual?"

Kernan laughed abrasively. "I don't know—why do you ask?"

Tennison opened the door and started to get out. Kernan backed away, making a negative motion. "I've got to go, Jane . . ."

Tennison did get out. Kernan's shoulders slumped as she confronted him. "Mike, I need to know because I think he is involved in this murder, the rent boy—"

"I've nothing to tell you." His face was a closed book.

Tennison gave him a hard, penetrating stare. She said in a low urgent voice that was almost pleading, "They're young kids, Mike, some of them eleven and twelve years of age—your boy's age. All I want is the truth."

Kernan glanced guardedly toward Dalton in the car, and moved farther off. He looked down on her, flat-eyed. "Do you want me to spell it out?"

"Yes."

"If you start digging dirt up again on Kennington," he muttered, shaking his head, "it'll be a waste of time. He may no longer be a big fish, but he'll have a hell of a lot of friends who still are. A whisper gets out, you'll tip them off and you won't get near them, and it won't help the kids, won't stop the punters. They'll all be still on the streets. You should back off this one, Jane."

"Even if he was a high-ranking police officer," Tennison said heatedly. "Even if there are judges, politicians, barristers involved . . ."

"Kennington's out of the force now," Kernan said heavily, trying to make her see sense. "Ignore it, that's the best, the only advice I can give you."

Tennison nodded slowly, but it didn't fool him. She pursed her lips. "There's a Superintendent vacancy up for grabs, you know which area?"

Kernan gazed at her for a moment. He held up his hand, fingers and thumb spread wide. Five. He gave a smirk and said out of the corner of his mouth, "Becoming a player, are you?"

Tennison nodded. She got back in the car and slammed the door. She revved the engine and put it in reverse. Kernan stood watching.

"Good night!" he called out.

"Thanks, Mike," Tennison said, backing up.

Kernan whacked his open hand on the car roof and she shot off, through the archway to the main road. He shook his head wearily, puzzled and pissed off. If he couldn't stick the woman at any price—and dammit he couldn't—why did he so admire the bloody bitch?

Twenty minutes later Tennison dumped her briefcase on her desk, flung her coat over a chair, and scooped up the sheaves of reports, internal memos, and phone messages that had piled up in her absence. After twelve straight hours on the job she was fighting off bone-weary fatigue with pure nervous energy. Her nerve ends jangled.

Dalton trailed in after her. He had a limp, wrung out look to him, the classic symptoms of bags under the eyes and pasty complexion, sweat trickling from the roots of his hair.

He stood, slack shouldered, making a great effort. "Can I say something, apologize really, but I didn't have much say in the matter and I've . . ."

His voice trailed away when he realized she wasn't listening, too preoccupied as she scanned through the messages. The silence sank in.

"What? I'm sorry?"

"I'm sorry, and, well . . ." His speech stumbled along. "I dunno where I am. It's like I'm in some kind of limbo . . ."

Tennison paid full attention. Dalton seemed to be cracking up in front of her eyes. He wasn't able to look at her, too embarrassed or fearful or something, and it all came tumbling out in a flood, a dam-burst of raw feeling.

"I can't sleep and, well, my girlfriend, I haven't told her. I'm even scared to have sex with her because . . ." He swallowed painfully. "It's just hanging over me all the time. What if I have got AIDS?" His eyes suddenly filled with tears. He choked down a sob, standing there forlorn and pitiful. "I'm sorry, sorry . . ."

Tennison went to him and put her arms around him. She gave him a strong, comforting hug. She could feel him shaking inside. She stood back, holding his shoulders.

"Listen, anyone would feel the same way. And, listen—I think it'll be good for you to sit and really talk it all out . . . and to someone who understands all the fears—and they're real, Brian." She touched his wet face. "You go and wash up. I've got the contacts here for you, okay?" She nodded to her desk. "Maybe you and your girlfriend should go together."

Dalton let out a shuddering sigh. "Yeah, thanks. Thanks a lot."

He wiped his face with the back of his hand and turned to leave. Tennison waited for the door to close. She pressed both hands to her face, covering her eyes. She held a deep breath for a count of five, and then snapped back into action, picking up her messages as she returned to her chair.

The door was rapped. Otley looked in.

"We've got Parker-Jones in interview room D oh three."

"What?! He's here?" Otley nodded. Tennison glared at him. "Whose bloody idea was that?"

"Mine," Otley retorted, sauntering in. "We got some kids that recognized Deputy Chief Commissioner Kennington's house. Plus, the property where we picked up Jackson, it's owned by him."

"What?" Tennison was on her feet.

"Jackson's been living in a house owned by Parker-Jones. It's all there . . ." He made a flippant gesture to the desk. "Full report."

"Who's interviewing him?"

"Haskons and Lillie."

Tennison swore under her breath as she scoured the littered desk for his report.

Otley's long gaunt face was looking distinctly tetchy. He'd worked his bollocks off on this case, and what did he get in return? Sweet F.A. Overbearing cow. "And as you weren't here," he said, not troubling to hide his sarcasm, "and we couldn't contact you, I'm just trying to close the case."

Tennison flared up. "*You*? I know what you're playing at, but you are just not good enough. Stop trying to demean me at every opportunity. This *isn't* your case!"

"I know that."

"Then stop working by yourself. I didn't want Parker-Jones brought in yet."

"You got a reason?" Otley said, insolent to the last.

She had half a dozen, but she'd be damned if she was going to rhyme them off, chapter and verse, for his benefit. She was in charge of this investigation, and Bill Otley had better wise up to it double quick.

"I'm not ready for him," was the only reason she—Detective Chief Inspector Tennison—felt obliged to give the cheeky toe-rag.

• • •

Edward Parker-Jones, quietly casual in a dark check sport jacket, collar and tie, green suede shoes, sat in interview room D.03. Haskons sat directly opposite him, with a beautiful shiner of a black eye and a cut lip. Lillie had a bruised forehead where Jackson had butted him and a bandage on his chin over the wound he had dabbed with TCP cream.

"Yes, the properties are mine. I have admitted that they are, and I would, if you had asked, given the information freely. I have nothing to hide."

He was one cool customer, Haskons thought. A real con artist, and he'd met a few. But, so far, Mr. Parker-Jones was completely legit, and had to be handled with care.

"Do you have the books?" Haskons asked, raising his undamaged eyebrow. "You are paid a considerable amount of money from not only Camden Council, but also Holloway and Hackney."

"They are very large houses, and yes, if you wish to see the books, then all you have to do is contact my accountant. Taking care of the homeless is not a lucrative business, far from it. Laundry bills, heating, electricity, water . . ." He looked pointedly at his watch, shaking his head and sighing. "Is all this really necessary? Why exactly have I been brought in yet again? Why wasn't this all asked before? I have been perfectly willing, and cooperative . . ."

The door swung open. It was as if an icy blast had swept in.

Lillie bent toward the mike. "The time is six-thirty and DCI Tennison has just entered the interview room."

Haskons took one look at Tennison's face and vacated his seat. She sat down in it. She wasn't afraid to let the silence linger as she settled herself, flipped open her notebook and unscrewed the cap of her fountain pen. She looked up.

"Could you please tell us about your relationship with Margaret Speel?"

Parker-Jones hooked a finger over one ear, pushing back a trailing strand of jet-black hair. "She's my fiancée." The question hadn't surprised him, or if it had he'd covered superbly.

"Did you, in 1979, run the Harrow Home for boys in Manchester?"

"Yes."

However closely Tennison scrutinized him, she couldn't detect a flicker of concern or unease.

"And in 1986 the Calloway Centre in Cardiff?"

"Yes."

"Do you know Anthony Field?"

A half smile. "Yes."

"And Jason Baldwyn?"

"Yes, they were both in my care."

Tennison pretended to jot something down. Eyes downcast, she said. "Do you also know John Kennington?"

Parker-Jones eased back in the chair. His body language gave nothing away. He tilted his head slightly. "Yes—not well, but I have met him."

"Could you tell me about one of your employees, James Jackson?"

"I wouldn't call it employed, but he did on the odd occasion do some repairs—caretaking, that sort of thing."

"How well did you know Mr. Jackson?"

"As I have already stated," Parker-Jones said, making it sound weary and pedantic. "I did not know Mr. Jackson on a personal or social level. He simply did the occasional odd job for me. Nothing more."

Tennison leaned her elbows on the table. "But he lived in a property owned by you, Mr. Parker-Jones."

Parker-Jones looked to the ceiling. He smiled very patiently, humoring her. "Again I have admitted this. I paid Jackson only a nominal amount, and in return for his room he repaired the property. I have no reason to know or even be aware of what Mr. Jackson did in his private life." He spread his hands. "I was also unaware if he lived there on a permanent basis, as he told me he had an elderly mother he took care of and spent a lot of time with."

Tennison decided to pass on the elderly mother. She idly wondered why he hadn't bothered to mention that she was white-haired, crippled, and had multiple sclerosis as well. Instead she said:

"What other names have you been known under?"

"I have two houses in the name of Edwards, and one in the name of Jones." Glib, straight out with it. As if he already knew the questions and had rehearsed the answers. "I have on occasions used both."

"Why did you use different names on the deeds of these properties?"

"I just did." The half smile appeared. "There is no law against it."

She'd started off gentle, tossed him some easy ones, and he'd batted them back without breaking sweat. She now got ready to lob a few grenades. Her voice went up a pitch.

"Would you like to tell me about the two charges for indecent assault. The ones in Manchester, and Cardiff!"

Parker-Jones fiddled with his signet ring. "Not really. In both incidents all charges were dropped." His deep-set eyes returned her gaze, measure for measure. "I can see no reason to discuss them."

"Did John Kennington assist or advise you in any way concerning these two sexual assault charges?"

"I don't recall."

"Have you at any time in the past months attempted to get monies from John Kennington?"

"What?" He blinked several times.

"Blackmail? Or extortion? Have you, Mr Parker-Jones, *attempted to get monies?*"

"Absolutely not." He laughed at the idea. "Ridiculous."

"Were you aware that John Kennington was considering bringing blackmail charges against—"

"I would obviously not consider attempting to extort monies out of someone who freely donated to my centre," he said caustically. He tapped the table with his manicured fingers. "I have, as requested, presented a detailed list of all those who forward charitable donations to the centre. I presume this information was passed on to you . . ."

Tennison cut across him. "Did you on the night of the seventeenth of this month call the emergency services?" she asked sharply.

He hadn't rehearsed this one, because he stared blankly at her for a second. "I'm sorry?"

"Did you call an ambulance? On the night of the seventeenth of this month?"

"No."

"Would you please state where you were on the night of the seventeenth from eight-fifteen P.M. to nine-thirty P.M.?"

"I have told you," Parker-Jones ground out. "I never left the advice centre." He threw up his hands. "This is really becoming ludicrous . . ." He looked at Haskons and Lillie, as if they might help him in dealing with this raving madwoman.

"You think so?" Tennison said, her voice as soft now as it had been sharp a moment earlier. Her tone implied that they hadn't reached ridiculous yet, never mind ludicrous.

"Do you know it is illegal to display false credentials?" While he was grappling with this change of tack, she switched again.

"We would like the names of the witnesses who you say saw you at the centre for the duration of the evening of the seventeenth."

Parker-Jones slumped back.

Not *again*.

He was beginning to get an inkling of what lengths ludicrousness could get to. He started off, lips thinning as he repeated the old familiar litany of names:

"Billy Matthews . . . Disco Driscoll . . . Alan Thorpe . . . Kenny Lloyd . . . Jimmy Jackson . . ."

The Squad Room was winding down. The last reports of the day were being written up. A skeleton staff would be on duty through the night, but most of the team had knocked off at seven.

Kathy was at the alibis board when Tennison wandered in. She looked dead on her feet. Hungry yet too tired to eat, she was hollow-eyed and ratty.

Kathy turned with a big beaming smile. "I think I deserve a bottle of champagne because . . ." She tapped the board with a felt-tip marker. "Billy Matthews's alibi is now withdrawn. Billy was not at the advice centre or anywhere near it. He was in fact in hospital, taken there by ambulance on the night of the sixteenth. And this is the best part—from the advice centre . . ."

Tennison stuck up a clenched fist. One more down. She looked at the list of names. "Martin Fletcher dead."

". . . Donald Driscoll, alibi withdrawn," Kathy went on. "Kenny Lloyd ditto. Just Parker-Jones giving Jackson an alibi and vice versa. The only other one out of the entire list is Alan Thorpe, and he has admitted he was drunk! If we'd been able to keep Jackson locked up, we'd have probably got them to admit they lied earlier on."

An aura of energy had transformed Tennison. Adrenaline pumping, she stared at the board, eyes gleaming.

"Where've they got Jackson?"

Haskons and Lillie had entered, and Haskons said, "He's with the Sarge and Larry the Lamb, room D oh five downstairs."

Without acknowledgment for Kathy's success, or even a word of thanks, Tennison did a smart about-face and marched to the door. A tight-lipped Kathy watched her go, hands on hips.

Passing Haskons and Lillie, Tennison said briskly, "You two. Divvy up a bottle of Moët for Kathy, in repayment for that fiasco . . ."

She pointed. On the notice board next to the door were two photographs of the pair of them, dug out of the files and blown up, their lips daubed with red felt-tip, flouncy dresses sketched over their outdoor clothes. The caption read, "FAIRIES OF THE WEEK."

"Bloody hell, who put those up?" Lillie snarled, flushing pink.

The culprit, Kathy, giggled behind her hand. Tennison shot one look back and went out. From the corridor came her full-throated, uninhibited bellow of laughter.

15

"What did Connie owe you this money for?" DI Hall asked.

"He needed to get some photographs, he needed some new gear." Jackson shrugged. "Well, that's what he told me, so I lent him the dough."

He looked up as Tennison came in. He nodded and smiled at her in a friendly fashion. For the record, Hall stated that DCI Tennison had entered the room, timed at 7:35 P.M. He went on to ask Jackson, "How much?"

"Two hundred quid. Then he disappears. So, I go out looking for him." Perfectly natural, nothing untoward, his tone implied.

Jackson's normally scruffy mop of spiky hair had been gelled and combed down. His face bore the signs of the previous night's fracas, but otherwise he looked quite presentable in a clean T-shirt inscribed with "Happy Mondays" and a brown suede trucker jacket. His jeans even had creases in them.

His brief, Mr. Arthur, had made no such effort. If anything, he was even seedier than before. A small attaché case rested on the shiny knees of his trousers, its cheap leatherette scratched and torn, one of the clasps missing.

Otley said, "You go to Vernon's flat looking for him?"

"Yeah, but in the afternoon. I spoke to Vera, she was there."

"And she told you what?" Otley asked.

"That Connie wasn't there!" Jackson exclaimed, the obvious answer to a dumb question. "I told you all this, I've said all this . . ."

Tennison had remained standing, next to the wall opposite Jackson, which meant he had to swivel his head as the interrogation switched direction. Her turn.

"Did Parker-Jones ask you to say you were at the advice centre?"

"I'm sorry, I don't remember."

"You don't remember? Tell me about the money. Did you often lend Connie money?"

"No. He usually had enough. He was always pretty flush." Jackson gave his thick-lipped smile. "I mean, sometimes I borrowed from him."

"When exactly did you give him the two hundred pounds?"

Jackson peered off into space, brow furrowed, in a credible performance of thinking hard. "Don't remember—I'm sorry."

"Did Connie live at the house in Camden Town?"

"Sometimes left his gear there, but he'd not actually lived—" He cleared his throat. "—lived there for months."

"Do you know where he was living?" Tennison asked. "Say for the past few months?"

Jackson shook his head.

"Please answer the question."

"No." Jackson answered in a drab, long-suffering voice. "I dunno where he was living."

"So where did you give him the money?"

"At the advice centre."

"But according to Parker-Jones, Connie hadn't been there for—quite a few months."

"Yeah, well, I don't remember where I give it him!" Jackson said testily. He glanced edgily at Mr. Arthur, and then his smile was turned on again, full beam. "I'm sorry, really I am. Just don't remember . . ."

"How well do you know Edward Parker-Jones?"

"I work for him, pays me a few quid to look after his property."

"Have you at any time attempted to extort money out of a man called John Kennington?" Jackson gave her a blank stare. Tennison moved nearer. "Blackmail, Mr. Jackson. Have you attempted to blackmail John Kennington?"

Jackson shook his head. "No, I dunno him."

"On the night Colin Jenkins died," Tennison said quietly, moving closer, "did you discuss anything with Parker-Jones?"

"Yes." He paused, deadpan. "Price of toilet paper. I get it in bulk for him."

"And after the death of Colin Jenkins, did you discuss anything with Mr. Parker-Jones? Not necessarily toilet paper."

"Like what?"

"You have stated that Donald Driscoll, Billy Matthews, Alan Thorpe, and Kenny Lloyd all saw you at the advice centre the night Colin Jenkins was murdered, is that correct?"

"Yes, that's right."

"You listed the exact same names as Mr. Edward Parker-Jones—so I am asking you." Tennison gripped the edge of the table and leaned over. "Did you at any time discuss this with Mr. Edward Parker-Jones?"

"No. No reason to." Jackson slanted his body away, trying to maintain the distance between them. His heavy-lidded eyes flicked sideways toward her. "They were there and so was he. So he's bound to say the same lads as I say, because I was there . . ."

Tennison straightened her back. "You are going to be charged with the attempted murder of a police officer, Mr. Jackson. You also refused an officer entry to the house in Camden and physically attacked another police officer." Jackson tried to interject, but she steam-rollered on. "You were holding a fourteen-year-old-girl against her will. You have been living off immoral earnings. You want more? Because we have more."

"I didn't know they was coppers!" Jackson held up his hands, palms pressed against an invisible wall. "On my life—I mean they just barged into the house and—that girl won't bring charges—she begged me to give her a place to stay—I didn't know she was fourteen!" He jerked his head, gulping. "And that other thing. I thought it was Red, that stupid old drag queen, didn't know it was a copper . . . just mistaken identity."

"Why did you want to kill her?"

"I didn't want to kill her, no way. I just wanted to . . . frighten her a bit."

"Why?"

Jackson was thinking hard now, and it was no pretence. He suddenly found himself in a hole, and instead of digging in deeper and deeper, he wanted to dig himself out. He licked his lips. "Well . . . Vera told me she'd been talking to the cops, and all I wanted to do was frighten her off."

"Why?" Tennison said. "Why did you want to frighten Rodney Allarton?" Jackson looked confused. "Red?"

Jackson wanted the help of his brief. Mr. Arthur had his head down, scribbling away on a notepad, using his attaché case as a desk. No help there. Jackson looked around, a bit panicky, and then said lamely, "Because I did. Look, I'm sorry, really sorry about that, it was all a mistake . . ."

"You must have had a reason."

"No, no, I didn't have a reason. And that is the God's truth!"

Tennison gave a little sigh, shaking her head sadly.

"Well, Jimmy, you are going away for a very long time—for no reason."

Jackson made a wild gesture, at last attracting Mr. Arthur's attention, who leaned over for Jackson to whisper in his ear. Mr. Arthur sat back. "My client is very tired, perhaps we can continue this interview in the morning?"

The punishingly long day had taken its toll on Tennison too. The lines around her eyes were etched in, the furrows in her forehead deeply ridged. She felt like saying, *Enough's enough, get this scumbag out of my sight,* but instead she merely nodded to Hall, who spoke into the tape, concluding the interview.

However desperately she might have desired it, the day was far from over.

They had Jackson running scared—no doubt about it—but he hadn't cracked, and until he did their case was long on suspicion, short on hard-clinching evidence. She was going to sweat that bastard and wring him out like an old dishrag.

Taking Otley along, she drove up to the house in Langley Road, Camden. From Otley's description of the place she knew what to expect, but it turned out to be even worse. The squalor of the poky bedrooms at the top of the house disgusted and depressed her. The smell made her nauseous.

They checked out the wardrobes and drawers, sorted through the kids' clothing and pitiful belongings. After ten minutes Tennison had had it. She slumped down on a narrow trestle bed, the one occupied by Billy Matthews, and picked up the physically challenged teddy bear and gazed at it with listless eyes. Some poor mite had clung onto this battered relic, seeking love and comfort. It felt damp, and she imagined they were a child's tears.

Otley slammed a drawer shut and looked at her over his shoulder. In a parody of Mr. Arthur, he muttered in his sardonic drawl, "My Guv'nor's very tired, perhaps we can continue this search in the morning!"

Scrawled into the plaster above the bed, in jagged capitals, she read: "MARTIN FLETCHER LIVES HERE."

Tennison rubbed her eyes. "I met a friend of yours in Manchester, David Lyall."

"Yes, I know, he called me," Otley said, leaning on the dresser. "I wondered why you were hot to trot to Manchester."

"Good that I did . . ." She gazed up at him, her hands limp on her knees. "It's like a jigsaw. I've got all the pieces and they just won't fit."

"Best not to push them into place," Otley advised, wise old sage. "Got to have patience."

"I've got that," Tennison snapped back, nettled, "just don't have the time." She added resentfully, "You jumped the gun with Parker-Jones—I wasn't ready for him."

Otley didn't think that merited a response. Anyway, he didn't give one, just wandered off into the next room. After a moment Tennison levered herself up and followed him.

There was a TV set, video recorder, porn videotapes and magazines, a crate of Newcastle Brown, half consumed, and a 200 carton of Benson & Hedges, the cellophane broken, just one packet gone. Jackson's room, quite evidently. His long leather coat hung behind the door, and there was other masculine tackle scattered around.

Otley was rooting through the wardrobe, taking stuff off hangers, going through the pockets, feeling the seams and throwing it on the floor. "They all stink, these rooms, used clothes, mildew . . ." He sounded puzzled. "If Connie stayed here, where's all the smart gear he was supposed to wear?"

Tennison rummaged through a chest of drawers, poking at Jackson's belongings with distaste. Otley was on his knees, feeling under the wardrobe. All he found was dust, so he moved along the linoleum to the smaller of the two beds. He lifted the corner of the stained eiderdown to look underneath the bed, and almost sneezed as the dust got to him.

"He must have had letters or a diary or something," Otley said, sniffing and pinching his nose. Crouching, he craned his head. "Hang on, what have we got here? If he was selling his story to that woman—what was her name?" Grunting as he reached under the bed.

"Jessica Smithy. That's what he said . . . ! And Martin Fletcher—'I can sell my story for a lot of dough.'" Tennison straightened up. Something had just clicked. "What if Jessica Smithy met him first, and Connie came second? Rent boys, not just one rent boy. She was writing an article on rent *boys*—plural."

Bent double, Otley dragged a small brown suitcase from underneath the bed. It was locked. He took out his penknife, and after a couple of seconds' fiddling that got him nowhere, lost his patience and used brute force. The clasps sprang open. Tennison looked over his shoulder as he flung the lid back. The two of them stared down at the jumble of whips, knives, blackjacks, rubber masks, leather jockstraps, bondage gear, and sundry other exotic sadomasochistic gear.

"Nice little away-day assortment!" Otley commented.

He shoved the case aside and peered under the bed again. Frowning, he got to his feet and leaned over, looking closely at the wall against which the bed was pressed. Dark stains and splashes. He whipped the eiderdown off the bed. The sheets were spattered with dried blood, and there were other discolorations that might have been vomit and diarrhea, going by the smell.

Together, Otley and Tennison moved the bed away from the wall. A pair of soiled Y-front underpants came to light, an odd sock covered in fluff. More dark red splashes. And something else. Lower down near the skirting board, bolted into the wall, an iron ankle bracelet on a chain, its edges crusted with blood.

Tennison recoiled with disgust, wrinkling her face.

"We better get Forensic in here, check the entire house over! And I want it done tonight!" She went to the door, sniffing Givenchy Mirage from her scarf. She said with grim satisfaction, "I don't think Jackson's brief's going to believe this—he's already worn his nasty little felt-tip pen out tonight, writing down all the charges!"

Outside, Tennison breathed in deeply, taking a lungful of wonderful evening air. She climbed into her car. Otley leaned in the window.

"I think we should have another go at our Vera," he suggested. "I mean, she's been living here." Tennison nodded agreement. "I'll hang around for the Forensic blokes, they could be a while." He snapped off a mock salute. "'Night. Mind how you go."

As the car moved off, Tennison gave him a look. "This is my case. Bill. Don't jump the gun again."

Otley's slitted eyes watched her drive off down the street. He wore his nasty little grin. "Your case? Yes, ma'am."

Ray Hebdon sat in the darkened viewing room, remote control in one hand, pen in the other, making notes as the tapes unrolled on the screen. Some of the stuff was pretty anodyne, some pure filth, and Hebdon wasn't watching by choice; he was forcing himself to sit here and endure it by an act of will, suppressing his repugnance.

He ejected the tape, stuck in another, and sat back in the chair, reaching for his lukewarm can of beer.

He'd seen this one before, but he watched it again. The classroom and the compliant pupils, the stern schoolteacher whacking his cane on the desk. From its innocent, even quaint, beginning, it degenerated very rapidly to the teacher meting out punishment and demanding penance in the form of spanking, masturbation, blow jobs, and buggery. Other "teachers" appeared on the scene, ready and willing to lend a hand, or some other part of their anatomy. Hebdon studied their faces and made notes.

"What the hell do you think you're doing?"

Hebdon turned. "I'm almost through," he said to Dalton, who had come silently into the room.

"What? Jerking off?" Dalton's expression was that of someone who's just got a whiff of a stale fart in a lift. "Are you into this kind of thing?"

Hebdon started to flush from the neck up. "Yeah, I'm off duty," he sneered, his eyes burning into Dalton's. "So shut the door when you leave, will you?"

Dalton hesitated, as if something was on the tip of his tongue and he couldn't bring himself to utter it. He coughed and turned to leave.

"G'night then."

As the door closed behind him Hebdon swung around and hurled his can of beer at it. Hot-eyed, he stared at the screen, his skin prickling with rage, and jabbed savagely at the remote control, freezing the frame on Kilmartin receiving the favors of Connie, Alan Thorpe, and Kenny Lloyd.

• • •

The hot water felt so good she could have stayed in another twenty minutues, but then she noticed her fingertips getting wrinkly. She dried herself, chucked sandalwood tale everywhere she could reach, wrapped herself in her Chinese silk robe, and stretched out on the sofa in the living room, glass of red wine within easy reach. She thought of putting on a CD she'd bought recently—Albinoni's Adagio in G minor—and then decided not to. The silence was too beautiful, and the peace and quiet too precious. Tennison sighed and closed her eyes.

The doorbell rang.

On her way to answer it she looked at the clock and saw that it was a few minutes after eleven. She pushed her hair back, still damp at the roots, tightened her robe, and opened the door.

"I'm sorry, I didn't wake you, did I?" Ray Hebdon said, genuinely apologetic.

"No, but I hope this is important." Tennison's look could have penetrated galvanized steel at twenty yards. He followed her in. She gestured for him to sit. Her half-full glass of wine was on the coffee table. "Do you want to join me?"

She went off to the kitchen and came back with a glass and a fresh bottle of wine. Hebdon had taken off his coat and was standing somewhat self-consciously rubbing his hands.

He cleared his throat. "I suppose you know I'm going back to my station?" She nodded. He smiled. "So I thought I'd do a bit of homework before I left."

Tennison handed him the bottle and corkscrew. "I've been watching the videos," he said, peeling off the foil. "You know Chiswick was after them? We've been shuffling them around until we'd had a good chance to check all the faces out. Maybe that's why the top brass want them!" He nodded behind him. "Look in my coat pocket."

Tennison picked up his coat from the back of the armchair. She found his notepad and flipped it open.

"Took me a long time, but I've listed all the faces I recognized. There's a judge, two MPs, a lawyer—big criminal lawyer, a barrister . . ."

"Any police officers?"

"None that I recognized." Hebdon uncorked the wine. He topped up Tennison's glass and poured himself one. "But that's quite a list!"

"Why?" Tennison was studying the names, frowning and shaking her head. "Why do they do it?"

"It's what they're into."

That didn't answer her question. "But to risk everything, their careers—for what? I don't understand."

"I think it gets to a point where they can't help it." Hebdon shrugged.

"Can't help it?" Tennison said with a grimace. "My God . . ."

Hebdon sat down. He sipped his wine and stared at the carpet, and struggled to explain. "Because . . . there's also the power, like they're above the law, untouchable." He looked at her. "Maybe because they are the law."

Tennison sat down on the sofa and reached for her glass. She said quietly, "Ray, who do you think killed Connie? One of these men?"

"I don't think it's as big as them—I mean, they might have instigated it, but they wouldn't dirty their hands."

"What about Parker-Jones? He's involved, that's obvious. Just as it's obvious he and Jackson cooked up their alibis together. But did he give Jackson the order to kill Connie?"

Hebdon drank, frowning into space. "That could be why he's covering his tracks."

"He'd also lose a lucrative business," Tennison pointed out.

But it seemed she was off beam, because Hebdon was shaking his head. "No, no, that's where you've got it all wrong. It's not the money." He leaned forward, elbows on his knees. "I think Otley and Co. have been off course—you know, looking for the money element. Those houses he owns—sure, they're cash in some respects, but it's not that. It's the power of being the supplier."

"What do you mean?"

"Call in the favors. It's obvious he had to have connections to have got off not just one charge but two. Parker-Jones must have big contacts. It makes him . . ." Hebdon pinged the rim of the glass with his fingernail. "Untouchable. I doubt if he'd want to mess it up with murder—or blackmail."

Tennison sloshed some wine into her glass and sat back on the sofa, grinding her teeth. "So we're back to Jackson." She took a swig and licked her upper lip. "If Parker-Jones sticks to his story, Jackson will get away with murder—*unless* we break it."

"Going to be tough, because that means you got to break Parker-Jones. If he ordered Jackson to kill Connie, no way will he back down."

The wine was getting to Tennison. But instead of making her more relaxed, she was feeling uptight and jittery. She said, "Do you have a cigarette?"

Hebdon shook his head and finished his wine.

"Time is running out on this one, isn't it?" Tennison brooded. She saw his empty glass. "Have another one—you opened the bottle, for chrissakes . . ." Her tongue slurred over "chrissakes."

Hebdon hesitated for a moment, and then refilled his glass. Tennison's head was back on the sofa, her eyes closed. She said slowly, almost mechanically, "I want to tell you something." Her lips felt numb. "I need to tell somebody."

Hebdon waited uneasily. He didn't know what to do, so he had another drink. He watched her, head back, eyes closed.

"I am pregnant."

Hebdon blinked, and filled the silence with a muffled cough.

"Congratulations."

"No, you don't understand," Tennison said, opening her eyes. She looked at him. "I am pregnant and I have absolutely no one I can talk to. I've tried, but . . . you tell me. Should I have it?"

"It depends, really." He shifted uncomfortably. "Well, on whether you want it or not," he added lamely.

"Would you, in my position?" The question wasn't just hypothetical, it was stupid. Tennison stared into her glass. "Hell, I could be out of a job tomorrow!"

"What about the, er—the father?"

"There isn't one—well, obviously there is, but not . . ." Her voice dropped to a whisper. "He doesn't know."

"Will you tell him?"

Tennison didn't have to think. She shook her head at once.

"We lived together for a long time and almost got married. But then I got cold feet and he went away and found somebody else." She threw the last of the wine back. "He is a very nice man, and I would like to be his wife . . . but it wouldn't be right." An expression of pain crossed her face. "No, it would be right, it was always right, just me that messed it up." She bowed her head, tightly clutching the stem of the wineglass in both hands.

Hebdon said cautiously, "Well, I suppose it comes down to whether or not you want it. Do you?" She was hunched over, hiding her face from him. "Do you want to be a mother?" he asked quietly.

Tennison's head came slowly around, her eyes bright and moist. A shy, radiant smile lit up her whole face. She said softly, "Yes. Oh yes, I do, very much."

16

Tennison was twenty minutes late arriving in the Squad Room. She had no excuses, except that she had a foul head and a thick taste on her tongue, and she wasn't going to offer those up in mitigation. When she finally made it, DI Hall had the 9 A.M. briefing under way. He had on a superb suit in dark olive green and a tie with so many swirling colors it made Tennison ill just to look at it.

She gave Hall the nod to carry on, while she took off her raincoat and tried to get her brain in gear.

"Parker-Jones owns a number of bed and breakfast stroke hotel stroke houses, under the company name 'Protega.' Mostly for children in local authority care." Hall referred to his notes. "As a registered charity he's got a staff of four, one administrator and two youth workers. Annual running costs of around one hundred and twenty thousand. He's on a number of grants, one hundred and sixty grand from Camden, another one from Westminster Council, that's for advice and support . . ."

Dalton came over and stood by Tennison's elbow. With one ear on the briefing, Tennison said, "They're still keeping you on, are they?"

". . . he's also got another fat one from London Boroughs Grants Committee," Hall was saying. "*Added* to all the grants, Parker-Jones receives from the local authorities a hundred and ten pounds per person. So far we've got eighteen registered to one house, another twelve in Hackney, and the one in Camden has eight."

He carried on, giving more details, as the team made notes and asked for a point of clarification now and then. The PA *bing-bong* chimed out. "DCI Tennison to Superintendent Halliday's office immediately, please."

Tennison glanced up to the Tannoy, a strange fierce light in her eyes. "This is it! I think it's charge or pull the rug time."

Dalton put his hand on her arm. "The doctor attached to the Calloway Centre, Cardiff. His widow, Joyce Ellis, two sons, aged fifty-two, in 1987 married John Kennington."

Tennison gave him a crooked grin. "What's this? Changing sides, are you?"

Bing-bong.

"DCI Tennison please return to her office immediately."

Dalton also looked to the Tannoy. "He doesn't know."

"Thank you," Tennison said, squeezing his arm. She headed to the door. Otley was there, beckoning urgently.

Tennison walked past him. "I know, Halliday wants me."

"Commander's with him!" Otley hissed.

She pushed through into the corridor, not waiting to see if he was relishing this or not, and caring even less.

Halliday was standing in front of her desk and Chiswick was sitting in her chair. The Commander had a crabbed look on his face, his small mouth tight and hard. He didn't give her time to shut the door.

"You have not one shred of evidence against Parker-Jones and his involvement in the death of—"

"Colin Jenkins?" Halliday edged out of the way as Tennison came forward, all fired up, ready for a showdown. "No, I haven't got him to admit his involvement, but I know he's covering up for Jackson and possibly for John Kennington."

"Drop it!" Chiswick said, icy quiet.

"Are you serious? In 1979 and again in 1986 both John Kennington and Edward Parker-Jones . . ."

Chiswick made a brusque sweep of the hand. "I am fully aware of the cases you are referring to."

"Then you should have made whatever information you had available to me!" Tennison said angrily. "I have wasted a considerable—"

"*Waste* being the operative word, Chief Inspector. You were supposed to be investigating the murder of—"

She was sick of his interrupting. It was her turn.

"The murder of Colin Jenkins. But if—*if*—I also discover evidence that proves Edward Parker-Jones . . ."

The bastard did it again.

"*This is not the Colin Jenkins case.*"

". . . is unfit to be awarded massive grants from four different councils, and is a possible pedophile . . ."

"Is this true?" Halliday asked Chiswick, but the Commander had no time for noncombatants. His sights were fixed on Tennison. It was a double-headed contest, two boxers slugging it out, attempting by sheer weight of punches to batter their opponent to the canvas.

"Chief Inspector Tennison, you give me no option but to warn you, that if you continue to investigate persons—"

"Persons?" Tennison was in like a flash. "One Edward Parker-Jones?"

"—against specific instructions, then disciplinary action will be taken."

Tennison took a deep breath and slugged on. "You take it, sir, and I will fight you every inch of the way." Her eyes flashed. She wasn't just angry now, she was blazing mad. "I have been fobbed off with 'stay clear of this or that person because of,' and I quote, 'repercussions to this department.' Well, this department has blatantly attempted to cover up my investigation into a murder, which has direct links to a pedophile ring—members of that said ring, and one member, John Kennington, who has been under a full-scale internal inquiry!"

"John Kennington was reinstated," Chiswick said, his voice trembling as he struggled to retain his composure.

"Yes—but six months later he's being blackmailed! The case never even got to court. What happened, everybody get cold feet, so retire him?" Tennison was filled with contempt. She was cutting in deep and raw, but what the hell, these were spineless excuses for officers charged with enforcing law and order. She thumped the desk, and Chiswick visibly jerked back.

"Retire him," Tennison raged on, "pay him off, and when another investigation touches on it . . . John Kennington is still alive, Colin Jenkins is dead."

"Just calm down," Chiswick said, raising his hand. "Look at it from our side, my side, the investigation into John Kennington—"

"Failed . . . and to the tune of over one and a half million. Next, Operation Contract!" Tennison shook her head, smiling bitterly. "How much did that set the Government back? You *knew* there was a leak—well, was it John Kennington?"

"Be very careful what you are insinuating," Chiswick warned her solemnly, playing the Senior Figure in Authority card.

Tennison closed her eyes for a second, breathing in deeply. She pressed her palms together. "All I want is to find the killer of Colin Jenkins. If it touches on Parker-Jones or anyone else, then that's the way it's got to be." She faced him squarely, looking him straight in the eyes. "You can lay it all on my shoulders. I take full responsibility. But I will not be anybody's scapegoat, and if you pull me off this case now, I won't go quietly."

Chiswick stared balefully at her across the desk. "Don't make threats, Detective Chief Inspector."

He rose ponderously to his feet and jerked his head to Halliday, indicating that the interview was at an end. As they reached the door, Tennison said coolly:

"I'd like to be put forward for the Superintendent vacancy on the AMIT Area Five. I am very confident that I'll make an arrest for the Colin Jenkins murder this weekend, and therefore, with the case closed, it will be unnecessary for me to continue any further investigation into John Kennington's connection with Colin Jenkins."

The two men were standing stock-still. They were both trying, as best they could, to take on board what Tennison had said.

Commander Chiswick opened the door and went out, stooping, not looking back. Halliday went meekly after him, pausing for a look at Tennison that was both guarded and puzzled before quietly closing the door.

Tennison heard them enter the next door office. She heard the rumble of voices through the wall. She closed her eyes and slowly sank back, needing the solid desk to support her.

Vera extended her tongue, delicately picked something off it, and wiped it on the handkerchief in her lap. She puffed on her cigarette and batted the smoke away. With soulful, heavy-lidded eyes she watched as Tennison took the packet of cigarettes, extracted one, and put it between her lips.

"You got a light?"

Vera struck a match and Tennison leaned toward the flame.

"Did James Jackson kill Connie?"

Close to her, Tennison saw the twin match flames reflected in Vera's eyes. She saw fear there, deep down. Deeper yet, stricken terror. She resumed her seat, breathing smoke through her nostrils. "He can't hurt you, Vera, he's going to be behind bars for a long time. So, tell me . . ."

"I don't know," Vera Reynolds said huskily. She bowed her head and smoked, looking down into her lap.

"Do you know a John Kennington?"

Vera shook her head.

Tennison sighed. "Vera, look at me. Come on, help me. Why was Jackson looking for Connie that night? He says Connie owed him money."

"Connie didn't need to borrow money from Jackson. He always used to have money."

"Did you know any of his clients?"

"No." Vera raised her head. She looked past Tennison to Otley, standing near the door, his arms wrapped around the shoulders of his wrinkled suit. She took a breath. "No, he was very secretive about them. Well, you give one kid a name, next minute they're offering themselves. You think he was just gay, don't you?" she said, a faint smile hovering. "Why do you think we got on so well?"

"I don't know how well you knew him," Tennison said gently. "Why don't you tell me?"

Vera swallowed, the prominent Adam's apple jerking in the long white throat. Above it, her makeup ended in a smudgy tidemark. Her blond wig wasn't on straight. She looked defeated and pathetic.

"He was the same as me. He'd go with gays, but he liked straight men better. He wanted money, needed a lot for the operation. They do the best in Rio. He would have had to pay for it, you see, there's no way the NHS would have given him the operation, he was too young. As it is you've got to go through six months of interrogation, analysts, and God knows what else, and then you're on a waiting list that'll take years . . . I know."

She took a deep drag, right up to the filter tip, and stubbed it out in the ashtray. She looked pensive.

"Always been my dream. I've been on the hormone tablets, but they're so expensive, and then I've got to buy costumes, pay rent. I just never had enough—but Connie, he felt ready." She tightened her lips suddenly, as if she was about to cry, turning her head away. "He was very beautiful, and . . . sometimes we'd talk, and . . . he understood . . . because we were alike, we were the same."

"Was one of his clients going to give him the money for the operation?" Tennison kept to her gentle tone.

"No." Vera's finely arched eyebrows went up. "Ten grand? More. You need a lot of after-care treatment."

"So Connie needed a lot of money—maybe ten, fifteen thousand pounds, yes?" Vera nodded. "How was he going to get all that? Blackmail?"

"Connie was capable of anything."

"Blackmail, Vera?" Tennison said more insistently.

"Yes, well, I think he was trying it on a few people—the famous ones. But I don't think he got very far. I think he got scared off."

Tennison jotted something down. Her cigarette smoldered in the ashtray. She mashed it out. "Do you know a Jessica Smithy?" Vera nodded. "Connie was selling his life story?" Vera nodded. "And?"

"I think she kept stringing him along, promising big money—he used to brag about it. But she wanted evidence. Names, photographs. Photographs."

"And Jackson knew about this?"

"Yes. He knew Connie had got a sort of file. You know, to show this reporter. He found out, because Martin Fletcher stole some things from Jackson and gave them to Connie."

Vera fumbled for a cigarette. Tennison waited. Otley shifted onto the other foot. Vera picked something imaginary off her tongue and wiped it on the handkerchief.

"That's why Jackson was looking for Connie. Not just to get back his things, but because he knew if Connie was selling his story, then he'd be in it. Connie had been one of his boys, you see, early on. Not lately, of course."

"Jackson got Connie on the game?" Tennison said. She made a note.

"Yes." Vera was nodding slowly. Her eyes were very sad. "He got him so young. He was only ten years old when Jackson found him." She looked at Tennison from under her eyelids. "But you got to understand, Jimmy was an abused kid himself. Didn't make any difference to him if they were eight or eighteen. They never stay with him long. Not once they get the hang of it." Her voice had become drab, lifeless; her whole behavior was subdued.

"Did you see what Martin stole from Jackson? What he eventually gave to Connie?" Tennison asked.

"No, I didn't see them, he just told me." Vera patted her chest, indicating that Jackson had concealed something in his jacket. "Probably pictures, photographs, maybe letters, I don't know. I never saw what Martin nicked from Jackson. But that's why Martin got beaten up. Because he stole the stuff from Jackson."

"If Connie told you about the 'stuff' Martin had taken from Jackson, told you about the press connection, did he also mention who he was going to blackmail with it?"

Vera shook her head. "He never told me, but he was kind of excited— you know, very pleased with himself. Said he'd get the money for his operation. He was very certain."

Tennison made a note and closed her notebook. She reached over and touched Vera's hand, a light firm pressure.

"Thank you, Vera."

Tennison stood up. Vera sat there, eyes clouding with confusion.

"You can go," Tennison said. She went to the door, pausing by Otley. "You doing anything lunchtime?" He shook his head. "See you in my office." She went out.

In her haste, getting to her feet, Vera had managed to drop her handbag, tipping most of the contents onto the floor. She got down on her knees, shoveling in lipsticks and tubes of makeup. Otley's face appeared beneath the table. "Get your handbag, Vernon, and you're out of here," he drawled.

Vera scrambled to her feet, clicking her handbag shut. She was palpitating, her eyes a bit wild. "That's it . . . ? I can go?"

Otley jerked his thumb.

She scurried to the door, heels clacking, clutching her handbag. "Vernon!"

Vera skidded and pitched forward. She whipped a frightened look over her shoulder.

Otley was dangling a hairbrush by its handle. "This yours?"

Alan Thorpe stood in the mustard-tinged gloom of the advice centre, idly glancing over the contacts board. He had a full carton of Rothman's King Size under his arm, and he was leisurely lighting up from the packet he'd just prized out of the cellophane wrapper. It was a little after 10:15 A.M. It was quiet, no one in the games room or the TV lounge.

Quiet for the next ten seconds until Margaret Speel came clattering down the stairs and barged through the door, frizzy black hair bouncing on her shoulders, her mouth taut as a steel trap.

She marched past the reception counter, did a smart right turn, and banged her small fist on the door marked "E PARKER-JONES. PRIVATE."

Parker-Jones opened the door. He stepped back and smiled, gesturing her in.

Margaret Speel didn't move. Her voice had a rasp to it.

"This won't take long. I intend to report you, get you blacklisted with every council, every government-run scheme that you have abused."

Parker-Jones had spotted Alan Thorpe, who couldn't help but overhear. He moved farther back, trying to draw her in. "What's brought this on?" he asked, quiet and steady, no histrionics.

"I trusted you, I may even have helped you—that is what is worst, worse than any of the lies you have told me." Her shoulders were hunched with the strain, fists clenched at her sides. Her usual pale coloring was now white as chalk. "I don't care if I lose my job—"

"Who's been talking to you, Margaret?" Parker-Jones asked, keeping his voice low. He reached for her hand.

"DON'T TOUCH ME!"

He swayed back, spreading his arms defenselessly. "Come in, at least talk this through."

Margaret Speel wore a bitter smile that made her pert face ugly.

"She knows everything—about you, and about John Kennington. And when I've finished you'll go to prison." Spittle flew from her lips.

Parker-Jones reached out and grasped both her wrists. "You don't know what you're talking about, Margaret. This is from that policewoman, Tennison, yes?" His face showed pain and bewilderment. He tugged beseechingly at her wrists. "Oh, Margaret, don't you understand? Please . . . just calm down." His hand touched her cheek. He implored her softly, "Just come in a minute. Let me explain."

She took a swift decisive step backward, pulling herself free. "Yes, I do. I do now."

And then she was striding off, past the reception counter. Alan Thorpe stared at her. She spun around, glaring at him, making a sudden grab for his arm.

"Don't come here anymore. Do you hear me? Don't come here. This is closed. *This is closed down!*"

Under the force of this onslaught Alan backed away from her. He wasn't scared, just bemused. Margaret Speel pushed him aside and started snatching down the letters and cards on the contacts board. She tore them off and ripped them up, scattering the pieces, and then she tried to drag the board itself off the wall. One corner came loose and she attacked it in frenzy, bringing the whole thing crashing down.

Parker-Jones came around the corner from his office. He leapt toward her, face livid, his hand grappling for her shoulder. Margaret Speel pivoted on her heel, her arm swinging, and caught him smack across his face, a stinging slap that split his lip. Her shoulder bag had come off. She swung it back on and stormed up the echoing wooden stairs.

From his breast pocket Parker-Jones took out a clean white handkerchief and dabbed his lip. He returned to his office, picked up the phone and dialed, dabbing his lip and looking at the spots of blood on the pristine white linen.

The connection came through.

He held the receiver close to his mouth, feeling the sluggish warm trickle on his chin.

"Mrs. Kennington? It's Edward Parker-Jones."

Jimmy Jackson was bent double in the chair, his hands locked across his head, tufts of hair sprouting through his fingers.

"All *right*. I never lent him any money!"

Mr. Arthur sat close by him, knees firmly together, fingers laced beneath the threadbare cuffs of his overcoat.

Tennison went on, "You were told by Martin Fletcher where Connie was. You then went to Vernon Reynold's flat."

"I didn't—I've admitted I was looking for Connie, but I wasn't the only one."

"Who else? Who else was looking for Connie on the night he was murdered? Jimmy, it's just five . . . ten minutes there and back from the advice centre."

"I never killed him. I couldn't have."

Otley put his hand on the back of Jackson's chair and leaned right over. "But you had to silence him, didn't you? Connie was going to tell about the way you kidnap underage kids. The room at the top of the house. We've seen the chains, the weapons, the knives."

"Did you torture boys up there?" Tennison said expressionlessly. She looked at his hands, the spiky hair sticking through. "Is that why we have, to date, fifteen separate blood samples, from walls, floorboards, bed sheets? What were you doing to those children?" She glanced at Mr. Arthur, and then inspected her fingernails. "Mr. Jackson, I would really try to be as helpful as possible. The charges against you . . ."

"Look, I did go to the centre, right?" His head came up, eyes bulging at Tennison, lips red where he'd been chewing them. "I told Mr. Parker-Jones I couldn't find him, right?"

"Edward Parker-Jones," Tennison said, looking at Otley.

Jackson nodded. "Yeah . . ." He sounded short of breath. He twisted around to Mr. Arthur, and twisted back again, plucking at his T-shirt where it stuck to him, one boot agitatedly thumping the carpet. He said hoarsely, "Martin Fletcher took my stuff out of the house . . ."

"What stuff?"

"Things, photographs . . . I wanted them back, right?"

"Photographs of you?"

"Some of them," Jackson said cautiously, "but Connie had nicked them, he got Martin to get them for him from Camden, right? You with me?"

"Who else was in the photographs?"

"I can't remember," Jackson said too quickly.

"You almost kill a boy for them," Tennison said, her voice brittle with disbelief, "and you can't remember who they were of? Who was in the photographs?"

Jackson shakily lit up. He dragged deep, crouched forward, elbows on his knees, blowing smoke at the carpet.

"Was Parker-Jones in these photographs?" Tennison said.

"No."

"How about a John Kennington? Was he in any of these photographs?"

Jackson tried to shrug it off. "Just kids, blokes dressed up . . . bit porno, that's all. Anyway, it got to about eight, bit later, an' I told Parker-Jones that I couldn't find Connie, an' he said go and get Martin Fletcher, he'd know where he was." He stared at her sullenly from under his thick brows. "So I did. Ask Martin Fletcher, he'll tell you."

"Martin is dead, Jimmy." Tennison allowed the silence to hang heavy. "So Parker-Jones wanted the photographs—why? If as you have just stated he wasn't in them, why would he want them?"

"I don't know. All I know is he wanted them, but so did I."

"But you were in the photographs." Tennison pointed her finger. "Are you sure there weren't any of Edward Parker-Jones?"

"I didn't have any pictures of him," Jackson said through his teeth.

"Was John Kennington in any of these photographs?"

"No! I told you before, I don't even know that bloke . . ."

"So they were just photographs of you? And you wanted them so desperately you were prepared to kill for them?"

"Look, when that fire started . . . I was over the other side of Waterloo Bridge." He waved his arm, indicating a vast distance, the backside of the moon.

Tennison rubbed the nape of her neck, trying to ease the hangover that was thudding in the base of her skull. Red wine was lethal bloody stuff. She felt rotten.

Otley saw her close her eyes for a second. He said, "So, who was at the centre when you were there?"

Jackson half-turned to him. "I was only there two minutes, no more," he said irritably. "Then I come out."

"Anybody else?" Tennison asked. "Did you speak to anyone else apart from Parker-Jones?"

"Yeah." Jackson sounded weary. "Vernon Reynolds."

Tennison and Otley exchanged looks. Vera? Since when was she at the centre that night? First they'd heard of it.

Head hunched down between his bony shoulders, Jackson stared miserably at his boots, blowing smoke at the carpet.

Tennison drove north along Highgate Hill, fuming at the traffic. Otley sat beside her, filling his face with a cheeseburger, a plastic cup of coffee held up in front of him to avoid spilling any. It was twelve-thirty. A soothing Brahms string quartet was on Classic FM, but it didn't help Tennison's temper any.

She swung the wheel, avoiding what she knew would be a totally clogged Archway and Muswell Hill, and took to the side roads on the eastern edge of Hampstead Heath.

"If Jackson is telling the truth, then he couldn't have done it," she said, turning right unexpectedly, so that Otley had to concentrate like fury to save his coffee.

He stuffed in the rest of the cheeseburger, cheeks bulging. "What about Vera, then? That was a turn up. I mean, she's never mentioned anything about being in or anywhere near the centre." He swallowed and took a slurp of coffee. "But she couldn't have started that fire—she was onstage at Judy's at nine-fifteen. She was bloody onstage."

The Sierra Sapphire came into the tree-lined avenue of large detached houses. Tennison leaned forward, peering through the windshield.

"What's going on here?"

There was an ambulance outside the gates, its rear doors standing open. Two attendants were wheeling a trolley from the driveway. There was a humped shape under the red blanket.

Tennison stopped the car and hurried forward. Otley took a peek through the gates, seeing the Panda car outside the front door.

"What's happened?" Tennison asked, showing her I.D.

The attendants were about to lift the trolley into the ambulance. She turned back the blanket. It couldn't be, she told herself, it couldn't be, but she was wrong. She clenched her jaw.

"It's John Kennington. Shit."

Otley glanced toward the house. "We'd better leave it," he advised, "must have just happened."

He looked around for her, but she wasn't there.

"Guv!"

Tennison was walking through the gates, heading up the gravel drive.

"Guv!"

17

Tennison stepped through the open front door into the parquet-floored hallway. To her left she could see a cluster of uniformed police in the study. There was a plainclothes officer kneeling on the carpet. Somebody else was taking flash photographs. She moved across the hallway toward them, and then stopped. The door to the drawing room was open. Mrs. Kennington was sitting on the sofa, her head downcast, a cigarette in one hand, a crumpled lace handkerchief in the other. A crystal tumbler, filled nearly halfway with Scotch, was on the coffee table in front of her. An open bottle of Macallan's Malt stood next to it.

Tennison put her hand on the doorjamb. "Mrs. Kennington? Could I speak to you a moment?"

The woman didn't move or look up as Tennison came in and eased the door shut behind her. The room contained an unnatural quietness, the stately ticking of the grandfather clock portioning out the silence.

"Are you all right?"

Mrs. Kennington stirred. "He shot himself, not me," she said, vacant and subdued. She turned her head. "You were here the other night, weren't you?"

"Yes." Tennison moved up to a winged armchair, set at an angle to the sofa. "I can leave if you want . . ."

"But then you'll want to come back, so ask whatever you want. Get it over with."

She happened to notice she was smoking. The cigarette was nearly done, and she took another from the box and lit it from the stub, very lady-like, little finger stuck out. She then noticed the Scotch, and drank a mouthful, little finger out. Tennison sat down. She put her briefcase by the side of the chair and folded her hands.

"I was in the front bedroom," Mrs. Kennington said. "We sleep in separate rooms. There was a phone call, I put it through to John's study. About half an hour later I heard the—well, I didn't know what it was, to be honest. I thought it was the plumbing. It's been making extraordinary noises. Obviously it wasn't. John had shot himself."

She blinked at Tennison, as if making an apology for some unfortunate social gaffe. She had bright, intelligent eyes, a striking light blue. Even under stress she maintained her poise, and Tennison was able to understand what an asset she must have been to her husband in furthering his career.

"Do you know who the call was from?" Tennison inquired after a decent interval.

"Oh yes, I know who it was from. His name is Edward Parker-Jones."

She didn't notice, or paid no attention, as Otley slid into the room. He moved behind Tennison's chair.

"At least this saves me getting a divorce." Mrs. Kennington smiled faintly, gazing at nothing. She delicately wiped the corners of her mouth with the wisp of handkerchief. "There have been obstacles in the way for almost a year . . ."

"I know about the investigations," Tennison said.

"Oh, do you?" Mrs. Kennington remarked, cool to the point of half frozen to death.

"You were a doctor, weren't you? Do you still practice?"

"No. My first husband died. We worked together, or in the same practice."

"In Cardiff?"

"Yes, in Cardiff. Why do you want to know about my husband's practice?" She peered closely at Tennison, frowning. "Why are you here?"

"When you were in Cardiff, Mr. Parker-Jones was running . . ."

"The Calloway Centre." Mrs. Kennington was now paying full, complete attention. She looked at Otley and then at Tennison, quite perplexed. "Why are you asking me these questions?"

"Did you examine a young boy called Jason Baldwyn? It was a sexual assault charge."

"Which was subsequently dropped. No, my husband examined the boy—" Her mouth fell open. "Oh, my God," she gasped. "You think I had something to do with that? My husband was critically ill, he was very sick, I had two small children, and . . ." She faltered, rubbing her forehead distractedly with the wadded handkerchief. "He had cancer, I only remember it because, because he died. Then there was this investigation about . . ." She stared, trying to recall the name, and failed. ". . . This boy. But there was so much confusion about whether his reports were stolen, or just mislaid, I really don't know."

The facade had cracked a little, and to repair it she took a drink, finger out, and was careful to put the glass down without making a sound. She dabbed her lips. "My first husband was a very decent human being. I can't say that about my second, I wish to God I had never married him. But I did," she added under her breath.

Tennison said, "Do you know if young boys were ever brought here?"

Mrs. Kennington rose and went to the white mantel. With her back to Tennison, she murmured, barely audibly, "Do I know if young boys were ever brought here?"

"Perhaps when you were away," Tennison said. She opened her briefcase and took out a photograph. "There is one boy I am particularly interested in." She got up and crossed over. "His name was Connie, Colin Jenkins."

Mrs. Kennington slowly turned. Her eyes were fixed on Tennison. They drifted down to the photograph. They flicked back, icy blue, sharp as needles.

"Get out of my house," she said, low in her throat, under iron control.

"Please look at the photograph," Tennison said quietly, equally controlled.

A shudder passed through Mrs. Kennington's whole body. She averted her face and stared at the row of silver-framed photographs on the mantel with a force that was almost manic in its intensity. Two fair-haired handsome youths progressed from grinning schoolboys to young adults with darker hair and engaging smiles.

"There were many young boys brought to this house, whether I was here or not." Her chin trembled. "I was at least able to protect my own sons."

Tennison slipped the photograph into her briefcase and snapped it shut. She nodded to Otley, and followed him to the door.

"I hope for their sake that you did," she said.

Tennison pushed through the double doors into the corridor, unwinding her scarf, and headed toward her office. As she reached the door, Halliday came out of his office and beckoned to her urgently.

"Have you got a moment?" He glanced up and down. "I want this kept very quiet, it's not official yet, but—" His voice dropped to a murmur. "John Kennington committed suicide this morning."

Tennison took a full pace back. "Good God!"

Halliday nodded darkly. He squinted at her: "That vacancy by the way, for Superintendent. It's Hammersmith, Commander Chiswick knows the Chief there; in fact they're playing golf."

Tennison widened her eyes, blinking owlishly. "I'd better charge Jackson then, hadn't I?" she said.

Halliday strode off and she entered her office. She tossed her briefcase down and hung up her coat. There was a mound of paperwork on the desk, and she contemplated it, spirits sinking.

First, though, she had a call to make. The call. But no joy. The receptionist promised to pass the message on immediately after Tennison had emphatically insisted.

Five minutes later there was a tap on the door and DI Hall looked in, dark eyebrows raised inquiringly. "You wanted Jessica Smithy? She's just arrived—and, was it correct you wanted Vernon Reynolds brought back in, only we just released her."

"Yes. And *you* keep your eye on Alice in Wonderland—Miss Smithy to you. Put her in interview room D oh two." The phone rang. She waved Hall out and answered it. Decision time. Now or never.

"I'm sorry to disturb you at home, Dr. Gordon, but I wanted to talk to you as soon as possible."

"I can make an appointment for tomorrow if nothing's wrong."

"No, it's just that I would like to arrange a termination," Tennison said. She heard her own voice, and marveled at its brisk impersonality. It was like listening to someone else, some other woman, strong and confident, without the slightest qualm.

"Are you sure?" Dr. Gordon asked after a pause. "This is a very big decision."

"Yes, I am aware of that." How calm, how collected! "It is a very big decision, but . . ."

"Obviously it is yours, Jane, but I think you should consider, or come in and discuss it with me." He wasn't hectoring, and she was glad about that, because she wouldn't have stood for it.

She toyed with her fountain pen. "I know it's a big decision, and I have obviously given it a great deal of thought." She pressed the nib into the blotting paper, testing it not quite to breaking point. "I want an abortion."

"It could also be a very final decision . . . considering your age."

"Yes, I know."

The door opened, Otley rapping with his knuckles when he was already halfway in. He hovered on one foot, motioning whether he should leave her alone. Tennison shook her head. She said into the phone, "I'll call you next week, to arrange a time and date."

"Think on it," Dr. Gordon advised her. "Good-bye."

"Good-bye."

Slowly she replaced the phone and sat staring at nothing. She took a sudden sharp breath, drumming her fingers on the desk. "I told Halliday we're ready to charge Jackson"—brisk and businesslike once more.

"You know something I don't?" Otley muttered, eyes narrowing suspiciously.

Tennison opened her mouth to reply, but nothing came out except a pitiful choking sob. Otley was totally transfixed, torn between embarrassment and disbelief. Numb with the shock of it, he watched as she burst out crying, tears pouring down her cheeks. She put her hand over her eyes, shoulders heaving, fumbling blindly for a tissue from the drawer.

"I'm sorry . . . sorry . . ." Tennison blew her nose, making it difficult for herself by shaking her head at the same time.

Otley stood like an empty sack of clothes, his face like a stunned rabbit's, arms hanging limply by his sides. For once his snide cynicism had deserted him.

Tennison wiped her cheeks. "I just feel as if I'm hitting my head against a brick wall." She sniffed hard, making a contemptuous gesture toward Halliday's office. "Get no help from him!"

"I could get the screwdriver, take off a few feet of his office and give it to you if it'll make you feel better," Otley offered helpfully, giving a gaunt ghost of a smile.

Tennison tried to smile with him, but this only brought on more floods of tears. Muffled behind a bunch of tissues, she croaked, "I have never done this before, I'm sorry . . ." She sucked in a deep shuddering breath. "He knows Kennington's dead."

"Good news travels fast," Otley remarked glibly. He gave a little uncomfortable shrug, hands spread. "Look, I can handle this afternoon."

"No!" Tennison wadded the tissues into a sodden ball and threw them viciously in the basket. "I give you an inch and you'll take a mile."

Otley sighed. "Do you want a cigarette?"

"No, I don't want a bloody cigarette!"

"Coffee?"

"No." Tennison straightened her shoulders, sitting upright in the chair, combing her hair back with her fingers. "Just . . . just give me a few minutes on my own."

She felt mortified. Not only about breaking down, but breaking down in front of Bill Otley, of all people.

Ye Gods, get a grip, woman.

When he'd gone she sat drained and empty, the muscles in her belly still quivering. Her chest ached, and she had to fight with all her strength to stifle the sobs that at any moment might engulf her.

But twenty minutes later, a transformation. Hair brushed, face washed, fresh makeup applied, she was in fine fettle for Vera. The momentary loss of control had somehow cleansed her, swept all her doubts and depression away, given her a steely, hard-eyed resolve.

She smashed the table with her fist, making Vera's hunched form jump and jerk, her stifled sobs turning into strangulated hiccups.

"And you *lied* to me—you never at any time even mentioned you were near that advice centre. Why? Why, Vernon?"

"You've always called me Vera," Vera wailed, raising a tear-streaked face, her eyes filled with childish hurt.

"Stop playing games with me!" Tennison barked. She spun around as Otley came in. "I said five minutes, Sergeant." She glared at him and bent toward the microphone. "Sergeant Otley has just entered the interview room at three-fifteen P.M."

Norma looked up from her pad, casting a hooded glance at Otley as one foot soldier to another; she's breathing fire and brimstone, keep your head down if you don't want it blown off. Otley leaned indolently against the wall and folded his arms.

"Did you or did you not see Jackson on the night Connie died?" Tennison demanded, returning to the attack.

"Yes," Vera said miserably.

There was a commotion outside in the corridor. Otley crossed to the door and half opened it. The strident tones of Jessica Smithy could be heard as Hall hustled her along.

"Just how long am I expected to wait? I've been here nearly an hour . . . she's doing this on purpose!"

Otley wafted them on and firmly shut the door.

Tennison paced up and down. She yanked the back of her jacket straight and without warning swept the file sheets off the table with such force that Vera cowered in her chair.

"You know what really sickens me about you?" Tennison rasped, leaning forward on her knuckles, face thrust toward Vera's. "That you said you liked Connie, understood him, that he was like you."

Vera ducked her head as Tennison leaned even closer, inches away.

"He wasn't though, was he? He wasn't like you. Because he was twenty years younger than you." Her voice was scathing, pitiless. "And he was going to get everything you always wanted, wasn't he? *Wasn't he?*"

Vera wriggled, her face collapsing in on itself, biting her lip to hold back the tears. Tennison resumed pacing. She stopped at the window, staring out. "What time did you get to the advice centre?"

"About eight-thirty." The answer barely crept out.

"Eight-thirty?" Tennison revolved slowly on her heel. *"Eight-thirty?"* She moved nearer. "Where was Connie?"

"In the flat."

"Alone?"

"Yes."

Tennison bent down to retrieve the scattered sheets. She dropped them any old how on the table. She folded her arms. "Well, your friend Red is now in trouble. He swore on oath that you were at his friend's studio at . . ."

Vera quickly jumped in. "Six-thirty—I was. He never knows the time, and I left to go to the club, just as he said."

"When you left your flat," Tennison said with ponderous deliberation, "was Connie there?" Vera nodded. "Suspect nodded his head." Tennison leaned in. "Alone?" Vera shook her head, eyes downcast. "Suspect shook his head. Who was with Connie when you left your flat at six-thirty?"

The Adam's apple bobbed in the long white throat. Vera's heavy-lidded soulful eyes came up, brimming with moisture.

"A journalist."

Tennison felt a jolt in her spine. She stared at Vera.

Jessica Smithy sat on the edge of the table, smoking, tapping her cigarette ash on the floor. Beside her were two empty cups of coffee and a half-eaten sandwich on a paper plate. With unconcealed impatience she was watching DI Hall, who a moment before had answered the wall phone. He was nodding. "Yes, she's still here."

He cradled the handset and turned to her, a deprecating smile on his lips, fidgeting with his tie.

"Choose them yourself, do you?" Her slender leg in its Gucci shoe swung to and fro like a relentless metronome.

Hall fingered his tie. "No, my girlfriend does," he responded brightly, beaming.

Jessica Smithy's hazel eyes flashed, sliding off somewhere. "I'd get rid of her." She blew smoke in the air, tapped ash on the floor.

"I tried—I told you—gave you all the clues. It was me that said the advice centre, even said Parker-Jones's name, and it was me that told you about Jackson, me who told you about the press. . . ."

Vera scrabbled in the box for another tissue. She discarded the sodden one and noisily blew her nose. She discarded that one too and wrenched out a handful to wipe her damp face.

"I went back to the flat because I'd forgotten a sequinned choker." The tears welled up again. "Connie was still there, talking—talking. I just listened for a second, I didn't want to interrupt, but I could see them, the door was just ajar, and he was showing her my album." Vera gazed up beseechingly at Tennison. "She was looking at my photographs . . . you don't understand, do you?"

Her arms folded, Tennison looked down at her watch.

"There were some loose pictures of me before, before . . . of my mum and dad, private pictures, no show business ones, just my mum and dad, my brother." Vera's face crumpled. She talked on through her crying. "I hurt them enough . . . I don't ever see them, so the pictures are very special. After all I had done for him, he was selling me, too."

She wiped the tissues under each eye, one at a time, and with a loud sniff straightened her back. Smoke trailed up from the cigarette in the ashtray but she didn't pick it up.

She said huskily, "I didn't want to make a drama, not in front of the press woman. I just called him out of the room, said I wanted to talk to him. He swore to me he wasn't letting her have a single picture. She left a few minutes later, and I went in to check my album. He lied. There were a lot missing, so I confronted him. He swore he hadn't given her anything, he said she must have stolen them, but he was such a liar, and, and . . . and I got hysterical. I hit him. With an ashtray, I think. I didn't mean to hurt him, but he fell down, I helped him to the sofa. And he—he gave me that smile of his, he had such a sweet smile. And, then, he closed his eyes, and I couldn't feel his pulse. He was—he was dead."

Silently, without expression, Vera stared in front of her, tears rolling down her cheeks and dripping onto her lemon yellow blouse.

"Did you call an ambulance?" Tennison asked.

"No, my phone's not working. I told Mr. Parker-Jones and he said he would . . ." She trailed off.

"What? Do what?"

"Take care of everything. Call the ambulance."

"Did he?"

"I don't know," Vera said, and in the same dead voice, "I want to go to the toilet."

"We are terminating the interview at three-forty-five P.M. in room D oh five as Mr. Vernon Reynolds has asked to use the bathroom."

Tennison switched off the tape and looked to Otley. "Take him with you."

Vera stood up, very tall and slender. "I was put in prison when I was not much older than Connie. That's what I am scared of. Inside they're all Jacksons. I was raped every night, that's what I've been so scared of." She clutched her handbag under her arm and went to the door. "I've wanted to tell you, but I was just scared."

She turned and looked at Tennison with large reproachful eyes.

"You're horrible. You just pretended to like me. Why can't you take me to the ladies?"

She followed Otley out.

• • •

Otley stood at the washbasins, attempting to flatten the recalcitrant points of his shirt collar. She was taking her bloody time. He sighed, glancing at his watch.

"Come on, Vera, love!"

A toilet flushed and Halliday emerged from one of the cubicles, buttoning his jacket. "Who's in there?"

Otley looked to the cubicle door, Vera's high-heeled shoes visible underneath it. "Sorry, Guv, it's Vernon Reynolds . . ."

He drew Halliday aside, speaking from the corner of his mouth.

"He's admitted that he struck Colin Jenkins. We just finished questioning him."

Behind them, beneath the cubicle door, a thick pool of blood was forming, spreading around Vera's spiked heels.

"So it wasn't Jackson after all," Halliday said, raising his eyebrows.

Otley turned. He snarled, pushing Halliday roughly out of the way, and dived for the cubicle door. "Get someone up here fast!"

Halliday dithered, old woman that he was, and looked around helplessly.

"She's cut her wrists!" Otley yelled, putting his heel to the lock.

Spurred on at last, Halliday slammed through into the corridor. By now he was running. "GET SOMEONE IN HERE . . . !"

He ran on as Tennison came out of the ladies toilet. Hurtling into the gents she came upon a bloody scene. Vera was propped in a sitting position against the tiled wall, legs stuck out, one shoe off, limp as a rag doll. Blood was spurting from both wrists. The front of her dress, her legs, the floor, were soaked in it. A smeared red trail led from the cubicle where Otley had dragged her.

Tennison grabbed the roller towel and gave it a fierce, frantic jerk, pulling the end loose from the machine. She kept pulling, unreeling a long white tongue, as Otley ran water in the basin.

Tennison knelt at Vera's side, her knees in the pool of blood.

"Vera, hold on! It's going to be okay—listen to me, can you hear me?" The blood was pumping out. She gripped Vera's upper arm, squeezing with both hands. "Hurry, she's losing an awful lot of blood . . ."

Vera's head lolled from one side to the other, her wig slipping askew. "Sorry, I'm sorry," she kept mumbling.

"Vera, listen to me! Can you hear me? You didn't kill Connie, do you understand?" The eyes were glassy, unfocused. "He was still alive." Tennison stared into the ghastly white face, streaked with blue mascara. "The fire . . . *it was the fire.*"

Vera looked at Tennison, eyelids drooping shut, and her head flopped forward onto her chest. Otley dumped the soaking roller towel onto the floor and began binding it tightly around Vera's arms.

Halliday barged in, heaving for breath. "There's a fifteen-minute delay on the ambulance call out . . ."

Tennison snapped, "Then get a car organized—"

She whipped her head around as it sunk in what Halliday had just said. Fifteen Minute Delay. Her lips thinned. "And one for me."

She looked to be grinning, but it was fixed in place, frozen to her lips, icy and implacable.

"I am bringing in Parker-Jones personally."

A furious Jessica Smithy marched along the corridor, Hall in close pursuit. "Half past two—I have been here since half past two!" she raged. Hall grasped her by the elbow and she gave him a withering look that would have scorched asbestos. "I want to go to the ladies."

Hall colored up and released her.

Jessica Smithy's eyes sparkled dangerously as she spied Tennison coming toward her. She plonked herself in Tennison's path, taller by several inches, her expression haughty and indignant.

"You have no right to waste my time," she stormed, tossing her head imperiously.

Tennison, her blouse and jacket cuffs, the hem of her skirt and knees caked in blood, let her have it. "I have every right, and I will hold you for as long as I want. You have lied. You have withheld vital evidence—and you have wasted *my* time."

Tennison swept past her, saying, "You wanted the ladies room, Miss Smithy, follow me."

She pushed open the door into the female staff locker room, and didn't hold it for Jessica Smithy, who nearly got her face battered. They went inside.

Otley appeared through the double doors at the end of the corridor, running. "Where the hell is she?"

"Toilets," Hall said.

Rubbing his face, Otley stood panting and fuming.

Tennison flung her soiled blouse into her locker and took out a short-sleeved navy shirt with breast pockets. She hadn't a matching jacket, so she had to make do with a double-breasted blazer in dark red with gilt-buttoned cuffs. No spare skirt or hose, dammit, she'd have to soldier on with what she had.

She ran water in the washbasin and was rinsing the blood from her hands when the toilet flushed and Jessica Smithy came out of the cubicle. There had been a subtle change. There was a dent in her haughty demeanor, her quick darting gaze not as brashly confident in the face of Tennison's grim single-mindedness of purpose, her firm authority.

Nevertheless, for the sake of appearances, she tried to rekindle her righteous indignation. "How long am I going to be here for? I am supposed to deliver copy for this evening's—"

"For as *long as I want!*" Tennison didn't need to raise her voice. The lethal sting in it was enough. "You were at Vernon Reynold's flat the night Connie died—did you make a third tape?"

The journalist had a sullen pout. "No."

Tennison gave her a searching look in the mirror and went over to the roller towel. Jessica Smithy's lean cheeks were slightly flushed. She stared at Tennison's back. "No, I only made two tapes. I swear before God, just two tapes. I never mentioned before"—clearing her throat uncomfortably—"I mean, I know I should have told you about me being at the flat . . ."

Tennison finished drying her hands. She picked up her shirt and shook it out. "Did you remove anything from Vernon Reynolds's flat?" She slipped the shirt on. "Did you?"

"Yes. They were just some snapshots—nobody famous. Just a few black-and-white photographs and drag acts. Nobody famous," she repeated anxiously.

"So, apart from these photographs you took, did Colin Jenkins give you anything?"

"Nothing, nothing . . . just some story about being picked up when he was ten or eleven. But I'm beginning to think he made that up." Her face had a strained, pinched look. "Oh God, it isn't the way it sounds—I didn't do anything!"

Tennison buttoned her jacket. "Oh, yes, you did. You stole photographs that meant a lot to someone, meant so much that Colin Jenkins died for them." She spared her nothing. "That's what you did, Miss Smithy."

Otley's head peered furtively in. Tennison gave her appearance a final check in the mirror and went over. "Kathy said you wanted to see me?" Otley murmured. "Something about an ambulance?"

"Yes." Tennison shot a look at Jessica Smithy. "Follow me."

She led the way to her office, Otley bringing up the rear. He could tell from her walk that she was a transformed woman, another person entirely from the one he'd seen weeping less than two hours ago. It was incredible. He couldn't fathom her. He didn't understand women as a species all that well, but Tennison absolutely baffled and amazed him.

Jessica Smithy was contrite, sitting in a chair, puffing nervously on a cigarette. "I tried to contact you, you know I did, it's not as if I didn't attempt to see you."

"Just stop the Doris Day act, it's getting on my nerves," Tennison said shortly, eyes narrowed. "Martin Fletcher?"

DI Hall came in and spoke over Jessica Smithy's head. "Car's ready and waiting, Guv." Tennison acknowledged him and beamed her attention back on the woman.

"He was the first boy I approached, and he introduced me to Connie." She gulped down smoke. "Then it seemed obvious to me that, well, Connie would make a better story. We were worried that Martin was too young and—"

"Martin Fletcher is dead, did you know?" Tennison said brutally.

Jessica Smithy's eyes rounded with shock. She felt she was being battered from all sides. The tough shell of blasé cynicism was falling to pieces, exposing a frightened woman floundering out of her depth.

Tennison looked at her watch. She was in a hurry to get on. She snapped her fingers, and Otley imagined he could practically see an aura of sparks coruscating around her head.

"So you drop Martin Fletcher and now offer Connie money, yes? Did you give him the money in Vernon Reynolds's flat?"

"Yes." Jessica Smithy nodded numbly. "He put it in his pocket, said it wasn't enough, he wanted more."

"Then what happened?"

"I said I couldn't give him any more, not until I at least saw what he had to offer. . . ."

"And did you?" Tennison demanded impatiently. "Come on, Miss Smithy, did he show you anything? Give you any names?"

"No."

Tennison looked again at her watch. "So then what happened?"

Jessica Smithy stubbed out the cigarette and wiped her fingers. "He left the room for a minute and there was this album on the coffee table. I'd just paid him five hundred pounds, so . . ." She blinked fearfully at Tennison. "I opened the album and just—I just took some of the loose photographs, and a few others . . ."

"Vera Reynolds's album? Yes?"

"They were just photos of a family," Jessica Smithy protested. "Couple of somebody in drag. They were no use, they meant nothing."

Tennison stood with her hands on her hips. "Wrong, Miss Smithy. They meant an awful lot to somebody, enough to . . ." She reached for the ashtray. "Make him pick up a heavy glass ashtray and hit Colin Jenkins with it." She emptied the ashtray, banging it against the side of the metal basket. "You have a lot to answer for."

Pale and stricken, Jessica Smithy licked her dry lips.

Tennison looked to Hall. She flipped her hand. "Take Miss Smithy and bring her back with Vernon Reynolds's photographs."

Jessica Smithy rose slowly to her feet. "Are you going to charge me with anything?" she asked tremulously.

"I'll let you know," Tennison glowered, wafting the bloody woman out of her sight.

There was a real buzz around the place. Everyone could feel it. Something big was going down.

Haskons and Lillie, infected like everyone else, hurried along from the Squad Room, in time to see Otley emerging from Tennison's office.

"Hey, Sarge, what's going on?"

Otley went past them. "She's picking up Parker-Jones," he said, not breaking his stride.

Hall came out and escorted Jessica Smithy to the main staircase.

Otley had halted, midway along the corridor, as Kathy rushed past him. She came up breathlessly, meeting a steely-eyed Tennison head-on as she marched out of her office.

"Emergency services have said there was a fifteen-minute delay that night, and all callers were informed that—"

Tennison punched the air. "I've got him! And this time I am ready for him." All fired up, she shouted to Otley, "Let's go!"

18

Otley went first, holding the door for Tennison to walk through into the reception area. She was alerted; it seemed unusually quiet. It was the dead time of the afternoon, but even so . . .

The door to the office was ajar, and Tennison peeked inside. The normally neat desk was a muddle of correspondence and document files spilling their contents, papers strewn everywhere. The desk drawers were open, and so were several of the filing cabinets, as if someone had been hastily rooting through them.

"Looks like he's about to do a runner," Tennison observed. "You think he's been tipped off?"

Otley stepped over the torn-down notice board. He gazed around at the address slips and contact cards, ripped up and scattered over the dank green carpet. He opened the door to the TV room and looked in. Empty. He turned back to Tennison with a shrug.

A sudden crash made Tennison jump. She spun around to find Parker-Jones looming over her, the door to the kitchen swinging shut behind him. He stared down at her, the black curtains of hair framing his sneeringly handsome face.

"Well, I hope you're satisfied. As you can see, the place is empty."

Tennison snapped erect. "Mr. Edward Parker-Jones, I am arresting you for questioning regarding the murder of Colin Jenkins. I have to warn you that anything you—"

"I want to call my lawyer," Parker-Jones said brusquely, striding on to his office. But then he turned in the doorway, all silky charm with a contemptuous edge to it. "Please continue, Inspector, you seem to like the sound of your own voice!"

Seething inside, Tennison followed hard on his heels. She gave the nod to Otley, who repeated the caution. Parker-Jones ignored it, his tall figure moving swiftly around the desk and reaching for the phone.

Tennison beat him to it. Her hand came down on the phone.

"We can do that at the station, sir."

A muscle twitched in his taut cheek. His long jaw was rigid with anger. Tennison stared up unflinchingly into the deep-set eyes. She beckoned Otley forward, there was a flurry of movement, two sharp clicks, and a moment later Edward Parker-Jones was blinking down in amazement, stunned and incredulous that these stupid thick morons had the nerve to slap the handcuffs on him. *Him!*

Halliday saw him being brought in. Standing outside his office he had an uninterrupted view the full length of the corridor to the double doors at the top of the main staircase. Two uniformed officers led the handcuffed Parker-Jones through. Even from this distance Halliday could see the dark glittering eyes, the suppressed manic fury in his stiff-legged stride.

The officers guided him toward one of the interview rooms in the adjoining corridor and he passed from view.

Halliday headed for the Squad Room. His shoulder blades felt clammy. He ran his finger inside his collar, clearing his throat as he pushed through the doors. Almost everyone was there, yet the room was eerily quiet. A telephone drilled through the silence and someone quickly answered it. Tennison was standing at her desk, calmly sorting through her interview papers. Damn woman was made of titanium. Halliday went over.

"Parker-Jones's brief is in reception." His voice became low and terse, a bit ragged. "You all set?"

"Yes, sir," Tennison's hand was nerveless as she slipped the sheets inside the document file. "Some developments this afternoon warranted my bringing in Parker-Jones."

"I know," Halliday said. He touched her arm, causing her to look up. "But you'd better nail him."

"I intend to." Tennison pushed her hair back over her ears, smoothed the front of her jacket, picked up the document file and snapped it smartly under her arm. She was ready.

Flanked by Halliday and Otley, she marched through the hushed room to the door. It was as if everyone was holding one huge collective breath. Eyes swiveled, watching the neat compact figure, seeing in the set of her shoulders and her raised head a ruthless compulsion, a chilling determination.

Nail him, Halliday had said. And by Christ she would.

Haskons stood near the door. He moved aside. "Good luck, Guv!"

Tennison gave a tight curt nod and went through.

The handcuffs had been removed. Edward Parker-Jones sat straight-backed in the chair, his manicured hands resting some distance apart on the table. If not relaxed, he seemed rather more at ease, the angry glitter in his eyes replaced by an opaque self-concealment, his face an expression-less closed book.

Perhaps the presence of Joseph Spelling, his lawyer, had worked the trick. Spelling exuded probity and restraint, from his starched collar and tightly knotted dark green silk tie to his pinstripe trousers and highly pol-ished black shoes. His pearl-gray homburg hat rested on his briefcase on the table, the initials J.D.S. stamped in gold in the burnished leather.

He regarded Tennison with a faintly quizzical air, prepared to tolerate her even though she was a mere woman doing a man's job. Seated next to his client, he leaned forward attentively, his bony beak of a nose in the deeply lined face thrust in her direction as she spread the papers out and unscrewed the cap of her fountain pen.

Tennison slowly lifted her head and gazed directly at Parker-Jones.

"On the evening of the seventeenth of this month you have stated that you were at the advice centre, Soho. Is that correct?"

Parker-Jones's face stayed impassive. "Yes."

"Could you please give details of who else was there on that night?"

Parker-Jones closed his eyes. How many more times? "Billy Matthews," he began wearily, preparing to repeat them all again, *yet again*, but got no farther.

"Statement withdrawn." Tennison's voice was quiet, devoid of empha-sis or emotion. "Matthews denies being at the advice centre."

"Donald Driscoll . . ."

"Driscoll has withdrawn his statement and denied being at the advice centre."

"Alan Thorpe, James Jackson . . ."

"Alan Thorpe has stated that he was, on the night of the seventeenth, at the centre." She paused, seeing in the depths of Parker-Jones's eyes a mocking triumph. She went on, "He was not only intoxicated from alcoholic beverages, but was also suffering from other substance abuse, and was, in his own words, unable to remember if he was actually there himself."

"James Jackson," Parker-Jones repeated steadily, his heavy dark brows knitting together as his eyes bored into her.

Tennison glanced down at the sheet in front of her. "Mr. Jackson made a statement this afternoon contradicting an earlier statement. He now states, under caution, that he was at the advice centre but for no more than two or three minutes." She raised her eyebrows. "Do you, Mr. Parker-Jones, have any other alibi witnesses that you wish at this stage to be noted?"

Erect in the chair, hands spread on the table, Parker-Jones was an edifice of cold contemptuous arrogance. He tilted his head as Spelling whispered in his ear. They conferred. Tennison tapped the table with her pen. Halliday and Otley, standing side by side against the wall, waited and watched.

"My client will answer," Spelling said finally, leaning back.

"I realize I have been very foolish," said Parker-Jones smoothly, and Tennison marveled at how his change in personality could be switched on and switched off at will, in a trice. Now he was conciliatory.

"I can only apologize . . . but I was trying in some ways to protect Vernon Reynolds. Vernon was at the centre on the seventeenth."

"Did you speak with Vernon Reynolds at all?" Tennison asked.

"No comment."

"But you do admit that Vernon Reynolds was at the advice centre on the seventeenth?"

A tiny hesitation. "I have just said so."

"Did Vernon Reynolds ask you to call an ambulance?"

"No comment."

Tennison looked thoughtful for a moment. She allowed her eyes to slide up from the desk to his face. "Mr. Parker-Jones, we are in possession of a tape recording made on the evening of the seventeenth, and it will be very simple for us to match the voice on the tape with yours. Did you or did you not call an ambulance?"

Tennison was lying through her teeth, and both Halliday and Otley knew it. They had such a tape, yes, but despite the best efforts of the technical people it hadn't been possible to identify the voice. Too much static and distortion. She was way out on a limb.

Parker-Jones was half turned away, whispering in Spelling's ear. Spelling replied, Parker-Jones nodding, and then he turned back.

"Yes, I did. Vernon's phone was disconnected and he was in a dreadful state. Said that Colin Jenkins and he had argued, and that Colin, Connie, needed a doctor. So, I did place a call to the emergency services. . . ."

Halliday and Otley exchanged relieved looks. She'd gambled and it had paid off. Yet her face betrayed not a flicker, not the slightest sign, and she carried on imperturbably, "What did the emergency services tell you, Mr. Parker-Jones?"

"That an ambulance was on its way."

"Anything else?"

He shook his head carefully. "No, I don't think so."

"Why didn't you leave your name?"

He smiled, somewhat ruefully. "To be perfectly honest with you, the advice centre has had to—on a number of occasions—place emergency calls. Some of the boys, well, they get deeply disturbed when they are diagnosed HIV positive. It's fear, you see, and then they refuse to go to hospital." He turned his hands, palms uppermost on the table, a gesture appealing for her understanding. "So I was afraid they might not be willing to respond—"

Tennison cut in, impervious to his smarm.

"Were you informed that there would be a fifteen-minute delay?"

He switched again, face stiffening when he realized she wasn't buying his bill of goods. "I can't recall."

Tennison was all patience and reason as she spelt it out. "But if you were informed that there would be a fifteen-minute delay, it would make sense, as the advice centre is only a few minutes' distance from Vernon Reynolds's flat, to . . ."

They were conferring again. Tennison sighed. She gazed at the ceiling, tapping her pen.

Parker-Jones faced her confidently. "I was unaware of any delays."

"Why didn't you call a doctor?" Tennison pressed him. "Or make that short journey?"

He had his answer ready. "At no time did he—Vernon Reynolds—make it appear there was a dire emergency, that Connie . . ."

". . . was possibly unconscious?"

"I was asked to call an ambulance or arrange for one to be sent. I have admitted that I did lie—or did not give you the information when I was asked before about this ambulance call out." Parker-Jones was back to being reasonable again, doing all he could to help the police with their inquiries. No doubt the influence of his lawyer, urging temperance and moderation. "I apologize, but surely you can understand my reasons—I simply did not want to get Vernon Reynolds into trouble."

It was neat and plausible and Tennison had no idea how to break through and expose his story for the pack of lies it was. This man was a filthy sadist, a vampire preying on the children entrusted to his care and leaving behind a wreckage of young lives. He'd been doing it for years, in different parts of the country, using Kennington and Margaret Speel and possibly countless others to aid and abet him and cover his tracks. He was a cancerous growth in society that long ago should have been cut out. Tennison was the surgeon, but it was as though the scalpel in her hand was blunted, or had been whipped away the moment she started to operate. He was a devious, clever, calculating, lying, perverted bastard with an impregnable sense of his own superiority. He had friends in high places, money to buy the services of a good lawyer, and sufficient power to put the frighteners on anyone who might be tempted to blow the whistle. He was above the law, that was the contemptuous opinion of Edward Parker-Jones, and

Tennison had a horrible, gnawing suspicion in the pit of her stomach that he might be right.

The silence in the room stretched on and on. There was just the rustle of papers as Tennison sorted through the file. Halliday eased his chafed neck inside his collar, his pale blue eyes loose in their sockets. Spelling cleared his throat ponderously. He leaned forward, his quizzical expression making his forehead a maze of corrugations.

"Do you have any further questions you wish to put to my client?"

"Yes, I do," Tennison said at once. "Mr. Parker-Jones, you have apologized earlier for lying. You lied about the presence of four witnesses that you said saw you on the evening of the seventeenth. One of these witnesses was Billy Matthews, is that correct?"

"Yes, but you must understand," he said loftily, in a patronizing drawl that infuriated her, "there are a number of them on any given evening . . ."

"But you were most specific about Billy Matthews," Tennison butted in. "You said you recalled him being at the advice centre because he was ill."

"Yes."

"But as it now transpires, Billy Matthews was not at the advice centre, he was in actual fact in Charing Cross Hospital."

He brushed it aside. "I'm sorry, I was simply confused as to the exact evening."

"Really? Even though you called an ambulance for him? That would be the evening of the sixteenth," Tennison stressed, and was charged with exhilaration to see, for the tiniest split second, a shadow of uncertainty flicker in the deep-set eyes. "On that occasion you did leave your name, and on that occasion you were informed that there would be a fifteen-minute delay. Is that correct?"

"It's possible."

"Possible." Tennison seized on this. "So it would also be possible that when an ambulance was called on the following evening you were fully aware there would be a delay." She stared him out. "Giving you perhaps even more time to leave the advice centre and go to Vernon Reynolds's flat. Did you? Did you go to Vernon Reynolds's flat?"

He was in a corner, but there was a simple way out, and he took it.

"No, I did not."

Back to bloody stalemate! She couldn't shake him, couldn't budge the arrogant bastard. They could sit here all night, her lobbing questions and accusations, and they would just bounce off that smug stone wall, that sneeringly superior shell he had built around himself. He was fucking fireproof. She felt like screaming and yelling and leaping across to tear out his eyes and rip the lying tongue out of his mouth.

Tennison was furious with herself. Not a snowball's chance in hell of nailing this shit if she allowed her emotions to veer out of control. By an act of will she quelled them. She looked up, her eyes cold, her voice without a tremor as she asked, "Mr. Parker-Jones, are you aware of the existence of certain compromising photographs that belonged to James Jackson?"

Parker-Jones leaned toward Spelling, but they didn't confer. The lawyer merely gave a long slow blink. Parker-Jones straightened up, wearing a smirk that Tennison wanted to smash from his face.

"No comment."

"That in many of these said photographs you are pictured with the deceased, Colin Jenkins?"

"No comment."

"That you were also photographed in various poses with a number of juveniles, and these photographs were taken from your home in Camden Town?"

"No comment."

"I think you knew of the existence of these pictures, and knew that Colin Jenkins intended to sell them."

"No comment."

"On the night of the seventeenth you had James Jackson searching all over London, desperate to track these photographs down." Her tone became thin and cutting as she replayed the scenario, telling the real story to his face, making him know that she *knew*. "To track Colin Jenkins down, but you just couldn't find him, could you?"

"No comment."

"And then Vera, Vernon Reynolds, came to you in, as you have said, a dreadful state . . ."

"No comment."

". . . telling you that the very person you were looking for was not only *in* her flat, but unconscious, alone, and with the said photographs."

"No comment."

"You said you would arrange everything. You would even call the ambulance—"

On his lips she saw the words forming and leapt up, slapped her hands flat on the table, her body arched tautly toward him.

"No comment?" Tennison hissed. "NO COMMENT AGAIN? Mr. Parker-Jones, you have admitted you were aware of the emergency services' delays during this period—"

"No comment."

"—You used that fifteen minutes to hurry from the advice centre, run over to Vernon Reynolds's flat. He wasn't dead, was he? Connie was still alive. And so you made sure, made sure he would never be able to tell anyone about you, Mr. Parker-Jones. *You* and your friends. It was so easy, wasn't it? He couldn't fight back, couldn't make any attempt to stop you as you set light to him . . . left him to burn to death."

She knew, at last, she had him. She was certain she had him, because he said nothing, his long face smoldering and sullen. Then he folded his arms, the corner of his mouth curling up in a little smirk, and she knew sickeningly that she hadn't.

Tennison stood outside the interview room. She felt so weary that she could have stretched out on the carpet in the corridor and gone fast asleep.

She looked away as Parker-Jones came out. "Good night, Inspector Tennison." His smiling glance passed over her dismissively. He turned to Otley. "Which way is it?"

Otley led him toward the main staircase. Tennison leaned against the wall. Spelling came out, carrying his briefcase and homburg, followed by Halliday. She watched the lawyer hurry along briskly to join Parker-Jones, who patted his shoulder and pumped his hand. Otley pointed the way and they went off.

Tennison sighed tiredly, rubbing her eyes. "I had to try, Jack."

Halliday nodded. She was drained, both physically and emotionally, he could see that. He said, not unkindly, "Supposition, intuition, really are worthless. Without hard evidence you didn't stand a chance in hell. Without a witness who actually saw person or persons unknown set fire to that flat, you will never have a case—especially not against someone like him."

She looked up at him with a strained mocking smile. "Does this blow my chances? Superintendent?"

"No. You'll get it. No strings."

"Guv!" Otley came up. "Jessica Smithy's back." He jerked his thumb toward Tennison's office.

Tennison touched Halliday's arm. He'd told her what she wanted to know. "Thank you," she said. She smiled at him, and kept smiling all the way back to her office.

Jessica Smithy handed over a buff-colored envelope. Tennison delved inside and looked at the snapshots of Vernon Reynolds and his family: little Vernon in short pants with his mum and dad, standing on a sunny promenade, the holiday crowd surging around them. Vernon as a lanky teenager in the back garden, one arm clasped around his mother's shoulder, both of them smiling. Other family snaps—school speech day, weddings, day trips, picnics—and three or four of Vernon, now Vera, as a very young man in a primitive drag outfit he must have compiled from jumble sales. Tennison slipped them back in.

"Is Parker-Jones going to be charged?" Jessica Smithy was anxious to know. She examined Tennison closely, keyed up, smoking rapidly with short little puffs.

In contrast, Tennison felt calm, wearily peaceful. "Still after the scoop, Miss Smithy?" she asked nonchalantly.

"I'm paid to expose the truth. It's my job, a bit like yours."

"No, Miss Smithy," Tennison corrected her, "your job is not like mine." And as if to demonstrate the truth of this, she opened a file crammed with statements, photostats, photographs, lists of names and addresses, phone memos and faxes, nearly three inches thick.

"But it is criminal that a man like Parker-Jones is able to gain access to young innocent boys," Tennison mused sadly. With her thumb she riffled through the contents. "All with the blessing of the social services."

Jessica Smithy turned her head to exhale smoke, but her eyes never left the file that Tennison was idly leafing through. Tennison detached a black-and-white photograph of Jason Baldwyn, holding it up.

"'Keeper of Souls.' This young boy said that was his nickname—good headline! Nice turn of phrase for a sick pervert . . ."

Tennison let the photograph slide from her fingers and drop onto the open file. She looked at her watch, and then reached behind for her shoulder bag. "Would you excuse me for a moment?" She came around the desk and went out, picking up the buff envelope on the way.

Her footsteps receded down the corridor.

In the silence Jessica Smithy slowly edged around the desk, craning her head. She nudged the corner of the file with her thumb, aligning it more directly into her field of vision. With a swift glance to the door and back, she took hold of the photograph and stared at it.

Several minutes later the door opened a crack. Tennison peered through. Her back to the door, Jessica Smithy was bent over the file in a cloud of smoke, microcassette recorder close to her mouth, sifting through the thick bundle of papers.

Tennison eased the door shut and released the handle from her clammy palm.

She was heading for the staircase when Otley emerged from the Squad Room, his wrinkled raincoat draped over his shoulder. He cocked his head. "You off then?"

Tennison nodded. "Miss Smithy's in my office. Give her another fifteen minutes, then get rid of her." She held out the buff envelope. "Oh, and would you make sure these photographs get delivered to Vernon Reynolds."

"Yes, ma'am." Otley tucked them under his arm. His head went back, watching her through slitted eyes. "Superintendent next, is it?"

"I think so," Tennison conceded, cool and poised.

"I guess my mate didn't have the right strings," Otley said. He made it sound casual and indifferent, but she could feel the bottled-up force of his resentment, the boiling anger.

"No, he just didn't know whose to pull," she told him.

"You live and learn."

"Not always the best man wins," Tennison responded glibly, matching his cliché with one of her own.

She walked on, feeling his stare burning holes in her back.

"Good night," she called out, not turning.

Otley's lips moved, spitting out volumes of silent abuse, calling her every stinking name under the sun, and he knew plenty—

Tennison whipped around, catching him in the act, a huge exuberant grin spread across her face. She crouched, aiming her finger at him, cocked her thumb and shot him dead. She blew smoke off the barrel and bounced down the stairs.

ABOUT THE AUTHOR

Lynda La Plante's fourteen novels, including the Prime Suspect series, have all been international bestsellers. She is an Honorary Fellow of the British Film Institute and a member of the UK Crime Writers Awards Hall of Fame. She was awarded a CBE in the Queen's Birthday Honours list in 2008. She runs her own television production company and lives in London and Easthampton, New York. A new American television series based on *Prime Suspect* premieres this fall on NBC.